THE VACILLATIONS OF POPPY CAREW

NOT THAT SORT OF GIRL

SECOND FIDDLE

Other books by Mary Wesley

A Dubious Legacy
Haphazard House
A Sensible Life
The Sixth Seal
Jumping The Queue
The Camomile Lawn
Harnessing Peacocks

MARY WESLEY

OMNIBUS II

THE VACILLATIONS OF POPPY CAREW

NOT THAT SORT OF GIRL

SECOND FIDDLE

MACMILLAN
LONDON

The Vacillations of Poppy Carew first published 1986 by Macmillan London Limited
Not That Sort of Girl first published 1987 by Macmillan London Limited
Second Fiddle first published 1988 by Macmillan London Limited

This omnibus edition published 1993 by Macmillan London Limited
a division of Pan Macmillan Publishers Limited
Cavaye Place London SW10 9PG
and Basingstoke

Associated companies throughout the world

ISBN 0–333–59692–7

1 3 5 7 9 8 6 4 2

A CIP catalogue record for this book is available from
the British Library

Phototypeset by Intype, London
Printed by Mackays of Chatham PLC

CONTENTS

THE VACILLATIONS OF POPPY CAREW

ONE

On parting with Edmund, Poppy Carew sank into a state of mind where physical need and emotion ceased as though she had been pole-axed. Instinct made her put foot before foot, directed the walk back to her flat, the insertion of key in lock, the closing of the door. Then she lay face-down on the bed, numb, tearless, cold; she did not even kick off her shoes.

Outside, lights came on in the street. London's Saturday night expended itself and, later, the dilatory quiet of Sunday morning expanded into a foggy dawn.

Pride, that ambivalent quality, roused her at her usual hour. She changed into track suit and trainers, let herself out of the house and trotted, zombie-like, towards the Park. As she ran she felt light-headed from lack of sleep, lack of food and surfeit of emotion. Pride forced her to lope, through the streets of Paddington, across the Bayswater Road into the Park. Habit led her padding feet towards the Serpentine, to turn right under the bridge as she usually did. It had not occurred to her that Edmund, also a creature of habit, would tryst his new girl exactly as he had trysted her years before, to meet and kiss in the shadow of the bridge, standing locked, their reflections wavering in the water a few feet away, broken by a passing duck, re-forming as they stood welded together by their fresh and enjoyable desire.

Poppy knew exactly what her successor felt like, knew the allure of the word "tryst" as used by Edmund. She was tempted as she ran past to catch them off balance, with a vigorous push to join their watery reflection. She resisted the impulse, knowing she would stop, reach out her hand, heave them spluttering out, be forced to find something apt to say. I look silly enough as it is, she thought as they stood oblivious of her brief presence. She noticed the wind lift the sweep of hair Edmund combed across his thin patch, remembered suddenly the voice in the night telling her that her father was in hospital. The message thrust swiftly out of mind.

Her father was critically ill, shorthand for dying.

No longer jogging, she raced through the park, forgetting Edmund, knowing herself guilty of purposeful delay in case her father should inquire after Edmund, say "I told you so". But I must allow him the last word, the pleasure of being right, it is the least I can do, she thought as she changed her clothes, checked whether she had money for the fare and took the tube to Paddington. The least, and I have never done much. Mixed feelings of resentment and love for her only parent superimposed themselves over grief and anger. She was in the unusual position, for her, of giving her father pleasure. It would make him well, cheer him up, put him in the mood to recover.

She bought a ticket.

But if I can get through this visit without telling him, I can think up something plausible later, she persuaded herself as the train drew out of the station: she felt she might be too raw and sensitive to apprise her parent of the parting.

Parting, she thought disgustedly as the train ran through the suburbs. To her mind, the act of parting was something that was mutual; there was nothing mutual about the parting with Edmund. He had left her.

TWO

The ward was a large one. Poppy had the impression of beds stretching to infinity, dwindling like the occupants' lives. In each bed lay an old man, grey-faced, white-haired, merging with the white sheets, grey blankets, cream curtains. Some had limbs encased in plaster hoisted by pulleys at improbable angles. Some lay turned away like sad children. Some eyed her with watchful, hostile eyes. Many slept, open-mouthed, oblivious, showing pinkish-grey tongues, putty-coloured teeth. At the foot of a number of beds, a notice clipped to the rail, "NIL BY MOUTH".

They had put her father in the geriatric ward.

"Here's your daughter to see you, Mr Carew. Isn't that nice? Wake up, Mr Carew," said the nurse, bosomy in her white apron over grey dress, strong calves, useful shoes. "He sleeps a lot," she said to Poppy.

"I was not asleep." Poppy's father swivelled eyes which had been fixed on the ceiling. "Hullo, pet." His voice grey, shadowy, faded, matching the environment.

"Dad." She bent to kiss his stubbled cheek, rough and dry. Why hadn't they shaved him?

"You may stay as long as you like," said the nurse, moving away, smoothing the sheet with a habitual hand as she did so.

"I'll get a chair." Poppy fetched an orange plastic chair from a stack by the ward door. She averted her gaze from the old men who followed her with their eyes. She felt embarrassed in her bright sweater and trousers. She put the chair by the bed, sat, took her father's hand, cleared her throat, tried to speak.

"What's all this Nil by Mouth then?" She mustered false cheer.

"They are for the chop. Going to be carved up, patched up for a few months, sent home until next time."

"Dad." Tears pricked behind her eyes.

"They stop you dying. It's against the rules. No use carving me up." Speaking tired him.

"Dad." Her nose hurt from suppressed tears.

"I never cared much for rules." He was, he implied, beating the system.

"Darling Dad." She held his hand, feeling it dry and illusive as it lay between hers. It was useless to deny the proximity of that which he had once jeeringly referred to as "The Great Combine Harvester".

"So, if there is anything you want to know or say," her father murmured, "now is the time. Now or— " A new nurse appeared, held his wrist, popped a thermometer into his mouth, chopped off the word "never".

Father and daughter's eyes met, gleaming with shared amusement. The nurse shook the thermometer, made a note on the pad at the foot of the bed, moved to the next patient who burst, on her arrival, into a lament of condensed acrimony. The nurse popped the thermometer into his mouth. "Now then, Mr Prule." The lament ceased abruptly.

"There's one small thing I've never asked you." Poppy watched her father, how thin his face had become.

"Yes?"

"Why did you call me Poppy?" A belated question; surely at a time like this there was something more pertinent.

"Poppaea." He breathed the name.

"I know, but you and everyone call me Poppy it's so . . . " Why worry about her stupid name now? She could not stop herself.

"She bathed in asses' milk; I was into the Romans just before you were born. I liked the idea. Then there was this horse. I bet on a double, The King of Love and Poppaea. Look them up in the stud book. Poppaea won the Oaks at twenty-five to one and The King of Love romped home at thirty to one. Bit of luck, eh? Then you came and we thought you beautiful, so Poppaea it was. All seemed to tie up. I was working as a milkman at that time. Your mother said nobody would ever spell it right and shortened it to Poppy which reminded her of a wallpaper she'd liked." He smiled faintly, pausing to catch his breath. "The other, The King of Love, if you'd been a boy she might have taken a bit more persuading, but she was content with the wallpaper. Not all that keen on horses your mother." He smiled remembering his wife.

Poppy watched her father. "I never knew you drove a milk float." She would resent her mother's frivolity later. To be named for a glorious racehorse was acceptable but wallpaper took some swallowing.

"A *lot* you don't know about me." There was satisfaction in his faint voice. He rested eyes closed, his breathing an effort.

Watching him, she tried to visualise him young, vigorous, driving a United Dairies van, clinking bottles on to doorsteps in the early morning while fellow citizens lay still asleep or drowsing in their lovers' arms as she and Edmund— Was her father asleep? His eyes were closed.

"I'm awake."

She tried again.

"And you, Dad. Is there anything you want to tell me?"

"Yes." His voice was weaker now.

She waited while he mustered his strength, his breath faintly whistling. Suddenly, the fingers, lying lax in her hand, clenched urgently.

"Poppy?"

"I'm here, darling." She leaned close holding his hand.

"Something I never told you. Didn't want it to influence you. Didn't want that bastard chasing after you because of it . . ."

"What?" He was tiring, he was a horrible dark grey under the eyes. What sad secret did he feel he should tell her?

"There's a lot of money for you."

"Oh Dad, please." His savings would cover funeral expenses, and there was always her holiday money. "You mustn't worry about. . . ." Her father frowned, tried to pull her closer as she leant towards him.

"We mustn't tire ourselves." The nurse was back, standing watchfully.

"We'd like a cup of tea, wouldn't we, Mr Carew?"

"Bugger off." His voice suddenly came out strongly. The nurse moved away, unruffled.

"How is that fellow Edmund, still nosing after you? Done a bit more than nose, hasn't he?" He was bitter now.

"I . . . er . . . we . . ." Surely Dad had not forgotten they lived together.

"He'll marry you for your money. Live off you, a sponger, a leech."

"But I have no money." Where was all that shredded pride?

"Wait until you see my will."

Poppy grinned at him. If that was her father's idea of a joke, OK, she would string along with him. "Did you win the pools then?" She tried to laugh, felt banal.

"You could call it that." There was an expression on his face she had never seen.

"You did not answer me about Edmund." Tenaciously he returned to his question, desperately his eyes pleaded. "Platt," he sneered at Edmund's surname.

If I tell him I shall break down, she thought. If I cry I will upset him. Oh God, this is horrible. Why did I come? I could have pretended not to get the message, caught the later train.

Effortfully, her father was speaking again. "Get that fiend to prop me up."

"The nurse?"

"Who else?"

Poppy signalled. Two nurses came, heaved her father up. Punched pillows, propped him up like some dreadful baby. One of them smoothed his hair with a possessive but offhand gesture. All about the ward, nurses tidied patients whose relatives and friends came bustling in with flowers, sweets, fruit, letters, books, get-well cards. Visiting hour, with its bonhomie, had begun, time to hide the bedpans.

"There's a fellow advertising in the *Field*."

She leant close to hear. "Yes?" This position was making her back ache.

"Furnival's Fun Funerals. You'll see, I've marked it."

"Furnival's Fun Funerals?"

"Yes." Her father's voice was fainter now. "I want one. Horse hearse, plumes, mutes, the lot, I want one. Something to look forward to. Think you could organise that?"

"I'll have a bash." Why have I never given him what he wanted while he was alive? she mourned.

"Pricey."

"That won't matter if you are so rich." Her voice sounded jocose.

"So what's happened to Edmund?" He was back on the track, remorseless. "Platt." His voice a hoarse whisper.

"He's found a rich divorcée. Very pretty. He's chucked me, Dad. He's going to marry her." There it is, out, like a bad tooth: I am giving him all he wants. Giving him my unbearable hurt and pain. Giving him something he wants while he's alive to enjoy it. Her eyes swam with angry tears, she hated her father.

"Oh, ho, ho, *ho*! How *lovely*! Ouch!" Bob Carew let out a rattling shout. His head fell to one side and his hand lay, lifeless, in Poppy's. He dribbled.

A nurse came up with a rustle and a swish, rattled the curtain round the bed with one hand, felt for the non-existent pulse with the other, frowned at Poppy. "Look what you've done," she hissed. "He should have lasted until after visiting hour."

"That will do, nurse." The ward sister stood now beside Poppy, who looked at her father with wonder.

"Is he dead?" He died laughing, she thought with satisfaction, at least I gave him that.

"Yes, dear."

"Don't you dare call me dear," Poppy shouted at the ward sister. "I am not your dear. I will not be called dear by you." She began to cry loudly, messily, unrestrainedly, her breath coming in angry hic-cups. She bent to kiss the dead face, her tears dripping into its open mouth. "He wanted me to have this." She snatched at a copy of the *Field* topping a stack of magazines on the locker by the bed. "Wasn't it wonderful that he died laughing?" She shouted, "Wasn't it marvellous? I made him die laughing." She stood by her father's bed, staring at the ward sister until tears blinded her.

"You'll upset my other patients." Sister had Poppy by the arm, was leading her towards the door.

"They are not upset. They are loving it. They are still *alive*," Poppy shouted.

An old man, destined for the operating theatre (Nil by Mouth) made a thumbs-up sign as the sister pushed Poppy towards the swing doors into the corridor.

"Nurse, bring Miss Carew a cup of tea in my office."

"I don't want your fucking tea," Poppy yelled.

"Good on you," croaked another old man.

The sister pushed Poppy into her office, forced her down on to a chair.

"Shut up," she said. "Be quiet."

Poppy sat. "I think I'm going to be sick," she said in her normal voice.

THREE

At about the time Bob Carew was dying, Willy Guthrie was crossing the Park to lunch with an old cousin who had offered to buy from him a house he had inherited from his mother who had died the previous year. The capital realised would enormously help the expansion of his present enterprise, relieve him of worry.

As he walked Willy compared the faded London grass with the sweet-smelling turf on his farm and looked forward to the day's end which would find him back home breathing country smells instead of petrol fumes, hearing country sounds instead of London's roar. He was a contented man, free – here Willy crossed his fingers – of emotional entanglements, happy with the life he had chosen to lead. Looking down his long Scottish nose at the citizens of London taking their lunchtime break in the park, Willy pitied them and marvelled that he had endured several years of city slog before opting for self-employment and the challenge of running a farm. He felt no regret for the large salary and safe prospects he had chucked in favour of agriculture and was even glad that his present profession was more robust and risky than the lyrical idyll he had falsely imagined it to be when he started. Even his ulcers, should he get them, would be, he felt, of a healthier sort than those of Lombard Street aficionadoes.

His cousin was waiting for him in the bar of his club, a double gin at his elbow.

"You look very well," he said resentfully, eyeing Willy's sunbrowned face, taking Willy's hard, brown hand in his pale city paw. "What will you drink?"

"Vodka." Willy subsided into a chair beside the old man who thought Willy horribly tall and healthy and that his dark eyes and springy hair made him look a gypsy in this discreet rather academic environment.

"This is rather an academic club," said the cousin hoping to make Willy feel bucolic. It was important to assume the upper hand, he lived in London and was of the opinion that people who lived in the country were less sharp than those in the capital.

"I wouldn't have guessed," said Willy grinning at his cousin who remembered rather belatedly that Willy's degree at university had been rather good whereas he in his day had gone down before taking his finals.

"You have your mother's eyes," said the old man uneasily. "Shall we go in to lunch and discuss her house, yours now of course. I had a soft spot for your mother."

First I've heard of it, thought Willy following his host into the dining-room, and it certainly was not reciprocated. Too late he wondered why he had let himself in for this meeting.

An old waitress handed him the menu.

"The Irish stew is good today," she said persuasively.

To please her – she looked weary – Willy agreed to the stew.

"The food in this club is disgusting," said the cousin, "but it's cheap."

Willy, who during his banking period had had occasion to learn his cousin's income and assets, stiffened at this parsimonious remark.

"Why do you want to buy my mother's house?" he asked, leaping to the point of the meeting without preamble.

His cousin flushed. He had prepared what he thought of as his orderly mind for other tactics, a long build up to confuse, ending with an astute offer the country bumpkin Willy would be grateful to accept.

Willy looked round the room while awaiting the Irish stew, listening with half an ear to his cousin who, deciding to ignore Willy's verbal jolt, set off along the route he had plotted.

The stew arrived.

To please the waitress Willy ate but asked for extra bread to sop up the watery gravy, refused wine, asked for lager. He did not wish to linger longer than the minimum time to register tolerable manners. There was an earlier train than the one he had planned to take. If he was nippy he could catch it.

Meanwhile the old cousin droned on (he was not all that old, years younger than Willy's mother). He had, Willy knew, a perfectly good house already. Through the verbal screen it became clear from what was left unsaid that the cousin would benefit greatly by moving into Willy's mother's house. It was nearer his club, nearer Harrods, nearer the favourite bus routes and the tube, it was SW1 rather than SW14, it would be cheaper to heat (cheap, Willy noticed, was a recurring word), needed no money spending on heavy repairs. If he sold his present house (there was an offer in the offing, he hinted) he would make a respectable profit.

As the old man rambled along his chosen course Willy plotted the future of his farm. He would expand, build more piggeries, fence more land eastward under the sheltered lee of the woods, he would pipe more water, increase the number of drinking troughs, build an annexe to the smoke-house, increase the insurance.

"How are your cows?" The cousin had noticed Willy's silence.

"I keep pigs."

"So you do, so you do, I forgot." He returned to his dissertation.

Now I come to think of it, Mother couldn't stand this man, thought Willy buttering his bread, she would hate him to have her house. I should have thought of that before. This stew is really revolting, all water, no dumplings, only one carrot and potatoes I wouldn't insult my pigs with.

"Of course the whole house needs redecorating," said the cousin brazenly. "One must take into account your mother has not touched it for years and Lord knows what I'll find when I take the carpets up."

"Rugs, parquet."

"What?"

"I said parquet."

"Oh really, I thought—"

"Never mind. I wonder, could I have some cheese?"

"Of course, of course." The cousin snapped his fingers towards the waitress.

"Bring the cheese board. I rather doubt the roof, you know, and the gutters and down pipes are, let's say, suspect."

Didn't he say earlier there was no fear of spending on heavy repairs? Willy helped himself to cheese, a surprisingly beautiful Stilton wrapped as it should be in a damask napkin. "What do you suspect the gutters of?" he asked.

"Dear boy! Your jokes, ha, ha, ha."

"They were all renewed when Mother had a new roof put on three years ago."

Willy was enjoying the cheese, its bite took away the flaccid taste of stew. There would be no time for coffee if he was to catch the earlier train. He let his eyes rest on the cousin's face. What an old fraud.

Catching Willy's thoughtful eye the cousin felt uneasy. Those dark eyes in the boy's mother had concealed a pretty sharp. . .

Behind the dark eyes Willy was now calculating just how much he could risk borrowing from the bank, how to spread the improvements to the farm over a longer period – no need to rush. "The Stilton's good," he said.

"Good, good, what about coffee? A brandy?"

"No, thank you."

"Are you in a hurry?"

"I have a train to catch."

"Of course you have. Back to the cows."

"Pigs."

"Pigs of course, how stupid. Now about the price, I was going to suggest—"

"I think there is a misunderstanding," said Willy. "I have not decided to sell."

Leaping into a taxi, speeding towards Paddington Willy hoped he had not been too rude, hoped on the other hand that he had. Then he thought, I can use Mother's house as collateral on the loan, she would far rather I did that than sell to the old cousin. The taxi driver, who enjoyed a joke, slid back the glass partition asking Willy why he was laughing.

"A near miss," said Willy getting his money ready and thrusting it through the partition into the man's hand. "Thanks. If I run I can catch my train – bye."

Saying goodbye on the steps of the club, crafty enlightenment had lit the old cousin's eyes.

"I *see*, the penny's dropped. You are getting married, want to keep the house. Very wise to have a London base." Cousin had looked wonderfully cunning.

"No."

"But you want to keep the house for – er – girls. Of course! There aren't many who'd want to dally on a pig farm. You did say pigs?"

"No girls."

"Ha, ha, no girls?" The rather pleased disbelieving expression on cousin's face had delighted Willy. "Boys?" he suggested, lowering his voice.

"No boys either. I am free, free, free." Willy had laughed as he said goodbye.

"Famous last words!" shouted the old cousin as the taxi left the kerb.

FOUR

"Yes," said the voice, "Saturday's OK, can do."

"Thanks," said Poppy.

"Do you want four horses or two?" asked the voice. "One could make do with two."

"Oh no, he wants, I mean I want, the lot."

"That's the spirit," said the voice. "Black and gold, or silver and black? Mutes? What coffin do you fancy? Oak? Black lacquer or red, tricked out in brass or plate? Loops?"

"Loops?" There was nothing about loops in the advertisement.

"Silk ropes, nylon actually. We do a good line in a sort of frogging round the box – the coffin I should say. You can choose from the catalogue when it reaches you: it suits military gents."

"He is not – was not – military. I gave you my London address, but I'm in the country in my father's house."

"Ah, not so easy then. Shall I send another?"

"I could come and choose for myself, then I would know he was getting what he asked for. You are not very far away."

"Fine. You do that. Pass the time until Saturday. Any particular flowers?"

"I will decide when I see you."

"We do a good line in laurel wreaths."

"He is not – was not . . ." was not the stuff of laurel leaves. "I'll come tomorrow." She put the receiver down and looked dubiously at the advertisement her father had ringed in red biro. (Get me this) "Furnival's Fun Rococo Funerals". Dad, what have you let me in for? Why rococo in death when, in life, his taste had run to restrained eighteenth century?

Time to get ready for Anthony Green, her father's solicitor, hers now, she supposed. She must change her clothes, have a reviving bath. She had not slept since leaving the hospital, had not slept the night before. She felt light, as though levitating, as she went up the stairs.

The house was full of her father's presence: she related to him in a way she had never managed in life.

Avoiding her old bedroom, she took her bag into a room reserved for visitors, which held no special associations of childhood. She ran a bath, found clean clothes, laid out black shirt and sweater, sensible skirt, clean tights. She must impress Anthony Green as sober and responsible. They had not met for years, although he was one of her father's oldest friends, had known her mother.

The visitors' bathroom was equipped with large towels, expensive soaps. Who had been her father's visitors during the last years when they had met only in London, in restaurants, agreeing not to quarrel, not to cause an irreparable breach? The breach, she thought as she soaked in the bath, wedged open by Edmund.

Enough of that. She left the bath, dried herself and went to dress. Picking up her discarded clothes, she looked for a laundry basket. One of her father's foibles had been that unwashed clothes should be out of sight until whisked into the washing machine. Seeing no basket, she braved her father's room, dumping her clothes into his basket.

There were signs of hasty packing for the departure to the hospital, drawers half shut, cupboard doors ajar. Illness had come like a thief. Moving to shut a cupboard, Poppy saw a parcel in festive wrapping labelled, "Happy Birthday, Poppy". My birthday, Saturday, on Saturday. . . She untied the ribbon, held up a dress, put it on, viewed her reflection in the glass, wondering where he bought this marvellous garment, composed of a multitude of triangles in bright colours. She brushed her hair, saw that the dress suited her, felt elation.

Outside the house a car crunched on the gravel, stopped, the door clunked shut. She ran down to meet Anthony Green as he let himself into the house.

"I see you found your father's present." He bent to peck her cheek. "He bought it in Milan. It suits you."

When had he been to Milan? She had not known her father's movements, nor he hers, carefully kept secret.

"Come in. Would you like tea or a drink?"

"Tea, please." Anthony followed her to the kitchen. "Feels odd," he said in his pleasant voice, "without your father."

"I feel closer to him than ever before." Poppy filled the kettle. "Don't mind me," she added, noticing Anthony's raised eyebrows, "I'm not fey or anything, just short of sleep."

"Ah."

"You know I killed him," she watched the kettle, "made him laugh."

"Not a bad way to go." Anthony found a tray, assembled cups, sugar and milk, showing Poppy that he knew the house as well as she, perhaps better.

"The hospital seemed to think it reprehensible."

"Hospitals." Anthony dismissed hospitals. "He was on the way out – his heart was a mess."

"I am ashamed. I shouted at the sister, she implied Dad's death was inconvenient. I apologised later. I saw him again when they had . . ."

They had moved him out of the ward, tidied him up, closed his mouth and eyes. His nose looked as though they had pinched it with a clothes' peg. She had preferred his expression in death, rather ghastly surprised amusement.

"Let's take the tray into the sitting-room." She poured boiling water into the pot.

They had also shaved him, brushed his hair, given him a parting.

"You forgot to put any tea in."

"Oh God." She felt displaced, inadequate.

"Let me."

She watched him make the tea, followed him when he carried the tray to the sitting-room. "I have nothing to offer you to eat."

"Not to worry." He sat on the sofa, legs apart, watching her. "I watch my weight."

Poppy sat with her back to the light. "This won't take long, will it?" She wanted to be alone. "Dad had nothing much to leave, had he? He wanted me to arrange this funeral, he seems to have set his heart on it. I rang the man. He wanted Furnival's Rococo Funerals, he . . ."

"What?" Anthony leant forward. "Who?"

"Furnival's Roco—"

"I heard you. I've heard of Furnival too. What will the neighbours say?" Anthony, discreet solicitor, was about to say it himself. "You can't . . ."

"I'm going over to fix it, it's what Dad wanted."

"So far only a pretty odd pop star and a member, well, it's said he was a member of the IRA, have used—"

"Dad wants . . . wanted . . ."

"It costs the earth to . . ."

"I expect I can pay by instalments."

"You won't need to do that."

"What?"

"There's rather a lot you have to know, Poppy." Anthony sighed. "Shall you pour or shall I?"

"Sorry." Poppy poured, remembering that Anthony liked one lump and a drip of milk.

"I've given up sugar."

"Oh." Poppy fished hastily with a spoon. "Sorry." She passed the cup. "Dad didn't even own this house."

"That's right." Anthony took a swallow of tea, testing it for sugar. "You do; he put it in your name soon after your mother died."

"Why? What an extraordinary . . . he never told me."

"He wanted to save death duties. As a matter of . . ." Anthony paused, the girl wasn't listening. What was she thinking? He watched her: she had a curious expression. He opened his briefcase, took out the will.

Laurel wreath, she thought. Why should Dad not have a laurel wreath? He would like it far better than a lot of rotting flowers, it had been a good suggestion from Furnival's Funerals: it would amuse him. He would have laughed, too, if she had told him Edmund's new girl was called Venetia Colyer, an upmarket name, far more sophisticated than Poppy. Poppy's mind wandered to Edmund holding Venetia against him under the bridge over the Serpentine, his face against hers, her naturally yellow hair blown across his eyes. Perhaps she should have pushed them into the water. It was an opportunity missed. His hand had been on what the French call the saddle, pressing her against his genitals.

"You are not listening, Poppy. I didn't come here to watch you daydream; pay attention."

"I am, I will." She sat up straight, fixed her eyes on Anthony. "You had got to death duties."

"I had got a lot further. I'll start again." Anthony blew out his cheeks. He had finished his tea; he poured himself another cup.

"Sorry, Anthony. I am all attention."

"Right then. It's all here in legal language." He tapped the will.

"Oh."

"I will put it into plain English."

"Thank you." Poppy assumed a trusting, expectant expression. Anthony wondered if she was as great a ninny as she looked.

"Your father put this house in your name to save death duties. You got that?"

"Yes, Anthony. How wonderful of him."

One had doubted the wonder of it at the time, thought Anthony. However, "So, should you want to sell it, you can; straightaway." He watched her.

"Sell Dad's house?" The house where she had first made love with Edmund? Not very successfully, they'd been expecting Dad back from a trip to Brighton. Edmund had enjoyed it; he was, she found herself admitting, pretty selfish in bed.

"That's something for you to decide later. I only wish to make the point that you may, if you want to sell, sell." Anthony suppressed a niggle of irritation.

"Thank you, Anthony. Point taken."

"You will find – I shall explain to you – that you have not only the house and all its contents, but quite a substantial income and considerable capital sums banked in your name."

"Gosh. Why?"

"Presumably your father did not wish to leave you destitute." Anthony could be acerbic.

"I knew nothing about his money. . ." Poppy was puzzled. "I mean, he never talked, he never . . ."

"Your father had a phobia that some man might want to marry you for your money. I used to tell him you had more sense."

"Thanks, Anthony." Poppy's mind strayed back to Edmund and Venetia. Venetia had money, Edmund made no bones about it, grant him that, "I fancy being kept, Venetia has a safe income." Would he be selfish in bed with Venetia, not bother whether she came or not, or would he feel he owed—

"Poppy!"

"Sorry, Anthony. I am paying attention, it's just that I don't understand. Dad was always rather economical, not mean, just . . ."

"Careful," said Anthony. "Wise in his way."

"Yes, yes, I see," but she didn't see. "Where did he get it, this money? I always understood my mother bought this house with her bit. I mean, he never earned it, he was always changing jobs; and for years he's done nothing at all, just travelled about. Where does it come from, this money? Are you his executor?"

"Well, no. Naturally he asked me – actually the bank is executor. As your father's friend, as his solicitor, I am here to tell you, to advise . . ."

"The bank. Nice and impersonal. Great!" Anthony compressed his lips. "I mean, you won't be bothered by me and a lot of trivia, that's all I mean."

"A substantial inheritance is not trivia." This girl is hopelessly unworldly, thought Anthony, even if she isn't stupid.

"No, no, of course it isn't." Poppy drew in her breath, dismissing Edmund and Venetia and their possible orgasms. "You haven't answered my question, Anthony. Where did this money come from? Do you know? I never had an inkling. Was my mother, after all, rich?"

"Certainly not your mother."

Why "certainly" in that tone of voice? What had Dad done? Anthony did not approve, whatever it was. "Then what?" asked Poppy, alert. "How?"

"Your father backed horses."

"So that's where he went, he went to the races, he was a betting man."

"Not to put too fine a point on it – yes."

"Bully for him."

Anthony frowned. "And, ah . . . he nearly always won, and he—"

"Spent it on women?"

This girl, his reprehensible old friend's daughter, was making light of what might so easily have been a disaster. Frivolity was, he supposed, in the blood.

"Yes. You could say in a way that he did."

"But he invested a lot of it?"

"He invested what he called Life's Dividends." Anthony's tone was repressive.

"Sounds like Dad. Where did these dividends come from?" Poppy fixed Anthony with her dark green eyes.

"Not to put too fine a point on it" (why does he keep repeating himself?) "these . . . ah, um . . . women." Anthony dropped his voice, muting his tone.

"How?"

"Sums, large sums, left in wills. Quite legitimately, I assure you."

Poppy let this pass. "Had he been their lover?"

Anthony poured himself a third cup of tea, now grown cold. "I have no idea," he said coldly.

Silly old goat, thought Poppy watching him sip his chilly tea. Perhaps Dad saw to it these ladies who made wills in his favour had delightful, splendid times in bed.

In a way I am glad, thought Anthony eyeing her, that I am not the executor. He cleared his throat. "Well, that's it, then. The bank will give you all the details. I have made an appointment for you with them tomorrow. I have put a notice of your father's death in *The Times*, and I will contact the undertaker for you."

"Furnival's Funerals?"

"No, no, my dear. The best round here are Brightson's. You will find them very efficient and discreet. Most helpful—"

"He wants – he wanted – Furnival's Fun—"

"I know, I know. Trying to keep his spirits up, a sick man's joke—"

"Dad's joke is sacred—"

"But—"

"I have a date to see them. More tea?"

"No, thank you." Anthony stood up, pulling his waistcoat downwards.

"A drink then?"

"No, no, I must be on my way." He made a last appeal: "It would be, well, in rather well . . . rather dubious, er . . . rather frivolous."

"So apparently was Dad."

Poppy watched Anthony drive away. Viewed through the back window of his sensible car, he looked huffy. He was trying to manipulate me, she thought. It was cheek to put an announcement in the paper without telling me. Cheek to try and thwart Dad's last wish. He probably wants to buy the house cheap, she thought uncharitably, for a client who has had his eye on it for years. Perhaps he isn't an executor because he tried to manipulate Dad. "It's OK, Dad, you shall have your wish," she addressed the spirit of her progenitor as she went in search of food, suddenly ravenously hungry, not having eaten since that awful catastrophic evening with Edmund. What a remarkably tiring scene, she found herself thinking, as she opened a can of consommé. She felt that, if she cosseted herself, she might just possibly recover, a possibility she had not envisaged since the humiliating parting, the death of the affair. The end, she thought histrionically as she twisted the can-opener, of an era. She reached up to grasp a bottle of sherry from the cupboard, uncorked it and sloshed a liberal dose into the soup.

FIVE

Victor Lucas tore the paper out of his typewriter, crushed it between both hands and threw it violently towards the grate to join a trail of similarly treated first paragraphs of Chapter Five of his fourth novel. Sourly, Victor viewed the mess of wasted paper, wasted effort. It was all too likely, at this rate, that novel four would join novels one, two and three in the shredder.

Blocked, stuck, Victor decided to try the trick of studied inattention which, before now, he had found could jostle his lethargic muse into coming up with an idea or two. He would go out, get some exercise, buy something to eat for supper. He snatched up his jacket, pushed his arms into the sleeves, ran downstairs, slammed the street door and set off walking fast along the street towards the shops. As he walked, he considered his ex-girl Julia who had recently, out of the blue, after months of silence, sent him a paperback cookbook, *How to Cheat at Cooking*, by a pretty girl called Delia Smith.

To win her back when the affair was unravelling he had invited her to dinner in his flat. Bloody Julia had not been won back, had not enjoyed the meal he had cooked with such trouble: clear soup, veal in wine and cream sauce, green salad, wild strawberries (costing the earth). "Too much Kirsch," she had said in that clipped voice, "you drowned the taste," and later adding insult to injury sent the cookbook.

He had hoped, now that they had gone platonic, that Julia would commission a series of amply paid articles for the glossy magazine for which she worked. "Not a sausage," Victor muttered, walking along, shoulders hunched. "Sheer waste of money, waste of time, bloody bitch." He headed towards the supermarket where he would buy himself a steak and Sauce Tartare in a bottle, as recommended by Miss Smith (or was she Ms? With a lovely face like that, more likely Mrs) or, considering his present economic state, some sausages.

Striding along, Victor passed the fishmonger where, on marble slabs, lay, on crushed ice and seaweed, oysters backed by black lobsters, claws bound with tight elastic, Dover sole, halibut, cod, herring, shining mackerel and – "Oh Christ!" exclaimed Victor, "it's alive!" as a fair-sized trout flapped among its supine companions, in a shallow indentation on the fishmonger's slab.

"It's alive," Victor cried to the fishmonger, a stern lady in white overall and fur boots. "The poor thing's alive."

"Come in fresh from the country," said the fish lady complacently, "from the fish farms."

"But it's drowning," cried Victor, desperate.

The fish lady nonchalantly picked up the fish and slid it on to the scales, which joggled as the fish threshed its tail.

"No, no, don't put it in newspaper. Haven't you a plastic bag and a drop of . . ." he fished in his pocket for money; the trout gasped, open-mouthed, "water?"

"Your change," said the fish lady.

"Keep it." Victor was racing back to his flat, opening the door, the key shaking between his fingers, tearing up the long flight of stairs, gasping in sympathy with his prize, running the cold tap in the bath, jamming in the plug, gently releasing the trout: watching its extraordinary miraculous revival. "How could anyone eat anything so beautiful?" he crooned to the fish which stationed itself, its head towards the fall of water, idly moving its tail and fins, keeping in position under the cold tap, its pink flanks iridescent.

Victor tried to remember what he knew about trout.

They needed pure running water. At this rate he would flood the house. He reduced the flow of tap water, cautiously let some run down the plughole. Who did he know who lived near, or had, a trout stream? Where could he take his protégé, where it would not be caught by some demon angler?

Presently, leaving the tap dribbling, he was telephoning his friend and cousin (more of late years an acquaintance) Fergus, explaining the trout's plight, imploring asylum.

"Well, well. Well, I never," said Fergus. "Yes, of course, bring it down, no problem. You can stay a night if you want, I've got a job for you."

"An article?" asked Victor eagerly.

"More of a manual job, not so cerebral as your talents deserve."

What does he want? Victor asked himself. I'm in no position to refuse. He strained to see how the trout was faring, but the telephone lead was not long enough.

"I'll pay you, of course," came Fergus's voice from the country, "and come to think of it, there might well be an article. Good for you, good for me."

"Oh thanks, I . . . what . . ."

"Put a lid on the container."

"A lid?"

"Don't want it jumping all over your car, cause an accident!"

"Should I feed it? What about fish food, where can I get maggots?"

"No need. It can last. Come down the motorway; don't brake suddenly or you will bruise it. See you."

"What's the job?" Victor shouted, but Fergus had rung off.

Presently, with the trout in a plastic bucket, holes punched in the lid, Victor wondered, as he drove past Chiswick to join the motorway, what Fergus had meant by "good for you, good for me". He had never entirely trusted Fergus since the occasion Julia had stood him up, preferring Fergus's company to his. "He's so enterprising," Julia had excused her conduct. Bet she went to bed with him, Victor mused as he drove carefully so that the water in the bucket should not slop. Not that I care now, he told himself truthfully: glossy mag Julia is not the girl she was, I can't stand what she's done to her hair. There was too the connection with Penelope which he preferred not to think about. Driving carefully, Victor wondered what enterprise Fergus was at present engaged in. He had last heard of him doing something in France, though what that something was his informant had forgotten.

"First things first," Victor addressed his passenger. "He has a stream through his orchard, he doesn't fish, your only risk will be an occasional heron."

SIX

Les Poole, bank manager, placed the Carew folder on his desk. He delighted in the gift he imagined unique to himself, of observing himself as others might, indeed must, see him.

The desk was cleared for action except for the framed photographs of his dog, his wife and his daughter, familiar props, part of the furniture, well worn, well loved, he supposed, never being exactly certain. Time, he thought, peering at Marjory's photograph, time she got herself done again. That hairstyle was old-fashioned and the hair had changed colour, from brown to auburn (she was good about weekly visits to her hairdresser, keeping the grey parting under control). The scene was set for his pleasurable interview with Poppy Carew. Had she, one wondered, been born on Armistice Day? The father (what a character, should one consider him eccentric?) had been capable, if not of anything, of much, as the content of the folder proved. Les Poole looked at his watch, spoke into his desk telephone, "Send Miss Carew in when she arrives."

"She's here now," replied Ida, pertly invisible in the outer office.

Poppy Carew came in, shook hands, sat down, smiled. "How do you do, Mr Poole?"

In imagination, Les Poole had expected a tall girl with black, tangled hair, gypsy eyes, dressed in red. The real Poppy Carew was slight, medium size, with plain, straight, fawn-coloured hair, dark green eyes, black lashes, large mouth with rather too many teeth. She wore no make-up and a black shirt and skirt. She looked sensible. She will need to be, thought Les Poole.

"It is a rare pleasure to give good news," said Les Poole, giving the folder a little shake, as though saying to it: wait until you are spoken to.

"Yes," said Poppy, looking intelligent.

"Yes. Well, then. We come to the investments. Your father used to call them—"

"Life's Dividends."

The bank manager frowned. "The best birthday present she will ever have had, is what he called them to me."

"My birthday is on Saturday," said Poppy, thinking, And so is Dad's funeral.

"Ah, indeed, yes, well. Here is the list." He glanced out at the late September sunshine. So much for Armistice Day. He handed a list from the folder across the desk. Poppy took it. She did not, he observed, paint her nails: he must tell Amanda (aged fifteen). "A rich girl like Poppy Carew," he would say, "does not paint her nails black." Amanda would answer, "So what?" At least he would have tried. He watched Poppy read the list, eyebrows rising.

"Gosh," said Poppy, handing it back as though afraid it might snap. "Gosh!"

"There are too some capital sums," said Mr Poole, bestowing his benison.

"So Anthony Green told me. What's it mean?"

"Your father meant it to mean that if you wanted, immediately, to buy a house, buy a car, go on holiday, you could do so without disturbing the investments which are your income."

"An income from investments." Was her tone derisory, or respectful? Hard to tell.

"Yes, Miss Carew." A girl like this should now say, Oh, do call me Poppy. She didn't.

I am stunned, thought Poppy. How did he come by all this? It's difficult to realise one's the child of a gigolo. She noticed the bank manager was waiting for her to say something. "I don't want a house. I apparently already own my father's. I don't want a car, Dad's just bought a new one. I might buy a little house in London." I never want to see my flat again, she thought. "A little house would be nice." And she added, to please this harmless man (bet he never jilted anyone, far too square), "It would be a good investment."

Has she really got too many teeth, or is it her jaw formation? Marjory would know. If I were younger, I'd call that mouth sexy, thought Les Poole, a generous mouth. "If the house is in a good neighbourhood it would be considered a good investment," he said gravely. "You might find one in an area which is coming up. I have clients who swear by Islington or Bow."

"I don't," said Poppy. "I'd just like to get away from where I live now. I'll look south of the Park."

"There's no hurry," said the bank manager. Somehow this girl looked capable of foolish impetuosity. It wasn't just the mouth which was sexy; those breasts, well, leave the breasts, pay attention, she was asking a pertinent question.

"How much, Mr Poole," she had taken the trouble to remember his name; quite a lot of people didn't, "how much exactly is my income?"

Les Poole made pretence of studying the list as though for the first time, then named the sum calculated on the computer the previous day.

Poppy said, "Wow! Shall I be stung for income tax?"

"I fear so. We shall, of course, always be happy to advise and help, Miss Carew – no charge of course."

"Do call me Poppy," said Poppy relenting, though not liking patronising avuncular men (I'm not *that* stupid).

"Thank you." He paused.

Poppy looked expectant. What other surprise did this old boy have in store, what shock? "Just one thing more. Your father left a letter for you, with us, in the event of his demise . . ."

Why can't he say death? Dad's dead, bloody dead, stiff.

"It's in our vault, Miss Ca— Poppy, shall I send for it?"

"Yes please." (Pompous ass.)

Les Poole spoke into the telephone, "Ida, ask Mr Dunne to bring me the letter for Miss Carew."

"Righty-ho, Mr Poole," Ida crackled.

"She's leaving us to get married," Mr Poole informed Poppy, who said, "Really?"

They waited. Poppy's eyes roamed over the desk, the photographs, the blotter, Mr Poole's feet in neat black pumps, his perfectly creased trousers, navy blue socks.

Les Poole decided that Poppy's legs were long in proportion to her body, and approved. Marjory's would be better longer.

Mr Dunne brought an envelope which he handed to Mr Poole, who passed it across his desk to Poppy.

Mr Dunne swept the discreet eye of a future bank manager over Poppy and left the room.

Poppy eyed the letter addressed to herself, "Poppy Carew", in Dad's large handwriting, with an exuberant "Top Secret" flourishing right across the envelope under her name. She put it in her bag. She stood up, holding out her hand.

"Thank you very much indeed, Mr Poole, for all your trouble."

"Delighted . . . of help . . . any time." Her hand was small, dry, firm (no rings, he must tell Amanda).

"Would you perhaps be kind and come to Dad's funeral, Mr Poole? And Mrs Poole, if she would bother?"

"We would be honoured." What a fool thing to say, the girl's father was nothing more than a—

"Saturday," said Poppy. "I'll put a notice of the time in the paper."

"I can find out from Brightson's—"

"I don't think you'd find out much, but there will be a notice. Goodbye, Mr Poole. Thank you so much."

She was gone, the letter hidden in her bag. It would have been interesting to know what was in it. One had some pretty funny clients, banking had its moments.

Pushing through the swing door into the street, Poppy was muttering: "Can't have him advising me on undertakers, like Anthony Green; it's too much. I'll read Dad's letter when I can find somewhere quiet, when I feel calmer."

She got into her father's car, adjusted the seat once more to get it right for her length of leg, checked the mirrors, fastened the safety belt and headed towards the point on the map where, hidden in a fold of the downs, Furnival's Funerals had its establishment. As she drove, she wondered whether Dad would like Mr Poole to be at his funeral, or, for that matter, Anthony Green. Now I come to think of it, she thought as she drove, he must have despised all those respectable people: not very nice of you, Dad, while you were laying up store in heaven, placing your bets, living it up with ladies. I wish I'd taken the trouble to know you, Dad, instead of panicking about interference. Perhaps you were too busy collecting Life's Dividends to interfere seriously. Wish I'd known you better, Dad: too late now. Never mind, you shall have your funeral. So she tried to stifle her feelings of guilt and remorse.

SEVEN

By the time Poppy found Furnival's, she was tired from driving up lanes which ended in farmyards, making three-point turns in the unaccustomed car, reversing when to turn was impossible, and when she stopped to ask the way at lonely cottages, the occupants were either out or professed ignorance. On the point of giving up, going home and ringing up Brightson's, as advised by Anthony, she spotted a painted board on a gate leading to a grassy track which said "Furnival's Fine Funerals". It led her gently up a valley, running parallel to a small stream until, rounding a corner, she came upon a group of faded brick buildings crouching, in secret isolation, under the downs. Parking the car beside a battered Ford, Poppy pushed through a door in a brick wall to find a yard, neatly cobbled, flanked on two sides by looseboxes, from each of which, benignly, stared a horse.

In the middle of the yard there was a stone trough and a pump. A very old sheepdog lay asleep in the sun. Poppy walked towards the dog, who raised his head, flapped his tail but did not rise. Poppy looked round for a bell or knocker, but found none. She crossed the yard to a barn which formed the fourth side of the yard, opened a door and peered in. It was dark, but sunbeams, striking through cracks in the tiled roof, showed what she took to be a tractor, covered by plastic sheeting. Crossing the barn, she ventured through a door into an untidy garden, a-hum with bees feasting on golden rod and Michaelmas daisies. A weedy path led to a brick cottage, its door propped open by a stone. Poppy knocked, knocked again and peered in. A large cat, lolling on a chair, one leg hanging nonchalantly towards the flagged floor, stared at her with insolence.

Poppy called, "Anybody there?"

The cat stared, Poppy called again. There was no response, only the sound of bees and rooks cawing, as they floated up the valley to a stand of beech. Poppy went back to the yard to wait. She presumed somebody would come, eventually, to tend the horses.

She idled round the yard, speaking to each horse, gratified by the friendly snuffling and whickering as they made her welcome. She breathed in the stable smell, enjoyed the silky feel of well-groomed necks and soft noses. The old dog lurched to his feet and walked beside her in amiable companionship. She began to relax from the pain of the last few days, appreciating the sunshine and the gentle animals.

One of the horses turned from nuzzling her face over its box-door, to lurch across and blow draughtily down its nose into a manger. At once, a baby caterwauled loudly. Startled, and unable to see more than tiny feet and fists, bunched in a reverse attitude of Muslim prayer, Poppy peered into the loose-box.

How to effect a rescue?

Gingerly, she opened the box-door. The horse swung round, laid back its ears and bared yellow teeth. Poppy retreated fast.

"What d'you want to wake him for? Bloody hell."

A thin girl in black jeans and T-shirt, ink-black hair brushed up spikily, appeared at Poppy's side, pushed past her into the loose-box, slapped the horse's rump, "Out of the way, there," snatched up the baby, who at once stopped bawling. "I told that sod not to put him there again." She banged shut the stable door and walked away. Over her shoulder, the baby stared reproachfully at Poppy with round black eyes.

"Well," said Poppy to the horse. "Well!"

The horse, calm again, made a huffle-wuffle sound and stamped its hoof. Poppy went and sat on the edge of the water trough, shaken by the girl's anger. The old dog flopped down at her feet and resumed its snooze. The yard was silent. Poppy did not feel equal to following the girl and the baby. The large cat sauntered through the yard to sit a few yards from her, and stare offensively, unblinking. Seeking solace, Poppy opened her bag and took out her father's letter.

Poppy love,

1. *Never lend, give.*
2. *Never marry unless you are certain sure you cannot live without the fellow.*
3. *Don't be afraid to back outsiders.*

Love, Dad.

She put the letter back in its envelope. There was no indication of when it had been written. She felt no wish to ask Mr Poole, it would show how little she had known her father. Nor would she ask Anthony Green.

Resentfully, she mulled Dad's advice. Had he guessed that she lent money to Edmund? Had she been certain sure she could not live without Edmund? She was, she thought ruefully, without Edmund as she sat here in this stable yard, still living; and what did Dad mean by outsiders? She considered her father. He had been kind and, she supposed, caring. There had been a housekeeper to keep house, she had been clothed, educated, fed. Had he loved her, had she loved him? She felt unsure. He had been away so much. She had been away so much, first at school and then, after the rows over Edmund, away for good, only keeping a tenuous connection – thanking belatedly for the postcards. He sent her postcards from all over England. Even in childhood the postcards had dropped through the letterbox. What had he been doing? – he had no job. He had been (she stared back at the cat), he had been at the races with those ladies who produced Life's Dividends, she thought censoriously, remembering that Edmund seldom repaid her loans, took money she could ill afford as of right.

"Sod Edmund," she said aloud, staring back at the cat, "sod him, sod him, sod him." At her feet, the old dog wagged his tail. "And sod you too, Dad," she murmured with amused affection, "landing me up in this place, miles from anywhere, to fix you up with a rococo funeral." I will miss him, she thought, miss the occasional lunches in London restaurants, when we chit-chatted of nothing and he pointedly refrained from mention of Edmund. Curse Edmund, she thought. If it had not been for Edmund she might have known her father, that small man with dun-coloured hair, bright brown eyes and engaging laugh. She remembered the laugh, totally without malice. Perhaps that was his charm. He had charm, she thought, and loved her father as she sat in the sun on the edge of the water trough. "Shoo," she said to the staring cat, who lifted a leg and began to wash its parts.

Her reverie was interrupted by voices. Several rather wet dogs ran into the yard, followed by two men. One man was mocking the other.

"You were never so tender-hearted when Penelope nearly drowned that time," he said, laughing.

"She could swim; besides, I wanted shot of her," said the other.

"So you did, and did get shot. What a pain she was. Aha, here's my client, Miss Carew. I expected you to be much older." He made a rapid inventory of Poppy's finer points. "Down," he said to a Labrador who was preparing a boisterous greeting.

"Sorry we weren't here to greet you. Victor – this is Victor, Victor Lucas – had a—"

"There was a baby . . ." stuttered Poppy.

"The infant Jesus, I'd forgotten. I put him down while we went to the stream."

"A girl, your . . ." Poppy hesitated to say "wife", though this man had eyes not unlike the baby.

"That's Mary, its mother, one of my grooms. Found it, did she? Keeps house too after a fashion."

"Yes."

"That's OK then."

"But the horse might have—"

"No, no, best baby-sitter in the place. Did Mary create? She shouldn't have left it with me. I told her I couldn't be bothered. My name is Fergus," he held out his hand, he wanted to touch this girl, "and this is Victor as I said." He clasped Poppy's narrow hand and held it a moment. "You've come about your father's do. Furnival's Fine Funerals, that's me, Fergus to you."

"Yes." Poppy did not dislike the handshake, but was shocked by the cavalier attitude to the baby. In her turn, she had visualised an older man, grey haired, dignified. This man couldn't be much more than thirty and struck her as altogether too light-hearted to run a funeral establishment, almost jokey. On the other hand, she knew instinctively Dad would have warmed to him.

"Let me show you round," said Fergus. "Sorry to keep you waiting. Victor had a fishy friend who had to be rehoused. You've met the horses, I take it. Come and see the tack room and the hearse, then we can discuss the rest in the house over tea. Be a good friend, Cousin Victor, tell Mary to put the kettle on and, if she won't, tell one of the others."

"They're out," said Victor, who had not taken his eyes off Poppy since their meeting. He made no move to carry out Fergus's request.

"Well then, you do it," said Fergus impatiently. "This way, Miss Carew."

He led the way to the barn. Poppy followed, taking stock of the tall dark young man not much older than Edmund but, unlike Edmund, magnificently fit.

"Do you jog?" she asked.

"Jog?" Fergus grinned. "No need to jog if you have six horses and are humping bales of hay and mucking out all day."

"I thought the girls did most of that," said Victor drily.

"Do you jog, Miss Carew?" Fergus ignored Victor, his dark eyes met Poppy's, his grin showed teeth Edmund would have envied, he being sensitive about his one gold-capped eye tooth.

"No," lied Poppy, "of course not." (Why must I keep thinking so nastily of Edmund?)

"Do you jog, Victor?" Fergus decided, since he would not go and tend the kettle, to include Victor. "You didn't jog from the fishmonger's, you ran like the clappers."

Victor laughed, catching Poppy's eye.

"Victor lives in London. You must get him to tell—"

The roar of a motorcycle drowned Fergus's voice, as a heavy Yamaha bounced through the door into the yard, coming to rest by the drinking trough. Two figures, wearing heavy boots, studded leather jackets, jeans and crash helmets, got off the machine.

"You are late, girls," shouted Fergus above the noise of the engine, as the rider revved it for the last time before stilling it. The riders took off their helmets and shook free a quantity of hair. "Annie and Frances," said Fergus. "My stable girls."

"Hi," said the girls, quite friendly. "Hi."

"Put the kettle on, one of you."

"Why can't Mary? It's still our time off."

"She's feeding infant Jesu, found him in the stable."

"His name's Barnaby," said the girl, Frances, wheeling the Yamaha towards a shed. In spite of her tough appearance, she sounded maternal.

"Poor little bugger," said the girl called Annie. "He'd be much better off living with the family. I can't see the grandmother leaving him in a manger."

Poppy made a lightning readjustment of the baby's parenthood. Fergus, noting this, said, "The father's called Joseph. The girls met on holiday on the Costa."

Annie and Frances laughed, exchanging sly looks. Then, returning to the point where he had been interrupted by the Yamaha, Fergus drew Poppy across the yard towards the barn. "As I was saying. Victor had this trout he brought from London. He knew it wouldn't last long in his bath; London water's passed through twelve pairs of kidneys before you drink it. Did you know that?"

"No," said Poppy bemused.

"No trout, Victor thought, could stand that. Wouldn't survive like you or me, so he SOS-ed me and brought it here."

"What was it doing in the bath?" Is this supposed to be a joke, Poppy wondered: perhaps Dad would find it funny.

Fergus explained the trout's career, Victor's dilemma, the mercy drive down the motorway. "We were seeing it settled in the stream in the orchard. Victor's tenderhearted."

"I am," said Victor, still studying Poppy (what a super girl).

"Couldn't let it drown, could I?" he said, contriving to catch her attention, pleased that she seemed impressed by the saga, hoping to tell her more.

"He was quite different with his wife," said Fergus, noticing Victor's attempt. "She divorced him."

"The trout was helpless," exclaimed Victor, "drowning, gasping." He gaped at Poppy as the fish had gaped on the fishmonger's slab, trying, at the same time, to indicate that his ex-wife Penelope was not the helpless sort.

"Well it's OK now," said Fergus, who had had enough of the trout. He took Poppy's elbow. "Come and see the hearse." He propelled her towards the barn. "Be a kind friend and pull the sheet off, Victor."

Victor gave a tweak to the plastic sheeting Poppy had observed earlier.

"That suit your father?" asked Fergus.

"Oh!" cried Poppy, overwhelmed. "Yes." Then, "Where did you find it?"

"In France," said Fergus, proudly. "Restored it, then I found the tack, the fittings, bought the horses, broke them in for driving, got them used to wearing the harness, plumes and so on. Come and see." Still holding her elbow, he led her to the tack-room.

"Oh," said Poppy, gazing at the ornamented harness, black ostrich plumes, the richly caparisoned rugs. "Dad will love it . . . would." She was moved almost to tears. "It's exactly what he would want."

Victor, who had followed behind Poppy and Fergus, thinking it was time Fergus let go the girl's arm, that her hair was rather nice even if it was mousy, and those were very nice shoulderblades, said, "What about that tea?"

"Ah yes," said Fergus, looking at his watch. "Tea, and of course . . . er . . . um . . . business."

"Business," agreed Poppy, pulling herself together, "of course."

"Come to the house, we'll have tea in my office," said Fergus, leading the way. "I take it your father's in cold storage?"

Poppy did not answer.

"You want the funeral on Saturday, don't you? That's what you said. Today's Tuesday."

"Oh," Poppy began to cry. "God."

"Oaf!" said Victor to Fergus. "Tactless oaf. Cold storage . . ." He stepped towards Poppy who, through her tears, noticed him properly for the first time. Long, thin, sinuous, so slender he could be drawn through a napkin ring; the shape of man poor Edmund would have liked to be.

Oh fuck Edmund, she thought, laying her tearful face against

Victor's chest. Victor gave her a brief hug with thin but muscular arms. (This is not the time, not in front of Fergus.)

"Tea first, and then business." He quickly wiped Poppy's eyes. "There." Perhaps she's one of those girls who are in love with their father, he thought. No, she can't be. "Tea," he said, repeating the formula.

"Actually," said Poppy, "I'm pining for a drink. Is there any whisky?"

EIGHT

The office, which was also the cottage kitchen and living-room, was crowded, having to fulfil more roles than there was room for. Kitchen equipment overlapped with typewriter, account books and stationery. A pile of freshly washed baby clothes took up room on the kitchen table. The dogs pressed up to the stove, edging away from the cat. A gun was propped in a corner, a game bag in another. There were two top hats occupying one of the chairs: a heap of horse rugs in another corner and pieces of harness in the process of being mended or cleaned occupied more room. There was a long row of rubber boots by the door and the door itself groaned under the weight of coats and waterproofs hanging from hooks.

"Sorry about this," said Fergus, "space is at a premium. We really need a much bigger house, but do come in and find somewhere to sit."

The girl with spiky black hair now shared the chair with the cat. She had hitched up her T-shirt and was suckling the infant Barnaby, who rolled lollipop eyes at Poppy without interrupting the business in hand. His mother stared stonily at Poppy. Victor, averting his eyes, muttered greetings which the girl, Mary, ignored.

"Hi, Jesu," said Fergus, moving towards a walk-in larder. Mary stuck out a foot, he tripped and nearly fell. "Ouch!" he said, regaining his balance. "Damn you."

Mary said, "Barnaby," with soft menace, "his name is Barnaby."

"All right, Barnaby." Fergus reached for a bottle of whisky. "Miss Coquelicot needs a drink. Miss Coquelicot Carew, esteemed client of Furnival's Fine Funerals." He poured a stiff tot into a tumbler and handed it to Poppy. "Sit down, sit down; please sit down." He smothered embarrassment with jocosity.

Poppy sat on a chair pushed forward by Victor and gulped the whisky which, travelling at speed into her system, began its revivifying effect. From a room above she could hear girls' voices and laughter, there was a sudden rush of water down a pipe by the cottage door, the scent of shampoo drifted into the kitchen.

"Out of interest," said Fergus, filling a kettle and setting it to boil on the stove, "why are you called Poppy?"

"Poppaea," said Poppy, aglow with whisky. "Dad was interested in the Romans." No need to tell them he was a milkman.

"Didn't she get hitched to Nero?" Victor had no intention of being excluded from the conversation, and considered his erudition more shapely than Fergus's.

"He treated her bad, kicked her when she was in foal," said Fergus, deliberately horsey to irritate Victor.

"Sod." Mary switched the baby to her other breast and resumed her silence, ignoring Poppy. Her anger double-wrapped about her.

"Did you ever kick Penelope?" Fergus asked Victor. "His ex-wife," he informed Poppy. "Very pretty girl."

"Would have liked to but didn't." Victor helped himself to whisky and watched Poppy.

"Soft-hearted," said Fergus jeering. He collected cups and saucers from a varnished dresser which had one worm-eaten foot supported by a brick. "Hence the trout," he laughed as he rattled the china. "Perhaps you are only a softie to cold fish: there must be a moral of some sort there. Don't you think so, Miss Carew?" He spooned the tea into a brown teapot.

"Do call me Poppy," she used the whisky's false courage, "silly name though it is."

"I like it," said Fergus and Victor in unison. Mary sniffed, narrowing fine nostrils, rolling supplicatory eyes at the ceiling.

Fergus found plates and knives. "Any scones?" he asked. "Or cake?"

"In the larder," said Mary, not looking up, devoting herself to the baby.

"You realise," said Fergus maliciously to Victor, "that on that fishmonger's slab were oysters equally alive and lobsters, alive too; I know the shop."

"They did not gape." Victor put an end to the subject.

Poppy remembered her father in death. If this goes on, she thought, I shall never get anywhere. I came here for Dad, not to listen to these men girding at one another. She cleared her throat. "Furnival's Fun Funerals—" she began.

"Aah!" cried Fergus. "It was a wicked misprint. I shall sue the editor." He put a plate of scones in front of Poppy. "It's Furnival's Fine Funerals," he emphasised the word "fine", thumping his fist on the table.

"Dad seemed to have taken to the fun part." Poppy felt embarrassed.

"Your dad must have been quite a character. Come on, eat your tea. Butter, jam," he produced these from the larder, "then we shall plot him a slap-up do, and Victor shall write an article which will be syndicated all over the country. You did not know Victor was a writer, did you?"

"Manqué," said Victor, deprecatory, modest. "Extremely minor."

"Only up to now. We'll get him launched, won't we, Poppy?"

Poppy said nothing, not having previously met anyone with literary pretensions.

"Just a humble journalist," explained Victor. "Freelance."

"Dad wouldn't want, I don't want, publicity," Poppy took fright. "I don't think . . ." but perhaps Dad would enjoy publicity; how was she to know.

"Of course not, of course not," cried Fergus. "Now then, to business. Time to stop fooling."

Mary put the baby against her shoulder and patted its back. It gave a prolonged burp.

Fergus said, "Oh God! Sick next."

Mary left the room, carrying the baby. Frances, her head wrapped in a towel, pushed past her into the room. "I must use the telephone—"

"No, you must not. Push off, use it later, can't you see I'm doing business? This isn't a madhouse."

"Not a bad imitation." Frances retreated in a waft of shampoo.

Fergus shouted after her through the open door, "When will you learn to wait for the boys to ring you? You frighten them away by your pursuit, you'll never have a lasting relationship this way."

Out of sight Frances riposted, "Your love life's not all that brilliant, and it's the telephone bill you fear for, not my single state."

Fergus closed the intervening door.

"That's better. Now then. Time. Place. Four horses, you said. Wreaths? Mutes? Would you like a special coffin for your father, or to have whatever he's in draped with a pall? I have a fine black velvet I found in Stroud, or would you prefer purple?"

"Black," Poppy whispered, beginning to shake.

"Black it shall be, and where did you say your dad is now?"

Poppy began to cry again, more from the onslaught of whisky than grief. (It's not Dad I'm weeping for, it's Edmund.)

"Butter her a scone, Victor," said Fergus; then, as Victor did so, he said gently, "I suppose he's stuck in the hospital morgue." Poppy nodded. "We can fetch him from there, you know, Poppy; would you like to have him at home until the funeral? We can arrange that too, he could lie in state."

"At home," said Poppy in a low voice. "Please."

"Right, I'll fix all that presently on the phone. Eat your scone now."

Victor handed Poppy a scone, ready buttered, which she obediently ate.

"Drink some hot tea, try." Victor was solicitous, pushing the cup towards her.

"All right." She drank the scalding tea.

The two men watched her with concern. Fergus ruffled his thick black hair. "I have so little experience," he apologised. "I know the rules and all that, but not how to behave to clients. We've only done two funerals. One was a pop person, bit of a shambles that, and the other—"

"Anthony Green, Dad's – I mean, my – solicitor said it was an IRA, he said—"

"No, no. It was a vagrant. We wanted a practice run. The poor devil had been sleeping rough. We gave him the works, it annoyed the Council who had to pay, it was not exactly the pauper's funeral they intended."

"He was a wino," said Victor, "Mary said."

"What if he was? He was entitled to something," Fergus was aggressive, "man in the image of God and so on."

"Oh!" exclaimed Poppy. "Oh!" She mourned for the vagrant, for her father, for the girl Mary and her baby, for Edmund, for the two men watching her, their expressions kind. "I'm not usually lachrymose," she cried, "I feel so guilty, I hardly knew him. I never paid any attention to what he wanted unless to do the opposite. Oh," she snuffled.

Wisely Victor and Fergus let her cry.

"I'm sorry," she said presently, "it's a whole lot of things, it's . . ."

"I apologise for clowning," said Fergus hoping to console.

"Me too," said Victor. "I am fundamentally serious."

"Everybody feels guilty when someone dies." He sat beside Poppy and offered a kitchen tissue. "Mop."

"What about your mum, is she . . . ?" Victor asked.

"Died when I was a baby." Poppy wiped her eyes on the tissue.

"So you can't feel bad about her."

"I suppose not." Poppy smiled weakly and blew her nose.

"That's better." Fergus grew brisk. "Now we plan. Come on." He reached for a notebook. "Name, address, hospital, parson or priest, church? Let's get the forms filled in."

Poppy supplied the information, signed where told to sign, drank her tea, watched Fergus fill in forms.

"That's about it." Fergus stood up. "The rest I'll do on the telephone. Now come and meet the Dow Jones."

"The who?"

"The average horses. It's a joke, you are supposed to laugh."

Poppy obliged. "I've met them," she said.

"Come and meet them again. They are what shops call 'seconds', not good enough to get into the Horse Guards or Police, but good enough for Furnival's."

"What about eats?" asked Victor, following them out of the cottage. "After the service people expect a binge."

"Do they?" Poppy was appalled. "I've never been to a funeral, don't know what's—"

"Like me to help?" Victor offered eagerly.

"Would you?"

"Love to. Will there be lots of relations, dozens of friends?"

"I don't know." Poppy thought of the providers of Life's Dividends, presumably dead. "Not many friends," she said, "and no relations, we had no relations."

"What a mercy," muttered Fergus enviously.

"I suppose the village will come. I live in London, I hardly know . . . we didn't meet often. I think his best friends are dead." I wonder who they were, she thought; clever old Dad.

Victor and Fergus exchanged puzzled looks.

"Tell you what," said Victor. "Now you've fixed everything with Fergus, suppose I follow you home and suss the situation, then I can arrange the catering. What did your father like?"

"Champagne." Certainly champagne. Had champagne celebrated all those winning horses? Poppy visualised Dad in company with shadowy ladies at candlelit tables in intimate restaurants.

"I see."

"And spicy Indian food, or Chinese." The memory of a lunch with Dad, and Dad shying away from the subject of Edmund as he bit into a particularly fierce chilli. He was so lovable in retrospect, she had hated him at the time.

"Tell you what," said Victor again. "I'll fix it all. The booze at least we can get on sale or return. I don't suppose your father's friends are great drinkers."

What makes you suppose that, thought Poppy. It was drink that caused Dad's coronaries. "I wouldn't know," she said evasively.

Fergus noticed Poppy's expression. So her pa was a boozer.

"That's fixed then." Victor assumed Poppy's compliance. "I have an Indian chum in Shepherd's Bush who does a super take-away."

"Come and meet the horses," interrupted Fergus, furious with Victor. How dare he plot to go off with the girl, leaving him to slave. Spitefully, he wished he had not given the trout house room.

"I'm coming too." Victor jumped up. "I'm already brewing a superb article for Julia's mag, she won't be able to resist it, she might even come to the funeral." He visualised a double spread, illustrated; he must alert a good photographer, and why not TV while he was about it or was that going too far?

Poppy, beginning to wonder whose funeral this really was, accompanied Fergus to the stable yard. Annie, Frances and Mary were filling haybags, removing dung and carrying buckets of water, watched by baby Barnaby propped against a bale of hay. Sparrows chirped, swallows swooped, a portable radio blared, bantams pecked round the stable doors. There was a smell of horse and saddle soap. The girls sang to the radio and called to one another in cheerful voices.

Fergus led Poppy round the yard, naming each horse. "This one has a white blaze and two of them have white socks. We dye those bits black for the occasion. Mary's got the dye. She's a natural blonde," he stroked an equine nose, "gets carried away and dyes her own."

"I see," said Poppy. "That accounts for her white skin. How thorough you are. Dad will – would – love this." She looked again at the hearse, the tack-room and the splendid harness, the sombre ostrich plumes. "Do you muffle their hooves?" she asked, remembering something she had read, was it Sir John Moore after Corunna?

"No," said Fergus, who had never thought to do so. "That makes the scene a bit macabre."

"How do you get to the, er . . ."

"Location?"

"Yes."

"I have horse-boxes and a lorry for the hearse. We get ourselves sorted out and hitched up half a mile or so from the pick-up or the church."

"Like a circus," said Poppy, giving mortal offence.

"If you say so," Fergus answered stiffly. Observing this, Poppy felt irritation: whose father is having this funeral, who is paying for this jamboree? She felt furious: who is hiring Furnival's Fine Rococo Funerals? "I expect you would like a cheque in advance," she suggested, putting Fergus in his place (I bet Brightson's wait months).

"Spot on," said Mary who was crossing the yard, baby on hip. She smiled brilliantly at Poppy, her previously hostile expression gone. Poppy caught a glimpse of the merry girl who had become entangled on the Costa.

"Certainly not!" exclaimed Fergus loftily. "Payment when the customer is satisfied."

"Ha, ha," said Mary, walking away, "ha, ha, ha," on a rising note.

Fergus exploded. "She's impossible since she had that child. Pretends to be unemployed. Draws single-parent benefit, knows all the dodges."

Poppy did not respond.

"That poor man is dying to marry her, writes to her every day, utterly lovelorn. What it must cost him in stamps – telephones. Fellow's a fisherman. But she's too grand, says the county would never accept him. You wouldn't take her for county would you?"

"I—"

"Her pa's probably one of your father's friends, he's my landlord, actually used to train racehorses here, gives her a colossal allowance, sent her to Westonbirt or Roedean I forget which—"

"Neither," shouted Mary, still in earshot.

"She enjoys slumming and playing the Gypsy Queen. I wish I'd never taken her on."

"Just for the ride," shouted Mary mockingly. "The ride."

Not thinking Fergus's relations with Mary her business, Poppy said, "All the same, if you don't mind, I would rather give you a cheque now. Let's say half. How much?"

Without hesitation Fergus named a hefty sum. Poppy gave a mental whistle but, fishing her cheque-book from her bag, wrote a cheque. It had better be good, she thought, underlining her signature. She handed the cheque to Fergus who pushed it quickly into his hip pocket.

Victor, breaking a thoughtful silence, suggested that it was now time they left.

"May I come with you in your car, I've run out of petrol?"

Poppy nodded.

As they drove away Victor looked back to see Fergus study the cheque, then wave it as though it had burned his fingers.

"He expects it to bounce," he told Poppy; or perhaps, he thought, he's waving it in triumph.

"It won't bounce." Poppy stopped the car. "You haven't run out of petrol, have you?"

"Just thought I'd try."

"Pretty feeble," said Poppy. "Run back for your car. I'll wait, and you can follow." She had recovered her cool and wondered why she had wept; she blamed the alcohol.

"OK." Victor got out of the car unprotesting.

"I take it Furnival's Funerals are short of trade." Poppy surprised Victor by her shrewdness.

"You could say that." He reassessed her.

"M-m-m." She drummed her fingers on the driving wheel. "What are you waiting for?"

"Sorry." Victor ran back to his car, the old Ford Poppy had seen when she arrived. While she waited, she thought of Edmund, the soul of convention, and how horrified he would be by the planned funeral, how he would have insisted on Brightson's, how he would, if asked, have prevented Dad lying, for his last days above ground, in his own house, how he would have implied this to be somehow insanitary. Oh Edmund, she thought, weakening, recollecting the feel of his body, the bristly hairs round his navel. Oh Edmund, impregnated with tact for all seasons, no wonder Dad did not like you. "This is Dad's funeral, not yours," she said out loud.

Catching sight in the driving mirror of Victor's car coming down the track, she put the car into gear, released the brake and drove on. How one wishes it were Venetia to feed the worms, she thought with venom; what a pity murder is illegal. She pressed her foot on the accelerator, deciding to wear Dad's festive dress in his honour. I am torn between the dead and the lost, she told herself histrionically.

NINE

Driving her father's car up to the front door of her home (she must get used to owning it) Poppy regretted her show of emotion. It had been ridiculous to cry on a strange man's chest, to give way to grief for Edmund. Naturally the two men thought her tears were for her father; it made her behaviour the more absurd. She decided to be businesslike with Victor, discuss the comestibles, show him the general layout of the house and nothing more. In decency she supposed she would have to offer him a drink. It occurred to her that if she searched carefully among her father's effects she might find some clues to his persona which now he was dead belatedly aroused her curiosity.

Victor, who had hoped to increase his knowledge of Poppy, found himself shown the ground floor of the house, the sitting-room with the French windows opening on to the garden, the kitchen where he would assemble what he called the eats, the cloakroom, and that was all.

Poppy offered Victor a drink. He accepted a vodka and tonic, and was put out when Poppy did not join him but stood plainly waiting for him to leave.

Victor took a swallow of vodka. "So," he said, "I will see about the drinks. Are you sure you want champagne?" If they discussed alternatives he could elongate the conversation.

"Sure," said Poppy. "Quite."

"Right," said Victor, "champagne it shall be. You have shown me your fridge."

"Yes."

"I had better hire glasses, you may not have enough."

"As you wish."

"The food I can get from my take-away friend in Shepherd's Bush. Will you leave it to me to make a choice of little eats?"

"Of course." Her flat tone indicated that they had been into all this already, no need to recap.

Victor sipped his vodka, spinning it out; she might not offer him another. He would have to leave if he put down an empty glass.

"If the weather's fine as it is today your guests can overflow into the garden."

"Yes." What guests? Who would come other than Dad's daily lady, Mrs Edwardes, a few curious from the village, local bores. She had invited Mr and Mrs Poole and Anthony Green. What a dreary party! She would have to invite the vicar. She tried to remember whether of late years Dad ever went to church. Had he not claimed to be quasi-agnostic? Was she doing right to have a church service? Oh Dad, look what you've let me in for.

"What about parking?" Victor sipped his drink letting it run back through his teeth into the glass.

"Parking?" Poppy was amused by Victor's ploy (does he think I don't notice?), watching her with his small pale eyes with dark pupils like a jackdaw's. "Parking?" she questioned.

"Yes. All the cars and for that matter Fergus." Grudgingly Victor mentioned Fergus.

"There's the road, the village green, there's the stable yard."

"Stable yard, could one see it?"

"Sure. Have another drink," she relented. "I will show you the stables." She watched Victor gulp the remains of the vodka, poured him another. "Across here." She led him through the garden. Victor, carrying his fresh drink, followed her.

"These are the stables, rather dusty and unused. The er – hearse horses could rest in them if—"

"Fergus has his horse-boxes, he can load up and go home after the ceremony. Get the horses home quickly after the job is what he'll want."

What makes him think that? He looked the sort to want to join in the champagne drinking, eat the eats. The girls too looked as though they would appreciate a party.

"I have to talk to the vicar," she said. "I've got a date." A grey lie, never mind.

"Right." Victor gave up, downed his drink. "I will ring you from London to confirm the logistics." Victor was fond of the word "logistics", brought to his attention during the Falklands War. He hoped one day to find a place for it in a novel.

"It's very kind of you." Poppy walked with him to his car. "It's extremely kind of you to be so helpful." Without this man could she have forced Edmund to help, appealed to his better nature? If he has one, she thought, sourly remembering the entwined figures by the Serpentine and other occasions when Edmund had not been altogether perfect. "Well," she said as they reached the car, "goodbye and thanks again."

"I'll be in touch. See you Saturday, 'bye." Victor waved as he drove off. She saw through me like a sieve, he thought with amusement. Glad she lives in London, it will be easier to get to know her there. "I won't live here," she had said in her father's house. "There may be a use for it, weekends perhaps." I wonder how I can stop Fergus seeing those stables, mused Victor as he drove towards London, unaware that Poppy, looking at the dusty buildings, had decided to ask Fergus for his advice about them, perhaps rent them to him if he expanded his business.

Fergus was the sort of man Edmund detested and another type he loathed would be Victor with his thin intelligent face. Edmund had no time for intellectuals. I wish I had stopped by the Serpentine and spat in his eye, she thought, and went to answer the telephone which was ringing.

"Hullo, Vicar." She recognised the hesitant insecure voice, not the sort to inspire confidence or lead one to higher things. Dad had once unkindly said "not enough spunk". "Hullo, Vicar. Yes please, it would be very kind if you would come round or we can discuss it now." She listened to the vicar, giving him half her attention while the picture of the girl with the spiky hair flitted across the other half. She supposed the baby's father was a Spaniard; if one went by the baby's face he must be a knock-out. The girl had been jolly rude. She must be unhappy to be so antagonistic. The vicar was talking about the grave.

"— the sexton says he can just fit it in the old graveyard with your mother."

"Dad will be pleased."

"— and the service? Have you any particular—"

"As simple as possible, he would, I would like, jolly hymns, sort of rejoicing."

"— ?" The vicar mumbled a doubtful query.

"Yes, Vicar, I do mean rejoice. He's had coronary after coronary, *he* will be rejoicing all that's over."

"If that's your – attitude."

"Yes, it is." Is he going to make difficulties?

"Most laudable. I – er—"

"It's not laudable, it's what Dad would feel so I must too. Surely you who believe in the after-life agree."

"I never knew your father well, ah – er – he never discussed his beliefs with me."

"I think he hedged his bets," said Poppy.

He would, wouldn't he, thought the vicar who, though he barely knew Bob Carew, had heard much said in the parish about Bob Carew's interests.

"To come back to the hymns," said the vicar, retreating to safer ground, "it's a bit difficult, it's—"

"No jolly hymns? Nothing suitable?" This vicar was eminently teasable.

"Suppose our organist, if I can get Mr Ottway to play – he's really very good – suppose we do away with hymns and ask Mr Ottway to play a lot of Bach."

"Brilliant idea."

"Oh good, then suppose, Miss Carew—"

"Poppy, please."

"Thank you. Suppose I come round tomorrow and we make the final arrangements. I can get details and fix times with Brightson's."

"Not Brightson's."

"What?"

"My father wished to have a firm called Furnival's."

"Oh." The vicar's voice dipped. "I see."

"I saw them this afternoon. They will be in touch with you, Vicar."

"Oh." The vicar sounded alarmed. "I see—"

"And I hope you will come back to the house afterwards."

"Thank you." On the other end of the line the vicar gathered strength. "Do I really understand that—"

"Yes, not Brightson's, Furnival's, it's perfectly legit, Vicar."

"Yes, yes of course. I'll telephone tomorrow." He sounded apprehensive, on the verge of protest.

"Thank you very much. Goodbye." Poppy waited for the vicar to ring off and presently telephoned *The Times*, the *Daily Telegraph*, and the local paper asking them to put in a notice of her father's funeral, spelling the name Furnival, making sure they got it right.

Left alone, Poppy walked about her father's garden, trying to visualise him as he used to be when she was a child. Mowing the lawn, sweeping up leaves, weeding. But she could not see him. Here behind the lilacs she and Edmund had kissed. Here, out of sight of the house, they had lain on the grass on hot summer evenings, their bodies touching. Dad, where are you, Dad? The leaves on the lilacs were now turned yellow, a hesitant breeze testing the quiet autumn air rustled the bushes, bringing back that moment when, sheltered from observant eyes by scented lilac and philadelphus, Edmund had pulled her down on to the grass, kissing her mouth, holding her body against his, hard, heavy urgent; had penetrated so that astonished she had whispered, "Go on, do that, don't stop," in her first exultant sexual success, "go on, don't stop, don't stop," with the selfishness of satisfied joy, and as it waned leaving her gloriously spent her father had called from the house and Edmund had frustratedly called her "you fool, you fool, you put me off" and then "damn your fucking father".

The breeze dropped as quickly as it had risen, a leaf from the lilac drifted crisply to the ground. Drily Poppy thought that never again had Edmund admitted her need before his own.

She bent down brushing the grass with her palm where this, her first sexual experience, had happened. Then the grass had been short dense deep green, springing, today it felt dry, brittle, rather dusty.

Poppy went back to the house. She would leave Edmund in the garden; the scenes she remembered were old anyway, seven, eight years old, an age of ignorance. She wandered through the empty rooms seeking her father, thinking now of the unhappy girl Mary, with spiky hair and the beautiful baby.

When the telephone rang it was Fergus.

"They will bring your father early," his voice was kind, reassuring, "tomorrow."

"Thank you. What time?"

"Nineish or even before."

Perhaps with Dad actually in the house it would be easier to find him. She felt very tired. Climbing the stairs to bed, she decided she would sleep in the visitors' room. Edmund, so disliked by Dad, haunted her room. Poppy dismissed her fanciful thoughts. Dad was in his coffin and would be brought here tomorrow. Edmund would now be tucked up snug with Venetia in Venetia's flat after eating one of her delicious dinners. She was an impossibly good cook, spent lavishly on food.

As she was getting into bed the telephone rang in Dad's room across the landing.

"Hullo." She stood in her nightdress and bare feet.

"It's me again I'm afraid." It was the vicar. "Sorry to bother you."

"Yes?"

"I just wondered thinking about the service on Saturday and your wish for a cheerful hymn whether you had thought of any particular one so that I can apprise the organist. It is usual to have at least one hymn." The voice was gently insistent.

"Oh, I—" Poppy stood barefoot holding the receiver "Um – I—" she searched her mind: "The race that long in darkness—"? "How dark was the stable"? "There's a home for little children—". Dad was no child for Christ's sake! "Colours of day"? "The King of Love—"? "Oh Vicar, I can't."

"Perhaps," the vicar's voice was mild, "perhaps you could leave it to me?"

"Please. If that's—"

"Nothing lugubrious, nothing mundane, nothing the Bishop would take exception to."

"The Bishop? What's he got to do with—"

The laugh was both deprecating and dismissive. "His job to criticise, Poppy."

"I see." I don't see, all I see is Edmund in Venetia's arms. Does he explore her teeth for stoppings with his tongue as he did mine? The vicar was still talking.

"— so if you leave it to me I will make sure you have something your father would like."

"Leave it to you?" First Fergus, then Victor, now the vicar. There is nothing left for me to do. "Do you know what Dad would like?" She felt doubtful.

"Certainly I do," said the vicar.

"All right, Vicar. If you are sure, I will."

"Good." He did not ring off, waited for her to thank him, end the conversation.

"Is there anything else?" he asked.

"No, no, nothing else. Thank you. I am sure you will make a suitable choice." The vicar laughed again in an affectionate way. "You have been so kind."

"— my job."

"Well good night, and thank you again."

Has Venetia found out yet how he picks his teeth?

TEN

Late in the afternoon, Mary, baby on hip, came up to Fergus. "Now you can pay the rent. And the feed bill." Her tone was sarcastic.

"In part perhaps—"

"Father didn't rent you this place for free."

"I wish your father would take a—"

"Running jump," said Mary. "I'm with you there." Her tone was quite hearty.

"Really?" Fergus was surprised.

She watched Fergus. "Have you thought about this place in winter?"

"Winter?" Her voice implied a catch.

"It gets snowed in. You won't find your business possible without a snow plough. Father's known it cut off for weeks, months, in some winters." She waited for Fergus's reaction with relish.

"So that's why he rented it so cheap, the crafty bastard." Fergus thought of Nicholas Mowbray's weather-beaten face, expansive gestures, fruity voice.

"He thinks I'll get over my horsey phase if I am frozen and uncomfortable."

"You can nip back to Spain to warm up in Joseph's arms," Fergus suggested.

Mary ignored this gibe. "He thinks you're a sucker. He doesn't mind if you go bankrupt; all he thinks is that I might decide to try a job he would consider sensible if this one packs up."

"Like secretary to an oil mogul?"

"I wouldn't last long." Mary let off a peal of laughter. "You should have checked the advertisement before posting it," she jeered. "You are not competent. You know I can hardly type."

Fergus eyed her without animosity: her typing error had brought him Poppy's father. I am a simpleton, he thought. I rather took to Mary's father and his bonhomie: he is using me, I shan't pay the rent, there are far more urgent bills. Ruefully he considered the pile of buff envelopes on the kitchen mantelshelf.

Forgetting Mary, he stood looking down the valley, seeing all too clearly how cut off he could be. He thought, I could get the horses out, but where would I take them? His enthusiasm for his project had led him to jump at the cheap rent suggested by Nicholas Mowbray. He flinched, thinking of the monthly payments on horse-boxes, Land-Rovers and the lorry. The horses are mine, he thought, seeking comfort, the tack and the hearse are mine. He looked round the yard for reassurance from the horses, as they watched from their loose-boxes. I refuse to be defeated, he thought, I must make a success of this. He said nastily, "What a bloody little Cassandra you are. There's no necessity," he cried angrily, "for your single parent situation. I understand Joseph would like to make an honest woman of you, why don't . . . ?"

"Do you want to get shot of me?" Her voice quavered upwards in thin defiance.

Fergus ignored the question. "Wouldn't it be better for Barnaby?"

"Why are you so keen on marriage for me? You steer clear of it. You are as bad as my father, you want to see me pegged down."

"I should have thought Barnaby quite a peg." Fergus met the baby's eye. Barnaby smiled gummily.

"I can travel with him; a child is a carrier bag, a husband is a trunk."

"You wish to travel light?"

"For the present." Keeping her options open, Mary shifted the child from one hip to the other with a sensuous movement. Fergus appeared to have erased from his memory the horse-buying trip to Ireland when, for months, she had shared his bed. From Ireland, she had gone to Spain and returned with Barnaby. She stood looking down the valley, bleakly considering her options. She was glad she had planted the seed of unease in Fergus: he's too bloody pleased with himself, she thought, remembering him in Ireland. And, before Ireland, Fergus had had something going with Victor's ex-wife Penelope and, later, with the magazine editor Julia. "You and Victor are pretty close friends, aren't you?" she said with sweet malice. "Great sharers, keep your girls in the family."

"So, so." Fergus was not to be drawn. He was remembering Poppy's slip; circuses, he consoled himself, have winter quarters – so?

Standing beside him, baby on hip, Mary shied away from the thought of the extended family ready with its octopus arms to gather her in, coddle her in its expansive bosom. I can't live in Spain, she thought, I could never get used to that crowd. I shall get no help from Fergus. Despairingly she looked at her child who looked back at her with his father's eyes. "Oh!" Mary yelled in frustration. "Oh!"

At this moment Annie and Frances joined them. Both girls now smelled of shampoo. Frances looked extraordinary, which was her intention, in a skin-tight mini-skirt which barely covered her pubic region, an immensely baggy black jersey worn under a man's string vest, on her wrists a jingling collection of silver bracelets. Annie, demure in a flowing black dress, bare feet, plethora of earrings, red caste mark between her eyes, a diamond clipped to one nostril, had not succeeded in disguising her Sloane Rangership. "Coming to the disco?" they asked Mary. "Help us sort out the local boys?"

"All right," Mary was obliging. "I'll come as I am," she said. "You do look an old-fashioned pair." She eyed Annie. "Are you from the bazaar or the souk?" Annie laughed. "You won't mind baby-sitting Barnaby, will you?" She held the baby out to Fergus.

"No fear," said Fergus, "you can take your carrier bag with you." He started walking back to the cottage.

"We can't squash three on to the Yamaha," Annie was plaintive, "and a baby."

"Take us in your car," cried Frances to Fergus, "be a devil."

Fergus went into the cottage and slammed the door, locking himself in with his dogs. He wanted his supper. Fetching some chops from the larder, he watched from the window as the three girls wedged themselves on to the motorbicycle, and proceeded slowly down the track. They would return in the small hours in some local boy's car, noisy, part-drunk, happy.

"Such nice girls," Fergus said to the cat Bolivar who wove silently through the casement window to sit, paws together, preparing to terrorise the dogs with basilisk stare and, hopefully, lick the frying pan when Fergus had finished with it. The dogs shifted uneasily on their hunkers, casting sidelong glances at the cat, licking their lips, unable, since he was a favourite of Fergus's, to attack as they would have liked. Fergus gave Bolivar a snippet of raw meat, respecting the cat, an entire tom, for having shown guile and agility in escaping the vet on the day of his intended emasculation. Something about Bolivar set him thinking of Poppy Carew's father, wondering whether there was any similarity. I must not make a cock-up of this funeral, ruminated Fergus, frying his chops. That's a lovely girl, she shall have what her dad wanted, and who knows, he thought optimistically, it may lead to other work. Eating his supper, Fergus thought about Poppy and was a mite uneasy of the feelings she engendered. For, like Mary, he had a penchant for independence.

Having eaten, Fergus spent a session on the telephone. Then, plans made, he whistled his dogs and walked up the valley to the downs. Bolivar came too for the first quarter-mile, spoiling the dogs' joy by his sinister presence. Since he had found the hearse mouldering in a barn in France, he had put his savings and everything he could borrow into his business, bought the horses, their harness, the vehicles. Rented the yard and the cottage from Mary's father and was only now, deeply in debt, ready to start in independent practice.

Overheads are terrible, Fergus shuddered, thinking of the pile of bills, the monthly payments, the rising bank interest. Treading the springy turf, he blamed himself for being so unsuspicious of Mary's father who had, long ago, trained horses here, out of sight of snoopers. He reached the top of the valley and looked along the stretch of downland where the horses had galloped. There was no evidence now, on the short turf grazed by sheep, of the unsound animals dosed with anabolic steroids, innocent collaborators who had displayed their paces to potential buyers. Standing on the sweet turf, hearing the ghostly breath and drumming hooves of horses long gone, Fergus felt lonely, afraid, vulnerable.

Mary's father now farmed in East Anglia, growing surplus grain for the EEC. He had not been specifically warned, but hinted, out of the racing world. The old boy network had netted him and, humiliatingly, let him go, as too small to fry. He saw me coming, thought Fergus ruefully, remembering Mary's introduction followed by the helpful offer at low rent of the cottage and stables.

"Any friend of Mary's . . . glad to help an enterprising chap . . . wonderful to be your own master . . . bound to make a success." At this rate, I am bound to the bank, nothing belongs to me, my Dow Jones are in peril. Fergus stooped to peer in the fading light at a harebell still in flower in late September, and was glad that his landlord was too mean to spray and spread fertiliser, kill the harebells, thyme and shepherd's purse. He felt sorry for Mary having such a treacherous father; he forgave her her careless typing and arrogance, guessing that she was warning him to be careful of her father by telling him what could happen when it snowed. Winter, after all, is the dying time, the boom time for undertakers. Had she not told Frances, a notorious blabbermouth, about the anabolic steroids and the end of her father's interest in horses? In Ireland buying horses, she had been invaluable, spotting defects he might have overlooked. He had been puzzled, at the time, by her esoteric knowledge.

Fergus straightened up as his dogs lit off in sudden noisy pursuit of a hare. He watched the hunt vanish over the hill, racing towards the moonrise, and waited for their panting, shamed return; standing on top of the quiet downs, watching the lights of distant cars on the main road and the sparkle of the town where Mary, Frances and Annie danced in the disco, almost he wished himself with them.

He knew Mary well enough to guess that Barnaby would be disposed of somewhere safe. And another thing, he thought, to Mary's credit. She had not tried to father the infant on him. It would have been possible, he would not have been able to disprove it. He had been galled and at a loss when shortly after Ireland she had vanished abroad without warning.

Many months later when searching for suitable stables he had run into her in Newbury. She had suggested her father as landlord. It had seemed natural to ask her to work with him again, she had brought with her Annie and Frances (to himself Fergus admitted that without Mary it was doubtful his venture would have got off the ground).

Watching the lights in the distance Fergus found himself hoping that it would be a long while before her love of travelling light inspired her to disappear a second time. A replacement would be difficult, well nigh impossible to find.

He recalled her hair had been long and thick-plaited like a corn dolly, oat coloured. Fergus winced at the thought of it now chopped short, often tinted an ugly black. He remembered the feel of the plait in his hand, the temptation to yank it like a bell pull. She had been more approachable then, less abrasive, perhaps less competent?

She did not speak of her year in Spain; what meagre information he possessed was gained from Frances and Annie's idle gossip, gossip which Mary made no attempt to elaborate, lurking behind her habitual reserve, a reserve which bordered on the inimical tinged with not unfriendly mockery. Cheered by thinking better of Mary than he normally did, and by the exhausted return of his dogs, Fergus ran back down the track to the stable. As he ran, his eye caught a glint of moonlight on the pool in the stream in the orchard, where, that afternoon, he and Victor had loosed the trout. He peered into the water, fearing to see it floating dead on the surface (as well it might after its vicissitudes) but, noting Bolivar sitting still and enigmatic, watching the water, he assumed its survival and went to bed, to sleep and forget his anxieties. It was only when the girls returned in the small hours, with Barnaby yelling and their boyfriends shouting raucous good nights, that he woke to worry as to whether Victor, going off as he had with Poppy, had stolen a march on him. Damn Victor, he thought, and damn those bloody girls.

"Shut up," Fergus flung open his window, "shut bloody up." The laughter trailed away then broke out again into bubbles of high spirits. Slamming his window shut, cracking a pane, Fergus thought they will wake the dead and the dead are my métier, as he drew the covers over his head to deaden the sound.

ELEVEN

Early the next morning, deserted by fickle sleep, Poppy lay in the visitors' bedroom thinking of her father. Although he had spoilt her as a child, never been angry, impatient or unkind, he had been much away leaving her with Esmé.

There had been between Dad and Esmé, a handsome woman referred to behind her back as "The Spirit of Rectitude", an uneasy truce. She insisted on brushed hair and washed hands, had been known to tell Dad to change his gardening clothes before sitting down to tea. Childhood had been punctuated by sharp commands: "wipe your feet", "clean your teeth", "go and have a bath", "don't bring that filthy thing into my kitchen, take it out at once". "Your mother" or "Mrs Carew" (depending on which of them she was addressing) "would not like that". When Esmé called on his wife's name for support Dad would laugh and say, "She wouldn't mind, Esmé. You are inventing her, building her in the image of past glories." Esmé had once been Nanny to a diplomat's children and was not averse to putting the Carews down a peg. Poppy had never been sure whether Esmé had actually known her mother, her own memories of her were hazy. There were the photographs in Dad's room, the recollection, vague, of Mum leaving on a trip abroad, of time passing and the eventual realisation that she was not coming back. That somehow she had been negligent, had died. Life had carried on, orderly, rather dull, with Dad constantly away. "Another card for you." Esmé would sort the post, picking through it with suspicion, sniffing at bills and appeals. Where were those postcards now? Restless, Poppy got out of bed, crossed the landing to her old bedroom, crouched down by the chest-of-drawers and began to search. What a lot of rubbish, old letters, broken toys, odd socks, snapshots of cats and dogs, school groups, junk jewellery and snaps of Edmund. Oh Edmund, did you really have your hair cut like that? And oh, I'd forgotten you tried to grow a moustache (it had been unkind of Dad to laugh). And the postcards, bundles of them, the message always the same, "Love from Dad, see you soon." Poppy turned them over, looking at the postmarks.

Cheltenham, Plumpton, Newcastle, York, Worcester, Wincanton, Newton Abbot, Chepstow, Brighton, Liverpool, Ascot. A litany of racetracks. He had been with those mystery ladies who dealt out Life's Dividends. Poppy sniffed the cards. Were the ladies beautiful, witty, sexy? Had Esmé known as she sifted the post what he was up to? Where was Esmé now? Alive? Dead? Esmé had liked Edmund, unlike Dad who had taken his instant dislike. She had encouraged Edmund, making him welcome, laying another place at the table (no trouble at all). She never did that for anyone else (can't have just anyone popping in without so much as a by your leave). Crouching by the drawer full of junk and memories, Poppy remembered Esmé's expression. She had been defiant, annoying Dad on purpose, getting a kick out of it. "Edmund will do you good," she had said. What had she meant by that? Had she meant Edmund will hurt you which was Dad's fear? I believe, thought Poppy, putting the postcards back in the drawer, I believe she fancied Edmund, how repulsive, eugh.

Soon after Edmund had become established as a fact, welcome or not, Esmé had retired, gone to live with her sister, showing no emotion at parting. Poppy remembered Esmé's voice, its rasping timbre. "My sister wants me. You are old enough to look after your father. I've arranged for Mrs Edwardes to come in and clean, she will do for you well enough." Esmé's voice had been contemptuous. Had the contempt been for the Carews or Mrs Edwardes? For us, thought Poppy, shutting the drawer, nobody could despise Jane Edwardes. At the time she had been shocked, realising that Esmé did not mind leaving, she and Dad had been a job, no more, she had wasted no emotion on them.

She didn't love us, thought Poppy, and to be honest we did not love her. Dad had suggested lunching out on the day of Esmé's departure. They had lunched in Newbury. Dad had raised his glass and said, "Let's drink goodbye to Rectitude." After another drink or two he had said, "I hope Mrs Edwardes won't moralise or encourage followers," a dig at poor Edmund. (Why do I pity him, the swine, tucked up with Venetia.) Briefly Poppy considered finding Esmé, asking her what she knew of Dad's life. Impossible. As impossible as to ask Mr Poole or Anthony Green exactly when the various dollops of dividends had appeared and in what quantities. It was extraordinary to have lived in the same house as Dad and not know what he was really like, shameful to have shown so little interest and to let him die a stranger. Am I too late? Poppy asked herself. Perhaps he did not mind, she thought hopefully, but if Dad had not minded he would not have been so inimical towards Edmund filling her life for ten years.

And now Venetia. "I hope she chokes him."

Poppy re-routed her search into Dad's bedroom. It was rather eerie going through his drawers and cupboards. Orderly, neat, smelling faintly of Dad. Shoes, socks, underclothes, suits, shirts, photographs of Mum smiling and one very sad and beautiful by his bed. She searched the dressing-table drawers. Indigestion pills, heart tablets, cufflinks, nothing to introduce or betray. Downstairs she searched his desk, fingering receipts, bank statements (might be a clue or two there, but the only ones kept were recent). A catalogue of a country house sale, writing paper, pens, paperclips, old indiarubbers, TV licence, dog licence (old Buster dead last year), racing calendars, snapshots of herself at school, on the lawn with her rabbit, in her bath (what a fat baby), none of herself with Edmund, Dad had not wanted any. (I don't need reminding.) Several drawers were empty. He must have tidied up, known he might die. Of course he had known. At another lunch – when, a year, two years ago? – he had said, "I might go any time, not to worry, it's the only certainty and I've enjoyed my life, I only grumble about one thing and that is beginning not to bother me." At the time she had thought he is coming round to Edmund, beginning to accept him. Now she realised, sitting back on her heels, feeling chilly in her nightdress, that what made Dad feel better were the first signs of Edmund's impending desertion. Clever Dad, you noticed before I did. Was it then you wrote me your letter and put it in the bank to wait?

And now for the locked drawer, the drawer Edmund had prised open with his neat bit of plastic, the drawer full of old letters.

"Other people's letters are a laugh. Lush, slush, sentimentality, let's see the sort of stuff they wrote to each other in their day." Edmund, giggling. Dad's letters to Mum and Mum's letters to Dad, tied in packets of ten or twelve with tape, the envelopes yellowed, the ink faded.

She had slammed the drawer shut, catching Edmund's fingers. He had black fingernails for weeks, months. He had hit her dancing about the room in agony. It was the first time he had hit her and she forgave him, crying, "Sorry, sorry, I'm sorry."

I'm not sorry now, she thought, pulling gently at the brass handles. She would find the key among Dad's things. The drawer opened sweetly, lightly, showing emptiness. Empty of Dad and Mum, empty of written evidence of their love. Dad had not trusted her, had withdrawn himself and her mother too.

She stood up remembering Dad coming into the house when he had been away, holding out his arms to hug her, "How's my Poppy love?"

★

Outside the hearse came to a discreet halt, the driver rang the bell, his mate stood by the hearse, waiting.

Poppy put one of her father's old coats over her nightdress and opened the door.

"Miss Carew?"

"Yes."

"We've brought—"

"Yes."

"Indoors, love?"

"Yes."

"A couple of chairs perhaps?"

"There are stools. Wait a moment." She must hurry to let Dad into the house. She ran to the sitting-room where his small television perched on a stool. "Here," she called, "help me with this." One of the men moved the television to the top of the desk, carefully displacing the silver photograph frame which held her mother aged seventeen. "There's another upstairs." The second man followed her, fetched down the stool.

As they carried Dad in Jane Edwardes drove up in her car. "Thought I'd come early, get you some breakfast." She put her arms round Poppy and hugged her. "Heard he was to come home. Still in your nightie, don't catch your death."

"I'm all right."

They watched the men settle the coffin on the stools. They were quick, expert, tactful, did their job and left.

"Go and pick a few flowers from his garden while I make your coffee."

Jane Edwardes handed Poppy secateurs. Poppy, walking in the dew listening to the birds in Dad's garden, remembered his favourite flowers and cut their stalks snip, snip, as he had done. A robin sang furiously asserting territorial rights. Edmund knew a lot about birds. Damn Edmund, don't come between me and my father, get stuck into Venetia.

Jane Edwardes had a bowl ready on the coffin. The house smelled of coffee. "That's better." She steadied a rose into place. "Looks nice. My nephew works for Brightson's—"

Oh, not that again.

"Tells me you are having Furnival's."

"Yes." (Must I be defensive?)

"The old bastards had the monopoly far too long, my nephew says. He's thinking, my nephew that is, of applying for a job with Furnival's, says Furnival's will soon be the 'in thing'. That's what the young ones are saying."

"Oh?"

"He, my nephew that is, my brother's son Bill, you know him?"

"Yes."

"He rang up Mr Furnival and offered to give a hand Saturday at the funeral—"

"How very—"

"He thought, well we all thought, the village would like it, you know just to show—"

"What?"

"We loved him, always had a joke your father. He gave them many a good tip in the pub too."

"Dad did?"

"Didn't you know?"

"No, no I didn't know." I didn't know the village loved him, I didn't know he went to the pub. "Thank you, Mrs Edwardes."

"Come and eat your breakfast, love."

"I'll come in a minute." Poppy stood by the coffin. This oblong box held the man with the unmalicious laugh, now silent. The capable hands which would never again pick flowers. "Pick flowers with the dew on them, they last better." She touched the flowers in the bowl, the late roses, rosemary, pink daisies, a few late lilies. I am making myself think these morbid conventional thoughts. Those hands, those fingers used a biro to mark many a race card, how I wish I'd known his companions at the races. Those strong fingers tore up all your letters, destroyed your past, wrote me that last short note. An appeal? An order? A warning, a suggestion?

"Fergus thought you would like these." She had not heard Mary come in. Did not recognise her at first. The black hair was washed clean and hung down as gold as Venetia's and as smooth. Mary looked prim in clean jeans and grey cotton jersey. She carried what looked like a black rug over her arm and held a wreath in her hand. "If you lift the bowl of flowers I will spread it for you, unless you want to do it yourself."

"Oh no." She drew back from the coffin.

"Hold this then a minute, it's the laurel wreath—"

"Oh."

As Poppy did not move Mary picked up the bowl of flowers herself. "These are nice. From his garden?"

"Yes." She watched Mary spread the pall over the coffin so that its edge, braided in gold, trailed down to the floor, replace the flowers. "Over his heart. Poor old boy, was it one of his coronaries?"

"Did you know him?" She was surprised.

"We used to meet at the races. I'd get him to mark my card. He had a nose for winners. Didn't know him well, people said he talked to the horses. There, that's better." She put the bowl exactly in the centre. "Of course he talked to the trainers too, and the wreath, how about that?" She propped the wreath at the head of the coffin. "Made it myself, worked for a short time at a florist's when I left school. It will smell nice when the room warms up." She looked sharply at Poppy. "It's bay, you know, not laurel. I pinched this lot from a garden I know. They won't miss it."

"I—" She longed to ask Mary who had been at the races with Dad.

"There we are." Mary brushed her hands together. "Do I smell coffee?"

"Come and have some."

"You been up all night?" Mary walked with Poppy towards the kitchen.

"Most of it." She could not question this stranger.

"Fergus sent me to take a look round the church, get the lay of the land, where to unload and hitch up the horses, that sort of thing."

"I see."

"I've done that. Nice church, nice village. Oh great, coffee." She took a cup handed to her by Mrs Edwardes and gulped it hurriedly. "Thanks a lot. Got to rush or Barnaby will be yelling for his feed. Many thanks." She put down the empty cup, "See you Saturday," and was gone.

"What a nice girl," said Mrs Edwardes, watching her go with an approving eye.

Poppy stood watching Mary walk to her car, get in and drive slowly past. As she drew level, Mary wound down the window and leaned out.

"Did you love your father?" Her eyes were questing.

"I hardly knew him." Why do I say that? It's the truth. Poppy met Mary's eyes.

Mary nodded. "It happens." She went on looking at Poppy, taking her in. "I can't stand mine." She smiled connivingly, slipped the car into gear, wound up the window and drove away.

TWELVE

Although he knew perfectly well that the trout was in Fergus's stream, on his return to London Victor looked in his bath to make quite sure it was gone.

The whole episode seemed out of context with his ordinary life. He screwed the bath tap, which was dripping, tighter. As he thought of the fish, his sympathy for its plight on the fishmonger's slab, he relived the comprehension in Poppy's eyes when she heard the story from Fergus. She had appeared to think his action natural, even reasonable, she had given Fergus an appraising look when he joked about it.

A girl like that, thought Victor, putting a clean sheet of paper into his typewriter, was not in the same league as his ex-wife Penelope who would have snatched the fish, gutted, filleted and grilled it for supper.

An occasion, buried in his memory, came hauntingly back. Staying with Penelope's parents – they had lately become engaged – he had been strongly tempted to backtrack, call the engagement off. Across the lawn a rabbit had struggled, pursued by a weasel. Fear paralysed the rabbit so that its limbs jerked, its eyes rolled, it could hardly move its legs. Penelope, leaping out of the window, had snatched the rabbit and wrung its neck. (Sitting at his typewriter Victor winced, remembering the crack of bone.) As Penelope leapt and ran towards the rabbit Victor had assumed she was racing to the rescue. He had been shocked when she wrung the rabbit's neck, had been too much in love to protest.

I suppose I was in love, thought Victor, setting the paper in position, testing the new ribbon. Good job all that's over, he told himself stoutly.

The ex-wife Penelope jumped nimbly out of the window and wrung the rabbit's neck, he typed.

I am a moral coward. If I had trusted my instinct I would have saved a lot of time, emotion, money. I didn't mind when she nearly drowned that time, I didn't mind when she slept around with a whole lot of people, Fergus included. I am damn glad to be shot of her, it wasn't love, it was lust, he assured himself.

Yup, this ribbon is OK, just lust. Victor tore the paper out of the typewriter, crushed it into a ball, threw it towards the grate, inserted a fresh sheet, started typing his article for Julia.

Two hours later he'd got it right, Julia would publish the article in her glossy mag, Julia's mag would pay. In no way could this interesting original piece hurt Poppy's tender susceptibilities. Victor experienced the euphoria of a man who has written consecutive paragraphs of decent prose. He looked up Julia's office number and dialled it.

"Oh, hullo Victor, I've—"

"I've got the article for you, Julia, you won't be able to resist it."

"Really?" She sounded quite friendly, the telephone suiting her contralto voice.

"Shall I come round with it and take you out for a drink? You're just leaving your office?"

"Yes, if you like. I've got a bit of—"

"We could go to that bar you like and if you like my article I'll stand you dinner afterwards."

"I'm trying to—"

"And then we could—"

"Victor," Julia shouted, "listen, I have some news for you."

"Oh Lord."

"It's good news, no Oh Lord about it."

"How's that?" Victor was suspicious.

"You know a year or so ago I said I'd show your manuscript to my publisher friend Sean?"

"Oh God. I'd forgotten. I'd rather forget."

"No you wouldn't, Victor. He got around to reading it. He likes it."

"What?"

"Likes it. Wants to publish it. He'll pay you an advance, Victor."

Victor was silent.

"Victor, are you listening? This means money."

"Julia."

"Yes."

"Is this novel about you know—"

"Your marriage to Penelope thinly disguised? Yes, it is."

"I thought I'd thrown away all the copies."

"You told me to throw it away when I'd read it."

"And you didn't?" Who can you trust, thought Victor with glee.

"I thought it was such a marvellous portrait of old Penelope" (Julia pronounced the name to rhyme with antelope) "that I kept it. She did give you a rough time, Victor."

"Well." Victor remembered the rabbit and the time Penelope nearly drowned. I could easily have helped her, he thought, but I didn't want to.

Julia was still talking. "Then the other day I showed it to Sean and he loves it, it's as simple as that. Screams with laughter."

"Laughter?" It's a tragic book, thought Victor, nothing funny about it. "Oh Julia—"

"So bring your article and give me dinner."

"What about libel?" Adjusting to having written a comedy (what's the difference, all great tragedies have a comic element) Victor remembered his novel. "I wrote that book with my pen dipped in cyanide."

"That's what Sean likes. He calls it stark. Penelope's far too vain to recognise herself, don't worry."

"Julia, I love you, I'm on my way."

As Victor walked jubilantly along the dusty late September pavement to the bus stop he thought about Julia. She will expect me to sleep with her after dinner, she will forget the brush-off she gave me, she'll forget she switched to Fergus. I shall tell her about my trout, Fergus's enterprise, well, the article is about that but I can tell her a few more details, Mary and her baby for instance. I am grateful for the introduction to Sean, he's a good publisher, well in a good publishing house, not afraid to take risks whatever that means, not that my novel's a risk. I could write a children's book about my trout or we could get it on television, a cartoon perhaps, bring in that fearful cat of Fergus's, Bolivar, no all that's been done. My luck has turned. Superstitiously Victor bowed to the new moon as he waited at the bus stop, turning round three times, jingling the silver in his pocket, wondering what to wish for.

He had a vision of Poppy's shoulderblades, mousy hair, long legs, funny teeth and tip-top tits.

But I call them breasts, he thought, climbing into the bus which had roared to an impatient stop. I shall take Julia to Shepherd's Bush and she shall help me choose the nosh, that will teach her to send me cookbooks. What a fool I am, thought Victor, as the bus jerked forward, how vain I am. Sean is Julia's current lover, I heard someone say so, sex with me doesn't come into it, we are platonic, have been for ages, I am just a writer with a novel she can lay at his feet, it costs her nothing. Better not wish too hard for Poppy, it might be unlucky. Victor glimpsed the crescent moon through a gap between high rise flats. I shall wish, he thought with a burst of generosity, I shall wish that Fergus makes a success of his enterprise, that my article brings me recognition and Fergus customers, that my book gets rave reviews.

Sitting in the bus on his way to meet Julia, Victor tried to adjust his mind to being a comic writer and mulled over some particularly felicitous turns of phrase which had tapped from his fingers. Rereading his article as he rode along, Victor was pleased with his afternoon's work.

As he got off the bus Victor felt a pang of conscience. Poppy didn't want publicity, might not be pleased with his article. Julia might be inspired to come to the funeral, she was incurably inquisitive, might even bring Sean. I shall discourage her, Victor told himself, it's a solemn occasion, not a raree show. Then thinking yet again of his article he decided Poppy couldn't possibly take exception; it was faultlessly written, in excellent taste, restrained prose. The sort of taste Penelope made fun of. There's a fine line between love and lust when one is very young, thought Victor, wishing now that when he'd wished on the new moon he had wished never to think of Penelope again. It still hurt.

One of the things which hurt most was the drowning episode frequently brought up by friends as an example of his heartlessness towards his then wife. The most favoured version, which he had grown used to believing himself since it was the one most often recounted, was of the quarrel in the cove in Greece witnessed by onlookers, of his slapping Penelope's face, of Penelope in tears, diving off the rocks and swimming out to sea. That he had sat, not bothering to swim out to help or call for assistance when she got into difficulties.

In actual fact Victor remembered it had been Penelope who had slapped him so that taken unawares he had sat abruptly and bruised his coccyx while Penelope dived gracefully off the rock and swam off without a backward glance. He had lain back, eyes closed, nursing his injuries, physical and emotional. When he opened his eyes there had been no sign of Penelope. Worried, he had scrambled up the cliff to a vantage point and seen Penelope loitering along the cliff in her bikini, picking flowers, stopping to chat to groups of tourists. She looked very lovely and strange with her long wet hair and sun-brown limbs. She obviously made her usual impression. Busy making it, she had not seen him. He had hurried back to where she had left him and when she eventually rejoined him he had said, "I wish you had drowned." He could still remember her mockery. "I don't drown easily."

Going up in the lift to Julia's office Victor thought, I never felt protective towards Penelope as I did for the trout and do towards that girl Poppy. It was I, he thought, making his way past Julia's pretty secretary ("Julia's expecting you, Victor"), who was in need of protection.

THIRTEEN

"Haven't you got a nice black?" Mrs Edwardes stood with her back to the window looking at Poppy in the bed.

"Not really." Poppy sipped the strong tea Jane Edwardes had brought her.

This was the fourth morning she had woken in the visitors' room. She felt rested after a night's sleep unmarred by memories of Edmund or pangs of conscience over her father. She felt positively cheerful. This, Dad's last night so to speak, had been dreamless. She had slept in peace in the visitors' bed, had felt that Dad after his fashion was at peace also.

It seemed a pity that he had to be disturbed from his position between the stools in the sitting-room, to be carted to the church, endure the service, be carted again to the graveyard and buried out of sight, soon to be out of mind.

The days spent by Dad in his coffin in the sitting-room had been friendly, pleasant, therapeutic. People had popped in to visit through the front door which she left open or in the case of some who were more intimate or perhaps shy (it was not possible to discern which), through the French windows from the garden. In almost every case these people, Dad's friends from the village and villages around, had something appreciative to say about him. They touched the coffin the way they would the sleeve of a friend. Some chuckled or laughed outright at some pleasing but private recollection. Some brought flowers, laying them by the coffin, promising a proper wreath on the day.

Poppy had grown used to Dad being there as one grows used to a new sofa after the first cultural shock, the replacement perhaps of a battered piece of Edwardiana by a new chesterfield from Habitat. She had grown used, too, to sprawling in this extremely comfortable bed, waking to the sound of sparrows chirping and the twittering of swallows ranged along the telephone wires in the road, gathering their wits, exchanging last messages before the long flight to Africa. They must go and Dad also. Today was the day, Saturday, Dad's funeral, her birthday.

"Haven't you got a nice black?" Jane Edwardes watched Poppy propped on her elbow drinking her tea in the large bed. The sheets slipped back as she lifted the cup, showing biscuit-coloured breasts with nipples Mrs Edwardes's grandmother would have called Old Rose. Jane Edwardes's grandmother had been a dressmaker and taught Jane the names of colours – Moss Green, Marina Blue, Nigger Brown, Old Rose, the fashionable colours of her day, the Thirties. Jane's grandmother would have run Poppy up a nice little Black Number for her father's funeral in a day if she had still been alive and no nonsense about wearing the dress Bob Carew had brought from Italy.

"It's my birthday. I always wear his present on my birthday." Poppy put the cup in its saucer, laid it on the bedside table and, leaning back on the pillows, smiled up at Mrs Edwardes, not bothering to pull the sheets up.

The dress from Italy hung expectantly on the outer side of the cupboard door flaunting its simple elegance, its amazing juxtaposition of coloured triangles. Glancing sidelong at the dress Mrs Edwardes noted Moss Green, Lilac, Old Rose, Red Carnation and a blue which in some lights looked purple; her grandmother would not have known it as Aubergine.

"Delicious tea. Thank you."

"There's a boutique in Newbury which has little black dresses—" Jane Edwardes tried again.

"I know it."

Jane stooped to pick up Poppy's white cotton nightdress lying discarded by the bed.

"Can't sleep in them." Poppy watched the older woman.

Jane shook the nightdress quite roughly, making her feelings clear.

"It's Dad's funeral, Mrs Edwardes."

Jane sniffed.

The sun streaming yellow into the room was blacked out by a momentary cloud.

"I must have a bath, wash my hair." Poppy slid out of bed and made for the bathroom.

"Bacon and egg for breakfast?" asked Jane Edwardes, accepting defeat.

"Yes, please," answered Poppy warmly.

The sun shone in again illuminating a buttock as she went into the bathroom.

"Girls these days, I don't know . . ." The older woman folded the nightdress, put it on the bed. "Only wears it to walk about the house."

Poppy turned on the taps. "I'm going to keep that room as mine from now on," she called above the rush of water.

"So that's how it is," Jane commented as she went down to the kitchen. If asked she would not have been able to explain what she meant but inside she knew and quite liked the knowledge. There were two shades of lilac in that dress, she thought, taking the kitchen scissors to cut rind off bacon. Clever people with colour, the Italians. She'd noticed it last summer on the tour with her cousin when they'd seen Venice, Florence, Rome and that other place in six days. There might well be two shades of red and green in that dress. If she insists on wearing it I'll check, thought Jane, reaching into the refrigerator for an egg. I wonder whether she would eat two? She should eat a good breakfast, it's going to be a long day. Jane hesitated. One egg or two? That dress, though. Any other day but at your father's funeral! She went to the hall and, standing at the foot of the stairs, shouted: "One egg or two?"

"One, please," Poppy called from the bathroom.

Milan, that was the other place they'd seen. The dress came from there. What had he been doing in Milan? No need to ask. Jane Edwardes, standing by the refrigerator holding the egg, thought with tolerant affection of Poppy's father Bob Carew, hearing his voice, "Like to flutter a fiver on the three thirty at Kempton, Mrs Edwardes?" He'd always called her Mrs Edwardes, never Jane. The egg was pale brown, the same colour as the girl's skin. I was always good with colours, Jane reminded herself, comparing the egg with Poppy's tan. Bathes topless, one can see that, but wears the bottom bit. Bit's the word, thought Jane, recollecting the thin streak of white slanting across Poppy's bottom when she walked into the bathroom. Barely enough. Jane picked up the kitchen biro and traced a double V on the egg. Barely enough to cover her fluff. I don't know, I really don't. Sighing, Jane Edwardes went back up the stairs to stand in the bathroom doorway.

"You want a nice black dress on a day like this." It was her last appeal.

"No, Mrs Edwardes, no, no, no." Poppy looked up at the older woman's disapproval. "I don't want," she said and burst out laughing as she lay in the bath.

"No laughing matter." Jane Edwardes was delighted to hear Poppy laugh. The first time she's laughed since he died. Laughs like him, she thought, remembering times when he would laugh. "That animal won the three thirty. I told you it would. You should have risked your fiver." What a tease he had been.

"Come and eat your breakfast," she told Poppy.

"Coming." Poppy got out of the bath. "It will be all right, you'll see, don't fuss." She felt a surge of unseemly mirth, remembering Dad's affectionate mimicry of Mrs Edwardes's Berkshire vowels. "It's what he would like." She reached for a bath towel. "You know he would. And I like it. For once we are in agreement."

Silenced, Jane went down to cook breakfast. Picking up the egg she doodled a bit more. "Quite rude," she murmured, giving the drawing a finishing touch. "I should have taken up art." She cracked the egg into a cup and crushed the shell, dropping it into the pedal bin, slightly ashamed of her lewdity.

Poppy came down in a white towelling robe, her wet hair screwed up in a towel. She sat at the kitchen table to eat her breakfast.

Jane poured two cups of coffee and sat across the table from Poppy. She was glad to see the girl sitting easy, tucking in to her bacon and egg. She would never have thought before this that Poppy would take her father's death so hard. For the last few days she had looked all twisted and screwed up, her face tense with misery. Better today, though. Jane sipped her coffee. That boyfriend, that Edmund. Why wasn't he here to help the girl? Now her father was dead there was no need to keep away. Jane considered Poppy eating her bacon. Those two had been a matched pair, met when Poppy was sixteen or thereabouts, the girl crazy about the man, always rowing with her father, row, row, row, until she upped and left home to live and work in London, share a flat with Edmund. Running a thoughtful tongue round her molars, Jane Edwardes wondered whether she should enquire.

"Have another egg? It's no trouble."

"No thank you, that was lovely." Poppy held her coffee cup in both hands.

"Edmund coming to help, is he?" The words slipped traitorously out.

"I shouldn't think so." Poppy stiffened.

"They didn't get on, did they?" The question needed no answer. Edmund was apparently consigned to the past.

"I must dry my hair and get dressed. Thanks for my breakfast." Poppy stood up tense and nervous. Jane watched her leave the room and, cursing her ineptitude, deliberately smashed a plate to vent her feelings. How was I supposed to know? Bending to pick up the pieces she became aware of a man carrying something heavy shuffling backwards into the kitchen.

"Easy, Singh, don't push or I'll topple over."

"Poppy," shouted Mrs Edwardes, catching sight of a jowly brown face topped by a turban suffused by the strain of carrying a heavy box, sharing the load with the first man. "Poppy!"

Shuffling backwards into the kitchen was not the way Victor would have chosen to present himself to Poppy who, answering Jane Edwardes's cry, came back into the room.

He was not to know that the laugh with which she greeted him was not mockery but surprise as she compared his unusually slender hips with the vast bulk of his companion.

"Where can we put this?" Victor gasped, his arms aching.

"On the table." Poppy hurried to clear a space. "What have you got there?" How long he was, how narrow, his legs must be a foot longer than Edmund's, well, not to exaggerate, half a foot. "Here." She spread her hands over the space she had cleared, "Put it here. Hullo," she said to Victor's companion who was averting his eyes from the cleavage rendered wider by her gesture.

"This is Singh, my take-away friend." Victor straightened his back, noted Poppy drawing the robe across her chest, tightening its belt. "The king of Indian nosh."

Poppy held out her hand. Singh took it in polite silence.

"He has no English," said Victor, grinning.

"Try not to be stupid," said Singh in a bass voice with impeccable pronunciation.

"Well, very little," said Victor to prolong the moment when he could watch this girl, her pale face topped by the white towel confronting Singh, dark bearded, blue turbanned.

"Enough to get an honours degree at the LSE," said Singh good-humoured, smiling with perfect teeth at Poppy who smiled back.

"But he doesn't like talking," Victor spun out the introduction, "so he took to take-away food."

"It pays better than teaching, stupid."

"So this?" Poppy indicated the heavy box.

"Thermos boxes, Singh's family's relics of the Raj, your eats for this afternoon. I thought if we unloaded now Singh could go back to London and I can return the empties tomorrow. Singh can't stay."

"Alas," said Singh, watching Poppy with shining dark eyes, "I cannot."

"Come on, Singh, two more boxes," exclaimed Victor. "They were used for tiger shoots when the Viceroy came to stay," Victor told Poppy, hoping to see her smile again.

"On railway journeys, stupid. We never entertained viceroys," said Singh rather nastily, belittling viceroys.

"How was I to know? Well, better get on with it, time is short, I have much to do." Victor clapped his hands together smiling at Poppy.

"Come on then, stupid. He is a clown," Singh said to Poppy as he left the kitchen, "but he means well."

"How can you be so cruel?" cried Victor.

"Can you manage?" asked Poppy. "I have to dress and dry my hair."

"Sure, leave it all to us, we have the booze in the van and glasses and plates and all that, actually it would be better if—"

"I were out of the way?"

"Well no, no of course not."

"I'm just going, I must."

"I'll help if they need anything," said Jane who had been standing watching by the sink. "I've seen photos of these things. The gentry used to use them at shooting parties and at races in the old days."

"Stand by for a flood of reminiscence." Singh came back carrying another box. "These Thermos boxes unleash a cornucopia of memories. I shall have to stop using them, a terrible time waster." He shot Jane a sultry glance. "Young stupid here knows how to look after them, not to shut them immediately when they have been washed, else they smell musty."

"I'll see to that," said Jane busily. Poppy left the room to dry her hair and dress.

They can manage perfectly well without me, she thought, pulling off the turbanning towel, brushing her damp hair. They could manage Dad's funeral without Dad. They have all the trappings, the food, the drink, the Thermoses, the horses. As she combed her hair she watched the stout Indian leave the house, get into his van and drive off. From the kitchen she heard voices, Jane and Victor.

I'm very quiet, she thought, brushing her hair, and Dad's very quiet.

An Interflora van drove up, a man and a girl got out, opened the van doors and began to unload wreaths.

Oh God! Poppy stood watching. More trappings. I wish I could run away. Why did she have to ask after Edmund? I was all right until then, now I feel sick. Would they notice if I left them all to it? Brushing her damp hair, she wished she could jump into her car and drive away. They are all happier without me, I am *de trop*. She stood by the window looking out at the swallows on the telegraph lines. She felt isolated as one standing in a fog, the sounds from the outside world muffled and indistinct. They are arranging all this without me. They do not need me. They are carried away by their plans for the ritual, using me and Dad as a rehearsal for the burial of their own loved ones when their time comes. I wish it were over.

FOURTEEN

Half awake, Edmund experienced a feeling of unease. He lay still, setting his sleepy brain to define the grounds for this sensation. His mind, clocking into gear, recognised the cause. It was not Poppy who lay warmly asleep beside him but Venetia Colyer, a longer version of womanhood than Poppy, quite a lot older and, he faced it bravely, cooler.

One of Poppy's assets had been her physical warmth. She had been lovely to cuddle on winter nights. It had been nice to feel her warm bottom in the small of his back as they lay back to back as he now did with Venetia.

Heigh-ho, thought Edmund, can't have everything. He consoled himself for his loss by enumerating Venetia's assets. She was beautiful, sophisticated, rich, well dressed. She had a marked talent for cooking, useful friends who were in touch with important people. Her flat was large, comfortable, finely furnished. For instance, the bed in which he now lay was perfectly sprung, something which could not be said of the bed he had shared with Poppy which, sagging in the middle, led to sexual encounters when he was too tired or felt he should have been too tired, having a fear of excess in these matters as do many keep-fit maniacs. Except that I am not a maniac, he told himself, I just mind my diet and exercise properly. Damn, thought Edmund, reminded of exercise. I must arise and jog in a few minutes and Venetia has now said that she will not jog with me. Only on occasion. Edmund recalled Venetia's upper crust voice which he revered saying "only on occasion", making the occasion sound like a rare benison, a medal for good conduct.

Beside him Venetia shifted slightly in her sleep, her feet brushing against his calves. Her feet were cool, even chilly, after hours in bed when they should have been warm and friendly like Poppy's. Edmund resented in retrospect the last few nights when, getting into bed, Venetia had pressed her cold feet between his legs saying "warm me, warm me", as though it were something he would enjoy. He wondered, while resenting the temperature of his mistress's feet, whether if he gave her bedsocks it would set off her other irritating trait, sudden gushing tears spurting unheralded by as much as a moan from her large blue eyes. Superstitiously Edmund wondered what the third irritation would be, simultaneously crushing the sense of loss he still felt for Poppy. One has not lost something, one has discarded, he told himself sarcastically as he prepared to slide out of bed. Venetia would sleep on for another hour while he jogged round the Park solo.

Outside it was raining. Poppy would have exclaimed "I feel chicken", but the rain would not have stopped her. Plucky little thing, Poppy.

Setting his jaw, Edmund trotted along Venetia's as yet unfamiliar street towards the Park, consoling his lonely state with the thought of Venetia's breakfast. Orange juice, crisp bacon, excellent coffee (she made much better coffee than Poppy, who made it in a tin jug), brown toast, Devon butter and Cooper's marmalade, which would be waiting on his return. "Have I time for a shower?" he would say, as he had these last few mornings. "Yes, but don't be too long," Venetia would reply, her gold hair brushed and shiny.

Forgetting the temperature of Venetia's feet and her tendency to sudden tears, Edmund swung north towards Bayswater, taking care to leave the Park by Lancaster Gate and not by the old gate as he had yesterday, his feet from long habit leading him towards Poppy and the flat they had shared for so long.

Passing a paper shop Edmund stopped to buy a paper. He had been shocked to find Venetia's daily paper was a rubbishy tabloid not *The Times*. "Buy your own," Venetia had said, "if you must have it." People like Venetia, he had often heard, were mean in small things, hopefully generous in large. Perhaps this was the third irritation, he thought with relief, in which case it was a blessing in disguise. Had not Poppy often taken his *Times* just to pore over the reviews, messing up the paper?

It had stopped raining. Edmund opened *The Times* as he walked the last stretch of pavement, running his eye down the column of births and deaths before turning to the City page. "What's this, what's this," Edmund exclaimed aloud and again, "What's this?" He stood in the street re-reading the small announcement. "Robert Carew, loved father of Poppy – suddenly – funeral Saturday."

"Saturday – today is Saturday." Edmund used the key Venetia had given him and went up to the fourth floor in the lift, infinitely preferable to climbing four flights as he had all these years, though climbing stairs kept one fit.

"I have to go to a funeral," he said, kissing Venetia absently as though they had been married for years. She had consented to marry him all right, no problem there, but stipulated she should keep her name. "I am fond of Colyer," she had said (her divorced husband was Michael Colyer). "Why don't you change yours by deed poll? Edmund Colyer sounds terrific." Edmund had answered jokingly, "I might well at that. I'll think it over." There was time to think, they were not married yet. Why not Edmund Colyer-Platt? That sounded good, making the deplorable Platt, so awful in its single state, positively *Who's Who*ish.

"I have to go to a funeral today," said Edmund.

"Whose funeral?" Venetia's ready tears spurted. "I'll come with you," she said, "and spread the load."

FIFTEEN

"Are you wearing this?"

Poppy did not know how long she had stood looking out of the window, hairbrush in hand.

Cars and vans had come to the house, flowers had been delivered, large sprays and small, brought by people coming up the steps, ringing the bell, handing their offerings to Jane who, invisible beneath the window, thanked and chatted before calling goodbye and closing the door. The sun moved round to shine directly into Poppy's eyes. Her hair was dry now. She had watched the young swallows make tentative flights, returning after each adventure to the communal safety of the telephone wire to twitter and preen, display flashes of white and chestnut against navy blue plumage. She had seen Victor leave the house to join Fergus, driving away in his old Ford, followed shortly after by Jane in her new Metro. Before leaving Jane shouted up the stairs: "I am going home to change into my black." Poppy had not answered. She remained by the window looking out at the swallows.

"Are you wearing this?"

Reluctantly Poppy turned towards a woman who stood in the shadow, holding the dress Dad had bought for her birthday.

"Yes." How had this woman got in?

"Good," said the stranger. "Perhaps you'd let me help you dress?" she suggested. "Your front door was open," she answered the unspoken question.

"I'm all right." Poppy was defensive.

"Of course." The woman was old but erect. Poppy saw that she had beautiful legs, narrow feet, she wore a heavy white silk dress and coat, black hat, bag and shoes, she gave the impression of confidence and authority, she smiled at Poppy, amused, she held the multi-coloured dress so that it seemed to move towards her, anxious to be worn.

Poppy faced the stranger.

"I am a friend of your father's, used to meet him at the races."

"Oh." Poppy reached for her knickers, pulled them on, let the towelling robe drop, pulled a slip over her head. "Tights," she muttered.

"Here." The tights were held out to her.

"Thanks."

"Shoes?" questioned the old woman.

"Will black shoes do?"

"Of course."

Poppy adjusted the tights, put on the shoes. "Now the dress." The dress was slipped over her head. "Beautiful, just as we thought," murmured the old woman.

"We?" Poppy stared at her. "We?" she questioned apprehensively.

"I was with him when he bought it." This woman had once been lovely, was beautiful in age. She smiled at Poppy. "I helped him choose it, he asked my advice. We had met at the races. I hope you don't mind."

"You are still alive." Poppy thought of the anonymous leavers of Life's Dividends.

The other woman laughed. "I was never in *that* category." She read Poppy's thoughts.

"I just wondered."

"Yes?"

"Are they all dead?" Here perhaps was someone who could enlighten, who had known Dad's companions, mistresses perhaps.

"I wouldn't know. Your father had lots of friends; some were lonely people afraid of going to the races on their own. Your father was kind to them."

"Did he, were they—" Poppy bit off the rest of the sentence.

"He didn't necessarily sleep with them." Life's Dividends were dismissed.

"There now, you look lovely, look at yourself." She indicated the mirror. "He would be very pleased, your pa," she said, smiling at Poppy's reflection.

Poppy envied the stranger's assurance, her elegant clothes, the jewellery she was wearing, the waft of unusual scent. She had not known that her father had friends like this. She had not known her father.

"Here they come." The old woman moved to the window. Poppy joined her.

Round the bend in the road into the village clip-clopped hooves, into view came the Dow Jones, rich harness gleaming, bits jingling, ostrich plumes waving. They drew the hearse, shining black and gold, its glass sides polished, its springs creaking, its wheels rumbling and crunching on the road. On the box Fergus, in black, tail-coated, top-hatted, rug wrapped tightly across his knees, held reins and whip, beside him Victor similarly dressed. Behind the hearse Annie and Frances in black also but hatless, while in front at the horses' heads Mary strode gravely.

"Beautiful!" exclaimed the old woman. "I shall certainly book him for myself. I must make a note for my executor. Where did your father find them?"

"An advertisement in the *Field*."

"Never missed a trick, your pa."

The hearse came to a halt. Mary stood by the horses' heads as they stretched their necks and blew down their noses. Annie and Frances went into the house. Fergus and Victor jumped down from the box.

"Time you went down," said the old woman.

"Oh my God!" Poppy shrank from what lay ahead, she shivered.

"Oh my nothing," said her visitor briskly. "You have to see him out of the house and follow behind him to the church. Brace up, don't be a ninny. Here, wear this." She took off her white silk coat and put it on Poppy. "I felt cold at my husband Hector's funeral. Look sharp," she said. "Play your part. Think how he's enjoying this." She pushed Poppy towards the door. "A bit of pageantry in this dark age, be proud. I can imagine him watching, can't you?"

Poppy walked down the stairs. She did not feel her father was there to watch.

Jane Edwardes had appeared wearing unmitigated black. Her husband John and her nephew Bill were with Fergus and Victor hoisting the coffin on to their shoulders. They carried it to the hearse. Frances replaced the laurel wreath on the coffin and helped Annie arrange other wreaths round the coffin and on the roof.

When the cortège started Poppy looked round for the old woman to thank her but she was gone. Obediently she paced behind the hearse carrying Dad's body through the village to the church. In later years when she smelled the smell of horses in harness she would sniff, reminded of that day but missing the elusive scent which impregnated the borrowed coat. She followed the hearse, her head up, glad now that Dad was having the funeral he wished. The half-mile to the church was the proper distance to walk in the September sun with the swallows twittering from the telegraph wires and rooks cawing as they flew up the valley.

While the hearse drew Bob Carew at a walking pace and Poppy followed, lonely behind, the church filled with people.

They paused in the porch to give their names to the reporters, blinked as they adjusted to the dimness, muted their voices as taught by their forebears, shuffled their feet, found seats, greeted friends discreetly, looked around, remembered to kneel, pray or appear to pray before sitting back to wait for the service to begin.

Calypso Grant observed the congregation, sifting the locals from those from further afield, recognising people who had once gatecrashed parties now become almost professional funeral-goers who, in youth, had known or pretended to know all the party givers. They now come, she thought, to watch their former hosts departing who knows where.

But, she thought, there are lots like me who really cared for Bob Carew, as his daughter does too late, while those who cared most for the dear man have preceded him. I wonder, mused Calypso, whether there is some splendid race meeting in the sky and they wait for him by the paddock rail to advise them which horse to back.

Beside her, her nephew Willy who had driven her to the funeral sat quietly, knowing no one, looking ahead at the pale stained-glass window behind the altar. He is thinking of his farm, the dear fellow, and is too nice to feel resentful of this boring afternoon I have let him in for.

I must register every detail, thought Calypso, so that I can tell Ros Lawrence what sort of job her son Fergus makes of being an undertaker. Ros makes no complaint but her new husband may not welcome Fergus's choice of career. Hector would have found it original. I've seen those stable girls before, Calypso thought. The fair one is old Mowbray's girl. What's the story? And I see he has roped in his cousin Victor to help. Without seeming to she docketed and placed the congregation.

The organist struck up gently and the people rose.

At the church gate Poppy stood, a slight figure, as the men unloaded Dad and carried him into the church. Somebody nudged her arm and led her in to settle her in the front pew alongside the coffin. She was unaware of Anthony Green and his wife, of Les Poole with his consort, of the eyes of the congregation watching her as she tried to concentrate on the service, on the words designed to consign her father to God's keeping. Did he believe in God? Did all these people, his friends believe in God? Why did I never ask him, Poppy wondered. Why did we never discuss serious matters? Why did we shy away and worry at the subject of Edmund? Oh, Edmund.

Beside his aunt Willy Guthrie suddenly stiffened like a pointer. She followed his glance.

The organist let rip a burst of Bach then it was over and the bearers were preparing to carry Bob Carew out to the hearse for the short trip to the grave.

There was silence in the church except for the shuffling of the bearers and the mass breathing of the congregation as they waited.

The vicar moved round the coffin ready to lead it out.

Oh my God, thought Poppy, there will be a hymn. I should not have left its choice to the vicar, how can he know what Dad liked, he will have chosen some awful muscular Christian tune which will set my teeth on edge. She gripped the pew in front of her. The vicar glanced at her sidelong.

From behind the altar came a pure high note. A blackbird sang joined quickly by mistlethrush, thrush, robin, tit, finch and wren in delirious joyful chorus filling the church. The vicar did indeed know what Dad would like. She remembered then her father telling her how the tape had been made one spring morning in his garden. I will get him to play you the tape, Dad had said, if you are interested. She had not been interested. Instead they had squabbled over her life with Edmund.

She followed the coffin into the September light slanting now across the green, her ears full of birdsong, feeling grief, remorse, gratitude to the vicar. She did not notice the congregation waiting for her to pass, watching her. She did not catch their eyes. Behind her in the church the birdsong ran on until the tape ran out.

Standing by the grave for the final words as the coffin was lowered Poppy felt relief that Dad had had the send-off he wanted, satisfaction that in this at least she had given him something he wanted. It rounded off Edmund's defection.

People gathered round her as she shook hands with the vicar and thanked him.

"You will come back to the house?"

"Thank you."

A heavy man in a tweed suit said, "Hullo, you must be Poppy." He smelled of alcohol and cigars.

"Yes."

"The birds were an inspiration."

"The vicar's."

"Not a church-goer your father, it was the race tracks for him." The man laughed fatly.

"Yes."

"Used to take my aunt to Chepstow and he took Archie over there's mother to the National every year. Kind to the old girls your father, never accepted any reward, most charitable chap I ever knew, free with his tips too. My name's Ebberley."

"Oh."

"Let us give you a lift? Get you home in a flash."

Yet again others were taking charge, knowing what she should do, doing it for her. She heard the strangers around her saying, "OK, see you in a minute at the house. Could do with a drink after that," "Hope there's something stronger than tea," "Sure to be some booze, Bob was never mean about booze." They all seemed to know each other, substantial men with their competent high-voiced wives mixing with the neighbours from the village and villages around. Their voices carolling up.

"Excuse me, would you mind if I took my aunt's coat?" A man's polite voice. "We have to leave."

Flustered by the noise around her, Poppy took off the coat. "Where is she, I must thank her? Won't you come to the house?"

"Over there." He took the coat. "Don't bother, we have to go." He sounded angry. "Goodbye." She watched him join the old woman waiting in the car. She smiled and waved. The young man got in and drove away.

"Who is she?" cried Poppy embarrassed not to know. "She was so kind, she seemed to know my father."

"Calypso Grant, used to be quite a raver when she was young. Here, jump in."

The man in the tweed suit was managing her, putting her into a car beside a wife who smiled a welcome, patting the seat beside her. "That was Calypso Grant," the man told his wife who said, "Oh, Calypso, one's heard of her of course," noncommittally.

Poppy, half in the car, hesitated, fighting suffocation. I am being killed by kindness, she told herself. She backed out, scrambling away. "Please go on," she urged. "I must just see – I have to speak – do go on up to the house—" She escaped, doubling back towards Fergus and Victor waiting by the hearse for the cars to move, the road to be free. One of the horses threw up its head and neighed impatiently. People were getting into their cars, slamming doors, starting the engines. Frances and Annie stood at the back of the hearse. Mary was chatting to a group of people she seemed to know.

"You will come back to the house?" asked Poppy, looking up at Fergus.

"Love to."

"I must, I'm doubling as waiter," Victor said smugly.

"Put your horses in the stables, Victor will show you." She needed to keep Fergus near her and Victor too.

"Stables? That'll be fine," said Fergus, surprised.

"Didn't Victor tell you?"

"Victor did not." Fergus shot a suspicious glance at Victor, who looked innocent.

"May I drive back to the house with you?"

"Of course you may, there's room on the box," said Fergus.

"You are the only people I know here."

"Stay with us then." Victor drew closer to her. He would have liked to put an arm round her but not in front of Fergus.

"What I'd really like is to be alone," cried Poppy.

"Have to wait a bit," said Fergus.

"We'll stand by," said Victor comfortingly.

Mary came up laughing. "At least ten people have asked for your phone number, Fergus. This has been a wonderful advertisement. Half the bookmakers in the south of England are here and lots of the hunting crowd. You are going to be the in thing, Fergus, if you are not snowed in," she teased, "but no fun then."

Fergus snapped "Do shut up, Mary," glared and muttered.

"What does she mean, snowed in?" Poppy looked up at the weather, set fair.

"My father rented him a pup," said Mary and sketched the trap Fergus might find himself in.

"Don't let it bother you." Fergus indicated the hearse. "Jump up."

Poppy scrambled up in her beautiful dress, showing a lot of leg in the view of the verger who was waiting to close the church and get home to his tea, not that he objected to legs but not at funerals.

Annie and Frances sat in a row with Mary, swinging her legs in the back of the hearse. "Walk on, gee up," cried Fergus cracking the whip.

The Dow Jones threw up their heads and lurched forward. Fergus drove through the village at a smart trot. People returning to their homes looked amused or disapproving at Poppy in her multi-coloured dress sitting on the box between Fergus and Victor.

"They don't look too pleased," commented Victor.

"How else am I supposed to get home?" cried Poppy. "I was offered a lift but it was with strangers."

Victor and Fergus felt jointly pleased not to be so considered.

"Why don't you rent my stables as winter quarters," suggested Poppy when they arrived, speaking as though the idea had just occurred to her. "I'll introduce you to my solicitor, you can fix it up with him. I shan't be here much," she added, dashing Fergus's spirits. "Do the place good to be used," she said. "You may have the house too, if you want it. Let us get this dreadful wake over." She must play host to all the people who had known Dad and very likely Life's Dividends too. It pleased her to think that it was Life's Dividends who were paying for the party, forking out for the champagne.

SIXTEEN

As the Dow Jones clattered round to the stable yard Victor acknowledged a shout from Julia Wake who, having parked her car, was heading towards the house in the company of Sean Connor.

"Who are they?" Poppy asked but who cares, she thought, the church had been full, strange faces outnumbering the familiar ten to one. With the funeral ordeal over came euphoria, sparked off by the novelty of the drive from the cemetery. High on the box between Fergus and Victor she was exhilarated by the horses tossing their heads, black plumes dancing, bits jangling, the snortings, the pounding hooves on the road, the eager canter quickly repressed by Fergus. "Whoa there, steady."

"That's Julia Wake, she edits the magazine I told you about." (Had he told her?) "The man with her is Sean Connor, he's in publishing, he is very interested in my novel." Victor hoped Poppy had been as distrait as she looked during the ceremony, had not noticed the photographers, not being sure how well she would receive his article when it got into print.

"A novel? How exciting. Are they coming to your party?"

"Your party," Victor corrected her.

"I hardly feel it's mine, it's been organised by you. Shall you rush ahead and pop the bottles?" Poppy jumped down from the box as Fergus drew up in the stable yard. "Run on," she said to Victor, "all these people will be dying for a drink." She waved towards the house. "I'll follow in a minute," she said, quashing his desire to linger.

Victor, host perforce in his role as caterer, went reluctantly ahead to the house.

"Now," Poppy switched to Fergus, "let me show you the stables."

They left the horses to Frances and Annie and toured the yard. Fergus, expecting shabby desolation, was astonished as he looked into loose-boxes, tack-room and coach-house. "It's in good nick, all it needs is a lick of paint and a few repairs."

"Dad would have liked to have horses here, it would have been one of his dreams. Like to rent them, what do you say?" She looked at Fergus.

Fergus said, "It would be a bloody miracle. You've no idea of the terror that gripped me since that bitch planted the fear of snow. If I were snowed in I'd go bankrupt."

"Her father took you for a ride; why?"

"He wants to muck up Mary's life, wants her to be respectable."

"Fathers do," said Poppy drily.

"He was getting at her through me. If I go bust she'd lose her job."

"Charming." Perhaps I was lucky with Dad, he only talked, she thought. "I'll introduce you to Anthony Green, he'll be in the house. Rent it for a year and see how things go," she suggested. "Oh!" she exclaimed as Fergus hugged her. "Ah!" she said as he kissed her mouth.

"Sealed with a kiss." Fergus kissed her again. "More?" he suggested, enjoying himself.

"Well," said Poppy. She had not been kissed by anyone other than Edmund since she could remember, not like this. Fatherly pecks on the cheek by Dad, avuncular cheek-touching by Anthony Green, certainly nothing of this sort. "Well." She felt cheerful and, to her surprise, roused. She smoothed her dress, shook out her hair. "No more," she said, laughing. Fergus desisted.

Poppy watched while the girls took the horses out of their traces and loosened their bits. They brought haybags from a Land-Rover. Mary watched also, holding the infant Barnaby who had materialised with the haybags. He held out plump arms to Fergus and said, "Dada, Dada."

"I'm not your bloody dada," said Fergus. "Wait till you are of age, I'll sue you for slander."

Mary looked down her nose.

"Dada," insisted Barnaby, bubbling spittle. Poppy felt happy, with Fergus and the girls watching the horses chump their hay, swish their tails, sigh gustily, break wind, phut, phut, phut of sweet-smelling gas. She was in no hurry to go into the house.

"There will be no booze left if you don't come in," Victor shouted jealously from the kitchen door.

"OK, we'll come." Poppy led Fergus and the girls towards the back door.

They were met by a wall of sound from the sitting-room, hall and overflow into the garden.

Friends from the village and neighbourhood raised their voices in competition with Dad's friends from the outer world. Bookmakers, gypsies, racing men, smart suited in tweed and pinstripe, shiny-shoed, boomed and bellowed while their wives and mistresses yelped and trebled as they snatched and nibbled at the Indian eats, gulped and swilled champagne, greedy for the life from which Bob Carew had so recently absented himself.

Poppy strained to hear snatches of conversation, hoping to piece together a picture of Dad through his friends.

"The last race at Doncaster was when—"

"Cast a plate at Plumpton so the second favourite won."

"You marinate it in white wine. Try it."

"Man cannot live by bread alone, he needs butter."

"Haw, haw, haw."

"Knew Furnival's mother, very pretty girl Ros. I shall book him for my exit."

"Don't you think it was in rather dubious taste?"

"Oh come on, makes a change from the usual humdrum do."

"Apprenticed himself to an undertaker, they say, rather enterprising."

"Went to France, found the equipage there—"

"Why France?"

"Why not—"

"A papist contraption—"

"But why?"

"Search me. Search *la femme*. Any more of that bubbly?"

"That chap over there drowned his wife."

"Victor something—"

"That's right. Writes. Wish I could drown mine. Victor Lucas, that's it."

"I keep forgetting names."

"Too much alimony. It's old age creeping up on you."

"Ha, ha, ha. You too."

"Isn't that girl Mary Mowbray, Nicholas Mowbray's daughter?"

"It's said she had a baby by a wog. That must be it. I say! Anything goes these days." (Mary was observed sitting on the stairs suckling Barnaby, glass of wine in hand, legs apart.) "Looks like one of those Virgins and Child in the National Gallery."

"Don't be profane, darling."

"The ones in the Gallery wore longer skirts."

"Something funny in her breeding, her grandfather is supposed to have slept with Tallulah Bankhead."

"Who's Tallulah Bankhead?"

"Oh come on. Yes please, just one more."

"No, no I mustn't, I'm driving."

"It's got a cough, been scratched."

"What about that horse he backed at Ascot? Wasn't it fifty to one?"

"You mean Epsom, funny thing that, Stewards' Inquiry as near as dammit."

"Steroids?"

"Well – one doesn't—"

"Beating about the bush—"

"What bush, whose?"

"Haw, haw, haw."

"No, I mustn't drink any more or my wife will insist on driving."

"Splint."

"There's always York."

"It wasn't a splint, it was—"

Hemmed in, Poppy looked round. She was trapped among the loud voices. She felt as invisible as her parent so rapidly forgotten by his friends.

Across the room an old woman plastered in pancake make-up with blue eyelids waved. She recognised Esmé looking like a man in drag. She had no wish to speak to Esmé, felt safer where she was.

Jane Edwardes shuffled to and fro through the crowd hospitably. "Let me refill your glass." She knew everybody. She laughed and chatted, she was enjoying herself wearing her black.

Victor, a tray of empty glasses in his hand, was pinned against a wall nearby. Poppy edged towards him. Near Victor, Julia and her friend Sean were shouting. (Impossible not to shout in this uproar.) Poppy strained to hear. Sean was giving Victor his opinion of the novel. Soon Victor would be known, up and coming, acclaimed. Julia shouted Sean down to give Victor a witty resumé of the characters in the book (surely he knows his own book, thought Poppy). Sean recaptured Victor's attention, dousing Julia. "I like it, I like it," he said. "A lot more than your first efforts. Come and see me next week, come to lunch, I'd like to publish, there are just a few things of course that need—"

"Such as?" asked Victor, hackles anxiously rising, glass halfway to his mouth.

"Nothing much. Well – er – once again as in the first book you've failed to check your foreign bits."

"Which?" queried Victor suspiciously.

"I'm no linguist of course but if Urdu or Armenian are hard to check the same isn't true of French."

"Oh, what—" hackles rising.

"Well, just glancing through of course, I noticed for instance '*compotes*' which takes a circumflex neither in French nor in English. And '*comme il faut*' with two intrusive hyphens, '*marché noir*' with two erroneous capitals."

"Aah—" Victor gargled.

" '*Tiree à quatre épingles*' written as it *shouldn't* be in the masculine and '*vieux jeu*' in the plural whereas that idiom always takes the singular, '*ceci n'empêche cela*' the '*pas*' left out – true, skipping the '*pas*' sometimes gives the distinguished touch but where you use it it gives a false note – and '*femme d'un certain âge*' with the circumflex missing."

"Oh," whispered Victor, outraged.

"That's just a few I noticed as I whizzed through." Sean took a long swallow of champagne. "I must read it more thoroughly before we—"

"Just a few. No linguist," breathed Victor, mortified, flushed.

"But I love it. It fits nicely into our spring list," insisted Sean extending his empty glass to Mrs Edwardes passing with her tray, taking a full one. "I love your book." He looked tenderly at Victor as though unaware of the pain he was inflicting.

"I—" began Victor, choking with spleen.

"And of course," Sean gulped wine, "it's the funniest book I've read for years. The way you've disguised the black humour with obvious sentimentality, pretending it's a tragedy is masterly."

"Aah—" It was hard to tell whether Victor was mortally wounded or exalted to the spheres. "Aah," he breathed deeply. "So glad you latched on to the hilarity," he said, almost choking on his bile.

With detached insight Poppy decided Victor was about to hit Sean, ruin his literary career, remain a writer manqué for the rest of his days. She flung her arms around Victor's neck. "Kiss me, don't hit him," she said in his ear, "quick."

Victor obliged, pressing his mouth hard on to hers. "This is because I once called him a poof," he said, catching his breath, "he's getting his own back." He kissed Poppy again.

"And is he?" She came up for air.

"Both, my darling, both hetero and homo." Victor kissed her yet again.

Fergus, watching from across the room, thought, Bloody hell, there goes the march I stole on him, and began to shoulder his way across the room.

"Artful little bitch," said Sean to Julia. "Doesn't miss a trick, does she? Who is she?"

"Our hostess," said Julia. "You've had too much to drink, nearly lost yourself an author."

"I couldn't resist a small tease. I abhor the ignorant use of Franglais."

"You are a snob because your mother was French," said Julia, laughing.

Poppy was interested to find how much she enjoyed kissing Victor, quite as much as Fergus who had a different technique. She was after all enjoying Dad's party.

Fighting his way through the throng Fergus reached Poppy. "What about that introduction to your solicitor?" He put his arm round her waist.

"Of course." Poppy disengaged herself and led him towards Anthony Green who had found an armchair in a safe corner of the room. "Anthony, this is Fergus Furnival. I want him to rent the stables for his business, and the house, too, perhaps."

Anthony struggled to his feet. "I say, I see. Is that wise?" he asked, peering cautiously at Fergus, reaching into his breast pocket for his spectacles.

"The stables are empty. They will go to ruin. My father would like Fergus to use them, so would I."

"We can of course go into it."

"Go into it tomorrow." He is going to delay, prevaricate, make difficulties. "Just work out a fair rent and lease the stables to Fergus for a year, then if we are both happy with the arrangement he can renew the lease."

"I shall have to—"

"Look sharp." Poppy finished Anthony's sentence for him in a mode he would never have used. "I want him to have them so make out a simple lease, dear Anthony, or shall we go to another solicitor? You do do leases, I take it?" Poppy sized Anthony up with her green eyes, looking, had she known it, exactly like her father Bob Carew at his most obstinate.

"We can make an appointment. There is no rush, I take it."

"There is a great rush, it may snow."

"I can pay the rent in advance," suggested Fergus, remembering Poppy's cheque lodged in his bank, not yet spent.

"Nonsense," said Poppy. "You'll be quick about it, won't you, Anthony? I want the horses in the stables as soon as possible. Cut the red tape or I'll put them in rent free without a lease." She put a daughterly arm round Anthony's neck and kissed him, aiming the kiss close to his mouth. Anthony squeezed her waist in a not quite avuncular way which made his wife, who was watching, decide that it was time to go home and that it would be safer if she drove.

Poppy helped herself to another glass of champagne from a passing tray and found she liked the party even better than a few minutes earlier. It seemed a pity that Dad, who was responsible for this happening, should not be here but no matter. Drink up, she could almost hear his voice.

She continued to enjoy the party until Edmund, coming unexpectedly from nowhere, took her roughly by the arm and dragged her away.

Accounts later varied.

Victor and Fergus maintained that their way had been blocked by intoxicated guests when they struggled to reach her. Annie and Frances differed as to whether Poppy had put up more than token resistance. Mary maintained that Poppy had passed her on the stairs where she sat nursing Barnaby shouting, "I *must* go to the loo first," before joining Edmund in the car quite willingly. Innumerable people saw Edmund bundle her into a car and drive off towards London.

What nobody present had noticed was Venetia watching Edmund both in the church and at the party, nor did they observe her, when Edmund drove Poppy off in what was Venetia's car, go to the kitchen, pour honey over the floor so that feet passing through the kitchen would carry stickiness throughout the house, working it into rugs and carpets. Minutes later she hitched a lift to London from a fellow guest, made agreeable conversation, and declined an offer of dinner.

Reaching her flat before Edmund was likely to arrive (she assumed he would take Poppy to a crowded restaurant where she would be embarrassed if she made a scene), Venetia set to work on Edmund's clothes. She stuck up the cuffs and flies with Superglue, folding each garment with precise attention, nor did she neglect the pants, socks and pyjamas. Then, packing a bag, she hailed a taxi and went to spend a weekend with her mother at Haslemere, from where she phoned the police to report her car as stolen.

SEVENTEEN

With surprise on his side Edmund held a tactical advantage. Not expecting him, she had not noticed him. Edmund congratulated himself. He noticed too that Poppy, who held her liquor weakly at the best of times, was rather drunk. She must be, he thought, kissing the undertakers, snuggling up to Bob Carew's sly solicitor, ignoring the dignity of the occasion by riding back to the house on the hearse. He waived the thought that the ride on the hearse was prior to the champagne. She might have had a fortifying drink before the service.

Telling himself that he must stick to the point, get Poppy away, wait until later to reproach her for the ludicrous horse-drawn hearse, the ghastly tape of birdsong instead of a decent hymn, the lack of dignity among the guests at the house. (The scene had resembled what one had read of Irish wakes, not that even they had Indian food and champagne, from what one had heard a slosh of the hard stuff was more probable.) Above all, he was disgusted by the wearing of that frivolous dress. Where on earth did it come from? The whole scene, thought Edmund, driving fast towards London, was one one would hope to forget, an undignified pantomime in the worst possible taste, making a mockery of a solemn occasion.

Edmund maintained a lofty silence, keeping Venetia's car in the fast lane, treading on the accelerator when challenged by other cars.

I must keep a clear head, he thought. He had restricted himself to one glass of champagne. I have to sort Poppy out. (For the moment he set Venetia aside.) Get her back to our habitual footing, she will need me when she sells her father's house and realises her assets. There are some quite decent pieces of furniture which will come in useful, the rest can be sold at auction. We can move into a larger flat now her father is dead. Now he is out of the way we can get married and start a family – if I want to.

I shall keep my options open, thought Edmund, think it over carefully. There is a lot to be said for the Poppy I know against the Venetia I am discovering.

Allowing himself a quick glance at Poppy, Edmund's mind strayed to Venetia's ready tears and cold feet.

No need for an immediate decision, thought Edmund, remembering Venetia's income. One should approach marriage with caution, divorce was by all accounts a financial disaster. One could keep Venetia as a mistress or vice versa. Poppy needs me, I must look after her, she probably feels a bit sad at the loss of her disreputable father but, he assured himself, she will get over it, she is a resilient girl.

Slumped in the seat beside Edmund, Poppy, aware of her intoxication, had the sense to keep quiet. If I speak I shall say something I regret, she told herself, something irreparable. I shall sit here in this infernal car which stinks of Venetia and wait. She stared ahead at the road waiting for her eyes to regain their focus, letting her thoughts stray.

She enjoyed the movement of Venetia's car, Edmund had always been a good driver. She wondered what he wanted.

Does he want to get me back? she asked herself; after all, he threw me away in favour of Venetia. Has he heard that I now have money? I shall not tell him if he hasn't.

He will be planning to sell Dad's house which may be worth quite a lot. He worked for years as a house agent, he will know its value.

Or is he just being dog in the manger? Is he furious that I organised the funeral without consulting him (not that he was there to ask)? He would not admit he wasn't there, he will say, "Why didn't you telephone when your father died?" be hurt, blame me?

"Why didn't you telephone when your father died?" asked Edmund, slowing the car as it began to rain, switching on the wipers.

Poppy did not answer.

"I find it extremely hurtful." Edmund sounded aggrieved.

Poppy bit her tongue.

"After all . . ." said Edmund, leaving the sentence to float between them.

After all, he left you, Dad would say if he were alive and Dad would laugh that chuckling laugh, not the shout of triumphant joy which had killed him.

"It was a coronary, I take it," suggested Edmund.

Poppy failed to reply.

She remembered Dad's note. What had it said? Give, don't lend. Don't marry unless it's impossible to live without the fellow. Back outsiders. What, in Dad's book, were outsiders? She could have asked any one of those friends of Dad's, those bookmakers, that woman who had lent her coat. The man who took it back. Fergus, Victor, were they outsiders?

"We will have dinner at Luigi's," said Edmund as they drove into London. "I've booked a table."

Poppy kept mum.

If Edmund had booked a table at Luigi's, their favourite restaurant for special occasions, it would have been for Venetia.

Poppy marvelled, rediscovering Edmund.

"I thought you would need a good meal and cheering up after your ordeal."

Does he take me for a doormat, she asked herself. A complete fool? What else have I been for the past ten years, she answered herself, an imbecile.

She felt despairing, lethargic. Without the energy to protect herself, she let herself drift as Edmund willed.

Arrived at Luigi's, she combed her hair and washed her hands in the cloakroom, smoothed her dress. It looked great by electric light, flattering her eyes, making the colour of her hair quite interesting and – the sign of a good dress – it looked as fresh as it had when offered to her by that old woman on its hanger.

Edmund sat waiting at a table in the middle of the room. In the space of a week it had become Venetia's favourite table, she liked to be in the centre of the restaurant to be viewed from all angles, no back to the wall banquette for her. Poppy joined him without comment. The waiter gave them each a menu.

Edmund ordered smoked eel, fillet steak, chipped potatoes and spinach. He would finish, Poppy knew, if he had a chink left, with Stilton. He must, she thought as she studied the menu, have borrowed the money from Venetia. As ever, his fear of putting on weight was defeated by his love of food.

Poppy ordered a dozen oysters (Edmund's eyebrows rose), grilled Dover sole, matchstick potatoes and a green salad. "Then I'll have an artichoke with sauce vinaigrette."

She chose on purpose so that I shall have to order both red and white wine. (Edmund prided himself on his knowledge of wine.) He consulted the wine list, recklessly ordered two bottles, red and white. Damn her eyes. She knows I can't stand the hours she takes eating an artichoke.

Poppy ate the oysters in slow appreciative silence, enjoying the salty juicy flesh as she bit the poor live creatures. She was beginning to feel rather cheerful, her alcoholic fog lifting. She wondered why she had never before tested the pleasure and power of silence. She watched Edmund tackle his eel, knew he expected her to offer him a glass of her white wine with it, refrained.

She sipped her wine, watched the room full of chattering diners.

Edmund started talking again. Getting on with her meal – the sole was delicious – she listened.

"This new job of mine means quite a lot of travel." He bit his steak, forked up some chips.

What new job? Ah yes, he had this new job in a travel agency, it had thrilled them both in those faraway days – at least two weeks ago – before he had left her for Venetia. He was to earn twice the money he made as a house agent and there were, he had said, excellent perks. Edmund was still speaking. "So I thought we'd go as I have the tickets. We fly from Gatwick. It will set you up, you will get over your loss, you can lie in the sun while I do what business I have to do. The climate's lovely at this time of year, still hot of course. I thought we'd go the day after tomorrow which gives us time to pack. I have to get some decent clothes suitable for the job."

You'll like that, commented Poppy in her silence. What marvellous nerve. He plotted this for Venetia, why the switch? Poppy started work on her artichoke, dipping each leaf in the sauce, letting the sauce smear her chin to see whether he would notice.

Edmund averted his eyes and went on talking (a week ago he would have hissed: "Sauce on chin, love, wipe it"), he described the African town they would visit, the sun, the sea, the beach, the food, the trips to visit the Roman antiquities, the Arab cities, the markets. He has done his homework thoroughly, read the brochure, Poppy thought, in her silence stripping off the last artichoke leaf, preparing to savour the last delicious bit, the heart. Edmund's new job was to plan tours for his new company, undercut, if possible, the opposition.

The waiter took away Edmund's plate. He had not the heart to order cheese, he crumbled a roll. He had run out of puff.

Poppy sipped her wine, dabbled her fingers in the finger bowl, dried them on her napkin. The oysters had been restorative, the sole delicious, the artichoke fresh and perfect. She felt very well. Glancing at Edmund under her lashes she thought, He doesn't look too good, he's got himself into a difficult situation.

Edmund had never before not savoured fillet steak. The last piece had nearly choked him. I should not have brought her to this restaurant full of memories. I should not have sat her at this exposed table where everyone can see us. I must not lose my nerve now. He said, "Poppy, listen. I love you. I cannot live without you. I have behaved—"

"Coffee, madam?" suggested the waiter. Poppy nodded and smiled at the waiter.

"I have behaved badly, please forgive me. The Venetia thing was mad, an aberration."

What nonsense, thought Poppy, how banal.

"I am very unhappy, quite dreadfully unhappy—"

That's right, lay it on with a shovel, thought Poppy in robust silence.

"Please, darling, let's begin again—"

Whatever for? She kept silence.

"I love you so much, forgive me and—"

The waiter poured coffee, rattled the cups, moving them unnecessarily, lending an ear.

"I will try and make it up to you, Venetia doesn't mean a thing. You mean everything to me, you always have. I love you so." Edmund stared at Poppy and to his horror, moved by his own eloquence, began to cry.

Raising his eyebrows the waiter moved away.

Across the table Poppy began to cry too. Edmund's speech was maudlin muck, patently fake, having the tear-jerking quality of massed bands, "God Save the Queen" or "A Hundred and One Dalmations".

Poppy did not produce the swift gush of tears that were Venetia's but two slow oily drops which hovered for a second before oozing economically on to her cheek. She wiped them away with her finger.

"More coffee," suggested the waiter, coming back.

"The bill please," said Edmund keeping his voice level with an effort.

"You had better return Venetia's car." Poppy spoke to him for the first time since the parting.

"You are quite right. I shall." He paid the bill, calculating the tip. I shall not give him extra because he saw my tears. Churchill wept and Wellington, dammit.

They went out to Venetia's car. He was too cautious to touch her, she might jerk away. They drove to Venetia's flat in silence then on arrival: "Come up and give me a hand with my packing," he said from force of habit. "It will be quicker," he added to placate her. "I cannot help my male chauvinist piggery," he joked feebly expecting her to contradict him, which she didn't.

Poppy followed him into the lift thinking he would have stood aside for Venetia, minded his manners.

Edmund let himself in at Venetia's door, put the key down where she would find it, making sure that Poppy noticed his action, laid the car keys beside it.

In the bedroom on the bed Venetia had stacked Edmund's clothes: "She's guessed," said Edmund, embarrassed. He fetched his suitcase from a cupboard in the hall and prepared to pack.

"What's this? What on earth?" As the full extent of Venetia's act became clear Poppy, who had up to now felt detached and ambivalent, made up her mind.

"OK," she said. "I'll come to Africa." Was it possible, she thought, as they went down in the lift, that Edmund qualified as an outsider? That Dad was, as she had always maintained, wrong?

EIGHTEEN

Anthony Green had not expected to see Fergus again, imagining Poppy's proposal to rent her house and stables an idea born of the effervescence of champagne, which would subside as fast as the bubbles and, the day after the funeral, be forgotten. He was not pleased when his clerk told him Fergus was in the outer office.

Agreeing to see Fergus, Anthony decided that the quicker he discouraged him the sooner he would be rid of him.

As Poppy's solicitor, though not the executor of her father's will, Anthony had anticipated advising her to sell the house and invest the proceeds while she thought through what she wished to do with her life. He had yet to discover whether she wished to marry or start a new career. With capital behind her, her horizon had altered. He would advise her to take time, make no hasty decision. He hoped that with the connivance – though connivance was the wrong word – of Les Poole they should between them steer the proceeds from the sale into gilt-edged harbours.

Still in search of a better word than connivance Anthony rose to greet Fergus, standing behind his knee-hole desk in his tweed jacket and corduroy trousers, it being market day in the town and many of his clients farmers or country people. Fergus's clothes, aged jeans, flannel shirt, none too clean jersey and torn leather jacket strengthened his resolve. They shook hands.

Fergus, with few illusions about the speed with which Anthony would be prepared to work, yet expected to discuss terms of a lease of Poppy's stables and with luck the house. He was not expecting the whole project to be blocked, which Anthony proceeded to do with a fine example of circumlocution delivered at ponderous pace while he fingered his pen and patted some papers on his blotter as though to say, "I have to sign these documents, you are wasting my time, please go away."

Fergus broke in, cutting him short. "Has Poppy changed her mind about renting me the stables? It was her idea, Mr Green. There was mention of the house, too."

Anthony hesitated. Naturally it was Poppy's idea, true daughter of

Bob Carew. He was here to stop such ideas coming to fruition. He must put a stop to the spirit of Bob Carew living on in his daughter.

"Why don't we ring her up, Mr Green, settle it one way or the other? She was perfectly sober when she had the idea, though possibly not when she told you about it. If she has changed her mind there will be no need for me to bother you any more. May I borrow your telephone, her number is—"

"I know her number, Mr Furnival." Anthony failed to conceal his irritation.

"Well, then." Fergus sat back smiling.

"There are er—"

"References? You need references?" Fergus queried.

"Of course." Anthony snatched at the proffered straw. The conversation was taking an annoying turn, but references will slow him down, put a brake on this indecent haste. A person with a mounted undertaker's business – for some reason he could not define Anthony saw Fergus as mounted on his black horses so irreverently called Dow Jones – no person proposing to run such a business would produce reputable references. Anthony smiled thinly at Fergus across the desk. "Of course we shall require references, that goes without saying." He let his tone hint at patronage.

Fergus reached a long arm across the desk for the telephone at Anthony's elbow and dialled Poppy's number.

"I say!" Anthony was beginning to be angry. This young man was impossible.

"Poppy?" Fergus was speaking. "Did you or did you not offer to rent me your stables and possibly your house?"

"Of course I did." Fergus held the receiver away from his ear so that Anthony could hear Poppy's voice.

"What's the problem?" asked Poppy.

"Your solicitor seems to have doubts."

"Silly old ass. I'll talk to him, I can't write, I haven't time, I'm going away, you were lucky to catch me, ten minutes more and—"

Fergus said, "I'm in his office, speak to him now. I shall give him references and so on."

"Don't bother about references—"

"I'd rather bother but I am in rather a hurry, winter is nigh."

"It's in my soul."

"What?"

"Nothing. Business looking up?"

"You could say that. Here's Mr Green." Fergus surrendered the telephone to its indignant owner and sat back, taking care that Anthony should see that he did not listen.

Anthony listened; he found it hard to get in more than the odd word since Poppy let fly in a voluble rush expressing her ardent definite wish to rent to Fergus, begging him to act fast before the weather closed in, elaborating on the dangers of snowdrifts and the duplicity of Nicholas Mowbray.

Fergus wrote three names, three addresses and telephone numbers on a sheet of paper and waited for Anthony to finish his conversation.

Anthony replaced the receiver rather flushed. How dare the girl who had sat on his knee as a small child (well, if she hadn't, she could have) be so peremptory. She had brushed aside his rearguard action, almost ordered – "She seems quite anxious to rent you her premises," he said cautiously. Fergus said "Good," keeping his eyes on his sheet of paper. "These are my references." He pushed it across the desk.

Anthony, still ruffled by the tone Poppy had seen fit to use, took the paper. The names of Fergus's references leapt from the page. "These are?" he asked keeping his voice in neutral.

"My stepfather, my godfather, my uncle. Should you require others—"

"These will do very well, I dare say." On no account, Anthony told himself, admit that you had not guessed Fergus was one of *those* Furnivals. How could one possibly be expected to connect an undertaker with such – well, not to put too fine a point on it – exalted people. God help poor old Brightson's, he whispered to himself. "Well now, suppose I make you a lease for a year and we review it at the end of that time with the prospect of renewal. Would that suit you, Mr Furnival?"

"Yes," said Fergus. "Fine. How long will that take?"

"Let's say a week since you are in a hurry."

Fergus extended his hand. "Thanks, I'd like to move in pretty soon."

"Of course," said Anthony, generous in defeat. "May I wish you every success in your enterprise. I dare say you will make your fortune—"

Standing up, a head taller than Anthony, Fergus said, "Success isn't just money, Mr G. Bob Carew's funeral meant his daughter felt better because she gave her father something he had wanted. She felt guilty about him. Taking the trouble to have me and my horses goes a little way to assuage the guilt."

"Guilt?" Anthony frowned.

"Didn't you feel guilty when your parents died?"

"No," said Anthony, who had never crossed his parents.

"How unusual, lucky you." Fergus looked at him with interest. "We could have a fascinating conversation on the subject of guilt but I won't waste your time. I must be off. Goodbye."

Watching Fergus go, Anthony thought that after all connivance had been the right word to use in that context; it would have been wrong to manoeuvre Poppy into selling her house. He would see to that lease right away.

He rang for his clerk.

Crossing the street to a telephone box with the intention of alerting his parent of the probable requests for references so that she, with her charm, could warn his stepfather, godfather and uncle, Fergus thought, What did Poppy mean implying that her soul was wintry? Was he imagining a hint of desolation in her voice, had he been optimistic in thinking that the funeral had cheered her? He remembered kissing her and wished he could do so again soon. He dialled her number but the telephone rang in an empty flat. "Going away," she had said, "lucky to catch me." Where? She had said nothing at the funeral of any such plan. He considered telephoning Victor and asking him, since he was in London, to go round and find out but dropped the idea feeling jealous. Victor had kissed her too, would be only too ready— He dialled his mother's number. "Hullo, darling," she said, "we were all thrilled to see you on television, all my friends are determined to have you when their turn comes."

"Not too soon, one hopes."

"Someone has to start or you'll go broke."

"Are you offering?" he asked laughing.

"Not yet, but it makes one think. Bob Carew wasn't that old, he drank of course and had a dicky heart."

"Did you know him?"

"Anyone who went to the races over the last twenty years would know him. He had a pretty daughter, I believe."

"Yes, Poppy."

"Is that her name?" His mother's interest quickened. Fergus would have liked to discuss Poppy with his mother but he ran out of change.

By the time he had got more change and reconnected himself with his mother he no longer wished to discuss Poppy, she was as yet too fragile an idea to discuss with his parent whom he quite erroneously considered robust. He therefore confined himself to the matter of references. His mother laughed and promised results. Thoughtfully replacing the receiver, she prayed that Fergus would not get hurt. Was he aware that Bob Carew's girl lived with that rather awful young man Edmund Platt? If not, it was not for her to volunteer the information.

NINETEEN

Looking down at the clouds from her corner seat, Poppy absented herself from Edmund sitting in the gangway seat which allowed him to stretch his legs as he sat half turned away reading the evening paper. The clouds did not look like cotton wool or whipped cream, just layers of cloud turning pink in the sunset. It had been raining when they left London, it would be raining still. "*Il pleut dans mon coeur—*" how did it go? Her mind wandered in search of poet and poem, she was too apathetic to concentrate. Victor would know or Sean Connor with his knowing superiority. She would certainly not ask Edmund, sitting beside her in his new suit. Was it "*pleur dans mon coeur*"? For a moment she conjured Victor with his thin face, jackdaw eyes. How could anyone be so slender without appearing scraggy? She glanced sidelong at Edmund's muscular legs. Victor merged into Fergus, black-eyed, burly, flat-stomached. Until he stood up one didn't see Edmund's slightly convex stomach, a convexity which worried him and was the cause of the jogging before breakfast.

Got it, it was "*pleut*" not "*pleur*". Cry, cry! Cry for what? I cried for Edmund, she thought, and here he is, here we are, I have him, snitched back from Venetia. Poppy's lips twitched as she looked down on the clouds. Venetia had no inhibitions, no false restraint. I never glued up his flies, she thought, I just let him go and wept for him. But here he is. She turned further away from Edmund, laying her head back, pretending to sleep. She would feel safer when Edmund put down the paper and buried himself in his Dick Francis. I paid for that too. She peeped under her lashes as Edmund folded the paper and reached for his paperback, cracking its spine in his strong fingers. I paid for the suit, the book and practically everything in his suitcase. He even bought new sunglasses, the French kind one is supposed to be able to stamp on with impunity (I must try it).

When he had spoken the expected words, "Will you lend me some money?", not "can" or "would you mind", but "will", expecting her to say yes which she (immediately, almost apologetically) had, she felt she had regained along with her lover her identity. Or, she thought, as Edmund turned the first page of his thriller, almost, almost regained, for never before would she have had the cheque-book ready and pen in hand. Always before she would have believed the words "I'll pay you back of course" carried credibility.

To be fair, she thought, glancing at his well-clad legs, sometimes he repaid her, sometimes he didn't, but this time she had not listened, not bothered, just written the cheque.

He thinks he owns me and everything that is mine, she thought resentfully, suiting her miserable mood to the thrum, thrum sound of the aeroplane. Yet, she thought, conscious of the man beside her, I suppose I love him.

A stewardess pushing a trolley along the aisle stopped. Edmund ordered a large whisky, jogged her elbow. "Drink, darling?" She kept her eyes shut. "I think she's asleep." Edmund reached for the wallet in his hip pocket. The smell of whisky, the desire to sneeze. She suppressed the sneeze with an effort. Who was it Dad had told her who maintained an orgasm was a sneeze, no more. Peter Quennell, that was who. What could he mean? How come Dad knew Peter Quennell; writers were not his line at all. Used he perhaps to go racing? With Dad gone it was too late to ask. I rate my orgasms higher than a sneeze, thought Poppy.

Edmund read his book, drank his whisky in measured gulps. A beautiful man, Poppy thought. It was not just the wonderful legs in the new trousers, the magnificent torso, the muscled arms, the thick neck (did I say thick?), the handsome face, the golden hair (ears a bit too small but one should not quibble), the whole man was marvellous, had he not been in the Olympic team, well not quite, almost, spare man or something. I love him, I've got him back, what am I to do now? she asked herself in misery.

Beside her Edmund snapped his fingers for attention, ordered another drink.

So indifferent had she been, she had not even asked exactly where they were going. "A place in Africa" might mean anything. Leaning back, feigning sleep, listening to the thrum of the engines, Poppy let her mind play back the last forty-eight hours.

She had been too astonished at Edmund's appearance at the funeral party, his whisking her away in Venetia's car to be either pleased or sorry. Edmund had never before been impetuous. She had been a little drunk, on the defensive. She perversely enjoyed the dinner at Luigi's, felt much the better for it, resolving in future never to order fewer than a dozen oysters.

On the way to Venetia's flat to return the car and collect Edmund's clothes, she had decided to leave him. Get shot.

The drive across London had been long enough for her to compose what she saw as a firm but unhurtful paragraph (she would later put it in writing to make doubly sure) of parting, civilised, definite, kind, final.

The parting words remained unspoken. Venetia's revenge put a strange gloss on the situation. She had felt sorry for Edmund, protective even, her instinct had been to comfort and console. In no time they had found themselves back in the flat they had shared for so long, lying in the bed which sagged in the middle, doing what they always did.

So, thought Poppy, as the aeroplane bore them through the night towards Africa, the wounds in the fabric of their relationship were mended, the holes cobbled together, preparations for the trip planned for Venetia (not that Edmund would have admitted it) kept them busy. Edmund borrowed the money, bought his new clothes, rushed her to the doctor for the necessary injections, made sure she too had the right clothes, took her to Boots to buy anti-diarrhoea pills and suncream, to Hatchards for a supply of holiday books. He was as attentive and caring as one could wish a lover to be.

Perhaps, thought Poppy, I am being ungenerous in thinking he is suppressing the things he would like to say, his objections to the funeral service, the horse-drawn hearse, the oddity of Dad's friends, the multi-coloured dress, the dawn chorus, Fergus and Victor.

Just one small sentence muttered under his breath had escaped as he made love to her. "That will teach you to kiss those yobboes," gasped as he reached his climax long before she was ready for hers.

Was he going to order another drink? Yes, he was, and the intelligent stewardess was ignoring him. Shortly there would be a plastic meal on a plastic tray, he would order wine. Poppy hoped the flannel disguised as bread would absorb the alcohol. Possibly she would pretend to wake, make herself agreeable. One providential thing, she thought behind her closed eyes, was that he had been in the lavatory when Fergus telephoned, had not heard her tell Anthony to lease Fergus the stables and the house.

Edmund jogged her elbow, put a hand on her knee.

"Wake up, darling, dinner."

She opened her eyes, kept silent.

"Might as well eat it, shall I order a bottle of wine?"

He ordered a bottle of wine.

He looks beautiful, poor fellow, when he has had a few drinks, she thought, carefree, pink.

The stewardess brought the plastic trays with plastic food in plastic packets. Poppy buttered a roll and handed it to Edmund who accepted it, munched.

The stewardess brought the wine, poured it into their plastic mugs.

The engines went thrum, thrum. Around them fellow passengers, keeping their elbows close to their sides, picked with urgent fingers at packets of butter, examined the secret parcels of food disguised as meat, cheese or whatonearthcanthisbe.

"I thought," Edmund gulped the wine, spoke close to her ear, "that when we are married I'd call myself Platt-Carew."

"What?" The wine halfway to her mouth rippled in its beaker.

"There's nothing to stop us now your father is dead."

"God," she murmured. (Threat? Exclamation? Prayer?) She swallowed some wine.

"You never liked my surname any more than I do, lots of people take their wife's name. You have a pretty name and will probably like to keep it."

"I shall."

"Good, that's settled, glad you agree." Edmund picked at one of the mystery packages and uncovered what appeared to be a wodge of beef.

"It's not."

"What?" Edmund half turned towards her.

"You never asked me to marry you."

Poppy bit on a roll, put it back on the plastic dish, buttered it and tried again adding some St Ivel cheese, could not swallow, gave up, spitting it into her paper napkin.

"Love! I took it for granted. You can't expect me down on one knee in a plane." Edmund laughed, drank his wine. "Shall we order another bottle, they have a way of shutting the bar."

"No."

"No more wine? Come on." Edmund drank.

"No."

I can't think what I am doing on this plane, thought Poppy. I can stop loving Edmund if I want to, it's not obligatory. Perhaps I only stuck to him because of Dad's objections, now that Dad is dead I am free. If Dad had died sooner I might have stopped loving Edmund long ago. Yet he is a very beautiful man, she thought weakly, turning towards Edmund, looking him over. Perhaps I can teach him to be less selfish. I must think this over, keep a clear head, wait until I am less tired.

"I'll think about it," she said.

"That's settled then." Edmund kissed her cheek, "Eat your dinner, darling."

Poppy pushed the tray away, feeling forlorn. She felt a longing to talk to another woman, found herself thinking of Mary and baby

Barnaby, wishing she knew her better. Normally she feared other women in case they might rob her of Edmund and Edmund for his part distrusted her female friends, subtly denigrating them so that she was more isolated than most women of her age.

That is not how I wanted to do it, thought Edmund, drinking his wine, but, he reassured himself, it will be all right. I hope I appeared more confident than I am. Better the girl that one knows, I dare say. Time has proven that I love her. He turned to take Poppy's hand in his, to hold it reassuringly but she had stuffed both hands in her pockets.

I shall get to know Mary, Poppy thought, and then it occurred to her that, improbable though it might seem, it might be fun to get to know Venetia.

TWENTY

Edmund had not been the only person in the church to concentrate on Poppy.

While most of the men in the congregation let their eyes stray discreetly, recognising friends they wished to buttonhole after the service while their wives took stock of their neighbours' clothes, state of health, stage of decrepitude, Calypso Grant's nephew Willy Guthrie, having sighted Poppy, was unable to take his eyes off her.

It was not, he thought, that she was particularly pretty, it was the general ensemble, even the imperfections which struck a chord in his heart. He had a full face view as she came up the aisle and a long stare at her profile during the service. He was pleased that his aunt had deputed him to retrieve her coat when the service was over.

"Once Bob's in his grave she will feel warmer." What exactly did she mean? "You can ask for it back, for by then it is I who will be feeling the chill." An old person being fanciful.

Willy looked forward to introducing himself, asking for the coat, finding something felicitous to say. He believed in the impact of words. He hoped she would smile at whatever he said and that later at the drinks party it would be possible to chat and pave the way for future meetings *à deux*.

He was therefore aghast when Calypso, on leaving the graveside, asked him to fetch the coat saying that she was cold as she had predicted she would be, tired and more than ready to go home. "You don't wish to go to an awful drinks party, do you?"

Willy made a faint unspoken protest, his aunt appeared impervious. "Think of all the noise, all those hearty men heehawing and their wives screeching. I am too old for that sort of thing, and champagne, for if it's anything to do with Bob Carew it will be champagne, upsets my stomach at this hour. Run for the coat, dear Willy, I shall wait in the car."

Forgetting his felicitous phrase, Willy mutinously went to get the coat. He was rewarded by Poppy's smile and a grateful flash from her green eyes which in the church he had thought to be brown. As he carried the coat, still warm from her body, back to his aunt Willy decided that what was always said about her was right, she was an utterly selfish old woman who had never been anything else. He started the engine of the car and drove off stifling his disappointment.

"An attractive girl." Calypso settled in the seat beside him.

"Was she?" Childishly Willy attempted to hide his chagrin.

When they arrived at his aunt's house Calypso stepped out of the car and slammed the door. "If you drive fast," she said, looking in at Willy, "the party will still be going on, the most boring people will have left, the fun beginning. Have a good time."

"But—" said Willy.

"I wanted to come home, you wanted to go to the party. Hurry." She was mocking him.

"How—"

"Go on, Willy, off you go and tell me about it later."

"Are you—"

"I am all right. I shall change my clothes, then take the dog for a walk. Off you go." Even with her face close to his so that he could count the wrinkles, he could see what people meant when they said she had been a lovely girl. "Not as selfish as all that." She was laughing now, teasing him.

"Thank you." Willy turned the car and drove back towards Poppy Carew. As he drove he whistled a Bach cantata and allowed himself to hope that in some neat way things would work out so that, the party over, he would be able to take Poppy out to dinner and who knows – or if this was too fanciful a scenario he would be on such terms that it would be natural, in a day or two, to telephone, fix a date, carry on from there. He forgot that a few short days before he had boasted of his freedom. As he drove he composed felicitous phrases and congratulated himself that there would be no overlap: his long affair with his late girl Sarah had ended not with a bang or even on a sour note, it had unstitched like a seam no longer able to hold together. He felt perfectly friendly towards Sarah, a very nice girl, but in retrospect surprised that he had ever felt desire. He felt the same towards several other girls who had occupied his time and his heart. Was it heart though, Willy wondered, searching, as he drove, for felicitous phrases, or merely sex? The sensations both mental and physical aroused by Poppy were utterly different. It is different each time, he told himself, but heretofore I have found things to say while now even imagining myself faced with the girl, hoping to impress, I am struck dumb, can't think of a thing and I have yet to speak to her. It was rather ridiculous, thought Willy, to feel like this when all he had to go on was her appearance, he had not even heard her voice properly. That at least, thought Willy, driving fast, can be rectified. What if she has a voice which grates on the nerves? Willy scotched the idea, it was too awful.

Reducing speed as he reached the village, he drove past the church and the graveyard where Bob Carew lay cool under a mound of flowers and along the village green. The line of cars which had stretched from the church to the house was nearly gone, a few people were standing chatting by their cars before driving away. Willy stopped the car by the house. The front door was open, the hall empty. He listened.

From the back of the house he heard a raised voice, a row of some sort was in progress, somebody was very angry, a woman's voice expostulating, a high keening coloratura.

"My rugs, my carpets, it's ground into the parquet, I'll kill whoever did it, my kitchen, the stairs, have you seen the landing? A whole pot *and a* tin of golden syrup, look at it, look! Don't move, you'll make it worse, oh, I could—" The voice drowned a muttered chorus male and female. Willy had the impression that the lament was repetitious, could it be Poppy making this gruesome racket? Mystified, he took a few steps towards the sound and peered into what proved to be the kitchen. At once the voice shouted: "Don't come in here, you'll grind it in. Who are you? What do you know about this? Was it you? Your idea of a joke?"

"Not a joke," said a voice from the chorus.

"Not funny at all," said another.

Willy felt the woman's blast of anger; an oldish woman was doing the shouting, three girls in the background and two men he recognised as the undertakers the chorus. There was no sign of Poppy.

Silence fell. Willy introduced himself. Interested faces stared. One of the girls was holding a baby. He was suspected of something malign.

"I came to see Poppy," he said bravely, "er – Poppy Carew."

"She's gone," said the larger undertaker.

"Evaporated," said the thin undertaker.

"Whisked away," said one of the girls.

"Dada, dada." The baby held out its arms.

The undertakers laughed, releasing pent-up merriment.

"What—" began Willy.

"Some joker has poured honey and syrup on the floor, it spread all over the house on people's feet. Mrs Edwardes is furious. This is Mrs Edwardes."

Willy smiled placatingly at Mrs Edwardes and said, "My name is Willy Guthrie." Mrs Edwardes looked unlikely to believe it.

"I am Fergus. This is Mary, that's Annie, Frances, the infant—"

"Barnaby." Mary jogged the baby. "And Victor." Fergus indicated Victor.

"How awful." Willy grasped the cause of the brouhaha. "Who did it?" He deftly cast the ball back into Mrs Edwardes's court.

"The Mafia," suggested Mary, grinning. Mrs Edwardes drew in her breath, she was off again unless—

"Why don't we clear it up?" suggested Willy. "I'd be glad to help."

"So who did spread the treacle?" asked Calypso later that evening when Willy had recounted his experience. "It was good of you to stay and wash the floors, it was not after all anything to do with you."

"I was able to talk to them, get to know them."

"Ah."

"Yes."

They sat on either side of the log fire he had lit to cheer the autumnal evening, Calypso, resting after her tramp through the woods (working off the depression engendered by the funeral), waited for Willy to tell her more. She would not ask again who had spread the treacle, she thought she knew, her eyes had ranged round the congregation, not got stuck on one object like Willy's.

They had washed the kitchen floor and mopped through the house cleaning the sticky footprints from rugs and carpets. Like a general with his troops, Mrs Edwardes had issued orders to her depleted workforce for as soon as Willy offered, Fergus and the girls remembered the hearse and the horses and the urgent need to load up and get them home which left Victor, who it transpired was only standing in as assistant undertaker, having no proper role in the Furnival outfit. As they worked Willy listened to Victor ingratiating himself with Mrs Edwardes; it seemed Victor too was interested in Poppy's whereabouts.

"I did see Edmund in the church," said Mrs Edwardes, emptying the bucket of dirty water down the sink, "but he was with another girl, not sitting as you'd expect with Poppy."

"Oh," said Victor, encouragingly tilting his voice to a questioning tone, "— is?"

"Since her Dad couldn't stand the sight of him, it may be that Edmund was being tactful." Mrs Edwardes made this sound improbable.

"Perhaps he was," Victor led her on, "being tactful."

"But I got the impression," Mrs Edwardes raised her voice above the sound of fresh water pouring into the bucket, "earlier today, this morning to be exact, that Edmund is no longer persona grata." She turned off the tap.

"Oh," said Victor, "why was that?"

"Persona grata he has been for a very long time, years, I should say, eight years to be exact, yes I'm right, eight."

"Ah," said Victor, "eight."

"But not with her Dad. Oh no, Edmund was persona *not* grata with him."

"Non," murmured Victor.

"I dare say you're right." Jane Edwardes was undampened. "I got that impression from Poppy this morning when she was eating her breakfast. Bacon and egg, didn't want two, I offered another, she seemed a bit off Edmund, if you get my meaning."

"Oh."

"Quite off, I'd say. If you knew girls as well as I do you'd know the signs."

"Of course."

"Then suddenly at the party, I don't suppose you noticed, you were all very busy talking. No, you didn't notice." Mrs Edwardes looked round. "Got any more of that washing powder? Carpet shampoo's what we need but I've run out."

"This do?"

"Thanks, that's fine, not much more to do now, is there, Mr . . ."

"Guthrie, Willy."

"At the party?" ventured Victor, manoeuvring the conversational wheel.

"Just this bit, that's the lot. I can check tomorrow when it's dry."

Willy admired Victor's restraint.

"As I say. All of you busy talking when in rushes Edmund, catches sight of Poppy, drags her off and in two jiffs they are gone. I don't know what happened to the girl."

"What girl?"

"The girl he was with. Came into the church with him, nice looking girl, a bit older than Poppy but as I say nice looking, wearing a decent black dress, very suitable, not like—"

"Like?" Victor dared.

"Well," Jane shrugged disloyally, "nobody could call the dress Poppy was wearing suitable."

"I thought it very pretty," said Victor rashly.

"Pretty all right." Jane Edwardes twisted a floor cloth in her strong hands, wringing it over the sink. "There. That's it then, that's the lot. Thank you very much both of you. I'll be shutting up now." It was plain she was waiting for them to leave. "Got a lift back with somebody else, I dare say."

"Who?" asked Victor who had lost the thread.

"The girl in the suitable dress," said Willy speaking to Victor for the first time.

Victor laughed. "Come and have a drink in the pub." He was convinced that Poppy would be returning to her father's house that night, wished to fill in time.

"No thank you, I have to get back," Willy declined thinking that if Poppy had been as it seemed abducted, she was not likely to come back. On the other hand it was just possible that his aunt might know where he could locate her in London. He was loath to ask Victor for Poppy's address and so declare his interest. Victor was clearly a rival.

"I am thinking of taking a few days off some time soon," said Willy casually as he prepared to leave for his farm, after supping with his aunt. He had decided to keep quiet about his sudden passion for Poppy; Calypso was used to a fairly rapid turnover of girls in his life and might class Poppy as just another of the many, not realising that she was unique, too precious to discuss.

Calypso, who had found Willy's company irritating during the meal, guessed that the sultry mood he appeared to be in could be attributed to the moment in the church when he had sighted Poppy.

"Your pigs will come to no harm, you have left them before," she said.

"Well—" said Willy.

"You have fallen in love with Poppy Carew, I saw it happen at the funeral. *Coup de foudre,*" stated Calypso, cutting short Willy's reluctance, tired of waiting for him to confide.

Willy laughed unconvincingly.

"It happens," said Calypso blandly. "If one can hate at first sight equally one can love. It runs in your family. Your uncle Hector got it when he clapped eyes on me. I thought all he wanted was a healthy girl to breed an heir by. Later of course I adored him."

Willy thought this was not the picture of his aunt painted by her peers and that anyway no comparison could be made between an old uncle he had barely known and himself.

"So what are you going to do about it?" pressed Calypso, assuming Willy's tacit agreement.

"I have to find her," said Willy, yielding.

"Ask if you need any help." Casually Calypso prodded the large dog who screened the heat of the fire from her legs. "Move." The dog flicked his ears back, settling his haunches more firmly on the rug. "Good luck," she said, as Willy bent to kiss her goodbye.

"Thanks," said Willy, "I may take you up on the help." There were times when he found his aunt extremely trying. This was not one of them.

TWENTY-ONE

As her ears began to pop and the stewardess made sure the safety belts were fastened, Poppy regretted her hauteur during the preparations for the journey. A new place in Africa might be anywhere. Judging by the length of the journey, North Africa was their destination. It was now too late and she was too proud to ask Edmund which country. If I had any wits I would have listened to the captain on the intercom, she thought, as the plane lost height, her ears popped and the engine whined then roared preparing to land, arriving with a triple jolt to taxi to the disembarkation bay.

Experiencing a spasm of fear, she thought of how beautifully birds came in to land, twisting their wings to brake against the wind, extending their feet ready for contact. She thought particularly of mallard measuring their descent exactly, their clever feet touching the water so that there was no bumping, jarring or shaking, just a long V of ripples on a still lake.

She looked out at lights, a glimpse of buildings, as the plane swung taxiing in a half circle. Fellow passengers raised their voices eager to get out of this metal tube, release the straps holding them, stretch their cramped limbs.

Edmund, stuffing his Dick Francis into his briefcase, was anxious to stand up and ease the new trousers cutting into his crotch.

"There's a fellow meeting me. Representative of the Tourist Board," he said offhandedly. Poppy did not answer. He would be nerving himself to think clearly: to be ready for his business talk, hoping to make a good impression. He should not have drunk all those whiskies.

"He will be waiting at the Customs, see us through," said Edmund, "he'll have a car." He checked their tickets were safe in his jacket pocket. "Got your passport?"

"Yes," she said, undoing her safety belt, giving Edmund a quick glance, noting with sinking heart his out-thrust lower lip, sure sign of too many drinks. Hope for the best, she told herself, standing up, collecting her hand luggage, following Edmund out of the plane into a dark North African night.

They waited with the other passengers by the carousel, yawning, tired, dousing the anxiety that their particular bag might have acquired a will of its own, gone elsewhere to a friendlier country, might not turn up whirling round on this piece of technological nonsense which replaced the human porter who might, just possibly, hoping for a tip, have greeted one with a smile.

Poppy looked round at hawk-nosed men, holsters on hip, watching them. Guards? Police? Customs men? She was not going to ask Edmund. Fleetingly she thought of Singh's bulky figure carrying the Thermos boxes of delicious funeral meats. Had he got them back, had Jane Edwardes cleared away the débris, tidied the house?

Was her home still there?

Her bag appeared lying upside-down, shaken by the carousel, the strap torn, the label with her name on it shredded. She grabbed it as it passed. Edmund looked irritated, thrust out his lip, the carousel went round twice more.

"Where the hell? Bloody inefficient—"

"There, it's coming, catch it—"

They pushed their trolley towards Customs. Haughty, expressionless men gestured at cases. "Open." Their fingers roughly probing among nighties, knickers, dresses, disarranging so that the case would be hard to shut, picked out books, ruffled pages, peered.

"We might be in Russia," a man complained.

"There's nothing subversive or even porn in my bag."

"Didn't like my duty free—"

"Muslim country," said another in explanation. "Dry."

"Pay attention to that, do they?"

"Wouldn't know, this is my first visit."

"That must be my man." Edmund hurried, lip back in place, smiling, expansive, to shake hands with an Italian-suited individual, dark glasses blotting his eyes. He introduced Poppy who shook hands, failing to catch the name as muttered by Edmund, not really listening, thinking it rash of Edmund to refer to this individual as "my man", it being more likely to be the other way about.

Their luggage was put into the boot of a black Mercedes. They sat three abreast on the back seat, Edmund in the middle, Poppy silent, ignored by the two men who talked immediately of the new hotel to which they were going, the prospect of opening the country up to the expected tourist boom, its troubles being now over.

Half listening, Poppy wondered which country in this part of the world did not have troubles. She was by now, as well as tired, hungry. She regretted passing up the meal on the aircraft.

They drove fast passing other cars with blaring horn, shaving close to contemptuous camels, terrifying cyclists wobbling out of the dark, nagging at lorries clinging desperately to the crown of the steeply cambered road, overtaking with a snarl and a howl, car lights briefly illuminating humble overloaded donkeys, errant goats, palm trees, dogs.

Poppy shut her eyes as a limping dog dashed across the road, the car bumped, the driver laughed a short yelp of glee. She strained her ears, heard nothing more. Dear God, let it have been killed outright.

Edmund went on talking. "How far out of town is the airport?"

"Some thirty miles. In a moment the road runs along the sea by the new boulevard and the beach where we build the Cabana complex among the palms which I show you tomorrow. They should be a great attraction, bring many tourists. We transplant the palms of course from the famous oasis."

"I see."

Had they not seen the dog, felt the bump? Poppy's mouth was dry, she no longer felt hungry, drawing away from Edmund into her corner.

"And there is our sea. See the waves are phosphorescent, see how they light up as they reach the sand, are they not beautiful, romantic?"

"Difficult to see, it's very dark." Edmund craned his neck to look out into the dark past Poppy.

"I think perhaps there will be a storm maybe, an autumn storm."

"Rain?" asked Edmund, not expecting rain, pained. "Really?"

"But not to worry. Storms are short. Here is the hotel, as I told you, not quite completed but it is superb. The other passengers on your plane go to the old ones, you only are complimented with the best. Under this archway, here you are, please, welcome."

The car stopped under a portico. "No doubt Miss Carew would like to mount straight up to the room?"

"I expect she would."

"And we go to the bar for your nightcap?"

"Great."

Poppy drew breath, breathing in a lungful of wet concrete-smelling air. She watched their bags collected by a servant in khaki uniform.

"You go ahead, darling, make yourself comfortable, I'll be up in a minute."

He was pretending not to have noticed the dog. Perhaps he had not noticed the dog.

She did not look at Edmund, said a polite good night to their guide, followed the servant with the bags to the lift. The room was large, airy, twin beds, fitted cupboards, bathroom. It might be any hotel room in any country. The servant put down the bags, she tipped him with English money, he left. She opened the window, looked out from a balcony into inky darkness, the sound of distant surf, palm trees rustling and with the smell of wet cement a whiff of jasmine.

Perhaps he had not noticed the dog, he was busy talking.

He had his work, it was important that he should succeed in this his first venture in the new job.

Perhaps he had not noticed. He could not have helped the dog.

Nobody could help the dog.

A few cars patrolled along the sea road. She watched their lights. Her watch had stopped, it must be pretty late. The hotel was silent, almost as though it were empty. She ran water in the bathroom, bathed her face, washed her hands, her hands would not stop shaking. Stupid.

Better to unpack and go to bed, be asleep when he comes up.

She heaved her bag on to the bed, picked out the lovely dress, Dad's present, carried it to the cupboard to put it on a hanger to hang it perhaps outside the cupboard where she could see it, be comforted. She opened the cupboard door, screamed a small controlled choking scream, shut the door in haste, bent to pick up the bedside telephone.

"'Allo?"

"A gentleman in the bar. Please find a gentleman in the bar. Mr Platt, Room Thirty-eight. Get him fast."

"*Comment?*"

"Oh – *Un monsieur. Il y a un monsieur dans le bar, appellez le vite, s'il vous plaît.*"

She waited, taking deep breaths.

"Plat?" a puzzled voice.

"Yes. *Oui*. Platt. P – L – A—"

"*Pas de messieurs.*"

"What?"

"No gentleman. Bar empty. *Fermé. Chiuso.*"

"God!"

"*Comment?*"

"Send somebody up, Room Thirty-eight. *Vite*. At once. *Subito.*"

"*Subito.*" The line went dead. This is ridiculous.

It seemed a long time before there was a knock on the door. Two servants standing, moderately interested.

Poppy showed them the occupants of the cupboard, a group of very large reddish cockroaches clustered halfway up the cupboard, fidgeting in the electric light, waving long sensitive feelers.

"Ah!"

"I want another room, I can't sleep here."

"*Comment?*"

"Another room. *Une autre chambre. Ein anderer – un altro*—"

Confabulation, shrugging of shoulders. One of the men flipped at the cockroaches with a towel from the bathroom.

"No. *Non. Nein.* Another room—" She pushed the dress back into the bag, zipped it shut, made herself plain by signs and single words. One man seemed to understand Italian, the man who had flipped with the towel. Now he craftily captured the cockroaches in it, shook them away out of the open window.

"*Ecco!*"

"I still want to move."

"*E pericoloso sporgersi.*" The man leaned out laughing, demonstrating the insects' departure, smiling ingratiatingly, expecting to please with his little joke.

"I—"

The man pointed at the bed. "*Allora! Dormez bien. Gute Nacht.*"

"*No.* Another room. The bloody things will come back." She knew she was being irrational. "*Un altra camera. Ein.* Oh God, I can't speak German. For Christ's sake move me."

"OK."

At last another room far down the corridor, the servants anxious to please, by now opening each cupboard door exhibiting its pristine emptiness. The drawers too pulled out, virgin clean, bringing more towels to augment those already in the bathroom, running the water (See it runs?), testing the lights, the telephone. Everything in order. "*Alles in Ordnung.*" Accepting tips. English money again. Good night. Good night. Poppy locked the door after them, washed her hands again, undressed, got into bed, covered her face with the sheet, prayed for sleep.

He *must* have noticed the dog.

Perhaps he had *not* noticed the dog.

Had Victor and Fergus helped Jane Edwardes clear up after the party? Perhaps the girls had helped? The girl with the baby, Mary? Why had she not telephoned from London, she was after all responsible, it was her father's funeral, asked Mrs Edwardes whether everything was all right, told her that she was letting the house and stables to Fergus. Yes, Mrs E., all those horses, yes, Mrs E., that's what I said.

Am I having a nervous breakdown?

What about her job? Had she or had she not made it clear when she telephoned them about Dad's death that she was not coming back? What had she said? Had she made herself clear? Memory failed her. Why worry about that now, a bit late surely.

No, I am not having a breakdown.

And Edmund? Not in the bar? There were other bars. There were always other bars. She had seen this film before.

What would Venetia Colyer do under these circumstances? Or Mary with her dyed and spiky hair pomaded into points, tiny upright striking spears?

Poppy switched on the light, took the dress Dad had given her for her birthday and hung it near her on a chair so that if by some miracle she slept it would be in view when she woke. Then she got back into bed, laid her head on the pillow, switched off the light.

Neither Venetia nor Mary would have got themselves into a dump like this boiling with cockroaches with a man like Edmund. When they didn't really want to.

We have no joint destination, she thought, Edmund and I.

Somewhere in the night a donkey brayed, expressing, as no other beast can, all the sorrows of the world.

TWENTY-TWO

In an empty bar Edmund sat with Mustafa from the Government Tourist Board, a half-full glass of whisky before him. He was aware that his host barely succeeded in hiding his feeling that it was a long time since he had met the plane, that everything that could be discussed between them that evening had been mulled over multiple times, that it was time to call it a day.

I have one more thing to say to him, thought Edmund, it is important. Why did I tell him the whole story of my life with Poppy, my love for Poppy? Edmund tried to remember. How did Poppy come into this important thing he had to say, ah of course, got it, here goes.

"I know the car's well sprung. Trust the Krauts to make a good car," he began.

"—?" Mustafa hummed.

"Yes. That's what I said. No, not better than a Ro— Ro— What? I said Rolls Royce, didn't I? Ro Ros are the very best, we all know *that*. You agree?"

"—" he sighed politely.

"Of course. Even Arabs – God – I've lost the thread. I was saying that we ran over a dog, you must have noticed."

Mustafa lit a cigarette, blew smoke towards the ceiling.

Edmund ploughed on. "Poppy noticed. Went stiff as a board with horror."

Edmund's host glanced secretly at his watch, caught the eye of the barman.

"Yes." Edmund answered Mustafa's silence. "As I say. Too polite, too tactful to protest of course, but horrified."

"A stray dog." Mustafa drew in a lungful of smoke.

"Grant you, a stray maybe, but your driver ran over it. I felt the bump even though we were in the second-best car. I say, that's funny. Second best."

"So?" Mustafa let the smoke drift out of his mouth finishing with a sharp puff.

"He should have stopped."

"Stopped. Why?"

"For appearance sake. Taken the dog's number."

"No use, no point, no number—"

"Of course no use to the *dog*, it was dead, wasn't it, but if you want to attract the British tourist you have to stop when you run over a dog, it's essential."

"Ha ha ha." The marvellously comic Brits.

"No laughing matter. Preferable of course *not* to run over a dog in the first place. The British tourist doesn't want to spend his hard-earned pounds running over dogs."

"You say—"

"I'm telling you. I say nothing matters, my precious Poppy says" (well she didn't, too polite wasn't she, a tactful girl) "nothing matters as much as dogs, better a child."

"A child?" Mustafa straightened from a lounging position.

"Yup," said Edmund wisely. "For some reason, yes. Herod is a secret hero with some sects in the UK."

"Ah?" He must make inquiries, sects could be a serious cause of disturbances. "So?"

"I say. What's the time? Lord, it's late. You've kept me talking while what I've been meaning to do is take my precious Poppy in my arms and tell her how much I love her. I've loved her for years."

"You will marry her?" Mustafa feigned interest, he was sick of the subject of Poppy.

"Of course. Her father died the other day. Didn't like me, influenced her against me or tried to. I told you that didn't I?"

"Yes." Twice over, thought Mustafa, in truth, in triplicate. Can't stand it again.

"Didn't succeed though, did he? Told you that too. Now then, look here, I can't sit up all night talking to you when I have to comfort Poppy. Shall I tell you—"

"No." Mustafa released a glint of impatience.

"Oh, I see. OK I won't, but let me tell you the British won't stand for killing dogs, it isn't done."

"She did not notice," unwisely Mustafa answered.

"Of course she bloody noticed. She noticed the *dog*, the bump, the shit driver laughed. Christ, that laugh could cost you all Thompson's Tours, much better Herod."

"Who is this Herod?"

"Wouldn't go down well here, he was a Jew as far as I can remember."

"So?" Bristle concealed by cigarette smoke.

"So," said Edmund with a flash of sobriety, "I must leave you. Meet you tomorrow in the hotel bar. We can get down to business then."

They drove back, conversation exhausted. Edmund knew they had arrived when he smelled wet cement. They said good night. The night was beautiful, moonless. Edmund looked up at the stars. He felt an overwhelming love for Poppy, he wondered as he went up in the lift why he had not insisted ages ago on marrying her. Soon he would be in bed, hold her warm in his arms, too tired tonight for more than that but her warm bottom in the small of his back held familiar allure. He would not wake her, just creep in (ah, here we are), no need to put on the light. He stood to accustom his eyes to the dark, moved forward, arms outstretched. "Oh hell, twin beds, creep into this one, tell her in the morning when my head has stopped roaring how much I love her." He pulled off his clothes, slipped into bed. He must not take Poppy so much for granted. He lay down, remembered his watch, wound it, put it on the bedside table, laid his head on the pillow. What had he told Mustafa? My love is a fire which inflames my soul. Oh dear God! I'm drunk. The classic way to make a fool of oneself. For some reason it seemed all Poppy's fault he had made a monumental cock-up of the job, first try.

TWENTY-THREE

When Calypso Grant's husband Hector returned from the 1939–45 war he bought land to plant his dream wood, an idea born in the treeless Western Desert which had become an obsession.

He found his location, a bowl of land with a stream meandering through it dotted with oak and limes. On the side of a hill overlooking the land a tumble-down house. He bought the land, restored the house and spent the rest of his life planting trees.

By the time Hector had planted wild cherries in a series of loops, circles and curves to spell his wife's name, Calypso, who had originally scoffed at her husband, became bitten by the bug. Together they planted beech and oak, chestnut, hornbeam, sycamore, pine, larch, rowan, birch and more limes to scent the air. They encouraged an undergrowth of spindleberry, blackthorn, hawthorn, hazel and wild rose. Among the scrub they set honeysuckle to ramp. In open spaces they encouraged gorse. When the wild cherries flowered spelling, as Hector intended, his wife's name, they had rivalry from hawthorn, rowan and horse chestnut. Between them they had planted clumps of box, philadelphus and lilac, planning that at almost every turn of the year there would be the reassurance of sweet scents. Forty years on, walking through the wood in the evening, Calypso doubted whether anyone flying over the wood would read her name spelled in blossom but there was no part of the wood which did not spell Hector for her.

To wild anemones, primroses, bluebells and foxgloves they added in open glades drifts of fritillary, spring and autumn cyclamens, windflowers, daffodils and narcissi.

In the centre of the wood they widened and dammed the stream to make a lake, bordering it with reeds to form a haven for wildfowl and warbler. The wood as it grew was colonised by innumerable birds and wild animals.

As she walked in the wood the day after Bob Carew's funeral Calypso thought of her husband, how he would have enjoyed the funeral, especially the tape of birdsong in the church, a dawn chorus comparable to the chorus in the wood which had delighted their springs.

Pausing by a clump of hazel wound about with honeysuckle, thinking of Hector, she breathed in to catch a last elusive whiff of honey. Instead, sneaking from the far side of the hill on a north-east breeze, she smelled pig.

Some years before his death, to protect his wood from an encroaching developer, Hector had bought the land over the hill and with it a group of derelict farm buildings. He restored the buildings and leased the land to a dairy farmer. To the dawn chorus was added the comforting sound of lowing cattle.

The lease expired, the farmer died and Calypso rented the farm to Hector's nephew Willy Guthrie who had chosen an agricultural career. Tiring of milking cows, Willy switched his attention to pigs and presently prospered, growing what his aunt referred to as Happy Hams, pigs who lived in comfort, lolling at night in deep straw in the barns, roaming freely by day in family or adolescent groups in large paddocks with ample fresh water piped to their troughs.

In exchange for not losing their tails, having their teeth extracted, sleeping on bare concrete, imprisoned in the sweatbox – conditions of the modern pig – the prospective Hams surrendered their lives after a period of cheerful carefree growth to become sides of bacon and high-class smoked ham similar to Jambon d'Ardennes which Willy smoked himself in a barn converted into a smokery. These hams under the brand name of Guthrie he sold at high prices to upmarket restaurants and delicatessens.

Calypso, scenting pig, forgot Hector, noted that the wind had swung to the north-east, the only and fortunately rare wind to bring hint of pig, remembered that she had news for Willy garnered from carefully selected telephone calls. She was fond of Willy, who reminded her of her late husband, not so much by physical resemblance but by genetic quirks. Hector had never been as Willy was, gangling as though his limbs were not only loose but double-jointed, giving his movements a disconnected quality which some people found irritating but which she found endearing. Where Hector's eyes had sparkled like jet, Willy's were brown velvet. It was the intonation when moved, the catch in his voice which made her stop, remember with a pang that she would never hear that voice again.

With her hand raised to pick the last honeysuckle and hold it to her nose, Calypso hesitated. She left the honeysuckle where it was and set off towards her house to telephone Willy. Her dog, who had been patiently waiting for her to make a move, followed.

"Willy?"

"Yes, Aunt."

"What are you up to?"

"Just about to stroll round the enterprise, scratch a few backs perhaps." His voice was depressed.

"Leave all that and come and see me."

"OK, I'll come, love to."

"Have you had supper?"

"Not yet."

"Come and share mine."

"Thanks, I'd like that."

"Good."

"I'll be over as soon as I've settled the pigs."

"Don't bring Mrs Future."

Willy laughed. Mrs Future, a sow of exceptional intelligence and charm, born the runt of the family, was, after being reared on a bottle by Willy, under the impression that she was entitled to accompany him wherever he went, tripping merrily at his heels, raising pleased smiles from the neighbours in her early and adolescent youth but now, a mature sow, her appearance in people's houses and gardens raised protests, complaints even.

"It's OK," Willy reassured his aunt. "She farrowed last night, she can't leave her piglets."

"I hesitate to worry you but there was a bit of a whiff when I was walking in the wood just now, of dung."

"Not to worry, that would be Harry Arnold who took a load away to muck spread it, suits his land, the pong is gone."

"Right."

Calypso uncorked a bottle of wine, setting it to breathe in the warmth of the kitchen, debated what to give her nephew to eat, decided on pasta with a garlicky sauce, the aroma of which would stifle any lingering hint of pig Willy might bring with him. In her youth, she thought with amusement, she would have sent him off to bath and change his clothes if he dared bring evidence of the byre with him. In age she was sensitive to young people's feelings. As she chopped onions and garlic for the sauce she debated whether or not to tell Willy the result of her telephonings. She was still undecided when he arrived, coming in by the kitchen door, stooping to kiss her cheek.

"Smells delicious, brought you a ham. I had a bath after your remarks and changed. Have I kept you waiting?"

"No. Hang it on the hook on the larder beam. You must let me pay you."

"No, no."

"I insist."

"No, no, I owe you."

"Whatever for?"

"Taking me to Bob Carew's funeral."

"I hope this doesn't end in tears," Calypso exclaimed as she poured the saucepan of pasta to drain in a colander.

"If it did it would be worth it," said Willy. His aunt drew in her breath with a hiss, reminded with a fierce pang of Hector. She watched Willy scatter Parmesan on his pasta, twirl it round his fork and eat. She was glad that love had not impaired his appetite. She offered a second helping.

"No, thank you." He sipped his wine, stared gloomily at his empty plate then, looking up at her, said bleakly, "What am I to do? I can't find her."

"Where have you looked?"

"I tried the daily woman, Mrs Edwardes, at her father's house. Not much joy."

"And?"

"She gave me Poppy's London address and the address of her work. She's left her job and her flat is empty. Nobody answers the door and the telephone rings and rings."

"Sad."

"It appears that Fergus Furnival and his cousin Victor are trailing her too, no luck for them either."

"Ah."

"And Poppy's solicitor who is arranging the lease for Fergus – he's renting her house and stables by the way—"

"Swift work."

"Yes, very. Well, the solicitor hasn't got her address, bit annoyed about it Mrs Edwardes says, complains of being rushed."

"It's good for solicitors to be rushed." Calypso offered fruit.

"No thanks." His appetite blunted, Willy sat looking glum. Thoughtfully Calypso peeled a peach.

Willy burst out, "I must find her. I've got to. Please don't laugh."

"I am not laughing," said Calypso as sharply as she could with a mouthful of peach. She swallowed. "It's not funny." It's quite possibly sad, she thought. He sits there reminding me of Hector behaving in this painfully old-fashioned way. Why me, why must he drag me into this? I am old, I manage to keep my equilibrium. Why should I be bothered with Willy in love?

"What about the man who swept her off, her lover?" she asked, conscious of her brutality.

"I don't think he matters," said Willy.

"She went away with him, you told me. You told me he burst in on the party and dragged her away."

"I don't think she went willingly."

"If she did not want to go she could have called for help, made a scene."

"Perhaps she felt embarrassed—"

"Come off it, Willy."

"There may have been a reason for going with him. I'm sure she didn't want to."

"What makes you think that? You weren't there."

"A gut feeling."

"Now we have guts. Extra-sensory perception next."

"Look, Aunt, if I had been there I would have stopped her. Victor and Fergus who could have stopped her were otherwise occupied, the one coping with the solicitor the other with a publisher – he's written a novel, I gather – it all happened very fast. If I had been there—" Willy looked distraught.

"So now you blame me for making you drive me home when you wanted to stay—"

"Not that. You needed to get home. You sent me back. I was too late, that's all, but I feel there was a reason to make her go with him."

"I can only think of one reason if she is not in love with him," said Calypso laughing. "She went with him to prevent another girl getting him."

"Aunt!" Willy was shocked.

"It doesn't mean she has feet of clay, it would be a very normal reaction, the sort of thing I'd have done at her age." Calypso chuckled.

"Oh." Willy was thoughtful, not sure he wanted Poppy to resemble his aunt when young.

"Coffee?" suggested Calypso.

"Please."

They were silent while Calypso made coffee. She was surprised to find herself anxious for her nephew, Hector's nephew, she corrected herself, it being her habit, of which she was proud, to let others, particularly the young, make their own mess without interference.

"How sure are you," she asked quietly, "that it's love?"

"As certain as I could ever be about anything."

"But you don't know her."

"Did you know much about Hector? Did he know you?"

"What has that got to do with it?"

"Just that I want to spend the rest of my life with Poppy. Uncle Hector must have felt the same about you."

"I didn't realise it at the time."

"But you did later. You said you did. Poppy can't realise it either. We haven't even spoken to each other or rather I said something about taking your coat back and she smiled. I didn't hear what she said."

Calypso stared at Willy whose voice as he spoke of Poppy waxed lyrical.

"She isn't a virgin; I was," she said, hoping to bring him to earth.

"You may have been a virgin but . . ." Willy flushed, hesitated, fell silent.

"But what?"

"Oh you know, the catty things people say about you being a – er – man eater. All those old women and—"

"The old men?"

Willy laughed. "The old men all wish they'd been in my uncle's shoes." He watched his aunt, they regarded each other smiling.

"So you are certain?"

"Yes."

"Very well. I think I can find out where she's gone."

"You can?" Willy's voice whooped up exultant.

"Not that it matters."

"Why not?"

"Because you will be lying in wait for her when she comes back."

"Oh no I won't. Wherever she is I shall go and find her."

"Oh my!" Calypso admired his spirit, refrained from asking whether this was wise.

"So how can you find out where she is?" To Willy it seemed wildly improbable that his old aunt could help him.

"By talking to the girl Poppy snitched him from."

Willy gaped.

"She was in the church with Edmund, she's called Venetia Colyer."

TWENTY-FOUR

When Edmund found Poppy on the terrace overlooking the swimming pool she had finished her breakfast and sat talking to Mustafa who was making himself agreeable.

Edmund felt at a gross disadvantage as they turned towards him, eyeing him through their dark glasses. Taking his own sunglasses from his shirt pocket, blotting out his hungover eyes, Edmund regretted encouraging Poppy to buy such dark ones, he could not see her eyes, her mouth gave nothing away.

Mustafa called out "Hi," smiling and, "Have you had breakfast?" snapping his fingers at a hovering waiter. "Refresh the tray."

"Just coffee please." Edmund sat beside Poppy. "Black."

"Delicious figs," said Poppy in neutral tone, pointing to bits of bruised fruit skin on her plate, bearing, Edmund saw with a pang, the marks of her teeth.

Mustafa called out "Coffee" and something in Arabic.

Edmund wondered whether Mustafa knew they had slept in separate rooms, did he perhaps know where Poppy had spent the night, there had been neither hide nor hair of her when he had surfaced. He was not going to ask Poppy where the hell she had been or what she thought she was up to, in front of Mustafa. He felt betrayed and bitterly resentful, he had had a terrible fright waking to find her gone, she might at least have left a note. He felt choked with whisky-fumed self-pity and love.

"I was suggesting Miss Poppy might like an expedition to the Roman amphitheatre while we do business today. There will be parties going in buses from the other hotels, easy to arrange. The amphitheatre and the theatre are interesting if you like that sort of thing."

"I'll think about it," said Poppy politely.

"The archaeologists who worked for our government were partially British."

"How partial?" asked Poppy gravely.

"From Cambridge," said Mustafa.

"Not Oxford?" (So that's how she's going to be, thought Edmund, little bitch.)

"A bit of both, no matter." Mustafa was careless of universities. He was aware from the servants of this girl making a fuss the night before, she had not mentioned the matter to him, it would be indelicate if he brought it up. The servants had been cringing but with a hint of mockery describing the scene. The girl had made a fuss over a few immigrating locusts, the servants said, calling them cockroaches. Mustafa realised that the offending insects probably were cockroaches yet preferred, as the servants did, to think of them as locusts. Clever beasts to get into such a new hotel, though in truth it had stood half built for a long time. Edmund had slept in the room too drunk to notice the girl's absence. The information on this score was reliable. If Edmund and Poppy represented what one must expect of the new wave of European tourists and their women it would be as well to make it clear once and for all that in this country visitors were expected to make use only of the room they had booked, not move around as the girl had done. Not that it mattered. Edmund was guest of the State and the hotel still empty, incomplete. The girl was talking, projecting her remarks at a point between himself and Edmund. Mustafa jerked to attention.

"Such extraordinary camber," she was saying. "That road we came along from the airport last night, so steeply cambered it was not like the roads you see in most countries, was it an old road?" She turned towards Mustafa, "Pot holes too."

A servant brought coffee for Edmund, collected Poppy's used cup and plates.

"Yes, an old road. The new road is under repair," said Mustafa, "it will soon be open again." That sounded all right, he told himself, no need to tell her the main road had been cleared for troop transport hurrying to take up station at the airport. These things happened, it was unfortunate but not necessary to inform visitors of every slight disturbance. Their currency was too welcome.

"And so crowded," continued Poppy, "so many people and animals at that time of night. Camels and donkeys and—"

"Travelling in the cool of the night," said Edmund, breaking into the chat, fearing mention of the lame dog; he remembered it lame.

"The weather isn't hot," said Poppy. "I'm wearing a jersey and what seemed rather funny was they were all travelling away from the town, it looked like the flight from Egypt."

"Your sense of direction!" exclaimed Edmund in sarcastic contradiction.

"You usually say how good it is," said Poppy saccharine sweet.

"Ah," said Mustafa lightly. "There is a tribal caravan trek at this time of year. Simple people, they move out to an oasis." The girl was likely to be ignorant of local geography and the explanation was in part true.

"Really," said Poppy. "I see." Politely sceptical.

"Forgive me a moment while I telephone," said Mustafa rising. "Then perhaps we start on our tour of the town, the beaches, the Cabana complex to be starting with, the Office of Tourism? You meet the Minister." Edmund should be impressed.

"Certainly," said Edmund. "I am ready." He was gratified.

"And you," said Mustafa to Poppy, "you like to join the bus to the Roman antiquities?" He was sure she would.

"I think I'll just fan about in the garden." She leant back smiling.

Mustafa went to the telephone.

"Garden," said Poppy with a laugh, "great piles of cement. The *garden*," she stressed the word contemptuously, "the garden isn't half made, the whole place reeks of wet cement. I bet the workmen pee in it."

"Shall you bathe?" asked Edmund. "The pool looks nice." Would Venetia have been more helpful?

"Very nice. If you weren't so pie-eyed you'd see it's empty."

"It will all be finished very soon." Edmund ignored the gibe. It was true, if he had looked he would have noticed the emptiness of the pool. He looked at it now. There was a suspicious-looking thing like ordure in the far end. "Soon all this will be peopled by tourists."

"Cockroaches."

"What?"

"Never mind."

"It would help me if you went to the Roman sights and let me know what they are like." It was as close as he could come to an appeal.

"I think I'll stay in the garden or I may explore the town."

Edmund swallowed his resentment. At least she had not brought up the squashed dog, he did not feel up to that just yet. They sat uneasily silent until Mustafa came down the steps from the hotel. He had missed the chance to find out what had happened to Poppy the night before. If he had not been so heavy on the booze there would have been no problem, no mystery.

"Well then," Mustafa rubbed his hands together, "everything arranged. We drive along the coast after visiting the Minister of Tourism."

"Oh, the Minister," said Poppy. "Oh."

"Will you be all right?" On his feet now, preparing to leave with Mustafa, Edmund lingered by Poppy. If only she'd take off those bloody glasses.

"She will be all right," said Mustafa, pleased with his telephone call. The airport was quiet now, they said, excitement over, arrests made. The road was clear, everything under control. We'll keep an eye on the girl, they said, there is nothing to see.

"Are you sure you don't want to see the Roman ant—" began Edmund.

"You know how I hate conducted tours," snapped Poppy.

"Well—" Edmund stood hesitating looking down at her lolling in the garden chair, her long legs crossed at the ankle. "Is there anything I can get you before I go?"

Poppy shook her head.

Edmund walked away with Mustafa. "Goodbye then," he called over his shoulder, hurt. She watched them go down the steps to the road, get into a car and be driven off. She wiped a tear with a finger before it could roll down her cheek.

TWENTY-FIVE

Edmund, introduced to the Minister of Tourism, took a violent dislike to him, loathing his thick greying hair, macho moustache, red lips, even teeth and above all his extremely healthy general appearance. Not having jogged for several days Edmund was pervaded by guilt. This emotion generated a sort of second wind which cleared his mind to such an extent that he was able to conduct his business with zeal, efficiency and dispatch, surprising the Minister whose information relayed from Mustafa via his secretary prior to their meeting had been to the effect that Edmund was to all intents and purposes a pushover.

Edmund's success with the Minister did Mustafa no good but no harm either since he was the nephew by marriage of the Minister's wife. He was amused by Edmund's transformation since it proved his grandmother's theory (she was partly French) that no Englishman was to be trusted. With this in mind he excused himself and went into the outer office where he arranged for a message to be transmitted to the Minister to the effect that it would be as well to take Edmund out of the town for a few hours, visit the Roman city perhaps, be usefully occupied a hundred kilometres away while the troop transports returned from the airport, one never knew with such perfidious people what interpretation they might put on what they saw. There was no need for Edmund to hear of yesterday's unrest. He returned to the Minister's office in time to watch him receive the message on his office telephone, accepting it with understanding calm.

Mustafa thought if the opportunity arose it would be amusing to test another theory his grandmother held about the English. Taking off his dark glasses he flashed an enigmatic smile at Edmund. Edmund remained expressionless, not wishing to show pleasure at having scored, from his employers' point of view, a variety of vital concessions. He was not bothered that Mustafa signalled that he was aware of his success, it was up to Mustafa to run with the hare and hunt with the hounds, he was that sort of wog. Thinking these thoughts he relented and returned Mustafa's smile.

The Minister was now suggesting that their official business over, minor points conceded on both sides thus showing a proper spirit hopeful for the future of tourism, it would be a pleasure and a joy if Edmund allowed him to drive him to the Roman antiquities, the city, the theatre, the amphitheatre, only a few kilometres along the coast by the sea; a few hours off from affairs of State would do no harm. Edmund found himself sitting beside the Minister in his Porsche, driving at speed along a road parallel to the sea while Mustafa followed at a more sedate pace in the Mercedes. Too late Edmund thought that it would have been possible to bring Poppy, then consoled himself that she had had the chance and refused. He set himself to listen to the Minister's description of the Roman city they were to visit, excavated, he assured Edmund, by archaeologists from London University. Edmund thought briefly of Poppy's earlier tease about Oxbridge.

The Roman city impressed Edmund enormously, it was so large it had swallowed up several busloads of Scandinavian tourists with their guides. The buses were parked, silent, glinting in the sun, while their drivers gossiped with a group of herdsmen who were building a fire of driftwood on a slight elevation on the dunes overlooking the ruins. They had with them several disappointed looking donkeys and some flop-eared goats whose charming little kids with enormous knees attracted Edmund's eye. Poppy would have loved them. He made himself listen to the Minister's historical dissertation on the city, its rise, its prosperity, its fall. Having eaten no breakfast and nothing since his meal on the plane, his attention flagged, hunger vied with intellectual interest. Would it be eventually possible, he suggested by way of a diplomatic hint, a good thing even, an encouragement to tourism if the Minister's government built a restaurant near the ruins where hungry tourists would spend their pounds, dollars, Deutschmarks, nothing vulgar naturally.

"Hungry are you?" asked the Minister who had spent a long time in England and was familiar with the expression "cut the cackle". "You English march on your stomach like Napoleon?"

"He was French." Edmund disliked the Minister more than ever. "A Corsican actually."

"Look." The Minister pointed towards the car park.

"I see. The buses are driving away."

"Not that. See, there is Mustafa. I sent him to arrange a desert meal in your honour. Can you see him?"

"Yes." Edmund followed the pointing finger in time to see one of the men hold up a kid by its legs while another man slit its throat.

"Delicious," said the Minister, "roasted with herbs over the open fire, you will never have tasted anything like it."

"I dare say not." Edmund's throat was dry. Thank God Poppy had not come with him.

"So while the lunch cooks we swim," said the Minister. "Work up an appetite."

"OK," said Edmund cravenly turning his gaze towards the sea.

"You don't have to eat its eyes," said the Minister, evilly mischievous.

Edmund said nothing.

They reached the beach, a deserted expanse of sand beaten by creaming rollers.

"Race you to the water." The Minister dropped his trousers, Edmund followed suit, running into the sea, diving under so that the water would drown the sound of the startled bleat, the vision of the exposed throat. It would be nice to catch the Minister by the foot, pull him under, drown him, but curse him, he swam like a porpoise.

Back at the picnic site the Minister excused himself. "Eat your lunch," he said, "enjoy the al fresco." Mustafa would be his host, he himself had urgent business, it had been a pleasure but now alas . . . He drove away in his Porsche.

"Now eat," said Mustafa.

The kid was delicious, tender, redolent of herbs. Not far off one of the men milked its mother. "You would not like milk to drink," said Mustafa, "the vessel is filthy, these are ignorant men."

"Oh, ah, I—"

"I have brought you something else." Mustafa produced a bottle of wine and glasses from the Mercedes. "They can make us coffee," he said, "we have work to do."

"So has the Minister, urgent business."

"If you call it business." Mustafa took off his glasses and stared at Edmund. "You look better," he said looking away.

"I was not ill." Edmund defended himself boldly, holding out his glass for a refill. "I take it the Minister has a beautiful wife," he said. One must not let these fellows get the upper hand.

"Very beautiful." Mustafa laughed, crinkling up his eyes. "You understand it all."

"Well," said Edmund, pleased, "one does—"

"Now coffee." Mustafa handed him a tiny cup of gritty coffee. "Then we drive back, inspect the sites for the Cabana complexes, visit the hotels we have already built, the site for the golf course, the tennis courts and the stadium. I will show you the plans for the stadium."

"You never mentioned a stadium." Edmund felt he might wilt. "Won't tomorrow do?"

"Of course. Have some more wine, finish the bottle."

"I think I have," said Edmund, surprised. "I rather like you without your glasses," he said, not guarding his tongue.

"So, to work." Mustafa let Edmund's remark drop. "And when we have done our work I will show you a private bar where you will—"

"What?" Mustafa's tone made Edmund suspicious. "What will I?"

"Nothing important. They have a pastis like in France, you will enjoy it in the cool of the evening. Arak."

"Maybe," said Edmund watching Mustafa's curious velvety eyes. "Put your glasses on," he said roughly, "and let's get on with it."

"OK, OK," said Mustafa, gently mindful of his grandmother.

TWENTY-SIX

"Are you listening, Willy?" said Calypso on the telephone.

"Yes, Aunt."

"Then take this down. I have the name of the country, the town and the hotel they are at. Shall I start?"

"Please." Willy wrote rapidly as Calypso dictated.

"Thanks," he said. "You are a perfect marvel."

"You fly from Gatwick, there are three flights a week, there may be one tomorrow."

"I'll soon find out." Then, "I thought," said Willy, "that they were entirely into oil in that country. This must be something new."

"They are enterprising people, they look ahead. When the oil runs out there will still be tourism to net the dollars."

"I see."

"What about Fergus and Victor? What are they doing? Were they not in the hunt? Perhaps they are not really serious," suggested Calypso.

"I checked. Fergus is moving his business into Poppy's stables, he wants to get settled before a rush of orders bogs him down."

"Is he expecting a flu epidemic or Legionnaires' Disease, or does he rely on *anno domini*?"

Willy laughed. "He's of sanguine disposition, he feels after the press and television coverage of Bob Carew, business will perk up. Did you read Victor Lucas's article in Julia Wake's magazine? There's mention too in *Horse and Hound* and *Country Life*."

"I did and Lord Hatchet's letter to *The Times*, objecting, is a marvellous advertisement. I wonder who put him up to it." Calypso chuckled. "And what of Victor?"

"He's bogged down by his editor who wants a mass of alterations to his novel done immediately so that the book can get into the spring list."

"Have you made friends with those two that you know so much?" Calypso was curious.

"No, no. I gave Mrs Edwardes, Bob Carew's daily lady, a ham, one of Mrs Future's nephews actually."

"Don't, Willy! I must have my hams anonymous. How *is* Mrs Future?"

"Terrific. So clever too, she gauged her last litter exactly a piglet to each teat."

"The result of hormones?"

"You know I don't give them hormones, she just is the perfect sow," Willy enthused.

"Who are you leaving in charge, Arthur?"

"Yes, he copes well if I have to go away."

"Will he control the smell?"

"Of course he will. Don't tease."

"Take plenty of money. Are you OK for money?"

"Yes, thanks. I can't thank you enough. I am eternally grateful. How, by the way, did you get all this information? Did you extract somebody's teeth by torture?" Willy was curious.

"I telephoned Venetia Colyer as I promised. She volunteered it."

"Good Lord!" Willy whistled.

"She's no slouch when she wants something. She wants Edmund Platt back."

"Good Lord!"

"One wonders what she means, almost one feels sorry for him."

"Good Lord!"

"Don't keep saying 'Good Lord', Willy, try a bit of variety."

"Sorry, it's hard to grasp this aspect—"

"According to Venetia this Edmund of Poppy's, although not a particularly nice character – who is when it comes to that and you really look among the debris – is very attractive. Girls would like to have had him rather in the way antique dealers like to have a collector's piece in their shop window."

"Oh."

"Venetia says Poppy's had the monopoly for far too long and she, Venetia, wants him before he goes off."

"Oh."

"Some girls are like that."

"Oh."

"Not Poppy of course." Was Calypso making fun of him? "So Venetia's not averse to getting him back, says she knows it's perverse but she would not mind keeping him permanently."

"Oh!"

"Don't keep saying 'Oh', Willy, you've no idea how irritating you sound."

"Sorry."

"When shall you go?"

"Tonight."

"Let's hope she's still there."

"That's a risk I have to take."

Willy's tone reminded her of Hector. "God speed," she said, replacing the receiver. "I hope I've done the right thing, not buggered up his life," she murmured to her dog who, wagging his tail and rolling his eyes towards the door, indicated that a walk in the wood at twilight would be the right thing for a dog.

Following her dog through the wood, it occurred to Calypso that by aiding Willy she was guilty of hindering Fergus.

When Fergus's mother Ros, a friend of years, had heard that she intended going to the Carew funeral Calypso had agreed to report on Fergus's enterprise.

"If you are going to this do will you let me know whether Fergus is going to make a success of his crazy idea, or a fool of himself? I am worried sick for him. I can't interfere, he is so touchy, all I can do is stand by and pray," Ros had vented her maternal anxiety. Calypso had agreed; the request was simple enough. I went to say farewell to Bob, she thought irritably. I can tell her the horses were beautiful, the turn-out impeccable, the hearse dignified, the service moving, that, as funerals go, it was a success. I can tell her it's the sort of thing Hector would have liked, that will reassure her. One does not anticipate the undertaker falling in love with the chief mourner or one's nephew, level-headed and sensible, to fall arse over tip for the same girl. I shall censor the news of Poppy, give her a glowing report, stick to the hearse and horses. "What she's really worried about is all those pretty stable girls," said Calypso aloud to the dog.

The dog thrust his head up under her hand, nudging for a caress.

TWENTY-SEVEN

As soon as Edmund and Mustafa had gone Poppy felt regret. She should have been nicer to Edmund, told him about the cockroaches, told him why she had changed rooms, why she was not there when he came to bed, enlisted his sympathy, he was after all supposed to love her. But no, she told herself robustly, he had gone off on a round of the bars with Mustafa, he was never loving or sympathetic when drunk, he had looked pretty poached when he turned up this morning.

So how to occupy her day?

She looked beyond the empty pool and the half-made garden to the sea, choppy and uninviting, and decided to change some money, explore the town.

The man at the desk explained in halting English that there were as yet no facilities to change traveller's cheques in the hotel. She would have to find a bank, the hotel was not yet geared for tourists. Poppy thanked him, looking round the empty hall, wondering whether she and Edmund were the only guests. The emptiness was a little eerie.

"Three months," said the desk clerk, holding up three fingers. "Finish in three months, *drei Monaten.*" This explained perhaps the smell of wet cement, the desultory work being done in the garden, the empty pool. Perhaps there had been a pause in the building of the hotel during which the cockroaches had moved in.

"Taxi?" suggested the desk clerk.

"Thanks, I'll walk," said Poppy.

Settling her sunglasses on her nose, she set off for the town. She had all day, she would do what tourists do, explore, buy postcards, find a museum perhaps, sit in a café.

Arriving in the dark the night before, she had not noticed the environs. Outside what was to be the hotel garden there was an expanse of ground where there had been buildings. Bulldozers were at work levelling the ground, earth-moving machines scooped and scraped, lorries churned up dust with their enormous wheels, turning the landscape barren. She looked back at the hotel and guessed that in the near future there would be other shoebox hotels, swimming pools, bars, all the complex thought necessary for travellers, but we are not travellers, she thought, we are tourists, packaged into manageable parties by people like Edmund and Mustafa. She picked her way across the waste ground to the road leading into the town and eventually found herself in a large square surrounded by municipal buildings, offices and banks.

The population did not seem very large. There was little traffic but armed men stood in groups at the street corners and as she looked about for a bureau de change a dozen army trucks drove through the square. In the trucks soldiers looked at her with lack-lustre eyes over the tops of their weapons. As she stood watching, several busloads of tourists passed the army trucks, overtaking them and driving out in the direction of the sea. Poppy surmised they were heading for the Roman city and congratulated herself on resisting Mustafa's plan to herd her with them. She located a bank and went in past an armed policeman to change her traveller's cheques. The clerk who attended to her asked whether she wished to change Deutschmarks or dollars and let his face fall when she admitted to pounds. He rallied however when she spoke to him in Italian and asked her where she was staying. When she told him he exclaimed and said that the hotel when it was complete would be the most magnificent on the North African coast. Poppy felt it would be unfair to complain of the smell of cement, the empty pool and the insect lodgers. He wished her a happy holiday and, slightly cheered by this brief human contact, she left the bank and its armed guard to buy picture postcards and find a café where she chose a table in the shade from where she could watch the passers-by.

Waiting for the waiter to bring her coffee she was conscious that people at other tables in the café stared at her with interested disdain. She became aware of being a woman alone; such women as there were in the café were old, caring for children, the majority of the customers male. Pretending not to notice Poppy addressed her postcards, sipped her coffee, taking her time to write a postcard to Jane Edwardes, another to a girl she was not particularly friendly with at her late job. There had been no camels for Venetia Colyer, a psychedelic view of a sunset with palm trees would have to suit. There was no possible message for the woman who had stolen your lover when you had got him back. She stared down at the blank card pondering this conundrum, wrote one word. Quickly she scribbled a card to Mary, care of Furnival's Fine Funerals, adding "much love to infant Barnaby" remembering his lollipop eyes. It crossed her mind that it would be fun to be here with Dad even though they would squabble about Edmund. They had never been abroad together, she had made an excuse the only time he had suggested it, inviting her, she remembered with a pang, to the races in Paris. If he were here would she be able to tell him what she now felt about Edmund (and what may that be, asked her inner self), would she feel tempted to ask his advice? The very idea amused her, she finished her coffee, paid and tipped the waiter. The clientele had stopped staring at her and were watching the people in the street who were all drifting in one direction, taking a street which led out of the square. One by one the men in the café got up, joined the crowd, drifted away with it.

An occasional gust of wind swept through the square stirring bits of paper, billowing out the robes worn by the older men. Poppy noticed that what women there were about were hurrying against the tide of men, dragging children with them. In casual search of a postbox she let herself be carried along with the crowd which, funnelling out of the square into a long colonnaded street, seemed to grow thicker by the minute. As she walked down the street on the look-out for a postbox she was puzzled that shopkeepers were putting up their shutters; was it perhaps a holiday or siesta time or was everyone going to a football match? All round her men spoke in low muttering voices or walked silently so that the street was filled with the shuffling slapping sound of feet. Far ahead there was the sound of shouting; the crowd hurried forward. Poppy began to wish herself elsewhere, having a claustrophobic fear of being hemmed in, suffocated by numbers. She tried to keep close to the side against the shop fronts, closed up now so that it was no longer possible to go into one and take refuge.

Suddenly noisily with shouts, hooting and cries two armoured cars forced their way through the crowds who were pressed and heaved against Poppy. She held on tight to her bag which held her freshly changed money and her passport. If I lose it, she thought, Edmund will be furious but at least he has my return ticket. A man trod on her heel, pressing up against her in haste. The pain as his foot scraped down her Achilles tendon was acute. She threw herself against the wall to get out of his way.

The street ended abruptly, opening into an open space with rising ground on the far side and a vista of palm trees on a road leading away to open country down which swayed what looked like the procession of the night before, women, children, dogs, donkeys, camels, the poor of the city on the move. On the corner of the street as it debouched on the open space was an iron pillar against the wall. Poppy held on to it while the crowd surged past her.

In the middle of the space under a plane tree, surrounded by the crowd, were army trucks, armed soldiers faced the crowd which murmured and muttered repeating a sort of groan which grew to a demanding rhythmic shout. The breath of the multitude stank and Poppy found herself taking quick shallow breaths, denying her lungs the odour of anger.

Quite suddenly the crowd hushed. In the silence from behind the trucks two men were hoisted up: ropes put round their necks thrown over the branch of the plane tree, they were pulled strangling up.

The noise the crowd then made was terrifying.

Stifled by the sour smell of the people, Poppy turned towards the wall, her clothes drenching with sweat, she began to claw her way through the crowd. As she fought her way inch by inch part of her noticed the postbox she had been looking for. She stopped, opened her bag, took out the postcards, dropped them into the box, struggled on.

Later she was running along the water's edge on the beach, her thin shoes soaking in the shallow waves.

A flight of weary swallows came in low from Europe to pause and recoup before continuing their journey across the Sahara.

Poppy tripped, stumbled, sat by the water's edge trembling, exhausted.

She bathed her sore heel as the sea advanced and receded over her feet.

She pushed her hair back, congratulated herself that she had not lost her bag, found a comb, combed her hair, remembered that she had written no message on Venetia's postcard beyond the one word, wondered what Venetia would think when she received it, wondered how long it would be before Edmund found her.

Time to get back to the hotel. She stood up, straightened her dress, looked about, found her bearings, walked limping along the beach until she reached the town. Here she climbed up to the road which circled the harbour. It forked and led her back into the town and into the square where long ago she had found the bank and cashed her traveller's cheques. In the square was a newspaper kiosk she had not noticed that morning. It sold foreign papers. She bought a *New York Herald Tribune*, went and sat in the café she had visited earlier in the day, ordered a brandy. People looked at her curiously as she lifted the glass with hands that shook. She felt better when she had drunk it. She stopped trembling and ordered another.

She opened the paper, found what she was searching for, an unimportant paragraph on an inner page.

An unknown sect had thrown a bomb. The airport had been occupied by troops in case of trouble. People from the desert in the town for the celebrations (what celebrations?) had evacuated by night, taking their livestock and goods with them, their camels – the dog, there was no mention of the dog – the main road into the town from the airport had been closed by the army, the old road was heavily congested. A few arrests had been made, everything was now calm, riots slight, no panic.

A few arrests.

A few hangings.

Poppy folded the paper carefully and sipped her brandy.

Sipping her brandy, steadying her nerve, she discussed with herself why she was more afraid here than she would have been at home. There are after all kidnappers, hijackers, rioters, terrorists everywhere these days, all sorts of innocent and ignorant people mixed up with such things. Don't be so silly, she told herself.

It is the not understanding the language just hearing the sounds which is so frightening, she answered herself.

That dreadful silence when the crowd grew still, that greedy silence while the soldiers put the ropes round the men's necks. The crowd holding its collective stinking breath, its lust. The roar of satisfaction when the dangling men kicked as though they were dribbling an airborne football.

Snap out of it, she told herself. Pull yourself together, she told herself in Esmé's voice of long ago. She had hated Esmé.

Edmund was going to be furious when he got back from his day's work with Mustafa and the Tourist Board and found her still out. She sipped her drink, looking about her, outstaring neighbours at the café tables with arrogance.

There was rather a jolly family party two tables away. A young couple, three well-behaved children, a much older woman, some sort of baby-minder and fond grandparents, very bourgeois, very sedate, happy. Poppy exchanged a secret smile with a little girl who looked about three.

What to tell Edmund?

Edmund was not the man to understand the almost sexual smell of the crowd observing death or their sense of appeasement when the soldiers—

Her hands were trembling again, she picked up the brandy with both hands, gulped.

A thin cat shot out of the inner café and wove its way through the tables to disappear with the speed of light. Poppy thought of the cat Bolivar's contempt as he outstared her in Furnival's yard.

*

Would Fergus understand?

Would Victor Lucas, so tender-hearted over his rescued fish? He was supposed to have drowned his wife. What was it she had overheard at Dad's wake? She sipped her brandy, one could not believe everything one heard.

One could not believe everything one saw either.

Poppy snapped her fingers for the waiter, finished her brandy, paid the bill.

"Get me a taxi."

It was so easy. The waiter found her a taxi, she told the driver where to go and in no time was on her way to the hotel.

It was almost dark as she drove along the sea front, past the waste ground to the hotel, dark enough to see the phosphorescent waves roll on to the sand.

Edmund had not yet come back.

Poppy went to her room and had a long bath, soaking in very hot water, easing the pain of her scraped heel, soaking away the sour smell of fear.

Edmund had not come back when she got out of the bath.

The multi-coloured dress was on its hanger in the cupboard. Poppy put it on the chair by the bed, got into bed and covered her face with the sheet.

TWENTY-EIGHT

Penelope Lucas met Venetia Colyer in Harrods Food Hall.

"Hullo," she said, kissing Venetia's tendered cheek. "Charging a few bits and bobs to your ma's account?" she joked, knowing Venetia's shopping habits, swift to deliver the first thrust.

"Paying for my own cheese actually, Penelope dear." Venetia laid her smooth cheek briefly against Penelope's. "And how is Penelope?" She pronounced the name to rhyme with antelope, having recently gossiped with Julia Wake on the telephone.

"You've been talking to Julia," said Penelope, good-humoured. "She wears her jokes to death. Did you see Victor's article about that super funeral in her magazine? A huge puff for Fergus."

"I was there actually."

"At the funeral?"

"Yes."

"Really! Did you see Victor? You must have, he couldn't have invented all that about the horse hearse, the horses dressed in feathers and the mutes."

"Victor was principal mute."

"Gosh! How did that come about? I know, don't tell me. The Furnival man paid him, he's fearfully strapped for money."

"He won't be strapped long. Sean Connor is going to publish his novel."

"Whatever next!" Penelope was genuinely surprised. "Is he getting a good advance, I wonder?"

"Ask Julia, she might know."

"Can't very well, Victor and I are divorced, she might think I was after his money."

"So you would be. Wait a sec while I buy my cheese, then let's go and have a coffee."

"Harrods is too expensive for me."

"What are you doing here then?"

"Just looking. It's all so pretty, a lovely still life. I like watching the Japanese tourists taking photographs in the butcher's department."

"I'll stand you coffee, wait while I get my cheese."

"And a bun," Penelope stipulated, accepting.

"Anything you like." Venetia moved to the cheese counter.

Penelope watched. Venetia's hair in the artificial light was the colour of Wensleydale. She bought Brie, Parmesan and goat. They repaired to a coffee bar and settled at a corner table. Venetia ordered coffee and cakes. "So what's your news?" she asked, scanning Penelope's face with her bright eyes.

"Nothing much." Penelope hesitated then, making up her mind, asked, "Did Julia tell you which of Victor's novels Sean is publishing, he's written three."

"His last I think."

Penelope let out a cry. "That one, it's his version of our marriage, I never thought anyone would publish it."

"Why not?"

"All our rows, almost verbatim, masses of four-letter words, abuse and some pretty intimate sexual revelations."

"You do let rip when cross." Venetia put two lumps of sugar into her coffee. "Sugar?"

"No, thanks. I'm trying not to. I could sue him for libel."

"Great publicity. How did you come to read it, he's written it since you parted company."

"I still have the key of our flat. I went to look for something I wanted and as the manuscript was there I had a quick flip through. I thought it well written and terribly sad."

"Julia says Sean finds it irresistibly funny."

"Other people's miseries are." Penelope sipped her coffee, made a face, weakened, put in a lump of sugar. "And what's with you these days?" She turned an appraising eye on Venetia. "Didn't I hear you had a new man, Edmund something?"

"Platt."

"What a name!"

"He can change it to Colyer." Venetia was equable.

"But Colyer was your ex," Penelope demurred.

"True, but it's a name I like, I shall keep it." Penelope raised her eyebrows. "It's nothing new," said Venetia defensively. "A contemporary of my granny's married a big title, rather a pretty one, then she married a Mr Jones but she kept the title. I shall stick to Colyer."

Penelope stirred her coffee, watched Venetia. "It's coming back to me. Your Edmund Platt is the man who's been living with that girl Poppy Carew for absolutely years. You must know who I mean, her father's the man who always backed winners."

"That's right." Venetia bit into an éclair. "Try one of these, they're super."

"A great judge of what horse would like which course, that's her father."

"Got it in one."

"The Poppy girl's father started life as a milkman then took to the turf, became the terror of the bookmakers."

"How do you know all this?" asked Venetia, mildly curious.

"An old friend of my aunt's used to talk about him, she went racing with him, I think. My mother swears she left him money but you know her stories, she gets carried away with her powers of invention, she should write . . ."

Venetia finished her éclair, licked her fingers.

"I *say*." Penelope turned to look at Venetia. "The penny's dropped. It was Poppy Carew's father's funeral Victor wrote about. He's dead."

"Would have to be—"

"And you went with Edmund," Penelope's voice rose.

"That's right."

"What a nerve. Did she see you?"

"Don't think so."

"Well!" said Penelope.

They sat thoughtfully stirring their coffee for some minutes.

"Has Victor put how he tried to drown you in his novel?" Venetia moved in to attack.

"Of course not." Penelope was momentarily tempted to defend Victor, to tell the truth about the famous drowning.

"Can't think how you went on living with him so long afterwards." Venetia started on a fresh éclair.

"I didn't leave him because of that—"

"These are too rich, I can't manage two." Venetia laid the wounded éclair on her plate.

One should think of the starving Third World, thought Penelope. "I've often seen your Edmund." She turned again to look at Venetia. "Big tall man, fearfully good-looking, fair, lots of muscles."

"That's the one."

"Jogs in the park, used to be some sort of athlete?"

"That's him."

"Drinks."

"What?"

"Drinks too much."

"Nonsense."

"Darling! It's coming back to me. I've seen him about with Poppy. He drinks too much and gets bad tempered, sticks out his lower lip like this." Penelope stuck out her lower lip.

"Only when he's bored. He's been too long with—"

"And he won't drink too much with you?" Penelope's eyebrows rose, her tone implied "Pull the other one".

"Of course he won't."

Penelope gave the shriek of laughter which had charmed Victor in their early days but engendered murderous feelings during the latter part of their marriage. Venetia felt that Penelope was venturing too far.

"That sort of man gets awfully fat, if he lasts," Penelope persisted, her tone foretelling heart trouble for Edmund.

"I like fat men who drink," said Venetia comfortably. "Edmund will last."

"I was only thinking of your happiness, darling."

"That's great of you." Venetia gave the discarded éclair a push.

"Is he around? Would one be allowed to meet him?" asked Penelope sweetly.

"He's abroad on a business trip to North Africa." (No, you would not be allowed to meet him.) Venetia helped herself to more coffee. "You needn't think I don't know Edmund's weak points – more coffee? Oh, I've finished the pot – where was I?"

"Weak points."

"Yes. Well of course he has weaknesses, who hasn't? One must balance them against, well—"

"Terrific in bed?" Penelope slipped a quick thrust under Venetia's guard.

Venetia laughed, leaving the question unanswered. "Oh Lord, is that the time? I must go." She waved to catch the waitress's eye. "Oh, I pay as I go out of course. What's this I heard about Victor and some old trout?"

"What?"

"Something about settling her in Berkshire near the Furnival man, I didn't catch it all. Must rush." Venetia gathered up her shopping, pecked Penelope's cheek. "It's been marvellous to see you, see you soon," and she was gone, walking fast back towards the Food Hall where she extravagantly bought a pound of smoked salmon, congratulating herself that she had not let slip to Penelope that Edmund was not alone in North Africa but accompanied by odious Poppy Carew, may she rot.

Stung by Venetia's thrust, Penelope sat on in the coffee shop. She could not visualise Victor with an older woman, had difficulty visualising him with any woman other than herself, it was after all her he loved, she who was irreplaceable. He had no right, no business with anyone else. Why, she asked herself dolefully, had she allowed Venetia the last word? She should have kept her, hinted of an Edmund with an interest in little boys perhaps, suggested that soon he would develop not only into a fat man but a fat man with the spongy complexion of a drinker, boozer's flush. Edmund was not likely to write a novel about Venetia. Penelope sought comfort in the thought that Victor had written a book about her, then remembering the parts she had read she was appalled that the quarrels, the memory of which had hitherto been privately dear to her, should be made public. Her eyes filled with an uncharacteristic rush of tears. She resolved on a vengeful expedition to Berkshire soonest.

TWENTY-NINE

Edmund woke. It was quiet, the bed was luxurious. He stretched out a hand, feeling for Venetia, moving his legs out of reach of her feet in reflex action. She was not there. He drifted back to sleep.

Below in the garden sparrows chirped, the wind stirred the fronds of the palms making a gentle scraping noise. He woke again.

A shaft of sunlight stabbed through the drawn curtains as the wind blew in to part them then sucked them closed again. He opened his eyes, looked round, sniffed, smelled wet cement, remembered.

He was at least in the right hotel but not with Venetia.

Steady, he told himself, take it easy, it will come back.

Moving his head with care, he observed the room in the half-light. It was not the room he had previously occupied, similar but a different shape.

Hanging over a chair he recognised Poppy's frock, the dress of many colours. What brilliant instinct had brought him safely to her room? Where was she? Moving with caution, Edmund rolled over. The adjoining bed was empty but had been slept in. There was a familiar dent in the pillow, sheets thrown back. Had she been in the bed when he came in? Take it easy, he told himself, it will unfold.

He lay on his back, eyes closed, cudgelling his memory. They had arrived, he remembered, waiting by the carousel for the luggage, he had been with Poppy not Venetia. Surely the idea had been to bring Venetia on the trip. They were after all getting married (this bit was muzzy). Why had he brought Poppy, something wrong there. Sort that out later.

So, he remembered their arrival, then something about a dog. Oh God yes, poor dog.

Meeting the Minister with Mustafa in the Office of Tourism, yes.

A picnic somewhere near the sea, a goat, a kid. Oh Lord, yes.

The swim, the Roman ruins, the meal, the wine, rather good claret. Why had Poppy not been there?

After the picnic the drive back to the town in the Mercedes with Mustafa. Quite a long drive through stony desert. Then what happened? It had been evening by that time, almost night, the sea had been phosphorescent along the harbour wall. Edmund lay on his back breathing deeply, filling his lungs; if his lungs cleared his head would clear. He cajoled his memory, come on I must remember, something must have happened.

A bar. Mustafa had persuaded him to try the local pastis, they called it something else here, right, he'd got that, he'd tried the pastis, well several, pretty potent, what then? (Arak, it's called arak.) A memory floated back. It can't have happened, he told himself, as the blood flooded his face, his heart thumped, his neck grew hot, his ears roared.

Jesus, it had happened, he knew it, Christ!

He remembered leaving the bar, getting into a car, not the Mercedes they had used all day, another older car which smelt of what? Got it, cannabis. There had been two youths, had they been in the bar? No matter, come back to that later, no don't, it's not important. He remembered them all in the car, the two youths not much more than boys, Mustafa and himself driving to a house somewhere outside the town and then all too clearly it came back, that room with the divan, the boys, Mustafa in a corner smoking a cigarette, watching.

And I enjoyed it.

Edmund lay with his eyes shut, trying to close his mind also.

At first in the car driving out of town he had thought that they must be kidnapping him, one of the boys was armed, the driver had a weapon beside him on the seat, had Mustafa by then been armed too?

The youths were beautiful, olive skin, softly curling black hair, sensual mouths.

Edmund was drenched with sweat as he lay thinking. He had his job to finish, the survey of tourist possibilities for his firm. There was the stadium to visit, the details of the hotels to note. The ultimate cost of tours to discuss with the Tourist Board, spy out what goes on with such tours from other countries already ongoing, loose ends to tie up, finish the job, write the report.

A sharp rap on the door made him jump, chilled the sweat on his body.

Poppy called from the balcony: "Come in – *entrez* – *avanti* – *herein.*" As she came through the curtains from the balcony she laughed, "I don't know what language they use so I use all the ones I know."

The sun illuminating her mousy hair from behind made a curious halo effect. She opened the bedroom door to let in a waiter carrying a tray. He took it through to the balcony, put it down on an iron table with a clatter. Poppy thanked him. "Thank you – *merci* – *grazie* – *Danke.*" There was the welcome smell of coffee.

"I left you to sleep," she said, "you came in late."

The servant went away closing the door behind him.

"Thanks," said Edmund, sitting up in the bed, pushing the hair out of his eyes, ignoring the pain stabbing his temples.

"Why don't you have a shower? I'm starving so I shall start breakfast," she said.

Edmund dragged himself out of bed, went into the bathroom, stood under the shower, let the water wash, wash, wash it all away.

She had been very quiet out there on the balcony, leaving him to sleep. What state had he been in when he came in during the night? What had he said? Had he said anything? Would she tell him what he had said supposing he had said it? If he had been legless he would hopefully though not necessarily have been speechless too. Venetia would tell him at once without hesitation. Poppy was quite another kettle of fish, close.

Listening to the swish of water in the shower Poppy poured herself coffee, hot, fragrant, civilised. Her hand shook as she poured. She added milk and sugar, lifted the cup with both hands, drank.

"Ah," she sighed, "that's better."

She buttered a roll, ate ravenously, wondered when she had last eaten. I shall not tell him what happened yesterday, he would probably not believe me, it would do no good, she shuddered, drank more coffee.

"Let's have a nice day," she said as Edmund joined her, wrapped about the waist by a towel; he was really a beautiful man to look at, even his feet were elegant. "Have you got to work or could we go somewhere together, swim perhaps, enjoy ourselves?"

"Why not," said Edmund accepting a cup of coffee. (I can't possibly tell her, never, never, never.) "I can take the day off, finish the job tomorrow," he said. "This is good, just what I need." He gulped the restorative liquid. "That fellow Mustafa is a bit of a bore in large doses, we can dispense with his services today."

"Lovely," said Poppy, looking across the palm tops towards the sea. I had better not suggest aspirin, she thought, it only irritates him.

"It's a long time since we spent the day together," said Edmund, who had lately spent his free days with Venetia.

"Ages," said Poppy thinking of Venetia, had she posted that card, did Venetia know what *chameau* meant? "Did you have a successful day?" she asked in the tone of voice which expects no answer.

"You could say that." Edmund chose a roll, buttered it. "How was yours?"

"So, so," said Poppy, "so, so." She put on her sunglasses, handed Edmund his, wondered whether anyone had yet trod on them. "Sun's very bright," she said. If we can keep this up nothing need have happened, nothing will have happened.

There was an English language paper by the breakfast tray. Edmund picked it up, glanced at it. "There seems to have been some political trouble just before we arrived. All quiet now it seems."

"Oh really?" said Poppy.

Edmund put the paper down, helped himself to more coffee, looked out across the palms towards the sea, burst out laughing. How could Venetia's feet be so permanently chilly, she must have a funny sort of metabolism.

"The cupboard in the first room they put us in was full of cockroaches," said Poppy.

"Oh darling," said Edmund, still laughing, thinking of Venetia's feet. "Why didn't you tell me?"

"You weren't there to tell," said Poppy lightly. And you weren't there when they hanged those men either. She clipped up her secret thoughts.

THIRTY

Willy Guthrie's intention of flying in search of Poppy on the first available plane got a setback when he found no airline called at the desired destination for two days. With mounting impatience he prowled his farm, trying not to drive his stockman mad with repetitious instructions for the duration of his absence. He sought solace watching the young porkers hop, skip, chase each other in short grunting rushes, root thoughtfully along the hedges, gobble their balanced diet from their speckless troughs. He found no solace. Communing with Mrs Future, admiring her aerodynamic Zeppelin shape, catching the beady intelligent eyes peeping at him from the shade of ears shaped like arum lilies, he sought comfort. It was some years since, tiny, pushed aside by her siblings, squashed almost to death by her mother, she had lain in Willy's arms feeding from a bottle. She had rewarded him with almost as much companionship as a dog, he had derived a lot of pleasure driving to market with a pig beside him. Walking the fields with Mrs Future was something he missed now that, full grown, she regularly brought litters of little Futures into the hard world of hams.

There was no trace of sentiment in Mrs Future's eye as she twitched her mobile snout, took from his hand a proffered carrot. Willy felt that Mrs Future would consider, were she human, his emotions *vis-à-vis* Poppy rather ludicrous, without place in the real world.

Scratching Mrs Future's flank with a stick kept specially for the purpose, Willy dreamed of Poppy as he had seen her standing alone in the front pew at her father's funeral. "You don't know what it is to be lonely," he said to the pig, lifting her large ear to peer into her little eye. The sow's eye gleamed red in the evening light. "When your litter have grown a bit we will take them for a walk under the oak trees," said Willy. "You love acorns."

Mrs Future turned away sashaying back to the litter in her byre. It was sentimental to think of her as any different from the other breeding sows lolling in their comfortable quarters, rows of piglets laid along their flanks in pale pink harmony.

To the uninitiated each sow identically resembled the next. Except for their past relationship Mrs Future might just be one of the many, indeed the pig's rather nonchalant attitude inclined to hint that now that she had better things to do their special relationship was at an end. Rebuffed, Willy experienced a fresh pang of loneliness, his mind veered away from the pig to speculate on his aunt in her house on the other side of the wood and her uncharacteristically helpful attitude towards his love for Poppy. Had she murmured something about risk? He searched his memory. Did she suggest love was a *risk*? Was that her opinion? Surely a risk worth taking? Uneasily Willy set out to walk off his fretful anxiety, tire himself so that he would not lie sleepless before his journey. As he walked he remembered Calypso visiting his smokehouse, inspecting the cadaver of a pig split neatly in half ready for smoking. "That is what I feel like," she had said, turning away. Willy had wondered what the hell she meant. As he walked along the wood path Willy discovered what she had meant for he felt he would never be whole without Poppy just as Calypso could never be whole without Hector. Here was the endemic risk in loving. There is no knowing, thought Willy grimly, whether I shall ever experience that wholeness. Pig farmers cannot afford to be morbid, he told himself.

I can perfectly well live without Poppy, I have up to now, he persuaded himself.

The word mawkish occurred to him. He had survived other loves, he thought robustly, there was no need to be mawkish.

In the fading light the wood grew dark, occasional yellow fern, precursors of winter, lightened the way. In the still hour when the night's inhabitants roused themselves, Willy waited under a giant oak, survivor of a long gone forest towering among the young trees planted by Hector. He promised himself to do some coppicing for Calypso during the winter. On the edge of the wood a cock pheasant cried, was still. From the oak a tawny owl flew out silent about its hunting. Willy sighed with satisfaction, walked back over the hill, came finally to his farm, turned on the harsh electric light, cut himself a sandwich, poured himself a beer, switched on the radio for the late news. "Terrorists, attempted plot uncovered, attempt on ruler's life, shots fired in the streets, two men arrested, executed, calm restored." He waited for the weather report, went up to bed, slept. The distant sound of a train rushing through the night blew in on the night air.

At cockcrow Willy woke, shaved, bathed, dressed, checked his bag, put passport and tickets in his breast pockets, ate a hurried breakfast, carried his bag to the car and drove across country to Gatwick.

Arriving early, he wandered round the departure lounge, drifted through the duty free shop, read the titles of the books on the bookstall, bought a newspaper and a couple of weeklies, impatiently waited for time to pass. Ruefully he envied the sangfroid and ease with which habitual travellers drifted along just in time to board their planes. In the past he too had been a carefree traveller. At last, time relented, he boarded the plane. Once airborne he felt elation; in a matter of hours he would find Poppy, what happened after that was up to the Almighty. In an attempt to keep calm he opened his *Spectator*, tried to read.

Halfway through the third article he realised with a jolt that he was reading about the country of his destination, went back to the beginning of the article. "The country's past record is by no means peaceful, the present troubles are due—" Frowning, Willy read on. Plot, counterplot, suppression, terrorists, kidnappings, bombs had a familiar ring, he was not unduly disturbed. Reading about trouble abroad, he had always understood, was quite different to being actually present where it took place. The odds were, if you were on the spot you would notice nothing. Uneasily Willy cast his mind back to the previous evening's news. Where and in what country had the reported trouble been? If it was in Poppy's country her man (even to himself Willy refused to think of him as her lover) would take care of her and all governments took care of tourists. Willy put down the *Spectator*, searched his newspaper, found nothing, no mention even in the stop press. Reassured, he dozed.

Roused by the steward for the midflight meal, he was picking at the packets on his tray when the intercom crackled and the captain made an announcement. The weather along the North African coast was of such turbulence that the plane must alter course and land in Algiers. The airport at their proper destination was temporarily under water.

Willy could not believe his ears. He checked with his neighbour who agreed; he too had heard the announcement. It was confirmed by the stewardess.

Willy shouted, "God damn the bloody plane I want to get off." His neighbour, much amused, ordered a large whisky and offered one to Willy who fretfully refused.

The plane altered course in the direction of Algiers. Philosophically the passengers ate their meal.

The captain apologised for any delay and inconvenience caused, promised that the passengers would be accommodated at the airline's expense in the best hotels. The plane would land in forty minutes.

Presently the plane lost height in a series of stomach-jolting jerks, groaning down through dark rain clouds. Willy watched the ground rush up, saw lashing rain, palm trees waving like dishmops.

"Much worse along the coast," shouted Willy's neighbour. How did he know? "Often happens in autumn, equinoctial gales—" What a know-all.

The plane landed, splashing on to puddled tarmac, taxiing through sheeting rain to the terminal, stopped. The aircraft doors open a voice hailed, "*Que messieurs les passagers descendent*—"

"Here we go," said Willy's neighbour. "Wonder what dump they'll put us in." Wretchedly Willy followed him out of the aircraft to Customs to wait dejectedly in line. Dispirited, sniffing the smell of Algiers, garlic, spice, petrol fumes, thirsty earth, listening to the mix of French and Arabic, thinking that at any other time he would have been amused, interested, pleased by this diversion in his proper journey, Willy let his eye wander across the Customs hall to a group from another plane standing by their baggage, queuing for the Customs officers. A man and his wife were squeezing shut their suitcases, each cursing the other's attempt to help. Next in line behind them a girl obeyed the Customs official, opened her case.

Willy exclaimed, shouted, leapt over a barrier, grabbed the girl, held her. "Poppy."

She looked at him astonished without recognition.

"I saw your dress, I knew it at once." The multicoloured dress lay on top of the case.

The Customs man poked brown fingers down the sides of the case. "OK." Poppy pushed the dress back, shut the case. The man moved on to the next passenger. Someone called to Willy, "Hey, monsieur."

"I think they want you back over there." She had a frightful black eye, she looked awful, her nose was swollen. She picked up her case, moved away.

"Monsieur—" An official harried Willy to get back where he belonged.

"Wait for me," Willy shouted at her retreating back, "*wait.*"

"We are all headed for the same hotel." Willy's neighbour from the plane knew even this.

"Your case, monsieur, open it." The man was impatient. Willy complied, craning his neck to see where Poppy had gone. The Customs man took his time. Willy memorised his face so that some day, even if it were in the after-life, always supposing there was such a thing, when he had the time he would come back and hit him. The man relinquished his futile search, moved away. Willy snapped the case shut, nipping his urgent fingers, ran. She was standing in the next hall.

"I waited," she said.

"Thank God," said Willy.

"Do I know you?" she asked.

"You will," said Willy. "Give me your case, let me carry it for you."

THIRTY-ONE

Having made sure by an unanswered telephone call that Victor was out, Penelope let herself into the flat. She wondered whether Victor knew that she still had a key, how much he would mind that she had quite often in the years since their divorce let herself in to pry. While she had a strong aversion to anyone poking their nose into her own affairs, she persuaded herself that her interest in Victor was excusable.

Inside the door she listened.

The tap in the bathroom dripped as it always had, defying DIY efforts and even the arts of a visiting plumber.

Outside the window on the parapet pigeons strutted and cooed as they always had. The noise of traffic passing in the street was deadened by the dry leaves rustling in the plane trees.

Penelope went into the bathroom to give the tap a futile nostalgic twist. Victor had filled the bidet with socks, they soaked in grey unappetising water, she was almost tempted to wash them. The bedroom had acquired an austere masculine air: pillows heaped against the centre of the headboard, the duvet pulled askew, suggested a solitary Victor. His clothes had edged across to her side of the hanging cupboard, he had left the doors open, a carelessness which had been a continual source of irritation during their marriage. Unable to resist interfering, she shut the doors.

In the living room she inspected the desk and was surprised at the number of receipted bills. Things were definitely looking up for Victor. She fingered through a pile of letters finding none of interest bar one from Victor's mother. Opening it she read, pursing her lips, breathing in, closing her nostrils in imitation of her former mother-in-law who had the haughty appearance of a llama. Victor's parent congratulated him warmly on the acceptance of his novel while hoping that it was not as autobiographical as the previous unpublished manuscripts. "Some hope," muttered Penelope. You were very unfair to poor Penelope, wrote Victor's mum. I know she can be irritating but so, my goodness, can you. "Hallelujah!" said Penelope loud in the silence. You get it from your beloved pa, wrote Victor's mother, and went on to give some routine and boring news of Victor's family. Penelope returned the letter to the pile.

In Victor's typewriter a pristine sheet of paper, Page One, Chapter One. "The day I decided to drown my wife dawned crystal clear."

"Hey," said Penelope, "this *is* fiction." She knelt by the grate to inspect crumpled sheets of paper. Victor had written, "The day I decided to drown my wife dawned grey and—"

"The day I decided to drown my wife dawned thundery—"

Penelope addressed herself to the desk drawers. "I must really clear out this mess," she muttered, momentarily forgetting her divorced status. "Oh bugger." She shut the drawer. There was no trace of what she feared, nor was there anything to indicate the existence of another woman in the kitchen, no alien garlic crusher, nobody's favourite knife. After a final look round she let herself out and drove west out of London, towards Berkshire, in search of Fergus.

Leaving the motorway at junction thirteen Penelope headed towards the downs. She drove slowly with only the vaguest concept of Fergus's whereabouts. Victor's article giving Furnival's Fine Funerals its splendid write-up had left the location of the enterprise enigmatically vague. "A beautiful secret valley in the Berkshire Downs" did not get one far. While hoping to extract information about Victor from Fergus Penelope was unsure how best to set about it. After their brief affair Fergus had moved, apparently jointly, with Victor into Julia's embrace, but now if gossip was true Julia was seriously committed to Sean Connor. Penelope was friendly with Julia who presented no threat; she was interested in the unknown quantity hinted by Venetia in Harrods. "Though why I bother—" Penelope talked to herself. "Victor is just an untidy habit I have given up, or should give up if I had it."

On the outskirts of a pretty village two workmen had just finished erecting a sign which read *Furnival's Fine Rococo Funerals* in large letters, in smaller lettering, *Director Fergus Furnival*. "What luck," said Penelope parking her car by the side of the road, peering up at the house, "but this village isn't particularly secret—"

The men who had put up the sign collected their tools, got into a van and drove off. Penelope stood hesitating in front of the house.

From a window on the first floor Mary, baby Barnaby in her arms, watched. Penelope walked round to the back of the house. Mary moved from the front bedroom to watch Penelope's progress from the bathroom at the back.

Penelope reached the stable yard and went round it, peering into the loose-boxes. Two Dow Jones put interested heads over their box-doors to observe her progress. Penelope, who did not trust horses, gave them a wide berth. She inspected the tack-room, opened the double doors of the carriage house, looked in on empty darkness, walked slowly back towards the house through the yard, hesitated outside the back door, went round to the front.

Mary ran downstairs and opened the front door with a jerk as Penelope was putting her finger on the bell. Penelope jumped.

Mary said "Yes?" on a note of query.

"Oh," said Penelope. "Ah, I am Victor Lucas's wife, Penelope Lucas."

"Yes?"

"We are divorced of course—"

"Yes?"

"I was wondering whether—"

"Yes?"

"Whether Fergus, I am a friend of Fergus—"

"Yes?" Mary was enjoying this.

"Whether," Penelope refused to be disconcerted, "whether Fergus knows where I can find – er – Victor?"

"Yes."

"Yes, he knows?" Was this girl half-witted or plain bloody-minded? "Does he know?"

"Yes."

"There is something I have to talk to him about, something I need to tell him."

"Yes?"

"I believe he has a friend somewhere near here who might – er – Venetia Colyer said that—"

"Yes?"

"Do you know Venetia?"

"Yes."

"Is Fergus out?"

"Yes."

"Perhaps you can help me." Penelope caught baby Barnaby's eye, round, black, appraising. Without deflecting his gaze from Penelope he stuffed a hand in the opening of Mary's shirt, grabbed her nipple and sucked. Penelope took a step backwards. "Isn't that baby a bit old to be nursed?"

"Yes."

"I thought so." Penelope held out a finger which Barnaby snatched and held in his tight infant grip. "Are you being irritating on purpose?" she asked.

"Yes."

Penelope laughed and waggled her finger in Barnaby's fist. He stopped sucking Mary's nipple and tried to stuff Penelope's finger in his mouth. Penelope snatched the finger away.

"You'd better come in." Mary pulled the door wider, jerked her head towards the kitchen. "We aren't settled in yet, we only moved the day before yesterday, Fergus and the girls are doing a funeral near Wallop."

"Oh." Penelope followed Mary to the kitchen.

"Sit down." Mary nodded at a chair.

"Thanks." Penelope sat. An old dog got to his feet, came across the room to sniff and wag, retreated to lie by the stove.

"So you are looking for Victor," said Mary. "He lives in London."

"Of course he does. It's a friend of his who—" Who? What? Who is this friend I am so het up about whose existence is hinted at by Venetia. Venetia never meant good. Must I ask this rude girl as Fergus is not here? Penelope regretted her impulsive journey. "If Fergus is out I can telephone or come another time—"

"Didn't you go for a spin with Fergus?" Mary's eye, though not dark and round like her child's, was more penetrating.

"What d'you mean?"

"Screw, didn't you screw with Fergus?"

"Well, really I—" Penelope got to her feet.

"Yes or no?"

"Well, yes – um – what business is it of yours what I – er – we. It wasn't for long."

Mary grinned. "Just placing you. Sit down, have some coffee." To Penelope there was something menacing about the offer.

"I – I ought to go."

"Oh come on, you can't come all this way for nothing." Mary put Barnaby on the floor, filled the kettle. "What do you want poor old Victor for, what's his friend to do with you?" As she spooned Nescafé into mugs Mary sized Penelope up. "I bet Victor never really tried to drown you," she said, looking at Penelope, amused.

"Of course he did," Penelope said defensively.

"And this friend?" asked Mary. "What's your interest?"

"Nothing, it's nothing." Penelope was harassed. "Just something Venetia said when we met the other day."

"I know Venetia." Mary handed Penelope her mug. "Sugar? Milk?"

"Just milk please. I thought Fergus's place was more isolated." Penelope took stock.

"It was. He's rented this from Poppy Carew. He did her father's funeral. You read about it?"

"Yes. I did. Victor's article and—"

"Poppaea has disappeared with Venetia's new man—" Mary chanted. "Poppaea!" mocking the name.

"Oh."

"This man is Poppaea's *old* man, he left her, I guess, an educated guess, for Venetia."

"Gosh."

Mary sipped her coffee watching Barnaby crawl across the floor to join the dog who licked his head. "There's an interesting connection if you are interested in Victor." She switched her eyes back to Penelope. "Both Fergus and Victor have their sights on Poppaea. They do seem to like the same girls those two, you, Julia and now Poppaea, funny isn't it?"

Penelope put down her mug. "Then what the hell is Victor doing installing some old trout in Berkshire?"

"Is that what Venetia told you?" Mary looked enchanted.

"Yes it is." Penelope was outraged. What business had this girl to pry? Why had she let slip Venetia's mischief? That she was herself prying did not bother her at all.

"And you think Fergus can tell you where to look?" asked Mary, deceptively mild.

"That was the idea," said Penelope stiffly.

"Are you jealous, do you want him back or just dog in the manger?" Mary teased.

"Of course not," said Penelope hotly.

"You go up the road a few miles, take the fourth turning on your left, the second on your right, follow that road until you get to a humpback bridge and a track which goes up into the hills beside the stream. It's possible you will find what you are looking for."

"Oh." Penelope got to her feet. "Thanks," she said grudgingly.

"Not at all," said Mary, picking baby Barnaby out of the dog basket, walking with Penelope towards the door. "If when you are there you should see a large tabby cat please catch him and bring him here, Fergus is frantic, misses him terribly. He was out hunting when we moved, Fergus has been back to look three times already, he loves that animal."

"But—"

"Surely you can catch a cat."

"I doubt it." Penelope loathed cats, longed to refuse, was afraid to.

"He'll be starving by now. Fergus will be eternally grateful." Mary spoke with enjoyment.

"I don't think—" protested Penelope.

"I'll give you a tin of sardines to entice him; not allergic are you?" Mary turned back to find sardines, opened a tin. "There, lure him into your car, keep the windows shut as you drive or he'll jump out."

"I don't know anything about cats," protested Penelope weakly.

"Then now's your chance to find out." Mary was propelling her out of the house. "You may also find out a lot about Victor, the great softie."

"I—" Penelope was out of the house and in her car.

"Fourth turning on the left," Mary pointed. "Then follow the track into the hills after the humpback bridge." She put the tin of sardines on the seat beside Penelope. "His name is Bolivar," she said. "Let me know about Victor's friend when you come back. I would be interested to hear your opinion."

Mary's mocking tone so infuriated Penelope that she leant out of the car window and shouted, "I'm not going to bother about a bloody cat, Fergus can catch it for himself."

"Oho, what spirit!" Penelope's tormentor leaned in through the car window to stare at Penelope at close quarters; from her arms Barnaby reached in to stroke Penelope's face. "Pitty, pitty." Mary snatched his hand away. Penelope flushed.

"You bitch. Why are you so bloody?" The two women glared at each other across the baby's head. Barnaby crowed, reaching pudgy hands towards Penelope.

"He likes me." Penelope pursed her lips, blowing a kiss towards the baby. "Is it Fergus's child?" she asked. "Those eyes—" Mary stared at her, stony faced. "And something about the mouth—" Penelope persisted dangerously. "When one's – well, you know what I mean obviously – one sees people from a different angle when one's—"

"Jesus," murmured Mary holding the baby against her face, staring down at Penelope. "Christ."

"Who are you anyway, what's your role around here?" Penelope felt a sadistic desire to wound this woman who would not let her touch her child.

"I'm part of the scenery." Mary was recovering fast.

"I didn't know Fergus was fond of scenery, that's not a side of him I know." Penelope reached back for the safety belt. "Is your baby teething?" she asked, looking up at Barnaby from whose open mouth trickled a stream of saliva. With her arm stretched up behind her, her hand fumbling for the buckle, she showed in her open shirt a pretty cleavage.

Mary dipped Barnaby forward so that his spittle dropped between Penelope's breasts. "You don't see much scenery when you're flat on your back," she said. "Mind you remember the cat," she called over her shoulder as she moved back into the house.

Penelope started the engine, put the car in gear and drove off. As she drove she composed apt rejoinders, tart replies, crushing last words she might have inflicted on the girl with the baby had she been fast enough on the rejoinder.

THIRTY-TWO

Victor, waiting to be served, watched a hurried spectacled youth buy mackerel, next a thickset woman hesitate between halibut and Dover sole, making vocal allusion to her husband, his penchant for shrimps or oysters with or without cream in the sauce. Victor costed her silk shirt, cashmere sweater, St Laurent jeans, gold bracelets, double row of pearls. How many advances for novels would pay for all that? Shifting his shopping basket from one hand to the next, he exercised his mental arithmetic.

The fish lady, apparently patient, ran a sardonic eye over the marble slab. The loquacious customer changed her mind, decided her husband would enjoy ray *au beurre noir* which, with out of season asparagus miraculously grown in Israel and new potatoes ditto, might deceive him now in October to believe it spring.

"Spring," said the fish lady, slapping the ray on the scales, naming the price, wrapping the fish. "Spring," she said with lofty contempt for the seasons, looking past the customer's head at the street and its passers-by.

The woman took a notecase from her Hermès bag. Victor goggled at a wad of fifty-pound notes; he opined that the metier of mugging would show greater dividends (always supposing one had the nerve) than writing.

Unmoved, the fish lady took the money, gave her customer change, handed her her fish, turned to the next customer. "Yes?" Victor had watched this man when in the early halcyon days of their marriage he had shopped with Penelope, unable to bear her out of his sight, carrying their shopping in the very basket he now held. The man now being served invariably bought lobsters, taking his time, discussing the particulars of each crustacean as the fish lady lifted them for his inspection, their bound claws forlornly semaphoring. Penelope had voiced the opinion that the man was homosexual, Victor thought not but in those early days rarely contradicted his wife.

The present loneliness of shopping sharpened his powers of observation so that he took note of people's dress and mannerisms in case they might fit into some brief paragraph of a future work.

"Yes?" said the fish lady, jerking him out of his reverie. "Yes?" Contempt in her voice.

"Oh! Half of unshelled prawns please."

Why should I be humbled, he thought indignantly. Not all of us can afford lobster and sole. Prawns with brown bread and butter make an excellent lunch with salad. "The salmon looks nice," he said for the sake of saying something. The salmon wore a leering expression and had an undershot jaw. "Cock," said Victor to illustrate that he wasn't a complete fool, could tell the sex of salmon, hopefully insult the fish lady.

The fish lady did not answer but weighed the prawns indifferently.

"All girls," said Victor, listening to the prawns tinkling frozen into the scales. "All the prawns I buy have eggs."

"Scotch," said the fish lady, referring to the salmon. "Iceland," she handed Victor his prawns, took the money he proffered. "Wait a minute," she paused by the till. "Or Greenland."

"I gave you the exact money," said Victor defensively.

"Your change," said the fish lady, handing Victor some coins. "Oh?" Victor was at a loss. "Why?"

"You neglected your change," said the fish lady, turning towards the next customer, "when you bought your trout," she tossed over her shoulder. "Yes sir?" She was already in spirit with another.

The old bitch, thought Victor morosely as he turned towards home. She used to call Penelope "ducks", now she pretends not to know me, doesn't call me anything. Feeling excluded from the human race he made for home, for his desk, to lose himself in his work.

As usual Victor approached his novel at an angle hoping to take it by surprise, to be at work on it before he or the novel became aware. He ate his lunch, buttering brown bread, sipping a glass of lager, peeling the prawns, crunching them, swallowing a lot of the shell as he ate. Penelope had said the roughage was good for him, she never bothered to peel her prawns thoroughly, sucked the contents of the heads, then licked her fingers.

Victor, eating his prawns, listening to the lunchtime news, thought of Penelope's fingers and other more delectable parts. By writing about her it was his intention to expunge her from his system so that he could the better concentrate on Poppy Carew. Finishing his lunch he tossed the débris into the pedal bin, washed his hands and went to the telephone where he dialled Poppy's London number. There was not, as there had not been for days, any answer. "Still away." Victor sat down at his desk. "Not back yet."

He read: "The day I decided to drown my wife dawned crystal clear."

He tore the paper from the typewriter, crushed it between both hands, tossed it towards the grate. He would answer his mother's letter lying in its envelope on top of the pile. The very act of typing would lead him smoothly into the novel by artful trickery.

Re-reading his mother's letter Victor felt mounting annoyance. What right had she to criticise, not for her to find Penelope irritating, not for her to denigrate her ex-daughter-in-law. Even though their divorce was several years old, Victor still had difficulty in thinking of Penelope as ex-anything. I shall exorcise her by writing about her, Victor told himself.

"Dear Mother," he wrote. "Thanks for yours. Are you coming up for the Horticultural Show or the exibish at the Hayward? We might have a bite and go together. So glad you are glad about my book" (two "glads" in a sentence but never mind, this is only a letter, she's lucky to get it). Victor tapped a little more about his novel, the advance he was to receive from Sean Connor, Sean's connection with Julia. His mother deplored Julia whom she had once accused of hooking him, did she know what a hooker was? Poor mother, he thought, as he typed, spacing the lines widely to fill the page, recommending a new novel she would enjoy (get it from the library), giving her a pungent piece of family news which might not yet have reached Somerset of a second cousin twice removed discovered in buggery. She would enjoy the use of the word "buggery", feel "with it", an expression she was fond of. I must telephone her soon, thought Victor as he typed "with much love as always—" Poor old thing, she wishes me to be happy, she always says "how lovely to hear your voice", she has no bloody business to find Penelope irritating, it's not for her— Victor tore the letter out of the typewriter, signed it, folded it, crammed it into an envelope, licked the envelope, addressed it. Now for the novel.

"The day I decided to drown my wife dawned clear and sweet—" Oh God what bilge.

How sweet had been Penelope in those far-off days when they decided to go to bed after lunch, take the phone off the hook – oh God, he was thirsty, those prawns, so salt. Victor left his desk and went into the kitchen for a glass of water, gulped it down as he looked out between the fat little pillars of the parapet at what they had laughingly called "our view", a view constricted to a piece of pavement at the corner by the pillar-box outside the paper shop. Often and often Victor had waited for Penelope to come into view, stand hesitating, looking left and right at the traffic before stepping off the pavement and out of sight. And Penelope had done the same. Lovers watching.

On the parapet the pigeons strutted and cooed. Victor flung the window up. "Fuck off," he shouted. "Fuck off." He slammed the window shut, drank another glass of water, felt even less like working, gave up. Hoping to expunge Penelope in another way, he ran down to the street, got into his car and drove.

As he drove Victor made slighting comparisons between his ex-wife and Poppy, hands, feet, fingers, noses, hair, eyes, teeth, arms, legs. The trouble was he had never seen Poppy naked so that comparisons stopped short. Were her tits brown or pink, was her bush mouse like her hair, or astonishingly dark and secret like Penelope's, darker than the hair on her head, or even her eyelashes? Penelope, who had not bothered him seriously for weeks or even months, imposed herself between him and Poppy.

When he got around to drowning her in his novel would she cease to torment him?

THIRTY-THREE

Willy walked with Poppy to the airport bus carrying her bag with his own. She walked stiffly, holding her head high, her shoulders unnaturally straight. He stood aside to let her climb on to the bus, blocking the way to the other passengers so that she need not hurry, then he followed her to where she settled in a seat next to the window, stood between her and their fellow travellers while he heaved the bags on to the rack, then inserted his bulk into the seat beside her. The torrential rain streaming down the window made it impossible for anyone looking in to see Poppy; within the bus he shielded her with his body. Her bruised face, dishevelled hair, the way she sat ravelled into herself reminded him of the rabbits dying of myxomatosis he had seen as a child, too stupefied, too blind to get out of the rain. Then he had joined his father in awful retching sorties to shoot or club the miserable animals, putting them out of their misery. Sitting with Poppy in the bus Willy experienced the rage of pity and fury he had had as a child magnified tenfold.

It was clear Poppy had not been in a car accident.

The passengers all seated, luggage stowed, the driver brought to an end an altercation he had been having with somebody out of sight, climbed into the driver's seat and started the engine. The bus trundled slowly through the downpour out of the airport, crawling through wind and flood towards Algiers. After a quarter of a mile the bus stopped to take on board a policeman whose cape and boots streamed water on to the floor of the bus. The policeman shouted and gesticulated at the driver who yelled back, released the handbrake and jerked onwards. The policeman continued to shout to make himself heard above the noise of the engine and the roar of the storm, the driver constantly taking his eyes off the road to confront the policeman, yelled back.

In the bus the passengers sat glum, barely exchanging a word, lighting nervous cigarettes, their collective breaths steaming up the windows.

Beside Willy Poppy made a small desperate movement, glancing up at the window.

"Want some air?"

She nodded.

Willy stood up, swaying with the movement of the bus, leant across her and forced a window open. In rushed wind and rain, there was a stormy protest from the seats behind in nasal American.

"Would you rather she vomited?" Willy shouted savagely. "That better?" he asked, resuming his seat. "Let them get wet."

She nodded slightly.

The drive was long, several times the road was blocked by floods and débris. The driver stopped, cursed, shouted, reversed. The policeman got out, got in again, directed a detour. Eventually the furious sounds of the gale altered their tone, they sloshed through partly built-up areas, then streets.

Willy said, "If you would like to give me your passport and so on I will see about rooms, then you can get to bed and rest."

Poppy did not answer but opened her bag, found her passport and handed it to him. Her knuckles and the backs of her hands were blue, he had the impression that she was near the end of her resistance, could not hold out much longer. He said, "Soon be there." She huddled in her seat like an old woman.

The policeman shouted, the driver changed down, crashing the gears, and drove in a rush up a steep hill. It was like driving up a watercourse, and floodwater whooshed over the bonnet in a muddy wave, the policeman stood beside the driver shouting encouragement. They proceeded thus for half a mile, then the bus stopped, the policeman and the driver slapped one another's backs, laughing. The bus had made it. Triumph. The fellow passengers, breaking out of their torpor, gave tongue, struggled with their luggage, urgent to get out.

"Wait till the rush is over." He was afraid she might be knocked down. Poppy waited. Willy lifted down their bags. "OK now, can you manage? Follow me." Between the bus and the hotel storm water rushed in a foot-deep torrent. "Wait." Willy splashed to the entrance, dropped the bags in the shelter of the portico, came back to where she stood on the step of the bus, held out his hands, led her through the water into the hotel lobby, noticed that she flinched, was lame.

Willy sat Poppy on a sofa beside their bags. "A little more waiting." Elbowed his way into the hubbub round the reception desk.

Twenty minutes later they were in a large room on the fourth floor with a panoramic view over the harbour where little boats tossed like corks and large vessels strained at their moorings.

Poppy's face under the bruises was grey, her lips bloodless. Willy searched and found whisky in the hotel refrigerator, held a glass for her.

"Sip it, try." She sipped, swallowed, coughed. "And again," he said, "good girl. Now I'm going to put you to bed, we'll see about a doctor later."

"No," she refused violently.

"OK. We'll see. Come on now, let's get these wet things off." He eased off her shoes. "Some joker's trodden on your heel." He helped her out of her clothes. "Afraid we have to share a room, lucky to get this one. The hotel is full of tours who thought they were going to trek across the Sahara, or go up into the mountains, and oil people diverted on their way to Libya, all stuck here until the weather clears, none of them meant to be here at all. There, let me ease this over your head, that's better." Willy went on talking as he extricated Poppy from her clothes, fetched a towel from the bathroom, wrapped it round her. There was a dark bruise on her collarbone. "Is your bag locked?"

"No."

"I'll find a nightie." Willy unzipped her bag, put the multicoloured dress aside, found a nightdress. "Here we are." Helped her put it on. "It would be a good idea if I bathed that heel and your face could do with—" Willy stopped, not trusting his voice.

Poppy stood up, holding on to the back of a chair. She was stiffening up. He helped her to the bathroom, sat her on the lavatory and bathed her face carefully. "Now your heel." She let him bathe it, winced with pain. "Fine. Strong enough to make the bed? No? Never mind." He picked her up carefully. "This is how I used to carry Mrs Future. Mrs Future is my prize sow, I brought her up on a bottle, I am a pig farmer. There you are." Willy pulled back the bedclothes, eased Poppy into the bed. He hoped that if he kept talking it would overcome some of the strangeness of the situation. "I'll put your dress where you can see it when you wake up. I always put something she knows near Mrs Future if I change her sty—"

"Oh," she was crying, "my—"

"Hey, hey, no need to cry, not now. You are safe, try another sip of whisky; that's better, lie back now." He gentled her as he gentled his animals when they were afraid or disturbed, concentrating on her need for rest and quiet.

"Don't—"

"I won't leave you. You go to sleep. I'm going to get out of my wet things, might even have a bath. If you wake up and I'm not here I shan't be far off, you will be perfectly safe." Willy went on talking in the reassuring voice he used for Mrs Future as he drew the curtains, blotting out the gale and the ugly churned-up sea. Then he moved a chair within Poppy's vision and laid the multicoloured dress across it.

In the dim light he peered anxiously down at Poppy's bruised face on the pillow. "By the way," he said, "my name is Willy Guthrie."

Poppy giggled.

"I thought you were in shock." Willy bent closer.

Poppy's bloodshot eye met Willy's. "Just knackered," she said.

THIRTY-FOUR

Ros Lawrence stood listening. The October sun warmed her back. She hesitated to ring the bell, the house was so quiet, but since the front door was open she supposed there must be someone about. With her finger by the bell she looked into the hall watching the dust dance in a shaft of sun. She felt an intruder.

Finding herself five miles from the village she had given in to an impulse she was now inclined to regret. It would have been politic to ring up, say she was coming, better perhaps to leave now, drive away, telephone, fix a date and visit later when expected. Having decided on this course a shuffling noise attracted her attention.

From the darkness at the back of the hall a baby crawled. Ros watched the effortful progress.

The child wore a loose T-shirt which inched itself up round his neck as he shuffled down the hall pushing himself backwards into the sun which lit a sunburned bottom, a roll of dimpled flesh at the waist, heavy head covered with dark curls. The baby pushed with determined hands, thrusting with plump legs, gasping and grunting with concentrated effort. As he came to Ros's feet he collapsed on to the floor, laid his head down, slid into sleep.

Ros watched the child, wondered whether she dared touch him, pull the T-shirt into a position less likely to throttle or whether to creep away without waking him. But if he woke he might continue his progress, crawl into the road, get himself run over.

Entranced, Ros watched the child, leaning against the lintel, her hand by the bell, counting the baby's soft breathing in the still October afternoon.

Down the road the church clock struck the hour. There was a clatter of jackdaws. The baby slept far away at her feet.

Ros bent down, carefully touched the baby's nape, he sank closer to the ground, splaying out tiny feet, lying like a frog. Ros was absorbed.

Then she noticed bare feet by the child's head, narrow ankles, brown legs disappearing into an indigo skirt. She looked up, smiling. "Yours?"

"Yes." Mary watched Ros warily squinting into the sun.

"He crawled down the hall backwards, he tired and fell asleep." Ros smiled at the dark baby's mother, admiring her hair bleached almost white by the sun, blue eyes startling, dark.

"He is learning, some days he can only manage backwards."

"Quite a long crawl."

"Yes."

"What's his name?"

"Barnaby."

"What a good name. I am Ros Lawrence."

"Fergus's mother?"

"Yes. Is he in?"

"Out. He's doing a funeral near Wallop. He won't be long if you'd like to come in and wait."

"I should have telephoned." Ros excused herself. "I found myself only a few miles away. I should have warned him."

"Should you?" Mary looked amused.

"I dare say he would rather I did. I don't like people dropping in on me unexpectedly."

"It depends who. Like some tea? Why don't you come in." Mary bent to pick Barnaby off the floor. He woke, stared at Ros with enormous black eyes, smiled.

"Oh." Ros stared back. "Oh, he's—"

"I expect," said Mary turning to lead the way to the kitchen, "that you need to see what your husband has given Fergus a reference for."

"It seems rather nosey," Ros apologised. Barnaby kept his eyes on her, staring over his mother's shoulder.

"No, it doesn't. Come in. I'll show you round. Like to hold Barnaby while I make us some tea?"

"May I—"

"Of course." Mary handed Barnaby over. "Half a tic, I'll give you a towel in case he pees on you."

"I wouldn't mind." Ros sat, made a lap, felt the round little bum settle against her thighs. "How old is he?"

"Eight months, nearly nine." Mary reached up to a shelf for the teapot. "I brought him back from Spain." Putting cups and saucers on the table, reaching for the milk, Mary continued casually, "The father's called Joseph." Ros watched her. "It was one of those accidents." Mary stood waiting for the kettle to boil. Barnaby chucked his head back hitting Ros's solar plexus with a thump. "The other girls, Annie and Frances, who work for Fergus too, found boys to go around with, I found this Joseph type." Ros said nothing. "He writes a lot, telephones, he's a lonely sort. Fergus thinks he's a waiter or a fisherman or something."

"Spanish?" asked Ros casually.

"No." Mary warmed the pot. "His family's Swedish, they run one of the hotels. Fergus calls Barnaby the infant Jesus, it's his sort of joke. My name's Mary." Mary made the tea, her back to Ros.

"Ah." Ros flushed with shame for Fergus.

"It's supposed to be witty." Mary set the pot down.

"I hope you clout him." Ros held the naked baby between her hands.

"I don't bother." Mary poured tea. Ros raised her eyebrows.

"Milk? Sugar?" asked Mary.

"Just as it is please." Ros bent to kiss the child's head, breathing the indescribable smell of the very young. "He's – er—"

"Yes?" said Mary on the defensive.

"Absolutely gorgeous." Ros let out her breath.

"Oh – well – when we've had tea shall I show you round? Two of the horses are here, the other four are out with Fergus. You would like to see it all, wouldn't you? The whole set-up?"

"Well – Fergus might prefer me—"

"He won't mind. I'll show you the house as well. Bit of luck Poppy letting it to Fergus, wasn't it? She's away somewhere, Fergus can't wait for her to come back."

Ros was silent. Then, filling in a pause, said, "I knew her father."

"So did I. A nice bloke, a genius for picking winners. They say he won a fortune." Mary laughed. "Others say that he was left money by women."

"He was kind," said Ros, "to lonely people."

"Yes. More tea?" Mary was suddenly wary.

"No thanks." Ros, sensing Mary's change of mood, kept silent, her hands stroking Barnaby's plump legs, tickling his toes. His nails were like pink pearls.

"Fergus is greatly taken with Poppy," Mary said flatly.

"And she with Fergus?"

"I wouldn't know. She has another sort of entanglement. Shall I take him?" Mary held out her arms as Barnaby began to whimper. "I'm still breast feeding." She unbuttoned her shirt.

"I nursed Fergus." Ros surrendered the child reluctantly.

"That was nice for you." Mary was distancing herself. "And for him," she said drily.

Ros stood up. "I think I won't wait for Fergus. Will you tell him I came? I'll telephone, let him ask me over." Ros bent to kiss the baby's head. "Goodbye, Barnaby. Don't bother to see me out, don't disturb him. He looks so happy."

"Thanks, goodbye then, it's been nice—"

"I'll see you again now I know the way. Goodbye."

Ros went out to her car. "What do they think they are playing at," she muttered. "What a fraud." She accelerated, driving away from the house in a mood of dangerous exhilaration. The smell of the child was in her mind, she felt a fierce longing to bath him, wrap him in a towel, stay with him, rolling him on a rug in front of an open fire on a winter's night, feel again the fierce joy of motherhood, hear the delighted chuckle and shriek of a happy baby. I shall box his ears, she promised herself, puzzling over the mixture of sensations, the turmoil which assailed her.

"I have not felt like this since first love at sixteen," she told her husband that night. He, being an understanding man, took off his reading glasses, turned out the bedside lamp and took his wife in his arms.

"It's all very well for you," she cried, bursting into tears, "to be so detached. You are only his stepfather."

"Amen to that," said her husband.

THIRTY-FIVE

Curled in a foetal position Poppy lay in the bed where Willy had put her. Demented rain slapped and smashed against the windows, gusts of wind whistled and howled, draught seeping in from the storm rattled the shutters which kept it at bay.

Her eyes hurt, her head throbbed, her hands ached. If she moved her arms the bruise on her collarbone was exquisitely painful. The pains of her body counterpointed the savagery of the weather.

Nothing broken, she reassured herself, just lie still, wait, and it will go away. This is nothing to the storm I left behind in cockroach country. Poppy groped for consolation, distancing herself from the last few days, from the unfinished hotel, the smell of wet cement, the insect infestation, the violence, the squashed dog, the hanging men –

With a glint of satisfaction she thought, The epilogue with Edmund is over.

Since she felt in no fit state to review the past week she dropped a closed portcullis over her mind. Start again at the moment where Willy Guthrie had materialised in the Customs. Last seen reclaiming the coat lent her by that friend of Dad's. What was he doing here, apart from being fantastically kind?

Arriving in this God-awful storm, Poppy thought, I'd just about run out of puff.

Was this man, she puzzled, part of Furnival's Funerals or a friend of Dad's? She did not remember him with Fergus and Victor. Would Fergus or Victor have gathered her up, brought her here, put her to bed without one question asked?

Putting aside the enigma of Willy, she considered Fergus and Victor, being kissed by Fergus and kissed by Victor. It had been agreeable, exploratory, loving; remembering the two men she was surprised by a twinge of desire (not done for yet) but curiously the desire was in essence equal for both. Poppy let her mind dwell on Fergus and Victor as potential lovers. It was so long since she had considered any man other than Edmund in such a role (never for more than a minute, never seriously). Fergus, she thought, would be a taker afraid to give, but an experience not to be ignored. And Victor? She thought of

Victor's extreme slenderness. The fit of bodies would be a fresh experience. Edmund's hips were wide and muscular (banish Edmund). She thought with tender curiosity of Victor. Sleepily, for she was growing sleepy, she cast her mind back to the afternoon that she had met the two men, remembering the old dog in the stable yard, the younger dogs, the offensive insolence of the cat, the girls who shampooed their hair in the room above the kitchen while Fergus worked out the cost of the funeral. And Mary, brooding, sulky and enigmatic, holding that lovely baby. Sitting there as aloof as the cat she did not fit with the girls who harassed their boys on the telephone. Then, sliding into sleep, Poppy remembered Mary sitting on the stairs in her father's house during the wake and the smile she had given her as she ran up to the lavatory before leaving with Edmund. "Watch your step," Mary had said, her tone conveying female solidarity at variance with her words. Had she or had she not called after her when she passed her going down, "Give the bugger hell"?

From a chair by the window, his back to the storm, Willy watched Poppy relax her foetal position, lay back her head in sleep, let her limbs lie free. He tiptoed across to look down on the sleeping girl before leaving her to go in search of arnica for her bruises. Even if he could find it she did not look the type to welcome raw steak on her eye. We are imprisoned here by the gale, he thought, she can spend its term resting while those bruises fade.

On his way down in the lift Willy considered ways and means of wreaking revenge on whoever had beaten Poppy up. Garrotting done slowly might be good for starters.

An American lady, also stranded by the weather, observing Willy's expression, pressed herself against the side of the lift and scuttled out to join her husband when they reached the lobby.

Returning presently with supplies Willy let himself quietly into the room, disposed of his parcels and stood looking down on Poppy sleeping now on her back, head thrown back, arms flung out, legs apart, snoring.

Willy bent to look at her. She reminded him in this abandoned attitude of Mrs Future as a piglet. The only human characteristic Mrs Future had acquired was the knack of sleeping on her back, trotters in the air. This in her now mature years she no longer did nor, Willy thought, his lips twitching, had Mrs Future ever snored.

Poppy opened her good eye: "Was I snoring?"

"Yes." Willy straightened his back. Poppy drew her legs together, folded her hands protectively across her chest.

"I got some arnica, there's a chemist counter in the hotel shop. I thought it might help your bruises."

"Thanks." She drew her hands under the coverlet.

"And he also – that's the chap in the shop – suggested some stuff to put in your bath, have a good soak he said, or I think he said, my Arabic's lousy, nonexistent actually."

"Mine too."

"That makes two of us. Anyway, I bought some. It smells nice, sort of aromatic, it might be worth a try."

"Thanks," she said again. "I'm sure it's marvellous."

Why must she be so bloody polite? "Oh well." Willy looked away. (That is the most awful shiner I have ever—) "Actually what I thought would be of immediate help is some booze. I nobbled a couple of bottles of champagne, it's in the fridge, and the barman's promised to keep us some more in case we are stuck here long. He'll defend it from our American cousins. There's a large party of them stranded *en route* from Morocco; it's OK. They really prefer Scotch."

"Oh."

"Like a glass now?"

"Please."

"Great. Got anything to put round your shoulders when you sit up?" (Cover that bruise at least.)

"No, no – I—"

"Try this." Willy fetched a cardigan given the previous Christmas by Calypso.

"Soft." Poppy fingered the material. "Cashmere."

"My aunt gave it to me. I'll open the bottle."

"The one with the coat?"

"That's the one."

While Poppy got her arms into the cardigan, wincing as she moved, Willy clinked glasses, uncorked champagne in the anteroom. He came back to hand her a glass, sat distancing himself from the bed so that she would not feel threatened.

Poppy sipped in silence.

"This storm has got itself into the newspapers." Willy broke what threatened to be too long a pause.

"That doesn't make it any better." She swallowed.

Willy refilled her glass. "You have one hell of a shiner." He took the bull by the horns. "Was it an accident?" (Of course it was no accident.)

"Not exactly."

"Oh."

"A fight, actually."

"Ah."

"He's got a broken leg." Poppy sipped her champagne, not looking at Willy, remembering the scene in that other hotel bedroom when Edmund— "He's in hospital," she said.

"I was planning to garrotte him."

Poppy laughed. "That's sweet of you." Laughing hurt.

"But since somebody's broken his leg—"

"I broke it."

"Bully for you."

"With a chair."

So with a vinous half truth Poppy joined the legendary figures of Victor, famous for drowning his wife, and Mary, known to all as the girl who had a child by a wog, to become celebrated as the girl who broke her lover's leg with a chair.

THIRTY-SIX

It began to rain as Penelope bumped up the track and a nasty little wind got up as she reached the group of buildings which had been the headquarters of Furnival's Funerals. She was tempted to turn round and drive back from whence she came. Only the memory of Mary's jeering voice and Venetia's fluting in Harrods prodded her on.

She switched off the engine, reached for her coat and got bravely out of the car.

Pushing open the yard door she found herself among empty loose-boxes where bits of straw shuffled into corners. An empty Coca-Cola tin rattled along the gutter; the doors of the boxes creaked.

She walked across the yard past the empty stables, sniffing the stale scent of horse. She kicked the Cola can which shot away rattling noisily, coming to rest against the water trough. The wind dropped, she listened. Nothing.

Leaving the yard Penelope shouldered open the doors of the coach house, walked boldly across its darkness and out into the garden, sighted the cottage, strode up the neglected path, seized the knocker, knocked.

Getting no answer, she knocked again. Above the door a window rattled on a loose latch. Penelope shielded her eyes, peered through the window into the kitchen trying to make out signs of occupation. Then she tried the door, found it locked. Exasperated she walked round the cottage peering in at the windows, unable to decide whether or not there was anybody living here.

I could write a note, she thought. Who to? she answered herself. You don't know who the woman is, who to address your note to.

The rain, up to now light, renewed its energies, slanting unpleasantly down from the top of the valley. She left the exposed doorstep, ran across to the coach house. As she pushed open the door there was a clatter and a crash, an ominous growl. Penelope's heart jumped into her throat. Something pushed against her legs, she shrieked.

"Oh God!" She was furious. "Fergus's bloody cat. I am supposed to catch you."

Bolivar pressed his bulk against her legs, purring throatily.

Penelope thought of all the trashy stories she had read where stupid girls were frightened by cats in empty buildings.

"Get off." She kicked at Bolivar. "Stop doing that. I hate cats. Follow me to the car and I'll give you your bloody sardines, then you can sit in the back and I'll drive you back to Fergus and that horrible girl. He should give me a reward for this," she said, opening the coach-house door, slamming it shut, crossing the yard to her car.

Bolivar ran ahead of Penelope, his ringed tail in the air, exposing a tender triangle of gingery fur round his anus, jauntily displaying his balls.

"Here you are, you beastly animal." Penelope took the tin of sardines from the car seat, laid it on the ground.

Purring loudly, Bolivar set himself to eat.

Penelope got into the car out of the rain and sat waiting for the cat to finish its meal. As Bolivar ate slowly after the first gulp she drummed her fingers on the steering wheel impatient to be off.

"Hurry up, for Christ's sake. I've had enough of this place, there's nobody here."

Bolivar paused in his eating to lick his chops, shake the rain off his coat, stare around. "If there is anybody here she must be out. I'm not going to wait." For some reason she felt very nervous.

Bolivar resumed his meal, crouching intent and thoughtful over the sardines.

"Buck up," ordered Penelope. Bolivar rasped his tongue round the tin, sucking up the last drop of delicious oil, then sat back and began his toilet.

"Oh for God's sake, you can do that in the car, jump in." Penelope opened the car door.

Bolivar moved away.

"Come on, get in, I'm not going to pick you up." Penelope made to shoo Bolivar into the car.

Bolivar stepped aside.

"Blast you, get in I said." Penelope reached down to pick Bolivar up. Bolivar scratched her.

"Bloody fucking beast." Penelope lunged to grab Bolivar. Bolivar skipped aside. Penelope gave chase.

Bolivar ran ahead, enjoying the game, cantering tail up, as before, beautiful tabby flanks gleaming in the rain. Had Penelope been a cat lover she would have appreciated that here in Bolivar was a truly beautiful specimen of domestic cat.

Penelope stopped running, altered tack. "Puss, puss, puss," she called in her sexiest voice.

Bolivar sauntered down a grassy slope to the stream, crouched like a tiger to drink, his pink tongue lapping the clear water, the tip of his tail twitching in rhythm with his tongue.

The rain stopped as suddenly as it had started. Bolivar sat on a flat stone and resumed his interrupted toilet.

"Bugger you," Penelope cooed between clenched teeth. "Come on, pretty puss. Puss, puss, puss." She approached the cat slowly.

Bolivar ignored her.

Holding her breath Penelope crept closer. Two feet from Bolivar she pounced. Her outstretched hands gripped empty air. The grassy bank overhanging the stream gave way. She crashed into the water, twisting her ankle in an agonising wrench, banging her knee on a stone, bruising it badly.

Stunned by the pain, Penelope hauled herself out of the water, sat on the bank, took off her shoe, watched her ankle swell and blood seep from her knee.

"Oh God, oh God, that woman will come back and find me like this," Penelope moaned, "I must get away." She snatched up a stone and threw it at the cat. Bolivar did not flinch, he watched, sitting still again, whiskers fanning outward. Now in her wretchedness Penelope remembered Mary giving her the sardines. "Lure him into the car," she had said, "lure him in." Not put the fucking tin down in the open.

Bolivar moved, he nudged up against Penelope weaving a sinuous caress. "Fuck off, piss off," said Penelope gritting her teeth, close to tears.

Bolivar repeated his gesture, catching Penelope's eye, pressing his arched back against her side.

Penelope ignored him. The pain in her ankle was growing worse, it was beginning to throb quite horribly. She dipped her foot, ankle and all, into the icy stream. "Oops!" Courageously she kept it there. She splashed water over her bruised knee. Bolivar was interested.

Holding her foot in the water, trying to keep still, breathing in shuddering gasps, Penelope felt disgusted respect for the cat who now sat out of reach on his stone, gazing down into the water trickling over a pretty little waterfall into the pool. From time to time Bolivar licked his lips.

Following Bolivar's intent scrutiny Penelope saw a fish idling in the current, lazily steering with its semi-transparent tail and fins. The water was so clear she was able to count its spots, view its pink-tinged flanks. Watching the fish, keeping her foot in the pool, she became aware of mud seeping through her clothes to chill her bottom and thighs, oozing icily through her skirt.

"I have to get away." Penelope withdrew her foot from the pool, tried to stand. Impossible, she crumpled, the pain was awful. She went down on hands and knees and began to crawl back to her car.

Bolivar, interested, kept pace.

Penelope had managed twenty painful yards when she heard a car coming up the track. Her first reaction was to shout "Help!" Then, no, oh no – that woman – I can't – won't. Penelope lay flat out of sight of the track. I'll get away when she's gone into the house, she thought, I can't possibly confront her like this. Conscious of her muddy and dishevelled appearance, painful ankle, bruised knee, Penelope lay face down on the wet grass.

"What on earth?" cried Victor, running down the slope to visit his trout. "I say! Oh God, it's you, darling. I thought the car looked familiar. What are you doing here? You are hurt. What happened? Who did this to you? Let me see. Oh my love, my poor, poor love, don't cry. It's all right, I'm here now. Here, use my handkerchief. Oh, my darling. Put your arms round me. That's right. I'll get you to a doctor. Gosh, you are soaking, you'll catch pneumonia. Your poor ankle, look at that knee. Jesus, it's swollen. How on earth – I say, what's Bolivar doing here – trying to catch my trout, the old faker. Don't cry, darling, it's all right now, I'm here."

"The cat did it," said Penelope viciously.

THIRTY-SEVEN

Victor helped Penelope into her car. "You'd better let me drive." He took off his jacket, rolled it into a ball. "Cushion your foot on that, then it won't get jarred going over the bumps."

"Thanks." Gingerly she eased herself into the seat.

"If you came to fetch Bolivar," Victor went on, "we'd better drop him off at Fergus's new place on our way to a doctor. Fergus will be able to recommend one. Bolivar can sit in the back, he'll be all right there."

Penelope, so lately rescued, felt it unpolitic to say "Just try and catch him." Remarks of that ilk had sparked off many a row in the past.

Victor bent down, picked Bolivar up. Bolivar pressed a sheathed paw against Victor's cheek, chucked him under the chin with his head. "Gorgeous animal," said Victor, "how come you got left behind in the move? You must have been out hunting or after the girls, you old rogue." He put Bolivar on the back seat. "Better wind the windows up in case he takes it into his head to leap out."

Penelope wound up her window, Victor closed his.

"Perhaps he doesn't like cars," Penelope ventured.

"Nonsense, I bet he drives everywhere with Fergus."

"What about your car?" asked Penelope.

"I'll come back for it."

"Are you leaving the keys in the ignition?"

"Yes," said Victor, who had forgotten them. "Why are you always right?" he asked bitterly.

Penelope sniffed danger.

"Nobody comes up here," Victor justified himself. "Right, let's be off." He started the engine, turned the car.

In the back Bolivar began to scream.

"I don't suppose he's ever been in a car," Penelope shouted.

Victor yelled, "The poor fellow's frightened, he'll settle down in a minute."

Penelope's answer, if she made one, was drowned.

Bolivar bounded caterwauling from side to side of the back seat.

Penelope shielded her head with her hands in case he took it into his demented head to leap over into the front of the car.

Victor laughed. "At least we can't have a row with this racket going on," he bellowed.

Penelope stopped her ears with her fingers.

For the ten miles to Fergus's new establishment in Poppy Carew's house and stables Bolivar kept up an ear-piercing, growling, panic-stricken yowl. The only thing which prevented Victor from stopping the car and letting Bolivar out was the thought of the many, many times in the future when, supposing they were re-united, Penelope would say "I told you so".

At last reaching Poppy's house, Victor stopped the car, switched off the engine and sat still, his ears tingling in the sudden silence. Penelope kept her ears blocked and her eyes shut.

On the back seat Bolivar now sat quiet and wary, his eyes brilliant with suspicion, his tail lashing.

"How clever you've been. I never thought you'd catch him. Sardines did the trick, did they?" Mary ran to greet them. "Hullo, Victor, what are you doing here?" she shouted through the closed window, cheerful and pleased.

"Went to visit my trout," shouted Victor, beginning to wind down the window.

"Don't do that! He might run away, he's never been here, he might be frightened. Keep it shut," shouted Mary. "Wait while I fetch Fergus, he's just got back." She disappeared into the house. They heard her voice still, "It was a very successful funeral, went without a hitch. Fergus, Bolivar's arrived!"

"Am I in hell?" muttered Penelope.

"That was Byron on his wedding night—" Victor, not one of those men who fancy themselves in Byron's shoes, waiting obediently for Fergus to appear, wished that there might be a time when he was not in perpetual disagreement with his ex-wife then, feeling an unwonted rush of affection for her, leant across and kissed her cheek.

"What did you do that for?" Penelope took her hands from her ears.

"Love," said Victor.

Penelope said nothing. In addition to the throb of her twisted ankle and her bruised knee she was trying to assimilate the revelation she had just been posed by Mary. Then: "I feel such an utter and complete fool," she whispered.

"Why?" Half expecting her to snatch it away, Victor took her hand.

"I *say*! Clever girl, found and caught my Bolivar." Fergus came out of the house, bounding down the steps, putting paid to any explanation

Penelope might see fit to make. "Thought you didn't care for cats, Penelope. Here, just let me get at him. Come along, my treasure, you've no idea how worried I've been." Opening the car door, Fergus gathered Bolivar tenderly into his arms. "There, there, what a dreadful time you've had. Never mind, it's all over now."

Penelope and Victor exchanged glances.

Moaning with joy, Bolivar nestled against Fergus, pressing his furry bulk against his chest, his purr rumbling fit to choke in his throat.

"It's Penelope who's had a dreadful time," Victor yelled in exasperation. "There's nothing wrong with your bloody cat. Penelope's hurt, I must get her to a doctor."

"Really? Why?" asked Fergus, distracted from Bolivar, sighting Penelope. "What on earth have you been up to, you do look a mess. Did Victor get around to trying to murder you again?"

"One of these days your jokes will get you into serious trouble." Mary pushed Fergus aside. "Shut Bolivar up somewhere until he's calmed down, butter his paws. You come with me," she said to Penelope, "you don't need a doctor. I'll fix your wounds. Help me get her up to the bathroom, Victor."

"Bossy boots." Fergus stood aside.

"And when you've shut the cat up, tell one of the girls to make a pot of tea. Come on, Victor. Lean on both of us," she said to Penelope. "Get cracking, Fergus, light the fire in the sitting-room while you are about it and find the whisky. Keep an eye on Barnaby while I'm busy."

"Christ!" Fergus, hugging Bolivar, watched Mary and Victor help Penelope into the house and up the stairs.

"And tell Frances and Annie they can't go out tonight, there's far too much to do," Mary called from the stairs.

Fergus gaped. "What's got into her?"

"Your mother came to see you this afternoon," Mary called from the landing.

"My ma? What did she want?"

Mary did not apparently hear. "Leave her with me," she said to Victor as Penelope sank on to the bathroom chair. "I can cope better without you."

"I—" said Victor.

"Go on, you're only in the way."

Victor looked at Penelope's face smeared with mud and tears. She made a tentative movement. Victor bent down, she put her hands on his shoulders. They kissed carefully, neither spoke. "OK, see you later." Victor straightened up and left the room.

"Cry into this." Mary handed Penelope a roll of lavatory paper. "I honestly think you'd do best by getting into a hot bath, you're soaked. Let me help you out of your clothes. I'll lend you some of mine."

"You're kind."

"Just interested in the boomerang effect of whatever it was Venetia started—" Mary turned on the taps, helped Penelope undress. "Have a good soak while I find a bandage to strap up that ankle. I'm sure she didn't intend you to meet Victor."

"It was a ploy, probably directed against Poppy Carew. Oh, that's lovely." Penelope lay back in the bath. "Didn't you say when I was here earlier on that both Fergus and Victor are interested in Poppy?"

"Exactly. Quite funny as things—" Mary began to laugh. Penelope joined in.

Fergus, in the kitchen buttering Bolivar's paws, looked up nervously.

"Listen to those two. What can they be laughing at?"

"Us, probably," said Victor. "Where d'you keep the whisky?"

"It's on the dresser." Fergus placed Bolivar in the dog basket. Bolivar shook his paws, sniffed, then started to lick them.

Victor poured them each a drink. "When did you move in here?"

"Few days ago. Mary's getting us straight. It's lucky we moved. I'm wonderfully busy. We buried a retired hunt servant today and I've got two funerals in the next six days, an industrialist whose widow aspires to be county and a gypsy's grandmother from near Romsey. Mary's wonderful on the phone with that voice of hers, she talks posh to some, cosy to others, can't think how I'd manage without her."

"What happened to Poppy?" Victor looked round the kitchen, reminded of her existence.

"No idea." Fergus sipped his whisky. "Her father's daily lady doesn't know either. Isn't she in London?"

"No," said Victor, "she isn't."

"Oh." Fergus looked at his cousin thoughtfully. "I thought—"

"What did your mother want, d'you suppose?" Victor headed Fergus off, not wishing to discuss his intentions *vis-à-vis* Poppy with Fergus or to hear Fergus's plans. If Fergus was busy he would have little time to spare chasing Poppy. His own intentions were ambiguous.

"I don't know," said Fergus, reminded of his parent. "She doesn't usually drop in unannounced, she's supersensitive to interference herself."

"Happy with your role as undertaker, is she? How does it fit in with the family image?"

"She persuaded my stepfather to give me a reference, it gave Poppy's solicitor a salutary shock."

"I should have thought—"

"What?" asked Fergus suspiciously.

"That he was used to all sorts with Poppy's father's friends. What a *bouillabaisse* at the funeral." Victor laughed.

"Not all of them fishy. Didn't you notice Calypso Grant?"

"Was that who it was? I wonder who spread the treacle. That was a fishy act if ever there was one. Must have been somebody with a grudge."

"We must ask Poppy when she reappears."

"Aren't you going to look for her?"

"How can I?" said Fergus. "I'm up to my eyes with work. Are you going to look for her?"

"I'm pretty busy with this book of mine at the moment."

"I see," said Fergus. "And Penelope?"

"Well—" said Victor. "I—"

The cousins paused like hunting dogs who have temporarily lost the scent.

"What were you doing up at my old place?" Fergus poured Victor more whisky.

"I was stuck in my work. I went to visit the trout, see whether it was still alive, get a bit of inspiration."

"And is it?"

"Yes, I think so. I forgot to look."

"Eh?" Fergus looked at Victor. "And you took Penelope with you?"

"No, I found her there—"

"What was she doing? Why did you push her into the stream? How did she find her way there?"

"I don't know. I didn't ask her. I didn't push her—"

From the bathroom above the kitchen there was a shout of feminine laughter, followed by a spate of chatter.

"She seems all right now," said Victor dubiously.

The laughter above them was renewed.

"Hilarious," muttered Fergus. "I wonder what the joke can be."

"Us," said Victor positively.

Listening to the laughter the two men felt threatened.

"I wonder what my mother wanted." Fergus skated rapidly round his conscience. "It's ages since I heard Mary laugh like that."

"Ganging up," said Victor.

"Pessimist." Fergus was robust. "Still, I'd better light the fire, as she said."

THIRTY-EIGHT

Willy's personal experience of black eyes and bruises was limited to an occasion in adolescence when he had been involved in a car smash. Watching Poppy sleep he tried to remember how long his bruises had taken to fade. He was anxious for Poppy, anxious too to get back to his pigs. All very well to leave Arthur in charge for a few days but the prospect of much longer irked him. He did not like the hotel, inefficient and sloppy with its resentful undertones of past French glories. The atmosphere created by fellow stranded travellers with their hysterical impatience to continue their interrupted tours made him jumpy. He worried about running short of money, and worse; now that he had found Poppy, there was a barrier of silence between them which he resented.

She was not, he thought, watching her sleep, capable of breaking anybody's leg. It was at least doubtful. This must be some sort of joke. Not knowing Poppy he could only guess at her idea of humour.

Since she was, he supposed, in the grip of some sort of trauma, it would do her good to unburden herself, break this stubborn silence, but how to bring this desirable effect about?

He must not force her.

Long ago in his early days of farming he had forced Mrs Future's great-aunt to move from a sty where she was settled and content into another where it was easier, from his point of view, to care for her. Mrs Future's great-aunt had retaliated by eating her entire litter, presumably acting on the theory that they were safer inside than out.

It was two days since he had found Poppy. During that time she had volunteered no information, had been politely grateful for his care but most of the time she had slept, shutting herself away out of reach.

Tired of watching the storm outside, Willy stretched out on his bed and tried to read the only paperback he had with him for the third time. The complexities of Len Deighton bemused him, the book fell forward on his chest, he fell asleep.

Waking in the dark, Willy listened for the storm; its frenzy seemed a little less. Next he listened for Poppy's breathing, heard nothing, sat up, reached for the bedside lamp, pressed the switch, it did not work.

Cursing, he blundered to the door, tried the switches, none worked. He opened the door into the corridor, that too was inky dark. Below in the hotel there was the confused sound of dismembered voices clamouring up the lift shaft. Back in the room he made for the window, looked out. There were no harbour lights. There was no moon.

Afraid for Poppy, he felt his way round the room, felt her bed, found it empty. Thinking he might have mistaken Poppy's bed for his own he searched the second bed. This too was empty.

Suddenly afraid, Willy shouted, "Poppy!" screaming "Poppy!"

"I'm here," she called, "in the bath. The lights went out."

"Are you all right?"

"Getting cold."

"I thought you'd run away." His fear was still with him. "I thought you'd gone." He felt his way to the bathroom. "I thought something had happened to you, I was terrified."

"I was soaking in that stuff you brought me, it's delicious, helps a lot. Can you find me a towel? There's a bathrobe hanging on the door."

Feeling for the robe Willy was surprised to find himself shaking. "I have it," he said.

"Thanks, heave ho, up I come." She splashed up out of the bath beside him. "Where are you? What's the matter?"

"Thought you'd gone." He felt for her wet body, wrapped her in the bathrobe. "God, it's dark. Am I hurting you?"

"No, it's all right."

"Don't get cold." He held her bundled against him, smelling her hair under his chin.

"When the lights come back," he said, "I'll tell you I love you."

They were pressed against the edge of the bath.

"Perhaps until then we could sit somewhere comfortable."

"The bed—"

"Yes, OK. Why don't we get in?" She was shivering.

They felt their way to the bed. Willy pulled back the bedclothes. They lay facing each other. Poppy put a hand over his heart.

"Your poor bruised hands," he said.

"They are getting better. Much better."

Why did I tell her I love her? Blurt it out like that in a bathroom. Clot. Enough to put any girl off.

Outside the storm whooped up with renewed vigour. Further along the hotel's façade a shutter broke loose, clattered in anguish against the wall.

Should he go down, try to find out why there was no light, when it would come on again, join in the confusion raging in the lobby? He held Poppy damp in the bathrobe. She was speaking, her breath warm against his throat.

"I was awful to Edmund on the plane. I should not have come with him. I did it to spite Venetia. It seemed a good chance when he snatched me away after Dad's funeral. A surprise, that, because he had left me the week before. He's in love with Venetia. He wants to marry her. He never wanted to marry me, we just lived together. I suppose he had this impulse – I didn't like to make a fuss in front of strangers and in a way it was a bit of a joke, a poke in the eye for her. I thought I'd say no in private, No, it's over, then when I saw what she'd done I was sorry for him and I gave in, came on this journey. It was sheer cussedness and stupidity, crazy, a colossal mistake. But he assumed I loved him, assumed I would marry him, started talking marriage. He must have guessed I have money now, it couldn't be anything else. It was so crass. There were these insects, awful things, we ran over a dog and then those men I saw. They hanged them, sort of hoisted them up—" Willy held her, said nothing. She went on— "He went out for the day, disappeared, came back so pissed he got into the wrong room, no, it was the second night he was pissed, no, both nights. Then in the morning I could see something terrible had happened to him, he was hangdog and hung over, so I said let's have a lovely day together and we did. We picnicked and swam and drove out to an oasis in the desert and made love. Just like old times. When we got back he started drinking again, he can be awfully disagreeable when he drinks. Well, we had this bust up, this row, he hit me, knocked me down, stamped on my hands – I got frightened." Willy held Poppy tight. "Then I broke his leg with a chair." Still Willy held her, she felt his heart beating under her hand.

Willy held his breath.

"I swung the chair with both hands. I heard the bone crack." She went on, "I was glad. I packed my bag, sent a telegram to Venetia and sent for Mustafa to cope, get Edmund to hospital or whatever. (Actually I did that before I packed my bag and alerted Venetia.) Oh, Edmund—" Poppy paused to feel the familiar pang, felt nothing. "Then I got a taxi to the airport and got on to the first plane out. That's how I landed up here." Poppy gave a long tired sigh. "Sorry to bother you with all this."

Willy held her, said nothing, content to piece the facts into some sort of sense later.

"It's remarkable," said Poppy conversationally, "how really nasty I become when I'm unhappy. It's not only me. Look at Venetia. She would never have done that to Edmund's clothes if she hadn't been unhappy. I can't help admiring her though. (He's such a beautiful man.) Then there's Mary, the girl with a baby, she's miserable, it sharpens her tongue. I dare say Venetia's happy enough now. Am I boring you?"

"No."

"Say if I do. I'd got cold in the bath, the water wasn't all that hot to start with. I'm nice and warm now."

"Good."

"Are you worrying about your pigs?"

"No," said Willy untruthfully.

"I wish the lights would come on."

Willy stirred. "I don't."

"Oh." She sounded sad, then, "It's true what I told you about Edmund's leg and the chair, but we did not make much love when we picnicked and it wasn't such a lovely day. It was a good try, that's all. I credit myself with trying. To be quite truthful it was one hell of an awful day. What are you doing?"

"Guess," said Willy.

"Wow!" said Poppy presently, "that was— Oh, I wish the lights would come on."

"I can tell you in the dark," said Willy.

"No, please don't. That's not what I want." Poppy took fright, she had no wish to get involved with the pitfalls of love. "Edmund never did it like that," she said.

"I'm not all that keen on hearing about Edmund's performance," said Willy huffily.

"No, I suppose not, how tactless, it was meant to be a compliment. Tell me about Mrs Future then."

"You remembered her name." He was amused.

"Of course." Poppy lay in Willy's arms enjoying herself. Suppose I take this man on as a pleasure man? It's ages since I experienced pleasure. I've never had this sort of delight. What would it be like with Victor? With Fergus? "Oh! Are we doing it again? It's nice like this in the dark, isn't it? Do you mind my talking?"

"No."

"I am enjoying this – mm – yes, go on doing that. Yes, yes. If it hadn't been for the power cut we might not have— Oh!— Yes!— Oh!— Do you suppose there are people stuck in the lift?"

"Oh, oh Poppy—"

"Sorry, I made you laugh at the wrong moment—"

"It's never the wrong moment." He had not heard her laugh before.

"Do you then think laughter and copulation are compatible?"

"Absolutely."

THIRTY-NINE

Frances and Annie leant against the kitchen door, sharing a packet of crisps, minding their business. This comprised waiting for Frances's latest man to telephone. Frances called him a man although he was still sixteen. "He has the requisite parts," she had said when challenged on his tender years by Annie, whose present choice was twenty-three, and dissolved into giggles. Frances was eighteen, Annie eighteen also. They were evolving from horsestruck chrysalises into boystruck girls.

They had finished work, fed and watered the horses, swept the yard, cleaned the tack, polished the hearse and now anticipated the evening's entertainment, lolling against the kitchen door, looking out at the yard.

"It's much better here than up in the hills." Frances smoothed the front of her dress. Her new man liked her in skirts.

Annie wore a kimono bought in a secondhand shop in Pimlico and baggy trousers *à la mode* from Miss Selfridge. She had slanted her eyes with eyeliner. Both girls' hair was freshly washed and set to look as though they had been drawn roughly through a hedge backwards.

"How long since Joseph telephoned?" Annie crushed the empty crisp packet between her hands. The crackle caused several horses to look out of their boxes hoping for lumps of sugar.

"Not since we moved down here."

"Perhaps she didn't give him the new telephone number."

"Perhaps she's tired of him telephoning."

"Is that what you think?"

"You know what I think." Frances rolled her eyes.

"Telephone!" Annie ran to answer it. She came back after a few minutes. "It was some woman wanting Fergus, said she is coming round."

"A client? Did you tell her he is out?"

"She said she'd come and wait for him to get back."

"Where is he?"

"Walking the dogs."

"Are you two going out?" Mary called from a window above their heads.

"Yes. Coming with us? D'you think she heard us?" Frances whispered.

Annie shook her head.

"No thanks," called Mary.

Bolivar came out of the kitchen swaying his body so that he brushed against the girls' legs without seeming to pay them attention. Frances bent to stroke his back, letting his upward waving tail run through her fingers. He sauntered on to sit in a patch of setting sun.

Lowering their voices the girls discussed what Annie thought of Joseph, then, bored by this overworked unrewarding theme, switched to Victor and Penelope.

"I wonder." Annie caught Frances's eye.

"I bet you," said Frances.

"But will they actually remarry?" Annie mused.

"Positive," said Frances.

"Rubbish," said Annie. "You were positive he was keen on Poppy Carew. He once tried to murder Penelope, he might try again."

"After or before marriage?"

Lolling in the kitchen doorway the girls gossiped about Penelope and Victor last seen driving off to London in apparent amity. They would come back later to retrieve Victor's car.

"Nothing like that happens to us, nobody tries to murder me," Annie complained.

"Our lives have barely begun." Frances was an optimistic girl.

They stopped chattering to watch Mary, carrying Barnaby across the yard, get in her car and drive away.

"She's not exactly sociable these days."

"Never really was."

"Telephone. I'll get it." Annie ran to answer it. Coming back she said, "They are on their way, let's wait in the porch." They moved to sit on the front steps. Annie tore open another packet of crisps. "Have one? Who's this?" A car drew up by the house. "A client, d'you suppose? At this hour?"

Annie and Frances watched Ros Lawrence get out and walk towards them. They assessed her clothes, her hair, lack of jewellery, excellent skin for her age. They sent out feelers to gauge her mood. Widow? Grieving parent? Friend of the deceased?

"Hullo," said Ros. "Is Fergus in?" She was nervous. "I'm his mother," she introduced herself.

"He's walking the dogs," said Frances.

"Oh," said Ros. "Oh. I had hoped to see him."

"He won't be long. They don't allow dogs in the pub so he'll be back. Won't you come in and wait for him," said Annie, politely welcoming. "We thought for a moment you might be a client."

"Not yet." Ros smiled, hesitated. "I should have telephoned or written perhaps." Annie looked at her curiously, recognising the voice on the telephone. I must sound odd, thought Ros, but surely it's perfectly natural to call on my own son, nothing to be frightened of. ("Mind your own business," her husband had said, "don't interfere, he's a grown man.") "I just thought I'd like to see him."

"Naturally," said Annie, puzzled.

"We work here. We are the grooms," said Frances, trying to put Ros at her ease (what a jumpy lady), "and the mutes if they are needed. I am Frances and this is Annie."

"Of course," said Ros. "I've heard all about you." He hasn't told me about them, did he tell me about mutes? I can't remember. They are pretty girls if they'd give themselves a chance. "It's nice here." She looked up at the house.

"Very convenient," said Annie.

"Much better than up on the downs," said Frances. "Why don't you come in and sit down, he won't be long." Annie waved Ros into the house. "We are supposed to be going out but Fergus will be back any minute."

"Here they come," said Frances, relieved, as the boyfriends drove up. "Will you be all right if we leave you? We are going to a party."

"Of course. Have a good time." Ros watched the young people go, went into the house, sat on a sofa in the sitting-room, got restlessly up, looked at the bookshelves, fingered a pair of field-glasses, remembered Bob Carew wearing them round his neck at Newmarket, missed him, not as a close friend but as someone she had always been pleased to see, always felt the better for meeting. Had he really named his daughter after a racehorse? Had he worried about her as she worried now about her son Fergus?

She listened to the empty house.

If I went upstairs I could pretend I'd gone to the lavatory, she thought. With a quick look round I could work out who sleeps in which room, with whom. God, how base! She suppressed her curiosity, resisted the urge to explore, moved to the safer ambience of the kitchen and on out into the yard to talk to the horses.

"Hullo my beauties, hullo." She patted necks, stroked noses. "And Bolivar, how are you, how do you like it here?" She caressed the cat who accepted her tribute offhandedly. She wished Fergus would come in, feeling increasingly nervous, remembering her husband. "I would hesitate to interfere," she had said.

"Which is exactly what you want to do," he had answered.

"But I must find out what is going on," she had said. "I am his mother."

"All the more reason," he had said, "not to poke your nose in."

"Oh Fergus," she exclaimed, as Fergus came into the yard with his dogs. "Thank God you are back."

"Why, what's happened?"

"Nothing, nothing. I've been here such ages I was beginning to think I'd better come back another time, let you know beforehand, warn you." She heard herself being querulous, tried to stop.

"I saw you arrive from up on the hill—"

"Oh, you did? Well, it seemed a long time." Ros was defensive.

Fergus bent to kiss her. "I'm back now, come along in and have a drink. Didn't the girls—"

"They went out, a party or—"

"Of course. Always on the go those two. They chase more boys than I have fingers or toes. Veritable Dianas. Isn't Mary about? She would look after you."

"The house seems empty actually. It was about—"

"Well, come on in." Fergus put his arm round her shoulders. "Have you had supper?" He reached for the whisky, poured Ros a drink.

"I must get back. Henry will be waiting."

"And how is my step-papa?"

"Fine, fine. What I came for – was—"

"Yes?"

Ros, courage evaporating under Fergus's kindly gaze, procrastinated. "Well, I came to see how you are getting on now you've moved." She sipped her drink. "Could I have a little more water in this, it's very strong?" Trying to sound normal she succeeded in sounding nervous.

"Of course."

"I used to know Bob Carew. Your father and I often met him at the races. This house was his, wasn't it?"

"Yes. We buried him. I'm renting it, from his daughter."

Fergus's face softened at the thought of Poppy, Ros noticed. "I saw it on the local television and somebody wrote an article about you which I read in a magazine at the hairdresser's," she said.

"Yes, Victor."

"Oh, oh yes of course." Ros sipped her whisky; it was still much too strong, drinks went straight to her head these days, some sort of by-blow from the menopause. "Of course," she said again, "it was Victor."

Fergus looked at his mother over the rim of his glass. What's the matter with her, has she repented of marrying Henry, is she afraid to tell me she's made a cock-up, she can come and stay here if she wants to think better of it, get shot of him. "What's the matter, Mother?"

"Nothing, nothing's the matter." Ros gulped her drink. Where's my sangfroid? Why am I afraid of my own son, my only child? Mind the whisky. "How are the dogs?" (Idiot question, the dogs are fine, sitting round us, wagging their tails, waiting for their dinners, it's a shame to keep them waiting.) "Would you show me round? I'd love to see it all." She made a circling motion with her glass.

"Of course. Come round the yard and see the horses." Give her time and she'll tell me what her worry is. I thought she was happy with Henry. In many ways he's a lot nicer than Father ever was, got more humour, hasn't got his filthy temper. Fergus frowned as he led the way out to the stables. "We had a good funeral a couple of days ago over at Wallop and I'm booked for two more this week," he said cheerfully.

"How splendid. Soon you'll have so much work you – oh, I thought that horse had a white blaze."

"He does. So does number three. Mary dyes it and their white socks."

"Oh Mary. Of course I was—"

"Sometimes she dyes her hair at the same time." Fergus laughed tolerantly. Ros looked at him sharply. "Come along and let me show you the house." Ros followed him in and up the stairs. "You looked round the ground floor, I take it."

"Sort of."

"I hope the girls haven't left everything in a mess." Fergus led her upstairs, began opening doors. "That's Annie in there, Frances here. Bob Carew's daily lady comes to us now, she's quite a dragon, keeps us in order. You must meet her some time, she's what your mother would have called a treasure."

"Oh."

"Good so far." Fergus glanced through a doorway. "Nobody daring to be untidy. Mary's in there with Jesu."

"Who?"

"Her child—"

"Fergus—"

"And I'm on the next floor out of harm's way. This room used to be the spare room. Mrs Edwardes – that's the daily lady – says Bob Carew's lady visitors used to stay in it; d'you suppose they were his mistresses?"

"I think—"

"Apparently Poppy has reserved it for herself or did before the funeral. I thought if she'd like to use it for weekends she could still have it. A lovely girl, isn't she?" Fergus's voice warmed.

"Never met her."

"But you knew her dad, the one we buried?"

"Yes, of course. Fergus, I came—"

"Yes?" Fergus turned his black eyes on her. "Yes?"

"Nothing. I wasn't—"

"Would you like to stay the night, Mother, have Poppy's room, have supper with me, I'm on my own?" Give her time to sick up whatever's bothering her, something is, it must be serious, I've never seen her quite like this. "You could telephone Henry." If my stepfather is ill-treating her I shall have to—

"No thanks, darling. I'd better get back." She took fright.

"Have another drink, then." Loosen her tongue. I must find out what the trouble is. Fergus, sensing his parent's distress, felt growing concern as he led the way back to the kitchen, poured her another whisky.

"I really shouldn't," said Ros, taking it. "I have miles to drive."

"Then stay the night."

"No, no." The prospect terrified her.

"Why don't we sit where it's comfortable in the sitting-room. I'll light the fire, come along." He led the way. Ros followed, panic constricting her throat, why, oh why, had she come? Damn Henry for being right.

"There, sit there." Fergus pushed her into an armchair.

Ros sat, reminded of a rabbit with a stoat, the part of the stoat was being played by Fergus, her only child.

"Well, now. What's really worrying you?" Fergus leant towards her, his elbows on his knees. "I don't see enough of you, Mother."

Somehow she must get herself out of this ridiculous situation. She took a large swallow of whisky. "Henry and I thought, well I thought of it and he agreed, well of course he agreed" (what he'd actually done was fall about laughing), "we—"

"Yes?" Fergus leant forward listening, sympathetic, caring, he was really very fond of his mother, no reason not to be.

"Would you like a coach?" Ros shot her inspiration out with a rush.

"A coach?" Has she gone off her rocker?

"Yes. I thought for your business it would – I mean with a coach you could—"

"I've got a hearse, Mother." He was patient.

"I know, darling, it's just this, I thought if I gave you a coach, I saw one advertised in Bath—"

"It's very generous of you but what would I want with a coach?"

"You could do weddings," said Ros inspired.

"Aha! It's out. You are snobbishly opposed to funerals." He felt betrayed.

"NO!" She flushed.

"Yes, you are. You don't like having a son who's an undertaker."

"No, darling, it's not—"

"Or my stepfather doesn't like having a stepson who's an undertaker. It lowers the tone. Well, he must bloody put up with it." Fergus's short-fused temper exploded. "He can stuff his coach up his fastidious arse. I thought you were embarrassed about something when I came in, had some awful worry you couldn't bring yourself to talk about. I see it all. You want to bribe me to chuck my business for a fucking coach for weddings." Fergus spat out the last word. "Well, you can tell him I am not interested in weddings."

"I can see that!" Ros too had a temper.

Ignoring her, Fergus went on, "I've worked my balls off to get my business off the ground. I'm beginning to do really well. I am not interested in marriages, they always fall apart, look at Victor reduced to killing Penelope—"

"She's still alive," shouted Ros, infected by Fergus's rage, choking on her own agitation.

"I am interested in burials, in death, there's money in death and I am making it," Fergus shouted. He was standing up now, towering above his mother.

"I am very glad for you," Ros too stood up, put down her empty glass, "delighted, though you may not believe me, you are so touchy."

"I am *not* touchy."

"I didn't come about offering to give you a coach, that was off the top of my head on the spur of the moment, an idea engendered by terror."

"What did you come about, then?" Fergus stood looking down at his mother.

"Your child," said Ros.

"My *what*?"

"Your child, Mary Mowbray's baby."

Fergus stared at his mother. "Mother, you must be mad." He spoke very gently. (A good psychiatrist, this looked serious.)

Ros said nothing, watching him.

"That baby's father is called Joseph, Mother, he's a Spaniard, in Spain, he's a waiter or a fisherman or something."

"A figment."

"You do not suppose I'd—"

"Yes."

"Come on, Mother, you have the wrong end of the stick. She brought it back from Spain, I tell you."

Ros sat down again. "And I tell you, Fergus, that that child is the spitting image of you as a baby. I should know, I am your mother. It was a great shock when I saw him the other day. I can show you photographs of yourself when you were his age which could have been taken yesterday of that child and—" She held up a hand as Fergus tried to speak. "I can also show you photographs of your father at the same age. Same thing, identical. The Furnival genes are mighty strong."

Leaving the house, Ros passed Bolivar on the doorstep sitting in the dusk, whiskers twitching in anticipation of the night's business. She kicked his flank.

"That's not like you, Mother," Fergus cried desperately.

"But that baby is like you." Ros jumped into her car and drove off.

"You will have an accident if you drive like that," Fergus yelled after the departing car. "You are insane." He shivered, feeling very cold.

FORTY

When Edmund saw Venetia tripping towards him he was amazed.

The hospital ward was long and airy, the beds widely spaced, his bed the last in the row. As Venetia advanced the heads of the bodies in the other beds turned to watch her progress. He had time to wonder whether the Muslim patients would be shocked by Venetia's dress of fine cotton speckled with minute yellow flowers, semi-transparent, so that as she approached, with the light behind her, it was possible not only to see her legs but her whole silhouette. As her breasts bounced in time with her stride Edmund was pleasurably stirred.

"Edmund." She took his hand in hers. "I came as soon as I could."

"Venetia." He watched tears gush, roll down her cheeks, drip on to his hands. "How marvellous, darling, don't cry."

"I can't help it."

"I love to see you cry but do stop." He reached up to kiss her wet face. "Sit down, he's offering you a chair. How did you find me?"

The young doctor who had escorted her was indeed offering a chair. Venetia thanked him profusely, sat. Her tears ceased. She tossed back her yellow hair. She looked like the Primavera in the Uffizi, beautiful, radiant.

"How did it happen?"

"How did you get here?" They spoke in unison.

"I had an accident."

"I got your message, caught the first plane." Edmund held her hands while she took stock of his predicament. His leg, heavily plastered, slung upwards in a sling, rendered him immobile.

"Is it painful?"

"Not now."

"How brave. Was it a car crash?"

"Not exactly."

The young doctor who had escorted her said something in Arabic, repeated it in English, "I screen."

"Not at the moment, thanks all the same. Oh I see, misunderstanding."

Venetia laughed and Edmund too as the doctor drew a screen round the bed, creating a zone of privacy before leaving them.

"Well?" She looked at Edmund. "What happened? Tell."

Edmund stroked her hands, watched her face, he loved her yellow hair, such a definite colour compared with Poppy's mouse. Her eyes were not as pale as he remembered. "Are your feet cold?"

"Of course. I am adapted to a warm climate. Come on, tell me what happened. Was it something disreputable?" She was not to be sidestepped into a discussion about the temperature of her feet.

Edmund looked past Venetia at the North African sky, the storm was over, the palms in the hospital garden still, in the distance a glimpse of quiet sea. He was trapped. "It's a long story, rather boring." He was guarded.

"Not to me," said Venetia. "The sooner you start the better. I didn't come all this way for a silent sulk. Shall I fill you in about me?"

Edmund nodded.

"Right. You go off with this girl Poppy. You bring her here instead of me. I was really looking forward to this trip, Edmund. Anyway, this is no time for reproaches, she must have had some sort of hold over you." (Oh she had, she had, cried a private part of Edmund. What have I lost?) "So I won't nag, not now, my love. Days pass. I get an impertinent postcard from the girl, nothing from you. Then two or three days later a message which merely says 'Broken leg' and the hospital address, signed Edmund. I take it you sent it?"

"No."

"She did, Poppy?"

"Must have." Edmund looked anguished.

"And where is she?" Venetia looked round as though to repulse Poppy should she appear round the hospital screen.

"Buggered off."

"Oh my. You'd better begin at the beginning, take it slowly, I have all the time in the world." Venetia wriggled, settling her haunches in the hospital chair. For no reason Edmund remembered a French tourist remarking to his friend "*en voila des belles fesses*". He had been disgusted at the time but now – "I'm still pretty confused," he said.

"Don't prevaricate."

"You won't like it."

"Oh come on, Edmund, don't be stupid. If we are getting married we can't have secrets. I know some people do but I like things clear cut."

"You may not want to marry me when I've told you." (Did a still voice whisper, "Make a bid for freedom"?)

"Let me decide that."

"You're a bully." Poppy had never bullied or badgered, it was not her style.

"I am." She accepted his tribute. "I'm lots of things. I was captain of hockey at school. I have cold feet. I cry easily but I am as hard as the nose cone of a rocket, so begin."

"Ah." Edmund squeezed her hand. He'd been pretty lonely lying here since Mustafa brought him in the ambulance. "I love you," he said. It was probably true, he thought, he had loved, perhaps still loved, Poppy but there were so many no-go areas in the girl, so much privacy, so much from which he had been excluded. Venetia on the other hand was much easier to love. She might be hard compared with Poppy but she was as clear as a bell, an open book (Any more clichés? whispered Poppy's vanished persona).

"Tell all, don't edit." Venetia jerked him back into her orbit.

"Of course not," said Edmund, who proposed to do precisely that. "I'll start."

"Right." She was alert.

"You know about the job? Yes. Well, it went quite well, very well allowing for the fact that I've never dealt with non-Europeans. My opposite number here is called Mustafa, very friendly fellow, you'll like him. I got the hang of the set-up, what the Tourist Board's proposals are. The Minister took me out to lunch and a swim by the Roman city. You might like him, he makes a good impression."

"Did Poppy go with you?"

"I thought it better to leave her behind. I needed to concentrate on work."

"What did she do?"

"Amused herself, I suppose. There was a pool at the hotel." No need to mention its emptiness.

"That must have been when she bought the postcard."

"What postcard?"

"Never mind, go on."

"Well, I dealt with the tourist officials and got the picture, where they will have a Cabana complex, what hotels there are, where they are building more, the stadium, how many tours they will accommodate at a time, and so on. What hotel are you staying at, by the way?"

"I came straight here from the airport, I was so worried about you."

"My darling, thank you." Edmund held her hand. "I'd better get you into one of the older hotels. The one they put us, me, I mean, in is not really finished, smells a bit of wet cement—"

Venetia laughed. "Go on, don't bother about my hotel, get to the drama."

"The drama, as you put it, is really very small." Indeed as he talked, holding Venetia's firm hand, gaining confidence from her presence, the hell of the preceding days was shrinking. "After we had finished our business, Mustafa took me out with some friends."

"Where was Poppy?"

"She wasn't feeling well, tummy upset, that sort of thing. The trots." (How am I doing?) "We did a round of the bars to get the local colour. I'm afraid the arak round here is pretty potent."

"You got pissed."

"You could say that. Yes, not to put too fine a point on it, I drank too much."

"Yes?" Venetia remembered somebody, who was it? Of course, Penelope in Harrods. "Yes, go on."

"Well then—" Edmund lowered his voice, pulled Venetia closer. "It was rather, well very embarrassing."

"Go on."

"Mustafa's friends – come close, I don't want the whole world to hear."

"I don't suppose they understand English."

"Even so. His friends, these two—" Edmund searched for a word, unwilling to call the boys boys. "These two chaps started making advances to me."

"Were they pretty?"

"Darling! They were boys." Hell, it had slipped out.

"What did they do? Did they fondle your cock?"

"Venetia!" Edmund closed his eyes, remembering the shocked delight, the caressing, the smell of musk (surely people only smelt like that in pornographic books), the light brown skins, lovely, yes lovely black loosely waving hair. "No, of course not."

"Did you like it?" She seemed to be enjoying this.

"Of course I didn't."

"Lots of people would."

"I hope you don't take me for one of them." Edmund, genuinely huffy, caught Venetia's eye, saw she was laughing. "Because I'm not." He dismissed the experience to the realm of non-event. If in future years there were moments of sexual nostalgia or plain reminiscent lust he would be able to handle them.

"So what happened?" Venetia felt vaguely disappointed.

"I am afraid when I got back to the hotel I simply passed out."

"Was Poppy better by then? Stopped trotting, no more squitters?"

"She was asleep. She was quite all right next day. We spent the day together, swam, went out to the oasis, picnicked, that sort of thing." (Made love.)

"Was that when you had the accident?"

"No. It's pretty idiotic. I broke it falling over a chair, Poppy—" Edmund stopped. This was too painful.

"Poppy what?" Venetia pressed him, "Did she get drunk or what?"

"I don't think I – I don't like to—"

"Come on, darling, she's gone, left you in the lurch, tell me what happened. She got drunk and then what? No need to protect her to me."

Edmund drew a deep breath. If anybody ever needed protecting it had been Poppy. "She was throwing herself about, making a scene, she abused me for leaving her alone while I did my job." He supposed this sounded all right to anybody who did not know Poppy.

"You couldn't help that." Venetia was indignant for him. "So what did she do? She must have known you were here to work."

"Well," Edmund passed a hand across his eyes, brushed back his fine fair hair, "I tried to calm her. She got hold of a chair and I tripped over it and my leg snapped. I heard the bone go."

"Oh poor you. She hit you with it."

"Stupid isn't it, actually she—"

"What a vicious thing to do, break your leg." Venetia sat holding Edmund's hand. "What a vile bitch," she exclaimed.

Edmund squeezed her fingers, she squeezed his back.

Edmund felt drained, exhausted.

Let it rest there, what did it matter now, she was gone, wasn't she, whatever he said would twist on his tongue.

"I don't see why you should linger here." Venetia switched her mind to more immediate matters. "I am sure I can get you home on a stretcher or in a wheelchair. I take it your company insured you?"

"Oh yes." Edmund lay now with his eyes closed. If Venetia could swallow the leg-breaking episode, absorb the boys, what were a few lies on an insurance form?

"Leave it all to me, I'll get us home in no time." She sounded incredibly competent. But Edmund still felt a niggle of fear.

"What I told you, the – er – party with Mustafa, the arak and—"

"Don't worry, love. *I* don't mind boys, it shows you have a rounded personality. Getting pissed released your nascent inhibitions, it was healthy to seduce the little catamites."

"But I—" Was a trap yawning?

"We'll keep it between you and me, it would not have happened if Poppy hadn't kidnapped you, forced you to bring her here and broken your leg—"

Edmund could not but admire Venetia, she was so sincere, sitting there in that lovely dress, fixing him with those baby blue eyes, holding his hand between both of hers, those hands which had superglued the flies of all his trousers. No mention of that, he observed ironically. She was still talking: "It was all that bloody girl – anything that happened – not your fault at all." She absolved him.

Edmund was glad to have the ordeal over.

In future years the tale of the broken leg would be perfected by Venetia, dined out on. His slight rather arcane limp which added so much to his attraction would be blamed on Poppy, boost his reputation.

FORTY-ONE

Poppy waking saw Willy standing with his back to her staring out of the window, his attitude one of leashed energy.

"Are you fretting to get back to your pigs?" She sat up pulling his cardigan round her shoulders.

Willy turned round. Earlier he had watched her asleep, calculated the length of the eyelashes which shaded her bruised eye, minimising by their length the damage. The backs of her hands which had been purple had faded to green blotched with yellow. She no longer seemed to feel her injured collarbone.

"I was watching the harbour."

"Thinking of your pigs."

"Yes," said Willy, "among other things."

"We must find out when we can get seats on a plane then. The storm is over, isn't it?"

"Yes, all over." Willy looked down at placid water mirroring the ships and boats barely rocking, a group of resting seagulls. We are no longer prisoners, he thought regretfully. "I went down earlier, the streets are drying up, we could look round the town when we've found a plane, booked our seats," he said.

"Why not?"

Without the storm to pen them in there was constraint between them. Willy felt resentful. While sleeping she had distanced herself from him, as though forgetting their shared delight.

They went down the stairs to the lobby – the lifts were still out of order – and joined the people clamouring round a harassed airways official attempting to make himself heard above a polyglot hubbub.

"Nothing will get sorted out for ages, let's find a café." He drew her out into the street.

From a stall Willy bought figs. "We can eat these with our breakfast. You like figs?"

"Yes." She remembered the figs she had eaten that first morning while Mustafa watched her, waiting for Edmund to appear in the half-made garden by the empty pool of that cement-stinking hotel.

They found a café, sat at a table in the sun. Willy ordered coffee and rolls. Poppy put on her dark glasses.

Willy peeled the figs, Poppy watched his fingers, very different from Edmund's, which were strong and hairy even though he was such a fair man. For so dark a man Willy, apart from his thick hair, was remarkably hairless. She remembered her father's voice, "Can't stand hirsute men." He had been referring to Edmund though he had not said so specifically. Willy looked up, caught her eye, smiled.

"I was thinking of my father."

"Tell me about him." Willy shared out the figs, putting the ripest on her plate, wondering whether, were he a painter, he would be able to capture the nuances between the peeled fruit and her bruised hands.

"I know so little about him."

"You loved him?" Willy remembered her at the funeral, solitary in the front pew beside the coffin.

"Yes, I suppose I did. I think I love him now. Before, I had such awful guilt."

"Oh?"

"He could not stand Edmund Platt."

(So that's the bastard's name.)

Poppy bit into a fig, swallowed. "Delicious, much nicer peeled. I raked the flesh from the skin with my teeth before. Dad so disliked Edmund that whenever we met we either quarrelled or we talked of things that didn't matter to either of us. If I'd known—"

"Yes?"

"If I'd known Dad was such a gambler I could have learned a lot from him. He was always away when I was small. I realise now he was at the races. He sent me postcards from Brighton, Chepstow, Newcastle, York, Liverpool, Epsom; he was racing mad. I am called after a horse which won the Oaks, Poppaea."

Willy laughed.

Poppy grinned.

"My favourite pig is called Mrs Future; some damn fool knowbester told me, 'There's no future in pig farming,' " said Willy.

"Good for you." Poppy took another fig, helped herself to coffee. "I would like to know who Dad went to the races with," she said.

"Why particularly?" Willy took the fruit from her and peeled it.

"He seems to have had friends who left him money when they died. Women."

"Ah."

"They must have been old, older than him, because women live longer than men and a number of these ladies made—"

"Wills in his favour?"

"They remembered him. He called them Life's Dividends. His solicitor, Anthony Green, let that slip or the bank manager, I forget which now. What I wondered was whether—"

"He slept with them?"

"Well, yes."

"Does it matter? Is that to do with your feeling guilt?"

"No, no. I feel guilt because I never talked to him properly, because I excluded him from my life, was not interested in his, because I refused to listen to him when he was right." (So she agrees he was right.) "Because if I had not been so pig-headed and selfish I could have known him, been friends with him, loved him."

"You might even have gone to the races with him." Willy, laughing now, watched her.

"Exactly," Poppy put down her cup, "even if he didn't take me racing I could have known him. At his funeral complete strangers came up to me, said they loved him, met him at the races, or that he used to take their aunt or someone they knew racing. I'd never met any of these people, hadn't the remotest notion who they were, didn't know their names, was too embarrassed to ask. I felt a fool, a stranger, me, his daughter. That girl with the funny hair who works for Fergus Furnival knew him, was fond of him, said he marked her card for her at the races, and even an old lady who lent me her coat knew him."

"My aunt Calypso."

"Of course. She is your aunt." Poppy looked at Willy as though he might turn suddenly into his aunt. "She knew Dad. She'd advised him when he bought my dress. She guessed that I wondered about all those ladies, she said something to the effect of not being in that league—"

"She wouldn't be. If she can't have my uncle Hector she doesn't want anybody." And if I can't have this girl I don't want anybody, Willy thought savagely. "I do not feel you have more reason than most to feel guilty." He watched her covertly.

"Well, I do. I would like things to have been different."

"Vain regrets."

"I would like this minute to hear him say 'I told you so'," she exclaimed.

"Retrospective generosity."

"You are mocking my guilt."

"My aunt could probably tell you about your father, she would give a fair picture."

Poppy swallowed the last of her coffee, looked across the pavement at the passing traffic, did not answer. Would it or would it not be a good thing to know Dad? "He left me a letter," she said, "more of a note really."

Willy did not enquire its contents.

"You are anxious to get back to Mrs Future." Poppy turned towards him. "We had better see about a plane." She stood up, putting an end to the conversation.

Willy paid the bill. "And where will you go?" he asked. "Your flat or your father's house?"

"Neither," Poppy exclaimed before she could stop herself. The thought of the flat she had shared with Edmund horrified her. "I have rented Dad's house to Fergus Furnival," she said, "I can't go there."

"Job?"

"I chucked it when Dad died."

"Why don't you," Willy kept his voice level, walking back towards the hotel, "stay with my aunt? It's just an idea, while you make up your mind. She will like to have you." (She will because she is fond of me.) Then, as Poppy said nothing, he said, "Stupid of me, you must have dozens of people you can go to, endless friends."

"No, no I haven't." Poppy stopped at a street corner as though she was interested in the people thronging the pavement, milling about them, crossing and recrossing the street, dodging the cars and carts, shouting, arguing, bargaining, jostling them as they stood, an alien pair. "Edmund was clever at keeping me to himself," she said. "I liked it in a way but it means I have no intimate friends. I can't really tell you about Edmund but I'll try," she said, standing close to Willy now, looking up in his face. "I was in love with Edmund and I lived with him for years." A fat man in a hurry bumped into her so that Willy put his arms round her to keep her balanced. "Edmund drank too much." Poppy spoke in a flat voice. "Only on occasion but when he was on a bender he got rough. Why am I telling you this?" she cried sharply, then, not expecting an answer, went on. "He started before we left London and he drank on the plane. When we arrived he carried on drinking. He went off without me on the first evening with Mustafa. That was when I met the cockroaches and after we'd run over the dog; it was lame. Then the next day he went off again, he was doing his job of course, he is an ambitious man, a beautiful man too. I said no I would not go with him, actually I don't think he asked me to, that was when the men were hanged—" Poppy clenched her fists on Willy's chest. "They were strung up, literally strung up on the branch of a plane tree, I shall never— I couldn't speak of it to Edmund. It was too— Then afterwards the next day we tried or I tried, perhaps we both did, to have a day together but I've never felt so apart from anybody. Poor Edmund, it was a pretty awful day for him, he was hungover and stuffed to the eyeballs with shock at what he had done the night before. He had buggered two Arab boys – I know, when in Rome, but you don't know Edmund, he's pure, he was terribly shocked. Well, I did not mind because by that time I knew what I'd really known for ages, that anything with Edmund was over, that I didn't love him, that I'd only come to North Africa to annoy Venetia, so why should I mind? Of course when he first left me for Venetia I was mortified, humiliated but by then I'd realised I'd been freed. But Edmund felt so guilty, so ashamed, he wallowed in shame like a born-again Baptist. He'd enjoyed himself, these Arab boys are lovely, look around you. That evening he got drunk again and rough – well, violent. That's how I got my black eye and so on, my heel had been trodden on earlier in the crush at the hanging. Where was I? Oh yes, he was quite anxious to kill me and I was frightened, he's big." Poppy paused, looking up into Willy's face, oblivious of the crowd about them scurrying about their business like ants or strolling slowly, in discussion. "He was coming at me again so I grabbed a chair to put it between us and he fell over it. His leg cracked like a whip. That's what happened. I did not intend to break his leg. He screamed, I sent for a doctor, an ambulance and for Mustafa. They got him to hospital. I sent a cable to Venetia. She really wants him. I packed my bag and caught the first plane out. Oh Willy, I would so dearly love to tell this to Dad, it would have made him so happy!" She looked round at the crowded pavement. "What a place to tell you, how extraordinary. I bet Mrs Future would never do anything so foolish." She tried to laugh.

Willy started her walking. Keep calm, keep sane, he told himself. Put off the garrotting until you have nothing else to do. "We had better get you on to the plane," he said, "I am taking you to stay with Calypso." He led her back to the hotel. Some day, if she wanted to, she could elucidate the little matters of cockroaches, lame dogs, hangings, what mattered was that she had unbottled, let it come pouring out. They went up to their room in the lift which was working again.

As they crowded into the lift Poppy said, "I was boasting when I told you before that I broke Edmund's leg, actually I was scared stiff, just trying to fend him off. The first way I told you made me sound quite brave and aggressive. I wasn't."

"Of course not," said Willy, amused by the expressions of their fellow travellers pretending not to listen. "I think if your father were alive and you were a racehorse he would put his shirt on you," he said.

FORTY-TWO

"Where do you want to go?" asked Victor as they got near London. "Where are you living these days?" It made him feel peculiar not to know where Penelope lived, it was embarrassing having to ask.

Penelope did not answer, perhaps she had not heard, she was probably living with some man she would rather he did not know about. Whoever it was had a lot to answer for, letting her go off by herself to have a lonely accident, he should cherish Penelope better, prevent her risking her life, almost dying of exposure. Penelope's predicament in the empty farm grew larger in imagination as anger at her imaginary lover's behaviour stirred his loins, making him bold. "Come and have something to eat with me before I drop you off," he suggested, "or are you expected?"

"I am not expected."

"So you will come?"

"Yes, I will."

"Good," said Victor, pleased. "We will buy something to cook on our way. I haven't got much in the flat. What would you like?"

They discussed possibilities and methods of cooking as Victor drove. Penelope was surprised at some of Victor's suggestions. When they had been married he had been barely capable of boiling an egg unsupervised, but now he was suggesting barbecued lamb chops, veal Marengo, Italian beef, a variety of risottos and several quite sophisticated pastas. Uneasily she wondered whether she had missed some clue on her clandestine visits to the flat, whether there were not, after all, another woman. "I think I'd like fish," she said, "is our fish shop still there? I hanker for shellfish; what about mussels?"

"Of course it is." Victor drove through the streets in silence until they reached the fish shop, drew to a stop by the kerb.

"Why," cried the fish lady at the sight of Penelope, "it's little Mrs Lucas! How are you, ducks?" She trotted across the pavement in her white overall and fur boots. "Where have you been this long time? Nice to see you." She looked through Victor.

"Super," said Penelope, "lovely to see *you*. We want something delicious for supper, what do you suggest?"

Victor was reminded that one of Penelope's talents was to deceive people into believing that they made decisions for her.

"You did like mussels when you had time to prepare them; have you time? Eating them tonight are you?" The fish lady ignored Victor sitting at the wheel, leaning into the car, speaking past him at Penelope. "I've some lovely sole, or there's halibut."

"Let's have mussels. Would you like mussels, Victor?"

"Yes," said Victor averting his gaze from the sad black lobsters and the bowls of trout on the marble counter. "Yes, I would."

"I've sprained my ankle," said Penelope to the fish lady, "slipped and twisted it, look it's all strapped up." She raised her foot.

"Shame," said the fish lady. "You should be more careful, ducks." She looked balefully at Victor, blaming him.

"I'd better get out and pay," said Victor. "Don't move, darling, rest your foot." The fish lady would talk to Penelope all night if allowed.

"OK," said Penelope, "buy lots, let's make pigs of ourselves."

Victor followed the fish lady into the shop, watched her weigh the mussels.

"How's the trout then?" she asked *sotto voce*, dropping two final mussels into the scales, ping, ping.

"What?"

"You know," she kept her voice low, "the one that was alive, gave you such a turn, ate it did you?"

"Certainly not," said Victor annoyed. "It's living wild in a stream in Berkshire."

The fish lady laughed. Victor had never before seen her laugh. "You're a writer, aren't you?" She spoke kindly as though he were mentally retarded. "There's your supper." She poured the mussels from the scoop into a plastic bag. "Enjoy them." She twisted a fastener round the bag's neck with strong fingers.

Victor paid.

Getting back into the car he said, "She's glad to see you, she's always very offhand with me."

"She doesn't like men," said Penelope. Victor supposed this was probably true. "She seemed to know I write, how the hell does she know?"

"Standing in that shop all day she must get to know everything there is to know about the neighbours." Penelope remembered a month or two before, when buying a modest mackerel prior to snooping in Victor's flat, she had told the fish lady that Victor was writing a novel. "We need brown bread and butter, a lemon, parsley and white wine," she said.

"I've got wine," said Victor. "If you wait I'll run to the supermarket. Fend off traffic wardens while I'm gone."

"OK." Penelope watched Victor run, his thin legs streaking down the street.

The fish lady crossed the pavement, leaving a customer to wait. "Never told you how he bought a live trout, did I? He tells me it's alive and well in a stream in Berkshire."

"I know it is," said Penelope.

"Oh," said the fish lady, disappointed.

"You've got customers waiting," said Penelope repressively and sat waiting for Victor's return from the supermarket. But as they drove away she waved and the fish lady waved back.

Victor helped Penelope up the stairs, his free arm round her waist, their parcels gripped under his other arm. Reaching the top floor he released her, fumbled for his key. "Same old flat," he said, standing aside to let her pass.

"That tap still drips." Penelope hobbled across the hallway into the bathroom to give it a twist.

"Sorry," said Victor.

"I rather like it," said Penelope standing with her back to him.

Victor smiled to himself, tipped the mussels into the sink in the kitchen and started scrubbing them.

Penelope came out of the bathroom, pulled the kitchen stool to the sink, perched on it to ease her ankle and joined in the scrubbing of mussels.

"If I had a carrot, an onion and garlic we could have them *marinières*, I've got bay and thyme, I've run low on veg, should have thought of it in the supermarket." He had raced round the shelves, hurried through the checkout, fearful that left alone Penelope would take the opportunity to scarper.

"Do you know how to cook *moules marinières*?" Penelope looked at Victor quizzically.

"Yes."

"Been giving dinner parties?" Who had he been cooking *moules marinières* for or with, who had taught him all these new dishes? Penelope jerked the plug out of the sink to change the water before Victor was ready. He dropped the knife he was using and, searching for it among the mussels, managed to slice his finger. "Sorry," said Penelope, watching him suck it.

Victor, sucking his finger, considered whether to say no he never gave parties or yes he often did, neither reply being exactly true although in a sense he was giving a dinner party tapping it on to his typewriter. He had not thought to give his characters either *moules à la Béchamel* which they were preparing now or *moules marinières*. It was an idea he must consider. The problem had been whether Penelope, who in the book was tentatively called Louise, should be murdered before or after dinner.

"You will have to make the sauce," he said, "unless you want my blood in it. Sauce Béchamel tinged with blood."

Penelope limped round the kitchen finding the ingredients. Victor put a large pan on the stove, adding a cupful of water, transferred the mussels into the pan. While they opened in the heat (poor things, what a way to die) he drew the cork from a bottle of wine, poured a glass for Penelope and one for himself.

"Penelope," he toasted her.

"Victor," at one time she would have added darling. "For God's sake, put an Elastoplast on it," she said.

They concentrated on their cooking, eating the mussels straight from the stove. Penelope's sauce was delicious. "I read your article about that funeral," she said, "it was very good. It made the affair moving and dignified when it could have sounded way out and funny. I thought it gave Fergus a jolly good puff without a hint of vulgarity."

"Thank you." Victor watched his ex-wife, comparing her with Poppy who had since the funeral occupied the forefront of his mind, had even twice wandered into his dreams. "I took part," he said.

"What do you mean?"

"I was a mute, I helped shoulder the coffin, and afterwards I organised the food. I got it from Singh in Shepherd's Bush. Do you remember him? I got lashings of champagne on sale or return for booze. I don't think there was much left over to return, it was quite a party."

"I haven't seen Singh for ages." Penelope reached for the bottle to refill her glass. "Saw him in the street once." ("What do you want to leave Victor for, silly girl?") "Tell me more. What part does that girl who strapped my ankle up play in Fergus's outfit, is she or are all those girls his mistresses?"

"I think they just look after the horses. I got the impression . . ."

"Yes?"

"That Fergus was interested in Poppy—" said Victor reluctantly.

"The corpse's daughter?"

"Bob Carew, whose funeral it was, his daughter, yes," said Victor coolly. His ex-wife's nomenclature, though technically correct, seemed rather offensive.

"So you are interested in Poppy, too." With feline agility Penelope made the deduction.

"I hardly know her," said Victor who was out of practice with Penelope.

"You sound as if you did." Penelope wiped her plate with a piece of bread.

"Have you finished with Fergus?" asked Victor catching up, rather enjoying this.

"Oh, Fergus was just a hop, skip and a jump," said Penelope, dismissing Fergus. "We never ate enough of these things." She dipped her bread into the last of the sauce. "Did we?"

Victor got up and peered out of the window along the parapet. It had grown dark while they had supper, Penelope had switched on the lamp. "They roost here now," he stretched his neck to catch a glimpse of the pigeons, "I rather like it."

Penelope remembered being waked by the birds' mating calls all year round, pigeons' sex life, similar to humans, is not restricted to the spring.

"I am writing a novel," said Victor.

"I heard that you had one accepted," said Penelope. "Congratulations. Which one is it? I was afraid to ask."

"The one about us."

"Oh."

"In the one I am working on now I murder you."

"Should I be flattered? Are you getting a good advance? Who is your publisher?"

"Sean Connor."

"Julia's beau? Are they getting married? You and she finished your little trot together?"

"What a lot you know," said Victor, wondering whether Poppy Carew gathered gossip as Penelope did almost with the speed of light. "I am going to wash the dishes," he said. "I can't stand getting up to a mess in the morning, it puts me off work. Why don't you rest your foot?"

"Thanks, I will." She watched Victor collect the used plates; he had become positively old-maidish under somebody's influence or was it living alone? Limping, she went to the bathroom to wash her sticky fingers and then into the bedroom to look out of the back window at the anonymous backs of the houses in the next street. There had been times when it was possible to catch glimpses of other people's lives. Truncated from the waist, women rinsed their tights to hang them over the bath, men shaving in the early morning, shadows of both sexes running past landing windows down to the street. Once they had had to complain to the police during a noisy three-night-long party, on another they had listened to ghastly screams and been too shy to do anything. On hot summer nights, there had been radios blaring from competing stations. She shut the window, bent to examine Victor's bedside books. Dylan Thomas, Graham Greene, Gabriel García Márquez, Alice Walker. A notebook full of scribbled ideas, many crossed out, and *How to Cheat at Cooking* by Delia Smith, much thumbed. Penelope smiled widely. Maybe, possibly, she would give him *One is Fun* by the same author.

When Victor had finished the dishes and put everything away, he took two glasses and the bottle of brandy given him the previous Christmas by an uncle and never used. They could finish the evening on the sofa watching the box.

But Penelope was not on the sofa. She was in the bedroom, in the bed.

"I've moved your clothes back to your side of the cupboard," she said.

Victor put the brandy and glasses on the bedside table and undressed in silence.

I shall pretend she is Poppy Carew, he told himself, as he pulled his shirt over his head and dropped his trousers. I can use this situation in my novel, he thought, feeling rather agitated as he pulled off his socks.

Or, he can kill his wife Louise, *then* sleep with Poppy Carew, he thought as desire made him lusty. I still don't know what colour her bush is, but for the moment – he got into bed – this discovery ("Move over a bit, darling, or I'll hurt your ankle,") must wait.

"Oh dear God," said Victor, "I am home."

FORTY-THREE

From the top of the hill Calypso looked down on the house she and Hector had restored. Faded pink brick striping through the wisteria leaves, yellow now after an early frost, a fit background for climbing roses, and the magnolia which still drenched the evening with the perfume of its flowers, its scent mingling with that of nicotiana planted under the windows. From the yard pigeons flew up with a clap to circle over the garden, then settle on the tiled roof, a variegated flock, the original too perfect white having long since mixed with wood pigeons.

When she walked down through the wood she would find the flagged terrace warm in the autumn sun, sit and plan for another year for the wood and garden, more bulbs, more flowers, more scented shrubs. Used now to living alone, she relished an uninterrupted evening. Before returning to the house she used field glasses to scan the wood, note where a tree ailed which might be replaced, where it would be politic to thin. Beyond the wood on the far side of a meadow between the trees and the road she would plant a triple line of Lombardy poplars to reinforce her privacy. "I can live to see them started," she said to her dog, conscious of the slight stroke she had suffered three years before which left her limping a little when tired but otherwise unimpaired. The warning stroke had not been repeated. She thought of it only when one of her contemporaries died or at older friends' funerals. She had been aware of it during Bob Carew's service, he being much younger than she, and decided to miss the party after (a decision she now regretted) and then been distracted from morbid thought by Willy's entrancement with Poppy.

Swinging round to scan the wood towards the farm Calypso remembered with amusement that her son Hamish, summoned from the Highlands, had believed her dying but Willy, smuggling a tiny Mrs Future into the ward under his jacket, had mocked his older cousin saying "Death blew her a kiss", making her laugh before being discovered by a nurse and sent packing.

"No sign," said Calypso to the dog as she adjusted her binoculars to watch Willy's stockman going about his work with the pigs, "no sign yet of the lovers." She put away the field glasses, went down through the wood to lie on her garden chair, soak up the last of the sun's warmth beating up from the stone-flagged terrace, listen to the pigeons and the distant sound of Willy's bantam cocks crowing from the farm. She was none too pleased when, comfortably settled, eyes closed, face lifted to the sun, she heard a car arrive on the far side of the house.

I shall not answer the bell, she told herself, but the dog, giving her away, rushed barking into the house and out to the front to greet the visitor rapturously.

"Bloody animal." Calypso lay still, hearing the bell ring, keeping her eyes closed, hoping whoever it was, seeing nobody but the dog, would, with luck, go away.

"Calypso?" a woman called. "Are you there?"

Calypso did not answer.

"Your dog betrayed you." Ros Lawrence came out on to the terrace through the French windows. "Am I disturbing you?"

"Yes," said Calypso, "you are."

"You are not doing anything," said Ros, confirming some people's opinion that she was not all that bright. "I'm sorry," she pulled up a chair, "I have come to you for help. For help," she repeated distractedly, "help."

"You should know that I am the most unhelpful person of your acquaintance." Calypso stressed the last word, lay looking up at her visitor who, although seated, gave the uncomfortable impression of hovering above her.

"And your advice." Ros looked down at Calypso, irritatingly reposeful. "Your advice."

"I never give advice."

"I know. Most people volunteer, press it, that's why I have come to you."

"Oh Lord." Calypso swung her legs off her long chair. "Come indoors." She did not wish to share the loveliness of her terrace. Ros followed her into the drawing-room. Relieved of her weight, the wicker chair on which she had briefly sat creaked in relief.

"Sit down if you can find a clean space." Calypso waved at chairs and sofa. "Dog hairs everywhere, mud, pig mess—"

"Shall I go away?" Ros drooped. She looked round Calypso's beautiful speckless room, no trace of dog hair anywhere. "I can see I'm not wanted, not welcome." She accepted the hint, refused to take it.

"I'll get you a drink, sit down."

Calypso left the room, followed by the dog. "I shall send you to the Lost Dogs' Home," she hissed at the wagging animal. "You may like uninvited guests, casual droppers-in, I don't. I shall send you back to Hamish, he had no business to give you to me. He knows I don't like dogs. Why must he interfere? I don't need guarding, I don't need protection, you are too soppy anyway. I never had all these people charging in before you came. I lay doggo until they went away." Resentfully Calypso put the whisky decanter and glasses on a tray, filled a jug of water, plopped in ice. She carried it back to the drawing-room where Ros sat perched on the edge of an armchair in woeful silence.

"Strong or weak?" Calypso asked.

"Strong," said Ros, "please."

Calypso poured the drinks, handed Ros hers, sat opposite, sipped, waited. Ros, recently remarried after being widowed, was now presumably regretting it.

"Aren't you going to ask me what the matter is?" Ros spoke with barely suppressed agitation.

"No," said Calypso. "You may later regret telling me."

"I have to tell someone. Henry won't listen, he says—"

Calypso sipped her drink. The dog now sat with his back to her, watching Ros with more sympathy than she. She kicked him gently with her toe. There was much to be said for the Catholic Church, a captive priest in a confessional under holy oath of secrecy, she thought, watching the younger woman. If not the new husband what could it be? She was not overly interested.

"I have made a complete and utter fool of myself and alienated my son," cried Ros in violent anguish, "my only child."

"Easy done." (So it's her son.) Calypso remembered remarks she would have rather left unsaid, made over the years to Hamish. "We are all guilty."

"He's my only child, Calypso. It's Fergus, you know what his father was like, Fergus is very like him."

"Of course, Fergus." The father had been notoriously irritable but who could blame him, married to Ros. "How is he? I went to Bob Carew's funeral. I have asked Hamish to have him and those super horses for me when it's my turn. I was impressed, I hope he will be successful. The times call for someone like him." Calypso forced herself to be kind. "He has style."

"Thank you." Ros drank her whisky, gazed round the room, jealously admiring the older woman's possessions, wondered now why she had come, wished she hadn't. Her pain returned with a rush. "What am I to do?" she shouted, almost choking in agitation. "What – am I – to do?"

Calypso raised her eyebrows.

Ros finished her drink, put down the empty glass, half rose to go. "I should not have come to bother you." She sank back in the chair.

"No bother," Calypso lied politely.

Ros leant towards Calypso. "Fergus has a child," she enunciated painfully, "it's there in the house he's rented from the Carew girl. He has the house and the stables, his horses, the hearse of course, and three girl grooms – Henry let him use his name as a reference for the Carews' lawyer – one of the girls has a baby!" Ros waited for Calypso to say something. Calypso stayed quiet. Ros continued: "It's beautiful, quite beautiful. The mother is Mary Mowbray, you know who I mean, her father Nicholas used to breed horses." Again Ros waited for Calypso to say something. Calypso, no baby lover, made no comment. Ros went on. "The child is called Barnaby. He is lovely, Calypso. Fergus refers to him as Jesus, it's a disgusting joke. You look puzzled?"

"I am."

"Apparently the mother Mary went to Spain and returned with the baby. She had a friend there called Joseph."

Still Calypso remained silent.

Ros gasped, trying to restrain tears. "It's the spitting image of Fergus at the same age and of his father as a baby. I am not inventing," Ros shouted as though Calypso had accused her. Her tears began to fall.

Calypso reached for a box of tissues from the table beside her, handed one to Ros, on second thoughts passed her the box.

"Thanks." Ros wiped her eyes, pulled a bunch of tissues from the box. "The thing is, Fergus seemed to have no idea. The girl had not told him. Can you believe it? I feel, oh God, I feel such a fool. I shouted at him, told him the baby is his, bellowed at him about the strength of the Furnival genes—"

Calypso burst out laughing. "Sorry." She swallowed her laughter. "Sorry."

"Well may you laugh," cried Ros in anguish. "I would laugh if this happened to anyone else, but it's my grandchild. I don't suppose Fergus will ever speak to me again. Why couldn't I keep my trap shut?"

Why indeed, thought Calypso, interested in spite of herself.

Still Ros wept. "Henry is no help, he says a century ago there might have been dozens of tiny Furnivals scattered round the parish. Thank God for contraception. What am I to do?" Blowing her nose, Ros stared at Calypso.

"Quite a surprise for Fergus," said Calypso drily.

"It was, it was. What am I to do?"

"Oh, don't ask me," said Calypso, bored by the repetitions. "I can't give advice. I try hard not to. I remember how tiresome and interfering my family were when I was young. Unsought advice is against my principles."

"I'm seeking it—"

"Fergus isn't."

"You are *not* helping me," cried Ros as though Calypso had offered to. "I know I should not have interfered but I did – I did."

Surreptitiously Calypso looked at her watch. She always meant to time Ros's stream of complaint. This was a good opportunity. No need to actually listen, just sit and let it flow, she had heard the gist; Ros could only repeat what she had already told with embellishments.

As far as I can remember, Calypso thought, on previous occasions it took a good half-hour before she ran out of puff when she was complaining about Fergus's father, his foul temper and infidelities. One had a certain sympathy for the man. Calypso lowered her eyes, suppressed a smile. Of course this was a little different. The girl Mary was a character worthy of investigation and Fergus must be wonderfully short of vanity not to recognise himself in the child. There were men without vanity; Hector, for instance, had always been a man unaware of his looks. Ah, Hector, Calypso slid into thoughts of Hector. Hector's lovely voice. Now Ros, pitching into her lament, had a very trying voice. She had had enough of this feast of boredom.

I wish she'd go away, thought Calypso, shrinking from Ros's dilemma, retreating into her protective thoughts. (We should have planted more sycamores, she thought, they are underestimated trees, they grow fast.) Why should I get involved with Ros's troubles? I hardly know her. I can't help her, it's bad enough to have to have Willy chasing wild goose after Poppy, he may get badly hurt, I shall mind that very much, my equilibrium will be upset. What a bore this woman is. "Have some more whisky." Grudgingly she remembered her manners.

"No, no thanks. I must go. You've been very kind, I knew you would help."

"Not kind at all." Nobody ever accused Calypso of lying.

"I suppose you're right." Ros attributed words to Calypso. "I have said too much. I will shut up and not interfere, let them work it out for themselves as you say. You are so right. I knew you would help me. You do though admit it's hard for me – my first grandchild?"

As far as you know, thought Calypso. "Oh, Willy." She jumped up as Willy came into the room. "When did you get back?" Her relief at seeing him conjoining with the relief from the embarrassment of Ros showed plainly in her smile.

"Just arrived," said Willy kissing her cheek. "May I have a drink?

Oh hullo." He noticed Ros crouching now like a frightened partridge in the armchair, tissue at the ready. "How do you do. Am I interrupting?"

"I am just leaving." Ros sprang hastily up, put aside the box of tissues. "I'm on my way." She was embarrassed. "Thank you, Calypso, for all your help."

"It was nothing," said Calypso gravely.

"I'll see you out." Willy walked through the house with Ros, watched her drive away. "What was all that about?" He returned to his aunt.

"Trouble." She put Ros aside. "Are you alone?"

"Alone." Willy helped himself to a drink, patted the dog who was craving attention, sat in the chair vacated by Ros, stretched out his long legs, stared into his glass. Neither of them spoke.

The dog lay down with a sigh, laid his nose on his paws, watched.

Calypso waited.

Willy put his drink aside, sat forward with his face in his hands. "I had hoped," he said presently, "to bring her back here. I thought perhaps you would have her to stay, she didn't seem to have any place she wanted to go. I thought you wouldn't mind. I thought she'd agree to this—" He stretched out his hand, stroked the dog's head. "But she changed her mind, decided not to, refused."

"M-m-m," murmured Calypso, "m-m-m."

"Well," said Willy, jumping up, "better see to the Futures," false heartiness in his tone.

Calypso winced. "Come to supper presently?" she suggested.

"Another night, but thank you. I have much to do after being away."

"Of course. You must see to the Happy Hams. I haven't heard of anything going wrong but you must check."

"I am poor company." Willy apologised.

"Take the dog. He welcomes uninvited guests. He needs a run, he's in disgrace." Willy bent to kiss her, started to speak, thought better of it, walked away, his shoulders despondent.

"Go," Calypso said to the dog, "run after him, you dumb animal, he can do with your company. Go."

The dog jumped up and ran after Willy, catching up with him on the edge of the wood. Calypso called, "Take the dog, keep him for the night."

Willy looked back across the garden. "I remembered Mrs Future's aunt," he shouted across the flower beds, "and what happened there."

Reminded of Mrs Future's aunt's malign act, Calypso laughed. "So?"

"So I left her alone. I was afraid of rushing her."

Willy and the dog disappeared into the wood. Calypso, resuming her place on the terrace, lay listening to the pigeons on the roof, the hum of the bees among the Michaelmas daisies. It was at odd moments like this that she most missed her dead husband whose family genes she thought with amusement seemed stronger in his nephew Willy than in his son Hamish. She had taken it for granted that Willy would find Poppy, hoped he would bring her back with him. She was curious to hear what had happened but too wise to ask. She did not need Ros's example to stress the inadvisability of family interference, however well meant.

FORTY-FOUR

In the train from Gatwick to Victoria, in the taxi to her flat, Poppy was ashamed of her vacillation. In Algiers she had agreed without reservation to Willy's suggestion that she should stay with his aunt. Looking out of the taxi window on to the wet streets of London and the umbrella-shuffling crowds, she felt again how easy to do what Willy suggested.

But in the plane things had become different. She had felt she needed to distance herself from him, go back to the flat she now hated, be alone to decide without pressure what, if anything, she wanted next.

In Algiers, wrapped about by the storm, she had jumped headlong into rapturous sexual pleasure.

In the foreign streets she had told Willy more about Edmund than she ever would in England. The circumstances of their meeting, the intimacy born of her injuries, the odd manner of their being together, had made her talk as strangers proverbially do in trains, safe in that there will be no future contact.

The trouble was that Willy had no intention of letting her go, for him their being together was no casual affair. If she only wanted him as a pleasure man he would rather back out than know her on such terms. "All or nothing," he had said. They had exchanged angry words on the plane sitting with trays of uneaten food in front of them, cocooned by the hum of engines, too close in their seats, unable to move apart, their very proximity a hindrance to calm discussion.

He had told her, turning towards her, his long legs cramped in the aircraft seat, his back half turned on a somnolent fellow traveller, that he had decided at her father's funeral that he loved her, that he must marry her, that this was, for him, final.

She had said, "You did not tell me this in Algiers, it is ridiculous. When you saw me in the church you did not know me, we had not spoken, you could not know you loved me. It was pure imagination." She shied away.

"It was and is love," he said. "A bolt."

"Just an idea," she scoffed.

"A great idea. I would call it inspiration."

"Absurd," she mocked.

"You have not found me absurd these last days and nights."

"You gave me great pleasure," she admitted stiffly.

"So?"

"Pleasure is not love."

"The two are knit."

"No." She had loved Edmund, hadn't she? How to tell Willy about life with Edmund without giving herself and, incidentally, Edmund away. She had already said too much.

"You thought you loved that bloody man who beat you. I bet you never shared delight. You just persuaded yourself you loved him. *That* was imaginary."

"It was not."

"You have been happier with me than ever with him."

She would not admit this, she was handling this all wrong; planes brought out the worst in her, had she not been sulky with Edmund on the outward flight? "I have a lot to sort out, things to do. My father's business," she had excused herself, trying to sound reasonable. "I left home in a rush, I need to be alone. Why are you looking at me like that? What's so funny?" She was puzzled and irritated that in the midst of a serious desperate discussion Willy should start laughing.

"I may tell you some day. Not now. OK, go ahead, be alone, sort yourself out, I'll wait."

They had not parted happily.

The taxi stopped outside the flat. Poppy paid the man, stood with her bags on the wet and greasy pavement, nerved herself to use the key, climb up the steps. Inserting the key in the lock she noticed that a shop on the corner had changed hands in the short time she had been away, changing from a small grocery into a rather brash branch of a well-known bookmaker. Would Dad have called in there, did he place his bets by telephone or did he only bet on the course? As she unlocked the street door she thought she knew Willy better than Dad and damn Willy for laughing, curse his private joke. Resentfully she let the street door slam, crossed the dark and shabby hall to climb the stairs carrying her bag up one flight, up another flight and another to the top. Had he guessed, she wondered as she toiled up out of breath, her arms aching from the heavy bags, had he guessed what a rotten selfish lover Edmund had been, had he guessed from her joyful reaction that she had never known any better?

There are other fish, Willy Guthrie, she thought, as she searched her bag for the flat key. Where the hell has it got to, not lost, surely? Other fish such as slender intellectual Victor or Fergus, travelled, debonair, kind, enterprising – ah, here's the key – both of these had looked at her with interest, had shown their inclination and intention in their kiss. What had pig farmer Willy Guthrie got that they hadn't got? What had he to laugh about? She unlocked the flat door, pushed it rustling across uncollected mail littering the floor, slammed the door shut.

A dying bluebottle struggled buzzing on its back.

She had not shut the refrigerator door properly, it hummed as it had all her absent days, ice frosting down on to the tiled floor, a freezing reminder of useless activity during her travels.

The flat smelled stale and dry. Worse, it was permeated by Edmund.

Quickly she switched off the refrigerator, ran to open the windows, began feverishly and at once searching the rooms for Edmund's belongings, throwing books, tapes, clothes, shoes, sports equipment into a heap, rummaging systematically through drawers and cupboards for anything, everything that was his. It was amazing what a lot of unvalued dross he had left, not feeling it worthy of Venetia Colyer. Off the wall came his Hockney print and a picture of the Lakes he had given her. Out of the drawers came clothes, from the kitchen plates, cups, saucepans, dishes he had contributed to their joint living, his tape recorder and radio from the bedroom.

While she exhausted herself limping about in a frenzy the fridge began to drip. She heated a knife over the gas on the cooker and prized ice from the sides of the cabinet, throwing chunks into the sink. From inside the fridge she snatched a lump of Cheddar cheese Edmund had bought. When? Weeks and weeks ago to make Welsh rarebit. Threw it among his possessions. Yuk!

She found suitcases that were Edmund's, packed them with his things, crushed them shut, set them out on the landing. For the rest she heaped it on to his sheets, tying great bundles by the corners, heaving and dragging them out of the flat. Out, out, out.

She swept up their joint mail from the mat, sorted it, sat at the kitchen table, took a pen, readdressed all Edmund's letters, bills and circulars c/o Venetia Colyer, ran downstairs and along the street to the pillar box and posted it.

Back in the flat she finished defrosting the fridge, wiped and swept the floors, shut the windows, turned on the bath.

While the bath filled she undressed, scattered drops of pine essence on the kitchen and bathroom floors, dolloped a generous gush into the bath, stepped in shakily exhausted, lay back in the fragrant delicious water, closed her eyes to appreciate relief and freedom. Opening her eyes minutes later she saw on the shelf above the bath Edmund's bottle of aftershave, leapt splashing out, snatched the bottle, threw open the window, cast the bottle out, heard it crash distantly in the street and a man shout, "Oi!"

Back in the bath she dipped back so that her head too went under the water and all of Edmund in the flesh in the flat was washed away. But she knew as she dried her body and rubbed her hair dry that it was not so easy. Her eyes were used to the sight of Edmund, her ears attuned to his voice, her body habituated to fit with his.

The episode, she told herself, the episode with Willy was an episode, no more. Clambering into her lonely bed she felt as miserable and bereft as she had on the night that she heard that her father was dying. Halfway through the night she woke thinking she heard Willy's laughter and found some comfort in his amusement. Thinking of Willy she ached with desire. Unassuaged she lay awake until a blackbird sang in the dusty little square at the corner of the street.

FORTY-FIVE

Across the roofs the harvest moon and Orion were bright, there was a touch of frost. Poppy leant out of the window while the kettle boiled for coffee, craning to catch the first hint of sunrise.

She had slept for two hours.

Drinking her coffee she was uneasily aware of Edmund's possessions lurking on the landing as though threatening to re-enter the flat. She would not be truly rid of Edmund until she had removed his things.

Her car was in the country, parked where she had left it when Edmund had whisked her away from the wake. She must get down to Berkshire, retrieve the car, bring it to London, load it with Edmund's leavings, deliver them *chez* Venetia – hand them to the hall porter. There would be no need to meet Edmund or Venetia – and that would be that. *Finis*.

She shrank from the task.

Hungry, she searched the bread bin, finding half a loaf as hard as a brick, greening with mould. There was no butter, no milk, no sugar. She poured herself more coffee, drinking it bitter and black and thought what she must do. She needed a tonic.

In childhood should she sniff or grizzle or pretend illness when confronted by boredom, when she exaggerated the pains and inconveniences of her periods, Esmé would look at her with contempt and say, "You need a tonic."

The tonic was never forthcoming but the word had evolved in her childish mind something other, indeed the opposite of Esmé who damped the spirit. Esmé was not capable of producing a tonic for a tonic meant pleasure.

Dad's rare company exuded pleasure; it angered and frustrated Esmé. Since he was so rarely at home the benefit was presumably shared with his friends on the race course, with Life's Dividends, after she had left home to live with Edmund, in that remarkably comfortable and luxurious bed in the visitors' room. Poppy thought about the bed and smiled.

I need pleasure, she thought. A meal of pleasure, a creative bout, a crash course. There had been precious little pleasure of late with

Edmund. If she admitted the truth it had always been a bit rare and if there was any going Edmund scoffed it.

The need was urgent. Drinking her bitter coffee, Poppy composed the prescription for the tonic. Agreeable company, laughter, frivolity, physical pleasure. A light diet and no commitment. A diet I can take for once without giving.

"I am sick of this eternal giving," she said out loud, pushing the intrusive vision of Willy to the back of her mind. "I want some fun, I want to laugh, I've had enough of love."

She smacked the coffee cup down on the table, the bitter coffee jumped and spilled. She picked up the coffee pot and, opening the flat door, poured the gritty grounds over Edmund's things.

Inspiration brought her to the telephone. She looked Victor up in the book, discovering him among the many other Lucases hopefully awaiting her call. She dialled the number, promptly Victor answered. "Hullo?"

"Victor? It's Poppy Carew, d'you remember me?"

"Of course." He sounded drowsy. "How are you?" Less enthusiastic than she expected.

"I'm fine. Sorry if it's too early, I've no idea of the time, I should have—" Disappointment in her voice.

"What is it? What can I – of course it's not too early, tell me—" He sounded now as she remembered him, kind, intelligent, caring.

"I'm interrupting your work." (All writers work in the early morning, I've put my foot in it.)

"No, no, no I wasn't working." He laughed. "What's up? What can I do for you?"

She explained her predicament, wondered whether he was free, was doing nothing else, would he drive her to Berkshire to retrieve her car. She had this load of a "friend's" things cluttering up the landing – actually blocking – she needed the car to transport them, move them away. In spite of herself urgency crept into her voice, in a minute she would be whining.

"Why don't we load them into *my* car, drop them round at whoever's, then we'll go down and fetch yours. How would that be?" Victor suggested. "Make a day of it, lunch in the country?"

"It's such a bore for you—" she demurred.

"Not at all, be round in a flash, 'bye." He rang off, cutting short her thanks.

Poppy's stomach rumbled with hunger, her insides felt full of gas. She pulled on a sweater, took the few pounds she had left from her bag and ran downstairs. If quick she could run to the corner shop which would be opening at this hour to cherish local Indian and

Pakistani neighbours on their way to work or coming off the night shifts, buy milk, bread, fresh coffee, sugar and butter and thus be able, when he arrived, to offer Victor breakfast, repay a little of his kindness in advance, staunch the aching void in her gut. It seemed a good idea. Who knows, she thought as she hurried along, it might be fun to have a whirl with Victor, see whether he lived up to the kiss he had planted at the wake. He might, she thought cheerfully, be even more skilled, more wonderful than Willy. She whistled as she walked in anticipation of Victor. Nice girls don't think these thoughts. She remembered the days of Esmé, mentally mimicked her. If so what else do they think about?

She was greeted by the shopkeepers, a Bengali family. Where had she been? Away on holiday? Ill?

"A Muslim country."

"They did not treat you well." Tender glances from under long lashes.

She made her purchases, paid Mr Bengali while Mrs Bengali packed them with delicate fingers into a carrier bag. Mr Bengali bewailed the passing of the rival shop into the hands of a chain of bookmakers. "Temptation, temptation." He rolled his eyes. "Our savings will be tempted." Poppy loved to hear about the savings which mounted with steady persistence, an example to all frugal, hardworking families.

"My father made his fortune on the horses. Don't worry, Mr Bengali, you will not be tempted." She counted her change. Mr Bengali liked his customers to count their change. "I must fly, see you tomorrow." She set off, hurrying up the street. Often and often in the years of jogging with Edmund they had stopped at the shop to buy little cartons of orange juice to sip through straws as they walked the last hundred yards home.

Oh, Edmund!

She waited for the familiar pang, took note that it was faint and frail.

Getting better, nearly well.

As she reached her door Victor arrived in a smart car, stepped out smiling.

"You have a new car. Your literary success! Congratulations." Poppy was delighted to see Victor, it had been an inspiration to phone him.

"It's mine. He's still got his old banger, we are going to sell it." Penelope eased herself on to the pavement, careful still of her strapped ankle.

Poppy tried not to gape. What a turn up for the book.

"You haven't met my wife Penelope." Victor happy, smiling.

"His ex-wife. He's writing a novel about how he murdered me." Penelope beaming.

"What have you done to your foot?" I must say something. Poppy eased her Achilles tendon, still, now she thought of it, rather sore where the man at the hanging had trodden on it. Mercifully the black eye had quite faded.

"Sprained it. This the way up?" Penelope, using a stick, started up the steps. Even limping she was graceful, no wonder Victor—

"Where's all the stuff you have to move then?" Victor, proud of Penelope, bright eyes looking down at Poppy, friendly, brotherly, taking her parcels from her.

"The top floor, I'm afraid. Can you manage or would you like to wait here? I was going to offer you breakfast."

"We've had ours, thanks. I can manage, it's nothing. Hurt like hell at the time but Victor rescued me, didn't you, darling?"

Penelope and Victor climbed the stairs following Poppy. She's got a neat little bum, thought Victor, but Penelope's has got more swing to it.

"We live on the top floor, too," said Victor. "Have you not had breakfast?"

"I can't remember when I ate last, on the plane, I suppose. I'm starving."

"Where have you been? Nice holiday?" Penelope was untroubled by the stairs.

"North Africa. Not exactly a holiday." What then? An experience, a nightmare? What?

"Oh."

"Here we are, top floor at last." Poppy found she was breathless, rather weak.

"Is this the stuff you have to move? All this?" Penelope poked with her stick.

"Er – yes."

"You are throwing a lover out lock, stock—" Penelope approved.

"Er – just a minute, I'll let us into the flat – Oh God! I've locked myself out. Oh Christ, what a fool I am. The key is in my bag." She felt she might panic, cry or something. She kicked the door.

"And the bag's inside the flat?"

"Yes. Oh bugger, my keys, the car keys, my cheque book."

Penelope sat on the top step and laughed. Victor laughed too, then controlling himself said, "It's not funny. She's hungry, poor little thing. I bet she's not properly up, has yet to clean her teeth and go to the lavatory. We shouldn't laugh. Who has a spare key?" he asked.

"Edmund."

"The owner of all this?" Victor prodded a sheeted bundle with his toe.

"Yes."

"Where does he live?"

"With Venetia Colyer."

"Venetia!" Penelope stopped laughing. "Good old Venetia, I know Venetia." She did not speak particularly kindly. "It's good riddance for you," she said ambiguously. "It is, I'm serious. It's another of Venetia's good turns." Victor, grasping the situation, looked down his nose.

"Victor shall fetch the key, won't you, darling? Now what's the address, let me think."

"Really I don't know – I can't – I don't think—"

"I remember where she lives, that posh block where somebody got raped." Penelope told Victor the address. "We will wait here, won't we, Poppy? Buck up love, rush. He might be out."

Victor disappeared down the stairs. They heard the door slam and the car start up in the street.

"Don't look so miserable, this is fun," said Penelope cheerfully.

"Not for me." (Bang goes that tonic.)

"Serve them bloody right if Victor wakes them up." Penelope was enjoying herself.

"He is probably jogging in the park, we always did." Poppy momentarily forgot the broken leg.

"That's one thing you're spared. Don't be so woeful."

"It's so stupid of me."

"I think it's quite funny."

"I don't." Poppy sat beside Penelope on the top step. "Do you mind if I drink some milk, I'm so empty."

"Feel free. We had breakfast early. Funny that, usually I sleep late but these last few days, since Victor and I got back together, we've worked up such an appetite we wake starving. We get up, get breakfast then most times we climb straight back into bed, have a fuck and sleep again. It's making me feel so healthy!"

"Oh." Poppy erased any tentative vision of a whirl with Victor.

"This morning," said Penelope, "you telephoned at the exact moment. We'd finished eating and not started again."

Not finding a suitable reply Poppy opened her carton of milk, drank from it, wolfed some fresh bread.

"That better?" Penelope watched.

"Yes, thanks." Poppy munched. There are lots of other fish, she told herself, the world is full of them; anyway Victor isn't all that terrific, he's too thin.

"If we want to pee we can pee on your sod's things," suggested Penelope. "I take it he is a sod?"

"I suppose he is – yes, on the whole – I hope it won't come to that." Poppy thought Penelope looked able, indeed capable of carrying out her threat, that she would enjoy— "How is Victor's trout?" she asked.

"You know Victor's trout?" Penelope was intrigued. "It's very well, even I have been to see it." Penelope minimised the first person, maximised her position as Victor's girl, his ex- (ludicrous to think of it) wife. "Fancy you hearing about Victor's trout," she said.

"I was there making arrangements for my father's funeral just after Victor had brought it down from London. Fergus and Victor had put it in the stream."

"It's thanks to that fish we are together again. Really, to give her her due, it's thanks to Venetia."

"How come?" How could anyone be grateful to Venetia? She was not the kind to inspire gratitude.

"Venetia and I met in the Food Hall at Harrods. She didn't mean to do me a good turn, quite the reverse—" Penelope, with many sidesteps and embellishments, regaled Poppy with the *histoire* fish. She was still talking when the street door opened and they heard men's voices. Poppy jumped up. "I wish I could disappear." She was near panic.

"Don't be silly. You are throwing him out, aren't you?"

"Yes, but I—"

"He won't be drunk at this hour."

"How d'you—"

"I've seen him about with you. Sticks out his lip. Warning signal. Venetia will limit his intake, she's a strong-minded lady. What's going on, why are they so slow?" Penelope leaned over the banister, peering down, her dark hair swinging down like seaweed in an ebb tide.

"Edmund has a broken tibia." Remembering the circumstances of the break, Poppy broke into a nervous sweat and backed against the door of her flat.

"Here they come. He's got lovely hair, your discard." Penelope looked down. "He's tremendously good-looking, a bit passé perhaps. Struggling up with his crutches. One might get a bit tired of him. OK, Victor?" she called.

"We're on our way," shouted Victor from below. "We have the key."

"Why don't you bring the key up, then Edmund needn't bother. Poppy says he has a broken tibia."

"Determined to deliver it himself." Victor sounded not far off laughter.

"Oh." Penelope drew back from the banister and looked at Poppy. "Are you afraid of him?"

"Of course not," lied Poppy.

Disbelieving, Penelope sniffed and went back to watching the slow progress below. "One could spit on his head. Stump – hop – stump – hop – there's no need to make such heavy weather," she jeered. "I made it with my poor ankle."

Edmund's head came into view as he climbed the last flight, putting his weight on his good leg, clutching the banister with his left hand, hopping with the crutch under his right arm, hopping one step at a time; Victor, following, carried the second crutch. Edmund's face was flushed with effort, his lower lip thrust out. He reached the landing, stood looking down at Poppy.

"Thanks." There was a cold stone in her midriff.

"Here it is," said Edmund out of breath.

Poppy took the key. "It's fortunate Venetia has a lift." Don't soften, don't look at him.

"Don't sneer."

"I'm not sneering, just stating facts." Stating facts was a favourite expression of Edmund's cast in her teeth over the years. Why am I being so utterly horrible? "All this stuff is yours, I want to be rid of it."

"You could have thrown it away, I don't need it," said Edmund offhandedly.

"If I had thrown it away you would have wanted it. I foresaw weeks, months, years when you would come round to fetch it, one bit at a time." Why be so bitchy? Edmund flushed angrily.

"Attaboy. Doesn't she know him well?" said Penelope in admiration, grinning at Victor.

"Don't be so militant feminist," said Victor good-naturedly. "We'd better start carrying it down, come on, darling." He hoped to stop Penelope's mischievous trend, there was no necessity for more trouble. Poppy looked as if she might fall apart.

"Yes, you two do that," said Edmund not taking his eyes off Poppy. "I have to talk to Poppy."

"But I don't want to talk." Using the key, Poppy opened the flat door and tried to nip inside.

Before she could close the door Edmund stuck his plastered leg in it.

Penelope drew in her breath admiringly. Quite a fellow, clever blackmailer, to use the leg, a crutch, though safer, would not have had the same impact.

"Just a word," said Edmund standing on his good leg, "it won't take long."

"Why doesn't she kick it?" Penelope whispered to Victor.

"Come on," said Victor picking up the suitcases, "come on, Penelope, help." He started down the stairs.

Penelope looked at Poppy at bay in the doorway. "You all right?"

"Yes." Poppy stood keeping Edmund out, her face very white. She wished the door had a chain.

Edmund leaned against the door jamb, managing to keep his plastered leg in position.

Penelope shrugged, heaved up one of the sheeted bundles and dropped it down the stairwell, listening until it plopped in the hall below. So successful was this manoeuvre that she repeated it until the landing was almost clear, Victor arriving back just in time to grab the radio and the last suitcase. "Come down and help me load the car," he said. "You've broken quite enough."

"Should I?" Penelope looked at Edmund and Poppy shadowed in the doorway.

"Yes, come on." Victor pulled her away. "Let them get it over with, it's best."

With a last look at Poppy Penelope leaned her stomach across the banister, pushed off and slid away down out of sight. "Whoopsie, here I come."

"Mind your ankle," Victor yelled, anxious, but admiring her juvenile behaviour. He hurried after her, jumping down three steps at a time, endangering his spidery legs.

"Poppy." Edmund tried to reach her hand. "Darling."

"No."

"Venetia's gobbling me up, Poppy."

"Good."

"It's not good. Save me. I want to come back, it was a terrible mistake."

"I don't want you."

"I love you." (I really love her, I love her, I love her.)

"Nonsense," said Poppy, trying to sound robust.

"I didn't mean to hurt you, I didn't know what I was doing—"

"And I did not mean to break your leg. I'm glad it's better. I apologise. Now please go, Edmund. Down the stairs."

"You know you love me. You are naturally jealous of Venetia—"

"I'm not actually, that's all over. I wish her joy. I am grateful to her."

"I want to marry you. I told you on the plane. You agreed." Edmund reached out. Poppy drew back. "You must remember."

"I did *not* agree. Stupidly I tried not to be unkind. You wanted to marry me and call yourself Carew-Platt. Nastily I thought you wanted my money. Venetia has a lot more than me, Edmund, mine's peanuts compared to hers. Her father made washbasins and loos. With all the guilt in the world people wash more than ever. My father was a gambler who backed outsiders and doubles whatever that means—" Nervously Poppy gabbled, straining to be eloquent, to get through to Edmund once and for all. "Why don't you marry Venetia, keep a girlfriend round the corner? No, no, *not* me, not *me*, call yourself Colyer-Platt, that's what you'd like, it's much smarter." Edmund winced. "It's not on, Edmund, there's nothing doing. Nothing. Please go away." (This is not frivolous. This isn't fun.)

"My darling—"

"I am not your darling. Go away, go back to Venetia, take all the mess you left here." Poppy felt rising hysteria, she began to cry. "I hope Venetia teaches you how to make love."

"What did you say?" Edmund rocked forward glowering, managed to catch her arm as she put up a hand to wipe her tears.

"Stop, Edmund, you are hurting me."

Edmund shook her, swinging her round by the arm, pulling her out on to the landing.

"I said – I hope – Venetia – teaches you – how to fuck. Ah!" Poppy yelled "Ah! Ow!"

"That's quite enough of that." Victor, reappearing, caught hold of Edmund and pulled him away from Poppy.

Losing his precarious balance Edmund swung round cracking the back of his hand against the door. "Ouch!"

"Come away now. Downstairs," said Victor placid but firm. "Down we go."

"I'm coming up," shouted Penelope bounding up the stairs, forgetting her injured ankle. "I'll stay with Poppy while you drive Edmund and his rubbish back to Venetia."

"OK," said Victor leading Edmund down. They met on the landing.

"I'm afraid some of the things in the bundles are broken," said Penelope to Edmund. "There's a terrible mixed smell of aftershave and cheese."

Clutching his shredded dignity, Edmund managed to ignore her.

FORTY-SIX

Victor drove Penelope's car with Penelope beside him. Poppy sat in the back listening to the loverly chatter in the front seat. This was an altogether different Victor to the solitary loose-ended man she had first met, who had eyed her with appreciation and kissed her with lust. Reunited with Penelope he was more stable, less attractive.

If she had had any mind picture of Penelope before meeting her it would have been of an uncaring bitch whom Victor had quite rightly almost murdered. The Penelope who had helped in the ousting of Edmund was a girl she could be friends with, an ally.

Even when Penelope exclaimed, "Watch out, you idiot, you are driving my car not your old banger," when Victor tried to overtake a juggernaut on a bend, and Victor answered. "I'll murder you yet, just you wait," she gave the impression of affectionate marital give and take and clearly Victor's joke was not vindictive.

They were on their way to the country, Victor and Penelope to retrieve Victor's car and, as Penelope put it, take it to the knackers, and at the same time visit the now famous trout. They lightly toyed with the idea of buying another from a hatchery to keep it company.

Poppy was to visit her father's house and belatedly attend to dull business matters such as the lease and her inheritance. At Penelope's instigation she had packed an overnight bag and telephoned Fergus to apprise him of her plan. Mary, answering the phone, had said that Fergus was away on a job but why not stay the night? Poppy, demurring, ready to stay in the pub, had been overruled. "Stay here." Mary had been firm. "Mrs Edwardes keeps the visitors' room ready for you, she says that's what you wanted."

Shattered by the scene with Edmund, Poppy let her day be organised by others, allowed herself to drift. She would visit Anthony Green, find out what he had done about her father's house, get him to sell her flat, spare her the business details. Temporarily cocooned on the back seat of Penelope's car she put off decisions, let her mind wander. Watching the back of Victor's thin neck she tried to remember the spasm of attraction she had felt for him, looked forward to the rediscovery of Fergus, whose kiss at the wake had been if anything more ardent than Victor's, more demanding, more – she toyed with words to describe Fergus – masculine? macho? lusty? Sitting in Penelope's car, driving down the English motorway she blotted out the period with Willy. What had happened in Algiers seemed strangely improbable, so remote that it was as though it had not happened. I am frail, she thought wryly, I need a tonic; how grey the sky is compared to North Africa.

Victor, startled by the suggestion of an unpleasant death as presented by the juggernaut, drove with more circumspection. "I was not showing off." He squeezed Penelope's hand in her lap. "A few weeks ago I wouldn't have minded dying. Now it seems crazy."

"Sean Connor liked your book, that gave you hope."

"What's the use of hope on your own?"

"I bet you were thrilled. I bet you went to bed with Julia. Do you know she jokes about my name, calls me Antelope?"

"Not exactly. I didn't go to bed with her, she only rhymes it with—"

"Only because she's fixed up with Sean. You did at one time, at least once. Confess."

"What's once? All that's long ago. She gave me a cook book, that's all. Pretty innocent, it wasn't much."

"I noticed the cook book," said Penelope. "I rather wondered about that. Who else," she asked, her latent jealousy reviving, "who else has there been while we've been apart? What other girls? What about Mary, she's bloody attractive, have you been making passes at her?"

"Don't be ridiculous," Victor laughed, relieved that Penelope was not aware of his fleeting interest in Poppy Carew now sitting neutrally on the back seat. "Mary was Fergus's province, she's never been known to look at anyone else. She doesn't seem to be attracted to anyone or anything other than the job nowadays."

"What about the baby? What about that?"

"I can't say I'm much interested; it's said she went off to Spain and had a child by a wog. I dare say there's a story there if one grubbed about a bit."

"Your journalistic mind," she said. "One notices the lack of interest."

Victor did not like the tone in which Penelope said this nor the way she went on laughing. Uneasily he was reminded of the laughter in the bathroom above the kitchen that he and Fergus had listened to on the day he had found his darling caked in mud, her ankle sprained, having failed to catch Bolivar. Penelope and Mary had found something very comical to laugh about while Mary strapped up Penelope's injury.

"I don't ask who you have been having affairs with," he said (I could not bear to know, I could not bear it). "If we travel that road," he said, "we will only get hurt. Let's leave it, shall we?"

"Glad to." Penelope drew the line on post-mortems, perilous quagmires.

"That poor man." In his happiness Victor was charitable. "That poor Edmund of yours. He loves you still, Poppy," he called over his shoulder.

Poppy on the back seat said "Oh" doubtfully.

"He said Venetia's got cold feet," said Victor, with Edmund's grumblings and moanings during the trip to Venetia's flat in mind.

"What does she have to be afraid of? She's got the bastard now and Poppy doesn't want him." Penelope had little kindness to spare for Venetia.

"Not that kind. Apparently her feet are froggy, physically so."

"Damp?"

"He said that in bed her feet are cold. He compared their temperature unfavourably with Poppy's. Her bottom too does not compare well."

"Do you hear that, Poppy?" Penelope looked back, laughing.

"It seems Venetia is not nearly as snug to cuddle as Poppy." Victor, disloyal to his own sex, elaborated. "And she cries."

"What has she to cry about?" asked Penelope.

"God knows, but it gets on his nerves. Sudden gushing tears. He says it's unnerving."

"You got pretty pally in that short time."

"A form of research. He chucks Poppy, saying he still loves her, and moves over to Venetia. It's of literary interest, but why?"

"Money," Penelope suggested. "Good old LSD?"

"Maybe. Useful for my novel anyway. I can give one of my less lovely characters chilled feet." Victor and Penelope giggled. They forgot Poppy on the back seat and discussed Victor's book and their joint future for forty miles, arguing as to whether the character based on Penelope who was to get murdered should have cold feet or whether he might not create another girl altogether based on Venetia. "And then, of course," said Victor in full creative flow, "there's the rabbit, I must not forget the rabbit."

"What rabbit?"

"Don't you remember? You wrung that poor little inoffensive animal's neck."

"Oh God, I remember. We had just got engaged, begun our romance."

"I nearly broke it off. I was horrified."

"I was showing off. I thought you wanted me to be a tough, hunting, shooting, fishing girl. It wasn't me—"

"You certainly are a nicer girl since living with me."

"Idiot."

"Much nicer," insisted Victor.

"I am the same old Penelope, it's you who have improved. I love rabbits."

"You do not wring the neck of the thing you love," said Victor drily.

"You are murdering me in your novel."

"We seem to be getting into deep water."

"Right, let's change the subject."

Listening to them Poppy realised that their happiness was fragile, that both Victor and Penelope cared for it enough to defend it from themselves.

"When we get to the turning to the village," she said, "drop me off. I'd like to walk."

"Sure?" Victor slowed the car.

"Absolutely. I'll walk across the fields."

"Your bag?"

"It's light. I'll carry it."

"Tell me when to stop."

"At the next turning."

Victor stopped the car. Poppy got out. "Thank you for everything." She kissed Victor's cheek. Penelope hugged her. "Take care of yourself."

"And you both."

She watched them go for a moment then climbed a gate and started walking across a field full of cows.

It seemed an enormously long time since she had walked these fields as a child. It seemed an even longer time since her father's funeral. The path she was following led across the fields to the church whose tower she could see in the distance and through the churchyard into the village street. She would pass the grave where Bob Carew had recently taken up his tenancy.

Strolling slowly Poppy enjoyed the silence of the country which is not silent. Her ears attuned to the roar of the motorway took slow minutes to hear the brushing of her feet through the grass, the munch of grazing cows, their heavy breathing, the caw of rooks in lazy flight, the autumn song of a robin in the hedge, the sound of a tractor ploughing over the hill. She stopped as she walked under a row of telephone wires, looked up and listened for the twitter of swallows but they had gone to winter in Africa, last seen flighting in across the sea from Europe on the days she had witnessed the mob, the hanging, had the drama with Edmund. She walked on.

The day which had begun cold held the warmth of the October sun in the churchyard and butterflies crowded a buddleia, flies and bees worked in the long grass. She left the path and approached her father's grave.

He lay near the boundary wall. The flowers and wreaths had been removed, somebody had turfed it over, all that was left of the mound of flowers was the laurel wreath still fresh at the head of the grave.

Poppy squatted beside the grave, idly brushing grass pollen from her legs. It was peaceful. Jackdaws clacked about the church tower, she could hear the clock tocking. She stretched her legs and, sitting propped against the churchyard wall, tried to think of her father.

She was too young to know that memories do not come leaping to order, it would take her years to discover that they are evoked by a smell, a glimpse of colour, a tone of voice, a note of music. She fell asleep, her head against the wall, her feet towards the grave.

The clop of horses' hooves woke her. She sat up. The horses stopped.

"Hullo," said Mary, high on a Dow Jones. "I saw you from up here. How are you?"

"I fell asleep."

"Why not? Nice day." Mary sat the horse easily, one hand round Barnaby who perched in front of her. The other held the reins and a leading rein attached to a second horse. "I was giving these two a little exercise, the others are away working. Coming up to the house?"

"I was on my way. Just thought I'd—"

"See your pa. Is he there?"

"No, no he's not—" Perhaps that accounted for not being able to conjure him up.

"He's at some heavenly race track. Like to ride up to the house? Can you ride?" asked Mary.

"Yes. Thanks." Poppy climbed on to the low wall and dropped down bareback on to the spare horse and rode through the village to her father's house, her house now. Barnaby, perched in front of Mary, kicked his legs out and chuckled as they went along.

Dismounted in the yard Poppy watched Mary put the horses away. Just as Victor had changed so indefinably had Mary. She was prettier, thinner, her hair was not dyed, she looked even more withdrawn. "How is Fergus?" Poppy asked.

"Just the same," said Mary. "Just the same," she repeated, shutting a horse-box door. "Come into the house." She led the way in through the kitchen. "I hope you won't find we've changed your house too much, your room is untouched."

"It was never my room."

"Ah." Mary looked her up and down. "You have changed," she said, "you look different."

"I'm free. Perhaps that's it. I'm free."

"Is that so?" Mary smiled. "It must be nice."

"It's super." Poppy watched Mary pull off Barnaby's jersey, put him down on the floor, give him a raw carrot to gnaw.

"He's on solids now." Mary looked down at her child. "Got several teeth, haven't you?" She poked Barnaby's stomach gently with her toe. Barnaby looked up smiling enormously, rolling his bull's-eye eyes.

In spite of her brave words Poppy, watching Mary, suspected that the state of not being in love might wear thin when the novelty wore off. How did Mary manage? She found herself looking forward to the return of Fergus.

"Shall we see whether your room's all right?" Mary led the way upstairs. "How is your Lochinvar?" she asked, pausing on the stair where she had sat nursing Barnaby at the funeral party. "It caused quite a commotion when he swept you off in Venetia's car."

"I have disposed of him," said Poppy coolly, resenting Mary's mocking tone.

"Aha! Thinking for ourselves now, are we?" Mary laughed outright. "Well, here's your room, nothing's changed."

But everything's changed, thought Poppy. The room, the house may look the same, but Dad's gone. Mary, for she blamed Mary, has altered the atmosphere. There's a dangerous sparkle about her, she's some sort of volcano.

When Mary left she paced the room, went into the bathroom, touched the bath towels, the soaps and bath essence, ventured across the landing to her father's room. Mrs Edwardes had tidied and cleaned it, the bed was unmade, the furniture covered in dust sheets, no trace of Dad remained. Poppy closed the door, went back to the visitors' room where Life's Dividends had reposed in the ample bed. She unpacked her overnight bag, put her sponge and toothbrush in the bathroom, opened the windows.

It will be much better when Fergus comes in, she thought, remembering his kiss, his tongue thrust urgently into her mouth. A whirl with Fergus would do no harm. Dad would have liked Fergus, she thought, more perhaps than Victor, been delighted at the disposal of Edmund, approved of the final parting. She stood at the window looking out at the road, trying to come to terms with Dad's absence, the change in the house's atmosphere.

After a while she left the room and explored, peeping in at bedroom doors. Girls' clothes, shoes, tights in the room that had been hers, posters of pop stars Blu-tacked to the wall, alien paperbacks on the floor. In the bathroom strange toothbrushes, shampoos, coloured towels. In another room a child's cot, a potty. No trace in any of these rooms of Fergus. Where did Fergus sleep?

"Fergus has taken over the top floor." Mary had come up, silent, barefoot, carrying Barnaby. "He's due for his afternoon sleep," she said, laying the child in his cot.

Poppy, caught snooping, flushed. "Are you all quite comfortable?" she asked, to fill an awkward gap.

"Sure," said Mary. She drew the curtains, darkening the room. "Go to sleep," she said to the child, "close your eyes."

Barnaby closed his eyes and opened them again immediately.

Poppy moved back on to the landing.

"There's Bolivar," said Mary, looking out of the landing window. "See? There he is sitting in the road. He knows Fergus is on his way home. Hey, Bolivar," she shouted. The cat neither twitched nor looked up. "Fergus will be back soon. I take it you've come to see him," said Mary obliquely.

Poppy did not answer. She looked forward to Fergus's return, he would lighten the atmosphere, put a stop to this lonely feeling, the sense of something lying in wait. She remembered him large, capable, kindly, above all, cheerful. Feeling curiously endangered by Mary she decided to rest on the Life's Dividends bed until Fergus's return.

"I think I'll have a nap like Barnaby," she said.

Mary went away.

FORTY-SEVEN

Poppy rested on the visitors' bed, she listened to the house, her childhood home, her father's house. Below the visitors' room where she lay on the bed was the room that had been Dad's study. It was silent. No occasional cough, no scrape of chair pushed back from the desk, no sound of his voice telephoning, no voice calling out as it had in her childhood to Esmé and latterly to Jane Edwardes, "Is my tea ready?" What silly little things she remembered.

How had he appeared to the ladies who had lain in this bed? As friend? Lover? Companion? What were they like? Were they old? Arthritic? Horsey women with tinted hair and windblown complexions? Had they and Dad lain here? There was no echo of their voices, she would never know them.

She got off the bed and prowled the room. The cupboards were empty, the chest of drawers also. Life's Dividends had left no trace.

Her overnight bag looked out of place, ready to take off elsewhere.

If Life's Dividends were not here, nor was Dad, it was too late now to give him joy, she must get used to permanent regret.

Another regret, not, she told herself, of much importance, was Victor – re-absorbed by Penelope – who might, if she had handled their first meeting differently, have been more than a friend. He had certainly given that impression. But that opportunity, if opportunity it was, was past. Penelope had him back, would keep him.

I would have liked to have slept with Victor, it would have been an experience, thought Poppy, even though he is too thin, not exactly my type. But there is still Fergus, Fergus would be good for a gallop. Wasn't that one of Dad's expressions? So-and-so and so-and-so had "a gallop" or, if the affair had been on the mild side, "a canter". There would always be echoes of Dad in her mind even if he had vacated the house. Sleepily considering the prospect of a gallop, canter or even a trot with Fergus, she decided that presently she would bath and change, go down looking her best to dally with him. His invitation at the wake had been extremely plain, plainer, she persuaded herself, than Victor's.

Amused by the prospect, Poppy listened drowsily to the new sounds which had taken over the house; Mary singing to her child, Barnaby answering with sharp chortling shouts, the back door opening, Mary calling "Bolivar, come boy, dinner", answered by a growling miauling; the neigh of a horse, a hoof stamped in the stables.

Only the sparrows chirping in the eaves and the jackdaws clacking were familiar. During her absence the house had changed gear; it answered now to Mary who sang in the kitchen. She would decide what windows would open, what doors close, what cooking smells would pervade the house, she was the mistress now. I am on holiday, Poppy decided sleepily, on holiday after the trauma of Edmund, I deserve a holiday, a respite.

She woke to the sound of engines, Fergus's voice answered by Annie and Frances, the sound of ramps crashing down from horse-boxes, the clatter of hooves on wood, then hooves on the road passing the house, the rumble of the hearse manhandled off its lorry, shouts of "Mind the gate, keep to your left, steady" as it was wheeled to the coach house. Fergus calling to the girls, their high voices answering, fading away round the house, then footsteps returning, the starting up of the lorry and the Land-Rovers towing the horse-boxes to move them away out of earshot.

There was a harsh note to Fergus's voice, a lack of cheer, which made her unwilling to hurry down and present herself. The jokes, the atmosphere of frivolity and hairwashing which she remembered when she had visited Furnival's Fine Funerals that first time was noticeable by its absence. They must all be tired to be so cheerless, perhaps the funeral had gone off badly, leaving unsatisfied customers. Funerals could not all reach the high standard of Dad's.

She heard the back door slam, Fergus's voice ordering abruptly, "See they put them all away OK. Right? I'm going to have a bath."

Mary made an inaudible reply.

Fergus's tread on the stairs, pausing on the landing, an aggressive shout, "Have you fed Bolivar?"

"Yes." Mary exasperated.

"He says *not.*" Fergus's footsteps moving up the next flight. "Come on, my puss." A throaty yowl, footsteps diminishing, the sound of taps being turned on in the bathroom, rushing water.

Remembering the capacity of her father's hot water tank, Poppy hopped off the bed and turned on the hot tap in the visitors' bathroom, immediately decreasing the flow into the bath above.

Fergus swore as the hot water diminished. "Who the hell is taking all my hot water? It will run cold, blast you. Have you been washing your hair?" he shouted down the stairs.

"I told you, you have a visitor." Mary, irritatingly patient, called up from the hall.

Poppy, aware of the exact capacity of the tank, turned off her hot tap, added cold, stepped into the bath. (Fergus sounded just as selfish as Edmund.)

Whether to instal a larger hot water tank or manage with what there was had been a question which Dad had debated with monotonous regularity over the years. Now that she was Fergus's landlord it behoved her to consider the problem, it was no longer academic. Washing her ears, she decided to discuss the matter with Anthony Green. "A larger tank would ultimately add to the value of the house," she would say. Anthony would prevaricate, she visualised herself quashing his objections, he would be sure to object to her spending the money. That was what solicitors were for.

Poppy got out of the bath and dressed.

Someone, Penelope perhaps, had put the multicoloured dress into her bag. She put it aside and dressed in clean jeans and shirt. The dress held too many associations. She thrust it back in the bag feeling, as she did so, that it was not the dress she was pushing out of sight, not her father, not even Edmund, but Willy and she did not propose to think of Willy now, she was going downstairs to meet Fergus.

She zipped up the bag, pushed it out of sight under the bed and left the room.

Downstairs Annie was laying the table, clattering knives, forks, spoons into careless position. Mary stood by the stove.

"Do you mind eating in the kitchen?"

"Of course not. What's for supper? Smells great."

There was an atmosphere of constraint. Poppy wondered whether she was unwelcome among the girls, tried to appear natural and friendly. "How have you all settled in?" she asked.

"Oh fine, fine. We love it here, it's brilliant." Annie glanced up as Frances came into the room. "Shall we get some booze from the pub?" she asked Mary. "Got any money?"

"There's plenty here, Dad had quite a good cellar, I'll go and get a bottle or two." Glad of something to do, Poppy left the room. It would be a friendly act, soften the stiff atmosphere if she contributed wine to the meal.

Coming up from the cellar carrying bottles, she met Fergus.

"Hullo, Fergus."

"Hullo. Nice to see you. Hope you are comfortable. That for us? It's very kind of you . . ." His voice had changed, he sounded older, he did not seem particularly pleased to see her, there was no trace of the letching look in the eye she remembered.

"I hope I am not a nuisance. I won't stay long. It's just that I have to discuss a few things with Anthony Green. I hope he hasn't bothered you."

"He's been very helpful, actually, thinks my stepfather's reference makes me respectable."

"I could easily have stayed in the pub." Poppy excused her presence, embarrassed by she knew not what.

"Don't be silly, it's your house." Fergus frowned and glanced across the kitchen at Mary, who stood at the stove stirring something which smelt delicious with a long spoon.

Mary lifted one shoulder in a curiously defensive gesture.

"You people ready to eat?" she asked. "Find a corkscrew, Frances, give it to Fergus." She pointed at the bottles with her chin as Poppy put them on the table.

"Right." Fergus took the corkscrew handed him by Frances and drew the corks. "This is very good of you." He poured the wine.

Mary dished up, heaping rice on to plates, adding generous portions of chicken.

"What's this, *coq au vin*?"

"Cock." Mary helped herself last, sat beside Poppy. "There were some telephone calls for you," she said to Fergus. "I wrote them down, they are on your desk."

Dad's desk—

"Thanks. Any orders?"

"Two definite funerals for next week, various queries. I said you'd ring tomorrow early."

"Thanks." Fergus ate hungrily. "Any callers?"

"What?"

"Anybody come to the house?"

"No."

"Where's Barnaby?"

"Asleep."

"Oh. He all right?"

"Yes."

"Oh." Fergus turned to Poppy and began talking to her, enquiring where she had been, had she enjoyed herself, was it a good trip, what was North Africa like, spacing his questions between mouthfuls of food, barely listening to her replies.

Nettled, Poppy said, "We spent a few days in Purgatory."

"Oh," said Fergus swallowing some wine. "What was the food like?"

Annie and Frances smirked.

Mary laughed outright. "Haha! Hoho!"

Fergus looked round the table, surprised.

"Did I say something amusing?"

"Oh no," said Mary, "not at all, of course not."

They fell silent, looked at their plates.

Outside a robin started singing in a lilac bush. Bolivar jumped up to the windowsill and out in a long flowing movement.

"Well." Fergus finished his meal, pushed his plate aside. "You two girls coming to the pub with me?"

"Well," Frances hesitated.

"Well," said Annie, also hesitant.

"Come on, then." Fergus pushed back his chair and stood up. "I expect you are tired," he said to Poppy.

"I will help Mary clear the table," said Poppy.

"Sure you won't come?" asked Fergus, as though he had invited her.

"Yes," said Poppy, already gathering plates. "I must get you a new dishwasher," she said to Mary, "and another thing, I think you need a larger hot water supply. My father had been thinking of it for years, it just never got done."

"Too busy picking the winners. Don't bother for my sake," said Mary vaguely as she watched Fergus go out, followed by Annie and Frances.

"What's the matter with him?" asked Poppy, unable to stop herself.

"Just a mood." Mary sounded unconvincing. "I have put a lot of things away," she said, "things that might get broken. Some of your parents' things."

"Oh, thank you. I should have done it myself." (There had been no time.)

"Your solicitor thought it would be a good thing, he sent a man to make an inventory."

"That wasn't necessary." Poppy flushed.

"I asked him to," said Mary. "We have so much clutter, hats, boots, bits of harness, Fergus's gun," she glanced up at the chimney breast, "books, cat basket, dogs. The girls make a lot of mess, too."

Poppy helped Mary tidy the kitchen then, excusing herself, went to her father's study, sat at his desk to make a list of matters she must discuss with Anthony. It was high time she showed herself more capable than scatterbrained. She felt the need to do something practical to dispel the shock of Fergus's snub, for what was it if not a snub?

Her fantasy of a gallop, canter or trot with Fergus was as much pie in the sky as her whirl with Victor.

She could hear Mary moving about the house, answering the telephone, talking to Barnaby in the bedroom upstairs, singing a lullaby as she put him to bed, then talking to the old dog and to Bolivar. She watched her walk past the window to pick flowers in the garden, her pale hair in sharp contrast to the brilliant zinnias she gathered. Dad had always grown these flowers, admiring their vigour and vulgarity. Mary, thought Poppy, watching her, belonged to the house and the house knew it.

When the telephone started to ring she jumped up and left the house. She needed to walk and sort her thoughts. There was the risk that the caller might be Willy Guthrie; she could not bring herself to talk to him. She crossed the field behind the house. The cat Bolivar kept her company for fifty yards before disappearing under a gate.

She had begun the day believing she could use Victor and Fergus as buffers between herself and Willy, it was plain now that she was bufferless. They would have worked too as a salve to cure the wound left by Edmund.

Taking the route she had always taken with her father she set out to walk off her resentment. She climbed up behind the house to the stand of beech and on, on to the downs to turn, catch her breath and look down on the village snaking along the chalk stream, the village hall, the pub, the church, the garage, her father's house, the post office.

The church clock struck the hour; the pub would soon close, spilling out Fergus and the girls. She had no wish to meet Fergus again that night, having so nearly made a fool of herself. She broke into a trot.

Trot, she thought as she jogged down the hill, any trotting must be done alone.

A hundred yards from the house she heard Fergus's voice. He was shouting. She slowed to a walk and approached the house cautiously.

In the kitchen Mary stood with her back to the stove. Annie and Frances stood on either side of the table, Fergus was in the doorway from the hall. The kitchen was brightly lit and the door open into the yard.

Poppy, fascinated, watched unseen. There was no problem about hearing, both Fergus shouting and Mary speaking quietly enunciated clearly.

The row was in full swing.

"Deceitful, sly, crafty, selfish, abominable. No man in his senses would endure such a trick."

Mary, very quiet and cold, "Who told you?"

"My mother, no less. I have to have my nose rubbed in it by an interfering parent whom I have hitherto loved, trusted and respected. I didn't believe her, of course, what she said was too utterly preposterous."

"Yes."

"Yes? It's not *yes*. It's true! What my mother says is true. I thought it was her wishful thinking, her imagination." Fergus gasped for breath. "She's always wanted me to have—"

Frances caught Annie's eye and jerked her head, indicating "Let's get out of this."

"You stay where you are," shouted Fergus, "you are my witnesses, don't you dare move," he threatened.

Frances and Annie froze.

"Oh," said Mary, cool but whitefaced. "So?"

"So she cast my genes in my teeth."

"Who? What?"

"My bloody mother. I told you. My genes."

"Genes?"

"Yes, genes, fucking genes. She said it looked exactly like—"

"*He*."

"OK. He looked exactly like me as a baby and even worse my bloody filthy-tempered father. Genes, she said, don't lie."

"No."

"So I have my witnesses. I take them out to the pub, ply them with drink several boring nights running, quiz them about the holiday you spent in Spain after leaving me, ask crafty questions about your boyfriend, Joseph the father, we are led to suppose – who telephones constantly we are led to believe. Funny that it's always you who answers the telephone— Where was I? I've lost the thread. Oh, got it. This boyfriend Joseph who is the father of infant Jesus—"

"Barnaby."

"Oh-bloody-kay, Barnaby, and I am not even consulted about his name." Fergus yelling now.

"What's his name got to do with it?"

"Nothing," Fergus screamed. "Call the little bastard anything you like."

"Thanks."

"So I make them drunk, don't I? Out pop the indiscretions. I make a few simple passes at these nitwits – thrilled, they were. Oh, yes you were. A grown man at last not a boy from the disco. They regale me with the goings-on on the Costa where they met you. *There were no goings-on!* Saint Joseph, it turns out, is no beautiful Spanish fisher lad, he's a rather old, very fat, heavily married Swede, with a wife he adores and a grown-up family, the manager and owner of the hotel. Don't laugh!"

"I am not laughing."

"And this Saint Joseph, this Swedish gent, is fair, has almost white hair and so have all his sons and daughters and grandchildren. Grandchildren!"

"And?"

"And so have you. Very fair hair. You used to wear it long in a pigtail like a bellrope. Why did you cut it off?"

"So?"

"So this is where the genes come in, where you slip up in your evil deception. It's not possible for two very fair people to have a very dark baby."

"No."

"So *I* am very dark, my father was very dark. My mother meets Barnaby, puts two and two together and tells me I am his father." Fergus loomed over Mary standing backed against the stove with her hands gripping the stove rail. She pushed herself away from it.

"It will not take me long to pack." She walked past Fergus and left the room. They heard her run lightly up the stairs.

Fergus slumped down on a chair by the table.

Frances and Annie edged towards the door. Poppy, ashamed of greedily listening, came forward into the light.

Nobody spoke.

After a few minutes Mary appeared carrying Barnaby wrapped sleepy in a shawl. She walked past Fergus without looking at him, snatched a bunch of car keys from the dresser and walked on through the house and out.

Poppy, Annie and Frances followed her on to the porch.

"She can't," said Annie.

"She will," said Frances.

Mary settled Barnaby in a basket cot on the back seat, got in behind the wheel and started the car. She was turning it in the road when Fergus pushed the girls roughly aside and shouted, "Don't!"

Mary paid no attention.

Fergus rushed back into the house.

"Is he drunk?" asked Annie.

"No," said Frances, "he didn't drink a thing, it was we who were drinking."

"Oh God," said Annie. "Oh God." She moaned. Both girls were crying.

Mary was finishing a three-point turn and putting the car into gear when Fergus reappeared with his gun.

Annie and Frances shrieked.

Fergus fired.

Mary's car slewed sideways into a flowerbed.

Fergus fired again. The car stopped.

In the ensuing pause Mary said, "Damn you."

Fergus dropped the gun on Poppy's foot.

Poppy yelped.

Fergus shouted, "I love you, you FOOL!" and rushed down the steps to the car.

"And now he'll wake the baby," said Willy, coming into the bright glare of the porch. "Why the hell didn't you answer when I telephoned?"

FORTY-EIGHT

Barnaby, waked by the shots, filled his lungs and began to scream like a steam kettle on a high-pitched, ear-piercing, bat-deafening note which terrified Poppy who was unversed in babies and paralysed Frances and Annie with fright.

Fergus, reaching into the back of Mary's car, took the baby out as Mary leapt furiously from the driving seat.

"Gosh, what lungs," exclaimed Willy. "The child is perfectly all right, leave them." His urgent voice carried conviction. "For Christ's sake, leave them alone. Here," he said, picking up the gun from where Fergus had dropped it, "put this back where it belongs." He thrust the gun into Frances's hands. "Hurry, it won't go off, he fired both barrels."

Arriving fortuitously to lure Annie and Frances to the disco, two youths now found themselves pressganged by Willy into pushing the flat-tyred car into the yard out of sight of the road. (Fergus, being an excellent shot, had hit what he aimed for, the back tyres.)

Mesmerised by Willy's authority, the girls' escorts asked, "What happened? What happened?" as they pushed, trying at the same time not to spoil their party clothes. "What happened?"

"Nothing, nothing happened," said Willy, pushing. "A couple of blow outs, it was nothing, nothing."

"Oh nothing, it was nothing." Annie, taking her lead from Willy, pushed the car also.

"It was all our fault." Frances returned from putting the gun away and stood with Poppy on the front steps. "Fergus teased and tricked us into telling him about kind old Mr Joseph who gave Mary a job when she was pregnant. He and his wife warded off her family, they wanted to keep Barnaby, wanted to adopt him. Mary had to tear herself away from them. They still write and telephone, they've got a thing about Barnaby. Oh, poor baby." Frances sobbed loudly.

"Shut up, stop that noise," snapped Poppy, furious in relief, wishing she had a second pair of eyes and ears to simultaneously watch the removal of the car and the taut drama between Fergus and Mary, who now stood in the road muttering.

Each time Fergus's voice rose to audibility it was drowned by shouting from the yard: "Put the bloody brake on, you git", and "mind my foot", and "watch it", as the car was pushed by willing hands to bump into a wall to the accompaniment of crunching headlights and yells of anarchic irrepressible laughter.

Fergus and Mary might have been alone on Mars for all the attention they paid to the outer world.

Mary took Barnaby from Fergus as he stopped shrieking. He leaned towards her talking and presently took the child back, muttering intensely, his voice low, grumbling like summer waves on a cobbled beach. Mary gently took the child again, holding him up near her face as she answered in a very quiet urgent voice.

The two were so preoccupied Poppy wondered whether they were aware of what they did as turn and turn about they took the child from each other with reassuring ritualistic movements. Fergus's voice, still inaudible, rumbled and fell lower. Mary spoke less and less. From time to time Barnaby crowed as he was handed from one to the other, staking his part in the game. He had reverted after his shocked surprise to his habitual humorous self.

"Amazing," said Frances, standing watching with Poppy. "Incredible," she sniffed, wiping her tears with the back of her hand.

"Did I hear a gun go off? Thought I heard shots." Jane Edwardes came up the road. "We thought we heard a gun."

"Oh, hullo, Mrs Edwardes." Willy came through from the back of the house. "Do you remember me? I helped you clean up the golden syrup."

"Oh yes, so you did," said Mrs Edwardes. "Honey too, such waste. We were watching TV and thought we heard a gun. Boring programme, silly old Party Conference. I told my husband I'd come and look, he's interested in politics, I'm not. Did you hear about the golden syrup, Poppy? Mr – er – helped me clean it up."

"What?" said Poppy, still watching the two figures with the child. "He's called Willy Guthrie."

"Yes, I know," said Jane Edwardes.

"Did you ever find out who did it?" asked Willy.

"No," said Mrs Edwardes, "I did not."

"Did *what*?" asked Poppy, irritated at not being able to hear what Fergus and Mary were saying.

"I wonder if that was a gun we heard." Mrs Edwardes reverted to the cause of her call.

"Why don't we go into the kitchen and make some coffee," suggested Willy, edging Jane Edwardes and Poppy into the house. "We can tell Poppy about the drama of the treacle," he said as they moved indoors. "And you," he turned to Frances, "are off to the disco, I gather."

"Oh, are we?" said Frances, latching on. "I'd better be off then. Bye," she called as she ran off to join Annie and the boys. "I'd been going to wash my hair." They heard her voice diminish, the visiting car start up and mixed-sex laughter as it drove away.

In the kitchen Bolivar lay on his back in front of the stove exposing his gingery stomach to the warmth, his hind legs splaying out from his furry balls, eyes closed, front paws dangling across his chest.

"If anyone had fired a gun that cat would have been up and away," said Mrs Edwardes, moving the kettle across to the hotplate.

Willy grinned at Poppy.

"I hope no nosey-parker has telephoned the police," said Mrs Edwardes, spooning Nescafé into mugs. "Reach me the milk, dear, from the fridge. Thank you. I heard their sirens as I came along."

"There's been a pile-up on the motorway, I had difficulty in getting past on my way over," said Willy. "I expect the police are all busy with that."

"That's all right, then," said Mrs Edwardes, pouring boiling water into the mugs. "Can't be everywhere, can they? Milk? Sugar?"

"Both, please," said Willy.

"I know how you like yours," Jane Edwardes said to Poppy.

"Thank you," said Poppy, "so you should."

"Thank you," said Willy.

They took their mugs, stood grouped by the stove. Willy caressed Bolivar's stomach delicately with his toe. Bolivar yawned, sneezed, went on snoozing.

"All the same," said Jane Edwardes, "it would be a sensible thing if he cleaned his gun when he stops being so busy." She jerked her chin slightly towards the road.

Willy laughed. "I'll do it now," he said. "He may be busy for quite a while."

"Got a lot to say to each other, no doubt," said Mrs Edwardes. "He keeps the cleaning things in that drawer," she pointed, "the one on the left."

"Thanks." Willy put down his mug.

Poppy watched him clean the gun and return it to its place.

"That's all right, then," said Mrs Edwardes, satisfied. "Didn't take care of your father all those years without learning a thing or two. I'll be off now, Poppy. I'll send young Bill up to change those tyres in the morning first thing."

"Oh," said Poppy, "you were watching."

"I wouldn't say that," said Jane Edwardes, "not exactly. I'll be getting along. They'll take some time getting it all said, I dare say. Well, good night, I'll be missing the news if I hang about." She kissed Poppy.

Willy went with Mrs Edwardes to the front door. Coming back he said, "And I have a lot to say to you."

Poppy said quickly, "Are they all right, Fergus and Mary?"

"Looks like it. They seem to have taken root in the road."

"What do you know?"

"Fergus's mother came and moaned it all out to my aunt when she rumbled the situation."

"Oh."

"They share the child."

"How?"

"As people do, the accident of procreation." It's different, thought Willy, with my pigs. *There's* family planning for you.

"Accident! Good God!" said Poppy.

Willy looked at her with careful eyes. Poppy flushed.

"Or," said Willy, "it was some convoluted form of love and Mary's pride got in the way."

"I admire and like Mary," said Poppy stoutly.

"So do I, so do I," said Willy. (Curious this little trick he has of repeating himself, said a little nerve in Poppy's head.)

"Where's your bag?" Willy was saying. "I am taking you home."

"Supposing I don't want to come?" she prevaricated.

"Not that again," said Willy. "Let's get cracking."

FORTY-NINE

Willy holding Poppy by the hand pulled her towards his car.

As they passed Fergus and Mary he squeezed her hand but got no response. If Poppy was not exactly holding back physically she was confused and recalcitrant.

Fergus's dogs, crouching in the vicinity of their master, uncertain of what was going on, jerked hurriedly aside, jumping to their feet to let Willy and Poppy pass. The oldest dog, who did not normally concern himself with anything much, gave the whisper of a growl. None of the dogs had barked when Fergus loosed off his gun; two of them had run to Mary, the third, who now growled, had stood looking from Fergus to Mary, a prey to indecision.

Passing by the silent pair Poppy wondered how long they would stand bemused, whether Barnaby would catch cold in the night air, whether she wanted to stay and watch the upshot of this curious scene, whether she ought to stay or would it be better to allow Willy to take her away as he was now doing.

Possibly she had counted on another night in the Dividend bed. As she thought of this it became almost certain that this was what she wanted and Willy was depriving her of it.

As they pushed past Fergus he took Mary's head between both hands and, leaning to kiss her, said, "Promise you will let it grow?"

Mary said, "All right, I will," laughing, putting the arm not holding Barnaby round Fergus's neck, returning his kiss. "You shall have your bellrope."

"Then let's go back and start." Fergus turned Mary towards the house.

Overhearing this exchange, allowing herself to be pushed into Willy's car, Poppy craned back to watch as Willy pulled the safety belt across to fasten her in.

"He wants her to grow her hair," she said. "That's what he means."

"And to let l-o-v-e grow too." Willy slammed the car door, irritated with his darling.

Poppy wound the window down the better to watch Fergus and Mary disappear into the house.

"I bet they sleep in the Dividend bed tonight," she said.

"The what bed?"

"It's neutral ground. My bed. Well, Dad's visitors' bed. Some day I'll tell you—"

Some day, thought Willy, starting the car, engaging the gears, some day I shall have learned much about her but never the whole of it. There is no way that two people can know each other wholly, nor do I want that. He switched on the headlights, accelerated.

Some day I shall persuade Jane Edwardes to tell me all she knows about Life's Dividends, thought Poppy, regretting the so comfortable bed, or would it be wiser not to ask, just be grateful to them for their money?

Edmund would search around, poke and pry into Dad's past, suggest Life's Dividends could be better invested, know better, interfere. Thank God that is not Willy's style. But, she thought, amused as Willy swung the car too fast out of the village, I am not sure Edmund is not the better driver. Willy is a bit erratic.

"The last time I was driven away from Dad's house without prior consultation or consent was by Edmund," she said. "I have a distinct feel of déjà vu."

"I am not interested in Edmund," said Willy, keeping his eyes on the road, "until I have a spare moment and can take time off to murder him."

"Oh my!" exclaimed Poppy mockingly. Willy, not keen on Poppy's mood, drove on in silence.

He is assuming possession, thought Poppy. He has not asked whether I *want* to come with him. I have not been *asked* what I want. Yesterday I wanted a bit of experimental fun with Victor and lo he was snitched back into Penelope's marital orbit. Today I had promised myself a trot, canter or gallop with Fergus and now it's clear that he and Mary love each other and have even gone so far as to have a ready-made child. As far as my love life goes those two men are non-starters. She resigned herself to Willy. Just for a while, she assured herself, it's purely temporary of course.

"Do you think it possible," she asked presently, "that Fergus really did not know Mary's baby was his?"

"Perfectly possible," said Willy. "I know other people who can't recognise what's going on under their noses."

"Such as?" Poppy resented Willy's tone which was sarcastic.

"Such as you," said Willy on the same note.

"In what context?" she asked sharply.

"In the context of love," said Willy. "You busily pretend that you do not know that I love you. I should have thought by now you would be fully aware of it. Cognisant, if we are being pompous."

"I resent – busily."

"Hah!"

"I haven't had time to think about it. I am still bruised and battered by Edmund—" (This whining is ridiculous and also false.)

"Come off it."

"I want time to think," she complained.

"You are not slow witted. You've had time."

"No, I haven't. When Edmund and I parted—"

"He left you."

"Agreed. But he came back—"

"You wanted to annoy Venetia. You told me."

"So I did – and I did." Poppy relished the memory of an unsurpassed act of annoyance.

"Well then," said Willy, his eyes on the road.

"Well then, when we'd parted, split up, finished, when Dad had died, I was deciding what to do with myself, sorting myself out, taking my time."

"I came along," said Willy cheerfully.

"That didn't settle anything, Willy."

"It did for me."

"But not me. I was thinking of selling my flat and buying a little house in London, starting all over—"

"That's what you are doing now, starting afresh with me."

"No."

"I am taking you home."

Home, thought Poppy, what is home? My flat, with its connotations of Edmund, is impossible, even though I have thrown out all his things, he will still be in the air I breathe. Dad's house, my early home, it's now, thanks to my own bright idea, Mary and Fergus's. Would a little house in London, always supposing I found one, be a better deal? To be honest, until a moment ago, when Willy acted so sure of himself, I had forgotten that slight conversation with boring Les Poole at the bank. I am not being honest with Willy but no need to let on just yet.

There is always the possibility of nothing, doing nothing, nothing happening. One night or three in the Dividend bed is fine, but what about longer? What about it?

There is no way I can start afresh, thought Willy. I have been clumsy. I was so sure of my own love I didn't take hers into account. Does it exist? Am I rushing her too fast? With other girls I have sailed ahead not really caring, felt so confident, so carefree. This is absolutely bloody. Surely that was love as well as enjoyment we had in Algiers?

Is it possible she was fucking for fucking's sake when she laughed and cried out for more? Is it possible it all means nothing to her? Am I making the most awful fool of myself? What does she think I mean when I say I am taking her home? If I told her her home is my heart she would call me a sloppy romantic and I am one, unashamedly, hopelessly so where she is concerned.

Willy began to sweat. He had wanted to surprise and delight her with the charms of his farm, see her fall in love with it, fit into it, love it as he did.

"Perhaps I had better tell you where I am taking you," he said tentatively. "My farm."

"You were keeping it as a surprise."

"I was."

"Tell me now then."

She had seen a pig farm once. Long concrete buildings with hard concrete floors crowded with pigs penned in cramped partitions, fed in long communal troughs, no peace, no room to move, no privacy, no dignity. She had been aghast, repelled by the questing snouts, the hot atmosphere, the squeals and grunts, the slopping sound as they souped up their food, hastening to grow to the correct weight for the bacon factory.

Edmund, having taken her (it was in his house agent days) to view a house near the farm, had reacted quite otherwise, approving of the use of minimal space, the speed of growth, the financial turnover achieved by modern farming techniques. For her part she had been so shocked by the sight of the degraded pigs that she gave up eating bacon for at least a month. (If I were honest I would remember it was only a week.) I must be deranged, thought Poppy, sitting here letting Willy take me to a place like that, out of my tiny mind.

But Willy was talking.

"There was this group of farm buildings, my uncle restored them in his day. When I took over I did a lot more. The buildings are rather lovely pink brick barns with tiled roofs. The principal ones are squared round a cobbled courtyard with a well in the middle. I keep a few bantams and ducks because I like the noise they make and they look pretty. I live in one wing I converted into a cottage. I have a very large flagged living-room with an Aga at one end, an open fire at the other. I can walk out either into the yard or into a walled garden. I made the garden but it still needs a lot doing to it. There's a dovecot, one of those conical jobs with a tiled roof. No doves at present, though." (Doves, white fantails, would be lovely, thought Poppy.) "Above the living-room I have a large bedroom with an open fire and bathroom and you can see across the fields to the wood. I use a second barn as my office and store." (Is she listening? I am being very boring, wouldn't it have been better to wait and let her see it, judge for herself?) "The pigs, the principal sows have the other two sides of the square, each has her own space; pigs need lots of space."

"What?" Poppy, adjusting her thoughts, felt as though they were in a tumble-dryer.

"I said pigs need lots of space. You see them lolling together in groups of course when they are feeling sociable."

"Go on."

"My sows all have their separate styes. Terribly clean animals, pigs, did you know?" (What does she know? She must have some clue, she's lived in the country.)

"Not enough."

"My breeding sows, most of them, well, all of them now, I bred myself. The principal, most important to me, are Mrs Future and her aunt. I admit that to the uninitiated they all look alike. The little pigs, when they are old enough, live in groups in deep litter."

"Not on concrete?"

"Good God, no!" Willy exploded.

"Oh."

"I believe you thought I was a factory farmer," Willy accused, furious.

"No, no, of course not." (That was it, that was what Edmund admired, a factory farm. Oh Edmund, what a lamentable mistake you have been.) "Go on," she said, "please go on."

"All the pigs are out in the fields when it's not raining, rooting about playing."

"Playing? What?"

"Pigs are humorous animals." Willy was quite huffy now.

"I had not realised."

"I believe in my animals having happy lives."

"And after? What about after?"

"After life is ham. I specialise in smoked ham, the trade name is Guthrie."

"I've seen it in Fortnum's catalogue." Poppy steadied the tumble-dryer.

"I have my own smokery."

"Goodness."

"They live cheerfully, die quickly without prior knowledge. They reward me with a fat profit. It's a lot neater than what happens to humans."

"We are not eaten for breakfast."

"You split hairs. Your father—"

Poppy remembered Dad in the hospital bed surrounded by those sad grey old men. He had not been cheerful there. True, his life had been pretty comfortable – very comfortable, if one remembered the Dividend bed – he'd obviously enjoyed himself at the races but what about all those coronaries and although laughter had killed him—

"Do they smell?" she asked, seeking something derogatory to say, trying not to surrender to the description of the farm which sounded bliss. She had always longed for a large bedroom with an open fire. "Do they smell?" she repeated as Willy did not answer.

"About as much as Venice and not all the time. A good pig farm should not smell." (One must be truthful, there were times the pigs smelled, times they did not.)

"Do you grow fond of them?" (Keep on doubting, do not yield to this insidious propaganda.)

"Of course I do. I am particularly partial to Mrs Future and her aunt. I love them." Willy laughed.

"What's funny?" There was something suspicious in Willy's laughter.

"They are pigs of character."

"Tell me about them."

"I brought Mrs Future up on a bottle, she was a runt, she used to follow me about like a dog."

"And her aunt?"

"She's something quite else. Once, to make it easier to care for her, I moved her and her litter. She ate the lot. You remind me of her."

"Thanks a lot," exclaimed Poppy.

"Oh *shit*." Willy trod hard on the brakes as the car was engulfed in sudden dense deafening fog. "Curse it. Can you see out your side? We seem to have hit a bit of road without markings or cats' eyes. Oh bloody hell, I hate fog."

"It's beautiful new macadam." Poppy peered down at the road. "So fresh I can smell it. Delicious."

"Fuck the new macadam." Willy reduced the car to a crawl. The car lights, drowned in the fog, came bouncing back. "You all right?"

"Yes, I think so."

The fog was dense and eerie. Trying to see, seeing nothing, they were quiet for a while, crawling in low gear.

"Can you see the verge?"

"Just. I'll keep my window open." Poppy leaned sideways, watching the verge. "It may only be a patch."

"And it may go on for miles; this road runs along a river." They crawled on, nosing into the fog which fingered cold and wetly into the car. Willy switched on the wipers.

"There's a foghorn," said Poppy.

"It's a cow, stupid. In a field somewhere near."

"Oh."

A motorbicycle came suddenly out of the fog, swerved to avoid them, the rider shouted something antagonistic before disappearing, its noisy engine silenced in the vaporous air.

Suddenly all around them loomed enormous shapes. Dazzled by the headlights a vast Friesian bumped into the car, lurching against it so that the chassis rocked.

Poppy gave a surprised shriek as another cow blew sweet breath in her face through the window, starting back, slipping awkwardly on the road as her nose touched Poppy's cheek, her bland eye rolling in terror.

"I can't see the verge any more," she exclaimed.

Willy edged the car back to the side. "See it now?"

"Yes."

Willy switched off the engine. "Some clot has let these cows out." He got out of the car, cupped his hands round his mouth, shouted, "Anybody with this lot?"

His voice echoed back, "Islot – islot—" "You stay there, I must get them back, find their field, otherwise there will be a smash. There will be a gate open. Sit tight."

Willy disappeared along the road they had come, following the cows. She heard his voice "How-how-how' and soon the cows lumbered past the car at a trot in the reverse direction. For a second she saw Willy following them. "Whoa there, steady there, no need to rush. Stay where you are, I won't be long," he called to her as he and the cows were swallowed into the fog.

For a few minutes the steam rising from the cows' bodies sweetened the fog, then it was back, swirling cold and inimical. There was a strong smell of cowpat and silence.

Curiously afraid, Poppy undid her safety belt and scrambled out of the car. She called, "Willy, Willy."

The fog replied, "Silly – silly", remote, impersonal. She strained her ears, heard nothing. It may be miles before he finds the open gate, hours before he comes back. Supposing this is it, suppose this is the nothing, supposing he is gone?

"Willy." Poppy shouted louder now, urgently, experiencing the acute terror Nature's vagaries can engender. "Why was I so detestable?" she cried aloud and then again, "Willy, come back."

"Ack," rejoined the fog laconically. She stood straining her ears, her hand on the cold metal of the car, beaded with droplets from the fog. Should she switch off the headlights to save the battery? No, they must serve to guide Willy back.

He must come back.

She felt as though she was alone on top of a high mountain in her fear, she felt exalted. She listened so hard she was deafened by the fearful blood thumping in her ears.

The transport lorry hit the car so suddenly there was no time to jump clear. It crunched over the bonnet and straddled the chassis with its giant wheels as it shuddered, clanked, crackled to a stop. Breaking glass tinkled and chinked, there was the smell of hot oil, mingling with cowpat and spilling petrol and the blare of the car horn jammed on by the accident.

Oh God, I've peed all over myself, I am lying in a cowpat. She was flat on her back pinned down.

Slightly concussed, too frightened to lose consciousness, Poppy expected her past life to flash by. At top level her mind rummaged around to locate broken bones and torn sinews, at a deeper level it seemed imperative to recall Dad's message about, what was it, money lenders, racing tips?

She tried to move her head and yelped with pain as the hair was wrenched from her scalp (I am trepanned).

She tried moving her legs but somebody had put them in a bag and bound them tightly.

Warm oil dripped on her face but she could not turn her head to escape it.

I shall drown in a sack, she thought, my legs are paralysed, if I survive I shall be a paraplegic. She tried to call out "Get me out of here" but her mouth filled with oil. She choked and gagged.

She remembered the terror and anguish of falling out of bed during nightmares as a child, all wound up in the bedclothes, and her father coming from his room across the passage to unravel her. She spat out the foul oil.

I have been run over by a lorry and am pinned underneath it.

I am soaked in oil and petrol and when it catches fire I shall fry.

I am paralysed.

I have something to say to Willy, it's important. I was forming a witty phrase when this thing hit me.

I wish someone would turn off the car horn, it is getting on my nerves.

I am too badly hurt to feel anything.

My central nervous system is gone.

I wish I could lose consciousness. I need to tell Willy I love him. This will teach me to prevaricate and play hard to get (not that he was taking a blind bit of notice).

All I want is to be safe in his arms for ever, oh dear God, I am so cold.

Shut up, you fool, stop whingeing and whining and pitying yourself. Listen, listen to hear if there is anyone there.

There may be some sound not drowned by the car's horn. It will stop when the battery goes flat.

This lot may go up in a whoosh of flame before the horn stops.

Somebody *must* have been driving the lorry.

I am alone.

Somebody must have been driving it. There must be somebody there.

Nobody.

The car's horn stopped abruptly.

Running footsteps circled the wrecked vehicles, men's voices, lights.

"The driver's dead."

"Have to cut him out."

"Got a torch?"

"Bring it here." "Who was in the other car?" "They dead too?" "It's empty, some damned fool left it parked." "There's a body here. Run over, looks like. Must have been standing by the car when the lorry hit."

A torch shone in her eyes.

Willy calling, "Poppy, Poppy. Where are you? Answer me." Running, running, frantic.

Poppy spat oil, then, keeping her mouth shut, managed a sort of mooing sound, "OOO—"

A scrabbling behind her head, Willy's voice hoarse with anxiety. "I'm here, darling, I'm on my way."

"Ooooo—" She began to weep.

Willy's face upside-down, his velvet eyes close to hers beady with anxiety, the oil from the crankshaft dropping on to his head now cloying in long trails down his cheeks, his hands reaching round her, exploring her plight, his mouth kissing hers briefly.

"This is a novel sort of Soixante-Neuf. Will you marry me?"

"I can't, I'm paralysed."

"Nonsense, don't be imaginative, your hair and skirt are pinned by the wheel of the lorry." Turning his head to one side Willy yelled, "Someone bring me a knife."

"A what? We're busy with the driver."

"A knife. A fucking knife, hurry up, or scissors."

"OK, OK, keep your cool."

"Better hurry, the petrol isn't safe. Here's a knife, what d'you want it for?" said a voice.

Then Willy speaking gently. "Sorry about this, darling, I'll try not to hurt."

Willy sawing at her hair, her head suddenly free.

"That's better, now let me get at your skirt. Keep still or I'll cut your stomach open. Right. Can you move your legs?"

"Yes." Amazed. "Yes, I can."

"How d'you feel?" His voice quite wobbly.

"The fear of death has sharpened my intellect."

"Great! Now keep still a moment then I'll haul you out."

Willy edged backwards.

"I was so frightened I peed and worse, Willy. Ouch, what are you doing?"

"Pulling you out from under, let me get hold of your arms." Willy heaved, Poppy kicked as she scraped along the tarmac.

"Get a blanket from the ambulance," said a voice bossily.

"Got the stretcher here," said another invitingly.

"Easy does it," said a third. "That was just in time, I'd say."

"Where do they all come from?" Poppy staggered to her feet. The fog was clearing.

"Police and ambulances left over from the pile-up earlier tonight on the motorway." Willy wrapped her in a blanket, kept his arms round her.

"Lie on the stretcher, love," invited a policeman.

"No thanks, I'm perfectly—" She put her hand to her head and felt her hair gone from one side. "Oh."

"You can race Mary growing it." Willy was laughing with relief, covered in oil, his shirt torn.

"What is that?" There was an inert body on a stretcher, they were pushing it up into the ambulance, it looked very dead.

"The lorry driver," said Willy, "don't look."

"Watch out!" cried a man. "Up she goes!"

There was a thump and a whoosh of flame as the entangled machines finally caught. Willy, clutching Poppy, threw himself backwards. They toppled, staggering down a bank into a ditch. As they splashed down Poppy shouted "What did you do that for?" indignantly.

"I don't want to marry a Roman candle." He pulled her along the ditch away from the blaze.

In the distance a fire engine raced, its siren blaring, spreading panic.

Presently, teeth chattering, wrapped in a dry blanket, she was in a police car with Willy. Somehow blessedly he had persuaded these authoritative people that there was no need for the hospital, they could skip it and after answering questions go home.

⋆

Aeons later, awash with sweet tea, still wrapped in a blanket, she was standing beside Willy watching the police car drive away.

Last night's fog was reduced to swags of mist circling round the willows along the stream running through the meadow. A pair of mallard flew up and away with a quack. A rosy sun was swinging up the sky. A bantam cock crowed in the barn.

Calypso's dog, loosed for his morning run, ran over the grass to greet them. A faint smell of pig, sounds of rustling straw, contented grunts and chomping jaws drifted across the yard.

"We both need baths. I'll put a match to the fires."

"Might I meet Mrs Future and her aunt first?"

"Of course."

Willy, watching her walk barefoot across the cobbles, almost choked with emotion. She was so filthy. She looked so comical. "Here they are."

The giant sows were spotless, their flanks pink, their sparse hair crisp and bristly. The row of pearly piglets ranged sleepy, each snout aimed at a teat ready for the next meal.

The sow rustled the straw with her trotters as Poppy leaned over and whispered into an arum lily ear, "Hello, there."

"Ham for breakfast?" suggested Willy lightly.

Poppy looked up. "I realise I should feel flattered at being compared to Mrs F.'s aunt," she said. "I had not realised it was a compliment."

Willy stared at her.

I must get this straight, he thought. She has taken my feeble joke as an insult. She's had a knock on the head, she is probably concussed. She looks too silly for words, I've made a terrible mess of her hair. I shall cut the other side to even it up, give her breakfast and a bath, borrow some clothes from Calypso and take her home. I should never have rushed her in this way. I can't even learn to behave from a pig. I have behaved exactly like that shit Edmund. I need my head examined. Well, there will be plenty of time for that in the years ahead, he thought bitterly. I've really loused this up.

"When I saw you at your father's funeral," he said carefully, "I fell in love with you. As far as I was concerned that was that. I realise I have behaved selfishly in trying to force you. Of course you have your own ideas about what you want to do with your life. I suggest you have a bath. I'll borrow some of my aunt's clothes for you and drive you home in her car as mine is wrecked. I hope you will perhaps remember you felt some of your time in Algiers was quite fun."

"What's got into you?" cried Poppy. "I don't want to borrow your aunt's clothes. I don't want to be driven anywhere in her car. If you want to get shot of me I'll hire a taxi." She raised her voice to a shout.

"Any feelings I had in Algiers were mere hors d'oeuvres, but oh, Willy, could I have something real to eat before we get on with dinner?"

"At once," said Willy, not trusting himself to say more.

As they crossed the yard to his cottage he looked at her sidelong. She looked so funny holding the blanket up to cover her breasts, nearly tripping as it trailed round her feet. She looked like some strange punk with hair chopped from the left side of her head.

"I trust you won't be chopping and changing your mind," he said. "I don't think my nerves could stand it."

"After this I shan't be placing any more bets," she said. "I'm not very good at it."

Willy bent to kiss her, pushing her hair aside, tracing the streaks of oil down her face to her neck.

"One thing we don't need is all this lubrication. Let's get ourselves a bath, see whether we can manage without drowning, then breakfast, how's that?"

Later, eating breakfast, Willy, watching Poppy dressed now in one of his sweaters, her hair still damp from the bath, was seized by a terrible twinge of fear.

"If you *don't* like it here," he said, "you may rather live in London, I have a small house there." He was prepared to give everything up, to sacrifice Mrs Future if Poppy would stay with him (he would of course never forgive her). Since lunching with his old cousin he had almost forgotten the house, his mind obsessed with Poppy; now he saw its value and offered it as a forlorn alternative.

Poppy flushed. "I don't need bribing. When I changed my mind, wouldn't come back here with you, I was under the delusion that what I wanted was a lover, a pleasure man. I thought I might try Victor or Fergus or both." She watched Willy (if I said anything like this to Edmund he would black my eye and be off to Venetia). "Stuck under that lorry I realised that it wasn't just pleasure I wanted, I want the lot. Right?" Have I said too much, been, as usual, a fool? She looked away, afraid of meeting Willy's eyes.

But Willy was laughing, ebullient with relief. "I foresee lots of pleasure," he said, "as well as the rest. Besides," he went on, containing his mirth, able now to tease, "those two jokers are fully booked."

NOT THAT SORT OF GIRL

For Kate

ONE

Nicholas Thornby peered needle-eyed into the delicatessen. The narrow shop was full of customers competing for the attention of servers behind the counter; he squinted in, his view partially obscured by his reflection in the glass door. Recognising several people he had no wish to talk to, he decided Emily's shopping list of smoked cod's roe, soused herrings, Tiptree cherry jam and truffle chocolates could wait until later. Before moving on, he smoothed a hand over his stomach, congratulating himself on its flatness, comparing his reflection favourably with his contemporaries inside the shop. There was no need, he thought disgustedly, to droop round-shouldered, bulge like pregnant women, lose sight of your feet. Pleased with his ghostly reflection, Nicholas moved on before he could be seen, hailed, button-holed, bored. He could guess what was being said inside the shop.

But as he entered the wine shop he found Ian Johnson behind him.

"Morning, Nicholas," Ian said, following him in. "I've only just heard of Ned Peel's death. Harold Rhys told me. Poor, poor Rose. How ghastly for her."

"I dare say he's left her pretty well off," said Nicholas cheerfully. "What price the Beaujolais?" He addressed the lady behind the counter. "I might take some round to the old girl to cheer her up. I'll take six."

"It's hardly a celebration," said Ian.

Nicholas laughed, showing no proper feeling. "Who told you? I thought you were away," he said. "I wonder what else we need?" He looked around the shop.

"I was. Harold Rhys in the delicatessen."

"It's in *The Times*, if you'd looked. Thanks for reminding me I have to go to the delicatessen. I am getting so forgetful. I'll get Rose some of her favourite pâté."

"You know her well?" asked Ian. "Still?"

"Since we were children. Yes, please," to the girl at the counter, "I'll take six. Can you give me a box, I don't trust carrier bags? We knew her long before she married Ned."

"Poor Rose. What did Ned die of?"

"The usual. Accumulation of years, that sort of thing. Will you take a cheque?"

"Of course, Mr Thornby."

"Poor, poor Rose. She will be lost," repeated Ian. Nicholas did not answer, he was busy writing a cheque. (Nicholas Thornby is so original, he refuses to carry credit cards, pays for everything by cheque.) Nicholas clasped the box of bottles to his chest, left the wine shop and headed for the delicatessen. I'll buy her some flowers, he thought. This is quite like old times. In imagination he saw himself buying wine, pâté and flowers for Rose in his bright and springy youth before her marriage: it did not matter that in reality this had never happened. What mattered was that he and his sister Emily had known Rose for many, many years. Piling his shopping into the boot of his car Nicholas smiled secretly and mimicked "Poor, poor Rose," in Ian's lugubrious accents. He remembered Rose shy but merry, easy to tease. Could she have done better than marry decent, honest, nice-looking, well off, unquestionably dull old Ned who was not even particularly faithful? She had been such a pretty girl. Nicholas Thornby drove the three miles out of the market town to Slepe, Ned and Rose's house; now, he supposed, their son Christopher's.

Taking his parcels from the car, Nicholas rang the bell and walked into the hall, calling as he did so, "It's only me, Rose, Nicholas."

Faintly, Rose answered from the floor above, "I'm in the bath."

"Can I come up?"

"Of course."

Nicholas put his parcels on the hall table, climbed the stairs to Rose's bedroom and went in, rapping his knuckles on the door as he did so. He walked across the large light room and looked out of the window at Ned's fat acres. Through the bathroom door he heard Rose splash in the bath: "I won't be long," she called.

Nicholas thought, When we were all young Emily and I would sit on the edge of her bath and gossip or she would sit on the edge of ours and gossip with us. In actual fact, Nicholas had not been there on the edge of the bath, but being so close to his sister he had been there in spirit.

"Do you remember the enormous bath we had at home?" he called over his shoulder to Rose, still invisible in the bathroom.

"Of course I do." Rose, wrapping herself in a robe, came in from the bathroom. "How daring you were; what would your sainted father have said if he'd known about you and Emily?"

Nicholas and Emily's parent had been the rector of the parish, later to evolve into a minor bishop when his wife, who had the undeserved reputation of holding him back, had died.

Nicholas evaded Rose's question by asking, "Rose, are you not asking for trouble leaving the front door open? What would you do if a burglar took it into his head to walk in while you lie there in the bath?"

"The dogs would bark."

"Oh, Rose . . ." Nicholas watched Rose sit suddenly on the edge of her bed and begin to cry.

"All of them in one week." She wiped her tears with the sleeve of her robe. "Pass me those tissues."

Nicholas obliged and watched her blow her nose. ("That stupid thoughtless Christopher," Emily had said. "Letting the dogs loose on the main road, he must have been drunk.")

"Was Christopher drunk?" asked Nicholas.

"No, squabbling with Helen. He has always been cack-handed with dogs, and Helen . . ." Rose stopped crying at the thought of her son and daughter-in-law.

"Are they still here? I didn't see their car," asked Nicholas.

"Went back to London last night, that's why I overslept. Christopher has a lot to do in London and Helen was anxious to get back to her job and the children. She has to plan her life."

"Ah." Nicholas drew out the word. "Aaah . . ."

"Actually, it's been rather marvellous to have the house to myself. Will you turn your back, Nicholas, while I dress?"

Nicholas turned to look out at Ned's acres, watching a slow flock of sheep drift nibbling from right to left. Behind him Rose dressed in faded blue jeans, cotton shirt and striped red and fuchsia sweater. At sixty-seven she was still nice-looking, with clear eyes and hair that had once been ash blonde and was now completely ash, with lots of lines round her eyes and rather large mouth. Her hands betrayed her true age.

"They will be back at the weekend," she said to Nicholas's back, stooped towards the view, his sparse white hair in need of a cut, "to take over."

"So soon?" Nicholas spun round, shocked.

"The sooner the better. What is there to keep me here?" She spread her hands. "I can't wait."

She was amused, laughing at Nicholas. He does not realise, she thought, watching her childhood friend, that when the dogs were killed I was finally alone, far more so than when Ned died. The dogs were the last strand of the persistent thread which has tied me here.

"Who arranged the funeral?"

"Helen, of course . . ."

"I thought Harrods . . ."

"She orders the best, she does her best, she . . ."

"Knows best?"

Rose laughed.

"Why do you let your son and daughter-in-law treat you as though you were half-witted?"

"It makes them happy. They feel useful. Besides," said Rose, justifying her young, "all this is theirs now. Helen might as well begin as she means to go on. She likes to be bossy."

"And Christopher?"

"Christopher is guided by his wife." Rose failed to keep the zest of acidity from her voice.

"What shall you do?" Nicholas asked. Then, sensing that she was unlikely to tell him: "I've brought you some pâté and Beaujolais from the town. Ian Johnson was in the wine shop. Harold Rhys . . ."

"It's their wives' day for the hairdresser."

"Harold Rhys had told him about Ned. He kept saying 'Poor Rose, poor Rose, what will poor Rose do?' Were they such great friends of Ned's, still?" said Nicholas, remembering Ian.

"Well, friends. Yes, I suppose they were in a way. They all played together, were in the war together and latterly fished together. They are poor old men."

"Not so much older than us," said Nicholas, smiling.

"But they know they are old, Nicholas. You and Emily never think of your age."

"And you?"

"Rarely."

"Were Ian and Harold" – Nicholas watched Rose, sitting now at her dressing-table, brush her hair – "your . . . ?"

"I did not meet either of them until I married Ned. Did you say Beaujolais and pâté?"

"Yes."

"Then let us telephone Emily and picnic in the kitchen, if that suits. Unless," said Rose, "you would like to invite old Harold and Ian?"

"You know we don't like them. What's more, Rose, they do not like each other. It was Ned who held them together."

Ned's death, thought Rose, has unleashed more than just me. "Then go and ring Emily, and what about Laura, would she like to join us?"

"I doubt it," said Nicholas. "I had thought of taking you out to that new restaurant on the river, it's said to be good; but I thought it wouldn't, so soon after the funeral, be quite *comme il faut*."

"Damn *comme il faut*. You sound just like my old father. No, we must eat here because I haven't time for anything else, I am going away as soon as I have packed my bag."

"So soon? Where to?"

"I haven't decided yet. Use the telephone in the hall, Nicholas. I need to concentrate on what to take."

Nicholas left the room.

Rose sat on in front of her mirror, her hands in her lap. Looking deep into the glass at the reflections of the room, she murmured, "You, I'll take you." She got up and took from the wall a small picture and, after wrapping it in a nightdress she took from a drawer, put it into an overnight bag, padding it protectively with underclothes and jerseys. Then, fetching her washing things from the bathroom and adding them to the bag, she zipped it up and left the room without a backward glance. Running down the stairs she met Nicholas on his way up from the hall. "She's coming," said Nicholas, "let me take your bag." Rose let him take the bag so that he turned to descend the stairs again. She had no wish for inquisitive Nicholas to note the picture's absence from the wall. "Is this all you are taking?" asked Nicholas. "It's not much."

"I shall not be much away."

"Where?"

"Just somewhere quiet. The telephone has hardly stopped. I need to be alone. I thought just for once the solitude of a good hotel . . ."

"You could come to us, dear Rose."

"But I would not be alone, dear Nicholas. Come now and use your expertise with Ned's frightful corkscrew while I make toast for the pâté."

"Perhaps, since Ned is no longer here, I could use one of the many efficient corkscrews I have given him over the years, or would that be tactless?"

"It wouldn't be tactless. But didn't you know? Ned made a habit of giving your corkscrews, so hintingly given, to friends for Christmas."

"The old swine!"

"No, no. He would not be drawn, that's all."

"He didn't like me, did he?"

"He never said so," said Rose, cutting bread for toast.

"Where will you scatter his ashes?" asked Nicholas spitefully.

Rose did not reply.

"What hotel shall you go to?"

"I'll find one, I haven't thought."

"How long will you be gone?"

"Only a few days, Nicholas. Do stop asking questions." Rose's voice trembled.

"Same old secretive Rose," said Nicholas. It angered him that whereas Rose knew most of what there was to know about his sister

Emily and himself, there was precious little either of them knew about Rose that was not public property since her marriage to Ned in 1939. "Here comes Emily," he said, waving towards a white Ford car coming up the drive.

TWO

"There she goes." Emily Thornby stood with her brother Nicholas watching Rose's car disappear. "Can you see which way she is going?"

"No. The hedge hides the crossroads."

"It would be nice to know where she has gone," said Emily wistfully. "Do you imagine she has an assignation?"

"Rose! At her age! All that sort of thing is long past, if it ever existed."

"So we believe," said Emily.

"And there never was anything of that sort. She has been the model wife, she will now make an ideal widow. Rose's love life never amounted to much, her life has been an open book."

Emily snorted. "That was one of your theories when you called her the ideal daughter . . ."

"When we were far from ideal," agreed Nicholas. "Mind you, I've always thought her father was preferable to ours, I rather envied Rose her father's death."

They had sat with Rose at her kitchen table and eaten the pâté provided by Nicholas. Emily had mixed a salad. Both women had watched Nicholas struggle with Ned's corkscrew to uncork the Beaujolais. He had only succeeded after breaking the cork and had to decant the wine, straining off the bits of cork through muslin.

Rose did not drink more than a glass, while Nicholas and his sister finished the bottle and opened another. Now moderately inebriated, they stood on the steps outside the door which Rose had locked as she left the house. In the hall behind them the telephone rang unanswered, as it had all through the meal, as it would until Christopher, the new owner, the heir, took over or Rose chose to return.

"I bet Christopher installs an ansaphone," said Emily.

"Ned's carefulness with money!" said Nicholas irritably. "No ansaphone is on a par with his manic use of second-class stamps and re-use of envelopes. Just listen to it! How could Rose sit there all through lunch and not answer?"

Emily laughed: "I never told you about Rose and the crabs, did I? I was sure that no one, not even you, would believe me, so I kept quiet about it."

"What are you talking about?" asked Nicholas, suspicious of his sister's tone.

"I am suggesting," said Emily, "that Rose has not been the ideal wife we have watched all these years. I am suggesting that there is more to Rose than meets our eyes."

"Let us sit on her doorstep while you tell me then," said Nicholas, lowering himself on to the stone steps warmed by the afternoon sun. He drew his sister down beside him. "We shall not sit here so intimately when Christopher and Helen are masters but for the moment there is nobody to bother about us." He smiled appreciatively at his sister, seeing in her delicately pointed nose, narrow-lipped mouth, high forehead and inquisitive brown eyes a feminine version of his own beloved self. I wish, thought Nicholas, that I could tint my hair as she does, then we might still be taken for twins. "The chaps in the town are saying, 'Poor, poor Rose, she will be lost.' " Nicholas laughed and Emily, sitting down beside him, laughed too.

"It's nice here." She stretched her legs out beside her brother's, admiring her neat ankles and small feet.

"So, go on. Tell me," prompted Nicholas, "about the crabs."

"Some years ago," Emily turned towards her brother, "I was taking the short cut through Bennett's passage into Waycott Street and up it, you know how steep it is, a Land-Rover was slowly towing a small trailer. The trailer was open and it was full of crabs destined, one supposes, for one of the hotels, or more probably the fish restaurant in Jude Street. Actually, where it was going doesn't matter. I came out into the street as the Land-Rover slowed to turn right into the High Street. There was nobody about except Rose walking up the hill ahead of me. As the trailer drew level with her, quick as a flash, she helped herself to crabs as they went by, putting them into her shopping trolley. Then the Land-Rover went on round the corner and Rose walked on with her booty."

"Were the crabs cooked?"

"Yes."

"She didn't see you?"

"She didn't see me."

"And?"

"That was it. But later I met those boring fishing friends of Ned's, Arthur and Milly, and they told me what a marvellous crab supper they had had *chez* Ned and Rose."

"Oh."

"And Milly said she was particularly impressed because usually she did not think Rose put herself out for them as they were so much more

Ned's friends than hers. Hadn't much in common, was how she put it."

"How marvellous, how absolutely marvellous." Nicholas, who had been holding his breath, let it out in a gust, then leaned his head back against the closed front door and whinnied with laughter.

Emily looked pleased, but Nicholas, recovering from his mirth, said, "If there were this side to Rose which was unknown to us during her married life . . ."

"Forty-eight years."

"Yes, forty-eight years! How can we be sure we really knew her before she married? Was there a Rose we did not know? Have we ever known her?"

"Of course we know her. We knew her as children, as we grew up. We knew the men, such as they were, who might have married her. We knew everything she did. She confided in us, we were her friends. We knew she was a cold fish. Not for Rose the adventures and risks we took. Rose is conventional, she always was, she played safe, got herself married to Ned Peel and all this." Emily nodded back at the house behind them, waved her arm towards Ned's acres. "Find me a better example of her breed and upbringing."

"But," said Nicholas, "with your crab story, you have been suggesting otherwise."

"It must be the exception, the slip which proves the rule," said Emily, feeling a little annoyed with her brother.

"All the same." Nicholas was intrigued. "I would give a lot to get back into the house and go through her things. There might be a ribboned packet of letters, a precious clue which would lead to the discovery of the Rose who would steal crabs, a Rose who has conned us."

"If you went through the house with a fine comb," scoffed Emily, "you would find everything in order, in its place. Ned's farm accounts perfect, their income tax paid. You would find bundles of receipts but no love letters." Now Emily wished she had not presented well-known old Rose to her brother in a new and intriguing light; she feared her tale of the crabs had in a sense boomeranged. "We know Rose," she said with conviction, permitting the smallest note of patronage into her tone.

"Maybe you are right." Nicholas stood up. "It's getting chilly, shall we go home?" Probably, he thought, knowing his sister as well as he knew himself, the crab story never took place. It's more likely Emily saw the load of crabs herself, was tempted to help herself and attributed a non-existent act to Rose. It is the sort of story I make up myself.

"Come on," he said, holding out his hand. "Time to go home."

Emily took his hand, pulled herself up and walked with him hand-in-hand to their cars.

As they walked, it occurred to Nicholas that Rose had deliberately let the telephone ring all through lunch to put a stop to conversation.

THREE

"Would it be possible to have a sandwich in my room?" Rose asked, handing back the pen she had borrowed to sign the register. "Or is it too late?"

The manager, who was also the owner of the hotel, flicked a quick glance at the book as he turned it back towards him, changing his mind as he did so as to which room to offer his guest.

"Would a smoked salmon sandwich and a glass of wine be all right?" (She looked exhausted.) "Half a bottle of Muscadet?"

"Lovely."

"And a little fruit? Peaches, grapes? Brown bread or white? Coffee?"

"Perfect. Brown, please, no coffee."

"I'll lead the way." He picked up Rose's bag. (Goodness, it looks tatty; I've been meaning to replace it for years.) "I will put you in a room on the ground floor. You look out on the creek and can step out into the garden. It has its own bathroom, of course."

"Thank you. I am quite tired." Rose followed the manager along the passage. "I shall enjoy the quiet."

"Would you like to be called in the morning?"

"No," said Rose. "No, thank you. I wake." The trouble is, she thought, unpacking her few belongings, I don't sleep.

She busied herself putting toothbrushes and sponge in the bathroom, laying her nightdress on the bed, keeping her thoughts at bay, as she had managed so successfully on the long drive from Slepe, a drive to nowhere in particular until at the end of the long afternoon she had seen the sign which said "Hotel", and followed a winding lane down a wooded valley to arrive at this place, hitherto unknown to her.

She opened the window and looked out on to a lawn sloping down in the dusk to the water. A swan, its head tucked under its wing, drifted close to the bank; further out the cob swam placidly. Across the creek she could just make out the silhouette of a heron, immobile on a branch overhanging the water.

"How long is she going to stay?" asked a woman's voice from further along the building, its tone of irritation amplified by the water. "I have just got that room ready for the Dutch couple who are booked for Tuesday."

"Then you will have to get it ready again, won't you? She didn't say."

"Why," a note of rising ire, "why did you not ask her?"

"Hurry up with those sandwiches, don't forget the lemon. I put her there because she looks the sort who will recommend us to her friends," the manager snarled.

Leaning out of the window Rose listened for a contemptuous snort, smiled.

"With those clothes? With that shabby bag?" asked the woman. "Why is she travelling alone?" Her suspicion was almost tangible. One of them, Rose presumed the husband, banged the window down. Out on the creek, a coot cried and was answered. There was a knock on the door.

Rose drew away from the window. "Come in."

"Your sandwiches." She recognised the voice. "Is there anything else you would like?" The woman wore good looks masked by an expression of martyrdom.

"No, thank you. This looks delicious. I will put the tray outside the door when I have finished. Have you had a very busy season?" The trick of making herself agreeable was automatic.

"You can say that again," exclaimed the woman. (For two cents she will tell me how she hates her husband, how overworked and unappreciated she is.) "Shall I turn the bed down? Have you enough towels?" The woman peered into the bathroom, assessing Rose's toothbrushes and Greek sponge.

"No, no thank you. It's all lovely; thank you so much for all your trouble. Good night." Rose sat by the tray that held the sandwiches. She was suddenly ravenous and began to eat as the woman went out and closed the door.

Outside it was now dark. She finished eating, poured herself wine, went and stood by the window. Shafts of light illumined the grass, the angry voices were stilled, a secret cat crossed the beam of light and rejoined the night. I am travelling alone, thought Rose, and waited for memories of Ned to crowd into her mind, but all she felt was a surge of heretical pleasure at being properly alone for the first time since 1939.

Sipping her wine, she looked out at the water glittering blackly and savoured her pleasure. Her wine finished, she put the tray outside her door, locked it, switched the telephone by the bed to "Off", undressed, brushed her hair, went to the bathroom to clean her teeth and wash, smooth cream into her face, slide the nightdress over her head.

Ready for bed, she reached into the overnight bag for the picture she had taken off her bedroom wall and put it propped on the dressing-table where she could see it from the bed. She got into bed, switched off the bedside light, pulled the bedclothes up to her chin, lay back, closed her eyes and courted composure. Then, remembering Nicholas and Emily's expressions of pain as she let the telephone ring loud, intermittent, unanswered all through lunch, she began to laugh so that under her the bed shook. The probability was that all the messages would have been more or less identical, safe enough for the pricked ears of Nicholas and Emily. Yet one of the callers might have been Mylo. The risk of its not being Mylo had been so great that she had left the telephone unanswered.

FOUR

"Have you definitely made up your mind?" Mylo held her against him, teasing her hair through his fingers, bending to nuzzle her neck. "Snuggle up close, then you won't feel cold." He leaned back against the tree, feeling the bark rough against his spine. "Answer me, Rose."

"No, no, oh, Mylo." She put her arms round his neck, reaching up to him. "It's so difficult, so hard." She pitied herself.

"No, no, you won't marry him, or no, no, you haven't made up your mind?" He pulled away from her, trying to see her eyes in the dark. "It's not hard. You don't love Ned Peel, you love me. He's an old man, you can't . . ."

"He's only thirty-one."

"And you are eighteen. It makes me ill to think of him touching you; you can't possibly marry him," said Mylo violently.

"My father . . ."

"Your father thinks you will be safe with him. I bet that's what he says." (He would say: I want to die feeling that you are safe, that you are provided for. Were it not for this "cancer" I would not press you to make a decision. I am anxious for you. There is going to be a war. Married to Ned, you will be safe and with my "cancer" I cannot ensure you will be. And so on and on, with the repetition of the dreaded word in inverted commas, the stress on security.) "He knows the man," Mylo went on, "he has this house in the country, he knows he is well off, he will have informed himself, spoken with Ned of marriage settlements. Of course he has, I've heard of his kind. He knows Ned's job, knows what he earns, knows the form. Has he any idea what being in bed with Ned will be like? Has he put himself in your shoes?"

Rose giggled. "I can't see Father and Ned tucked up together."

Mylo shook her. "Rose, stop it. You know you love *me*, *me*."

"Yes," she said, "I do."

"So what's so difficult?"

"It's all difficult," weakly, for she was tired. Rose began to cry. Impossible to repeat her parents' opinion of Mylo. (A nice boy, of course, but only nineteen, no prospects, no money, no family, no job, hasn't even been to university, good looking in his way, speaks French. The speaking of French was somehow derogatory, louche, dangerous.) Their argument had gone on the whole evening, all through dinner in the restaurant and in the car driving out of London to the relatively quiet spot where they now stood on Wimbledon Common. She felt that all she wanted was to go to bed and sleep, forget her father, forget Ned Peel, even forget Mylo. "He is dying," she said, as she had said several times before, "he has cancer."

"I don't believe he has cancer. I think he is using a rather unsubtle blackmail. I think your father is a snob. He is impressed by Ned Peel and his worldly goods. It's a very old story. He'd like to boast about 'my son-in-law, Ned Peel', look him up in *Who's Who*."

"He'd never say that."

"Not in so many words. It's the elevation by implication . . ."

"Anyway," Rose said bitterly, "he couldn't say it, he'd be dead."

A car passed along the road; the tears on Rose's cheeks glittered in its headlights. The driver, a happy man, seeing the lovers, gave an appreciative toot on his horn.

"I bet you he will live for years and years," said Mylo nastily, "the old fraud."

"Mylo!"

"He will, like to bet?"

"You are calling my father a liar." She swung away angrily.

"I am. You wouldn't be so angry if you didn't know it's true. Your father would absolutely panic that you would ruin your prospects – that's how he'd put it – by marrying me. He knows I have no money, he'd think me far too young, nothing alarms a solicitor more than insecurity."

"Take me home." Rose walked to Mylo's little car parked on the grass verge. "I've had enough of this, I shall do what I please. I do not belong to you; all you do is make me miserable. It's terribly late and I promised I would be in by twelve. The aunt I am staying with is extra respectable and quite strict, she thinks late nights are immoral."

"One can also be immoral by day," said Mylo caustically, "not that you go in for it, silly little prude."

Rose said nothing, biting back a mixture of hurtful and/or loving, joking retorts. How on earth, she asked herself, have we got ourselves into this misery?

Mylo drove back into London. He had said too much, gone too far. "I am off to France," he said. "I've got a job."

Rose's heart turned over.

"I wanted it to be a surprise," said Mylo. "Now I shan't see you again. I wanted to take you with me. We could have managed; it would have been fun." (It was unlikely he would be allowed to take Rose, but never mind.)

Rose sat beside Mylo saying nothing, feeling a void opening in the heart that for the whole year had overflowed with Mylo.

"It's pretty stupid," said Mylo conversationally, keeping his eyes on the road, "we haven't even slept together. There has never been anywhere to go and I do so terribly want you . . ." He gripped the wheel tightly. They were crossing Putney Bridge, a flock of gulls flew down river. "It's all right, I shan't drown myself or anything. It just seems so wasteful that I have never held you naked in my arms, never spent a whole night with you, never learned with you how to make love. We could have learned together." He guided the car into the King's Road, past the World's End. "World's End," he said. "Well, our bit of World looks like ending. Where are you staying, I forgot to ask?"

"Chester Street."

"I dare say Ned Peel knows how to book in for a night at an hotel with a girl without curling up with embarrassment in inexperienced agony. He is not nineteen, he's an experienced man of thirty-one. It's possible, though he doesn't look the type, that he's done it often. He really does look reliable and safe, one can see the charm he holds for your father. I dare say your respected pa is absolutely right. Here's your aunt's street, what's the number?"

The bitterness in Mylo's voice was dry and crisp as the east wind.

"Twenty-two. The green door, by the pillarbox, just here." Rose got out of the car. "It's dreadfully late. I must creep in and not wake her. Good night." They did not kiss.

"I'll wait and see you safely indoors," he said.

"I have a key."

"I'll wait."

Rose fumbled in her bag for the latchkey, put it in the lock, turned it, pushed the door. "I'm locked out," she said incredulously.

"Ring the bell." Mylo watched her.

Both were astonished when the door suddenly flew open and Rose's aunt let fly.

"I hadn't realised she was like that," said Rose presently, standing by the coffee stall at Hyde Park Corner sipping boiling tea from a china mug, still so shocked by her aunt's invective that she had to hold the mug with both hands for fear of letting Mylo see how they shook. "What a surprise," she attempted a joke, "she slammed the door like an expert chucker-out."

"I thought whore, prostitute and tart all meant the same thing; her vocabulary isn't exactly original," said Mylo. "Where did she get her ideas about sinful and loose-living youth?"

"Father says she was unhappily married, distrusts men."

"Perhaps her husband had lots of outside sexual encounters. Where shall I take you now? What about Nicholas and Emily, aren't they friends of yours? You could come with me to France, of course."

"No, I can't go to them." Rose shied from the suggestion of the Thornbys, ignored the allusion to France.

"They don't seem the type to think I'd robbed you of your virginity in Park Lane."

"She didn't say Park Lane, she said 'dingy nightclub'. I said I'd rather not go to Nicholas and Emily's."

"She implied every conceivable indecency, suggested things I'd never heard of." (As though there could ever be indecency between me and Rose.) "Don't let's think about her, she's a nasty old woman," said Mylo.

Will she write or telephone my father? Rose wondered. He is so ill, it would be the last straw.

Mylo read her thoughts. "She won't bother your father; that sort of person keeps the hatch on her sewer. More tea, my love?" Rose shook her head. "I am staying with an aunt too, another sort of aunt, I'll take you there. She will give us breakfast and lend you money to get home. Come along, it's across the Park, she lives in Bayswater."

As they drove across the Park, Mylo said quietly, "Rose, don't rush into marriage with Ned. He's a nice chap; I'm jealous, that's all. There's nothing really wrong with him, but you are only eighteen. Even if you don't want me, you may find you want somebody else. There's the whole world, Rose, all your life."

Rose did not answer.

Mylo stopped the car by the Serpentine bridge. "Let's be quiet a minute and watch the water."

The Park was empty at this early hour, nobody about, London as still as it ever is.

"Shall we walk a little way?" Mylo got out of the car and held out his hand to Rose.

They strolled by the water, watching the water fowl. Ducks cruised, coots paddled in desperate haste to reach the reeds, calling to each other with sharp querying cries.

Under the bridge Mylo stopped and kissed Rose gently.

"I warn you, I shall have at least one more try before I give up," he said, "in any case even if we never meet again I am in your bones. It can't be helped. I know it, and you would too if you were honest. We can't escape. I will go to France. You may marry Ned. However unhappy we are, and I hope we won't be, we shall always have each other. Tell you what," said Mylo, laughing now, "I will telephone from time to time all through our lives."

"All down the years?" Rose mocked, yet felt a lift of spirit.

"You never know," said Mylo. "But the first time will be soon, you won't have long to wait."

Rose was uncertain how to take this. "Is that a threat or a promise?"

Mylo grinned. "I shall marry too, perhaps find myself a beautiful girl, kinder than you."

Rose drew in her breath.

"You can't have it all your own way," mocked Mylo. "I can't delay my sex life indefinitely, can I?"

Rose did not answer.

"Besides," said Mylo, walking her briskly back to his car, "there are more things than marriage to worry about. There will be a war soon; that will keep us busy."

"Ned is in the Territorials."

"Ned would be; his future role tidily arranged. My darling, do you realise what an utterly conventional life you are letting yourself in for?"

"I may enjoy it." She was defensive.

"We were going to travel the world, I seem to remember. Visit Russia, explore the Balkans, discover Greece, cross the Andes, explore Tibet."

"I shall travel with Ned."

"I dare say you will and at the back of your mind you will always be wondering whether it would not be more fun to be with Mylo."

"Shut up."

"Get into the car, my love."

Mylo drove slowly towards Bayswater. By the look of the sky it was going to be a beautiful day.

"And, in bed with Ned, you will wonder whether this curious act of sex would not with Mylo turn into something sublime."

"Shut up."

Mylo stopped the car outside his aunt's home.

"Promise me one thing, Rose, you owe me that."

"All right."

"When I send for you urgently to come and meet me, you needn't do anything you don't want to do, but just come."

"How can I?"

"You will manage." Mylo had confidence.

FIVE

Stretching her legs down into the bed, Rose tried to remember Ned. Easily she visualised his upright figure in greenish tweeds. The ancient but beautifully cut coat. The knee breeches he affected, ribbed stockings, brogue shoes, if it were fine. If wet or cold, he would wear a green quilted waistcoat, green gumboots and a greenish waxed rainproof jacket with poacher's pockets. Round his neck the soft scarf she had given him, dark red this, underneath a checked Viyella shirt and either a knitted tie or his old school tie, which he wore as unashamedly as had been the mode when he was a young man; topping the lot would be a checked cap or a tweed hat with flies stuck in it.

Ned's face was harder to remember than his clothes. A narrow-lipped mouth, watery blue eyes giving the impression that he drank, which he did not, a thick reddish nose which by its coarseness spoiled his otherwise rather distinguished appearance. His chin, a good feature in his youth, had mysteriously doubled, mysterious since he was not a fat man, more on the spare side.

More on the spare side, Rose repeated to herself while she waited for the memories which should now come flooding into her widowed mind.

Since no memories came, she tried dressing Ned in his London gear (they had after all lived much of their life in London), but although she could see Ned well enough in his navy pinstripe, his charcoal – almost black – suit, his Prince of Wales check, his camel-hair overcoat, even in his boring old striped pyjamas, Ned steadfastly refused to come to life. Which, thought Rose, as she lay in the strange hotel bed, is quite natural since he died ten days ago and is cremated.

She got out of bed and padded to the window, opened it to let in the night. The air rushing in was chilly; getting back into bed she switched on the electric blanket. This hotel was a lucky find – every comfort. "*Tout confort.*" Who said that? Mylo, of course. "*Tout confort,*" he had said, holding her tightly in his arms that first time in that fearfully uncomfortable hotel in the shabby little port where they had their first rendezvous.

Suddenly Ned materialised in her widowed mind's eye. Ned

watching her read the letter from Mylo with its neatly worked-out instructions for the intricate journey. "You take the boat as usual from Dunoon to Glasgow; from Glasgow you take the 11.30 train to Crewe. At Crewe you wait an hour, then catch the train for Holyhead. I shall be waiting on the station platform, You need do nothing you don't want to, but I absolutely must see you before I leave the country. This may well be our last chance to meet." Had Ned, watching her read Mylo's letter, also heard her answer the telephone two days before? The unexpected, for she had taken care not to tell him the Scottish address, call from Mylo, long distance. He had said, "I am in Dublin. I have written the trains and boat you must take to meet me. Do not fail me." And, clever Mylo, he had rung off before she could prevaricate or protest or get his number to ring back.

She had felt unease that he was in Dublin when she had believed him to be in France. Her thoughts when they strayed to Mylo had crossed the Channel, even caught the boat train to Paris. What was he up to in Dublin?

What had Ned been thinking as he watched her read the letter? Her heart jolting in her chest, she had said, keeping her voice casual, "Oh, damn, I had quite forgotten, how awfully rude of me. The Wigrams are expecting me on Wednesday. I shall have to leave a day early. They are my father's greatest friends" (well, they might be, if they existed). "I am so sorry, how maddening." She had held the letter out to Ned as though it was a nothing letter, a letter from an expectant hostess, taking the risk that Ned would take it, read it, but more probably not since he read with difficulty without his glasses and with luck would have left them upstairs. With her heart in her throat, Rose gambled on Ned's eyesight and good manners.

"Of course you must go," he had said, "but this means I cannot drive you home."

"Oh," she had said, "I'll take the train – she says I have to change at Crewe."

"I promised to give Nicholas and Emily a lift home and we cannot make them cut their visit short, they are relying on me."

"Of course. Never mind. It's not for long. You can't let them down, they can't afford the train." Gratefully she thanked God for the Thornbys' sponging habits, their continual cries of poverty.

"Poor you. How boring for you." Emily with her usual needle eye had noticed nothing. "The separation," said Emily, "will add spice to your engagement and, who knows, some good may come out of your duty visit, a sumptuous wedding prezzie, perhaps?"

Ned had proposed to her the evening before, walking along the river valley. Weighed down by her father's cancerous wish Rose had accepted him to the sound of curlews crying in the bog further up the hillside.

It was not an entirely fraudulent thing to do, thought Rose, lying alone in the strange hotel, part of me wanted to marry Ned. Much of me longed for the security, a house in London, the house in the country; the big wedding was tempting, the clothes I had never been able to afford. I was almost in love with Ned in August 1939 in Scotland at the house party for the grouse shooting, surrounded by his approving relations who thought I would do very well for Ned. (A nice little thing, quite pretty, she'll shape.) They had known, those relations, what was required of Ned's wife. At eighteen, thought Rose, I hadn't the remotest idea.

Lying in the dark Rose thought she heard a curlew cry and into her mind's eye came Ned's face, not as it had been when he died, but as he was in 1939 before his hair thinned and greyed, before his face grew lined. He was an awfully nice man, she thought. I was very fond of him, what a lovely friend he would have made; I must have been mad to marry him. I did not hear a curlew cry, I imagined it.

Ned had driven her to the boat at Dunoon, giving up a day's shooting to do so. Her future aunt- and uncle-in-law had pressed upon her two brace of grouse to take to her imaginary hostess, Mrs Wigram. Rose remembered gulping back laughter, a tearful attack which was assumed to be sorrow at the parting with Ned. "No need to cry, dear, you will see him in a few days." Her future aunt-in-law had pressed her against her large and rather squashy breasts, smacking her lips in the air with a parting kiss. "There!"

Nicholas and Emily had come for the drive and to do some desultory shopping in the town. Even then, thought Rose amused, they were prying inquisitively into my life. Ned's relations had stood on the front steps waving goodbye, pleased that Ned's future was settled, regretful that she must depart a day early but, good manners apart, impatient to be off for the day's shooting; a group of ghillies and beaters were waiting. And who else, thought Rose, peering back down the years, who else was there?

Ned's cousins, two soon to be killed in the war, and yes, of course, Harold Rhys and Ian Johnson, jolly high-spirited bachelors in those days, Ned's friends. It would not be long before they too married and began the long decline towards arthritis, piles, deafness, obesity, operations for this and that, collections of grandchildren, irritating sons-in-law, the decline which turned them into what they were now, dull old men. But, in those days, Rose remembered, they felt it their right, their duty, too, to make a pass at every girl in the house party and they expected the girls to be flattered.

Why did I tell Nicholas this morning that I did not know Harold and Ian until after Ned and I were married? He was hinting, was he not, that I might have flirted, had an affair with one or both of them. Poor Nicholas, he is obsessed, as is Emily, with my secret life for which there is no evidence. They sniff the air, they ferret from force of habit. I was careless, upset thinking of the dogs, my dear dogs crushed by the lorry. He will remember Ian and Harold were there in Scotland, for he was there too. My mind slips as I grow old.

She saw herself sitting beside Ned in his open car driving over the hills to Dunoon. She watched herself boarding the boat carrying the grouse, the boat drawing away from the quay; Ned, Emily and Nicholas waving; Ned shouting that they would choose the engagement ring when they met soon in London; she had waved back, and then alone at last on the boat she had faced the day-long journey to Holyhead with a mixture of trepidation and joy.

Only a very naïve person would get away with what I did, thought Rose. It would not have occurred even to Nicholas and Emily that I was not on my way to stay with the Wigrams, a duty visit to my father's friends, but that I was travelling to meet Mylo.

The charm of the situation had been that Nicholas and Emily hardly knew of Mylo's existence in her life, and neither did Ned. Remembering the journey Rose relived her fears. The fear of discovery by her parents or Ned, but principally the fear that at the end of the journey Mylo would not be there.

Rose remembered putting the grouse on the rack on the train from Glasgow to Crewe. At Crewe she had deliberately left them there, but a fellow passenger had shouted as the train drew out of the station, gesticulated, thrown the dead birds to a porter. Oh, those bloody birds, thought Rose, and tried to remember how she had rid herself of them, and could not. (The gaps in the memory as one grows old.) My fears, thought Rose, remembering vividly, my fears were so great.

And then at the end of the everlasting day as the train drew into the station at Holyhead, Mylo was on the platform, his face drawn and strained: "I thought you might not come," he had said, and later in the awful little Commercial Hotel they had gone through the brownish hallway which smelled of stale tobacco and beer, of years of vegetables cooking and failure, up the straight stairs to a room with a double bed. He had shut the door. "It's pretty shoddy, I'm afraid." Then holding her, sitting on the bed, bouncing to test it, he had said, his voice rasping, a little husky, "*Tout confort*," trying to lighten their situation, their love, their fear, their ignorance.

Who in these days, Rose wondered as she listened to the night sounds, the small breeze which now whispered through the reeds by the water, who in these days would credit that a girl of eighteen and a boy of nineteen should both be virgin? For that fear, the exquisite fear of the actual act of making love, terrified them, she remembered, though Mylo who assumed he knew how to set about it pretended not to be afraid (and so, to be fair, did she).

"What did the man at the desk think?" Rose had whispered. They had signed the register with trepidation.

"Thinks us a honeymoon couple," answered Mylo stoutly.

"Arriving separately?" Rose had jeered. "Oh, Mylo."

"It doesn't matter, forget him. You are here now. Kiss me."

They had hugged and kissed. Then, Rose remembered his arms round her, that his ribs were quite painful against her chest. They had drawn apart breathless, laughing.

"The bed's pretty lumpy," Rose had said. Then, "Shall we go out before it gets dark, go for a walk along the cliffs?"

They jointly put off what was to come.

I have never been back, thought Rose, the town must have doubled, trebled in size, perhaps even the cliffs where we walked have changed since that summer nearly fifty years ago.

They had wandered along the clifftop hand in hand, listening to the seagulls, meeting no one, leaned over looking down and watched the seals bobbing innocently below them close to the rocks, their faces turning this way and that on thick necks, rolling their oily eyes.

In the late afternoon they had clambered down to a stony cove and Mylo said, "Let's swim."

"No bathing things," she objected.

"Naked then, nobody to see us."

Greatly daring, she undressed near the water's edge, waded quickly in, the stones hurting her feet. The water was ice cold. She looked back, saw Mylo naked, magnificent. She had never seen a naked man, was aghast at the size of his sex.

She swam a few strokes out, turned, came back, climbed up the stones raking up and down in the swell, dried herself inadequately with a handkerchief, dressed.

But Mylo, confidently treading the cobbles, dived shallowly, swam out strongly. She watched his body gleaming silvery through the green water.

The seals had gone; she climbed the cliff, watched Mylo swim, waited for him to return.

He had said "You needn't do anything you do not want," but she knew, want to or not, she would do it.

Oh, poor us, moaned Rose, nearly fifty years later. What a shambles in that lumpy bed. How ironic the "*tout confort*". How frustrating for Mylo, how painful the whole experience.

"You are nervous, my sweet, try and open up, be happy."

"Happy," Rose murmured, now in recollection. Happy, she thought wryly; what was needed was a tin opener. If I was hurt, what about Mylo, what about him? He too must have been sore. Funny, she thought, now in the present lying alone in recollection, I never asked him whether he hurt himself. Eventually he had slept, his head on her breast, his arms around her body and she, wakeful as now, listened to his breathing, as now she listened to the night and smiled at their tragi-comic abortive attempt at making love.

Mylo had left in the very early morning on the boat to Dublin and she had caught the nine-thirty train to London where three days later Ned took her to Cartier to buy the engagement ring, putting on his glasses to inspect it.

Three days after that, Mr Chamberlain declared war. They were married at the end of September.

SIX

Mr Chamberlain's declaration of war delighted Rose, it relieved her mind, put paid to the possibility of questions such as How was the journey to the Wigrams? Had she enjoyed herself? Who else was staying there? Had they been pleased with the grouse? Nobody was interested in her mythical visit, everybody was adjusting to the war; those with the more active imaginations, for imminent death. For Rose the war was of secondary importance; filling her mind was the paramount question – was she or was she not pregnant?

The relief after ten days of crippling fear at the arrival of her period was so great that she was slow to take in the movement set in train by Ned and his family conjointly with her parents towards a wedding, hers to Ned. Ned insisted on an early date. He was joining his regiment immediately, he would get leave for his marriage then install Rose at Slepe, where she would live while he was away. She was not consulted, her agreement was taken for granted.

Ned, with his sensible orderly mind, had, it seemed, not only anticipated the war but made his preparations. Deploring the idea of evacuees in his beloved house, he had months before arranged for the greater part of it to be taken over by a branch of the Ministry of Information, only keeping a minimum of rooms for his own use and now, of course, for Rose.

Emerging from her fog of secret fear, rejoicing over her blood-stained knickers, Rose discovered that a lot had been going on without her. Her parents and the Peel contingent brushed her lovingly aside. "We are managing very well." The words "without you", while not actually voiced, were implied. The advent of war demanded short cuts, fast action, no hanging about. There was no time for prevarication on the bride's part; it would be best for her to keep quiet and let those who knew what's what to get on with it. Rose could usefully answer the telephone and relay messages, said her mother. So she fidgeted about the house waiting for the telephone to ring, answering it breathless in case the caller was Mylo: it never was.

If Mylo had got in touch, if I had heard his voice, Rose asked herself fifty years later, would I have gone to him?

The question nagged intermittently over the years, receiving no clear answer. A second question for which she had no answer was how and why had she so weakly – as she thought in the strength of old age – allowed herself to be steam-rollered by that inexorable tide of goodwill? Why had she not spoken up loud and clear, said quite simply, "I do not want to marry Ned"?

While dallying with the idea of getting engaged to Ned she had dreamily anticipated a long engagement during which there would be pleasurable shopping for a trousseau, time to acquaint herself with Ned's friends and relations, time to decide whether his ideas and hers agreed in principle (did I have any ideas?). Whether their tastes were similar, time to get to know each other. Above all, time to change her mind, time to break off the engagement.

It seemed, though, that during the ten days of what she later thought of as her phantom pregnancy an unstoppable juggernaut of family custom had started to roll. She and Ned would be married in the church where all Peels got married (no time for the banns to be called, a special licence was obtained). A bishop who was also a Peel would officiate, on condition he skipped the reception and caught the train at Liverpool Street to dash back to his diocese. She was to wear a veil of Peel family lace and round her neck the Peel diamonds whipped out of the bank for the occasion. Ned's aunt Flora's French dressmaker was willing to run up the wedding dress in record time provided the design was plain (Rose later had it dyed black and wore it for years). The honeymoon would not be spent in some exotic location but at Slepe, the marriage beginning as it must go on, at home.

Rose spoke up once, her voice squeaky with nerves, to her mother busy writing the wedding invitations; "I can't think what you want *me* for, couldn't you hire a model for the day?"

Without looking up, her mother had replied, "Don't be difficult, darling. If you've got a pain go and lie down with a hot-water bottle; if not, you can make yourself useful addressing these envelopes. Here's the list."

I lacked gumption, thought Rose in old age, I dithered. The parents and Ned were so enjoying it all it would have been wicked to spoil their pleasure, deny them their wedding.

And still during those long hot September days, while Whitehall wrapped itself in sandbags and the population of London began to dress in khaki and blue, the telephone rang, but it was never Mylo.

Hard as it is to credit now, thought Rose, I was moulded by custom and family pressure, by what was right and proper for them, by what was expected of me from the moment of my conception: not unlike an animal, a pig, a racehorse, a prize winner at Cruft's.

Yet there was Mylo who did not conform, and Nicholas and Emily who even then could scarcely be accused of conformity.

Rose turned on her side in the strange bed, pressed her cheek into the pillow remembering Emily's sharp nose, bright inquiring eyes when she pottered in to ask, "What are you going to do in the war?"

"I'm getting married."

"I know that, I mean war work."

"I hadn't thought. What shall you do?"

"We are considering possibilities, finding out what will be the most amusing for us."

"Us?"

"Nicholas and me."

"Won't he join up?"

"Nicholas does not want to do anything dangerous, neither of us do. We leave that to the Hoi Polloi." Emily managed to give this description of her fellow-men capital lettering. Rose remembered being jolted by Emily's honesty.

"There are lots of reserved occupations, we shall stay together," Emily had said.

"Oh," Rose had said. "Oh," rather shocked by Emily's independent spirit which about that time was beginning to show itself openly.

But Emily had switched her attention from herself and her brother to Rose. "Rose," she had said. They were sitting in the hall of Rose's home attending to the telephone which was at that moment idle. "Rose," lowering her voice slightly, for Rose's mother was reputed to have the hearing of a bat. "Rose, do you know anything about sex? We are worried for you." She leaned towards Rose, looking her straight in the eye. "Do you?"

"Of course I do." Rose had flushed. "I am getting married, aren't I?"

"That's why I asked, why we worry. I bet you know nothing. That's why I came round especially to see you, we . . ."

"We?"

"Nicholas and I. We don't think you know the first thing. Have you for instance ever seen a naked man?"

"I have." (Oh, exquisite Mylo!)

Emily laughed. "Rubbish. Statues perhaps. The real thing is different. Statues have very small cocks. Honestly, Rose, we are concerned about you. What has your mother told you? I bet she's told you nothing. I bet I'm right."

"She said she supposed I knew all about such things."

"What things?"

"I supposed she meant – you know."

"And you said?"

"I said, yes, I did."

"I bet you did." Both girls went off into a fit of high-pitched giggles. Rose's mother called from upstairs, where she sat at her desk addressing the last of the wedding invitations. "What are you girls laughing at, what's the joke?" not expecting an answer. Emily, recovering her composure, whispered, "She didn't even tell you to buy a pot of vaseline?"

"Whatever for?"

"Oh, we were right! You know nothing, nothing at all. Nicholas and I have a bet on it."

"I suppose you two know it all," Rose had said huffily. (Never, never would she divulge about Mylo.)

"We thought we had better tell you before you get too great a surprise, getting married might be quite a shock."

"No thanks, it's no business . . ."

"We don't want a repetition of when you started the curse," said Emily relentlessly. "If your mother couldn't bring herself to tell you about that she won't have told you what happens in bed with Ned or any other man for that matter, though Nicholas swears you will never commit adultery, we have a bet on that too."

"I . . ." Rose remembered the humiliating experience of getting her first period while staying the night at the Rectory. Nicholas and Emily had been surprisingly informative and kind, they had not mocked. Her mother, when she returned home with the news, had said awkwardly, "I had meant to tell you some time." Perhaps, Rose remembered thinking, perhaps some time after her marriage to Ned her mother would break to her the rudiments of sex. "All right," she said grudgingly to Emily, "fire away."

Listening to Emily she was amazed by Emily's powers of invention. Some of it may be true, she had thought, but she's crazy if she thinks it's fun. When Emily stopped for breath Rose asked, "How d'you know all this?"

"We . . ." began Emily, then stopped, laughed in what for her served for embarrassment, altered course. "We have made you an appointment with Helena Wright."

"Who's she when she's at home?"

"The contraceptive doctor, she's famous," Emily whispered.

"Oh."

"We thought we'd give you that as a wedding present. Something practical to remember us by."

"How thoughtful." Rose was overwhelmed by their interference. Even for Emily and Nicholas this was going too far. Could they have guessed at her phantom pregnancy? "No, thank you," she exclaimed. "Please don't." She realised that to accept such a present would connect Emily and Nicholas for ever with her every sexual experience, making of them some sort of godparents. Five decades later Rose thought she might not have been sufficiently grateful for their imaginative suggestion. She had postponed making an appointment for herself until after her honeymoon when she had become more brusquely aware of what Emily referred to as "the facts", a belated act which might if she had married some man other than Ned have cost her dear, precipitating Christopher into the world before his time. But Ned, so sensible, was also cautious; just as he had prepared for war so he prepared for marriage.

I remember little of my wedding, thought Rose, lying solitary in the hotel bed. My mother chose the hymns, Ned's aunt Flora chose the flowers (I hated gladioli then, I have hated them unforgivingly since). I remember Ned's bishop uncle gabbled the service; was he afraid of missing his train? I remember walking down the aisle on Ned's arm with the Peel veil tossed back so that I was able to see, as I had not been able coming up it with my father, searching the congregation for Mylo, but he was not among them and he was not in the small crowd which had gathered to gawp outside the church. He was not there.

SEVEN

"I think that went off very well." Ned took his hand off the wheel and felt for Rose's hands folded in her lap; he squeezed the fist they made. "Happy, dear?"

"Yes."

That might have been the moment when she could have told Ned that she detested being called "dear", simply loathed it. Being called "dear" made her curl up. But it was already too late. She would learn to smother her irrational dislike of this endearment and be glad that "darling" belonged to Mylo. When Mylo said darling in the voice which sounded like honey kept so long in its jar it had become gritty, her whole being responded.

So in late September 1939, driving out of London on their way to Slepe when Ned squeezed her hands and said, "Happy, dear?" Rose answered brightly, "Yes."

Thanks to Ned's planning the wedding had gone off without a hitch. Ned liked planning; his attention to detail would presently stand him in good stead in the army just as it already did in business. By the end of the war he would be a staff officer. He congratulated himself that his decision to get married put in train by a conversation with his Scottish uncle was working out so well.

Some time previously, on a bitter January day, Ned had sat with his uncle Archibald Loftus on the sofa at the top of the stairs in the vestibule of the Hyde Park Hotel watching the people coming in and out from Knightsbridge. They had lunched at his uncle's club, where over potted shrimps and steak and kidney pudding Uncle Archibald had suggested that now Ned had reached the age of thirty and come into his inheritance it might be advisable for him to marry. It was Uncle Archibald's habit to tender some piece of useful advice to his nephew on the rare occasions when they met. Ned had already agreed in principle and they had returned to the hotel where his uncle and aunt were staying on a foray south to the capital from their home in Argyllshire. Now they sat amicably digesting their lunch and mulling over Uncle Archibald's views on the relinquishment of celibacy.

"Find a girl," he had said. "She need not be particularly pretty –

that can be a nuisance – from a decent family, of course, she needn't have money, you have plenty, this widens your field. Healthy, of course, no skeletons in cupboards, and as young as possible."

"Why?"

"It's like buying a puppy or a horse," said Archibald Loftus impatiently, "you train 'em to your ways. If you take on a girl who has had the time to have other affairs she'll make comparisons, derogatory, unflattering. No, no, the younger the better. It's like buying fish, you look for the sparkle in the eye and make sure the sparkle is for you. Ask your aunt Flora."

"Was that how you set about it?"

"Practically snatched her from the schoolroom." Archibald Loftus stretched out his long thin legs, thoughtfully lit his cigar. "Like a brandy?" he asked. Ned remembered that while accepting the brandy he had realised his uncle had something more to say. Some pearl of wisdom, he had told himself, amused. "Your aunt won't be back for a little while," said his uncle, confirming Ned's suspicion. They had sat in silence until the waiter had brought the brandy and gone away. "There's one more thing you may find useful," said Uncle Archibald, warming the brandy between his hands, sniffing it with his long predatory nose. "You may remember that my mother originated in Austria, was half Viennese?"

"Yes?" Ned, puzzled by this tangent, sniffed his brandy, waited for his uncle to go on.

"Well, her uncle – we are going back to my marriage to your aunt Flora, dear boy – my mother's uncle, a good chap wholly Viennese and a great chap with women – but I digress – gave me a priceless piece of advice. Would you like me to pass it on?" He swivelled a glance at Ned.

"I shall be grateful."

"Needn't take it, of course; it's a bit, shall we say, continental." Uncle Archibald had laughed.

"Oh." Ned had hoped that he did not sound doubtful; there were times when his uncle could be rather too robust.

"Shall I go on?" Ned nodded. "I don't know how you feel about foreigners; being a Scot I have a soft spot for them, feel more at home with them than you people down here in London do."

"Make yourself clear, Uncle Archibald."

"I will, Ned. I am not a politician; when I make something clear it is clear, not some damn euphemism for muddle."

"Please go on." If he goes on like this I shall be late back at the office. "Go on, what was your mother's Viennese uncle's advice?" Better listen to the old boy, Ned had thought, I respect his advice as a rule.

Uncle Archibald lowered his voice so that a group of people passing on their way to the lifts should not overhear. "On the morning of your wedding you fuck another woman." He breathed in at his cigar. "If you have a mistress it's easy of course, but if not, fix yourself up with someone handy."

"Why?" Ned remembered asking stupidly.

"Dear fellow, think." Uncle Archibald was exasperated. "If you've already had a go you're not in a rush, you don't spoil your wedding night by fruitless impatience, you can afford to wait, take it slow. You are, one assumes, marrying a virgin."

"Oh," said Ned, getting the gist. "Ah."

"Naturally if you are marrying a widow it doesn't apply. No need to take my tip, of course. I just pass it on in case it's of use." Ned's uncle had sipped his brandy, puffed at his cigar.

"Did you act on this tip?" Ned had inquired.

Archibald Loftus had laughed. "Flora and I have been happy. Ah, here she comes." He got up to greet his wife, Ned's aunt Flora, coming in from the cold street laden with parcels but wonderfully fresh surfacing from the January sales.

"My uncle Archibald and aunt Flora are a good example of a happy marriage, aren't they?" Ned broke the silence between himself and Rose as he drove her towards Slepe and their wedding night.

"Yes," said Rose.

"Are your parents happy?"

"I've never really thought about it," said Rose. "They don't quarrel, so I suppose they are."

"We shall be happy," said Ned, driving along feeling grateful to his uncle Archibald. "I want you to be happy and I want you to love Slepe."

"I am sure I shall. I've only seen it from the outside, as you know."

"I want it all to be a beautiful surprise," said Ned.

"It will be," she assured him. "It looked lovely in the distance; I saw it from across the valley when I was riding with Nicholas and Emily."

"How well do you know those two?"

"More or less all my life, it's propinquity. Their father was our rector. My father is his solicitor. I haven't seen so much of them since he became a bishop. They are neighbours. Why? Don't you like them?"

"So you wouldn't have chosen them as friends?"

"Maybe not. I've never thought about it. Why? Don't you like them?" Rose asked again.

"They're all right," said Ned, "not exactly my sort. I thought since you asked them up to Uncle Archie and Aunt Flora's that you were close."

"They invited themselves," said Rose, "it was nothing to do with me." (Nicholas and Emily are not close to me, thought Rose, nobody is close except Mylo.)

"Oh," said Ned, rearranging his thoughts. "Oh," and "I see." He drove without speaking for several miles while he stilled a faint feeling of unease. "I have arranged that the fires will be lit for us when we arrive and I thought it would be nice to find supper left ready for us, something simple we can heat up ourselves. We have no servants as you know, just the Farthings."

"The gardener and the wife who cleans?" Rose hoped Ned would not tell her yet again about the Farthings who had cleaned and gardened for the distant cousin from whom he had inherited Slepe. She was already rather in dread of them or the idea of them, having recently read about malign old retainers in one of Daphne du Maurier's novels.

"Yes, them," said Ned. "We shall be alone. Nobody knows we are here, I told everyone we would spend our first night in the Ritz."

"So did I," said Rose, who had been looking forward to the Ritz, never having stepped inside its portals, but was, she hoped, too tactful to show Ned her disappointment.

"So here we are!" Ned had said, swinging the car off the road and up the drive. "There's the house, there's Slepe."

"Yes," said Rose, looking at its seventeenth-century charm. "Does it know we are coming?"

"Nobody knows except the Farthings. I hope you will be pleased."

"I trust the house will be pleased," said Rose, running up the shallow steps, pushing open the front door, crossing the flagged hall to the log fire, looking round at what was to be her home for fifty years, "and of course *I* am."

Ned carried in their bags, slammed shut the door. "Alone at last," he said. He took Rose in his arms: "Welcome to Slepe, Mrs Peel." He kissed her; "Mrs Peel." (He had rehearsed this sentence in his mind and was pleased now to voice it.) "There's a parcel for you," he said in irritation, looking over Rose's head towards the hall table.

"Oh?" Rose detached herself, looked at the packet: "It doesn't look important," she said, keeping her voice uninterested; "I expect it's just something I've left behind." Ned did not seem to notice the ineptitude of this remark; he was adding logs to the fire. "These seem a bit damp, I would have thought— Come, dear," he took her arm, "let me introduce you to the house so that you get to know each other."

"I am coming," said Rose, feeling that the house would have to get to know Mylo as well as herself. She was unaware that beside her Ned ungratefully felt a third party present. Someone "handy", had been Uncle Archibald's expression.

"Isn't it marvellous to be on our own at last," said Ned on a rising note.

"Yes," said Rose, "isn't it." As she walked past the parcel on the hall table she idly turned it over. She noticed that the stamps on it were French. So he's reached France, she thought, retrieving her thoughts from Dublin and sending them on a swift journey across England (he must have passed within a mile of me and I did not know), across the Channel – was the crossing rough? – and on to Paris. "Show me everything," she said, slipping her hand into Ned's. "Show me the house and show me the garden before it gets dark and then let's have supper . . ."

" . . . and go to bed," said Ned.

"Ah . . ." said Rose (would it be better here than in the Ritz or worse?) "and . . ."

"And a bottle of champagne with our supper," said Ned. (Somebody had said "prime her with booze": Uncle Archie probably.)

"I think I had enough at the reception," said Rose.

"Oh, no, dear, you didn't," said Ned.

Now, lying in the hotel bed, listening to the night sounds whispering through the open window, Rose tried to remember her wedding night.

Ned had been gentle. His ears had been cold. He had fallen asleep quite soon. Why do I only remember his cold ears? she asked herself lying wakeful as she had fifty years before. If I wrote my autobiography no reader would find the temperature of Ned's ears particularly enthralling.

EIGHT

Rose on her wedding night was grateful that Ned was a kind and caring man (he had that reputation). Aware of her inexperience, she crossed her fingers and hoped. She was anxious to cooperate, to make things easy for him, start on the right footing – though how feet came into what she vaguely termed as "things", still shying from the word sex, she did not know.

Although she had put off a visit to the birth-control doctor, she had not been idle. On an afternoon when she was supposed to be running errands for her mother, she had searched the shelves of Foyles bookshop, found a sex book for beginners. This manual she had perused locked in the lavatory, puzzling over the diagrams which bore no resemblance to her memory of flesh and blood Mylo. She looked up words she did not know in her father's dictionary, but was left little the wiser. Having memorised the necessary information, she disposed of the book in a rubbish bin in the Park, not trusting her mother's cook general who had a way of throwing kitchen implements, even silver forks and spoons, into the waste bin and later retrieving them. The book left her half mystified, half repelled, but she approved its lack of romance. Romance, joy, delight was left to the reader to practise and discover in his or her own good time. Rose felt she must rely on Ned to show her how this aspect of sex, this happy state, was achieved.

In bed with Ned, his arms around her, she tried to stop the nerves bunching her body into the stiffness of a cadaver. She bore in mind that the book stressed the need of relaxation for both participants. "Take your pyjama trousers off, Ned, you will get wound up in the cord." He had laughed, freed himself from the trousers, switched off the light, said, "That's better," relieved, kissed her, she had kissed him back, felt him relax.

"Where d'you get your hair oil?" She sniffed at him, an unconscious delaying tactic, nuzzling his neck.

"Trumpers, sometimes Penhaligon's. Why?"

"I like the smell. Smells matter to me."

Ned stroked her, gently running his hand down her flank, pausing on her hip, letting his thumb halt near her sex. Had Ned also read the manual? Rose stifled a laugh, her tense muscles loosening. "You can't be a very faithful man if you go to both shops." Still she put off the inevitable.

"But I am faithful." Ned stroked some more. "Is that nice? Tell me."

"Yes." And it was quite nice.

"If we stick a pillow under your bottom, it will be more comfortable."

He *had* read that book. She reached for a pillow, fumbling in the dark, shaking with a mixture of amusement and fear. "That better?"

When Ned slept, Rose lay listening to the magnolia which grew against the house rustling and scraping its stiff polished leaves against the old stone wall. In her mind a voice spoke, ". . . and in bed with Ned you will wonder whether this curious act of sex would not with Mylo turn into something sublime."

She was assailed by a sense of desolation.

Anguished, she had carefully got out of bed, leaving Ned deep in his private sleep, and leaned from the window feeling the night air cool on her hot cheeks, smelled the piercing scent of magnolia flowers, felt rather than seen the moths fluttering about them, felt pity and tenderness for Ned, shivered as the magnolia leaves stirred, climbed back into bed.

Half waking, Ned had clutched her. "Who? That you? Is it Rose?"

"Yes. Yes, it's me."

"Where have you been?"

"Just to the window . . ."

"Rose, don't leave me."

"Why should I?"

"Promise never to leave me, promise . . ."

"Of course not."

"Swear." He was sitting up now. "Say it, say: I swear never to leave you."

"Don't be silly, Ned, you are half asleep." She felt protective, maternal.

"No, I'm not. I am very much awake. Swear, say: I swear never to leave you."

"I did, at our wedding, in church . . ."

"You weren't paying attention, you were distracted, your mind was miles away." (How had he known?) "Come on, swear it to me now." He was insistent, almost bullying.

"All right." She felt afraid. "I swear never to leave you. What about you? What do you swear to me?"

"No need for me . . ." He was content, slipping back into his sleep, leaving her later, much later, to find her separate sleep from which she woke to a sunny morning with Ned up and dressed, confident and cheerful, bringing their breakfast into the room on a tray. "Wake up, Mrs Peel, we have this one day to explore . . ."

"And the other days?" she asked, pouring coffee, handing him his cup.

"The other days I must spend putting you in the picture for when I shall be away."

"And I am to stay here alone?" She knew this, had she not agreed, liked the idea, seeing freedom from her family, insisted that she would manage, would be all right.

"You said you would rather be on your own, but it's not too late. We can find someone to live with you, a girl friend to share . . ."

"Who, for instance?"

"Emily."

"Why do you suggest Emily?"

"Isn't she a friend?"

"Not particularly. What I'd like is a dog, or two dogs." Rose visualised a pair of companionable animals.

"Or a pack!" Ned laughed. "Remember the war, dear. We shall have food rationing soon; one dog should be more than enough."

"Oh, rationing," said Rose, privately deciding to have as many dogs as she wished.

"Yes, rationing," said Ned, "we shall have to learn to live with it. Which reminds me, I must show you where the petrol is."

"What petrol?"

"I've hidden a lot of jerrycans in a shed in the copse."

"Isn't that illegal? You have a hoard?"

"I did it before rationing started." Ned sensed disapproval. "I foresaw rationing so I laid in a store." (This may not be strictly true, he told himself, but she is not to know.) "If we are invaded, we might have to make a quick getaway, or you might if I am gone."

"Are you suggesting the Germans will invade us?" she said incredulously.

"If things go badly," said Ned, who had listened to talk in his club.

"Golly."

"It will come in useful anyway," said Ned. "This isn't going to be a short war, whatever people say, but what I am sure of is that everything will be in short supply; sensible people are stocking their store cupboards."

"Rich people! Well," said Rose, "I shall hoard tinned dog food for my dogs."

"You should have a dog," said Ned, as if the idea was his. "I would be happier when I'm away if you had a dog. I will buy you one."

"Let me find my own dog . . ." cried Rose before she could stop herself, knowing that Ned's choice of dog would not be hers.

"All right," said Ned, "if you insist." He felt cheated, rather hurt, feeling that he had planned to buy her a dog, an Alsatian or a Labrador.

Feeling the drop in temperature, Rose said, "More coffee?" holding up the pot (George III, recently inherited along with the house). Ned passed his cup. "Yes, please." Why not let her choose her own dog, he thought indulgently; it was a lovely day, last night had gone off well, he felt contented, luxurious, Rose looked very pretty sitting up in bed with the tray across her lap. He had enjoyed last night rather more than he expected. This marriage, entered into with care and consideration, was off to a good start. Uncle Archibald was a wise old bird. "We will choose a nice puppy," he said, "if you promise to be careful of the rugs."

"Rugs?" She pretended not to understand.

"When I take you on a tour of inspection, Mrs Peel, I will show you the rugs, some of them are very valuable, they should really be hung on a wall."

Rose wondered how long it would amuse Ned to call her Mrs Peel. "I've read," she said, "that in Turkey they pen geese on new rugs to make them look old, then, when they've been thoroughly shat on, they are washed in the Bosphorus."

"I don't like you using that word," said Ned.

"All right," said Rose, "I won't. I'm going to get up now. There's no hurry about the dog. I think I'll have a bitch. A dog might lift his leg against the Chippendale chairs. Don't look like that, Ned, I'm only teasing. Here, take the tray." She thrust the tray towards him. "Let me have a bath and then I want to be shown round the house, introduced to every stick of furniture, every picture, every rug." She laughed, pushing the bedclothes back, exposing her legs. Her nightdress had ridden up her thighs; Ned could see her dark bush as she kicked clear of the bedclothes. "Give me half an hour, I'll meet you in the garden."

Ned would have liked to catch hold of her but his hands held the tray; he watched her skip into the bathroom and close the door, shutting him out.

Carrying the tray downstairs, Ned told himself that Rose was very young, malleable, that loving him she would also love his possessions. He put the tray on the kitchen table where Mrs Farthing would find it, then walked through the house and out into the garden.

While delighting in his inheritance, Ned did not feel passionately about the garden. Flowers were insubstantial, they faded, got eaten by slugs, died. It was natural to feel strongly about pictures, furniture, silver and rugs. Ned winced at the memory of Rose's vulgar use of English. The garden, while aesthetically beautiful, was of no intrinsic worth apart, of course, from its value at so much an acre. Ned had a sneaking feeling that here he was lacking in sensitivity, that he ought to feel as passionately about the garden as he did for the house and its contents. Sitting on a stone seat in the sun, he tried to puzzle out this lack in himself, to pin it down. He picked up a stick and swished at a late wasp buzzing near some Japanese anemones. The wasp put on a burst of speed. Ned watched it go. Putting a value on his garden, he ruminated, was as slippery – slippery being the unwelcome word which came to mind – as setting a price on Rose. But surely not, he thought, kicking at a pebble on the path at his feet. He had picked Rose, chosen her with care, taken advice, used his judgement, his wits. I kept my wits about me, thought Ned, sitting in the warmth of late September watching butterflies swoop and hover over a clump of Michaelmas daisies. I decided to have her, I picked her out of the crowd at that party, made up my mind.

"What are you thinking?" Rose joined him sitting at the end of the stone seat, turning towards him: "You look so serious."

"I was thinking of the Malones' winter tennis party where I first met you and . . ."

"And?"

"And I fell in love with you."

"Ah," said Rose disbelieving, and then, "I remember, I remember it well." She let out her breath in a sigh.

They had sat, the newly married pair, each remembering the winter tennis party.

NINE

Ned remembered Uncle Archibald had said, "You have to start somewhere," holding out the invitation to the Malones' tennis party. "There may be some possible girls. I know the Malones, they are old friends, they built that indoor court just after the war. Their winter tennis party is an event. They get people down from London and mix them with the local talent. It's an annual do not to be missed, a compliment to be invited." He was enthusiastic.

"I am asked because I have inherited Slepe." Ned turned the invitation this way and that with suspicious fingers.

"Quite so, and I am asked because we are old friends. We played tennis before the war. His standard was high, almost Wimbledon."

"Does he still play?"

"No, too arthritic, but he likes to watch the young people. Flora and I always go if we are down south. We will come along with you, if you like. Motor down for the day."

"I'm not fearfully keen."

"Come on, Ned, you have to get to know your neighbours at Slepe. The Malones have sons and there will, as I say, be girls."

"Oh."

"The sort of girls you should be taking out in London, suitable girls," said Aunt Flora.

"I sense a trap," said Ned amused.

"Good God, Ned, the girls won't bite you, you play a decent game of tennis, you have to make a start, it's a year since I advised you to marry, this tennis . . ."

"On Boxing Day? In midwinter? So soon after Christmas dinner? I am more used to a Boxing Day meet or a day's shooting."

"It's an indoor court, Ned, marvellous to play on. It's wood, makes the game very fast, even quite poor players put up a good show. When you are playing in there and it's blowing and sleeting outside, you will be pleased you came. See more of the girls than muffled up to the eyes and miserable on a shooting stick or bouncing along on a horse they can't hold when all you see is their bums. I've nothing against bums, of course, but a tennis dress in the warmth shows them off better . . ."

"Honestly, Uncle Archie . . ."

"I shall accept for you," said Ned's uncle. "I have to ring him up anyway. You get a good lunch," he added consolingly, "as well as the exercise, and there's a dance in the evening for those who stay on."

There had been a men's four, Ned remembered; he had been partnered by Richard Malone against Nicholas Thornby and a visitor from London. The court, as his uncle had said, was marvellous; he found himself playing well.

There were, beside himself, George and Richard Malone, three men from London staying in the house, four vivacious girls, friends of the Malone sons, Emily and Nicholas Thornby, and a very young, very shy Rose, brought in as a stop-gap to fill the place of a girl cousin who was down with flu. Ned enjoyed himself presently, partnering Emily in a mixed doubles. She played a spirited game. Ned noticed that she did not wear a brassière; he was used to girls wearing brassières and found its absence a little disturbing. Twice he missed an easy backhand while thinking about this. Nevertheless, or because of it, he later suggested she might come out to dinner when next she was in London, he not yet being properly installed at Slepe; would she like to dine and dance or go to a theatre?

Later, when Emily and three of the girls from the house party played a women's doubles, Ned watched while Richard Malone sat whispering into his favourite girl's ear, reducing her to fits of giggles. Of the women's four, Emily had been by far the keenest player, leaping up and showing a lot of leg as well as the disturbing breasts, reaching up to smash difficult balls which did not necessarily land in court and might well have gone out if she had left them. Ned noticed Emily again when partnering one of the girls from London; he played against her and her brother Nicholas. They made a curiously cohesive team, giving no quarter.

Of the girls from London, Ned got to know two, later taking them out and receiving invitations back into their milieu. Emily came to London often and when she did she rang him up so that over a period of months he grew to know her fairly well. Imperceptibly she latched on to the group of friends he now saw most often.

It was quite untrue that he had, as he now told Rose, fallen in love with her at the winter tennis party. He had barely noticed her. In any case, during much of the tennis Rose, already rendered invisible by shyness, had absented herself.

It was much later, at another party – Ned had by this time become friends with the Malones – that Ned overheard Mrs Malone say to a friend, "Isn't it extraordinary that a plain little thing like Rose Freeling should suddenly blossom into a positive beauty."

"She must be in love," said Mrs Malone's friend, staring across the room at Rose.

"The boys say not. They say she has no one in particular; both George and Richard find her unapproachable; they both find her extremely attractive."

"Who is she?" asked Mrs Malone's friend.

"Nobody much," said Mrs Malone, "the family is all right, I suppose, but there's no money. The father is a solicitor, not successful, rather ill, on the way out, they say. The mother is a stick. One feels sorry for the girl, she doesn't have much fun. We asked her to the tennis last Boxing Day when some girl fell out. She didn't seem to make much of a mark, but we thought we'd give her another chance and then the boys found her quite ravishing."

Mrs Malone's friend said, "Being ravishing isn't everything. One needs money to carry it off."

"True," said Mrs Malone, watching Rose across the room standing with a group of men. "It's funny, though, she was so shy as a child, she was quite ugly, but now . . ."

"I thought Emily Thornby was supposed to be the local beauty," said Mrs Malone's friend, "not that she is exactly beautiful."

"There's not much money there either," said Mrs Malone, "but she and that brother of hers have lots of push."

Ned, overhearing this conversation, began to watch Rose and presently took the opportunity of asking her to dance, preparatory to getting to know her better.

Rose was not wearing anything under her dress, neither brassière nor knickers, but since she did not think about it Ned did not notice, yet he was suddenly anxious to make an impression. The ease with which Rose had stood among the group of men had annoyed him.

So it came about that when for their annual house party for the grouse shooting in Argyll, Uncle Archie and Aunt Flora invited two of Ned's friends, Harold Rhys and Ian Johnson, to form a leaven of young people among their middle-aged friends, Aunt Flora added two of Ned's cousins and let Emily and Nicholas fish successfully for an invitation. It was Uncle Archie who had noticed Rose at the Boxing Day party and been astonished that Flora had not added Rose's name to the list. Although getting to know Rose, Ned was not moving fast enough. "Quiet girls like Rose Freeling slip through your fingers," he said, "get her under the same roof as Ned."

"But she has no money," said his wife, who had had none herself and knew this disadvantage.

"In Ned's case it doesn't matter. I thought we were agreed."

"Very well, I'll write," said Flora, who had only brought up the lack of money to test her husband. "You may be right," she added. "Ned is the sort of man who gets hooked by an unsuitable girl; I am not sure I should have invited the Thornbys."

"I find them a lively pair," said Archibald Loftus, "the girl makes me laugh."

"A bit too lively," said Flora, "though I can't put my finger on why I think so."

Touched by his relatives' machinations for his welfare, telling himself that their anxiety was superfluous, Ned after considerable havering had decided to pick Rose from the choice presented to him. He was never in any doubt that she would accept him.

Thus, sitting on the stone seat in the garden at Slepe, the morning after their wedding, Ned honestly believed himself when he told Rose that he had fallen in love with her nine months before at the Boxing Day tennis party.

TEN

Rose's recollections of the winter tennis party bore little relation to Ned's; perhaps all that they had in common was their initial reluctance to go to it.

Mrs Freeling had answered the telephone and accepted Mrs Malone's last minute invitation on Rose's behalf

"That's extremely kind of you," she enthused. "I am sure she will be delighted. Oh, yes, she plays a reasonable game, though that sounds boastful on my part. Be there by eleven-thirty? Yes, of course she can. The Thornbys will give her a lift? How kind of you to arrange it. Of course, my husband would have brought her, but he's not very well at present. Rose will be thrilled."

"I am not thrilled," said Rose, overhearing.

"You should be, you have never been invited there before. The Malones' winter tennis is an event," said Rose's mother.

"As a stop-gap," said Rose. "Barrel-scraping only."

"What does that matter?" snapped her mother, who felt perpetually guilty that she had not got what she thought to herself as the nerve to launch Rose socially. Rose made no effort herself. "You make no effort, here's a chance to meet new people. You know how difficult it is for me to give parties for you with your father so unwell and . . ."

"So little money." Rose knew the litany.

"Really, darling!"

"I don't want to go," said Rose. "Tennis in midwinter is ridiculous."

"It's a covered court. I've heard it's beautifully warm. There will be a house party from London. Nice young people."

"Don't I know it." Rose already felt her toes curling with horror at the prospect of meeting sophisticated strangers from London.

"And the Malone boys, Richard and George, you hardly know them since they've grown up. This is a chance to get to know them better."

"They have had every chance to get to know me all these years, Mother, and they haven't bothered."

"Rubbish, Rose." Mrs Freeling stifled her agreement with this statement. When they were little she had invited the Malone boys to the children's party she forced herself to give once a year for Rose, her only child, an enormous effort this, after which she would relapse into her habitual lethargy, feeling that she had done her duty.

"The only time they ever came to this house George Malone threw jelly at the other children and shouted that this was the bloodiest party he had ever been to," said Rose.

"Well, yes, darling, but he was very young, only eight or ten. Mrs Malone rang up and apologised. She did. I remember it well. The poor little boy was over-excited and had a temperature."

"Ho!" said Rose. "Ha!"

"Rose!"

"They made excuses for ever after when you invited them, they never came again."

"Well, darling, they are grown up now, it's quite different."

"So am I," said Rose. She had admired George's action, remembered it with glee, pink and yellow jellies had flown through the air, splattering against the walls of the dining-room, and lodged in nice little girls' hair. George had been right: her mother's parties were of an extreme awfulness. "He's grown up jolly boring," she said, "more's the pity."

"You don't know him well enough to judge," said her mother.

"I have no tennis clothes," said Rose.

"That is not true, you bought new shoes in July."

"No dress."

"Rose, you are being difficult."

"No racquet."

"You can borrow mine," said Rose's father, looking up from *The Times*, hoping to put a stop to the argument. "I shall never use it again," he said with self-pity.

"Oh, Father," cried Rose, "don't!"

"Just go to the party; please your mother; you will find you enjoy it."

"So you want me to go?"

"I should like to think that my racquet is being used," said Rose's father, spoiling his otherwise generous offer by his tone of voice, wringing his daughter's heart.

"All right, I'll go," said Rose. (And why must he wring my heart with his bloody racquet? Why must he thrust his cancer down my throat, she cried to herself as she watched her father fold his newspaper and limp from the room. Why does supposed cancer of the stomach make him limp?) "I am not going to wear white," she told her mother.

Mrs Freeling did not answer. Let Rose go wearing every colour of the rainbow, so long as she went. People as rich as the Malones did not invite inconspicuous, shy and – let's face it – moneyless girls like Rose a second time. It was not often one of their guests went down with flu at the crucial minute, leaving a Heaven-sent gap. Fate, Mrs Freeling told herself as she made her way to the kitchen to make her shopping list, was not always malign.

If there should be some personable young man at the Malones' party, he might just possibly be attracted to Rose. Ask her out when they got to London. Perhaps Rose was not destined, as she felt herself to have been destined, to be crushed by life. I never had any real opportunities, Mrs Freeling told herself as she planned the day's meals; I have always been crushed.

Mrs Freeling at that time felt particularly harassed since the specialist had said that her husband's only chance was an intensive course of treatment in London. In a week's time they were to move into an expensive flat for half of every week so that Rose's father could receive this treatment, returning to the country at intervals to keep a toehold in his ailing practice.

What harassed Mrs Freeling even more than her husband's probable cancer (there was no certainty yet that he had it), their impecuniosity and Rose's rebarbative shyness was her subconscious wish that her husband would quite simply drop dead, that her long sad unsatisfactory marriage would come to an end while she was still of an age to have some fun. Naturally Mrs Freeling did not know she harboured such thoughts; they milled about in the recesses of her unconscious.

Sulkily, Rose went to the cloakroom where her father's racquet hung in its press. She took it out and twanged the strings.

Upstairs, she fished her tennis shoes out from the back of her cupboard. She had put them away dirty, they were stained green; she laid them aside to blanco. She pushed aside her winter clothes, and pulled out the only summer dress she liked, a simple cotton dress in a deep rose colour made by the village dressmaker the previous summer. Her mother had misjudged the amount of material, bought too much; there had been enough left over from the frock to make matching knickers; it was this that made the dress her favourite. Her mother had bought the material for her and for once she had not questioned her mother's taste. Laying the garments on the bed to be washed and ironed, Rose almost began to look forward to the party.

"My mother," she said to her reflection in the glass, "hopes I shall meet Mr Right. God, my hair's a mess!" She went to the bathroom to wash it. "It's greasy and the ends are splitting." She was still at the age when girls dramatise their hair; her hair was not in the least greasy, nor were the ends split.

"What are you doing?" Her mother's voice floated up the stairs.

"Washing my hair," Rose shouted, her head in the basin.

"Don't use all the hot water."

"It's automatic, it's automatic, she doesn't even think!" Rose plunged her head down in the basin so that water sloshed out on to the floor. As she came up for air, she heard her mother's voice again. "What?" she shouted. "Can't hear. What did you say?"

"I said," Mrs Freeling stood in the bathroom doorway, "I said Ned Peel is going to be at the tennis party. Oh, look what a mess you've made of the floor. You will mop it up, won't you?"

"Who is Ned Peel?" Rose worked shampoo into her hair.

"Is it good for your hair to wash it so often? You only washed it two days ago. Ned Peel is the man who has come in to Slepe, old Mr Peel's heir."

"So what?"

"Don't be rude, Rose. I was making sure Emily and Nicholas will pick you up tomorrow. Emily told me that he is to be there."

Rose said nothing, rinsing her hair, rubbing her head with a towel, jerking a comb through the wet hair. "Don't do that, darling," said Mrs Freeling, "let your hair dry naturally; wet hair is so brittle."

"Mother!"

"All right, darling, I will leave you. I only want you to enjoy yourself . . ." Mrs Freeling retreated. Rose ran after her, flung her arms around her and hugged her. "Oh, darling, you are making me all wet," said Mrs Freeling.

"Oh, oh," whispered Rose, watching her mother go down the stairs, "neither of us ever gets it right." She watched her mother's diminishing back with pity. "Poor Mother, am I supposed to be gobbled up by this Ned Peel?" She began filing her nails, waiting for her hair to dry. I'd better shave my armpits, she thought. And what about my legs? She pulled down her stockings and eyed the soft almost invisible hairs on her legs. No, leave the legs hairy. She went back to the bathroom and stole one of her father's razor blades. After shaving her armpits, she took the blade out of the razor and put it in her purse. A desperate idea had occurred to her.

ELEVEN

One of the mysteries about Nicholas and Emily was that in spite of their perpetual cries of poverty, they always managed to look chic; they exuded an aura of confidence and one-upmanship which Rose found unnerving. Arriving to fetch her in their father's respectable old Morris, wearing immaculate white tennis clothes under twin camel-hair coats, they jumped out to greet her, showing themselves off.

Rose often thought of them as saplings planted too close together, growing up entwined. She grinned at them posing, their arms round each other's waists. "Willows," she said, "wand like, unpollarded."

"What?" asked Emily.

"Nothing," said Rose.

Nicholas cried, "How pretty you look, Rose," meaning: Look at us, are we not pretty?

"Shall I sit in the back?" asked Rose, drawing her old school coat around her, muffling it over the pink dress. "What are the suitcases for?" she asked, squeezing into the back seat, pushing aside tennis racquets and suitcases.

"There's usually a dance in the evening," said Emily, getting back into the car. "We've brought our evening clothes to change into."

"Oh," said Rose, surprised.

"It's for the house party, but we are prepared, if asked, to stay on for it," said Nicholas, settling himself in the driver's seat. "Come on, you old rattler." The car shot forward.

"I see you've got your father's racquet," said Emily, whose beady eye missed nothing, "his new Slazenger. What happened to yours?"

"Bust," said Rose, feeling inferior. If they had told me about the dance I would have cried off, she thought, seeing in her mind's eye people dancing in evening clothes while she still wore her pink cotton. (She would have sweated under the arms by then, or spilt something down her front.) She said, "Nobody said anything about dancing to me."

"Never mind," said Emily, who had discussed with Nicholas whether to tell Rose and voted not to. (Nothing worse than an odd girl to upset numbers.) "Nicholas or someone can run you home. We got our racquets in the end of summer sales," she said, "they are brand new."

"They smell nice." Rose sniffed the leather on the racquet handles. "Delicious."

"Father is letting us have this car for ourselves from now on; the diocese are providing him with a new one now he is a bish," said Nicholas.

"Oh," said Rose, impressed. "A car for nothing."

"We will swap it soon for something more dashing; it looks a bit too churchy, don't you think?" said Emily. "We want a red sports."

"One could have guessed," said Rose.

"A *soupçon* of vulgarity suits," sang Nicholas.

"And," said Emily, leaning over from the front seat, "Father is sinking his savings in the Rectory."

"What do you mean?"

"The new parson wants a smaller house. Father is buying the Rectory from the Church Commissioners and putting it jointly in our names. He's heard this will save death duties."

"Very thoughtful is Father," said Nicholas.

"We are going to live in it, just us two," said Emily.

"The real reason is he would find us an embarrassment in the Bishop's Palace," said Nicholas. "Not that he actually says so."

"Why," asked Rose, bewildered, "should he?"

"If you don't know, we shan't tell," said Emily in the tone of voice which would lose her many a friend through life.

Nicholas sniggered.

Rose wished fervently that she had not let her father work on her feelings. "Have you been to this winter tennis before?" she asked dubiously.

"Oh, yes, often," said Nicholas.

"Several times," said Emily.

Once, perhaps, thought Rose.

"I hear Ned Peel is going to be there. I hope we shall like him as a neighbour," said Emily. "I plan that he shall be an asset."

"I quite took to him when I met him," said Nicholas, who had happened to sit next to Ned on the London Underground on a brief journey between Knightsbridge and Piccadilly and seized the opportunity to introduce himself. "I met him in London not so long ago. Of course, he never came down to Slepe before his uncle died."

"The old man was a recluse," said Emily, "never entertained. Ned hasn't opened the house properly yet, let's hope he's not like his uncle."

"Oh, no, he's not at all like the old man," said Nicholas, "he's entirely different."

"All the old man liked was his garden, they say," said Emily. "He kept a full-time gardener but no proper servants. I bet the house is in a state."

"Supposed to be full of lovely things," said Nicholas, double de-clutching around a corner. The Morris, unused to such grand treatment, screeched its gears like a demented turkey and stalled its engine.

"Poor old dodderer, outlived his welcome in this world," said Nicholas, restarting the car. "High time there was some young life at Slepe."

What a lot they know, thought Rose, wondering whether the skirt of her dress was the right length, sure that it wasn't, fingering her father's racquet as it lay across her knees. It's too heavy, she thought, it's a man's racquet, I shall never be able to play with it, I shall look a fool, I wish I had not come. Then she thought, Nobody will notice me, they never do, they will notice Emily who is so lively, she will hold her own, outdo the girls from London, why the hell should I bother? Then again, she thought, they will all wear white. I shall stand out like a sore thumb. My pink dress will make me obvious when I do something awkward, I don't want to be noticed, and Emily does, they will notice Emily if only because she is wearing white and has a new racquet, I wish I had the nerve to ask Nicholas to drop me by a bus stop to find my way home. (There is no bus stop.)

Nicholas drove the old Morris up to the Malones' front door. "Here we are, girls, let battle commence."

They had arrived too early.

George Malone, coming round the house from the stable yard, found them grouped on the doorstep waiting for the bell to be answered.

"Hullo, hullo," said George, "you are early birds, we don't start play until twelve, but do come in. Everybody will be changing. I bet some of the girls are not even up yet, there were faces missing at breakfast; we went to a party last night and got to bed in the small hours, but, tell you what, I'll get Betty to take you round to the court, you'd probably like to knock up or something, get your eye in. Will you show them the way, Betty?" said George to the maid who had appeared to open the door. "You haven't been before, have you?" he said to Emily.

"It's Rose who hasn't been before," said Emily quickly, "I know my way to the court. Come on, Rose, I'll lead the way."

George smiled at Rose and said, "Does your mother's cook still make those stupendous jellies?" And to Nicholas he said, "I must rush up and change. Mother likes us to be ready to greet our guests."

This is where if I liked Nicholas better I would feign a pain and ask him to drive me home, thought Rose, but he would see through me. Why, oh why, do he and Emily make me feel so provincial? She followed Nicholas, Emily and the maid through the house, out through a side door, across a stretch of garden to the building which held the covered court. Here the maid left them.

Nicholas and Emily took off their coats; Nicholas measured the height of the net, adjusted it, bounced several times on the balls of his feet, swung his racquet serving an imaginary ball.

"Isn't George an old comic," said Emily, swishing her new racquet. "What was that reference to jellies, Rose?"

"I don't know," said Rose, remembering with relief that Nicholas and Emily had not been at the party where George had disgraced her mother, but been in bed with mumps.

"Let's knock up," said Emily, swishing her racquet again. "Where are the balls?"

"Here." Nicholas opened a box of new balls. "Come on, girls, I'll take you both on."

"No, you and me against Rose and her father's wonder racquet," cried Emily, "let Rose Freeling take on the Thornbys."

"Why not," said Rose, fiddling with her shoe laces, standing up to confront Emily, gripping her father's racquet. The handle was too thick, intended for a man's hand. It occurred to her that one reason she had so enjoyed George's awful performance with the jellies was that Emily and Nicholas had not witnessed it; life unwitnessed by Nicholas and Emily was tolerable. Nicholas was already on the court practising his service. "Why don't we play a single and let Rose ball-boy?" Nicholas was furious with George for belittling his sister, snubbing him for his ineptitude at arriving early, and for having secret knowledge of Rose (what's this about jellies? I must find out). He knew George only pretended to think this was Emily's first visit; he had once overheard George tell another man that Emily was a pushy little tart who could do with taking down a peg. Hitting the ball as hard as he could, Nicholas vented his anger. Rose could be whipping boy.

Stepping on to the court, Rose felt Nicholas's enmity linked with Emily's malice; she mistrusted them. She felt the spring in the wooden floor communicate itself to her legs. She swung her father's racquet, returned Nicholas's serve, enjoyed the whizz of the ball, the impact on the strings of the racquet, the feel of the sinews in her wrist reacting. "I'll take you both on," she shouted on a rise of spirit.

"Ho! Listen to her! All right, little Rose, we take you at your word. Shall you serve first?" Nicholas patronised.

"No, you." Rose stood ready near the back line.

"No quarter," said Nicholas.

"No quarter," answered Rose.

Emily danced from one foot to the other near the net, looking mockingly at Rose.

Nicholas served, putting all his strength into it.

Rose returned the serve, flukily driving the ball hard and low. The strings of her father's racquet parted with a twang. The ball, driven across the net with the combination of Rose's strength and the weight of the racquet, thumped into Emily, hitting her hard between her breasts. Emily yelped. "My breast bone!"

"Sorry!" cried Rose. "Oh, look what I've done to Father's racquet. Oh, bother, I'll go and see whether I can borrow another from somebody." She ran lightly from the court, making her escape. Behind her, Emily groaned and Nicholas sympathised. I must get away, thought Rose, running across the garden and into the house. She doubled along a corridor and opened a door at random, shutting it quickly behind her. She was in Mr Malone's library. There was a log fire burning in the fireplace, the smell of hyacinths dotted about the room in large bowls, no sound except the faint ticking of a bracket clock on the mantelshelf and the rustle of ash as a log settled in the grate.

Rose put the broken racquet down on a table, leaned forward on her hands and let furious tears fall on to the polished wood. She stood thus for several minutes, drawing her breath in long shuddering gasps, loathing Nicholas and Emily.

Presently she wiped her eyes with the back of her hand and straightened up.

A yard from her nose across the table were a pair of men's feet, bare, high-arched, long-toed. The heels rested on a copy of the *Field*.

Rose said, "Oh, my God," and froze.

The feet disappeared as the legs they belonged to were lowered. A young man stood up, holding the book he had been reading against his chest.

Rose stared. He was not much older than she. Tall, thin, dressed in clothes she had only seen worn by French workmen, baggy cotton trousers in faded blue, a baggy jacket to match over a dark flannel shirt, collarless, fastened at the neck with a bone stud. He had thick, almost black hair worn rather longer than most people, a thin eager face, longish nose, wide mouth and black, intelligent eyes.

They stood staring at each other across the intervening table. On the mantelshelf the clock ticked on while their eyes meeting measured, assessed, questioned.

Then he smiled. "I must put on my socks. *Je m'appelle Mylo, et vous?*"

"Rose," said Rose.

"Lovely," said Mylo, sitting down on the sofa which had hidden him from Rose. "I have a bloody great hole in the toe of my sock."

"Oh," said Rose.

"Why don't you sit down," said Mylo. "You could mop your tears with this." He reached across the table to a blotter and eased out a sheet of blotting paper. "*Comme ça*," he said, blotting the tears which marked the table. "Salt isn't good for furniture or cheeks. Salt dries and becomes uncomfortable." He handed Rose the blotting paper. "Try it."

Rose took the sheet of blotting paper and dabbed her face. "Thanks."

"Excellent, and now the socks. Just look at that for a hole." He wiggled his toe through the hole.

"Are you French or English?" Rose moved round the table, nearer the fire.

"Both," said Mylo. "French mother, English father. And you?"

"English."

"Come for the tennis?"

"M-m-m."

"Bust your racquet on purpose?"

"I had a razor blade with me just in case, but it broke anyway. It's my father's. I was annoyed with somebody."

"You will have to go back . . ."

"M-m-m."

"But not just yet. Come and sit here." He patted the sofa.

Rose sat in a corner of the sofa and drew up her legs. "Are you going to play?"

"Lord, no. No fear. Not me. I am only the tutor."

"The what?"

"Tutor. I am here to babble French at George to help the final hoist into the Foreign Office. I am paid for my pains on condition that I don't let a word of English pass my lips. That colour suits you."

"Oh? Thanks."

"And you don't really belong in that *galère*. Not for you the marriage market, not for you the auction."

Rose looked at him in silent question.

"You know that's what it is, don't pretend. I bet your mother or your father pressed you to come to this party."

"They did," Rose admitted, "I suppose."

"An opportunity to meet . . ."

"Oh, yes," said Rose impatiently. "Shut up."

Mylo manoeuvred the sock so that his toe was no longer exposed, put on its mate. "It happens in the best societies," he said, "a marriage of convenience is a marriage that is often convenient for all, parents, children, everybody. In France where I've lived, it's out in the open, everybody knows. It's decent. In this country it's wrapped up, disguised, cocooned in things like winter tennis parties. I wonder why you were invited."

"I'm a stop-gap," said Rose, "some girl has flu."

Mylo laughed. "That explains it." He began fumbling around to find his shoes. One shoe, after the malicious manner of inanimate objects, had hidden itself under the sofa. Rose observed the back of Mylo's neck while he reached for it. His hair grew down in a point. "Got it!" He sat up and laced the shoe.

Watching his long fingers lace the shoes, Rose felt inexplicably consoled, then a swift spasm of pleasure. Mylo sat back, straightened his legs stretching them towards the fire, turned towards Rose and observed her.

Rose, sitting with her legs tucked under her, let her eyes travel from Mylo's feet, now decently shod, past his waist where the too wide trousers were belted in by a leather belt, up over the heavy cotton jacket, going slower now, to his eyes.

"There now, said Mylo, his lips twitching into a smile. "We could marry?" he suggested.

"What?"

"What is your attitude to marriage?"

"Trepidation."

"Both intelligent and beautiful. What do you say, though? Yes or no?"

No one had ever supposed her intelligent; the suggestion coupled with beauty made her laugh. Mylo laughed too. "My French side is practical. I have no money, we shall have to wait, but there is nothing to prevent us loving meanwhile, is there?"

"Are you making fun of me?"

"No, I am not. There is nothing funny about love. My father told me. He also told me that it can be extremely painful."

"Ah." She had not considered pain in relation to love. "Oh."

"I think, before they miss you, you had better go back to the tennis. Then, after a decent interval, come back. You can tell me about yourself and I will tell you about me. Go on, Rose, go." (I need a moment to think.)

"Must I?" (This is a lunatic conversation.)

"I fear so." (What am I letting myself in for?)

"All right." She stood up. "I'll go." (Perhaps he's not quite right in the head?)

"But come back."

"Yes," she said, "of course." She knew she would.

As she turned to go Mylo said, "This person who annoyed you just now . . ."

"Two people. Nicholas and Emily Thornby."

"Are you afraid of them?"

"Of course not."

"What do they do to you?" He did not believe her.

Rose was irresolute. Why expose her frailty, why clarify the Thornbys to this stranger? "I've known them all my life," she said defensively. "Their father was our rector; we were expected to be friends."

"Give me one example that explains why you are afraid of them."

"I am not," Rose denied hotly.

"Come off it."

"All right. Years ago . . . it was a joke. We were all about six or seven, I was at a convent day school, they were at a progressive school down the road."

"Yes?"

"I don't see why I should tell you, it's all forgotten years ago," she back-pedalled.

"You seem to remember."

"It's pretty silly."

"Go on . . ."

"They boasted that my nuns were dull and that at their school they learned lots of jokes and funny stories which they brought home to tell their parents and they all laughed at the stories together."

"That sounds all right."

"I thought so."

"Go on."

"I've never talked about this since it happened. I don't know why I'm telling you now."

"Do get on with it." (She looks distressed.)

"Well. They told me their *best*, actually I paid them sixpence for it, they said if your nuns laugh you'll get your sixpence back, I said, Of course my nuns would laugh, they often laughed, they were on the jolly side, those nuns. I thought that I'd try it on my parents first and if they laughed, the nuns would be sure to, my father and mother never laugh much, you see. So I paid my sixpence and Nicholas and Emily told me their story."

A flash of suspicion. "Did you understand this story?"

"Of course not, but I couldn't say so, could I?"

"Tell it me, if you remember it."

"I remember some of it."

(I bet she remembers all of it.) "Go on, then."

"It was about a man and a girl in a punt. They get in the way of a barge and the bargee shouts, 'Seeing as how you've a cunt in your punt, I won't say what I was going to say but what I will say is . . .' I really have forgotten the rest . . ."

(Liar.) "But you told your parents, you remembered it long enough for that."

"Yes. They had some people in for drinks."

"And?"

"My father whipped me, and my mother kept me in my room for two days."

"So the nuns never heard it?"

"No."

"The nuns might have been kinder."

"They might not have known the words either." (It's a funny thing that my mother did.)

"And you were still expected to play with these charmers?"

"Of course. My parents thought I'd heard the story from a rude Catholic child; they complained to Reverend Mother and took me away; there was a hell of a shemozzle."

"And you never let on?"

"I couldn't let Nicholas and Emily crow."

"What charming innocent children."

"Perhaps they did not cry at their baptisms," said Rose.

"Perhaps you will get your revenge one day."

"Perhaps I shall," said Rose, grinning. "It would be worth my sixpence."

"I love you."

"Pulling my leg."

"No."

Rose turned again to go. It was too early to tell him that she still did not know the meaning of the offending words; she had not been able to locate them in a dictionary. She had risked her naïvety far enough.

Mylo watched her move towards the door; by the door she looked back. It struck them both that they had not touched, their hands had not even met when he gave her the blotting paper.

"Later?" she said, looking across the space between them.

Mylo nodded.

"And the dangers?" she asked, as though she had previous experience of love, of life.

"We brave them together," he waved her on her way with his book, "all of them, Emily and Nicholas, the lot."

Rose laughed.

"Tell them, out there at the auction, that you have a reserve on you," said Mylo.

"Then I shall not mind the dangers," she said. Then, "Is the reserve a large one?"

"Limitless."

TWELVE

Mylo tried to switch his mind back to his book but it was no use; he laid it down. I will make George read it aloud, he thought, pounce on his terrible accent. While he reads, I can dream. He stood up and paced the room; he felt threatened. A hitherto independent future had become in one instant fused, interlaced with that of the girl in the rose-coloured dress who had burst into the room, disrupting his solitude.

As he paced Mylo remembered his father philosophising on love, on its aspects tragic, comic, pleasurable, painful. A lecture on love as they sat at a café table under plane trees in Provence, his father drinking pastis, his mother stitching to mend a rent in his shirt, his best, which he hoped to wear at the fête that evening. Now and again she stopped stitching to bite a thread and smile quizzically at her husband lecturing their son of ten years on the pitfalls and delights of love, urging him to enjoy but to take it lightly. He must have been a little drunk, thought Mylo, remembering the clouded pastis in the glass, the dappled sunlight slanting across his father's face, lighting his mother's eyes. "Beware," his father proclaimed, "love can alter your whole life, make you change direction, trap you."

"*C'est juste*," said the café owner, pouring his father another drink.

"Your father, of course, never changes direction," Mylo's mother said, mocking her husband whose chief characteristic was volatility.

"There you go, mock me, sweep the ground from under my feet," Mylo's father had caught his wife's eye, smiling at her with complicity over the rim of his glass, "as usual."

Mylo's mother blushed, returning his father's glance. The café proprietor flapped his napkin remarking, "*C'est un beau discours*," and went back inside the café chuckling. Watching his parents Mylo had realised with shock that his parents were in love. He was amazed. Amused by his stunned expression, his mother had said gravely, "Listen to your father, Mylo, he warns you of this terrible danger which you must avoid at all costs."

"It is only right that he should be made aware of the risks," protested his father, "when he meets . . ."

"This girl like me?" She had let the hands which held the sewing fall into her lap. "Remember that, Mylo, when the trap closes, *gare à toi*, take note of your papa's warning."

"But it will be too late," cried Mylo's father dolefully. "*Il sera foutu*," and his parents had laughed, watching his puzzled face.

The wonderful thing about them, thought Mylo as he paced Mr Malone's library, had been that their love for each other had buoyed him up, included him, carried him with them. (A stupid unnecessary accident had killed them both, leaving him to face the future by himself at sixteen. There had been enough money to finish his education at the lycée, but none for university. He learned to consider the years spent with his parents in France, England, Germany, Italy, and briefly South Africa, travelling with his father, a peripatetic freelance journalist, as important experience, the University of Life – that humdrum cliché. Bilingual in French and English, he could get by in three other languages.) He had seen his mother insulted as a Jew in Germany, watched the fascists in Italy perform their deadly pantomime, accompanied his father to illicit political meetings in Spain, to incipient Marxist get-togethers in the black parts of Cape Town, grown up to think of himself as English, "Even though," as his mother would say, unable properly to pronounce her "th's", "they are slow sometimes, they are your people. *Je te donne ton pays.*"

She was an Anglophile, his father complained, who longed to live permanently in the filthy English climate rather than that of her native France.

Mylo stopped pacing to stare out at the Malones' garden, neat clipped hedges, raked gravel, orderly flower beds. What would have happened to my mother, he wondered, in the war that is coming? How would things have gone for her as a Jewess in France? Jews are not going to have a very nice time. There is the possibility that unless there is a miracle the villages of England and France will have notices at the crossroads prohibiting Jews, as there are in Germany. And my father, thought Mylo, who wrote exposing the false tricks and hypocrisies of governments, how would he have fared? Could he, would he, have adapted? Most unlikely, thought Mylo, smiling in recollection of how his father had been, if not exactly evicted, asked none too politely to leave South Africa. As he looked out at the frosty garden Mylo hummed the song he had helped his father record, a song sung at those secret meetings:

Tom blows hot,
Tom blows cold,
Ev'ry time poor Tom gets so-old,
Therefore, brothers, black and white,
Workers of the World unite!

He wished as he sang the words softly that there was a way of indicating to his parents that the hitherto academic experience of which they had laughingly warned him had hit him. "Bang, smack, wallop," he said out loud.

"What?" asked Rose, coming into the library.

"What a long time you've been," he cried.

"I had to play two interminable sets, every time I thought I had nearly lost, my partner won a rally."

"It's getting dark outside."

"Yes." She moved towards the fire. "I must go home."

"Not yet!" he cried with pain.

"Mrs Malone said that if I looked in the library I would find a young man called Mylo Cooper. She didn't know that I already had."

"And?"

"To ask you whether you had had any lunch . . ."

"I haven't."

"And, if you had not, to drag you away from your books, take you to the kitchen, and get cook to give you tea on a tray. I don't notice you buried in your books."

"I was thinking of you."

"Oh, good – and she said you were funny about meeting people."

"It's she who is funny about my meeting people; it's my clothes, I disgrace her socially."

Rose laughed. "I thought so. I like them. Then she said that I was to ask you to drive me home, when you've had some tea, that is."

"And you, too."

"And she said to take her car, not her husband's."

"Right. When are you expected home?"

"Not at any particular time. If my mother knows there's a dance, she will hope I will be asked to stay on for it. I do know and I don't want."

"So we can get ourselves tea, take as long as we like, and you can tell me the story of your life."

"It's very short and dull." They stood looking at the garden in its winter sleep. A blackbird alighted on the grass, stood listening, then ran a few paces. A second, stronger bird came flying down and ran aggressively towards the first bird, who flew off cackling.

"I still have not touched you. I am putting it off," murmured Mylo.

Rose shivered. "Do you think I'll explode, disappear?"

"You might. This whole thing frightens me," said Mylo. "Let's get some tea. I have so much to tell you. I feel faint with love."

"If you've had no lunch your faintness may be due to hunger," said Rose, reaching for the mundane.

From the warmth of the Malones' kitchen they had brought a tray laden with teapot, buttery crumpets, bread and butter, strawberry jam, wedges of Christmas cake and mince pies. In the light from the log fire and the frosty starlight of the winter's evening, they ate sitting side by side on the sofa.

It did not seem necessary to talk – the whole of the rest of their lives stretched ahead.

When they had finished Mylo took the tray back to the kitchen. Rose sat waiting for his return, listening to the distant sound of the house party, no longer playing tennis but fooling and flirting in the drawing-room at the other end of the house. Emily and Nicholas had knit themselves into the company, making their mark with the girls from London, consolidating themselves with the Malones, forgetting her. Waiting for Mylo, Rose felt an elation and trepidation which was entirely new to her, scary.

Mylo, coming back, switched on a lamp, bringing light to pry into dark corners and illuminate Rose's eyes and mouth. He knelt beside her on the hearth rug. "*Elle est belle à la chandelle*," he quoted.

"*Mais le grand tour gâte tout*," she carried on.

"So you know Molière?" He was surprised.

"A little. Nicholas taunted me with those lines when I was fifteen . . ."

"I was not going to quote further than the first line. Shall I get even with him for you?"

"I think life will do that. Tell me about you."

"Where to start?"

"Your parents, perhaps. People always seem to docket one by one's family – it is not always fair."

"They are dead," said Mylo.

Rose said nothing.

"I will try and bring them alive for you. While you played tennis I was thinking of them. They once, when I was small, tried to tell me about love. I will tell you what they said some day, but not now."

"They warned you?"

"They could not warn me against something they cherished so . . ."

"Oh, fortunate people," Rose exclaimed.

Mylo stared at Rose. "Yes. My father was clever, rash, impetuous. A burster of bubbles, a reporter of uncomfortable facts. He loved ideas. He was traveller, linguist, lover. He adored my mother, and she him. My mother was Jewish, beautiful, French, determined; she built around us a barrier of love. They had great ups and downs," said Mylo, "because my father would not compromise, nor would my mother have allowed him to."

"And they made you happy?"

"Very happy. You would have loved them, and they you."

"Thank you for telling me about them."

Mylo put logs on the fire, stacking them in the glowing ash so that the draught would reach them and they would flare up. "And you?" he asked gently. "Shall you tell me about your parents?"

Rose drew a long breath. "My father is dying of cancer, at least he thinks he is; I find it hard to believe, but that's the general idea. He is a solicitor, not successful, I don't know why. Yes, I do, I must be honest. He is unsuccessful because he is all things to all men, and people don't really like it. He tries to please people when they want plain facts, even nasty ones, so they do not trust him (and nor do I, she whispered). Then he is a snob. It matters very much to him who people are, how much money they have. Why are you laughing?"

"I am not laughing," said Mylo, who had gasped at the pain in Rose's voice.

"My mother is much the same," Rose went on, "but she is shy and awkward. When she has people to the house, she infects them with her embarrassment. I have never spoken of my parents like this before. She is desperately anxious that I should get married to a man with money. She forced me to come to this tennis today; she thought I would meet someone suitable. You *are* laughing."

"You have met *me*."

"In her eyes or my father's you would be a calamity," cried Rose in anguish, "and awful though I have made them sound, I suppose I love them but," she cried, "they do not love each other. The idea of cancer is a plot to escape each other."

"Oh, my love." Mylo put his arms round Rose. "There," he said, kissing her, "there, I have touched you at last." Locking her in his arms, consoling her. "Oh, my love." He did not know whether he consoled her for her parents or for his love.

"Mylo, Mylo, Mylo," Rose loved his name, her arms round his neck, her face against his.

"Listen . . ." he said.

Trooping from the drawing-room through the hall they heard the house party in high-pitched badinage, George's laugh, Richard shouting some fool joke, Nicholas sniggering, the girls answering with coos and yelps, abrupt screams. "They are going up to change. There is to be a dance."

"Not for us," said Rose smugly.

"Shall I drive you home? Fetch your coat and meet me in the back drive by Mrs Malone's car."

"I must say goodbye and thank her. I'll be quick." She could not bear to part with him.

"Goodbye," she said to Mrs Malone, sitting tiredly in the drawing-room, "and thank you for a lovely day."

"Pretty boring, I'm afraid, you did not play much tennis. You must come again." Mrs Malone's head ached; she planned a drink of stiffish whisky while she had her bath. The Freeling girl seemed anxious to leave. And I don't blame her, thought Mrs Malone. All the boys do is work the girls up until they become noisy and shriek, high time they got married, this one seems quiet enough.

Rose fled through the house to join Mylo. "You will have to remember the names of the suitable people you played tennis with," he said.

"Tomorrow. Not now." She slammed the car door shut, sat beside him.

Mylo kissed her, holding her face in his hands. "Who else have you kissed, Rose?"

"The only person who kissed me did it for a laugh under the mistletoe. He had a wet mouth and a moustache; it was horrible."

"I can't be jealous of him."

"There will never be anyone for you to be jealous of . . ."

"Oh, Rose . . ."

How innocent we were, thought Rose half a century on, lying in the hotel bed. Pathetic in a comical way. Embarking on the rapids which crashed us together, tore us apart. In the stillness of the night, from the woods across the creek, there was the sudden shriek of a vixen calling for a dog fox, the blood-chilling scream which has terrified many a city dweller into fits (somebody is getting murdered out there). Rose stiffened in sharp recollection. The vixen screamed again as her ancestress had screamed the night she first met Mylo. Rose lay back, straining her ears. Who am I listening for? Ned? Mylo? Poor Ned, gone. Ned, cremated, dust, dust.

"I won't come in with you," said Mylo as they drove, "I will come and see you as soon as I can escape my tutorial duties."

"It would be better not," Rose agreed. "They will not like you," she said. "I don't want this day ruined." My mother, she thought, or my father could sully Mylo with one derogatory glance. I shall feel stronger tomorrow.

"You can regale them with your exploits at tennis."

"I broke my father's racquet and can't remember who I played with."

"You will remember by the morning. Shall you tell them about me?"

"Oh, no, they would try and spoil you, you don't know them. I will tell them nothing. I know it is best so."

"I could shout my joy from the housetops."

"Better not. When you meet them, you will understand. You could have told your family. I cannot tell mine. They are destructive."

"Then we shall be secret to one another."

"Promise?"

"I promise," said Mylo who, young as he was, knew the dissipating power of gossip. "It may not be for very long," he said, "but I shall keep mum."

"Stop here," said Rose. "There is a short cut through the wood."

They got out, leaving the car by the side of the road and walked up a grass ride, their feet crunching on the brittle frozen grass. They held hands, walking in silence, then a full moon dodged suddenly from behind a cloud, lighting the bare branches of the trees, exposing their faces to each other so that they stood and stared and examined each line and hollow, every curve of lip and cheek, taking note for their future. Then Mylo held her close and hugged her, and Rose discovered the joy of pressing against him, warming her cold nose against his neck as he nuzzled and kissed her. It was then the vixen screamed. Clinging together, they whispered, "Hush, listen, will he answer?" And again the vixen screamed.

"Oh, Mylo," said Rose, "I hope I never call for you and get no answer."

"Only death would stop me, although," said Mylo, laughing now, "in the nature of things I might get delayed, my love, but I will come, I won't be long."

How long is fifty years? Rose asked herself, lying sleepless in the hotel bed. How does one calculate the passage of time and retain one's sanity?

THIRTEEN

Mrs Freeling woke early, as was her habit, and heaved herself up on one elbow. Two yards away, her husband slept on his back, his mouth open, his breath going in-out-in-out in lugubrious rhythm.

At this hour before she had collected them, her thoughts wandered stumbling along the route beyond the noticeboard which said, No trespassing. The first unformulated thought said: I wish, if he is going to die, that he would, not hang about like this.

The second said: At least in London we can have separate rooms that will lead without quibble to separate rooms here. Then, if he should die, I could sell this house and move into something smaller, easier to run. Or a flat.

And next: If Rose would only get married, I could live alone.

Then she thought: I did not hear her come in last night; I wonder whether she got to know any new people at the party? She's pretty, it should not be too hard to marry her off to someone suitable. I really must do something about it. I wonder how one begins? I'm so bad at that sort of thing.

Here Mrs Freeling permitted her dream to present her with a son-in-law who, besides taking Rose on, would gratuitously produce a rent-free house or cottage for his mother-in-law. But that was going too far, too fast. Just let Rose marry.

Mrs Freeling sank back on her pillows and breathed deeply and slowly from her stomach in-out-in-out thirty-six times which should, she had read somewhere, induce beautiful thoughts and peace of mind. Perhaps, she thought, marriage would be all right for Rose; perhaps she would not mind the physical part – so messy at best, so painful at worst. There were women who did not seem to mind. It must be terrible to be raped, thought Mrs Freeling, thrusting into her unconscious the belief that her husband had raped her on their wedding night (and subsequently), and that Rose's birth, another agonising incident, was its direct consequence.

Time to get up.

Mrs Freeling swung her legs over the side of the bed and felt for her slippers. I was stupid, she told herself, getting into her dressing-gown, to put up with a double bed all those years. It's been much better since we had twin beds. If Rose marries, I shall advise twin beds from the start.

Mrs Freeling set off to the bathroom.

As she cleaned her teeth, Mrs Freeling thought, Rose should be able to find a husband; if she were ten years older, it would be another story, she would be up against the shortage of men since the last war. There had been "ten million surplus women, ten million surplus wives" in the words of the music hall song. They didn't know their luck, thought Mrs Freeling, spitting into the basin, rinsing her toothbrush under the tap.

As she dressed, Mrs Freeling shed her waking thoughts, resumed with vest, knickers, suspender belt, stockings, shoes, tweed skirt, blouse and cardigan, her proper persona. Then she knelt briefly by her bed to say her morning prayers, Our Father forgive us our trespasses, before trotting briskly downstairs to see whether the maids had her husband's breakfast tray ready.

"Morning, girls."

"Morning, madam."

"I will take it up to him," she said, supervising the lightly boiled egg, toast, butter, marmalade and China tea, "he likes me to be there as he wakes. I like to see him."

"Yes, madam," said cook.

The house parlourmaid said nothing; she had had a letter from her mother in Wales and felt homesick.

Mrs Freeling carried the tray upstairs. As she passed Rose's bedroom door she rapped on it smartly. "Time to get up," she called, "breakfast is ready."

Rose groaned, a groan she had perfected during adolescence, knowing the groan was expected. On no account could she let out the shout of, "I'm in love, I'm in love, I'm in love," which welled up. Damp it down, treasure it, keep it secret.

"Here we are, darling, here's your breakfast. How did you sleep? Let me plump up your pillows. Wait a sec, here are your teeth – how do you feel this morning, my poor darling? Is that all you need? Yes, I'll ask her at breakfast and get her to come up and tell you all about it. Oh, you'll be up? That's good. Feeling better today? How wonderful. Soon be in London and get started on the treatment. Sooner the better. I'll just open the window a crack, it's a bit fuggy in here. I'll get you a shawl to put round your shoulders . . ."

"Don't fuss me. Leave the window as it is."

"Oh, very well. I'll send Rose up for the tray presently . . ."

"I'm getting up. Why don't you listen?"

"Of course you are, sorry. It's a lovely morning. I can't wait to hear how Rose got on."

"I can. She broke my racquet."

"What? How do you know?"

"Couldn't sleep. Got up and went downstairs to read for a bit. Saw it on the hall table. Brand new Slazenger."

"Oh, dear, I wonder how it happened?"

"Broke it over some young fool's head."

"Nonsense, darling, Rose would never . . ."

"Where's *The Times*?"

"Oh, sorry, I forgot to put it on the tray. I'll send Rose up with it, then you . . ."

"Don't bother, can't read the paper properly in bed, uncomfortable."

"I wish. I wish." Mrs Freeling trotted downstairs to her own breakfast in the dining-room. She would have been horrified if anyone had told her that what she wished was her husband dead. "We have been married nineteen years," she often told people, "and never a cross word."

"Ah, Rose, are you there? Did you have a good time? Don't come into the room yawning. Was the dance fun?" She offered her cheek for Rose to kiss.

"I didn't dance."

"Then how was it you got home so late?"

"Oh, Mrs Malone – you know how it is – there were a lot of people – a lot of waiting about – then her car . . ."

"Didn't the Thornbys bring you home?"

"No, Mrs Malone got someone who is staying there to drive me back in her car."

"How kind of her. One of the young men staying there?"

"A tutor person," said Rose astutely.

"Oh, really." Mrs Freeling's interest dimmed. "You must tell us all about it. Pass the milk, darling. Do sit up, don't slouch, it's so ugly. Your father says you broke his racquet."

"Yes, I did this tremendous drive. I hit the ball so hard the strings bust."

"Oh, oh dear."

"Does it matter? He won't ever need it."

"Rose, how can you!"

"Oh, Mother, don't cry – please don't cry."

"It's just, it's just all so awful."

"Oh, Mother, stop. Please. Look, I'll tell you about the tennis party.

George Malone asked if cook still makes her jellies, and the new man at Slepe, Ned Peel, was there . . ."

"Ned Peel, did you talk to him much?"

"Not really, no. Not at all, actually." Rose, hoping to comfort her mother, was sorry to disappoint her.

FOURTEEN

I usually managed to disappoint my mother, thought Rose lying in the hotel bed. She had propped the window wide now and thought she could really hear, was not imagining, the rustle of the reeds as they swayed in the still night.

I disappointed my father also, she thought, but not so much. He had his work to think about and his supposed cancer. I wonder whether he did have cancer? Whether it might not have been ulcers or something of that sort? He died of a stroke. I remember my mother's resentment when the bill for the cancer treatment had to be paid. Had all that money been wasted? It's curious how little I know about my parents. Rose abandoned sleep, surrendered to a wakeful night.

They disliked each other, those two, she thought. It was rather dreadful the way they pretended not to.

Presumably they never had any fun in bed. If they had, there would have been ups and downs in their relationship. Lively shouting matches to break the monotony. Their rows were tamped down, never allowed to surface, just the sort of thing to produce ulcers.

Those quarrels, thought Rose, yearned for a bout of healthy fucking. I bet my mother never had an orgasm. My poor pa would not have known how to set about giving her one. An orgasm for a woman of my mother's generation was a matter of chance. She almost certainly went to her death with an undiscovered clitoris. She always said she was unlucky. I wonder, mused Rose, how much the younger generation's aptitude for guitars has contributed to sexual bliss. I must inquire of Christopher. No, I can't, he would find my question in poor taste. There is too much of Ned in Christopher. No wonder Helen has such a grip.

The least disappointing time for my parents, thought Rose, was the period between the winter tennis party and my marriage to Ned.

It was extraordinary in retrospect how Ned had insinuated himself into the Freelings' lives. Had there been a moment when it would have been possible to put a stop to Ned, choke him off without irreparably hurting him? Dear kind Ned. Was there a moment when

I could have cried halt? It was my fault, thought Rose, I was inattentive, I should have seen that his strength was his apparent vulnerability. I used him to deflect attention from Mylo. I trailed Ned as the lapwing trails her wing.

She tried to remember when it had become unremarkable, accepted, for Ned to come constantly to the house.

At first it had been George and Richard who came on one excuse or another on their way to the Thornbys, or bringing some message from their mother to hers in a friendship destined for an early demise, blossoming briefly, to die when Rose married Ned.

Sometimes George and Richard brought Mylo, practising their French. At other times Nicholas and Emily would be there and other young men whose names and faces now eluded her. I was in love, thought Rose, that made me attractive to other men, that is the way it works, just like the animal world.

Mrs Freeling had been delighted, made references to moths and candles, causing her daughter to wince. The advent of this modest number of young men had excited her, increased her subtle pressure for Rose to marry. She picked over the young men deftly. This one's father drank, that one had an uncle who was an undeclared bankrupt, another's mother was rumoured to have Indian blood. How had she discovered these things, to which grapevine did she connect? For an unsociable, retiring woman, she was no slouch. She shuffled the pack, conjuring to the fore the two Malones (the jelly incident forgotten), only to push them aside when Ned appeared and re-appeared, became constant.

She never really noticed Mylo, thought Rose. No warning bell sounded. Rose chuckled forty-eight years later.

Mylo came, dressed now as were all the others in the dress of the day. Tweed jacket and grey flannel trousers, a uniform as ubiquitous as jeans. There had been a brief parental bustle. Wasn't he rather foreign? Jewish, perhaps? No family. No money (poor boy, how worn his shoes). No proper job. No university degree. Frightfully young.

This quasi-invisible put-down, which applied in varying degree to lots of people, was enough for Mylo to steer clear, for them to meet secretly where they could be together unobserved: in the woods in fine weather, in churches when it rained. They pretended an interest in brass rubbing if anyone chanced to interrupt them absorbed in talk, sitting entwined in the most comfortable pew or reading aloud to each other. Our love, like prayers, must have soaked into the walls of those churches, stirred the loins of the long dead under the brasses, thought Rose.

Mylo had acquired his little car so they travelled far afield. It had belonged to a friend of Mylo's father who, owing him a favour, repaid it to the son.

When the Freelings moved to London for Mr Freeling's cancer treatment, they met in the museums, picnicked in the parks, strolled hand in hand in Kew Gardens, lolled in Richmond Park. Mylo by this time had finished his stint at the Malones (George never acquired a good accent, but was famous for fluency) and was looking for a job.

While Rose floated on cloud nine, Ned grew closer. Kind and friendly to her parents, consistently attentive, taking her to Quaglino's, the Écu de France, to dine and dance at the Berkeley, to lunch at the Savoy. To the regatta at Henley (surprising in his pink socks), to the Eton and Harrow Ball, to the Air Show, to Wimbledon, to theatres and cinemas, displaying the kingdoms of his world. Had she played him off against Mylo, had she been seduced by Ned's offerings?

If only I had not been a virgin, thought Rose. If only I had known what I learned later, that the hungry coupling of the young which failed us in that smelly little hotel could become a glorious leisurely indulgence.

How had the trap closed? Was there a day when Mylo gave up? Did he stand back, angry? When had she decided to opt for safety and pleasing her parents? (Be fair, I was pleased too.) Impossible now to put a finger on it, enough that she had said, "Yes, all right," walking with Ned in the dusk, in his Uncle Archibald's glen with the curlew crying.

It was then, Rose thought wryly, that her parents had stopped feeling their disappointment, had quite liked each other, basking in a joint glow of parental success.

I was so young, Rose excused herself, and Mylo was so young too. If only we could have waited.

My parents' liking for each other did not last. But the trap closed and I, thought Rose, grew fond of my jailer. Mylo, angry and estranged, absorbed by the war, disappeared; he might, in his silence, have been dead, so totally did he withdraw.

The telephone had rung while she was in her bath before dressing for her wedding.

"Somebody wants you on the telephone, he won't give his name" – her mother had been irritated – "won't give a message."

Wrapped in her bath towel she had heard his husky voice: "Meet me at the corner of the street. It's not too late. Come quick, don't stop to think. I've got the car."

"How can I? I'm in my bath. I . . ."

"I shan't bother you again, then." He was furious.

"Oh, please, please, don't go, don't say goodbye," she had screamed, regardless of her mother listening on the stair.

"I am not saying it . . ." He had rung off.

One of Ned's secrets was a sense of insecurity. He needed to be reassured, pampered. Something of a parvenu – he was only a distant cousin of the old Peel, had not grown up expecting to inherit – he enjoyed obsequious waiters bowing to his money as they pulled out chairs, flapped napkins, proffered menus, and I, thought Rose, was too young, too naïve to observe this until later. Poor Ned, I no longer mind but there were times when I deeply resented the asking and the giving of that promise. Poor old Ned, poor Ned.

I wonder, thought Rose jerking awake before she finally drifted into sleep, where I put Ned's ashes?

I am growing so forgetful, she thought worriedly, I am forever losing things.

Then, How stupid of me. How could I forget? Helen took charge of them. Helen would, thought Rose, smiling none too kindly in the dark. One wonders, does Helen pleasure Christopher? He wears such a discontented expression. He was such a dear little boy. Now he has a sad look to him. Does Helen look covertly at me and wonder how Ned and I got on in bed? Will she care for Slepe as I did? Where will she decide to put Ned's ashes? Is Ned, in ash, feeling more secure? There was never any need for Ned to worry.

Through the open window came the hotel cat, viewed on his way to hunt the night away. Now he sprang on to Rose's bed, stepping on to her body to tread and purr, pressing down his claws to clench the bedclothes, catching and extracting them, purring and rumbling in ecstasy and Rose, released by surprise, wept for Ned for the first time since he had died.

FIFTEEN

"So," Ned said, relinquishing his imprecise memories of the winter tennis, "shall I show you round the house? Shall we do the grand tour?" He was impatient, proud of his possessions, anxious to show them off, present Rose with her future.

Rose jumped up. "Could we walk round the garden first?"

"If that's what you'd like." He would indulge her. "I know nothing about gardens," he said, striking at a passing bee, swishing the head off a Japanese anemone.

Rose retrieved the decapitated flower. "Nor do I know much, but I am ready to learn." She walked ahead of him.

The paved path led through the garden to wrought-iron gates leading into a second garden. "How lovely," Rose exclaimed, two walled gardens, what riches, what wonderful flowers." She looked around, pleased.

"It's very disorderly." Ned looked about critically.

"That's what's so exciting," said Rose. "I like it."

"There's a third and larger garden for vegetables and fruit," Ned said. "It should be useful if food gets short as it did in the nineteen-fourteen war. I hope Farthing knows his onions. Ah, there is Farthing – we'd better say hullo." He took Rose's arm above the elbow, "This is my wife, Farthing, Mrs Peel."

"Ah," said Farthing, looking Rose over (as though I need pruning, Rose told herself). Farthing was a man of sixty with leathery outdoor skin, small bright eyes, a puckered mouth and obstinate chin. He was a very small man, no taller than Rose.

Rose took his hand. "Your garden is gorgeous."

"Who did that?" Farthing's eye seemed to slide down Rose's arm to the flower head in her hand.

"An accident." She would not betray Ned.

"I saw him," said Farthing. "Bees is useful animals." He had witnessed Ned swish at the bee.

"He missed." Rose grinned. "Do you keep bees?"

"Two, three hives, depends."

"How are the vegetables, has it been a good season?" Ned felt excluded.

"Veggies is all right." Farthing was studying Rose.

I wish he'd call me sir, thought Ned. "We should concentrate on vegetables from now on," he asserted his authority.

"But not to the exclusion of flowers, Ned, bees need them and honey is frightfully important; sugar is going to be rationed, and without disturbing the flowers, there are lots of vegetables which can be grown among them, aren't there, Mr Farthing?"

"Hadn't thought to do that, miss, good idea. Farthing will do, miss, just Farthing."

"Mrs," corrected Ned, "since yesterday. Mrs Peel."

"Ah," said Farthing, "um."

He is teasing Ned, thought Rose. "Will you teach me to work in the garden?" she asked Farthing. "When I'm on my own."

"Ah," said Farthing, "veggies is through there." He nodded towards a door in the wall. "Nice crop of onions and shallots; my old gentleman was fond of garlic too."

"Good," said Rose. "Come on, Ned, let's look." She led the way into the kitchen garden. "This is all jolly orderly," she said, pointing at the rows of vegetables. "What a lovely man; isn't he nice, Ned?"

"He will have to get used to me," said Ned, "he misses my uncle." Lovely was not, he felt, an applicable word for the gardener.

"Of course he does. One can read his feelings, his love in the gardens."

"I can't say I can, but he seemed to take to you . . ."

"Come on, Ned, don't be grumpy, just look at that crop of onions! They would win prizes anywhere."

(I am not grumpy.) "I'd rather show you the house, come along . . ." Ned walked her past the rows of onions ripening in the sun, turning his eyes away from the fruits of Farthing's labours. "Fortunately Mrs Farthing has looked after the furniture rather well. The house needs a lot doing to it, but we shall have to wait until after the war. All I've done so far is to put in an Aga. My uncle made do with a monumental Victorian range. It all needs modernising."

"Is Mrs Farthing pleased?"

"She should be. Of course she is. Here, come this way into the house, by the side door." Ned led the way. "When you get to know the house you shall help me decide what needs doing to it. This is the kitchen. Hullo, Mrs Farthing, this is Mrs Peel."

Rose and Mrs Farthing shook hands. "How do you do," said Rose.

Mrs Farthing, thin, wiry, tall and energetic, stood defensively by a kitchen table scrubbed pale. Rose could imagine Mrs Farthing's bony hands wielding the scrubbing brush which had worn the grain of the wood into almost parallel lines. At the moment Mrs Farthing made show of making pastry; Rose felt she intended to be found at work. The legitimate occupier. Newcomer keep out. "A lovely kitchen." Rose genuinely liked it.

"We must modernise it," said Ned, looking round, "get advice."

"I expect Mrs Farthing can tell you what needs to be done, she would be the person to know." She had noticed the older woman flush.

Mrs Farthing did not relax. "Our cottage kitchen is as we wanted it, our Mr Peel did that for us."

If she snubs him as hard as that, there will be out-on-your-ear trouble. "Do you have a cat in your cottage? A kitchen should have a cat; there should be a cat here, shouldn't there, Ned?" Rose burbled nervously.

"Do you want a cat?" asked Ned doubtfully.

"We have our cat in the cottage, miss, expecting kittens, miss."

(Another one calling her miss; she's a married woman, I made her so last night. Ned tingled in recollection.)

"Would you let me have one, or two, perhaps, to keep each other company?"

"Yes, miss, if you like, miss. Farthing was going to drown . . ."

"Oh, no!"

"Steady on, I said I'd let you have a dog, we'll be eaten out of house and . . ."

"I love cats. My mother never let me have one. They earn their keep, don't they, Mrs Farthing?"

Mrs Farthing's mouth semi-smiled. "Of course, miss."

Ned siphoned air up his nose, as Rose had known her father do when particularly irritated. (I bet her cat is fat as butter, and no great mouser.) "Show me the house," she said quickly. "Come on, Ned. I want to see everything, the pictures, furniture, silver, glass, rugs, the lot."

Mrs Farthing watched them go. "She may do," she said to her husband coming into the kitchen with a trug of vegetables. "Wipe your feet."

"Ah," said Farthing, "give her one of they honeycombs for her tea."

"Oh, my," said his wife sarcastically, "charmed already!"

"Makes a change," said Farthing, kicking off his boots, "we must learn to call him sir, if we want him happy." Farthing was sardonic.

"And her Mrs?"

Husband and wife doubled up in wheezy mirth.

★

"I shall be alone in the house when you are gone, with the Farthings in their cottage, just me with my dog and my cats," said Rose.

"Shall you be nervous?" Ned was uneasy.

"I like being alone." (Surely Mylo will be here sometimes, if only in my thoughts.) "What is this room?" Rose opened a door.

"The drawing-room. When you have the lay of the house, I want to decide what rooms to keep open. When the Ministry people move into the back, they will have their own entrance, but everything from that part of the house must be stored. So Rose, pay attention, there really isn't time to look at the view, this is not an ordinary honeymoon . . ." He let irritation escape.

"No." Rose turned back from the window. "It's not." She stopped looking out at the garden which she would grow to love. (He has already decided what rooms to keep in use, where to store the furniture.) "What's the matter, Ned?"

"I want you to like it here, it's yours as much as mine, you know it is." He caught hold of her and held her.

"No, it's not." She drew away.

Ned curbed his irritation. I am not doing this right. She doesn't know what this house means to me, she has no idea of the sanctity of inheritance. "It's ours, dear, and will be our children's."

Rose turned back towards the garden which enchanted through the window; unbelievably she had not envisaged children (why must he call me "dear"?) "Oh, Ned." She looked away.

"I had so hoped you would like it."

"I do. I do. Give me time. It's such a lot to take in. Start telling me. Who, for instance, is the privileged gent above the fireplace watching us now?"

"Augustus Napley. He married Angelica Peel. They did not get on. My uncle moved her matching portrait into the dining-room, said they looked much happier apart. My uncle was inclined to be whimsical, a fanciful old man." Ned was disparaging of his relation.

"I would have liked him."

"Maybe you would. Shall I go on?"

"Do."

Ned led her about the house explaining, naming, and describing his treasures. Rose stopped listening, content to wear an intelligent expression; later, by herself, she would get to know the house, develop her own rapport.

After lunch they strolled across the fields to the farm so that Ned could introduce her to his farming tenant and his wife. "The Hadleys have farmed here for years; you will not go short of milk, butter, eggs and cream."

"How you harp on about food."

"I thought you might like to send me hampers when I'm with the regiment," said Ned huffily.

"Ensuring your popularity."

Ned looked at her sharply. He had not realised that she was so, so un-meek.

The Hadleys, John and Tina, were both large and friendly, their several children friendly also. Ned talked farming with John Hadley; Rose saw that he was at ease with them, quite knowledgeable on farming. He expanded in the farmhouse atmosphere and made earthy jokes which made the Hadleys laugh, but not Rose; she did not understand them. Watching Ned with the Hadleys she wondered whether they were as bucolic as they seemed, or putting it on to please Ned. When they left, the Hadleys told her to come over whenever she pleased, there would always be a welcome.

Walking back to Slepe, Rose said, "I like them, but they are not as interesting as the Farthings. The Hadleys are open, the Farthings closed."

"I can't say I find the Farthings likeable, but they do their job; everything is above board at the farm; the Farthings are different."

"That's what I like," said Rose.

"I hope you will not be bored when you are on your own."

"Of course not. I shall find plenty to do."

"You are only twenty-five miles from your parents."

"Yes."

"And five from the Thornbys."

"Yes."

"And ten from the Malones."

"I'm not madly sociable, Ned."

"I shall be able to get home whenever I get leave, so long, that is, as we are in England."

"Of course."

"There is talk, strictly between ourselves, of France."

"When?"

"Soonish."

"France!" (Mylo is in France. That parcel . . .) "How soon?"

"Any time now, I fear. Damn, who is that over there in the drive waving?"

"Emily Thornby."

"One would have credited her with more tact," exclaimed Ned, furious, "than to call on the first day of our honeymoon."

"You did say it was no ordinary honeymoon," said Rose unkindly.

"Hullo," shouted Emily, advancing. "I was just passing, thought I'd stop and see how you are getting on."

"Very well, thanks," Ned said with chill.

"I shan't stay," said Emily laughing, "I can see I am not welcome." Her eyes danced brightly from Rose to Ned and back to Ned.

"Come in and have a drink," suggested Rose.

"Thanks. I've our wedding present in the car. Nicholas and I were late buying it, couldn't make up our minds or raise the cash. Like to fetch it from the car, Ned?"

Ned moved off towards Emily's car, grudging every stride.

"Eventually we managed to charge it to Mrs Malone's account," said Emily, grinning. "It's all right, she'll never notice." She watched Ned's back. "How are you? What's marriage like?" Emily lowered her voice an octave. "Do you think you can manage?" Her eyes swept over Rose from head to toe, then up again.

"What's the present?" asked Rose, feeling herself flush.

"A lamp from Peter Jones, Fortnums wouldn't charge to Mrs Malone. It's a Tiffany copy guaranteed to give a soft glow. Nicholas tried it, it's quite sexy. Are you all right?" she persisted.

"Of course I am," said Rose, stung into replying.

Emily made a move and giggled. "That's good." She was watching Ned's return with a cardboard box in his arms. "We hoped you would be, Nicholas and I . . ."

Ned put the box down beside Rose. "I'll walk you to your car, Emily."

"Oh," said Emily. "Rose has just suggested a drink."

"Some other time," Ned had her by the elbow, "not today."

"Oho," said Emily, tossing her narrow nose upwards, "so that's how it is."

"That's right." Ned opened Emily's car door and started pushing her in.

"What's she like then, Ned?"

Ned smacked Emily's bottom hard.

"Ouch!" cried Emily.

"Be off," said Ned, good humoured, and slammed the car door.

"That's better," murmured Mrs Farthing, watching from a window, "maybe he will do."

"What did you want to do that for?" asked Rose as Emily drove off.

"She had it coming," said Ned, rubbing his hands together. "I quite hurt my hand, she has a hard bottom."

"I thought men like you never hit women," said Rose, wondering why the curious little scene with Emily disturbed her.

"It depends on the woman." Ned closed the subject.

"I know I am very naïve," said Rose.

"Bless you," said Ned. He put his hand, which still stung, around Rose's waist and drew her towards the house. "Come indoors, it's getting chilly. Your naïvety is part of your charm," he said.

As she walked towards the house, Rose wondered whether in similar circumstances Mylo would have smacked Emily. I do not know why Ned should want to hit her. She is irritating, but surely – and would Mylo? In the hall Rose stood still and suddenly she shivered. I must stop thinking of Mylo, stop making comparisons. It isn't fair. I have promised Ned. Promised. She was hit by a wave of anguish. I must keep Mylo separate, or I shall go mad.

"What's the matter, Rose, are you cold? Are you tired? Why do you shiver? A goose, is it a goose?" Ned, unnerved by Rose's distraught expression, tried a joke.

Rose shook her head. "No goose," she said, "no grave. It's nothing, perhaps I need a jersey."

"Are you sure?"

"Let me take it easy, Ned. I hadn't realised how much there is to this marriage business. Your house, your possessions, your people . . ."

"Well, dear . . ."

"I will work it out, I will, I won't let you down." Rose held her hand out to Ned. "I am being silly."

"Yes," said Ned, puzzled, "you are."

She wondered whether he was being obtuse on purpose, whether he was trying to protect her as already she found herself protecting him. Last night, she thought, I tried to pretend it was Mylo; it didn't work. There is no way being in bed with Ned could ever resemble being with Mylo. He is gone anyway, she told herself bitterly, all that talk of phoning was just eye-wash.

"I think I'll have a bath and warm up," she said.

"You do that. Then come and join me in a drink." Ned moved towards the drinks in the drawing-room. We must shut up this room, it's too big, he thought, stack the furniture, use the old man's library for the duration. He let his mind snake through the rooms, deciding what furniture to move, what to store, which rooms to keep in use. He poured himself a drink, wandered back into the hall, shouted up the stairs, "Don't take too long, I need you with me." Listened for Rose's faint answer, wandered slowly back to the fireplace. I need to imprint my house on Rose, he thought as he stood listening for her return, but all he heard was the mocking clack of jackdaws coming down the chimney. He struck a match and bent to light the fire. "That'll put paid to you." He watched the smoke curl up.

SIXTEEN

The Farthings watched Ned enjoy his honeymoon with detachment. It amused them to observe the satisfaction he derived fitting Rose in among his property. He manipulated her with the same care that he lavished on the Sheraton desk, the sofa table, the Regency commodes, the sofa, armchairs, bookshelves and rugs with which he furnished the room that had been his uncle's library, moving and removing until he was satisfied that each piece was in an appropriate position.

He led Rose about, showing her every room, satisfying himself that she belonged in it, then walking her through his fields, showing her the boundaries of his property, bonding her to his land.

Just as they had noticed him adopt with his uniform a military persona, so, surrounded by his inherited possessions, they watched him cherish them and with them his appendage wife, making complete his role as landed gentleman. For a man who had until lately scarcely put foot outside London, they granted that Ned did not do too badly.

It entertained the Farthings inordinately when Ned took an almost womanly interest in his household, making lists of stores which could be hoarded prior to rationing and probable shortages, ordering, besides groceries, large stocks of coal and anthracite, arranging with the Hadleys to stockpile logs for winter fires. He even, much to Mrs Farthing's delight, checked and criticised Rose's meagre trousseau, telling her that she must as soon as may be get herself more warm clothes, thick sweaters, trousers, fur boots to overcome the absence of decent heating at Slepe, a draughty house with several outside doors.

"Thinks of everything," said Farthing, laconic.

"Grocery list as long as your arm," said his wife, extending her arm in sardonic gesture.

"Knows it all," said Farthing.

"Not quite," said Mrs Farthing and waited until Ned had come back with Rose from depleting the stocks in the market town, to suggest a fresh list of stores, without which she maintained the war could not be weathered. Olive oil, cans of golden syrup, rice and sugar.

None too pleased, Ned took Rose on a second foray and was even less pleased when she, entering into the spirit of things, added to the list lavatory paper, candles, dog food in tins, and Roget et Gallet bath soap.

"But there is no dog . . ." protested Ned.

"There will be . . ."

"She'll grow up," said Farthing, taking time off from the garden to help his wife stack the stores in the pantry cupboards. "Fact is, her's begun." Farthing liked to talk yokel on occasion.

"My poor back!" Mrs Farthing straightened up, groaning. "We'll teach her when he's gone to put butter down in salt and pot eggs *and* he's made no provision for ham and sides of bacon." Mrs Farthing eased herself, her hand pressed against the small of her back.

"A pig?" suggested her husband.

"Too soft-hearted, I'd say."

"Um. Farm pig, then?"

"That'll do."

"Who's it all for? Won't have evacuees."

"Wants to have his fellow officers to stay. Heard him telling her."

"What did she say to that?"

"Yes, Ned, why don't you. As though she's not to live here herself."

"She's only half here. Think she'll settle when he's gone?"

"Dare say she will find her own way; hers is not his, that's for sure."

On the last evening of Ned's leave he led Rose to an outbuilding in the copse behind the garages. "It's in here," he said, unlocking a padlocked outhouse. "I will show you where I keep the key. The petrol is in those tanks." He showed her two large galvanised iron receptacles. "You will see, if you climb up those steps, the petrol is in the jerrycans stacked inside them, a hundred gallons."

"Golly!" Rose peered down from the steps. "What a lot."

"I got one of the chaps from the regiment to help me put it there; the Farthings do not know, of course."

No "of course" about it, thought Rose, watching her husband lock the door.

"You are only to use it in case of dire emergency," said Ned, "it's not for joy-riding."

"What would dire emergency be?"

"A German invasion."

"So I could hop it to Scotland?" Rose was amused.

Ned did not care for her frivolity. "It's more than a possibility, from what I hear from the War Office."

"Do you have a direct line?" Rose teased.

"One gets one's information," said Ned.

Does one indeed? thought Rose.

"Should I be posted overseas, I shall lay up my car; it eats petrol; I am getting you a small Morris of moderate consumption."

"Oh. How moderate?"

"It's a surprise. The garage will bring it tomorrow."

"I am surprised. Thank you, Ned."

"It's not new, it's second-hand."

"Good enough to bolt from the Germans in a dire emergency."

Ned was not sure what to make of his wife's tone. He looked at his bride sharply, trying to read her thoughts.

A dire emergency, Rose was thinking as she turned smiling eyes on her husband, would be if I had to rush to Mylo, but I cannot rush as I do not know where he is; I cannot rush into a void.

"I am sad," she exclaimed with sudden passion.

"I am only going as far as Aldershot." Ned misunderstood her. "I am, too, but I shall be home whenever I can. One gets leave. I shall bring people to stay. You will not be lonely long. I will ring up."

"You will ring up?"

"Of course I shall. I shall telephone often, every day probably."

"Oh, Ned. Yes, of course. I had not thought of that." (And Mylo? When will he telephone?)

"If you find you're lonely, there's your family. The . . ."

"I shall be all right, Ned, I am looking forward to being alone," she said hurriedly. "I don't want . . ."

"That's nice!" exclaimed Ned, hurt.

How did I let that slip? "You know I don't mean looking forward to being without you. I mean that I am quite happy on my own, I am used to my own company. I am an only child, Ned."

"Dear," said Ned, "it's my last evening." He put his arm around her. "Come to bed."

Tomorrow, thought Rose climbing upstairs, when he is gone, I shall open the parcel. Perhaps it will tell me where Mylo is. There will be a message. There is bound to be a message. "All right, hurry up," she said to Ned to hasten his departure.

Ned took her hand and ran up the last few steps with her, misunderstanding. In the large rather lumpy fourposter Ned took Rose then, assuaged, lay sleepily considering his honeymoon which had passed so swiftly and busily. He was content as he reviewed the rearrangement of the rooms, the storing of the stores, the plans of what he had yet to do when he came on leave. "It's wonderful," he said drowsily, "how well you fit in to Slepe, it's as though you had been here for ever, you belong here."

Rose gritted her teeth, biting back the rejoinder, I am not one of your Regency commodes. "I think one of the things I must do is get a new mattress for this bed," she said. "It's bloody lumpy."

"It seems all right to me." Ned was nearly asleep (he must teach her not to swear).

Rose lay wondering what was in Mylo's parcel. Perhaps there would be a message to come at once and she had already waited seven days to open it. Perhaps she would go in the car Ned was giving her, treating her flight as a case of "dire emergency". But I cannot, I promised not to leave; promises cannot be broken. Had Ned, poor kind Ned, sleeping now, an inkling of what he had done by extracting that promise?

Do I like or loathe Ned? Rose asked herself, and unconsciously kicked her foot towards him, jerking as a dog jerks in his dream, withdrawing her foot in shame as her toenail grazed his calf. Ned did not stir.

In the morning when he had dressed in his uniform, buckling his Sam Browne belt, brilliant with polish, when he had jerked the tunic down to lie flat over his chest as yet bare of medals (those would come), put on with the uniform his military air, driven away in his car to join his regiment, and with it after many false alarms the war, Rose, barely waiting for him to be out of sight, bounded upstairs three at a time to take from where it lay hidden in a drawer under her nightdress Mylo's parcel.

Mylo had sent her a Bonnard lithograph.

Tearing away the wrappings, turning it over, she found no message, no hint of an address.

She sat staring at the picture, disappointed. Then as she looked she became aware that there was no need of written word. The tenderness with which the lover in the picture encircled the girl with his arm, the way she looked down into his face told her all that was needed.

Thus we sat in that glade in Richmond Park, so we lolled on the lawns of Hampton Court, it was like that in the gardens of Kew, in the country round my home, so it will be, said the picture Mylo had sent her, for us two, for our lives, for ever.

Her promise to Ned must be kept, but it would in no way alter the love she had for Mylo.

Presently, carrying the picture, she went down to the kitchen to borrow a hammer and beg a nail from Mrs Farthing. Then to her bedroom to hang the picture where she would see it last thing at night and first thing on waking.

"Looks happier now," said Mrs Farthing to her husband. "Don't bring in all that mud, wipe your feet."

"Hang that picture?" asked Farthing, aware as was his wife of everything new coming into the house.

"Looks so," said Mrs Farthing.

"M-m-m . . ." muttered Farthing, satisfied that his swift brain and X-ray eyes had deduced the content of the foreign parcel to be a picture.

SEVENTEEN

The prospect of exploring her new home without Ned held considerable allure. There were parts of the garden where he had prevented her lingering, a room opening out of their bedroom she would like to turn into a sitting-room for herself and furnish with small pieces of the furniture he had covered with dust sheets; she would extract them from the sad mass in quarantine for the duration. There was also the Farthings' pregnant cat to be visited.

When the car Ned had promised her was delivered she would drive up to London to choose a new mattress for the bed. I have nothing against the bed *per se*, she told herself, it is the mattress which is bloody awful. I want to be rid of the mattress Ned just fucked me on. (I will use words he deplores if I wish; he is mealy-mouthed.) All the same he is thoughtful to give me my own car, I should be more grateful. The sooner the car is delivered, the better.

As she waited for the car she wandered about the garden, then sat watching a pair of blackbirds gorging on fallen mulberries scattered like clots of blood under a tree. "What a mess," Ned had remarked disgustedly, "something must be done about that." The blackbirds were doing something.

The driver of the car hooted as it drew up at the house. Rose ran to meet it. She was disappointed to see Emily; she had expected a mechanic from the village garage. "Brought your surprise." Emily stepped out of the car which had been her father the bishop's. "Ned's present."

Hard on Emily's heels came Nicholas driving a shiny MG. "Hail the bride!" Nicholas shouted, bringing the MG to a halt beside his sister. "Is Ned gone? Does the bride grieve for her groom? Actually," he said, stepping out of the car, "we know he is gone, we passed him on the top road."

"He looks very fine in uniform," said Emily. "Larger, somehow. Don't you find him larger than you expected, Rose?"

"No," said Rose, watching her neighbours' (she did not at that moment look on them as friends) faces. This is some trick on somebody's part, she thought, but I shall not delight them by letting on and rising to their bait. "I see you have acquired your slice of vulgarity," she said, gathering her nonchalance about her, managing to ignore Emily's *double entendre*. "I trust you have filled the tank with petrol, topped up the battery, checked the tyres? Have you brought its insurance papers and so on?" she asked coolly. "Or did you give them to Ned?"

She walked round patting the bishop's car as though she was pleased with it. "Dear old thing," she said, "it reminds me of the Malones' winter tennis where I first met Ned" (and my darling Mylo) "and we fell in love. If you didn't know Ned as well as I do, you would not credit him with sentimentality, would you?" Rose looked smiling at Nicholas and Emily standing now by their red sports car. She began to laugh, forcing herself. "Sorry I can't ask you in," she said, "I was only waiting for you to bring it to be off to London. Let's see you drive away in your new-found vulgarity – oh, I must not be unfair to the car. I have a whole day's shopping and I'm late already. We were expecting you earlier, but Ned couldn't wait." (How am I doing?)

Nicholas and Emily's eyes met.

They were not expecting that, thought Rose, they now don't know whether I knew what Ned had done or not. Maybe I shall like the bishop's car, he is a rather nice old man. Later I may be able to work out whether Ned tricked me, or they tricked Ned.

"Are those its papers? Thanks, Nicholas." She took the car papers from Nicholas.

The way Ned smacked Emily's bottom has something to do with this, she thought, but it doesn't matter, it is not as though I were in love with Ned, none of them know how safe I feel.

Rose stood contemplating Nicholas and Emily, who growing uneasy under her amused scrutiny now wished to be away. What had seemed a splendid jape had in some peculiar way backfired. It was not Rose who stood surprised, disappointed and cut down to size, but themselves.

From the open window of the library, the telephone pealed. "I must answer that, it will be Ned," Rose exclaimed. "Goodbye, thanks, see you soon." She leapt up the front steps into the house and shut the door, leaving them in the drive.

"Oh, God, let it be Mylo," she prayed as she ran, but God was not answering prayers that day; it was Ned.

"Rose, I should have told you about the car."

"Should you?"

"It occurred to me as I drove that I should have explained to you that I had bought the Thornbys' car."

"Did it?"

"Yes. I thought you might . . ."

"Might what?"

"Might have expected something better, I . . ."

"Oh?"

"It's in frightfully good nick. The bishop . . ."

"And ultra-respectable."

"What?"

"Everyone will expect me to wear gaiters."

"What?"

"What?"

"Are you disappointed? I rather wondered as I drove along whether you were expecting something better."

"Oh, no, Ned. Why do you repeat yourself?"

"They had set their hearts on . . ."

"I know, Ned."

"So you don't?"

"No, I don't."

"Well then, I . . ."

"Where are you, Ned?"

"Halfway to Aldershot, why?"

"Then go the whole way. I am going to London to buy a mattress and swap a few wedding presents."

"Oh, Rose, which? We didn't discuss . . ."

"Nicholas and Emily's, for a start; they charged that lamp to Mrs Malone's account."

"I can't believe . . ."

"I can."

"Your time is up," said the operator, bored.

"Oh, Rose!"

And did they charge the MG to your account at the garage? Rose replaced the receiver.

EIGHTEEN

Life which had been as it were nibbling at Rose's edges took off.

During the first six to eight months of the war she grew up.

The tide of evacuee children from London which engulfed the neighbourhood at the outset of war ebbed and retreated as the expected mass bombing and poison gassing of major cities failed to materialise. Of the first exodus, only two waif-like children remained to lodge with the Farthings and grow, by 1945, as countrified and robust as any local child.

Ned, who his neighbours had been inclined to vilify for his selfishness (and foresight) in making over the major part of his house to the Ministry of Information, was now envied for his perspicacity in avoiding the problem of giving houseroom to children who might have infested heads or wet their beds. That nobody had actually had experience of such children was neither here nor there. The whole country was rife with horror stories of evacuees, just as later it would be with personal bomb experiences. During the lull known as the Phoney War householders with spare rooms filled them with old aunts or maiden cousins who would join the Red Cross or WVS and make themselves useful to their hosts, as domestic servants vanished.

Rose, new to her role in the neighbourhood, was barely aware of the discussion and general upset, accompanied by self-justification, that went on; she was occupied learning to run a house as large and inconvenient as Slepe, catering for Ned's friends when he brought them on leave clamouring for drinks, hot meals, hot baths, warm beds. At night Ned would expect what he called his "roll in the hay", regimental life having the effect of making him much randier than had been his pre-war mode.

Lying in Ned's uxorious embrace Rose tried not to listen for the telephone. As the months passed she disciplined herself to listen less, not to run when it did ring, nor lose her breath as she snatched up the receiver.

The Finnish war began and sadly ended. Winter grew vicious. It snowed and froze, pipes burst when it relaxed temporarily before freezing harder. All over England plumbers who had not joined the forces became the kings of society.

Ned and his regiment were moved at short notice to France.

Rose was alone at Slepe, listening to the radio, gleaning news of a frozen Maginot Line, of ice-bound northern Europe. She brought two of Mrs Farthing's kittens into the house and stocked up with hot-water bottles. Huddling in her bed with the cats and hot bottles she shivered as the wind howled round the house and whoofed down the chimneys. Still the telephone failed to deliver Mylo's voice. Seeking comfort from the lithograph he had sent her, she staved off loneliness.

There were times waking in the night when she questioned whether he had sent the Bonnard. There had been no written word inside the parcel. Almost his last words, she remembered with desolation, had been, "I shall not bother you again."

From time to time, mindful of soon-to-come petrol rationing, she drove to London to pay a duty visit to her parents who since her marriage remained permanently in town, her father concentrating on his cancer treatment. (It did not seem to be doing him much good, nor did he appear worse.) She drove into a London whose streets, parks and squares were deep in frozen slush, stained grey and brown with grime.

She brought her parents cream and butter from the farm and on occasion a fowl. ("I fear," she warned them, once, "that this is the last time I shall come by car; it will be more difficult to bring you things by train." "Nonsense," said her mother, "you are a strong girl; your father needs a bit extra.")

She stayed with them for as short a time as was decent. Visiting her parents confused her. Then she fled their probing eyes, their unspoken questions. When she reached the street she muttered her answers: "No, I am not pregnant, and no, I am not happy."

After one such visit, walking down Sloane Street, she ran into Mrs Malone. The older woman was struck by Rose's pinched appearance. She stopped, chatted, invited her to lunch near by. "The Cordon Bleu is still functioning."

Rose was about to refuse, say that she had a full day's shopping ahead, that she was not hungry. They were standing down-wind from the Kenya Coffee Shop; a customer coming out brought into the icy street a waft of coffee. Rose's mouth filled with saliva. "Thanks," she said, "I'd love to."

They sat in the restaurant and ordered their food. Rose told Mrs Malone that she had been visiting her parents, so explaining her presence in London.

"I hear that they have let their house," said Mrs Malone, "for the duration of the war, and might sell."

"They have not told me," said Rose, surprised.

"Not wanting to bother you." Mrs Malone buttered her bread; she was hungry and could not wait for the waitress to bring the ordered dish. "Your mother," she said munching, "would rather live in London, she expects your father to die."

Rose, who also expected this but had never voiced the eventuality to anyone other than Mylo, said nothing; she did not feel she knew Mrs Malone well enough to discuss death.

"You should call me Edith," said Mrs Malone, "that's the name I'm stuck with."

"Oh," said Rose. "Edith, thank you."

The waitress brought their order. Edith Malone began to eat. "Go ahead, eat. It is easier," she said, "to talk about your father dying to a comparative stranger than to your mother."

"I suppose . . ." Rose took a mouthful of food; it was good, its goodness made the topic of her father's demise worse. "I suppose . . ."

"Of course, your mother's trouble is that your father is not dying, he has not got cancer."

"Oh."

"I know his physician. This situation is tough on your mother, she had hoped to become free . . ." Mrs Malone munched on.

"How do you . . . ?"

"I know, but I do not suppose your mother does." Edith masticated slowly. "If she does, she suppresses it. Your mother tries to be good, she had a Christian upbringing no doubt, is repressed, and is constipated."

"She is continually dosing herself." Rose could not help her laughter.

"There you are. I wonder whether they have any profiteroles, so delicious, or has the war put a stop?"

"A stop," said a passing waitress who seemed to know Mrs Malone.

"Then, coffee for two," said Edith. "Black. Your mother now hopes that if they stay in London the god of war will oblige with a bomb and remove your father."

"There are no raids." Rose was convulsed with merriment.

"There will be," Edith assured Rose, delighted to have made her laugh.

"Then what does she do?" Rose warmed to this new version of Edith Malone.

"Oh, then she will start *living*," said Edith, sipping her coffee, "but," she was suddenly sad, "she may find that life when lived resembles coffee in that the smell is more delicious than the liquid. You didn't know I was so wise, did you?"

"No." Rose grinned at her. "I didn't."

I wish, thought Edith, that stupid George or idiot Richard had snapped this girl up before letting Ned Peel get her. Why did I never notice her properly? I could have done something about it. "If you have nothing better to do," she said, "come with me to Harrods. I want to stock up with toys."

"Toys?" Rose was mystified. "Why?"

"There may be a shortage presently, bound to be. Already this morning I found there are no glass balls for the Christmas tree. All made in Germany by our *enemies*! Ridiculous, isn't it, what brings home the reality of war."

"Yes," said Rose (the reality of war for me is no Mylo).

"When this Phoney War is over, there will be another wave of evacuee children. I plan to fill the house. I did not want them any more than anyone else. I am now rather ashamed. I am stocking up with toys and presents for them. Will you help me, give me your afternoon?"

"I would love to."

"Good," said Edith, paying the bill. "We can house ten children; they can use the tennis court as their playroom."

"I didn't know . . ." began Rose.

"Didn't know a woman like me could have a social conscience? Don't be fooled. I am going to enjoy those children just as much as your mother will enjoy her widowhood."

Rose, shocked and pleased, asked, "What about Mr Malone? Does he know?"

"He will enjoy them. I haven't told him yet. He never had much time for George and Richard when they were small, too busy making money. It's much easier to enjoy other people's children, one isn't ultimately responsible. Come along, we are wasting time. Have you a car?"

"Yes, the bishop's. Why?"

"I can load you up with my parcels."

"Of course, but wouldn't you rather have Harrods deliver?"

"There might be a raid which would prevent them," said Edith hopefully. "Rather fun, is it not, not knowing from one moment to the next whether or not we are to be raided?" Then, noting Rose's puzzled expression she said, "Come, my dear, it's no use being glum, it's better to get the maximum enjoyment out of every situation – in this case, the war."

"I had not pictured things that way."

"Then do start. Enjoyment is good for morale. Good morale wins wars. By the way, did you say the bishop's car? The Thornbys'?"

"Yes. Ned bought it from them."

Or they sold it him, thought Edith. "See a lot of those two? Nicholas and Emily?"

"Not all that much."

"You'll get a fresh insight into life there too, I gather. Something that boy we had to tutor George in French said about them rather interested me. An observant fellow, that."

Rose looked away, biting back her longing to talk of Mylo to this new Edith Malone, but it was risky, she must not. She followed Edith into Harrods thinking that if Edith was able to present her with a novel view not only of herself but of her parents, she might well be capable of unveiling a new Mylo, but he is all mine, she thought, only I must discover him.

Presently, loading Rose's car with her parcels of toys – she herself would be returning to the country by train a day later – Edith Malone thought it would not be wrong to suggest to George and Richard that they should take Rose out, enliven her grass widowhood. "Come over to supper one day," she said. "I will ring up and fix it. George and Richard will be on leave soon, they would like to see you."

Rose rather doubted this. "I have not seen them for ages. What are they doing?"

"George is soon to be posted abroad, and Richard has at last got himself into the Wavy Navy. You will come, won't you?"

"I'd love to," said Rose.

So life nibbled a little further, but reserved its fiercest nips for later.

NINETEEN

Rose caught a bad cold towards the end of the winter. She would have shaken it off if she had, as Mrs Farthing suggested, stayed in bed or in one room in an even temperature; but this she would not do. She moved, sneezing, from the kitchen which was warm through icy passages to the library, which was too hot near the log fire but refrigerating if you moved six feet away from it. She tramped about the garden making plans with Farthing, although she knew he would only pay lip service to her and carry on in his own way. She visited the farm where she got in the Hadleys' way. She needed to acquaint herself with Slepe as she saw it, not as Ned had shown it her; she was not used to the responsibility thrust on her, and would take time to bear it. In Mrs Farthing's book she crowned her stupidity by going to London to meet Ned coming on leave from France, hanging about a draughty station waiting for his train. It was an hour late after a mine scare in the Channel.

Their journey home was slow, the train crowded and cold.

Ned wanted her with him every moment of his leave, whether in the house or tramping the estate. He was gloomy, depressed and unusually silent. The campaign in Norway was raging disastrously and he was convinced that when the weather broke there would be fighting in France. He was pessimistic about the war, derogatory about the government. He confided his fears to Rose, snuffling in his arms. He did not like the new mattress she had bought at Heals and did not hesitate to say so. He banished the kittens from the bedroom, refusing to let them in when they scratched temperately but persistently at the door in the watches of the night, causing Rose to screw up her toes with suppressed fury. He was afraid too of catching Rose's cold. "I shall give it to everyone in the mess," he grumbled.

"I am sorry, Ned. I can't help having a cold. I didn't plan it on purpose."

"You've no idea how cold it is in France. I shall probably develop pneumonia," Ned grumbled louder, shifting his position and snatching the bedclothes round his shoulders and away from his wife.

"Then you can get invalided out of the war," she tried to cheer him as she pulled the sheet back.

"I shan't catch pneumonia until we are overrun by the Germans. Then it will be too late . . ."

"Ned, do stop moaning, you haven't caught my cold yet, you may be immune to my germs. What's the matter with you? I've never known you like this, tell me for God's sake."

Instead of answering Ned rolled over her and made love, climaxing with a grunt and collapsing on top of her so that her face was squashed against his shoulder and with nasal passages blocked with mucus she nearly suffocated.

"For Heaven's sake get off." She dug her nails into him.

Ned shifted a little. "What's the matter?"

"You are squashing me. I can't breathe, move over. These acrobatics are supposed to be pleasurable and romantic. Oh, God, where is my handkerchief, where's it got to?" She found it and blew her nose violently.

"Damn you, blast you, fuck you, bugger you and your cold," cried Ned and began to weep with great gulping sobs. "Oh, shit."

"Ned!" She had never heard him swear. "What's the matter? What is it? I'm sorry about my filthy cold." Nor had she ever known a man cry.

Ned went on crying.

Rose sat up and cradled his head against her chest. "Ned, tell me, what has happened to you?"

Ned's sobs subsided; he circled her with his arms, pressing his face against her breast, his copious tears soaking her nightdress. Presently he fumbled for her handkerchief and ignoring her germs blew his nose. Then he lay back with his head on his arms drawing himself away from her. "The truth is," he said, "I am afraid. I am afraid of the war. I am scared. I lie awake in France imagining what it is going to be like, what it will be like to be wounded. What it will be like to die. I can't discuss it with anyone. I wish I had not told you. You will now, I take it, want nothing more to do with a coward."

Rose felt a rush of affection for Ned. "Ned, darling, I love you. I swore I would not leave you, don't you remember?" (I could let her off her promise, thought Ned, no, no, I couldn't.) "I am sure you won't get wounded, why should you? Everyone says this war is going to be quite different to nineteen-fourteen, no casualties."

"That's what they say . . ."

"You won't get killed. I'm sure of it. You are not a coward. We are all frightened, all of us, I am afraid all the time and especially at night, that's why I have the cats for company." In speaking of fear she dredged up terrors as yet suppressed, she would share them with him, offer them to him.

"You use your cats as hot-water bottles. How do you know I won't get killed?"

"I just know it." She sought to be robust.

"I may be maimed. I may get my legs blown off. I may be blinded. I may be deafened. There's a fellow who trod on a mine near the Maginot Line who had his legs blown off and is now both blind and deaf."

"How near are you to the Maginot Line?"

"About a hundred miles."

"Oh, Ned . . ."

"I am glad you are afraid, too. I thought it was just me. There's no need for you to be afraid here at Slepe." Almost he was jealous of his fear, unwilling to share it.

"We are all afraid. We wouldn't be human else."

"Sure you won't leave me?"

"I promised."

Ned sighed, turning towards her: "I can hear those fucking cats scratching at the door. Shall I let them in?"

"Yes, please, Ned."

He got heavily out of bed, crossed the room and opened the door: "Come in, you little bastards." He closed the door on the feline entry and got back in bed, bringing with him a cold draught. He lay holding her hand.

"What started all this bad language, Ned? It's not you."

"What is me? What am I? Everyone swears, with the men every other word is fuck or bloody, it's catching."

"Like my cold."

Ned laughed. "Everyone . . ."

"They are afraid, too. They have the horrors, too."

"Glad, glad to hear it." Ned fell asleep breathing deeply, absorbed by his sleep. Rose listened wakeful to Ned's breathing, felt the cats' stealthy approach, the light leap on to the bed, the rhythmic treading of paws, the soft purr in kitten throats as they settled in the hollow between husband and wife.

Three days later at the end of his leave she went with Ned to London. He was cheerful, almost exuberant. They went to his tailor and ordered a new uniform, then on to Wiltons for lunch. They ate a dozen oysters each and Ned made a tasteless joke about the waste of the sexual effect now that they were to part. Rose was not hungry and watched him eat her brown bread and butter with his own and drink two pints of Guinness. She went with him in the taxi to Victoria and was still chatting from the draughty platform when the guard blew his whistle. She tiptoed up and kissed him goodbye. The train drew out. She waved until it was out of sight.

There had been no further mention of Ned's horrors. She felt extremely ill.

She crossed to Paddington in a taxi and caught the afternoon train home.

When Mrs Farthing sent for the doctor he came two days later; he was rushed off his feet, both his partners had joined up. He took Rose's temperature and listened to her chest.

"You've got bronchial pneumonia; I fear there is no available bed in the hospital."

Rose croaked that she was glad to hear it, she would rather die in her own bed in her own good time. The doctor turned the cats out of the room. Rose crawled to the door to let them in again while Mrs Farthing saw the doctor out. When Mrs Farthing came back with a fresh hot-water bottle and a hot honey drink she raised her eyebrows. "What you want is for Farthing to make a hole in the door, then they can come and go as they please. Won't make a mite of difference to the draughts."

"Thanks," Rose whispered.

"Farthing's taking the bishop's car to fetch you your medicine."

"Thanks."

"What you need in here is a nice fire going."

"Lovely . . ."

During the days that followed Rose listened as she fought for breath to the radio announcer describing the retreat from Norway and was glad good kind Ned was not there. Once she woke in the night screaming that Mylo was drowning in a cold fiord. She put on the light and keeping her eyes on the Bonnard lithograph knew that he had sent it even though he sent no word. She decided that as she was so near death, she must do something about it. She made up her mind to think positively about life after pneumonia; it was just possible it would be worth living.

When the train pulled out of Victoria Ned pulled up the window and straightened his back, cricked from the drawn-out farewell to Rose. It was amazing how plain a head cold could make a girl look. He undid a couple of uniform buttons, sat back and shook out his evening paper. By some fluke he seemed to have the carriage to himself. He felt very well after his lunch of oysters and wished retrospectively that he had taken more advantage of his marital rights while on leave. It had been irritating of Rose to have such an awful cold.

When the door from the corridor slid open and a girl backed in Ned put down his paper and stared. She was adjusting a notice on the glass door which said "Reserved". She stepped over his legs and stuck a similar notice on the window beside him.

"Hullo, Ned," said Emily.

"What are you doing here?"

"Same as you. Travelling to Dover. My job is peripatetic."

"Where did you get those notices?"

"We had an uncle on the board of GWR, Nicholas pinched them when he showed us behind the scenes at Paddington. We find them jolly useful in wartime." Emily now pulled down the blinds on the corridor side of the carriage.

"What are you doing that for?"

"The blackout."

"It's still daylight."

"I thought it would be nice for us to be private." Emily looked as alert as a blackbird listening for a worm. "Ghastly cold poor old Rose has got, hope you haven't caught it. I was watching you from along the train."

"You are not really going to Dover to work."

"How did you guess?"

"You followed me."

"Flattered?"

"Why did you?"

"Ask a silly question," said Emily pertly. "I thought it would be nice for us."

"Oh." Ned edged away as Emily settled on the seat beside him.

The train rocked over some points, gathering speed. Emily edged back closer.

"I'm a married man," said Ned stiffly.

"So you are," Emily agreed.

"I'm in love with my wife, she's very much in love with me."

"If you believe that, you'll believe anything."

Ned raised an angry hand.

"No need to hit me." Emily let her hand rest in Ned's lap. "What have we here?"

"Emily, do behave." Ned began to laugh.

"Why don't we behave as we feel? Why don't we have an enjoyable journey, fill in the time usefully?"

"In a train? One can't . . ."

"There's precious little one can't do in a train."

"Emily. No."

"Come on, Ned – by the way, what made you hit me like that the other day? You hurt me."

"I meant to. I hurt my hand. What *are* you doing, Emily?"

"Unbuttoning your flies. Oh, look!"

"Where d'you learn all this?" asked Ned presently.

"Never you mind."

"I'm sure this position is a sexual deviation."

"Suitable for trains."

"Really, Emily, I . . ."

"If your boat to France gets delayed by mines in the Channel, we could put up for the night in that lovely hotel. Last time Nicholas and I were there we stuffed ourselves with oysters. Isn't it marvellous, they aren't rationed?"

"Rose and I had oysters for lunch."

"Rather wasted on Rose. Will she be faithful to you?"

"Of course she will."

"You sure?"

"Of course. We're married. She promised."

"And men are different?"

"Men – well, yes – men have different habits."

"In that case . . ."

"I warn you, Emily, I shan't let you become a habit," said Ned firmly.

"Who suggested such a thing? What a silly idea," said Emily, putting on lipstick, powdering her nose, combing her hair. "I'm not a habit. Not me. I'm a pastime."

"A passing fancy," said Ned hopefully.

"Possibly." Emily licked her finger and smoothed her eyebrows, peering at her reflection in the looking glass above the seat.

Ned patted her behind as she adjusted her skirt. "Perhaps there will be mines in the Channel," he suggested.

But Emily had found the journey to be just the right length. "I have to meet a chap from the Min. of Ag.," she said. "Sorry." She kissed Ned lightly. "Goodbye, Ned. Thanks a lot. I really do have a job," she said. "He's one of the loonies who want to plough up the South Downs, but you try the hotel if you are delayed." She slipped out of the train as it drew into the station and ran towards the exit.

Ned wondered as he took his luggage down from the rack and struggled into his greatcoat why he tolerated Emily's behaviour, why he found her wantonness amusing. Thank God, he thought, there's nothing like that in Rose and smiled as he summoned a porter at the recollection of Rose's red and swollen nose. A bad cold is better than any chastity belt, he thought, following the porter along the platform and, pleased by his wit (could he call it an epigram?), decided to store it and air it in one of the conversations which tended to arise on guest nights in the mess.

The crossing to France was cold and rough. Ned sheltered from the wind in the lee of a funnel, preferring to stay on deck wrapped in a sense of well being. He thought fondly of Rose. As he passed through Paris there might be time to buy her some decent scent. (Emily had smelt rather nice.) As Uncle Archie had predicted, an inexperienced bride was what was needed; he was grateful to the old rascal. My marriage is working out well, he thought, remembering Rose with more tenderness than he had felt when he was with her. He slept in the train to Paris, huddled in a crowded carriage, and woke feeling calm. Somehow his leave had kitted him out for the war. He forgot the terrors he had confided in Rose and congratulated himself on the episode with Emily, thinking that he had handled her rather well. It did not occur to him that he owed his new confidence to one or other or both girls; he was too nice a man to go in for much soul-searching.

TWENTY

George Malone, sent by his mother to invite Rose over for the weekend, was horrified to find her so ill.

"Lord, Rose, you do look a dying duck!"

Rose wheezed, coughed, struggled to hitch herself higher on her pillows, flopped back fumbling for her handkerchief, her mouth full of phlegm.

"Here, wait . . ." George bent, heaved her up, piling and patting the pillows behind her. "That better?"

Rose spat into her handkerchief, nodded. Her face, George noted, was grey, translucent. "Who is looking after you?"

"Mrs Farthing." Her voice was a hoarse whisper.

"What about your mother?"

"Sent a message – can't – Father's ill, too."

"That old chestnut!" George had heard of Mr Freeling's poor health for years and was disinclined to believe in it. His father had often remarked, Whenever Freeling has something he wants to do, especially if there is money in it, he becomes quite well. "We've all heard that one." He pulled up a chair, took Rose's hand and rubbed it between both of his. "What does your doctor say?"

"Bronchial pneumonia," whispered Rose and was off again, coughing, wheezing, fighting for breath.

"You should be in hospital." George was alarmed.

"No. Hate them . . ."

"Surely it would be . . ."

"No, bossed about . . ."

"True." George looked around the room. "Are you warm enough?"

"Yes." Rose lay with her eyes closed. "Cats, hot-water bottles . . ." she smiled, "wouldn't be allowed in hospital."

"They would not." George's eyes, getting used to the lumps and bumps in the bed, noted the cats staring across Rose's body with a mixture of apprehension and insolence. "The passages in this house are like a morgue," he said. "Let me make up your fire."

"Thanks," she said croakily.

George poked the fire, laid on fresh coal and logs, watched it flame up. "I'll just go and see Mrs Farthing."

"They are not well either."

Finding Mrs Farthing in her cottage, George said angrily, "Mrs Peel is bloody ill."

"No need to swear. Farthing is ill too and so are the children, I'm doing all I can."

"She shouldn't be alone in that cold house."

"Listen," said Mrs Farthing aggressively, "to that." She pointed to the ceiling and George listening heard a coughing chorus. "Can't cut myself in two," said Mrs Farthing. "Her mother won't come, she doesn't like her anyway. Doctor says it's an epidemic and the last bed in the hospital is gone. She wouldn't go, said she was waiting for a telephone call. I could have sent Farthing or one of the little girls."

"From Ned?" George was not interested in the little girls.

"Didn't say. Don't think so. She won't let me tell him."

"I heard on the radio this morning that all leave is stopped; he'd only be worried sick," said George. "They must be expecting some movement over there. A push, perhaps."

"Huh," said Mrs Farthing, "might do him good to worry."

George let this pass. "What does the doctor say?"

"Keep her warm. Give her her medicine, lots of liquids and hope for the best."

"And your husband? The children?"

"Same thing, but it's only flu; she's got pneumonia."

Mrs Farthing, George realised, was near exhaustion. "I'm sorry I was so abrupt," he said. "What about you? You don't look good." Upstairs one of the children began to cry. "Would it help if I stayed?" he asked. "I can keep the fires going, give her hot drinks. I'll telephone my mother."

"You could, I suppose," Mrs Farthing admitted. "If the fire was lit in the hall, it would warm the house a bit and there's the Aga in the kitchen." She sounded more grudging than grateful. "It's worrying when she's delirious."

"Delirious?"

"Looks so, keeps saying, 'I should have been more tender' over and over."

"I'll go and telephone my mother."

Back in the house George built up the Aga, lit the fires in the hall and in the library, went back to Rose's room and stood watching as she slept. She looked awful, he thought, remembering her cheerful and pretty. She was not pretty now.

He telephoned his mother.

"Oh dear! Your leave. Never mind, it can't be helped. I'm waiting for Richard to arrive, then we'll come over and take it in turns."

"I can manage."

"Don't be silly. Did you say the girl's mother won't come? Really, that woman! All she wanted was to get Rose off her hands – I'm sure her husband is not ill – well, we had better be neighbourly. I wonder whether the Thornbys would help. They live much nearer. No," she answered herself, "much too selfish."

Too ill to notice what was going on, it was days before Rose realised that the Malones had come *en bloc* to care for her. Edith sent Mrs Farthing away to care for her own family, dealt with the doctor, miraculously organised warmth in the house and nursed Rose, bashing up her pillows, blanket-bathing her, overseeing the intake of medicaments while her husband and sons answered the telephone, ran errands and stoked the fires. Since it was Richard's leave and George was expecting to be sent abroad, the Malones kept together, the anxiety of war giving the family even greater unity than usual.

Edith allowed herself a number of uncharitable criticisms when she thought of Rose's neglectful parents. If I was her mother, she thought, or if I was her mother-in-law, and she looked reproachfully at her bachelor sons, blaming them. Slow in the uptake, slow off the mark, she thought.

After four days the doctor pronounced Rose out of danger. The elder Malones withdrew with Richard, who was due in Plymouth to join his ship. George was left to fetch, carry and tempt Rose to eat.

George sat with Rose and read aloud passages of *War and Peace*. While she lay ill, one of the telephone calls had been for him; he was posted to Moscow; must leave in two weeks. "One should know something of their literature . . ."

"Do you speak Russian?" Her voice was gaining strength.

"Only French. My French is pretty good. You will not remember, but I had a French tutor."

"Did he telephone?" She raised herself on the pillows.

"The tutor? Why should he? Oh, you mean Ned. No, he didn't. Too busy, I expect. If one can believe the news, things are on the move over there or will be soon."

No telephone. "Send me an Astrakhan hat." Her voice drooped.

"I'll try."

"There's the telephone!" She struggled to sit up, to get out of bed.

"Lie still," he pushed her back, "I'll answer it." George left the room.

Rose listened, straining her ears. "Who was it?"

"Nicholas and Emily asking whether they can come over and have a bath. After much grovelling they've got the plumber to mend their burst pipes, but he's making a meal of it, he's cut off their water. What shall I say?"

"Let them come."

"Selfish beasts, they could have come before, I told them you were ill."

"It doesn't matter."

George went slowly down again. He did not want Nicholas and Emily to come over. He heard himself telling Nicholas that it wouldn't be possible for them to come that day: "Come when I'm gone," he heard himself say. "I'll leave a list of jobs for you with the Farthings." This is my last afternoon with Rose, he thought. He was halfway up the stairs when the telephone rang again. Rose should get an extension put by her bed; all this haring up and down stairs was ridiculous. "Hullo," he shouted unnecessarily loud. "Who is it? Rose is ill in bed."

"Tell her," said Mrs Freeling, "that her father is dead."

"Wolf, cry wolf," George murmured as he went back to Rose.

"Who was it?"

It occurred to George that she was expecting a telephone call; he remembered a lovesick teenage cousin wearing just such an expression. "Your mother, she . . ."

"Is my father better?"

"Dead," said George, embarrassed.

"Oh." She lay back. "Cancer?"

"Doesn't sound like it. She said she went into his room this morning with his breakfast tray, his usual lightly boiled egg, and found that he had died in his sleep, a stroke. A coronary, perhaps?"

"What else did she say?"

George debated whether to gloss over what Mrs Freeling had said. "If you give me your hot-water bottle, I'll take it down and refill it," he prevaricated.

Rose fumbled for the bottle, come to rest under the cats, pulled it free and handed it to George. "What else did she say, George?"

"What a waste of an egg when they are in such short supply." George snatched the hot-water bottle and left the room. His laughter exploded on the stairs.

Bringing the fresh bottle after a decent interval, George apologised. "I should not have laughed. I'm sorry."

"How could you help it. Oh, George!" Rose too began to laugh. She reached up, caught his hand. "Oh, ho, ho, ho. Hold my hand a moment. My mother has been hoping for this for so long. What a shock. They are not like your parents, George, they don't get on, he was so difficult to please. I never – oh, where is my handkerchief?" She was crying now, her abrupt laughter changed to tears, runny nose, sobs. "I never pleased him, I was a rotten daughter. All he ever wanted was for me to be safe, he kept on about it, he was so glad when I married Ned, he thought all that mattered was safety, I never loved him much. I feel so guilty . . ." The rest of Rose's declaration was drowned by sobs. George saw himself gathering her in his arms to comfort her, lashing out with his foot to kick away the scalding hot-water bottle, pushing aside the cats. It seemed simpler to console Rose in her bed; she would not catch cold that way. Rather warm though. Easier if he took off his trousers. This is not really my style, he thought, but all the same it's pretty good and my word it's oh, ah, oh. "Heavens, Rose, I did not really mean to do that. I hope you don't think I set out to – I hope I've not made your pneumonia worse – here, hang on while I retrieve that hot-water bottle, oh, good, it's still warm, oh, Lord, look at the cats, what an unfeeling . . ."

"Stop burbling." Rose straightened the bedclothes as he got back into his trousers, pulled her nightdress down and the sheets up, settled the hot bottle by her feet, reached for a comb, ran it through her hair "Could you bring me a hot sponge?" She was startled into feeling almost well. George ran the hot tap, squeezed the sponge under it, brought it to Rose, watched her wipe her face, erase the tears, wondered what he should do or say.

"Oh, George." Rose looked up at his anxious face, handed back the sponge. "I'm so hungry."

From time to time through life George would be tempted to tell the tale of how he had found the barrel of oysters left for Rose's convalescence by his mother. Of how they had feasted together, she in her bed, he sitting beside it. When people remarked jokingly on the aphrodisiac qualities of oysters, George would say he wouldn't know about that but he had heard they were wonderful for convalescents. In old age, if reminded by the taste of oysters of the episode with Rose, he would puzzle as to whether it had really happened, whether he had mixed fact with fiction to make a good story. Was it likely, he would ask himself, that he would find oysters fresh in a barrel in such circumstances? Or probable that he would seduce a friend's wife when she was ill with bronchial pneumonia? In any case it was not the sort of story one could tell anybody. Was I that sort of fellow? he would question, looking at his beloved wife, splendid sons and daughters, charming grandchildren. "When I was posted to Moscow in the war," he would say, steering his train of thought into safer waters, "I spent a lot of time trying to find an Astrakhan hat for the wife of a friend of mine."

"And did you succeed?" one or other of them would ask. "Were you in love with her?"

"I can't recollect. I don't suppose so. One had many more serious worries; there was after all the war – no, it wasn't love."

But Rose remembered.

When people discussed tonics, pick-me-ups after severe illness, she kept to herself the prescription of a quick dip in bed with someone you liked but were not in love with. A short shock of sexual astonishment which could make you feel surprisingly well and high spirited.

After her little brush with George she found herself well enough to attend her father's funeral, console her mother for never noticing that he had a bad heart, help her find a convenient flat in which to spend her widowed days.

In actual fact the funeral and Mrs Freeling's move from Kensington to Chelsea took place over a period of months with many visits from Rose during the summer of 1940. But memory being what it is, her mind concertinaed the funeral and her mother's move into briefer space. What she chiefly remembered in age was returning to Slepe after the funeral with a sense of liberation, and her extreme annoyance at finding Nicholas and Emily in occupation, having invited themselves while the plumber sorted out their burst pipes.

TWENTY-ONE

The first indication that her privacy had been invaded was the sight, as she drove up the drive, of the MG parked askew at the front of the house.

"Damn." Rose parked what she continued to think of as the bishop's car beside the MG. She hefted her bag and went in. She stood in the hall listening. There was no sound. The bud of a late camellia fell with a plop on to the hall table. The water in the vase was low and the flowers Edith Malone had arranged two weeks before were browning and dead. Farthing had resentfully watched her cut the camellias, making it plain by the twitch of his nose that camellias lasted longer left where they belonged. After the fall of the flower, the silence was absolute.

Rose looked in the library. Nobody. Nor was there anyone in the kitchen.

She carried her bag upstairs, anxious to change from her funeral clothes. She supposed the Thornbys to have gone for a walk while waiting for her. She would offer them tea then pack them off home. They had not bothered to come to her father's funeral. They could, she thought resentfully, have made the effort. Other people had. Ned's uncle and aunt from Argyll, for instance, who scarcely knew her parents.

Crossing the landing to her room she saw the door of a spare room ajar and moved to shut it, but first she glanced into the room in case the cats had strayed; shut in, they might make a mess. She was surprised to see clothes thrown casually about, an open book on a chair, brushes and combs on the dressing-table. The bed dishevelled. She closed the door, frowning.

Then from across the landing, from the visitors' bathroom, she heard a gurgle of laughter, Emily's laugh. What bloody cheek. She strode into the bathroom, furious.

"Oh, Rose." Nicholas reached up from the bath to grip her wrist. "So you're back. How did it go? We knew Ned would want us to make ourselves at home, so we've done just that. Sit and talk to us, sweetie. This is the first bath we've had for weeks – can't tell you the bliss of a good wallow after washing in parts and boiling water in a kettle – one gets so cold – one feels so deprived." He pulled Rose nearer the bath. "Sit down, lovey, while we tell you about our resident plumber; he makes surreptitious eyes at Emily and she encourages him." He jerked Rose down on to the chair by the bath.

"Hullo, Rose." Emily lay in the bath facing Nicholas. She had put a cushion from the spare room to protect her head and shoulders from the taps; its fine brocade was soggy. "Keep us company," drawled Emily, "tell us the latest." She grinned gleefully up at Rose. "Remember how we all had our baths together as children? Pity there isn't room for you now. Weren't you a coy little thing!"

"You cried, didn't you, Rosie?" Nicholas kept hold of Rose's wrist.

Rose remembered her agonised embarrassment when, an only child, she had found herself expected to share the bath with the Thornby children, stranded with them for the night after a party (her father's car had broken down; he had not been able to fetch her home). She had reacted violently, made a scene, refused to undress, screamed. Nicholas and Emily's nurse had teased her for hiding her body, mocked her infant modesty. "What have you got to hide?"

Nicholas and Emily had followed suit, chanting, "What have you got to hide," in loud sing-song. "Take off your knickers. What have you got to hide?" They were not hiding much now.

Rose snatched her wrist free, remembering how Nicholas, excited, had threatened to pee in the bath water. The nurse had smacked him twice, once on each buttock; she had been shocked and curiously excited.

She stood up. On no account was she going to betray her surprise at seeing them together in the bath, lay herself open to taunts of lack of sophistication. "Ned couldn't get back for the funeral," she said, not prepared to endorse or deny his possible invitation. (I do not yet know Ned well enough, she thought.) She forced herself to look calmly down as they lay in the steaming water, Nicholas caressing his sister's neck with his toe, she idly soaping her leg, then her brother's. Apart from the obvious difference in sex, they were remarkably alike.

"Ned didn't exactly invite us – to be honest," said Emily, laughing, daring Rose to be shocked. "Notice the difference?" she asked, following Rose's glance.

Rose realised with fury that one part of her mind had been noting that Nicholas, unlike Ned, was circumcised. "Oh, I shouldn't bother to be honest, Emily, it's not you, is it?" She bent and removed the cushion from behind Emily's head with a jerk, at the same time pulling up the bath plug. "This had better dry off in the hot cupboard." She ignored Emily's squeal of protest as she dodged to avoid the hard taps against her head and neck. She squeezed the cushion over the bath. "When did you arrive?" she asked, keeping her voice casual. "Or should I say move in?"

"Yesterday," said Nicholas quickly. "Mrs Farthing said . . ."

Told her we'd invited them, thought Rose. "Maybe you'd do better to keep an eye on your plumber," she suggested, watching Nicholas get out of the bath, noting his weedy legs, making it plain as she ran her eye over him that his compared ill with Ned's physique. "Ned wasn't exactly the soul of welcome last time you called, was he, Emily?"

"Not on *that* occasion." Emily got out of the bath, hinting that there had been other occasions (and I don't care, thought Rose, if there were). "Don't let me hurry you." Rose watched Emily look around for a bath towel. "I remember now, I told George to tell you you could come over some time. How silly of me to forget. Oh, d'you want a towel?" she asked, as though to need a towel was somehow remarkable, that ordinary people shook themselves like dogs when they got out of a hot bath.

"We should have brought our own." Nicholas had ceased to enjoy the situation, was beginning to shiver in the prevailing Slepe draught.

"Oh, no, no, no," said Rose. "I'll fetch you some," she said graciously as she went out, leaving the door open, letting the draught increase, taking her time to cross the landing, open the hot cupboard door, place the damp cushion to dry, extract two of the least good bath towels. "Here you are," she said, strolling back. "I'd ask you to stay," she said, "but I'm expecting Ned at any moment and we will want to be on our own, you know how it is – or perhaps you don't?"

"Thanks." Emily snatched a towel and wrapped herself in it.

"And Nicholas . . ." She held a towel out to Nicholas. "My poor Nicholas, you are all goosefleshy." She looked despisefully at his exposed person. "There," she said, "I'll give you tea before you go. I'll go and put the kettle on." She forced herself to walk out of the bathroom slowly, go steadily down the stairs. Halfway down, her rage at their solipsistic behaviour overwhelmed her; she was affronted that they had come uninvited, shared the bath, and by the look of things the bed also.

"Emily," she shouted up the stairwell.

"Yes?" Emily, half dry, leaned over the banisters. "What is it?"

"Clean the bath before you go, strip the bed and put the used sheets in the laundry basket." To suggest disinfectant would be overdoing it.

"Oh," said Emily, "the famous Slepe hospitality!" But she went obediently back, and Rose heard her splash water in the bath and use a disagreeable tone to Nicholas.

Rose put the kettle to boil and laid out two cups and saucers; she would not join Nicholas and Emily to drink tea. She was amused to find herself as fiercely possessive of Ned's Slepe as though it were her own.

Mrs Farthing came in from outside. "Glad to see you back. They invited themselves, said Mr Peel had . . ." her nostrils twitched, "and that you said . . ."

"Don't worry," said Rose, "they are on their way."

"H-m-m-m."

"I'd rather Ned were not told."

Mrs Farthing relaxed a few folds round her mouth into a smile. "Shall I get the cake out?"

"Certainly not."

"Honeycomb?"

"For you and me later."

"Hah!"

"And we'll make that bed up fresh. Ned may come home; he might bring someone with him."

"Worried, are you? About the war?"

"I think the war is hotting up. Yes, I *am*."

"They do say," said Mrs Farthing, dodging away from Rose's anxiety, "that vicars are given to having funny children, maybe bishops is more so."

A car hooted in the drive. Rose ran out to find Uncle Archibald stepping backwards out of the station taxi. At the sight of his reassuring back, Rose gave a shout of joy. "Oh, Uncle Archie." She had never called him uncle before.

Archie enfolded her in his tweedy arms. He smelt of heather and whisky. He hugged her close and patted her back. "Flora suggested I should come and see you before I go back north; she's gone ahead."

"Kind, kind. Come in and have tea." Joyfully Rose hugged the old man. "Oh, I am glad to see you."

Renewing his hug, holding Rose with one arm while he fumbled in his trouser pocket for change to pay the taxi, Uncle Archie watched Nicholas and Emily slink out of the house, get into their MG and drive away.

"Got visitors?" he asked.

"Some neighbours who came for a bath; their pipes burst in the freeze-up; they have only just got the plumber."

Leading Ned's uncle into the house, Rose put the Thornbys out of her mind. "Come in. Mrs Farthing is making tea, and we have one of Farthing's honeycombs. You will stay, won't you?"

"Glad to, just for the night." He liked the way Rose led him into the house, holding his hand. The girl had changed, he thought, grown up, matured; she must be in love with Ned; good show.

Rose was interested by the way she led Ned's uncle indoors, that she made much of him for her own sake, not Ned's. I am turning into Ned's wife, she thought. "Tell me what you have heard about the war," she said. "I'm sure you know more about what's going on than what's on the radio or in the papers."

"Ah," said Uncle Archie sitting down to his tea. "Yes. France. Can't say I know more than you, my dear."

Rose sighed. Quite irrationally she had hoped he would have news not necessarily of Ned, but of Mylo.

"I only half trust the French," said Uncle Archie.

Mylo is half French, thought Rose forlornly.

"Flora wondered," said Archibald Loftus, accepting his cup, "whether you might not be lonely with Ned away and your father just dead and so on. Wondered whether you would come back with us and stay for a few weeks?"

"Oh, I can't go so far. It's terribly kind; I'm not lonely. I have to wait. I don't think I'd better go further than London – my mother and so on – I'm waiting for news."

"He writes, of course?"

"No. Yes, I mean yes. Of course he writes."

"But can't give news? Censors are over-zealous. Yes, please, I'd like some of that." He helped himself to honey, stirred his tea, drank, wiping his moustache with a silk handkerchief. She's not worrying about Ned in the way one would expect, he thought. Is it her father's death that's bothering her? She wasn't close, from what one's heard. Boring sort of fellow, not our type at all. "This war jangles people up," he said. "People will feel better when it's really started. They're all feeling a bit disappointed at the lack of action; when it comes they'll perk up no end; it's like waiting to have a baby."

Rose laughed. "I wouldn't know about that."

So she's not pregnant; about time she was. "He will be back soon," he said. Better do his stuff then, he thought, I could drop him a hint.

"Could someone just disappear?"

"No, my dear, oh, no, don't start getting fanciful ideas. The Army's got its head screwed on, it's good at its paperwork, Ned won't disappear."

But Mylo *has*, thought Rose, not a word since that last telephone call when he was so cross, and he's not in the Army.

Uncle Archibald started telling Rose what friends at his club had told him about the Norwegian campaign. "Most unfortunate, but a great deal of gallantry. Lucky Ned wasn't there. If he had been, there really would have been cause for worry." As he munched his bread and honey, moved on to Mrs Farthing's cake, Archibald Loftus thought, This Rose of Ned's is a dark horse; it's a waste of breath wondering what's going on in her head; what could she mean "disappear"? People like Ned don't, far too solid and mundane. He resigned himself to enjoying what he knew of her and his tea.

"What you need, my dear," he said, "if you won't come up to us in Scotland, is some fun; try and combine some fun with visits to your mother."

"I shall take your advice," said Rose, "if opportunity arises. Meanwhile stay here with me for a night or two, come and look round the garden."

"I'd like to listen to the news first."

"Very well . . ."

TWENTY-TWO

Listening to the news, Archibald Loftus became seriously worried. (Why was bad news worse in beautiful surroundings?) The Slepe garden was awash with spring, the smell of Farthing's wallflowers pervasive. Archibald did not, as Rose did, study the flora; he fretted. The news was not so much serious as potentially disastrous. Rose strolled peacefully, sniffing at flowers, picking little bits off herbs, bruising them with her fingers, adding her quota of scent to the evening. She kept Archie silent company, made no attempt at conversation, leading him away from the house out of reach of the radio.

Archibald appreciated silence in a woman; he was married to a chatterbox. But tonight he wished this girl of Ned's was not quite so reserved. This surely showed some pent-up emotion and fret? How was it that he got the impression that whatever was bothering her was not bother on behalf of Ned? He broke the silence: "I don't think you should stay here on your own."

"Why ever not?"

"Things look very black over there." He jerked his chin in the direction of France.

"It's difficult for me to make out what's going on," she said.

"There is every likelihood that our armies will be defeated. I distrust the French," he said, as he had said before.

"Ah." She was not paying attention; she was listening to a blackbird singing its heart out on the branch of a flowering cherry.

"The Germans may invade," said Archibald bluntly, "it's more than a probability."

"That's what Ned suggested," she agreed.

"Then he is cleverer than I thought."

Rose felt tempted to mention Ned's hoard of petrol but thought better not, he's a magistrate or something up in Scotland, and Ned said to keep it secret. She thought with amusement of her husband and his secret hoard supposedly unknown to the Farthings.

"You are not listening," said Ned's uncle.

"Yes, I am."

"What did I say last?"

Rose laughed.

"I was saying, Rose, that if and when the Germans invade you would be better off up north with Flora and me. Please be sensible and come."

"I must look after Slepe, Germans or no Germans. Besides, Ned will get back. I have to be here when he arrives."

"Let us pray he does." Archibald could not shake off his gloom.

"Of course he will." Of course. People like Ned don't get lost, but Mylo, what of Mylo?

"Come up to London with me," said Archibald urgently. If I can get her as far as London, I can persuade her on to Argyll, he thought.

I wonder what he would look like without a moustache? Rose was thinking. I have never kissed a man with a moustache, except for that scuffle under the mistletoe. I have not kissed many men. It must be like kissing a doormat. "I must stay here." She looked at Ned's nice uncle (I hope Ned is as attractive as that when he's old). "I would like to, but I can't, thank you. It's very kind of you and," she added, "Aunt Flora." (I wonder what she would say if I was suddenly planted on her?)

Archibald Loftus, admitting defeat, grunted.

The following day he left. On his journey north he sat in the train watching the fields rush by and thought that it would be nice to be young again and seduce Ned's wife, that she was just the sort of girl he could have left Flora for, that perhaps it was as well she had not been born when he met and married Flora, they had been pretty happily married. He had never had a mistress like his Viennese uncles (missed something there, no doubt), there had never been enough temptation. All the same, he thought – does Ned realise? Does he treat her properly? Does he? I am jealous of Ned, he thought with amusement, jealous! He left his seat and walked up the train to the restaurant car and ordered a large whisky. As he drank he let his mind dwell on Rose and speculated on whether she would be one of those rare women who are as attractive in age as they are in youth. And would she know it, and profit by it? He felt the prick of desire as the train rushed north, and watching the speeding fields he noted that he was not done for yet if a girl like Rose could make him feel like this and although it was in a way uncomfortable, it was also pleasurable. Then he thought of his dear wife Flora, grown thick-set and bristly in her tweeds and brogues. Desire evaporating, he ordered another drink.

Alone once more Rose wandered about the garden, played with the cats, came restlessly in and listened to the news. While Uncle Archibald travelled north to Scotland, the collapse of France already under way was admitted. There was congestion on the roads, the Belgians asked for an armistice, the French and British were encircled as they retreated towards Dunkirk, and the evacuation began as lovely day followed lovely day and the birds sang.

Mrs Freeling telephoned to say that she was taking a gamble (Mrs Freeling!) and buying the leases of two flats, not one. If one was to get bombed, she would move to the other.

"And if neither gets bombed?"

"I shall rent one to the Germans and take lodgers in the other."

"Oh." Mother making jokes! What next!

"As everybody who can is getting out of London, I am getting the two flats dirt cheap. There will never be such a chance again."

"I had not realised you had such a – a -- perspicacious business sense." Rose was amused.

"Nor had I. Isn't it fun?"

"Fun?" Rose was amazed at this new version of her mother. "Aren't you afraid of air-raids? Of getting killed?" she inquired.

"Of course I am, but I can't let that stop me. I have been dammed up too long."

"Where are these flats?"

"One in Chelsea, the other is in Regent's Park. I had thought of Hampstead, but then someone said there are a lot of Jews there and the raids may be directed at them. If I can sell the house in the country, well, I might try and find one in the Holland Park area. It shouldn't be difficult."

"A *third* flat?"

"Why not? Nothing ventured . . ."

"I wish you luck," said Rose respectfully. So that's what she's been, dammed up. Well I never, thought Rose, and went again into the garden where now the syringa was mingling with the wallflowers and a mistlethrush sang with heart-rending sweetness. Will my spirit be dammed by Ned as hers was by Father? She pondered the prospect as she paced the stone path. When the telephone rang at last, she ran.

"Hullo?"

"Rose?" A man's hoarse voice.

"Yes?"

"It's me, Ned. I'm at some bloody place in Kent but getting a miraculous lift home."

He arrived hours later exhausted, sunburned from his wait on the beaches, still damp from wading through the sea to the rescuing boats, in high spirits.

"Weren't you frightened?" she asked tentatively.

"Terrified by the bombing. It was really scary because my tin hat was full of gooseberries I had picked in an abandoned garden. I wanted to bring you some but the chaps ate them on the ship."

A new mother, a new Ned.

"What is it? What are you thinking?" He was pulling off his uniform sticky with salt. "Oh, I know. No, it's all right," he said, "I am not afraid any more. Once it begins, there's no time and when there is time it is never anything like what I expected or imagined. Piece of cake, really."

"I'm glad."

"Run a bath for me. Luckily I haven't much imagination, I think I've spent what I had these last weeks."

She brought him a drink as he lay in the bath. "Mrs Farthing is keeping food hot for you."

"What I need is sleep."

"Eat first."

She watched him eat, thankful to see him whole. Fond of him, rather proud, liking him in a comradely way, not at all jealous for Mylo. (All this is separate.)

Ned slept for fifteen hours. Then kissed her goodbye, hurried to rejoin his scattered regiment like a boy to a football game.

Rose went back to listening to the news. France collapsed. Paris fell. Mr Churchill flew to and fro. The evacuation of half a million men continued from Cherbourg and St Malo. Mr Churchill made his blood and beaches speech. Rose's mother furnished her flats, moved out of the flat her husband had died in (what a waste of money all that cancer treatment, had he ever had it?) and sold the house in the country at profiteer profit. Oranges vanished from the shops. Evacuee children streamed out of London and the big cities for the second time. Mrs Farthing joined the Women's Voluntary Service. Ned's regiment was sent to re-form near Catterick. Farthing joined the Home Guard. Nicholas and Emily rang up to say that their plumbing was all right now, would Rose like to come to lunch? Rose said, "No, thank you." Nicholas said, "Too bad, we have both got jobs with the Ministry of Agriculture locally. Nice and safe. We can go on living at home and get a good allowance of petrol." He sounded extremely chipper. By midsummer England faced the long hostile coastline of Europe and Rose would have felt, along with the rest of the population, rather exhilarated if only she could have heard from Mylo.

To stop her constant nagging anxiety she went to London for a few nights to help her mother and go out with Ned's regimental friends, Harold Rhys and Ian Johnson. They took her to dinner at the Czardas in Soho and to dance at the Café de Paris. They told her how brave Ned had been in the fighting, that he would surely get decorated (they were right; not so long afterwards he was awarded the Military Cross). Their vicarious pleasure in Ned's gallantry and courage mitigated the extreme boredom of their company. She felt like an adult listening to prattling children and gave them only half her attention while the unoccupied part of her mind mulled and digested the feelings she had for Ned since he confided his fear to her. She felt protective and was glad that he was brave. She tried to persuade herself that it would be sensible to forget Mylo and concentrate on her husband, that if she tried hard enough she would succeed.

Driving home through St James's Park, she passed banks of tulips lifting their heads to the moon and was reminded of waltzing hand in hand with Mylo the year before, of picnicking with him on a park bench, eating rolls, pâté and an apple between them, for they had not the money to go even into a pub, and her heart was wrenched back on course.

TWENTY-THREE

Rose paid the taxi and greeted the cats, lissom in adolescence. They twined in and out of her ankles, mewed, ran towards the kitchen, indicating that they were hungry, had not been fed. She followed. Two perfectly good cat dinners awaited their eating. They crouched down and ate, needing her company, needing an audience. And I need to be here, she thought, standing in the kitchen already grown familiar; it is after all easier to bear anxiety in my own environment. She admitted that Slepe was her home.

Farthing crossed the yard carrying a shotgun. He wore a Home Guard armband on the sleeve of his working jacket and his Sunday hat.

"Look a lot less foolish when you gets your uniform," Mrs Farthing's voice from the cottage borne on the still air. Farthing shouted back, "I shoot with the gun, love, not with uniform." He sounded stalwart and jocular. Rose heard him mount his bicycle and clatter across the cobbled yard to the accompaniment of shrilly shrieked goodbyes from the little evacuees. She cupped her hands and shouted from the kitchen window, "I'm back, Mrs Farthing."

"Good. I fed the cats. Want anything?"

"Nothing, thanks, let you know when I do."

"I'm going to have a big wash tomorrow. I won't be round for a day or two, if you can spare me."

"I can spare you." Enough to know the woman was there. From the back of the house she heard the Ministry of Information telephone pealing unanswered. The clerks kept office hours, they also kept to themselves, casting doubtful looks at Rose if they crossed her path, as though she had no right, did not belong. Ned had been irritated to find that they had fitted new locks on the communicating doors. He frowned when Rose said she neither minded nor cared. "They should have asked permission," he had grumbled. "It's my house, dammit."

What does it matter? thought Rose, amused by Ned's prickly attitude.

She found bread and cheese in the larder, ate standing in the kitchen, drank a glass of milk, poured a saucerful for the cats and went out to the garden.

A combination of dust in the atmosphere and evening mist coloured the moon like a blood orange. She stood on the steps leading to the walled garden and watched. In the distance she could hear the rattle and creak of harness, the rumble of wheels, the snort of carthorses as the Hadleys lifted the last load of hay by moonlight. Their lives were not much affected, thought Rose. They would not change as the Malones would be changed by their evacuees, and Ned and his friends by the Army. Even Farthing would change in the Home Guard, she thought, and smiled as she contemplated the self-importance already worn by Air Raid Wardens in the village. London was full of men joining the Fire Service or Ambulance, girls too. Uncle Archie and his Flora, to hear him talk, would run Scotland single-handed. Even her mother had said that the moment her flats were complete she would join the Red Cross. Rose wondered at all the activity, the stern enjoyment.

I want nothing to do with the killing, she thought, as she wandered under the lilacs, watched the cats crouch, freeze, leap after moths, miss. Yet I must do something; looking after Slepe and being wife to absent Ned is not enough to prevent me thinking. I must fight despair.

"The evacuation is over," she said out loud. "There will be no more news. It is over, over, over. I must do something to still my mind." She walked through the door in the wall to the vegetable garden.

I will help Farthing here. Grow food. Perhaps the Hadleys will let me help on the farm? I will tire myself to sleep, prevent myself thinking, teach myself to forget. When she went up to bed the moon had lost its rosy look, resumed its gold. She drew back the curtains undressed by its light, looked out at the cats still cavorting in the garden, got lonely into bed, supposed she would lie sleepless, slept.

Jerking awake she listened for a repetition of the sound. A pebble winged in through the open window to land with a skitter on the polished boards.

Springing to the window, she leaned out. Dark in the moonlight stood a man and a dog. The man, his face in shadow, stared up. The dog wagged, gently expectant.

"Rose?"

"Aah – Mylo," she whispered. "Mylo!"

"We will climb the magnolia," he said. "Come, Comrade, up you go." He set the dog to climb, steadying her from below as he followed. The dog scrambled, scrabbled, the magnolia leaves clattered, man and dog came in over the sill in a rush. "Are you glad?" Mylo held Rose in his arms.

"I had so nearly given you up."

"You knew I would come."

"I hoped, how I hoped – the telephone did not . . ."

"France is cut off for the duration."

The dog flopped down on the floor with a sigh. Mylo, his arms around Rose, his face in her hair, swayed with fatigue. "Get into bed," she said, helping him off with his clothes. "Are you hungry?"

"Later, later. Come close, take off that nightdress thing, let me feel you close." She lay beside him, he put his arms around her, buried his face in her neck, fell suddenly asleep.

Overwhelmed by joy Rose gulped great draughts of air sweetened by new-mown hay, sweetened far better by Mylo's sweat. While Mylo slept exhausted and the birds in the garden tuned up for the dawn chorus Rose knew the intense happiness of relief. Curled up beside him she catnapped, waking to the delight of feeling him with her. She listened to his breathing, laid her hand on his heart, feeling its beat under her palm. On the floor the dog whimpered in its sleep, scratched on the boards with dreaming paws.

As the mistlethrush led the birds in noisy crescendo Mylo woke, turned, held her close, kissed her eyes, found her mouth, made love tenderly with fluent passion, lay back laughing.

"We managed it right this time."

"Exquisite."

What had she done, so wifely with Ned, so friendly with George? Not this, nothing like this.

"And again?"

"And again and again."

Beside the bed the dog sneezed politely, craving attention.

"My poor Comrade. I brought her for you. I said if you must come with me, you will have to settle with Rose. She is probably hungry. We have travelled far."

"I will take her down and feed her, let her out. Where does she come from?"

"France."

"How?"

"She latched on to me. Followed my bicycle. I had a bicycle some of the way. She wouldn't go home. Has no home. She followed me from Conches to Perros-Guirec, leapt for the boat, fell in the water. I fished her out, she sneaked ashore with me at Brixham unnoticed and we came on here. Will you keep her?"

"Of course. I have been waiting for the right dog. I stocked up with tinned food. Ned would have liked me to have a Labrador. What do you suppose she is? Or an Alsatian."

"A French mongrel."

"I will feed her. What's her name?"

"I call her Comrade . . ."

Rose slid out of bed. "Come, then . . ."

"Stand still a moment, let me see you properly." Rose stood in the early light smiling.

"When you are old, you will look no different. Who is here? Are you alone in the house?"

"Yes. For the moment. The Farthings live in the cottage; he gardens, she helps when she feels like it; Ned's regiment is at Catterick." She must mention Ned. He exists, she told herself without alarm.

"Got back from Dunkirk, did he?"

"Yes."

"One wouldn't want one's worst enemy to be taken prisoner. I'm glad."

Rose pulled on her nightdress and dressing-gown. "Must you?" Mylo protested.

"I will take them off when I come back." (Mylo lay back.) "Don't you change, either . . ."

"Hurry back."

"I will. Come, Comrade." Rose ran downstairs with the dog, let her out into the garden, watched her trot through the dew, crouch thoughtfully. I shall tell Ned she is a stray, that I found her lost. The dog scratched the grass, kicking little clods of earth behind her, came back to Rose full of cheer. In the kitchen she put the kettle to boil, opened a tin of dog food. While the dog ate, she laid a tray, made coffee, boiled eggs, made toast, found marmalade, butter and honey, carried the tray upstairs. The dog followed at her heels, ignored the cats staring balefully through the banisters.

Rose pushed open the door, carried in the tray. Mylo was asleep again. "Come in, all of you," she said. The dog lay down by the bed while the cats, every hair on end, their tails like bottle brushes, sprang for safety on to the windowsill, baring needle teeth, gaping with silent mews.

Mylo woke. "Rose?"

She put the tray on the bed. "I must keep you secret; I only brought one cup for us."

"Take those things off."

She dropped the dressing-gown and nightdress to the floor, rejoined him in bed. They ate breakfast sitting close, sharing the cup. Then they made love again without haste, delighting in one another.

"You would think to see us now that we got it right the first time in that dismal little hotel." He stroked her flank. "I love you, love you, love you."

"And I you."

"You should see the expression of boredom on the faces of the girls I have regaled with my love for you. One yawned in my face."

"Many girls?"

"You should not ask questions. How is Ned?" he countered.

"Ned is all right."

"Isn't that *nice.*"

"Now then . . ."

"You are right, neither Ned nor other girls have anything to do with us."

"No, nothing." (Almost nothing, very little.)

"And do you speak of me?"

"Never. If I did, if I began, I should not be able to stop. I would go on and on and my love might dissipate in the process."

"There is that risk."

"Not really," she said, "how could it?"

"Ah, my love," he murmured, kissing her, "and yet in the nature of things it is better to keep me secret, nobody must know – my job."

"What job?"

"To-ing and fro-ing."

"What? Where? Not . . ."

"Yes. I shall be going back . . ."

"No!"

"I must. I shall come back often. Don't weep, Rose, don't weep. Nothing is easy."

It was later she felt resentful.

TWENTY-FOUR

Those precious days had set a standard difficult to adhere to, Rose thought, waking in the hotel bed, listening to the slap of water against the hotel jetty. The weather had been perfect; they had been so happy in their love, finding one another with passion, merriment, satisfaction. There had been no room for doubt or jealousy. They had resolutely shut out fear. The memory of those days in the midsummer of 1940 would endure strongly enough to bring the prick of tears, give courage in times of doubt or boredom, keep hope alive through disappointment, irritation, jealousy and anger. Do I dare hope, she asked herself; is hope a neglected habit which was strong in youth when I feared Mylo was gone from my life, had stopped loving me, loved someone else, was dead? There certainly had been times when hope guttered pretty low.

As a robin began to sing in a bush outside she looked across at the Bonnard hanging in view of the bed. "I hoped you would keep it in sight," Mylo had said that summer morning. "You guessed that I sent it. You knew, of course?"

"Even though you wrote no word."

"What is that garment she is wearing? A shift?" Propped on his elbow, he examined the picture.

"Camiknickers," she said.

"Shift is a prettier word."

"She has broken a shoulder strap."

"Do you break yours?"

"I remember one snapping when you hugged me in the Park. I thought if I protested it would spoil the moment . . ."

Mylo had laughed at that. "Look at our Comrade," he had said and they leaned together from the bed to stroke the dog's silky ears as she looked up at them, puffing out her lips with a whimper of devotion in the effort to express her affection, poor dumb animal.

I remember every moment.

"I feel like that about you. I am as inarticulate as the dog," he had said.

"You are not doing badly," she remembered saying with satisfaction. (Only temporary satisfaction, of course.)

We walked across the hayfields by the light of the moon. We lay on the grass in the walled garden under the lilac and syringa, we brought our meals out to the garden, we swam naked in the river. Why were we not interrupted or disturbed? I remember. Farthing was busy with his Home Guard; it was soon after that that he got his uniform; and Mrs Farthing had her big wash, an annual event of stupendous dimensions when curtains, covers, even rugs, were scrubbed clean; she probably made the little girls help her, so preventing them spying on us.

We lay in the bath and I told him about Nicholas and Emily; he said, "Do not let them hurt you, keep them at arm's length; they will try to insinuate themselves into your life."

"All very well," she remembered saying; "they have a gift of some sort."

"A talent for finding your sensitive spot and prodding it?"

"Yes," she had said. "You put it exactly."

"Then hide your sensitive spots."

"I only have the one, you."

"So?"

"So I hold my tongue, keep you secret. I shall not bore strange men telling them of you as you did those girls."

"Now, now."

"Who were they, anyway?"

"Does it matter? A girl in the Metro, another in a café, nothing to worry about – only girls."

"But I do."

"You must not be jealous; it would make more sense if I were jealous of Ned. I am, come to think of it."

"How could you be?" she had said, amazed.

"How can I not be?"

"Oh, Mylo, stop. Ned – well, Ned thinks too much about food; he is afraid of not having enough. He is really only interested in himself, not in me, except as a possession of some sort like the furniture, don't you see?"

"Nothing to fear, then?"

"Of course not."

"But you have promised him . . ."

"He was afraid."

"Hum." Mylo was unsure.

"I cherish you, my secret."

But was he so secret? She tried to remember. Had there not been a scene with her parents before she got engaged to Ned when she had suggested carelessly, to see what they would say, that she might marry

Mylo? Was it imagination? Did she invent her mother's snobbish put-downs, her father's acid remarks? If it did not take place, it well might have, so the effect was the same. There might have been a scene even worse than she thought she remembered, blotted from her mind. Why else her mother's sneering remarks, "people affecting workmen's clothes", "people of mixed descent", derogatory remarks made by an envious insecure woman. Funny that they ceased when she read an article about Mylo in the newspaper lauding something he had done. But that was years later, just before she died. (I know where *her* ashes are, thought Rose, I tipped them into the Serpentine.)

So those few days, if not completely perfect, came pretty close, Rose remembered, stretching her legs in the hotel bed.

"Ow! God! Ow!" She is seized with cramp in her old age. Cries aloud and struggles out of bed to stop the muscles bunching in her calf, treads down to relax the agonised tendons. I never had cramp when we walked along the hedgerow hand in hand and Comrade startled partridges and their chicks from the long grass verges. She massages her legs to relieve the pain which, stopping as quickly as it came, leaves an echo in her mind. "I suppose I am grown old," she says out loud. Is joy still possible? There had been so many times when joy was in abeyance. And hope? What about hope?

Hope had been hard put to it when she had waked to find herself alone in her bed. The silence told her he was gone; only the dog Comrade leaping on to the bed to lick her face and grieve with her proved that he had been there at all.

TWENTY-FIVE

Presumably, thought Rose lying in the hotel bed, the anguish of her cramped calf an echo, presumably it was during the late summer of 1940 that she plotted her future. Whatever she decided had been as deliberate as an act of taking out a life insurance policy. The surprise of finding Mylo there one minute, gone the next was something she was not prepared to endure.

She had once, as a child, bouncing as children do on her bed, bounced at an angle, hit her head against the nursery wall, concussed herself. Mylo vanishing left her equally stunned, she had not believed him capable of leaving without a word.

The first thing she had to do finding Mylo gone was to lie about the dog. She had found it, she told the Farthings, collarless, lost. It seemed quite an engaging dog, it did not chase cats.

"Got fleas?" inquired Mrs Farthing.

"Not so that you'd notice."

She drove to the police station on her way to the shops, reported her *trouvaille*, arranged that if it were not claimed she would keep it. The lies tripped easily.

"That animal?" The sergeant looked dubious. "I like a bit of class myself."

"I like her."

"It'll need a collar and a licence."

"I'll see she gets both." She drove back with Comrade on the back seat.

Ned, arriving on a week's leave, bringing Harold Rhys and Ian Johnson, found Comrade installed. Quiet, house-trained, trotting at Rose's heels.

"What an appalling mongrel. What on earth can it be? You can't want a creature like that. I've never seen anything like it. Where did you find it?"

"She appeared. I found her in the garden, she attached herself."

"You can't want to keep it?"

"I do."

"I wanted to give you a decent dog. A Labrador or an Alsatian. That animal isn't anything."

"A lot of things, I'd say," said Ian Johnson. "It looks like a scruffy sort of beagle mixed with terrier and a touch of spaniel." Ian mocked Comrade.

"I wanted," Ned exclaimed angrily, "to . . ."

"I know you did." Rose smiled at her husband, ignored Ian Johnson (not only boring, tactless also). She would keep Comrade's heroic retreat across France, her valiant leap from the quay to reach the boat (had Mylo intended leaving her?), her swim in the filthy dark water to be fished out by Mylo, her illegal entry at Brixham, to herself.

"If we were near the coast," said Harold Rhys who, never famous for brains, yet had the knack of striking the nail on the head, "I'd say it might be a French dog. There are dogs with a strain of hound in them all over France, supposed to be descendants of Wellington's foxhounds. I read a letter in *The Times* recently which said the French and Belgian refugee trawlers were bringing dogs and even cats across. Grandmothers too, apparently. It was calling attention to the dangers of rabies. One lot even brought a priest."

"Rabid grandmothers, promiscuous priests," mocked Ian Johnson.

"We are too far from the coast," squashed Ned, staring at the dog. "It does nothing for my home" (it was on the tip of his tongue to say ancestral), "for Slepe," he compromised. He had visualised, when Rose talked of having a dog, something elegant, pure bred, posing for the *Tatler*, Rose in tweeds, himself with gundog at feet.

"Oh, snobbish," mocked Rose. Ned flushed. "I was joking, only joking." But he failed to keep the anger from his voice.

"Darling, of course. Come with me. I want to show you my war work. You won't mind, you two?" She led Ned away.

"Your what?"

"Work. I am helping Farthing on a regular basis in the garden and I'm working on the farm. The Hadleys say they can use me."

"I don't think I . . ."

"It's so that I shall always be here when you come home, Ned." She popped a plug into his objections.

"Oh," said Ned, "I see," mulling the pros and cons. "Oh, all right, if it's not too much for you, if that's what you want." He wasn't sure he liked this but realised he could not stop her.

"If you don't approve I've been offered a job in the War Office." This was a lie, but how was Ned to know?

"I don't want you in London, you are much better here, safer."

"That's what I thought you'd say. And, Ned, when the war is over, we'll get you a Labrador."

Is she learning to manage me? Ned wondered as they walked through the vegetable garden. I must have a chat with Uncle Archie.

And, Rose thought, putting her arm through Ned's, as soon as I am sure Mylo is gone for good, I shall get myself pregnant. Mylo should have told her more, given her more hope, a child would be a sheet anchor through this dismal war, lessen her fear and insecurity.

It was years before Rose admitted she had opted as her father would have wished her to for safety, but at the time, since she was not completely ignorant, she also wondered resentfully where Mylo had learned to be such a good lover. She knew such things did not come naturally; had she not herself had to learn the mechanics with Ned? She discounted George, and bitterly resented Mylo's silent disappearance.

TWENTY-SIX

Far from subsiding, Rose's anger grew as weeks turned to months during the long summer of 1940. She resented Mylo's secretiveness, sneaking off without a word of farewell. He might have trusted her, she thought, as she hoed the vegetables, trundled her wheelbarrow, weeded the onion bed under Farthing's supervision. I would not have delayed him much, just enough for one last hug. Maybe he was hurrying away to other girls. The thought of other girls filled her with rage as she squatted among the onions, tearing up the weeds, filling her fingernails with grit. She gave small credence to his work, if it existed.

When Ned telephoned she babbled of her doings, giving him news of the farm, the garden, the village, making him laugh at the advice she received from Edith Malone. "She wants to turn me into a lady of the manor; fortunately your uncle set no example. I can't see myself in the role. Some of her ideas are positively feudal." She mocked Edith.

"Then keep a low profile," said Ned, laughing, glad that Rose appeared happy, under the delusion that he would shape her to fit Slepe as he wished. And Rose enjoyed those conversations, looked forward to Ned's distant voice which distracted her from her hurt. But, at night, with her body lusting for her lover, she cursed Mylo, decided to forget him, sweep him clear. Then, leaning from her window at night, she breathed the scent of magnolia, remembered his climb, pushing the dog up ahead of him, heard the stiff leaves clatter and saw his gleeful, exhausted face.

(Why the hell had he not behaved like an ordinary person and rung the bell at the front door?)

When in late September Ned came on leave she surprised him with an affection which he took for love, with tenderness he mistook for lust, with friendship which was genuine. In her anger and grief for Mylo she saw nothing odd in turning to Ned for comfort. In later years she would consider that she might have exaggerated her search for consolation in the conceiving of a child. She did this on Ned's last night, simply ceasing to use the outfit provided by Doctor Helena

Wright. She deluded herself that a child would erase Mylo from her mind. (Which goes to show, she would acknowledge in old age, what an idiot I was.)

Ned, driving down from Yorkshire in his large car so hungry for petrol, spent his leave hoisting it on to blocks, oiling and greasing it, disconnecting the battery, covering the whole with tarpaulin. From now on, he told Rose, he would use the railways and her car, should he come home on leave, economise on petrol. "Shall you be all right with this little car?" he had asked. She guessed that he felt a twinge of guilt over its acquisition. (Nicholas and Emily could be seen speeding about the roads in their MG with petrol supplied by the Ministry of Agriculture.)

"I shall be perfectly all right with it," Rose reassured him as she walked with him across the fields she had walked with Mylo, paused by the river where they had swum, watched Comrade flush partridges from the long grass as she had flushed them for Mylo. She held Ned's hand as they walked, daring herself to compare it with her lover's.

They sat, Ned's last evening, on the stone seat where on the morning of their honeymoon they had remembered diversely the winter tennis. Ned was to leave on the evening train. Across the fields John Hadley called his cows for the evening milking, "Hoi, hoi, hoi," his cry drowned suddenly by the roar of a plane.

"An enemy bomber?"

"No, a fighter. A Hurricane or a Spitfire. I cannot tell the difference."

"The Farthings' evacuees can," said Rose.

"Ah, children, children . . ." Ned looked across the garden where the first frost had yet to nip the dahlias. "As soon as this is over I shall want children."

"And not before?" Rose found her husband's selfishness amusing. "I might want one before. Or never," she teased, catching Ned's startled eye, "or are you leaving me out of this caper?"

Ned flushed. "You know I . . ."

"Should the war stop procreation?" Rose's voice was suddenly harsh, shouting at her husband.

"It's hardly the moment – with this battle going on – there's another plane, is it in trouble? – to my mind there is still danger of invasion . . ."

"Churchill is saying the battle is won . . ."

"So many pilots lost. I wish I had learned to fly."

"I'm glad you didn't."

"I am too old."

"Are you too old to have a child?" Rose snapped.

"Don't let's squabble my last evening."

"All right." Partly she regretted her impulse of the previous night (perhaps nothing would happen). "You will be on leave again soon."

"I didn't want to spoil our time together so I did not tell you that I am on embarkation leave." Ned stared at the dahlia, orange and red.

"*What*?"

"We are under orders for the Middle East."

"Another one who does not trust me."

"What?"

"Nothing, nothing. When do you go?"

"We don't know; it may not be for weeks, but tomorrow in London I must kit myself out with light uniform, visit my lawyer . . ."

"Lawyer, what for?"

"To check my will."

"Oh, God, you could have trusted me not to spoil your leave," she was bitter, "you treat me like a child, a thing . . ."

"I am sorry . . ."

"I should bloody well hope so . . ." A future without Mylo and now Ned. "I like you, Ned," she said ruefully.

"And I love you."

"I said like, not love." Rose was sharp.

"I heard you. It's important to like the person you love. I both love and like you, dear."

Rose breathed in, let speech out in a rush: "I know it's silly, I know I should have told you before, but I cannot bear being called dear, Ned, it makes me feel quite sick."

Ned looked at Rose astonished; in a secret crevice of his mind there wriggled the suspicion that she did not love him. Rose went on, flushing as she spoke, "Dear is what nurses call their patients, dear is what my parents called each other in hatred, dear to my ear is horrible. I'm sorry, Ned, but I simply can't stand being called *dear*."

Across the garden the dahlias glowed orange and blood-red. "I'd better get a move on," said Ned, "or I shall miss my train. I had not realised . . ."

Rose stood up, ashamed. (What a moment to choose.)

Ned went to fetch his luggage, his mind full of doubt. He had assumed that his feeling for Rose was reciprocated. Not usually given to introspection, he nevertheless thought as he drove Rose's car to the station that liking lasted longer than love, which to hear people like Uncle Archie talk was a flash-in-the pan business. He was glad that Rose liked him, the thought amused him, and he laughed out loud. Rose forbore to ask, What's the joke? The train was puffing into the station; they had to run to catch it, Ned scrambling aboard with barely time to kiss goodbye.

When Rose went back to the car she had to adjust the driving seat which Ned had moved to suit himself. Manoeuvring it, Rose thought, Give him credit, if he had had time, not had to run for the train, he would have put the seat back without being asked, he was that kind of man; he would move car seats for her, but when it came to starting a family, he would only consider himself. Driving back to Slepe, Rose in her turn laughed, pleased to have stolen a march.

TWENTY-SEVEN

Restless in the hotel bed, listening to the chirrup of dawn birds, Rose was undecided whether to read her paperback until breakfast or opt for an early walk.

She thought, I miss the routine which formed life at Slepe. It had begun working with Farthing, digging, weeding, sowing, gathering. Increased with work on the farm, with its closeness to animals, the smell of cows at milking, the cluck of hens, grown with her gradual interest in the house, sharing Ned's pleasure in the pictures, furniture, porcelain, silver, and even rugs, as she evolved from ignorant girl into wife and mother. All the multiplicity of small jobs, recurring responsibilities, interests and irritations which added up to security and contentment snatched away by Ned's death.

But this is what I have looked forward to, she mocked herself, eventual freedom.

She got up, dressed in jeans and sweater, let herself out on to grass drenched with dew.

A brisk walk to "stimulate the faggocites", her father's expression used in turn by herself, passed on to Christopher. What on earth are faggocites? She questioned the word as she set off along the creek. "I hope," she said to the hotel cat returning from its night foray, "to walk off my gloom." The cat dodged the hand she stretched to stroke it, proceeding indifferent on its way. "So much for hope."

As she walked she considered hope and what its loss let one in for.

Christopher, for instance?

Was Christopher the result of loss of hope? Probably. Blame him on Mylo? A plug against loss of spirit, fear, anger, jealousy, loneliness, or the result of a fondness for Ned and a maternal instinct stronger than herself?

Not that. She had never pretended to be excessively maternal, but how had Christopher, that lovely roly-poly baby, that delightful little boy, grown into the man chosen by Helen as husband. ("Let me take charge of that; I can see it upsets you. I will deal with it," taking the urn with Ned's ashes which she had put momentarily next to the sandwiches on the dining-room table while she fumbled for a handkerchief to blow her nose. Interference or kindness? Don't think of Helen; she cannot help being like that; Christopher loves her; enjoy your walk.)

It had never been easy to unravel the skein of motive and emotion which resulted in the advent of Christopher.

Had it been something to do with the dog Comrade?

This is ridiculous, dogs are sympathetic to humans, not the other way about. And yet when she had realised that Comrade was in pup, must have been in pup when she followed Mylo across France, running by the bicycle, leaping to catch the departing boat when he might or might not have meant to abandon her. There had been fellow-feeling between herself and the dog when, Christopher little more than a pinhead in her womb, Comrade gave birth to puppies, one of which survived to sire the first of a long line of engaging mongrels which terminated abruptly when Christopher, squabbling with Helen, let them get squashed by a juggernaut on the main road.

First the dogs, then the urn.

Will this make Christopher feel guilty towards me, as I always felt towards my mother, my father?

"One hopes not," Rose said out loud as she followed the path which led now through a wood.

There was the little matter of Mrs Freeling's ashes. (The official at the crematorium had called them Mrs Freeling's ashes, not your mother's or your parent's ashes, handing her the parcel.) Ned would not have understood her feelings of guilt towards her parents. In his book, the dear uncomplex fellow, you loved your parents, even loved in-laws. Neither Ned nor Helen would have understood why she had tipped her mother's urn into the Serpentine, watching the ash drift down like a sash towards the water. It was done to placate Mrs Freeling's spirit, to keep her happy in death, separate from the husband she had outlived so cheerfully. Rose spared a breath to laugh as she puffed up the path as it turned uphill away from the water. It had done no harm to let Ned and Christopher bury the empty urn beside Mr Freeling. Not expecting her to lie, they had taken it that Mrs Freeling's wish had been not to have her urn opened. Christopher, taking the urn without much reverence, had said, "Funny old Granny."

She can't have been more than forty-five when I discovered just how funny she was, thought Rose. Forty-five and she had seemed so old!

She had discovered her mother's funniness when, on impulse the day after Ned's embarkation leave, she went up to London and took her mother out to lunch. It had certainly distracted her mind from harping on Mylo. Across the table she had seen a new Mrs Freeling.

She no longer looked downtrodden, saintly, patient and forbearing, she looked lively; being widowed suited her.

As they ordered lunch, Rose observed her mother. She had had her hair properly cut; her hands were cared for; she wore new clothes. There was a rumour, she told Rose, that the government would ration clothes. "I am stocking up," she said. "You should do the same."

"I don't need much in the country, just lots of warm things. Slepe is pretty chilly."

"I hope you won't let yourself get stuck in the country all your life as I did."

"I thought . . ."

"You should get yourself something to do, like me. I have made a lot of new friends in the Red Cross. What are all your neighbours up to?"

"Mrs Malone has filled their house with evacuee children."

"God help her, but perhaps she likes children? Have you noticed how delightful London is without them? I enjoy the quiet of the Park without perambulators when I walk across it in the mornings."

"What about air raids?"

"I have not much time for them, too busy by day and I sleep like a top at night. First time for years."

"Really?"

"I get tired. There's the Red Cross, and I am still furnishing my flat. Did I tell you I have a lodger?"

"No?"

"A major who works in the War Office. He is mostly out, no bother, he pays his rent and keeps out of my way."

"Oh."

"You should come up oftener, I can put you up when I'm finally settled. There is plenty going on, concerts and now the theatres are open again, plays – you mustn't let your brain atrophy."

"I hope not."

"And I have taken up bridge, formed a regular four. My major plays when he's in, should one of us fail."

"You seem to be having an interesting time." Rose assessed this new parent who dressed smartly, went to concerts, played bridge.

"About time," said Mrs Freeling with force, "after all I endured with your father." Rose had sat open-mouthed as there followed a diatribe against her defunct parent. His failure, his selfishness, his boringness; he was picked over bit by bit, no facet left unpecked. Once started her mother could not stop: she tabulated a lifetime of resentments. Her father's table manners, mean economies, treachery to friends, his assumption of gentlemanly Christianity, his sucking up to social superiors, his bitterly resented illness, the wasteful cost of the treatment for non-existent cancer, his snores, his impecuniosity.

"Mother . . ."

But Mrs Freeling had not finished, out came her horror of sex, her husband's insistence on his marital rights – brutal rapes.

"Mother, please . . ."

"And then," Mrs Freeling made no effort to lower her voice, "the unspeakable process of procreation!"

"I thought marriage, the Bible . . ."

"Written by *men*." Mrs Freeling swept the Bible aside. "Sensitive women like me should not be subjected to such – fortunately for you the process of childbirth is academic."

"Is it?" Rose was astonished.

"Of course. A nice man like Ned would never . . ."

"Mother . . ."

Her mother's voice was clear; people at neighbouring tables munched with ears pricked. "It's beyond my comprehension that women still put up with it," said Mrs Freeling.

"The human race," suggested Rose bravely.

"It's men who want it to go on. Sheer vanity. Give me one reason why it should."

"I . . ."

"If it must," said Mrs Freeling, "the people who in earlier times had wet nurses should have gone the whole hog and let the husband couple with the wet nurse."

Is she drunk? Rose looked surreptitiously round at masticating jaws.

"I trust you are not proposing to let yourself be hoodwinked by Ned into enduring the agony and humiliation of having a child? My dear Rose, the thing jumps about inside you, you have no control; your body is not your own, you cannot escape, it *heaves*!" Mrs Freeling's voice rose in disgusted recollection.

Crimson-faced, Rose muttered, "Sorry, Mother, so sorry," in apology for her foetal antics.

"Take my advice and make a stand." The peroration was over. Mrs Freeling ate her pudding while her daughter wondered whether the exhilaration of widowhood had affected her brain. "You must think I have changed." Mrs Freeling put down her spoon, wiped her mouth with her napkin.

"A bit," she had murmured cautiously.

"I have been bottled up all these years."

"I wish I'd known."

"What could you have done?" her mother asked sharply. "You are just like him, you only think of yourself."

"I could have . . ."

"You can do one thing for me. When I die, I do not want to be buried with him. Have me cremated and scatter me over water. I would like that. Can I count on you?"

"Of course."

"Right. Is that the bill? Let's go Dutch."

Mrs Freeling had never referred to the conversation. Rose sometimes wondered whether she had imagined it. The outburst had been cathartic; she remembered her mother's serene expression when they parted.

How grateful I am now, thought Rose, panting as she climbed the hill, that she refrained during my childhood and adolescence from alerting me to the horror of sex as she saw it and left me to make my discoveries with Mylo. (And of course Ned.) There had been an air raid, she remembered, as she left London and she had hastened to get back to Slepe where now, as she looked back over the years, she realised she had just spent a happy week with Ned.

TWENTY-EIGHT

Ned left his lawyer's chambers and set off on foot towards his tailor. There was an air raid alert; he had listened to the siren while discussing his will. His solicitor, already blasé, had said, "You don't want to pop down to the shelter, I take it, it's the most fearful waste of one's time."

"No, no thanks." (He would charge me for time wasted in the shelter, knowing him, he's fly.)

"Good, then let's get on with it."

"Right."

"Your family trust makes it pretty plain sailing; it doesn't leave you much chance to settle old scores." The solicitor had laughed.

As he walked Ned ruminated resentfully on the terms of the trust which had brought him Slepe. Thanks to the laws of primogeniture and entail he had inherited Slepe from a distant cousin, so far so good. But should he die without a son, Slepe would pass to another cousin. Perhaps, thought Ned as he strode along, he had been wrong in his approach to starting a family. Suppose one had a quiverful of girls, didn't manage a boy first shot? Rose had been angry, had not been easily mollified; he was not sure why she had been angry, but it made him feel guilty. When the war is over and she does produce my son, I will give her a jewel, he thought. Then he thought, turning into Bond Street, Why wait, why not give her a present now? As he walked he glanced in at the jewellers' displays. If he bought her a jewel, she would at least have something to sell, should he get killed before she bore a son. He had practically no savings apart from monies tied up in Slepe. Rose had no money of her own. (The damn solicitor had tut-tutted about this at the time of his marriage.) All the jewels seemed tremendously expensive, but wouldn't their value increase? To buy or not to buy? Ned batted the idea back and forth. The principal snag in the family trust was that every penny, as well as the house, passed on his death to this imaginary son. Until this morning Ned had not taken much account of this clause. "How would Rose manage?" he had asked.

"The usual thing is that your son makes your widow an allowance."

"But suppose they don't get on?"

The solicitor had said, "They'd better," his voice crisp and legal.

Poor little Rose, thought Ned tenderly, why don't I buy her a jewel now? Give her pleasure, something she can flog if I leave her a widow; she doesn't get on with her mother, not liking parents may be hereditary. Ned idled along, coming to a stop outside Cartier. (My God, I can't afford any of that! Our engagement ring was too pricey, one pays for the bloody name.) He walked on. Yet, he thought, I would like to give her something to remember me by. But suppose I did and she flogged it for no particular reason? Better to give her jewels when she's had my son, a reward, a thanksgiving. She hasn't done the job yet; it would be silly to give her jewellery now, especially if there were all those girls first and one had to keep at it.

And yet some sort of present? She likes pretty things, she has a good eye, she picked up that Bonnard she has hung in our bedroom, said she acquired it for love, to give it a good home. He had said, "Like the dog?", joking, and she'd laughed. The dog was a pretty awful mongrel, but the Bonnard might easily turn into a canny investment. All the same I don't want to give her jewellery and have her flog it to buy pictures, you can come a cropper with pictures. The Bonnard might be just a lucky fluke.

He had arrived halfway up Bond Street and stared sightlessly at the window of the White House. "God!" he focused, "that's what the girl in her picture is wearing. Rose has no exciting underclothes, perhaps she bought that picture as a hint; my problem is solved."

Ned went into the shop and chose six pairs of cream satin camiknickers, arranged to have them sent to Rose, writing, "With all my love, Ned", on a card provided by the saleslady. He came out into the street relieved and generous. As he walked the All Clear sounded. He put thoughts of Rose aside and concentrated on his lightweight uniform. Should he go to Huntsman or Gieves? Just as he was in the habit of patronising two barbers, so it was with tailors, favouring now the one, now the other. His feet led him through Burlington Street to the corner of Savile Row and Vigo Street, and up the steps into Huntsman, the euphoria of his generosity making him decide on the more snob of the tailors.

Emily, sauntering down Savile Row, spied Ned emerging from the portals of his tailor, pausing to draw a satisfied breath, then running down the steps to the street with springing step.

"Ned, hi, Ned," Emily shouted, breaking into a trot. "Ned!"

Ned, recognising Emily, waved, waited for her to come up to him. "Hullo, Em. What are you doing here? Long time no . . ."

"I was on my way to . . . what are you up to?"

"Having fittings for lightweight uniforms. Come and have lunch."

Ned surprised himself by his impulsive invitation. "You are not doing anything, are you?"

"Just shopping," said Emily. "I'd love to. Thanks. Where shall we go?"

"Quaglino's? Why not?"

"Why not indeed." Emily put her hand through Ned's arm, giving it a familiar squeeze.

They walked through the Burlington Arcade, crossed Piccadilly and descended into Jermyn Street.

At Quaglino's Ned was greeted with obsequious bows and scrapes. The maître d'hôtel inquired after Rose and watched Emily from the corner of his eye while he handed Ned the menu. "A drink while you wait?"

They sat in the hall for a pre-lunch drink.

"And how is Rose?" asked Emily.

"I have been buying her a present, six presents actually, she's in great form."

"Oh, lucky Rose." Emily smiled at Ned as she sipped her drink; Ned regarded her with quizzical eye. He wondered vaguely why there had been no time to get in touch during the past months.

"This is nice," Emily sipped, "isn't it?"

"Yes, indeed." Ned stretched his legs, drew them back to let a couple in naval uniform pass, the girl in WRNS uniform looked a trim little piece. He swallowed his drink, ordered another. Emily refused, still busy with her first. He felt pleased with his morning, pleased with his uniform; part of the charm of joining the Territorials had been the uniform; he felt a better, a different man in uniform.

"Nice uniforms?" asked Emily.

"Mind reader. Yes, lightweight. I am posted overseas."

"Oh, Ned, are we to lose you?"

"Not permanently, I am not gone yet."

"What *will* Rose do?"

"She's working full-time in the garden growing food, and on the farm too; it's rum sort of war work but that's what she wants, it keeps her safe."

"It will ruin her hands, but keep her out of mischief," said Emily, spreading her fingers, inspecting her red nails, neat cuticles.

Ned laughed. What mischief could Rose get up to? "Let's have lunch."

They moved into the restaurant, sat on a banquette facing the room.

Emily scraped her nails on the white tablecloth, gritting her teeth at the thought of Rose's nails splitting and full of grit. "What present did you buy her?"

"I bought her underclothes at a shop I found called the White House."

"Underclothes!" Emily crowed with laughter, tossing back her head. "Camiknickers, I bet."

"Actually, yes," said Ned stuffily. "Come on, what are you going to eat?" He tapped the menu, bringing it to Emily's attention. Brought to order, Emily chose. "And what are you and Nicholas up to these days; still the Ministry of Agriculture?"

"Yup. Still the Min. of Ag. It suits me, lets me travel, as you know." Emily slid a glance at Ned, who failed to respond. "Tell me," she said, "about Dunkirk. I haven't seen you since. Everyone's saying how brave you were, got a medal, didn't you?"

"The MC."

"Go on, tell me all about it, I really want to know. Rose told me about the gooseberries," said Emily. This was not strictly true. Rose had told Edith Malone about the gooseberries in the tin hat; the tale travelled from mouth to ear by telephone, finally reaching Nicholas who had told his sister. (Imagine old Ned in danger, whatever next.) "I should like to see you coolly reacting to danger," said Emily, distracting Ned from thoughts of Rose. If anyone mentioned Dunkirk, he remembered standing in the queue in the sea, the hot sun on his head, the feeling that his legs were shrinking, the noise of the bombs. He had prayed to get back to Slepe and Rose, of course. "I thought you never saw Rose," he said.

"What makes you think that? I'm her neighbour, there's the telephone. Come on, Ned, tell me about being in danger, you are the only person I know who was at Dunkirk."

"I'm in danger now," said Ned, grinning.

"Ned, you are flirting." Emily turned towards him, pressing her knee against his leg.

Ned put his hand on Emily's thigh, digging his nails in. "Where are you staying?"

"Are you not going back to Slepe?"

"Up north on the night train."

"I'm staying with a friend."

"Is the friend out?"

"Away," said Emily.

"Finish your lunch. I'll ask for the bill."

"All right," said Emily.

"I love Rose," said Ned.

"Of course."

"Bill, please," said Ned to the waiter.

They sat in silence waiting for the bill; when it came Ned put notes on the bill and the waiter took it away to get change.

"I'll just telephone Euston and check my train," said Ned.

"All right," said Emily.

Ned went away to telephone.

The waiter brought the bill folded over Ned's change on a plate.

"He'll be back in a minute, just gone to telephone," said Emily.

The waiter went away.

Since nobody was looking, Emily helped herself to some of Ned's change, putting it in her bag.

"Right," said Ned, returning. "We've got several hours before my train." He pocketed the change without looking at it except to leave a tip commensurate with the splendour of his present to Rose.

Emily read his thoughts.

"I wonder whether she'll wear them gardening?"

Ned laughed, following her out of the restaurant, waving a taxi to stop. He handed Emily in. Emily told the driver the address. Ned sat with his arm around Emily. "I wonder what it's like in Vienna these days," he said.

"Why ever Vienna?"

"I was thinking of my uncle Archie and his Viennese uncles."

"Why?"

"They had quite a lot of fun, I gather."

TWENTY-NINE

Emily found Rose breakfasting in her kitchen, Comrade at her feet.

"Hullo," said Rose. The dog wagged her tail.

"I am on my way to your farm to get some Min. of Ag. forms filled in," Emily said. "My word, Rose, you do get up late. I had breakfast hours ago," she said virtuously.

"I help with the milking and feed the pigs, then after breakfast I work in the garden. I'm up before six," said Rose, matter of factly.

"I apologise." Emily sat opposite Rose.

"Let's see the forms," said Rose.

Emily put a protective hand on her briefcase. "They are for John Hadley."

"In Ned's absence I'm his landlord." Rose held out her hand. "Give."

Reluctantly Emily brought a sheaf of forms out of her briefcase, put one back and handed the rest to Rose.

"Help yourself to coffee." Rose perused the forms. "Not too tiresome," she said, "they want us to grow more wheat. We shall have to plough another meadow, otherwise it's OK. Now show me the other."

"What other?" Emily looked innocent.

"The form you put back, the one you didn't want me to see."

"You won't like it." Emily hesitated, then produced the form.

Rose read, eyebrows rising. "No," she said, angrily tearing up the form, "certainly not."

"You'll only get sent another," said Emily with mock patience.

"Tell them it's not on," said Rose. "They can take me to court if they like. I am not having our rooks shot; they eat hardly any grain, they eat leather jackets and do a lot of good. You Min. of Ag. people are an ignorant lot. I love our rooks and so does Ned."

(Has he ever said so?)

"Tell that to my Ministry." Emily was patient.

"I certainly will," said Rose forcefully. "Who is your boss?"

"Nicholas."

Rose burst out laughing. "Nicholas? Really?"

"Yes." Emily was laughing too. "Tell you what, we'll cook the books; nobody is going to check that you've complied with the order."

"Cheat?"

"If you like. There's a war on, we're busy . . ."

"A war within a war. Have some toast and marmalade, more coffee?"

Emily refilled her cup. "Actually you are not the only one to protest. The Malones nearly shot me. Then dear Mr Malone promised me two brace of pheasants a month throughout the season." Emily drank her coffee, watching Rose over the rim of her cup.

"H-m . . . and what bribe can I give you?" Rose eyed Emily with suspicion.

"Moral support," said Emily gravely.

What's her game? Rose wondered. "Me, give you moral support? Are you joking?"

Emily said, "No joke. I'm pregnant."

Rose was silent, absorbing this news. Then she asked quietly, "Getting married?"

"Out of the question."

"Is he dead? Married already?"

"It's not a question of that . . ."

"Then what? Oh, Em, you're not . . ."

"I had an abortion once. Two years ago. There's a clinic in Munich. Nicholas came with me. We had a rather jolly time in the end. It cost the earth. We sold one of father's teapots; he's never missed it so don't breathe, but now with the war one can't get to Munich, can one?"

"Of course not." Rose had an absurd vision of Emily and Nicholas infiltrating into Munich by parachute.

"I'm not in favour of back streets and knitting needles. I've tried gin and hot baths to no avail. You know us. Nicholas helped, he nearly boiled me alive, nothing!"

"There must be something, someone . . ."

"I've decided to have it."

"Emily! How splendid!"

"I don't know what's so splendid about it." The words were deprecating, but Emily looked pleased.

Rose had never received a confidence from Emily; she was tempted to confide in return, to expose herself, but long association with the Thornbys prevented her. She told herself that she was still not absolutely certain of her own pregnancy; she might be six weeks late or something.

"I notice you don't ask who the father is," said Emily demurely.

"It's not my business, is it?" said Rose.

The two girls thoughtfully drank their coffee. Comrade stretched out on the floor and yawned. She was heavy with pup.

"Do you feel sick?" asked Rose cautiously.

"Mornings," said Emily. "It's not too bad."

"Does Nicholas know? Does he know you want to keep it, I mean?"

"Of course Nicholas knows. He thinks it's a great joke; he's already making plans for its future."

"Oh." Rose considered Emily. Emily with so many boyfriends, Emily's visits to London, her popularity at parties. Then she thought of the brother and sister's closeness; was Nicholas perhaps pleased that Emily could not marry the baby's father, that she would not be leaving him? It was a lot to take in all at once. "What shall you do?" she asked. "Do you think Edith Malone would be helpful?"

"I told you. No abortion. If I turned to Mrs Malone, she'd think I was fathering the child on George or Richard."

"Surely not, she's so kind."

"It would be the first thing I'd think of in her shoes," said Emily. "No, no, we've decided to let people think and say what they please and have the baby. I shall ask my father for money. He can't refuse, he'd disapprove of abortion and he won't approve of the baby, but he isn't mean. Good Lord, bishops are supposed to be Christian."

"I think you are most courageous, Nicholas too." (Nicholas will love the drama.)

"Not really." Emily stirred her coffee, then helped herself to more sugar. "Sorry, I crave it, keep forgetting it's rationed."

"Couldn't you say the father was a fighter pilot, shot down and killed?"

"Oh, Rose, how respectable you are," Emily shouted angrily, "the little soul of convention! I can't be bothered to lie. If it bothers you and people ask, just say you don't bloody know. I am not the first girl to get caught like this."

"But . . ."

"I'm lucky," Emily yelled, "to be living with Nicholas in our own house. We've both got jobs, nobody's going to turn little Emily out into the snow. It will be a nine days' wonder. With the war going on, people have more interesting things to talk about. I wish now," said Emily passionately, "that I hadn't told you. You're so bloody pure, there's nothing disreputable about you, is there?"

On the floor Comrade whimpered in her sleep, flapped her tail against the flagstones.

"I'm glad you did tell me, didn't wait for me to wonder whether somebody was pumping you up with a bicycle pump."

"Well, all right, let's shut up about it, shall we?"

"There's no need to be touchy; of course I'll shut up."

"I'm not touchy," shouted Emily, banging her cup on the table. "Oh, curse it, I've cracked it, was it one of Ned's best?"

"No." Rose fetched a fresh cup from the dresser, wiped the spillage, poured Emily fresh coffee and sat down to finish her breakfast.

For a while neither girl spoke, then Emily said in her usual tone of voice, "When did Ned go?"

"He sailed from Liverpool nearly three weeks ago. It was cold and wet. At least he's gone to where the sun shines." (It's funny how I miss him, that matter-of-fact voice.)

"I saw him in London, we met in the street, he gave me lunch," said Emily.

"He told me, said you were most amusing, he's got a soft spot for you. Did he tell you," asked Rose, "that he'd gone bravely alone and bought me six pairs of camiknickers? From the White House, too, think of the cost!"

"Yes, he did. It made me laugh."

"I would have thought him too shy and proper to do such a thing."

"Much too shy, but he's brave, look what he did at Dunkirk; one would never have credited it. I made him talk. All that rearguard action before they got taken off must have been scary."

"The war seems to bring out fresh facets in people; have you heard about my mother? She's settled herself in London, changed her appearance and become a bridge fiend. She's so changed, Emily, that she might turn out to be somebody who would help you."

"I don't want help. I thought I'd made that clear," snapped Emily.

"Yes. Well. Sorry." Rose picked up her plate and cup and moved towards the sink.

"Ned told me when I met him in London that he loves you." Emily reverted to Ned. Was the Ned she knew the same man who was Rose's husband, inheritor of all this? Emily looked around the large rather dark kitchen with its stone floor, draughts and inconvenient clutter. She felt no envy of Rose.

"I believe he does." Rose rinsed her cup under the tap, not wishing to discuss Ned or dissect his love with Emily.

Emily watched Rose's back, the baggy corduroy trousers, the plain shirt under the thick sweater; when would she find occasion to wear the camiknickers? Not while milking, feeding pigs or gardening. "Well," she said, gathering up her briefcase, snapping it shut, regaining her poise, "I must be on my way. Any chance," she asked as they walked towards the red MG, "of some extra butter now and again?"

Rose laughed. "Blackmailer. Butter is rationed, pheasants are not. No chance."

"Worth a try," Emily said amiably. She kissed Rose's cheek and got into the car. "The moral support will do." She drove away.

Rose joined Farthing in the kitchen garden where he was trenching and manuring, preparing the ground for winter frosts. "Shall I help?"

"You don't want to do this. It's too heavy. The cold frames need sorting out, you do that. They are full of weeds."

"What's in them?"

"Parma violets and lilies of the valley. Come spring, you can post them up to Covent Garden or a posh shop like Constance Spry and make a packet."

"What a lot you know." Rose fetched a fork and trowel and began work, squatting by the frames. Does sly old Farthing guess that Emily is pregnant? Does he guess I am? He's heading me away from heavy jobs. Did it occur to Emily, or is she too absorbed in herself? Was Emily hinting, wondered Rose, her thoughts still on her friend, that Ned might be the father? Ignoble thought, she tried to push it aside but it turned this way and that in her mind. Emily would, but would Ned? Rose pulled up handfuls of chickweed, dug deep to extract a dandelion. Would Emily, if Ned? Would Ned, if Emily? Emily would, but would Ned? She pulled hard on the dandelion root which snapped, leaving a residue of root in the soil, buried deep to pop up later as persistent as Rose's suspicion of Emily. Would I mind? she asked herself. Mind much or mind a little? Not at all? The question does not arise, she scolded herself. Then she thought with surprise that Emily had looked vulnerable and then, even more surprised, she thought, I liked her this morning. I've never liked her before. "What do you think of Emily Thornby?" she asked Farthing as he wheeled his barrow past her.

Farthing stopped, smiled: "She's got spunk. They both have."

"Ah."

"Mind you, between ourselves, I wouldn't trust either of 'em round a razor blade." Farthing gave his barrow a heave and moved on. Rose laughed, sitting back on her heels. "Not a very flattering observation."

"She'd be a bit of all right in a tight corner," Farthing called over his shoulder, "and her brother would too."

"Their father is a trustworthy bishop, Farthing."

"And who's he descended from? There's funny blood somewhere."

"Are you suggesting pirates?" asked Rose, extracting a grub from among the weeds and throwing it in the direction of an attendant robin. "Or gypsies?"

"I ain't suggesting nothing." Farthing tipped the load of manure on to the ground by his trench.

Rose, remembering Emily's attack on herself, asked, "Would you describe me as bloody conventional, Farthing?" rather cherishing Emily's description of herself.

"Wouldn't say bloody," said Farthing, forking manure into the trench. "The word conventional varies according to what you're doing in which social circle, I've heard."

"What a philosopher you are," said Rose. "I think you and Mrs Farthing would be pretty splendid in a tight corner."

"Might be at that," Farthing agreed.

THIRTY

Mylo hoped to smell land. He stood, legs apart, balancing with the bounce of the ship. It was pitch dark and extremely cold. His fellow passenger, his charge, huddled below to keep warm; probably he slept.

Mylo strained his eyes across dark water, inimical waves leaping to mix their salt with rain sheeting from the west in a relentless torrent. The last words his fellow passenger had uttered before going below had been: "*Quel climat maudit.*" This in answer to the skipper's shouted information that they were two-thirds across the Channel, two-thirds towards their destination. Useless to point out that the weather had been equally foul in France.

Mylo fixed his eyes on a cloud, denser than the rest, trying to get his bearings. Afraid of showing his anxiety and fear, he refrained from joining the skipper in the wheelhouse. There had been an invitation, but Mylo judged it half-hearted. The skipper's job was to deliver them safe, not to entertain; if he was not happy on deck, he could go below. Staring into the mesmeric dark, ears buffeted by the wind, eyes watering from the cold, Mylo allowed himself to think tentatively of Rose as he had last seen her, curled in her bed, one hand pushed up under the pillow where his head had lately rested, the other flung wide across the bed. He had bent to kiss her, breathing the scent of her skin and hair; forcing himself to leave he had crept to the door, put out a hand to stop the dog, Comrade, from following, signalling her to "stay", opened the door with stealth, gone swiftly downstairs and away.

For three months he had rationed his thoughts of Rose, lest day-dreaming he might drop his guard, speak a word of English, turn careless, risk capture, death, betrayal.

Had she been angry or sad? Had she understood? Could he or should he have warned her? Whichever way he left, it would have been painful; he had taken the mode least painful for himself. With his eyes fixed on the bank of cloud Mylo thought now of Rose, wished he could hear her voice, feel her body, taste the salt on her eyelids. In his heart he expected to find her exactly as he had left her. He would climb back into her bed; she would wake in his arms.

His mind jeered at the sentimental vision; months had passed since the parting.

"That's Start Point." The voice startled him, banished Rose.

"I thought it was a bank of cloud."

"We'll be in Dartmouth before daylight. Like some cocoa? Join us in the wheelhouse." The voice was cheerful pitched against the wind, jolly even, gone the clipped accents used when he had taken them on board; it had been a nervous rendezvous. The tide had been too strong, tempers had frayed, almost there had been failure. Failure would have led to arrest, arrest to . . .

Mylo followed to the wheelhouse, accepted cocoa, answered smile with smile. "Relax now, we'll be ashore in time for bacon and bangers. The crossing was a piece of cake." The young officer was immensely relieved, tremendously pleased; so he, too, had been frightened. He hid it well, thought Mylo, drinking his cocoa. "Your Frog's asleep; I looked in on him. Would he like some cocoa?"

"He's pretty tired, let him sleep."

"They'll be meeting you, I take it?"

"Someone will be meeting us, yes."

"Got a lot of nerve, you chaps."

"I'm just a *commis voyageur*," said Mylo, half offended by his own modesty, inwardly ridiculing it.

"What's that?"

"Commercial traveller," both men laughed, "and I am half Frog."

"I say, sorry, I didn't mean . . ."

"We Frogs call you Rosbifs."

More laughter, the young officer laughing alone this time.

As the land reached out to block the wind, Mylo, back on deck, sniffed, hoping to catch the smell of home soil, a field under plough perhaps where seagulls swooped and foraged fresh-turned clods. Presently they anchored offshore; he woke his fellow traveller and they were taken off by a launch which whirled them away from the ship to land them at a jetty far up the harbour. They stumbled up slippery steps into the arms of waiting officialdom.

Mylo's companion showed no inclination to kneel and kiss British soil in the manner which years later would become de rigueur for His Holiness Pope John Paul. He gave a hoarse imprecation as his foot slipped on a scrap of seaweed which might have been construed as relief at reaching dry land if he had not before starting on the journey already made his dislike of things British clear, a dislike superseded only by his loathing of things German. They were led across a cobbled quay into a building which smelled of soap, damp uniforms and cups of tea, sifting through a cloud of cigarette smoke. Dazzled by the glare of unshaded lights, Mylo thought it would be at least forty-eight hours before he could attend properly to thoughts of Rose; his charge spoke no English, was still his responsibility.

They were offered tea by an attractive Wren. Mylo's charge accepted, sniffed in disbelief at the contents of his mug and put it aside.

Their escort disappeared through a side door while an Army officer wearing Intelligence Corps insignia came from an inner office carrying a sheaf of papers to shake Mylo by the hand and greet his charge.

"Does your friend understand English?"

"No." Mylo followed the officer into an inner office.

"Bit short of interpreters at the moment, actually; our one and only is down with flu. No matter. We shall be sending you to London to be debriefed and when your passenger leaves Patriotic School he will be the Free French's responsibility. They insist on running their own intelligence."

"Who will he be dealing with?" Mylo asked innocently.

"Chap who calls himself Passy, came over with de Gaulle. Haven't met him myself, of course. Do sit down, that pew's comfortable."

"I have," said Mylo. "Extreme right wing."

"Does that matter?"

Mylo shot a glance of wonder at the intelligence officer. Now I know I am in England, he thought, and burst out laughing.

"Joke? Did I make one? Cigarette?"

"No, no, it must be the relief at having got here." Mylo leant back in his chair.

"Yes. I see. Dare say your job gets a bit hairy." He picked up a telephone. "Won't be a minute. I'll just rustle up your transport." He spoke into the telephone, listened. "Well, wake him up, Sergeant! Now, where were we? Your friend will be all right out there with Margaret, she's a bright girl." He went back to the door which stood open. "Keep an eye on our guest, Margaret, there's a good girl." Then, raising his voice, "You'll be all right with Margaret, Monsieur – er – Monsieur – er – forgive me, what's your name?"

"Picot," said Mylo. "Sit down," he said to his charge, "I won't be long; they are sending us to London by car."

"*Tiens.*" Picot sat on a chair offered by the shapely Wren and looked about him. The intelligence officer closed the door. "Not exactly forthcoming, your Frog friend."

"Doesn't like the English."

"Well, we don't like them, do we? Give me Jerry any day, he's not an hereditary enemy."

"Well . . ."

"Yes, I know," said the intelligence officer catching Mylo's eye.

"My name's Spalding, by the way. Not supposed to ask yours, am I? All this secrecy reminds me of my prep school days, games we used to play after lights out after reading too much John Buchan. Some of it makes a nonsense, though. I was dealing with a super secret chap last week, told to keep my trap shut by the powers that be. They didn't know we were cousins, did they, and been to the same school? Both of us did what we were told and kept mum, couldn't even make a date to meet for lunch on our next leave, wouldn't have done to make my brigadier look a fool. The Navy aren't half so stuffy. That's why I've wangled myself a Wren, by the way. Now then, mustn't run on; let's get the bumf work done, shall we?"

"Fine by me." Mylo waited while Spalding shuffled through his sheaf of papers.

"Came to meet you carrying these, didn't I? I'm supposed to keep them locked up. Here we are, this is what we want. These are for you and I keep this and this. I'm supposed to ask you a lot of damn fool questions which you will be asked all over again in London, in triplicate I shouldn't wonder, and your friend Picot too, so I won't bother you now. Such a waste of time, God help the lot of us. Thank him, thank him, thank him, I'm due for a spot of leave. You two go up by car, but I go by train; it wouldn't be ethical to hitch a ride. Right? All done." The intelligence officer smiled at Mylo across his desk and stood up.

"Thanks a lot."

"I hear that Passy chap is a bastard, by the way," said Spalding as he lit a cigarette.

"I've heard it too."

"If your friend is a communist, tell him to keep it to himself."

"——"

"The Passy chap, calls himself a colonel, isn't so much extreme right as blazing fascist, if you ask me, but please don't. I'm only here to do my modest job. You did say extreme right, didn't you?"

"Something like that."

"Get the nuances right. Tip your friend."

"I will."

"There's a game within a game and it is not cricket. Am I being indiscreet?"

"Not at all. Of course not. What an idea."

"Well, then. Right we are. Your car should be here by now." Spalding shook Mylo's hand. "I was never much good at hints." They walked back to the outer office.

The shapely Wren was exercising her schoolgirl French. Picot was laughing as he corrected her accent. The Wren who was laughing too straightened her face and saluted Spalding. Picot got to his feet.

Mylo and Picot said goodbye and followed a military policeman who had materialised to a military car.

"Wish we could give you a lift," shouted Mylo, but the intelligence officer wasn't there any more. He got into the car with Picot, and they were driven off.

Picot watched the countryside of Devon, wet, brilliant green and ploughed, for half an hour, then turned to Mylo, "Well?"

"You will, as I told you, be taken to Patriotic School and after that the French take you over. There's a snake called Passy."

"Not a grass-snake?"

"No."

"Thank you."

"Eats communists for breakfast."

"*C'est un flic, c'est tout.*" Picot, much less glum than on arrival, laughed. "For an English girl that one was pretty. She moves soon to work in London; we are to lunch at a restaurant she likes, the Écu de France."

"If you escape the Deuxième Bureau."

"They do not bother me. And you, shall you be my escort next time? Shall we make a habit of this? Make rendezvous at your aunt in Paris and cross together to Dartmouth?"

"Possibly." Mylo did not want to talk any more; he wanted to think about Spalding's fake asininity, he wanted to think of Rose. With an effort he dismissed both from his thoughts and concentrated on the report he must make on arrival in London. Try to make sense while protecting his back. My back is in France, he thought. All those friends and acquaintances continually at risk. How dare somebody as safe as Spalding be so frivolous? Shall I try telephoning Slepe from London? What happens if Ned answers, if Ned's on leave, what then? Well, here I am not concentrating on my report. I shall mention as few names as possible. Was Spalding planted there to look silly and drop a hint, when in London they play it straight? Not easy to switch quickly from the Gallic and Teutonic mind to the Anglo-Saxon.

"She says, that girl Margaret, that the food is not too terrible in London and that the rationing is fair."

"Yes?"

"With us it is not so fair. I promised to bring my wife soap when I return; she has given me a list of things she wants."

"I have two Camemberts I bought in Normandy as we journeyed."

"There is no shortage there, the farmers do not suffer. Look at this country. Nothing is happening to your people, you do not suffer at all." Picot waved his hand towards the pasture and plough they were passing.

"The towns have been bombed."

"My friend, you have been listening to the German radio; your country is untouched; it is we who suffer, the workers."

Let him wait till he sees London, thought Mylo; sometimes, listening to the Picots of this world, I think fuck the workers. Mylo pulled up his coat collar, leaned back and tried to sleep.

THIRTY-ONE

Mylo woke from an uncomfortable doze and recognising the contours of the hills realised that they were passing within a few miles of Slepe. He was furiously tempted to ask the driver to stop so that he could telephone, hear on the line Rose's hesitant, cautious, "Hullo? Who is it?" When he said, "Mylo," her voice would swoop, bubbling up. But, he thought, looking at the driver's back, I shall do it later. The driver may have orders to report anything I do. I must wait until I am free, the job finished, then I can telephone or, better still, arrive quietly as I did before, find her asleep, let her wake in my arms and we shall be back where we left off.

It was getting dark when they reached the outskirts of London. The driver switched on dimmed lights and drove slowly. "Raid's started, sir." He sounded pleased.

"How d'you know?"

"Glow in the sky, sir. Very punctual, the Jerries come up the river same time every evening, can set your watch by 'em."

"What does he say?" asked Picot.

"There is an air raid."

"Can one see it? Is it dangerous?"

"No doubt we shall find out."

Picot grunted, leaning forward in his seat to watch the glow in the east, the occasional flash, the lingering searchlights.

They were flagged down near Chiswick. "Going far?" asked a policeman.

"Neighbourhood of Knightsbridge," admitted the driver.

"There's a landmine in the Cromwell Road, an unexploded bomb in Queen's Gate, the Old Brompton Road's blocked. You will have to re-route via King's Road and Sloane Street."

Mylo translated.

"*Tiens,*" said Picot, "so it's true you do have trouble, what a mercy it is not Paris."

"When you are free from your reception committee I will take you on a tour, show you the mess," said Mylo.

"Good, we can invite the girl Margaret who has incidentally already offered and my little cousin Chantal who works with the French Navy. The girl Margaret knows her and I have messages for her from Maman."

"Not written, I trust."

"Of course they are written . . ."

"Idiot," exclaimed Mylo. "If we had been caught the letter would have led the Gestapo to the mother and then . . ." (I should have searched the bastard, what a fool I am.)

"But we were not caught." Picot was amused.

"Your Colonel Passy will not be pleased to hear this."

"Shall you tell him?" Picot was amused by this too.

"I don't expect to meet him, but in future no written messages. There is no need to take idiotic risks." Mylo was angry.

"They did not search us at Dartmouth."

"That will happen in London."

"The Germans would search us before we left, halfway there, and on arrival," said Picot, hating yet admiring the enemy.

"Why were you so careless? I cannot understand . . ."

"My cousin Chantal wrote to say the English are amateur."

"Wrote? You got a letter?"

"We are not the only ones to cross the Channel, you must know that."

"Is your cousin a Party member?"

"If she was, she would not have been so readily accepted by the Gaullistes. Her father was a naval officer, she has the *entrée*."

It's useful that he has this cousinship to protect him, thought Mylo, he will need it; the Establishment's suspicion of communists is inbred, but so fortunately are family ties.

Separated on arrival from Picot, Mylo spent the following days being interviewed, questioned, requestioned, debriefed by the people who had sent him to France and by others he did not know. He felt resentful of these men who paced their offices or sat relaxed behind desks able to step out from Broadway, walk across St James's Park to lunch in their clubs, return to ask of their girl staff, "Any messages, Diana, Susan, Jenny, Victoria?" (All the girls in all the offices bore the genetic stamp of colonels' or captains' (RN) daughters, safe fodder for Whitehall, the War Office and Broadway.) Not for these men and girls in bed at night the fear of the knock on the door. These are my people, yet must I protect my back, thought Mylo, they cannot know how it is for my friends in France; there are names and addresses they need not have.

"Now we come to your friend Picot," said the man behind the desk. "How would you rate him?"

"High."

"Possibly, possibly. Party members are supposed to be more disciplined than your Free French enthusiast."

"Certainly." Mylo thought of Picot's cousin Chantal and her open letter borne by hand to Maman.

"He has, it seems, a cousin called Chantal in their Navy. Works for Soustelle. Did he mention her?"

So the bastard is at least well informed. "Yes. Says he is looking forward to seeing her."

"I dare say. Well, yes. We would like you, if you agree, to spend an evening with Picot and this cousin of his before we let the Free French have him. He also made friends with a Wren called, let me see, yes, Margaret, when you came ashore at Dartmouth."

"A plant?"

"You could make a foursome. Show Picot London as it is, go out for a meal."

"And?"

"Report to us, unofficially of course, whether Picot is working for others besides us and the French."

"The Party?" Mylo put innocence in his tone.

"That's the sort of thing, yes."

Mylo laughed. "He told me his cousin is the daughter of an officer; she would be the same sort of girl as the girls you have here."

"They are not as silly as your tone suggests." There was a snip of huffiness.

"What exactly do you want to know?" (I hate this man, I hate his kind.)

"Anything that doesn't quite fit, you know the sort of thing." (Non-committal, yet insistent.)

"Is this an order?"

"I should call it a request." (Smiling now, bland.)

Mylo stood up. His questioner rose, too, walked with him to the door. "Wasn't your father a communist at one time?"

Mylo grinned. "My father thought all party politics ludicrous. He was not a joiner."

"Wasn't there something he did in South Africa? I seem to have heard . . ." (The voice trailed.)

"He was asked to leave. He went to one or two Party meetings, he liked the songs."

"Songs?" (Puzzled.)

"They were better than the Whites', the Black and Coloured songs."

"Oh, dear. Here we get into colour." (Pained.)

"Uncomfortable thing, colour."

"Uncomforting too. Well! Have a good time, show him around. Let me know how you get on with the girls and so on." (Hearty now.)

"I am not in the business of betrayal."

"My dear fellow! What an idea." He was pained.

"And expenses?" suggested Mylo.

"What? Oh, expenses. Oh, yes, well now. Victoria is the girl you need." (Expenses are beneath me.) "Victoria, sweetie?" They had reached an outer office. "Yes, sir?" Victoria (a brigadier's daughter, perhaps) showed no pleasure at being addressed as sweetie.

"Fix Mr Cooper up with the proper forms and so on, he needs expenses."

"Very good, sir," snapped Victoria.

"Goodbye, Mr Cooper."

"Goodbye," said Mylo. They shook hands, watched by Victoria.

"This way," said Victoria, "follow me." She led.

"Do you know whether the Hamman Baths are still open?" Mylo asked Victoria's back.

"People do come out of that office feeling they need cleansing," said Victoria over her shoulder. "Unfortunately the Turkish baths are closed, a stick of bombs fell across Jermyn Street a fortnight ago and demolished the baths and everybody in them."

"Ah me!"

"It's all in the mind," said Victoria cheerfully, "nothing an ordinary bath can't cure. When I get that besmirched feeling, I buy myself a cake of expensive soap, that helps."

Mylo laughed. "I'll try that."

"Used I not to see you at the Malones'?" asked Victoria. "Aren't you a friend of George and Richard's?"

"It's a small world. I tutored George."

Does she know Rose, too, Mylo wondered, has she heard her voice lately? He walked back to where he was staying, stopping on the way to buy sandalwood soap. On reaching his lodgings he telephoned Picot to invite him and his cousin Chantal to spend the evening, do some sightseeing first. He was not surprised to hear that the Wren, Margaret, had turned up in London and would join the party. What do the buggers take me for, he thought, as he lay in his bath before keeping the rendezvous. No amount of soaping washed away the feeling of grubbiness engendered by the smooth-talking man who had toyed with him in his office in the building in Broadway.

They met early, while it was still light, having planned to make a lightning tour of bombed London for Picot's benefit. Mylo hired a taxi (Victoria had been generous with her promises to reimburse).

They drove through the city as office workers streamed away, anxious to get home before the air raids started. Picot leaned forward in his seat, staring at the faces of the crowd, trying to read their mood. "They show so little; is it already a habit?" He chatted with his cousin, exchanging family news while Margaret sat silent on his other side. Why must we all spy on one another; it is unreal. Mylo longed for Rose, comparing her favourably with these self-assured girls.

As they drove round the docks Picot fell silent, stayed silent at the spectacle of the ruined Guildhall, smashed Wren churches, blocks of offices where firemen still hosed the smoking ruins of the previous night's raid, their faces grey with fatigue. Through the open window they smelled the stink of fire. Chantal, wrinkling her nose, asked for it to be shut. Mylo watched her sitting back in the taxi, looking unmistakably French in her perfectly cut uniform, her white shirt speckless against her young throat, her face so carefully made up.

Beside her Margaret in her uniform looked scrubbed and British. Mylo sitting on the jump seat wondered which of the girls would be best in bed and laughed inwardly at even asking himself the question. Bed was one thing, he told himself, but Margaret would make the most intelligent report on the evening. I wonder what soap Chantal uses, he mused, or is she spared any sense of guilt?

They dined presently at the Écu de France (spared by the stick of bombs which had demolished the Hamman Baths). The restaurant was Margaret's choice. Chantal sulked; she had wanted to go to the Café de Paris; it was safe, she said, it was underground, no need to fear in the raids which she confessed made her nervous. One could dance, she wanted to dance. "It is the food I am after." Margaret demolished the French girl's protest. When later that year there was a direct hit on the Café de Paris, the bomb falling through its glass roof and slaughtering many people, Mylo remembered Chantal on that first and only meeting.

As it was they dined pretty well. Margaret enjoyed her food. Picot celebrated his reunion with his cousin and his first visit to England. Mylo drank steadily and too much to dull the impression of smashed London, to rid himself of the taste of betrayal and doublecross which he realised now to be endemic in the corridors of his masters. What the hell, he thought, as he grew bibulously cheerful, what the bloody hell. Coming out into the street he burst into song and seizing Chantal in his arms danced with her as he sang, "Hitler has only got one ball/ Goering's are very very small/ Himmler's are somewhat simmler/ but Goebbels has no balls at all." As they whirled along the pavement, Chantal pleading in French for a translation, an air-raid warden called to them good-humouredly and Margaret climbed into a taxi with Picot and drove away, shouting that it would be wise to take cover.

When a bomb fell within earshot Chantal took fright and begged to be taken home. In the taxi Mylo put his arm around her and kissed her; arriving at her flat she invited him in until the raid was over; she feared to be alone, her flatmate was away. Mylo followed her indoors. He had by this time reached the stage of intoxication when it was habitual for him to bore whoever he might be with with a description of Rose's charms and his love for her, and then since Chantal seemed an accommodating girl he would reward her for her charitable listening by making love to her; it would take her mind off the air raid.

When he woke, Chantal was already up and dressed in her uniform and offering restorative coffee. "*Vous etiez soûl mais gentil.*"

"Yes, thanks," he took the cup. "Nothing a ritual bath won't cure." He sat up. "Ow! My head! Ouch! Oh, Christ!"

"*Au revoir, je vous quitte.*" Chantal tripped away; he heard her heels click and fade on the pavement outside, looked at his watch, reached for the telephone, asked when a voice answered for Victoria.

"Tell your boss I did what he asked. There is nothing to report. The answer is nix."

"Write in . . ."

"You joking? It was *unofficial.*"

"Margaret said you had a good time."

"She reported in?"

"Two hours ago. Never mind, I'll tell him."

"Can one still get American pick-me-ups at that chemist in Piccadilly?"

"Like that, is it?" A genial girl, Victoria.

"Don't tell me they've been bombed, too?"

"Heppells? No, they're still there. Did you sleep with the Free French Navy cousin?"

"What does *she* say?"

"She hasn't reported; we aren't on those terms with the French."

In the unease of his hangover, Mylo was not sure whether Victoria was joking. Collecting his clothes, searching unsuccessfully for a razor (doesn't the girl even shave her legs?), he set off for his lodgings to soak in a hot bath, soap himself with sandalwood soap, forget about Chantal and Broadway, the trickiness of intelligence, and dream of Rose, soon to be in his arms, back where they left off, a joyful reunion.

THIRTY-TWO

Standing in Heppells, watching the white-coated chemist mix the concoction known as an American pick-me-up, Mylo was filled with self-disgust. What had possessed him to try and sleep with Picot's cousin? She had yawned during his description of Rose, shown herself an unenthusiastic bedfellow, clearly only requiring his company to still her fears of the air raid.

Mylo took the nauseous brew handed to him in a tiny medicinal glass and gulped it down. As the liquid hit his stomach his system registered a revivifying shock which brought tears to his eyes; he remembered with humiliation that he had been too drunk to come, had fallen asleep, probably snored. He fumbled for money, paid the man behind the counter and stepped out into the street.

The sun shone as he walked along Piccadilly; he belched violently, startling a passer-by. The pick-me-up was working. His spirits began to rise, he was on leave, free to do whatever he liked, what he liked was Rose, but first to settle his mind as well as his stomach he went back to the office in Broadway to deal with his debriefer of the previous days.

"I want to see your bastard of a boss."

"He's busy. Will you wait?" said Victoria. "His name is Major Pye, Peregrine Pye."

"I know his name, find out if he'll see me, there's a dear."

Victoria went away, came back. "In about ten minutes," she said non-committally.

"For a genetically trustworthy girl, you are rather nice."

"A what girl?"

"Uncorruptible, bred full of patriotism, a colonel's daughter."

"Brigadier, actually."

"Genetically safe."

"Oh." Victoria latched on. "I see." She smiled. "It does help with the Official Secrets Act. Did you go to Heppells?"

"Yes."

"Feeling better?"

"Yes, thank you."

"So glad." Victoria picked up a folder, opened it and began to read.

"I got stinking drunk in the restaurant last night, then I sang and danced in the street."

"Do you get drunk often?"

"It would be suicidal in my present occupation."

"I imagine it would," said Victoria.

"That's to say, I feel a bit foolish this morning."

"Reaction to the strain in France? I'd say that's what it was – if I was asked." Victoria had beautiful hazel eyes in an otherwise unremarkable face.

"What a sensible girl you are," said Mylo. "Do you ever get drunk? How do you know about pick-me-ups?"

"I have a brother and a fiancé in submarines. People have to let off steam." Victoria stood up. "Major Pye will see you now."

"Hullo, Cooper. What's the trouble? What can I do for you this morning?" This morning Major Pye was genial. Mylo wondered why he had feared him during the previous days; he was ordinary, even nondescript in his blue pinstripe suit, gunner tie, horn-rimmed spectacles.

"Can it be quite clear that I do not spy on the people I bring across? That I am *not* interested in politics? That I am simply and plainly a guide?"

"My dear fellow . . ."

"Can it . . . ?"

"Rather an odd request, but I suppose so, yes, can't see why not if you insist."

"Thanks. That's all I wanted to know, just to have it clear."

"Right, right. I'll circulate the news. You extract the people or persons, and have no interest after delivery. Can do. Happy now?"

"Thanks."

"You are on leave now and will report in during the week?"

"Yes, I'll telephone."

"Fine, fine. Goodbye."

They shook hands. Mylo left Major Pye's office, went down in the lift and out into the sunshine.

Major Pye looked down into the street from his office window and watched Mylo cross the street and dodge into St James's Park Underground. "I wish we had more like him," he said to Victoria. "Bit of an oddball."

"Half French," said Victoria. "I've been reading his file. His mother was Jewish."

"Both parents dead. Do we know where he spends his leave? Did he tell you? Did you ask?"

"No, sir."

"You think it's not our business, do you? I wish you wouldn't call me sir, Victoria."

"It distances me from the dirty tricks."

"We can't all abjure politics like your friend."

"Just an acquaintance, sir."

"A good acquaintance?" pried Major Pye.

"You split hairs, sir." (If Peregrine didn't pry so hard I would tell him Mylo Cooper tutored the Malone boys.)

"I thought I detected a *soupçon* of protectiveness."

"I would imagine he's well able to mind his own back, Peregrine," Victoria relented.

Jolting along in the Underground, Mylo gleefully counted the days of his leave, seven whole days with Rose, seven nights. Half a day wasted at Heppells and fixing Major Pye was no waste but a precautionary measure, and every minute now was bringing him closer to Rose. He would not, if he caught a train now, arrive to find her asleep as he had planned; no matter, arriving in daylight there would be the garden where they had strolled in scented twilight, the river, the woods, the fields; soon he would hear her voice, touch her, smell her, feel her.

At Paddington he jostled through the crowds to the ticket office, inquired the time of the trains, kicked his heels for an impatient hour before at last the crowded train pulled away from the platform and, gathering speed, carried him away from bombed London through undamaged suburbs into the Thames Valley. From the corridor he watched the ploughed fields, the copper and sulphur woods of autumn. The train stopped at every station, passengers crowded on and off, soldiers *en route* to Salisbury Plain, sailors to Plymouth, airmen to widely scattered airfields. Mylo watched, comparing them to the population of France with its expression of the watched and the watching; none of these Englishmen gave the impression of watching anything further than their noses, and why should they, Mylo thought in admiration, they had no need to. As the flat valley country changed to rolling chalk downland and again to brown plough and steeper hills Mylo's spirits soared. He arrived at his destination, left the train and boarded a country bus which carried him along familiar lanes to Rose's village; here, shouldering his pack, he set off to cover the last mile on foot.

As he walked he pictured Rose unaware of his imminent arrival, yet waiting for him. Comrade (until this moment he had forgotten Comrade) would recognise his step, bark with joy and alert Rose, who would hurl herself into his arms and then the hugs and kisses, cries of joy. Mylo walked faster, hurrying through the late autumn afternoon; it was clouding up, going to rain, he had left his mackintosh in London. Approaching the house from the back he felt uneasy, he was watched from a window by a woman with iron grey hair and suspicious eyes; he had forgotten the Ministry of Information. He waved a casual hand; the woman stood up to stare, a man came to stand beside her; Mylo could see their lips move. He waved again. They followed him with their eyes. Slightly disconcerted, wishing he had not taken a short cut but come the longer way up the drive, Mylo skirted the kitchen garden and arrived at the side door usually used by Rose. He opened the door, stepped into the stone-flagged passage, listened. Hearing voices in the kitchen he tiptoed forward, stopped in shadow to peer in unseen. There was a loud burst of feminine laughter.

With her back to him Rose sat at the kitchen table, at her feet Comrade in a basket suckling two puppies, across the table Emily Thornby laughing loudly at something Rose had just said, her head thrown back, eyes half closed, in her hand a cigarette. As she laughed she ejected little jets of smoke from her nose.

Rose was laughing, too. She did not see Mylo, spring into his arms with cries of joy, nor did Comrade like Argus recognise him with glad barks.

Since Emily was about the last person Mylo had hoped to see, he sidled quickly past the kitchen door across the hall to the library where he sat down on a sofa in a fury of disappointed rage.

It was forty minutes before a car drove up to the front door and Nicholas came running up the steps calling, "Emily, I'm here, sorry I'm late. Rose, are you there? I've come to collect Em. Rose?"

"Here, we're in the kitchen; d'you want some tea?"

Mylo ground his teeth.

"No, no." Mylo hated Nicholas's blithe voice. "We must go. Come on, Emily, buck up." Another ten minutes and a lot of laughter before Rose waved Nicholas and Emily goodbye and turning saw in the gloom of the hall a man. She sucked in her breath. "Oh!"

"Rose?"

Rose stepped backwards. "Who?"

"It's me, you idiot, Mylo."

"How long have you been here?"

"Nearly an hour, I didn't think you'd like the Thornbys to see us together."

"Mylo," Rose whispered. "Mylo."

"You don't seem very pleased to see me," said Mylo disagreeably. "Perhaps you are not. Perhaps I'd better go. I seem to be labouring under a delusion." His disappointment was whipping him into a childish rage. "I thought, I . . . I thought we . . . What the bloody hell was all that laughter about?"

They were standing yards apart, both white-faced, now staring, shocked.

"We were laughing about the father of Emily's baby, a sort of guessing game, she's pregnant, she pretends not to know the father."

". . ."

"And so am I."

"You? Pregnant? Who is the father?"

"Ned, of course."

". . ."

Rose drew herself up defensively, then whispered, "Oh, darling."

He did not hear her, just stood looking at her. She, growing aware of his fatigue, harsh disappointment, jealousy, anger, became afraid, dared not speak.

Comrade, disengaging herself from her puppies, came pattering into the hall to join Rose. She pricked her ears at the sight of Mylo's back, went up to him, sniffed his ankles, threw back her head with a warbling yowl, stood on hind legs to paw him, thrashed her tail, ululated with joy, making little upward ineffectual jumps.

Still Mylo stared at Rose. "I wish it was mine, oh, God, I wish it was mine." His voice bitter.

"I was so angry with you. So lost when you sneaked off without saying anything, so lonely, I thought . . ."

"And Comrade?" He stroked the dog's head.

"She must have been in pup when you brought her here."

"So we don't know the father of the puppies, and Emily doesn't know the parent of her . . ."

"Nicholas says he knows, teases her."

"Nicholas would."

Rose put out a hand. "Mylo, why are we standing here like strangers? Mylo, please."

"Rose."

They were laughing, crying, kissing, hugging while Comrade danced around them barking. "I thought," said Mylo between kisses, "I thought I'd come in the night and begin where we left off, climb into your bed. Oh," a kiss, "my love," a kiss, "it would have been pretty funny if I'd climbed in with Ned."

"He's in Egypt."

"Then I can . . ."

"Of course! Come in, let's shut the door, it's icy. This is the coldest house . . ."

"I didn't want the Thornbys to see me."

"I should hope not. You, we, are secret."

"And the baby?" He held her away to look at her. "Are you well? Shouldn't you be careful? Are you all right?"

"It's not an illness."

"I wish it was mine. I wish . . ."

"I'll have yours next." She was laughing, half serious. "Come and get warm, your hands are freezing."

"Darling, I was so excited at getting back, I got drunk last night, I . . ."

"Are you on leave?"

"Yes. A week."

"A precious week."

"I shall have to ring up, but yes, I have a week."

"And then?"

"I shall go back."

"To France?"

"Yes."

"Oh, Christ. Must you?"

"There are people there I have to help. It's what I can do. It isn't killing people, it's not political."

"Curse this bloody war," Rose cried with passion.

"Oh, Rose, I do so want you." He held her.

"Mylo, your tummy rumbled."

"Sorry, I'm bloody hungry. I haven't eaten today, I had this hangover."

"Come along, then. I'll get you a meal, then we'll go to bed."

"Should you? Won't it hurt the little . . . ?"

"No, it won't. A baby isn't measles, it's not dangerous, it's normal, lots of women do it."

"Are you certain?"

"Yes, yes, yes. Come and eat."

"Then I can pretend I arrived as I dreamed I would and we'll carry on where we left off?"

"Is that what you thought?"

"Yes, stupid of me. What was all that laughter I overheard in the kitchen? You and Emily . . ." (Suspicion creeping back.)

"Are you jealous?"

"I suppose so. Yes, I am. I felt so left out."

"There is no need," said Rose, leading him to the kitchen, making him sit down while she found him food. "Neither of us should ever be jealous."

There is no need to tell her about that bitch Chantal last night, she might not understand. I was, after all, drunk, thought Mylo. "Of course, you are right. Oh darling, this looks delicious," he said as Rose gave him a plate of food.

There is no need, thought Rose, watching him eat, to tell him what we were laughing at. If I told him we were laughing at my poor mother's horror of sex and particularly of pregnancy, her revulsion at the recollection of me in her womb heaving (Rose suppressed a giggle), it might put him off me in bed. "Let's get to bed as quickly as we can," she said.

THIRTY-THREE

They would remember four perfect days, four nights spent loving by the light of the fire. Falling asleep. Waking to make love again, then to lie close, each telling tirelessly, gently, of the immensity of love felt now, experienced now, to be cherished for ever.

Mylo would slip out of bed, put coal on the fire, balance another log on the coals, pat Comrade's head as she lay in her basket, puppies' noses pressed against her belly, stroke the cats purring in a ball on the hearthrug, return to hold Rose, lie listening to the breeze whispering round the house, to a restive cow lowing in the meadow, the shriek of a far-off train, the distant drone of a bomber. (The war stayed far away, did not impinge.) Time, though not standing still, passed with enchanted slowness. They loved, they slept, they woke to breakfast in the kitchen under Mrs Farthing's unsurprised eye.

"What have you told her?"

"She seems incurious so I say nothing, explanations can bog one down." Indeed Farthing, Mrs Farthing, the evacuee waifs treated Mylo as a natural phenomenon, no odder than Ned's visiting friends or the Malone family when they came to care for Rose in her illness, treating him with reserve, a reserve more stringently applied to the Ministry of Information people, should they come round from their offices at the back of the house confessing that they had forgotten to order milk for their mid-morning cuppas, or, worse, had run out of sugar. (We will pay you back tomorrow when we get our ration.) They were given sugar, made to feel they had stepped out of line, should have organised their sugar from their billets in the village.

On the fifth morning Mylo woke to hear rain smacking at the windows, rattling the leaves of the magnolia, wind whingeing and whining round the house, Comrade whimpering restless at the door asking to go out, and the knowledge that today he must telephone London.

Wrapped in a blanket, he went barefoot down to let the dog out, waited holding the door while she hurried out to squat, ears back, eyes slitted disgustedly at the rain, then finished, to scamper back into the dry, shake and patter fast up the stairs to her puppies. Creeping back into bed Mylo woke Rose.

"What is it? Your feet are cold. Where have you been? Why didn't you borrow Ned's dressing-gown?"

"I don't want his fucking dressing-gown. I have to telephone London, report in."

"Oh, God! So soon. Oh, must you?"

"Yes. Yes, I must."

"It's raining. Oh, Mylo, does this mean . . . ?"

"No, no, three more days. Keep calm . . ."

"How can I possibly?"

"You must, my darling, we must."

But the spell, if spell it was, was broken.

"If I drive you to wherever you have to go we can be together a little longer," catching, snatching at time as it meanly accelerated. "There's a hoard of petrol made by Ned for use in dire emergency. This is dire all right, of course it's dire. I can fill the tank, drive you to wherever, be with you a little longer."

"It won't work. I am not allowed to tell anyone where I go."

"Not even me?"

"Not even you."

"Damn, damn, damn. Go and telephone, then," she cried in fury.

Mylo telephoned, shutting the library door so that she could not overhear.

Returning, he said, "We are all right until Saturday, three more days."

"Two and a half."

"I shall go up by train."

"Can't I drive you to London?"

"No."

"Why not?"

"Don't be silly, you know perfectly well that what I do, where I go, is secret. I have told you."

"You haven't."

"I am telling you now, then."

"It's ridiculous."

"It's the war. Come on," he said, "cheer up. Don't let's spoil our last days."

"Could have been more happily put," Rose said.

Mylo laughed, but the days were spoiled. Each tried to hide from the other that they counted time passing. Rose found herself comparing Mylo unfavourably with Ned. Ned had made no mystery about his doings, had been quite open about his posting to North Africa, why else would he need to stop in London *en route* for the north to buy lightweight uniforms? He wrote regularly, true, boringly, but he wrote. Mylo made it plain that there would be no communication once he was gone, no letter, no telephone, silence.

"How shall I bear it?" Rose wailed in petulant grief. Almost she enjoyed this grief, voiced it without let.

"You bore it before." Here Mylo let the irritation up to now suppressed by the days of joy and love surface. Rose had changed since their last parting, grown assured. She was no longer the shy uncertain girl he had met at the winter tennis, she was mistress of Slepe, people responded to her, did what she asked, she took part in the farm, the gardens, village life. He had listened to her talk on the telephone, give orders disguised as suggestions, heard her gossip with Edith Malone, inquire after George and Richard, call Edith by her Christian name. He had seen her with the Farthings and the Hadleys; she had the strength and confidence given her by Slepe, she was happy in her environment, she had been happy without him.

When he arrived secretly to surprise her, she had been happy. She would laugh and be happy when he was gone. "Don't spoil our three days," he said harshly.

"I won't, I won't," she cried passionately. "How could I? They are ours, let's treasure them."

But that night when they made love, she said, "Don't do that, it hurts when you do that."

He stopped kissing her breast, saying, "What hurts? This?" and nibbled.

"It is because I am pregnant, my breasts are quite sore."

He flung away from her, turning his back. And she not knowing what to say or do said, sniffing, "I wish the baby was yours."

"But it's not mine, it's bloody Ned's. Since you wouldn't leave Ned and come to me, you have his baby, not mine."

"You've made it pretty clear I can't be with you. Don't be illogical," she shouted in unhappy exasperation.

"I am not illogical, I am half French."

"Besides," Rose cried, desperate now, "I promised Ned. I promised not to leave him. I can't break my promise, I'm funny that way."

"You should have promised me, then there would not be this fuss."

"You never asked me, you never asked for my promise."

"There was no need. I assumed we loved each other. Ned only extracted your promise because he was unsure of you, he obviously felt he must pin you down." Mylo was shouting now.

"Why are we quarrelling?" she remembered asking.

"Because we love each other." Mylo pressed his face between her breasts, listening to her heart.

"We have got ourselves trapped, haven't we?" She held his head in her hands, kissing his dark hair. "Perhaps we shall live to get out of the trap. I cannot wish Ned dead, though."

"Ah, never."

"Perhaps you will stop loving me, it's possible, people do fall out of love, wake to wonder what it was all about."

"What about you?"

"I shall not change." (But she has changed.)

"And nor shall I."

"We are stuck, then," she said with satisfaction.

"Yes," he said. "What about a little fuck?"

"What, now?" She pretended surprise. "Oh, Mylo."

Later she said, as the fire flared up and outlined his profile, "When I am alone and miserably missing you, I watch your picture and remember your voice and the feel of you. I get terribly randy."

"Thinking of me?"

"Of course, who else?"

"Ned. It would be reasonable for you to think of Ned."

"He doesn't make me randy."

"Some other lover you haven't told me about?"

"There is nobody but you."

" . . . m-m-m."

"Have you lain between other girls' thighs?"

"Silly girl."

"Did I tell you about Ned's present just before he went overseas?"

"His sperm? Yes."

"Not that."

"What then?"

"He chose and had me sent six pairs of camiknickers from the White House."

"What's the White House?"

"A grand shop in Bond Street."

"So?"

"Mylo! Don't be dense. Camiknickers like the shift the girl wears in the picture. Do you think he noticed your picture is like me? Of course, I haven't worn them."

"Why not?"

"Because the picture is you, yours."

"Let me see those things."

"Now?"

"Yes."

Rose hopped out of bed, opened a drawer and brought the satin garments to Mylo in the bed. (Would he leap jealously out and cast them on the fire? The smell would be awful.)

Mylo felt the silk, slid it through his fingers.

"Lovely. Put one on, let me see you in it."

She stepped into the garment.

"Exactly like." Mylo smiled at his love by the light of the fire. "I didn't know your husband had brains," he said.

"Of course he has brains."

"And imagination."

"I'm not so sure of that. Shall I wear them, then?"

"Yes, why not. Come into bed, keep it on. I want to compare the texture with the real thing."

So, curiously, from his distance, Ned healed the rift between his wife and her lover, eased their last days, made the parting less agonising.

"How long will you be gone?"

"Don't ask, I don't know."

"All right, I'll be good."

"Take care of yourself and Ned's baby."

I shall have yours next, she thought. "If you send for me, I will come at once," she said. "You can promise me that much."

"I shall come back," he said with more confidence than he felt. "I won't need to send for you."

"Don't ever again creep away without telling me, that's all."

"Don't nag."

"I'm not . . ."

"Even if it spoils it for us, knowing the parting has to come?" he asked.

"Yes. This I can bear."

"All right, all right, all right." He rocked her in his arms. "If I find a decent corkscrew in London, I will send it to you for Ned."

"What a strange idea, has this some esoteric Freudian connotation?"

"It is just that he has no decent corkscrew. If I send him one, it will even out the camiknickers."

"I love your jokes," she said. She found the impending parting so painful she wished it was over so that she could apply herself to grieving, stop pretending to be cheerful.

THIRTY-FOUR

When Mylo went away she had made herself busy, Rose remembered, as she stood on the hill letting her eye follow a flight of rooks as they wheeled and cawed down the valley. That was the trick, keep busy, keep occupied. Rose Peel working at the farm and garden, answering Ned's letters, caring for his friends on leave, learning to cook, clean, take an interest in the war, bear his child. That had become the norm. It used up time, energy and thought that might have been spent on Mylo, protected her from missing him physically, mentally, emotionally for long periods while she concentrated on her work, her child. It had not been possible, she thought, drawing her coat about her, turning away from the chill wind, to pine away. Just as well since the gaps between seeing him, being with him, were so varied, so long; and now she thought bleakly I have, in age, to think. It's hard to remember when I saw him last.

I used, she thought, letting her eye follow the distant birds, to believe we would always be in love, but now I don't know, I really don't.

Watching the rooks, blinking as the wind made her eyes water, she was reminded of her row with the Ministry of Agriculture, who had in spite of Emily's assurance arrived in a car armed with guns to shoot the Slepe rooks. She had hurried out, heavy with unborn Christopher, shouted at the men, ordered them away, made a considerable scene. Enjoyed it. Enjoyed embarrassing those men in a strident, authoritative voice, planting herself under the rookery, bulging with Christopher, born a fortnight later, ordering the men to "get off my property", Ned's in fact, Christopher's now.

She had written in triumph to Ned, desk-bound by then in Cairo. He had replied, "I can't see what the fuss is about; rooks do a lot of damage, you shouldn't interfere with the Min. of Ag.'s work." (She tore the letter up.) Nicholas and Emily had boasted around the neighbourhood of Rose's prowess. So unlike her mother, they said. "Rose behaved like an old county warhorse, you'd never guess now she is mistress of Slepe that she is not true *hochgeboren*." (Nicholas in the war liked to annoy by airing a meagre knowledge of German, reverting to the odd French expression on VE Day.) "Our Rose's vowels are perfect, unlike her ma's which betray her lesser origins." It was at this time, Emily being also pregnant, that the Thornbys cultivating Rose took to visiting her even without an ulterior motive. Emily's infant of unknown parenthood borrowed respectability from its mother's proximity to Rose, ponderously great with the child who would be heir to Slepe.

When Laura, a neat little baby, was born a week before Christopher it was natural that the mothers should be assumed to be friends as previously the same thing had been assumed of their mothers, although in actuality the only catty remarks ever uttered by Mrs Thornby when she was the rector's wife had been directed at Mrs Freeling; while Mrs Freeling, grown bold in widowhood, often lamented the tedium of hours passed in the company of Mrs Thornby. Lucky, thought Rose, watching the rooks disappear, that nothing came of Christopher and Laura's teenage scamper when they had thought for a day that they were in love and boasted of consummating their passion. Too soon the story had altered, their mood soured, Laura found Christopher boring, Christopher said Laura smelt!

Christopher takes after his father, thought Rose, yet he was such a darling little boy. She turned her back on the view and walked on. He had been a good and lovely baby; she had enjoyed his babyhood, enjoyed watching him grow into a delightful little boy. Had Ned been a charming infant, an adorable child? There had been no one to tell her, just a few photographs discovered by Aunt Flora at the back of a drawer when she was moving house, of Ned simpering beside his mother, of Ned looking sulky in baggy shorts aged about ten off to his prep school.

And Laura? Laura, looking exactly like Emily, had disappointed the curious who had laid bets, guessed at her paternity, run a sweepstake, naming all the men Emily was known to go about with, even including George Malone who at the time of her conception was in Moscow. Laura showed no likeness to anyone; her appearance gave no hint, nobody won the sweepstake. Christopher resembled Ned, there was no hint of Rose in his appearance; he had, as it were, rented her womb, taken nothing of his mother. I am quite prepared to accept that he is boring in bed, thought Rose dispassionately, as was Ned. If he slept with Laura so did Ned sleep with Emily, why he bothered to pretend he didn't defeats me. There are still people who think Laura may be Ned's child; somehow I have never thought so. Ned was quite fond of Nicholas. He was devoted to and proud of Christopher when he was small, maddened by him when he grew up.

Oh, the parental grumbles, thought Rose as she walked. She could hear in her mind Ned's voice droning and snapping down the years. "Can't you teach your son to shut doors? He messes my newspaper before I have touched it." (Ned, who never opened his *Times* until after lunch.) "Can't you teach your son not to smoke? He stinks the house out with those filthy Gitanes." (Like many who have kicked the habit, Ned was hard on smokers.) "He's left an enormous turd in my lavatory, and now he wants to borrow my car." What a fuss he had made when Christopher married Helen. "Who *is* this girl, do we know?" What would he say if he knew she had taken charge of his ashes? Turned in the urn?

At times like that her promise to Ned sat like a lump of indigestible dough; she remembered Mylo crying, "You can't bugger up our lives for a promise," and regretted her insistence that she could, she must.

Yet Ned was a kind man. Kind to animals, kind to neighbours, considerate to his cars, he paid his bills, did not fall about drunk, made a success of his wartime career, loved an Opel motor car he acquired in occupied Germany (or was it the driver he loved?), was successful in the City when he returned from the war, was a consistently good landlord. He blamed me for his discontent, thought Rose; he needed choice, everything in pairs: two bankers, two tailors, two women (there was always a second woman, not necessarily Emily; several had appeared at the funeral with their husbands), two houses, two cars. He never said, but made it clear by hints, attitudes and chance remarks that life would have been "all right" if he had had two children.

I had managed to forget Ned for several days, thought Rose, was quite successful handing responsibility to Christopher and Helen. I must not start thinking "if only" and "things would have been better or different".

"All that crap!" she shouted out loud, startling a wheatear from a gorse bush. Ned was not all that kind; he was on occasion accusatory and cruel. His permanent absence will not be so very different from his absence at the war, his frequent absences on business trips.

Just nicer.

THIRTY-FIVE

The telephone woke Rose. "Is that Mrs Cooper?" asked a distant voice.

"Who?" Her head came up from the pillow with a jerk. "Rose Cooper? Am I speaking to Rose Cooper?" The voice was faint, furtive, impossible to tell how far away.

"I am Rose . . ." Only minutes ago she had given Christopher his last feed, she struggled awake from heavy sleep. "What did you say, who?" Her heart was pounding.

"Your husband," droned the voice, "Mrs Cooper . . ."

"My *what?*" She was waking fast.

" . . . asked me to phone you. It strictly isn't . . ."

"Who – are – you?"

"Well, now, that's asking, let's say Truro General Hospital." The man began to sound irritated, nervous. "I'm not allowed, not supposed . . ."

"My husband?"

"Look. He asked me to ring you; brought in last night . . ." the line went dead, then the voice, reedy now, continued ". . . wounded." It said, "Nothing serious."

"Wounded? Badly. *Not* serious?"

A high nervous laugh. "You should have seen the others, they were dead."

"Who are you?" shouted Rose, as if it mattered, but the line was dead now, blank. Half an hour later she got through to Truro General Hospital.

No, no information about new patients. Sorry. No, there was no doctor she could speak to, sorry, no matron, no sister, sorry. No, no, and again no. Quite polite but suspiciously guarded.

Why should they be guarded?

What were they hiding?

Mylo. Wounded. Mutilated. Dying?

"Only one way to find out," said Rose to the sleeping baby. "We must go," she said to Comrade watching from her basket. "I can take you," she said to the dog, "but not your puppies or the cats."

She ran to the bathroom and bathed her face, she was trembling and drenched with sweat. Her hands shook as she dressed. "Calm, calm, keep calm," she muttered, pulling on her clothes. "Must look respectable," she exclaimed, tearing off the slacks she had put on, "you never know who . . ." She took a coat and skirt from the cupboard, a shirt and jersey, combed her hair back, pulled on her last pair of silk stockings and best shoes, viewed herself looking respectable in the cheval glass. "Right." She had stubbed her toe pushing right foot into left shoe, the pain made her face look drawn.

She gathered the baby's things, stuffing spare nappies, clothes and shawls around him. Anchoring him in the deep basket, she carried him downstairs. "Stay with him," she said to the dog, "stay".

She ran round the house, her respectable heels clattering on the stone terrace. Reaching the Farthings' cottage she knocked, shook the door handle, shook some more, "Oh, wake up, please . . ."

"Who is it?" Farthing, gruff.

"Me, it's me," she shouted.

"Coming."

Then Farthing was opening the door, as he buttoned his flies, the toes of his bare feet were widely separate, agile. "What's up?"

"I have to go – now – at once to – to a – a friend, can you – hospital?"

"Want the car? Taking the baby?"

"Yes, yes, and Comrade – I . . ."

"Want it filled up, that it?" He had put a sweater on, inside out and back to front.

"Oh, yes, how did you . . . ?"

"Half a mo, just get me shoes on . . ."

"But, do you know . . . ?" Her voice was a suppressed scream.

"Where the petrol's hidden? Course I do." Farthing laughed. "Watched 'the master' hide it, didn't we?" (Oh poor Ned, parenthesised master, mocked, and such a kind man.)

"Want some help, love?" Mrs Farthing descending the stairs in an extraordinary sexy nightdress, pink feathered mules on her feet.

"It's the cats and the puppies and . . ."

"I'll mind them, don't worry." Mrs Farthing pulled a sensible overcoat over the nightdress. "Come in while Farthing . . ."

"No, I must . . ."

"Where shall I say you've gone?"

"Oh, Mrs Farthing . . ." Rose watched Farthing disappear around the house with a torch. If only he would run.

"Got to have something to tell people when they ring up, and the Hadleys."

"Oh . . ." She found it hard to think. There was Mylo dying, what the hell did anything else matter? "Oh, hurry . . ."

"I'll come and see you've got what's needed for the baby; Farthing won't be long."

"I have everything. I must hurry, I . . ."

"I'll just check." The woman was remorseless.

"Oh." Rose clenched her fists.

"And if you are going far, you'd better take sandwiches and a Thermos. You never . . ."

"Never?" Rose snatched at the word.

" . . . never know when you'll want a meal or something hot." Mrs Farthing was walking Rose back to the house, her arm around her shoulders. "He might like something hot."

"He?"

"Don't be a muggins," they had reached the kitchen, "sit down while I get you a hot drink to set you on your way."

"I don't want a . . ."

"Won't take a minute. Farthing hasn't got the tank filled yet." Mrs Farthing poured milk into a pan. "Tea or coffee? I'll give you chocolate for the Thermoses."

"Anything." Rose's teeth chattered.

"Listen to your teeth chattering. Got enough money?"

"I hope so."

"Hope." Mrs Farthing handed Rose a steaming mug. "Drink that up, all of it." She reached up to a jar above the stove, "Now, here's fifty pounds, you won't need it all, but you never know."

"I can't take your . . ." she was appalled, "savings."

"Yes, you can, Farthing and I will be happier if you will. Finished your drink? Good girl. Now take a few really deep breaths. That's right. Better now?" Rose nodded, she no longer felt clammy.

"Filled her up?" asked Mrs Farthing of her mate entering the kitchen.

"Petrol tank's full. I checked the oil, water and tyres, and put two jerry cans in the boot. You should be all right," Farthing grinned at Rose, "for a dire emergency."

I wonder how much they listen to us, how much they guess. "Thank you," said Rose, "oh, thank you."

"We'll tell the Hadleys and anyone who asks that you were called away to help Mrs Malone with one of her friends, she couldn't manage on her own with all her evacuees, et cetera. That do?"

"Mrs Farthing! The brilliance of your mind." Both Farthings smiled. They are my friends, she thought, they do not judge.

"Take care of yourself and the baby, now."

Rose put her arms around the older woman and hugged her. "Now, now," said Mrs Farthing.

Farthing said, "Shall I stow the baby in the car?"

While Farthing arranged the baby basket on the back seat, Mrs Farthing said, "I don't really like being called Mrs Farthing by people I am fond of. My name's Edwina. It's not as if Farthing and I were married." (Rose swallowed the second statement to digest later, feeling she would cry if she thanked Mrs Farthing for liking her.)

What extraordinary people, she thought, driving away. They seem to enjoy – she said she liked – they must approve of me, nobody's ever done that. She drove west along the roads of England passing the occasional Army truck and early farm cart.

When Christopher whimpered she stopped at the side of the road and fed him, changed his nappy and drank from the Thermos. Fancy them not being married, she thought. I must remember to call her Edwina. What a privilege. She's even remembered Comrade's dinner. She put the dog's dinner on the grass and watched her eat while she held Christopher against her shoulder, waiting for him to burp.

She made no plan. She prayed that when she arrived at the hospital she would know what to do. She prayed that when she arrived she would not find Mylo dead. What had the man said, had she heard aright?

She reached Truro in the early afternoon, found the hospital, parked the car and stared at the lugubrious building.

Mrs Malone would know what to do, how to behave in these circumstances, not that she was the sort of woman to have a lover, but supposing it were George or Richard who was in there?

My mother wouldn't know, she never brought me up to deal with such a crisis. She was the cringing type, socially inferior, afraid of putting a foot wrong with authority; she's changed now, of course, but she never taught me the necessary oomph. What, thought Rose, would Mrs Malone do?

Walk straight in as though it belonged to her, right?

Leaving Comrade in the car, Rose checked the straightness of the seams of her stockings, squared her shoulders and marched in, carrying Christopher.

"I have come to see my husband," she said to a man at the desk.

"What name?" He did not look up, she could see no face, only a smooth, bald, pink skull.

"Cooper."

"Cooper. Cooper." He ran a slow finger down a list. "He'd be in ward seven by now unless he was one of the RAF with the flu, oh, they are in seven. You try ward seven."

She climbed stairs, walked corridors, passed wards full of women, another full of children. Wards one, two, three and on to six, where was seven? She did not want to ask the nurses squeaking along on their rubber-soled shoes, starched cotton aprons, clacking voices carrying clear enough to echo in the long institutional corridor. Ah, ward seven.

She stared through a glass-panelled door into a long ward full of active young men in pyjamas and dressing-gowns. Laughing, talking, wandering about, hugely restless, none of them looked ill or wounded. The noise was worse than the parrot house at the zoo. About to turn away, nerve herself to ask, she spied a still lump in a bed in the far corner. She pushed open the door and walked in.

As she walked between the double row of beds, the volume of noise decreased, the tempo of conversation changed. There were one or two whistles, quick exchanges between the men as they totted her up, following her with their eyes. She felt the blood rise traitorously to her neck and face. She held the baby as a shield, stiffened her back. She was afraid of the men who turned and stared, some of them stepping forward like curious cattle in a field. None of them looked ill or wounded.

Just as she felt her nerve might crack and her impersonation of Edith Malone desert her, she recognised Mylo.

Reaching the bed, she stood staring down at him.

"Sister's off duty." One of the men had followed her; he was bolder than the others, smoking a cigarette. He stared openly at her breasts, large with milk, straining at her blouse.

"Thanks," said Rose. "Are you allowed to smoke in here?" she asked coldly in the spirit of Mrs Malone. "Fetch me a chair."

A chair was brought; she sat. The walking wounded retreated to resume a slightly muted brouhaha at the far end of the ward.

It was eight months since she had seen Mylo. They must have been rough months. He lay on his back, deep green smudges under his eyes, his cheeks thin, the colour of cheese. She could trace the curve of his jaw under the stubble of his beard, see the presage of lines running from nose to mouth. His brows were knit in pain, he had a large bruise on his temple, his lips moved as he muttered something. Rose bent close to listen.

"I will shoot the . . ." He was reaching a hand up under his pillow, gripping a hidden object.

"Mylo," said Rose very quietly, "it's me."

Mylo's eyes opened with a snap. "Rose?"

"Yes."

"So you got here?"

"Yes."

"I was just going to shoot them, the . . ."

"Why?"

"The noise, the fucking noise. I have a revolver."

"I'll ask them to be quiet."

"They don't know what quiet means. They are all quite well, they only had flu. Young RAF servicemen bursting with health and high spirits." Mylo's voice was venomous. "How long have you been here?" Why was he not washed and in pyjamas like the others? Had he persuaded authority that he had a revolver? This was no time for games and the spirit of Edith Malone. "We were brought ashore the night before last, got our lines crossed with another party. The other fellows were killed in the cross fire. Get me out of here, darling." He shut his eyes.

"How badly wounded are you?"

"Nothing much. Leg wound and concussion, it's the bloody noise I can't bear . . ."

Somebody whooped at the far end of the ward, a chair was knocked over. "Pack it in," said a voice which might have been male or female. There was a succession of, "Sorry, Sister, sorry, Sister, sorry . . ."

"What's going on here? These are not visiting hours. Who are you?"

The sister was short, brisk, intimidating, busty and strong. She wore a watch pinned to her chest like a medal, she glowered at Rose, took Mylo's wrist to feel his pulse. Mylo snatched his wrist free and reached again under the pillow for what appeared to be a revolver.

It was a revolver.

If Rose had had difficulty in recognising Mylo, he was frankly incredulous of the woman who now appeared. Gone was the shy girl he had met at the winter tennis, reduced to tears by the Thornbys' teasing, ill at ease in company, afraid of the Malones' guests, scared of her parents' disapproval, immature, a prey to indecision, constantly in need of his protection. This new Rose drew herself up and spoke to the sister in a clipped authoritative voice. She asked, nay demanded, that Mylo's bed should be moved into a side-ward. (Do you want your other patients shot?) She walked beside the bed in which he lay holding the revolver. Two nervous nurses pushed and pulled. Away from the noisy ward she bent close to Mylo and in a low voice asked, "What's your boss's name? Quick."

"Pye, Major Pye, but don't . . ."

"Right. Shan't be long. Don't speak to anyone, hang on to the revolver." She went away. As she went she handed the baby to a nurse. "Hold this, please," and "Take me to Matron," she said to the Sister.

Mylo was left alone in the side-ward. He felt bemused and very weak. From the ward he had left he heard renewed shouts and baying laughter. Poor devils, he thought, they feel perfectly well, they have only had a touch of flu, they have not encountered fear.

Then there came the clack of heels, the crackle of Matron's starch, the pinched nose of Sister holding her breath in disapproval. The amused yet grave expression of a white-haired doctor who inspected the dressing on his leg, courageously felt the pulse in the wrist of the hand which held the revolver (chauvinistic bravura in front of the nurses, he looks at least sixty-nine). The doctor nodded and smiled, turned to speak to Rose standing there remote and dignified.

Then two orderlies were easing him into a dressing-gown (their breath hissed as he changed the hand that held the revolver, watching it with swivelling eyes), transferring him from the bed to a wheelchair, propelling him down the corridor to the lift, down, out through the hall, out of the hospital, to help him into the front seat of Rose's car, wrapping a blanket around his legs.

While this was going on he was aware of Rose beside him. She had at some stage regained the baby, which she put into a basket on the back seat beside Comrade who was furiously wagging her tail and moaning in pleasurable recognition.

"Don't faint yet," Rose murmured, leaning into the car. "Are you comfortable, darling? Where's the revolver?"

"Here."

"Better give it to me now." She took it from him. "Goodbye," she said to Sister (Matron had not come out with them), "and thank you so much. What?" She leaned towards Sister, who was explaining something in a low voice. "No, of course you couldn't, no, I understand perfectly," and "Goodbye." She shook the old doctor's hand. "Thank you for all your care and help." She got in beside Mylo and started the engine. She put the revolver into the glove compartment and drove. As she drove she let out a crow of laughter. "That poor Sister said they hadn't dared wash you because of the revolver." Mylo did not answer. "You can faint now," said Rose after half a mile. Mylo closed his eyes. After two more miles, Rose said, "I think they thought it was loaded."

"It is."

"Good God." Rose pulled in to the side of the road. "You might have killed somebody."

"I meant to shoot those yahoos. I would have if you hadn't arrived, they were driving me crazy."

"Unload it at once." Rose reached into the glove compartment and fished out the revolver. "You must be out of your mind."

Meekly Mylo unloaded the revolver. Rose threw the bullets into the ditch. "Really, Mylo," she was trembling, "I thought you were averse to killing people." She was near tears.

Mylo was interested to see that her hands shook. This was the Rose he knew. "I'd rather like to kiss you," he said. Then he said, "How the hell did you find me?"

"I got your message; a man rang up."

"So I didn't dream it."

"No."

"Whose baby is that?"

"Mine."

Mylo felt confused; he had forgotten that she had been pregnant. "The man said he wouldn't telephone you unless I paid him. I had no money."

"He must have thought better of it."

In his basket on the back seat Christopher began to scream.

"Sorry," said Rose, "he's hungry. I must feed him, won't be long." She moved the car closer to the side of the road and got out. "You'd better have a run," she said to Comrade.

Mylo watched the dog sniffing about in the grass, then Rose was sitting beside him with the child, undoing her blouse and thrusting her nipple into its violent mouth, silencing the screams. Her breast was swollen, marbled with veins. "Will they recover?"

"What?"

"Your breasts, will they . . . ?"

"Back to normal. When I wean him."

"So that's how it works."

"Yes."

"Ah." So peaceful. Only what, two days ago? The violence in the dark on the rough sea, the pain, fear, seasickness . . . and now. "This is all rather unreal."

"I don't think you should talk. That doctor said you should be kept quiet at home, and rest."

"Is that so?" (Soon I shall be able to laugh. Home.)

"Yes." She moved the baby from left breast to right.

Mylo watched the child's gums bite on her tender nipple. "You said it hurt when . . ."

"One gets used to it. You mustn't talk. I'll give you a hot drink in a minute. Mrs Farthing lumbered me with supplies. She asked me to call her Edwina and, guess what, she and Farthing are not married, isn't that a turn-up for the book?"

"Nor, alas, are we."

Rose did not answer. He watched her burp the baby, change it and settle it back in the basket, then as they sat drinking hot chocolate he said, "Excuse me asking, but where did the extraordinary bossy act you put on with the nurses and doctor come from? You ordered those dragons about and twisted the old doctor around your little finger."

"It's not an act. It's me. If sufficiently frightened or enraged, it comes naturally. I found I could do it when the Min. of Ag. sent people to shoot our rooks."

Mylo noted the our.

"And what did you tell them that allowed them to release me into your charge?"

"I said you were top secret, working hush-hush for General Pye (I promoted him), and that since you were fit to move, it was better all round for you to be at home with me. Your revolver had rather unnerved them, they are not really a military hospital."

"Did they think you were my wife?"

"Of course."

"You are not far wrong."

"How so?"

"The intelligence bit. I shall have to contact the bastard, let him know I'm not dead."

"Let him go on thinking it for a bit," said Rose. "I'm in no hurry to lose you again."

"The war."

"Let the war wait."

Rose screwed the top back on the Thermos. "Now shut up and let me get you home before Christopher starts screaming again. He's terrible when he puts his mind to it, he's been good so far."

Some time later, waking from an uneasy sleep, Mylo asked, "Did we eat the Camembert?"

"What Camembert?"

"The Camembert I brought you last summer when I brought Picot over . . ." She did not ask who Picot might be, but she remembered the cheese. Delicious, a little squashed on its travels, overripe. They had eaten it in bed, washed down with a bottle of Ned's claret, what a peculiar thing to remember now. "Yes," she said, "I remember. I remember it well. Try to sleep, darling, it won't be long now, we are nearly home."

Home, thought Mylo wryly. What home, whose home?

THIRTY-SIX

Time was, thought Rose, pausing out of breath to sit on a granite boulder, when I would have reached the top of this hill without effort. But then, she thought as she stretched her legs, I would hardly have noticed the view.

Noticing the view comes with age, she thought, looking down the valley where mist still laced around the tops of the trees she had walked under, drifted across the waters of the creek, reluctant to give way to the sun which now warmed her back. It was going to be a perfect autumn day, blue and gold, no breeze to ruffle the water, pewter flat and deep, or loosen the leaves of oak and beech on the turn from dark green to rust to gold. Unaware of the view, one missed a lot in the hunger of youth, one wasn't prepared, one was taken by surprise, she thought, casting her thoughts back to the day when in weather of sleepy beauty she had arrived back with Mylo from the hospital in Cornwall to cherish and heal him in privacy and love.

What possessed me, what gave me the nerve to kidnap him from the hospital, over-ride the objections of the staff? What did I think I was doing? It is difficult at sixty-seven to recall the emotions of twenty. I wish I still had the nerve, the mix of bloody-mindedness and innocence. Have I quite lost it, she wondered? Am I blunted, am I too aware?

She had not that day been aware of anything other than Mylo's need. It was vital that he should have peace and quiet, to protect him. If his nerves were shaken by whatever embroilment had resulted in his wound, she would heal them. They would be together, her passion would revive him. Had he not in distress sent for her? Beyond this she had no plan.

It was a shock and surprise to be met on arrival by Edwina Farthing wearing an air of warning, drooping the corners of her mouth, raising her eyebrows, whispering, "Watch out," as she leaned into the car.

"What's up?" asked Rose, startled, pulling on the handbrake, switching off the engine.

"Mr Loftus and Mrs Malone," hissed Edwina. "I have made up the gentleman's bed in the yellow room," she said loudly, "and the other gentleman, the young chap from Down Under, the pilot, is quite happy in the blue room. Mr Loftus and Mrs Malone think that will do very well. That's what you ordered, isn't it?"

Blue room? Yellow room? What was the woman up to putting on this air of servility? Rose was amazed to see Edwina semaphore with her eyebrows, hiss breath in through her teeth. She had not previously particularly noticed Edwina's teeth. Large and slightly crossed, they brought to some errant corner of her mind a likeness to the evacuee waifs when they would not admit an urgent need to leave the room and go to the lavatory in case they missed something of interest. Edwina's act of an old retainer was putting a message across: she was under strain.

But then Archibald Loftus had come hurrying from the house: "Rose, my dear! Good girl! Great minds think alike." He had kissed her as she got out of the car. "When Edith told me – when I suggested – when we found you had thought of the same scheme and gone to fetch – it *is* young Cooper, isn't it? That's what Edith said. I wasn't quite sure myself. We'd better get you into the house, my dear fellow, let Mrs Farthing give me a hand with you, you look just about done in, they should have kept you a while longer, shortage of beds, I dare say. Ah, here is Edith – now give me your arm – oh, I see, you can manage with a stick, jolly good." (Had Mylo winked as he caught her eye?)

As Edith Malone embraced Rose she watched Mylo hop and hobble into the house between Uncle Archie and Edwina. He did not look back as he adapted himself to the unexpected. (This is how he survives doing whatever it is he does in enemy France.) Rose let Edith press her to her breast. "I *thought* I had sent you all the particulars of the scheme, you must have answered but in my usual stupidly vague way" (Edith vague? Come on!) "I mislaid your letter. I was so enraged with Emily and Nicholas I tore their letter up. I must have destroyed yours with it." (Oops, clever one.) "They really are too selfish for words; they have at the very least two spare rooms in that house of theirs; people with far less convenient houses have joined the scheme and are putting themselves out, and look at you, living alone and willing. Nobody will persuade me that one small baby and part-time work – she's only part-time now at the Ministry of Agriculture, I took the trouble to find out before asking her – take up all her time. Why, look at you with Christopher, you took him with you to fetch – oh, by the way, my dear, don't take me amiss, but it was a *little* over-zealous to fetch him yourself. Where, by the way, did you get the petrol? Another time, leave it to the ambulance people, it is their job, you know, all the forms and so on. Never mind, you'll know another time . . ."

Tactfully, a quality he lost as he grew up, Christopher had begun to scream. Comrade, anxious to be of use, licked the baby's face, switching Edith Malone on to another tack. "Do you think it's a good idea to let the dog lick him? I know there is a school of thought which says it doesn't matter, but when you think where dogs put their noses and the things they pick up and eat – please don't think I am interfering . . ."

"Oh, no, of course not, not at all. I think he is hungry." Rose had picked Christopher out of his basket, grateful that he saved her the necessity of answering Edith's flow. (She is gabbling to hide her embarrassment, to save me from mine. Why should I be embarrassed?) "Gosh, he's soaking, rather overdone his jobs too, needs changing, would you like to hold him a minute?" She had offered Edith the bundled, stinking baby.

"No, thanks, my dear. I am no good with babies." Edith backed away. "I had Nanny for George and Richard; I like children when they are older."

"House-trained?"

"That's it. I think you girls who look after your own babies without help are wonderful."

"Emily?"

"Most extraordinary, that brother Nicholas helps her, baths the baby, I hear . . ."

"They are keen on baths." Rose shouted above Christopher's yells; he was working himself up into high gear. "How are the evacuees?" she bellowed. "Hush, hush, won't be a minute." She held hungry, smelly Christopher as a shield between herself and Edith.

"Marvellous, my dear. Tremendous fun. They all go to the village school, bright as buttons, they don't get on with the village children who simply loathe them, but all ten are pretty well behaved, bless them, that's why I haven't a chink of room for the chaps on leave. I started you off with an Australian, by the way, he's a nice young man, broke his leg learning to fly. Such a shame, though it's probably saved his life, they say far too many bombers are getting lost. I'll just go and see he is settled now you are back, then I must fly, Archie has our only spare bed. He was coming back by bus after talking to you, but perhaps you could run him back, you seem pretty flush with petrol?"

"I . . ."

Edith Malone hurried ahead into the house, mistress of the situation.

Rose took the baby to her room, changed him and sat down to nurse him. Mylo had been taken from her, she was afraid to protest.

Alone with the child, she found herself trembling with a mixture of anger and fatigue. She tried to compose herself while Christopher sucked and nuzzled at her breast, fat tears wet on his cheeks. He looked old and pathetic; he snatched and grabbed at her nipple, strenuous with hunger and anxiety, reminding Rose of Ned when he feared the war and its unknown consequences. "Hush," she said, "there, quiet baby, quiet. Don't be in such a hurry, you'll get wind. Take it easy. Take it slow." When Edwina put her head round the door, she said, "Come in, tell me what the hell's going on. Is this a plot?"

"Got it in one." Edwina came in and shut the door.

"Sit down and tell."

Edwina sat. "Your fellow's all right. He got straight into bed without a word. Wants sleep, I'd say, and quiet."

"Thanks. And?"

"People are more observant than you give credit," said Edwina.

"What if they are?" snapped Rose.

"Someone, some busybody in the village maybe, sees you and him together the last time or the time before, it doesn't matter who. They talk. Talk spreads, see? The master's Uncle Archibald . . ."

"I wish you wouldn't call him that . . ."

"Just our joke, Farthing's and mine. Well, his Uncle Archie gets a sniff, smells a rat. When he called by chance, he said it was by chance, and found you gone. You follow me?"

"Oh, yes."

"He didn't say anything, nor will he, but he acts, takes advantage of this scheme of Mrs Malone's for officers and men from all over on leave with nowhere to go and, what ho, bingo, it's done. He pops an Australian into the house, and you've got yourself a chaperon."

"Damn him, curse his guts," said Rose.

"He's protecting your name from gossip. Instead of playing with fire and singeing your reputation, thanks to him and Mrs Malone you are doing important war work." Edwina cackled with laughter, "Can't say it's not funny."

"Most droll. Bloody hell, how could . . . ?"

"You are so wrapped up in yourself, you never think anybody notices what you are doing, do you? You are too young, they think, to be on your own with him overseas. They watch . . ."

"Curse them."

"They commune."

"They what?" Rose laughed now and the child at her breast eased perceptibly.

"They commune," Edwina repeated, enjoying the word, "that means nothing gets said, but a lot gets thought and with those sort of crafties, they act. Sort of sly." Rose could see that Edwina admired Archie and Edith.

"Does Mr Malone play any part in this?"

"No, no. Driven out of the house by the evacuee children's noise, he spends a lot of time in London these days, says he'd rather have the air raids."

"What a lot you know," said Rose sarcastically.

"Well, Farthing and I are over the initial stage, you might say. We can see beyond our noses. Hear too, stopped being blind."

Rose giggled, she held the baby up to pat and stroke his back. "Come on, my pretty, don't go to sleep. Burp for mother." Christopher obliged so violently a mouthful of curdled milk trickled out. Rose wiped his mouth and put him to her other breast. "So we have an Australian lodger. What's his name?"

"Jack Bowen. He's harmless enough. I think, on the whole, those two did right."

"Traitor. Tell me one reason," said Rose in fury.

"You don't want to burn your boats so far from land, that's one."

"I believe you and Farthing want me to be respectable, to conform to . . ."

"There's such a thing as compromise, too."

"Ugh."

"He's not exactly offering you security, is he, your young fellow? You have the baby to consider."

"I do . . ."

"The house. The farm. The place . . ."

"You and Farthing?"

"I didn't say so." Edwina flushed.

"Oh, Edwina, I'm sorry."

"It's got to be said; he comes and goes, you never know where you are with him; let's face it, one of these days he might not come back. You don't even know where he goes, do you?"

"I do," said Rose bravely.

"Somebody had to say it, love."

When Edwina left her, Rose sat on with the child dozing on her knee. She had felt trapped, she remembered in age, sitting in the sun near the top of the hill looking at the view. She had viewed the trap she was in with sorrow and, she admitted now but not then, with resignation. Even if Uncle Archibald and Edith Malone had not interfered to frustrate her by the tacit use of their social act, she would have been self-snared by her promise to Ned. We had enough obstacles without them butting in, she thought. I hope I am wise enough not to interfere between Christopher and Helen.

She remembered that she had put Christopher down to sleep, washed her face, brushed her hair, and gone down carrying the dirty nappies in a pail. Archibald Loftus had been hovering in the hall. "Hullo, everything all right?" he had asked, rather bluff.

"Yes, thank you. I'll just get rid of this lot, then I'll drive you home," she had said.

"Oh, yes, ah well, thank you."

One supposes, she had thought unkindly, that he wants to have his say too, otherwise he could perfectly well have gone home with Edith; I shall not ask him to stay for tea.

He had settled himself beside her in the car; Comrade had leaned from the back seat to sniff and breathe on his neck. He had winced and Rose had not restrained the dog, taking petty pleasure in his annoyance. "You're a cat lover, aren't you?" she had said pertly.

"Would you stop in the village, I want to buy a *Picture Post* for you to take back for your visitors."

"That's kind of you. They must not be allowed to get bored," she had said crisply.

"Don't be like that." He had shown a tinge of weakness and for a mile or two she thought he might withhold whatever he had that he wanted to say, but in the end he had circumnavigated his indecision: "I am not saying you are unwise, I am saying that you looked as though you might be, which amounts to the same thing."

"Yes, Uncle Archibald."

"Your friend Emily appears to have been a great deal more indiscreet than you (a touch of bad luck there, one assumes). Edith, an old old friend you know, Edith knows and I know you have done nothing reprehensible. Of course not, of course not! But it looked wrong."

I wouldn't call it reprehensible, Rose had thought, you silly old man; if you think I am an innocent ninny, think away. "Is that all, Uncle Archie?" she had asked sweetly.

Uncle Archie had shot her a look which had she been older and more experienced she would have interpreted as an invitation to something very reprehensible indeed, but being only twenty at the time all she said was, "We can buy a *Picture Post* at the newsagent," and Archibald Loftus thanked her. Now at sixty-seven Rose chuckled in recollection. Uncle Archie was such a devious old man, he could not imagine her other than straight. He was funny that way. Or, she thought, frowning at the view, looking back along the years, was he even craftier than I thought? Did he guess I was tempted by security?

THIRTY-SEVEN

Mylo woke sweating. The weight of the bedclothes oppressed his wounded leg. He was handicapped. Visions of police, Gestapo, suspicions of unreliable friends raced through his mind, then, fully awake, he remembered where he was. He lay back, perspiration cooling on his chest as the heart which had thundered in terror slowed its pace.

He looked at his watch. He had slept seven hours since Edwina Farthing undressed him, manoeuvred legs and arms into pyjamas and rolled him into bed. He lay listening to the silent house, then cautiously got out of bed, limped to the window. A full moon lit the garden; across the fields an owl hooted. Under this moon he had held Rose after the winter tennis, kissed her as they listened to the vixen screech.

Pricked by desire, he hobbled into the passage, listened again. A board creaked as the house cooled; from a neighbouring room the Australian snored; he remembered his arrival with Rose, her expression, mixed astonishment and irritation, as Mrs Farthing imparted her news, her eyes wild as Archibald Loftus helped him into the house, the old man's grip firm, compelling, her expression changing to hopeless resignation as command of the situation was whipped from her. He had guessed that she was outmanoeuvred, was best left alone, but now – he made his way along the passage, opened Rose's door and walked in.

She lay as he had left her that first time, her hair tousled, one arm flung across the side of the bed he had just left.

From her basket Comrade thumped her tail as she had when, departing, he had told her to "stay". On the rug the twin cats curled entwined, emerald eyes watchful. It was the same, everything was all right, nothing was changed.

In his cot Christopher sighed, whimpering in his sleep.

Ah. That . . .

Mylo hesitated as the events of the last few days surged back. The fear, the chase, the pain, the grotesquely noisy hospital, the rescue by Rose.

"Darling." She was awake. "Get in." She held out her arms. "Careful with your leg. Can you manage?"

"I can manage." He struggled out of the pyjamas.

"You manage pretty well," she said contentedly when they had made love. "Very well, I'd say. Shall we do it again?" She kissed his throat, feeling his pulse under her tongue, while he breathed the scent of her hair. "Oh, my love, I have missed you so."

"If I were blind, I would know you by smell."

"If I were blind, I would know you by feel."

"Your voice."

"Your dear voice."

Christopher waking, wet nappies cooling around his parts, raised an aggrieved yowl.

"*His* voice! I have to feed him." She sat up.

"At this hour?"

"Yes."

"Tyrannical." He watched her get out of bed, snatch a wrapper around her shoulders, pick up the child, change it, bring it back to bed, sit propped by pillows, put it to her breast. Watching, Mylo felt a surge of jealousy, a murderous rage against Ned who thus in the guise of Christopher imposed himself, wedging him apart from Rose. "What does your husband think of his heir?"

"He hasn't met him yet."

"But he knew you were pregnant?"

"Oh, yes. I wrote. Yes, I wrote and told him."

"Wasn't he delighted?"

"He had gone overseas when I wrote, so . . ."

"So he was delighted?" (Why do I insist?)

"Not exactly," she answered carefully. "Pleased. Yes, I suppose he was pleased."

"You suppose?" Mylo was puzzled. "He knew it was his."

"Of course. He would not have supposed otherwise."

"He trusts you." Mylo lay on his back, put his hands behind his head.

"Of course."

"So he must have been enchanted, proud, delighted." (My wound is throbbing in time to the baby sucking.)

Rose glanced at Mylo over Christopher's head, his dark eyes looking at the ceiling glinted in the moonlight. I can hardly tell him having a baby was my idea, my decision, not Ned's, that Ned played no part, well, very little, was not consulted.

"I wrote and told him," she repeated.

"And what did the happy father say?" Mylo hoped the jealousy did not sound in his voice, knew his choice of words was unfortunate, too late to retract them. "He must have been thrilled to bits," he amended.

"He said, Let's pray it's not a girl." Rose kept her voice neutral.

"Primogeniture?" Shocked and appalled, Mylo sensed her pain.

"Yes," she said, "exactly."

"So, when he was born, what did he say then?"

"Thank God it's a boy. I trust it's strong and doesn't squint or anything."

"Anything?"

"Some distant Peel was born with a harelip," she said.

"He telegraphed this?"

"He didn't telegraph. He wrote."

"Bastard."

"He can't help it," she defended absent Ned, "he's a man of property, a kind man."

"So you say."

"So they say."

"Look, he's had enough, he's falling asleep. Put him back in his cot, come back to me." (One should not dislike an innocent infant.) Propped on his elbow, Mylo watched Rose settle the child in his Moses basket, stoop to kiss the top of its head.

"He can't help his nature," she said.

Did she mean the child or its father? There was something in the tone of her voice which filled him with elation. "I believe," he said laughing, "that you are a survivor."

"I hope you are too," she said.

Rose back in his arms, he stroked her hair, pushing his fingers up her scalp, cupping her ears in his palms, bending to kiss her mouth. She heard the roar of the sea as one does when holding a conch to one's ear and shivered close up to him, reminded of the Channel which so recently separated them.

"When I am about my business in France," he said, "on the rare occasions I allow myself to think of you, I see us as those two in the Bonnard." He raised himself to peer at the lithograph.

"We have already grown older than those two," she murmured.

"Not in our hearts, never that."

"Of course not," she agreed robustly.

"She has no husband to come between them," he said enviously.

"He has no job to take him away from her," whispered Rose. "Away, to get shot in the leg."

"All her attention is for him. She has no house to look after, no farm, no garden, no handsome Australian visitor to care for."

"Is he handsome?"

"Stunning. I caught a glimpse as I was frog-marched to bed. She has no interfering in-laws and friends, no baby. If she had a baby it would be her lover's."

"Oh," Rose turned away, "don't. That *hurts.*"

"My darling, I wouldn't hurt you for the world. I only beef because I am so lucky to be here at all, I love you."

"And I love you, but I don't suppose," she too looked at the lovers in the picture, "that they spent all their lives he naked, she in camiknickers."

Perhaps what held me most strongly to Rose, Mylo would think in later life, was the laughter we shared. It was a stronger tie than promises of eternal love, more lasting than jealousy, more binding than lust.

THIRTY-EIGHT

Rose was angry with Ned's Uncle Archibald and Edith Malone. She had not felt the interference of relations and friends so strongly since she had been manoeuvred into marriage. Now all her resentment came flooding back. Later she would learn to frustrate her elders' benign force, recognise and mock their divine right to know what was best for her. She would learn much from the Thornbys who, thick-skinned and selfish, yet managed to appear compliant and agreeable should it suit them, while doing the opposite of what was suggested.

The imposition of an Australian visitor, which infuriated Rose at the time since it deprived her of her privacy with Mylo, was to lead via Edith's scheme to other visitors, French, Dutch, Polish, Canadian, Belgian, American. For the rest of the war Slepe was seldom free of guests; Mylo faded from people's minds, was lost in the crowd. If it was hinted that she might be having an affair with one of her visitors Rose would laugh, guessing that the suggestion came from Nicholas, put about as a smokescreen for his sister, for Emily soon latched on to the hospitality scheme, offered their spare rooms and was not above poaching the more attractive and sensual of Rose and other hostesses' visitors, leaving the more boring and boorish for hostesses less spry than herself, so that by the end of the war it was general knowledge that Emily received more CARE parcels, was better stocked with cigarettes and nylons than anyone in the county, and that, in this the period of dried egg, spam and whale steak, she learned to cook from her polyglot guests (and other less tangible arts).

But all this was to come later. Coming in from her morning's shopping, aglow with the beneficence of the night's love-making, her mind busy with plots to get Mylo to herself during the day as well as at night, Rose was furious to find Emily, Nicholas and baby Laura making free with her tea ration in the kitchen, talking and laughing with the Australian pilot who dandled Laura on his knee while Nicholas drew a naked lady on his plaster cast. ("This is my sister Emily at her best.")

Rose was even more furious to find that without telling her Mylo had telephoned London and informed Major Pye of his whereabouts and was even now closeted in the library with Victoria. When Mylo introduced them she shook hands; meeting Victoria's remarkable eyes in her plain bun face, she felt a premonition of doom.

"Victoria is from my outfit, come to do a spot of debriefing," said Mylo.

"It's very good of you to have Mr Cooper to stay, you rescued him for us before we could get around to it." Victoria's smile was friendly, showed more than passable teeth. (Who does she think she is? Who are "us" and "we"? He's mine.) Victoria re-seated herself beside Mylo and looked up at Rose. (She expects me to leave them together. I am *de trop*.)

"I have to brief Victoria with the results of my trip," said Mylo. He did not want her to stay, did not call her darling, was distant.

"Then I'll leave you to get on with it," said Rose, then forced herself to say, "I hope you can stay to lunch?"

"I should love to, but I must get back to the office and I mustn't impose on your rations." Victoria's manners were as perfect as her eyes.

"But you must stay, I insist," said Rose. "We have a broken-legged pilot who needs cheering up and we have masses to eat since we have a farm. Please stay." Perhaps, she thought wildly, this girl will succumb to the charms of the beautiful Australian.

In the event Victoria stayed and was amused by Nicholas and Emily who entertained the lunch party, telling them that their father, the bishop, refused to baptise Laura, making a good story of their parents doubting the validity of baptism when the child was of father unknown. "Isn't it barbaric? Isn't it a typical churchman's attitude? He's a bishop and yet so unchristian."

"He's a nice old man and I bet he hasn't refused to baptise Laura. You've invented the story to be snobbish and show off" (What am I saying? I'm behaving like a child back in the nursery.) "that your father is a bishop."

"No, no, we haven't invented. He makes all sorts of excuses. Emily doesn't know who the father is, either. What would you do Down Under? You wouldn't be beastly to a little Pom bastard, would you?" Nicholas drew Rose's guest into his net, enjoying signs of embarrassment. "Come on, Rose, you must help us."

Rose backed away from what she suspected was a Thornby trap. "I never knew your father all that well," she excused herself.

"Then can you lend us a gallon or two of petrol?" Nicholas revealed the real reason for their visit.

"No," said Rose, "certainly not."

"Oh, come on, Rose, I'm sure you can spare some. Our friendly blackmarketeer has dried up."

"What about your Min. of Ag.?"

"They are being a little difficult."

"It's still no."

"What must you think of us blackmarketeers with illegitimate babies?" Nicholas turned to Victoria.

"It happens," said Victoria calmly, then, "I must go, I'm afraid." She turned to Rose. "Many thanks for lunch." Mylo limped with her to her car while Rose followed. "Goodbye," said Victoria, shaking Rose's hand, and, "I'll have you fetched tomorrow," she said to Mylo as she got into her car. "Can you be ready by ten?"

"Yes, of course." Mylo watched the car go down the drive. "Nice girl that," he said, "very capable."

Rose felt a fierce pang of envy. "You can't go tomorrow, your leg isn't fit enough."

"I'll get it checked in London."

"You can't leave me, I've only just got you back!"

"I must go . . ."

"Why?"

"You know why." He was not going to argue or explain his job, was forbidden to anyway. That night they had a row.

It began, as rows do, over a matter on which normally they would have agreed, Edith Malone. Rose, smarting at being jumped into hostessing a number of strangers for an indefinite period, complained when Mylo joined her in bed of Edith Malone and Archibald Loftus's interference. There would be a constant interruption of precious privacy, a crowd of visitors with unknown needs. The imposition was outrageous.

During the day she had fuelled her annoyance, letting her mind run over the occasions, real or imaginary, that her life had been impinged on by her elders. Forgetting that, had it not been for her mother's persistence, she would never have met Mylo at the winter tennis, she dwelt on the meeting with Ned. If it had not been for her mother and Mrs Malone she would never have met, never have been cajoled into marriage with Ned, would not now be trapped, lassoed into this hospitable role. She would like to be at peace, to be alone with Mylo, her love, her darling, to copulate. (This word, sometimes used with effect by Nicholas and recently added to her vocabulary, she tried now on Mylo who appeared unmoved by it.) Hurrying on, she said she would be bored and bothered by the uninvited guests, foresaw much irritation from Nicholas and Emily. "Look how they barged in on us today," she grumbled. "It is all Edith's fault, our day ruined." She dared not voice her real fears, Mylo's imminent departure. Where to? How long for? Would he be killed next time? Might she never see him again?

And Victoria.

Since the morning she had been devoured by a jealousy so intense it upset her milk, which in turn upset Christopher who now whinged with stomach ache, drew up his legs, clenched infant fists, and either could not or would not sleep as was his usually angelic mode. If Mylo was on these terms (she could not, of course, define *what* terms) with Victoria, who might there be in France to draw him back like a magnet? One girl in particular? Many girls? All that talk of boring French girls with expressions of his love for her, Rose, was obviously all my eye. So her thoughts and fears raged as for the umpteenth time she soothed Christopher, hopefully spooned gripe water into his mouth.

"Edith Malone is an old busybody. Since Mother went to live in London, she has appointed herself watchdog over my morals. I wish to God she would mind her own business instead of poking her nose in to mine and dragging Ned's uncle along. Why can't they leave us alone? How on earth did she guess about you and me, we've been so utterly secret?"

"I don't think she has the remotest idea about you and me," said Mylo equably. (If only Rose would get that baby to be quiet, we could cuddle up in bed and listen to the night.)

"What do you mean by that?" snapped Rose.

"Mrs Malone is a snob, it would not occur to her that you would sleep with her son's tutor."

"What nonsense. She's not a snob," (Of course he's right, she *is*) "that's nonsense," Rose repeated.

"It is not. She's kind. You have told me how kind she has been to you, how she looked after you when you were ill, sent George – by the way, what about George?" A wisp of doubt slid across Mylo's mind, but he went on treading the track of Edith's kindness. "She was kind to me when I worked for them, she even bought me clothes when she couldn't stand my French workmen's blues. I never told you that, did I? She is being kind to all these homesick servicemen you are going to entertain – don't go over the top with them, will you? – she just happened along with old Loftus in tow because he is staying with them. He possibly smelled a rat, she didn't."

"Don't be silly."

"I am not. As far as your glossy reputation is concerned, it's safe with Edith Malone, and Loftus won't gossip; it wouldn't be in his nephew's interests."

"How wouldn't she? Why?" Rose, tired and already irritable, resented Mylo's tone. She laid Christopher back in his cot.

"As I said, I'm her son's tutor, a servant, not someone a person like you would sleep with."

"How can you talk such rubbish! How can you be so ridiculous?" Rose's raised voice roused Christopher, who had been on the point of sleep. He rallied his strength, filled his lungs, whined, changed gear, screamed.

Sitting on the side of Rose's bed Mylo clenched his fists in exasperation. He didn't blame the baby, he told himself, he blamed Ned. During the lonely months in France when he dreamed of Rose, gentle, pliant, gloriously roused to passion, he forgot Ned's existence, but now – he eyed the screaming infant with distaste. He had wanted to make love to Rose as he had the night before, he had come to her room full of erotic anticipation, he felt choked with jealousy and frustration. "If that were my child, I'd drown it," he said.

Rose grew quite pale.

"What I meant," said Mylo, "was that I wish I could drown your husband Ned."

"No, you didn't. You want to murder my innocent baby." She had to shout to make herself heard above Christopher's screams. "And, if you must know, I love my husband," Rose yelled. (What devil possessed her to voice this patently obvious lie which Mylo, gorged with jealousy, chose to believe?)

There followed charges, counter-charges, tears, remorse, apologies, forgiveness, explanations and, since Christopher tired before they did and hiccoughed himself to sleep, fucking.

Next morning Rose shivered as she watched Mylo being driven away. What happened to us? she asked herself. We must never let such a thing happen again. She felt quite sick and ill as she stood on the steps and waved to Mylo; then the car turned the corner and was out of sight.

THIRTY-NINE

During the following weeks Rose suffered. The words and tones of the row reverberated and echoed through her mind. They had been too shattered by their own violence to have a satisfactory love-making. Mylo, hampered by his wounded leg, climaxed too soon. Rose was too tense to have an orgasm. They lay wakeful for the rest of the night, too distraught to sleep, clinging together in silence.

When he left her bed in the morning Mylo looked sourly at the Bonnard and the ideal it represented.

Watching him drive away in the car sent to fetch him Rose felt an astonishing spasm of relief.

During the next week she attended assiduously to her Australian guest, telephoned the person in charge of the hospitality scheme to arrange for a succession of visitors, re-arranged the house to make room for them. By filling her life to the brim she thought she could endure Mylo's absence. She worked harder than ever in the garden, increased the hours spent on the farm. Attended by her dogs, she carted Christopher about with her so that for ever after he would wonder why in times of stress he would smell the scent of cow-byres and think of his mother.

When Mylo telephoned she felt their separation fiercely. Listening to his voice, she craved his physical presence. When their short conversations ended she was more lonely than before. The conversations were of necessity brief, most of the three minutes allowed by wartime restriction, in retrospect, wasted. When next he telephoned she knew by his voice that he was leaving the country.

"You are going away again?"

"Yes, darling, tonight."

"Your leg, how is your leg?"

"Quite healed. However long I am gone, don't forget me."

"As if I could. I love you."

"And I love you. Keep watch over the girl in the camiknickers for me."

"I will. I will."

What else did they say? Take care of yourself . . . come back soon . . . come back safe . . . don't forget, oh, don't forget . . . I could never love anyone else . . . Words, just words. Did he hear the catch in her voice? She thought she heard a hint of uncertainty in his. Did she doubt him? How was she to know that he was to be dropped by parachute into France that night and the prospect turned his bowels to water?

"When will you be back?"

"I don't know. I can't tell you. Don't worry."

What a bloody stupid thing to say: don't worry.

She put the receiver back and went to the kitchen. Edwina was making tea for the postman. The Australian visitor was peeling apples to make apple rings for apple pie in the coming winter.

"Hullo," he said. "Come and join us. Mrs F. doesn't believe in idle hands."

"Good morning," said the postman.

"Cup of tea?" suggested Edwina. "Here's your post. Three letters from his highness."

The Australian looked up. The postman snubbed a grin.

"Don't call him that." Rose took the letters. "His highness is worse than 'the master'."

Edwina raised her eyebrows. The postman put down his empty cup, muttered goodbye and left.

Rose slit the airmail letters open with a knife. "I have written," said Ned, "to put my son's name down for my old school. It is important to get his name on the list for a good house. I have written to Uncle Archibald to find out the best housemaster for when my son is fourteen, if he is bright, thirteen. I have also provisionally put his name down for my old prep school."

Rose picked up the rest of the letters and left the kitchen. In the library she sat on the sofa and reread the letter. Her eyes had not deceived her. Ned wrote, "my" not "our" son, not Christopher, nor even "our baby". He wrote "my son" twice. Comrade, sensing that there was something wrong, leaned against Rose's leg. Her pup, still juvenile, lay on his back, exposed his stomach and wagged a beguiling tail.

In the next letter Ned gave news of his health (excellent), that of various friends (passable), hinted of imminent promotion to major (excellent also, since he was not a professional soldier) and "now for the good news, it is highly probable that I shall be back with you ere long".

Rose wondered whether her heart, already ebbing, could sink any lower. She opened the third letter. "Dear Rose," he wrote, "my bank manager is worried . . . you seem unaware . . . before spending so freely you should . . . while I am away fighting for my country . . . (Fighting? At a desk?) . . . not earning as much as in peacetime . . . now I have a child to . . . Is it necessary to cash such large . . . try to be economical as . . . is it, for instance, necessary to buy so many books? Hatchards account is . . . try please to imagine what it is like for me out here to . . ."

She was grateful for Christopher's cries. Time for his mid-morning guzzle.

"I don't seem to satisfy him," she said presently to Edwina. "He's fearfully collywobbly and he has not been fretful before."

"Being worried dries your milk. How about a supplementary feed?"

"A bottle?"

"Yes. Shall I mix him one?"

"If you think it will help."

The older woman went away. Rose brought up Christopher's wind. Squinting with indigestion, the baby looked remarkably like his father. "He's putting your name down for Eton. His son! Poor little sod." Christopher belched. "That's better. Ah! Here's Edwina with an itsy bitsy bottle, try it." Rose put the teat into Christopher's mouth. "My God! He loves it! I've been starving him. Look, he's uncrossing his eyes."

"Loves it . . ."

"In that case I shall wean him, and the major can complain of a remarkably heavy bill from Cow and Gate."

"The major complaining of extravagance?" Edwina, latching on, let her eyes swivel towards Ned's letters. "Been promoted, has he?"

"About to be."

"Send on the bills from his tailor, then. He told me to keep them back when he went overseas; re-address them, shall I? They are in the kitchen dresser drawer."

"Edwina!" Rose was lost in admiration. "Yes. Please do."

"All right. Leave the baby with me for a bit. The children can push him round the garden. You take the dogs for a walk, you'll feel better when you've been on your own for a bit."

"Shall I? Do you really think so?"

"Give it a try." Edwina swooped on the baby. "Come with old Edwina then, we'll push your pram to the post and shovel Dada's billsy-willsies into the postbox." Christopher chuckled as she carried him off.

Rose pulled on rubber boots and a jacket, whistled up the dogs. Walking up the river, watching the trees shed golden leaves into the water, she tried to imagine Ned in Egypt. His letters brought no mid-Eastern vision, he might as well be writing from his London club, she thought resentfully, and anyway what I want to see is France, Mylo in France. Will he be wearing his workmen's blues, melting into the French crowd? Will he be singing as he sings in his bath: *Par les routes de France/ de France et de Navarre/ Je fais ma révérence/Je m'en vais au hazard*. Will he sing? Watching the leaves fall, running to catch one and missing it, she heard Mylo's voice in imagination and cried out in the empty meadow, startling the rooks feasting on acorns in an oak tree. "I am lonely, lonely, lonely." But she was not to be lonely long. Five weeks later she realised she was pregnant.

FORTY

Having believed the old wives' tale that it is not possible to conceive while breast-feeding Rose could not at first believe her predicament. She left Christopher with Edwina Farthing, travelled to London for the day and had a pregnancy test in a hospital, giving an assumed name and telling glib lies. A week later she received an intimation through the post that the test was positive.

Mylo was gone, there was no means of communicating with him. He had volunteered no address; she had been too proud to ask whether messages could be transmitted via Victoria. She had no means of knowing when he would be back or, coldly she faced up to it, whether he ever would come back. She must manage alone.

Who could she ask for help?

If she asked for help it meant she thought to get rid of the child.

No need for help if she had it. Ned would be home soon. She could, with a lot of luck, present him with a little brother or sister for Christopher (born prematurely). He would speak of "my" daughter, "my" younger son. This scenario was ridiculously and improbably silly.

She could not bring herself to involve childless Edwina. The permutations of help which could be offered were endless.

Emily? Would Emily be the right person to ask? Had she not recently presented the neighbourhood with Laura and had not "the talk" already died away? Emily had Nicholas's backing. People feared Nicholas, kept on the right side of him. Rose too feared Nicholas, shrank from putting herself in his power. Neither he nor Emily had rumbled Mylo, nor must they.

Should she confide in Edith Malone? No, said her inner voice, she is too close a neighbour. She would be too kind, too bossy, she would gobble me up, baby and all.

When last year she had told him she was pregnant Mylo had cried, I wish it were mine; in her mind's ear she could hear his voice. She daydreamed that she had not married Ned, that Mylo had not vanished into France, that she had money of her own. Sleepless at night, her thoughts plagued her; however busy she was by day the fears, the arguments for and against pursued her.

Her milk dried up and Christopher prospered on Cow and Gate baby powder, growing chubby and contented.

It is cowardly and ridiculous to be afraid of "talk", Rose argued in robust mood. What have I to lose?

Everything, said the voice of sense. Husband, home, child, work, good name (whatever that means), security. Oh, ah, security! "Fuck my good name, fuck security," she said out loud.

At the sound of her voice the dogs looked up, wagging their tails. "I might even lose my dogs," she thought.

On impulse, in desperation, she telephoned Flora Loftus, the most improbable person she could think of.

After inquiring after Flora's and Uncle Archibald's health, she said, "I need your advice. We only have three minutes. Our landgirl is in trouble. So tiresome – yes, that kind of trouble. What?"

Flora Loftus's voice fluted from Argyll, clear, confident, cheerful. "Funny thing," plump laughter, "Archie's landgirl had the same thing; it's all the fresh air, these town girls are not used to it. I'll send you the address on a postcard. She'll need eighty pounds in cash, that's the price apparently, take it or leave it. Archie grumbled but, as I told him, a good landgirl's price is above rubies. You telephone the man for an appointment and the service is immediate, I gather. How is your darling baby? I long to see him. What a bore the war is, everything so difficult and – oh, dear, are we about to be cut off, these telephone operators could teach Hitler a thing or two, they enjoy their power, I'll post the address . . ."

"Oh, thank you . . . so sorry to bother you . . . with Ned away I'm supposed to be responsible . . . you are always so kind."

"Not at all, my dear. Not to worry, Archie will catch the evening post for me, he's just off to his Home Guard. What fun the old boys are having! Did I tell you the man is in London? Archie grumbled about the fare down there. It'll be less expensive for you, of course, than for us . . ." This time they were cut off.

Three days later in the train to London Rose looked out at the passing landscape and thought bitterly, "Put your trust in the Establishment, for sheer hypocrisy they are peerless, unbeatable." Then she thought, "I can't beat them, I am joining them."

She counted the telegraph poles as the train thundered past, one, two, thirteen, eighteen, twenty, forty . . . one hundred, one hundred and one. A man opposite her who had been reading *The Times* watched her lips move, thought her eyes sad: "I watch the fences, this lot are well cut and laid, and think myself on to a good hunter and jump them effortlessly behind the hounds who are in full cry, the fox only a field away."

"I don't hunt. I'm afraid of horses."

"Ah," he said, "surely not." A pretty girl like you, he wanted to say, should never need to be afraid, but being English he merely said, "Ah," again and picked up his newspaper defensively.

"I am afraid. Full stop," said Rose distantly. "Here we are in the suburbs. Your ride must end. My telegraph poles go on and on."

"Ah, yes," he said, "I see."

"You don't see *anything*. Do you see, for instance, that I am about to drown in Establishment soup?" Rose hissed.

The stranger was glad when the train drew into Paddington; it was folly to speak to strange girls, one should have remembered.

★

The man in the white overall put the money in a drawer, washed his hands at the basin.

"If you will take your knickers off," said his assistant, "and lie back on the chaise." (Why did she call it a chaise?) "Have you brought some STs? You will need some STs."

"Yes."

"Open your legs wide," said the assistant, "while I swab you with antiseptic. You like the smell, yes?" She too wore a white overall. It all seemed very clean and efficient. The surgical instruments cooking in that tray thing. He was pulling on what looked like new rubber gloves. Full marks for cleanliness.

"There will be just a little prick of local anaesthetic, it won't hurt, takes a minute or two to work. Take a taxi home and go to bed for at least twenty-four hours; if you have pain or excessive bleeding, take these pills. Two, every four hours. Now, just a prick." It stung.

"I tie your legs apart like this so you keep quite still," said the assistant.

She had yelled, "No, no, no." Sprung off the chaise, grabbed shoes and stockings, pushed the assistant aside, rushed to the door, opened it, torn down the passage, put shoes and stockings on in the lift as it went down, run clattering out into the street.

It was dark, she couldn't see a taxi, she walked fast over the bridge into Chelsea, into the King's Road. She struggled on to a bus. She was numb, her vagina was numb, there was no feeling there, none at all, local anaesthetic he had said. I wish he had pricked my mind.

"Oh, the bloody buggers," said a woman beside her. "Here we go again, another fucking raid."

"Knightsbridge. Everybody off," shouted the bus conductor. "Into the Underground with you." He sounded glad.

She was swept along with the crowd down steps on to the moving staircase. Warm air blew up her legs from far below. (I left my knickers in that place.) She let the crowd sweep her with it on to a train. She stood, held upright by the press of people, struggled free at Piccadilly. I'm feeling funny, she thought. If I could get some air, if I could sit down somewhere – all these people. She walked slowly, picking her way. The crowd frightened her. People were getting settled for the night, wrapped in blankets, cramped several together on mattresses, reading books by torchlight, drinking out of Thermoses, playing cards, singing, snoring. A drunken man whooped. The tube trains chuntered into the station – "Mind your backs, mind the doors" – and out again. She craved air. Halfway along the platform the wrenching pain began. She was outraged, cried out. (How *can* it? I didn't *let* him, he didn't *do* it. I *saved* it. I haven't *had* an abortion.) She doubled up, bending over. (Oh, God, this is awful, what a place to – Oh, my knickers, I'm not – oh pain, the pain.) She felt blood oozing out of numb vagina, pouring, streaking down her legs. (I left my STs in that place, oh, Jesus Christ.)

"Look, Nance! That girl – I call that disgusting," said a voice. "I mean. Look here. In the tube with people trying to sleep, taking shelter like decent . . ." And other voices said other things. Her legs were not helpful, not managing the one foot in front of the other job, quite simple really.

"Needs help," another voice, a young sailor. Then she was being wrapped in a blanket and was this a stretcher? Try everything once – and an ambulance, bright light, voices, "Don't try to stand, just lie quietly, we'll soon . . ." and rumble, rumble on rubber wheels, very fast along a corridor. "The raid's over, jolly good." And an icy swab on her arm, an injection and away roaring in her head, woom-womb-woom-womb. Those bills, what was he worrying about in his letter? The lovely smell of new books, oh, Hatchards, obviously Nicholas and Emily had been up to their usual tricks charging books to Ned's account, rather comical, quite a joke. What or who else had they charged to his account? one wondered. She was talking out loud now. "I wonder what he'll say, whether he'll notice that last cheque cashed for eighty pounds. Did you put it on a horse?" she gasped.

"She's coming round now. It's all right, dear, all over, you're OK now. Try a sip of water, bad luck, getting caught in a raid like that, poor dear. You've been nicely tidied up." Tidied up, is that what they call the baby who escaped life into the Underground, running down my legs in a slodge of blood? Tidied? That was my baby, his name was Tidy, funny name for a boy, well, perhaps it was a girl, it didn't wait for me to see. (I was nearly born in the Piccadilly tube station.)

There was a grey-haired doctor in a white coat standing by the bed;

he looked very tired (well, everybody does these days, it's the war).

"I am afraid you lost it, Mrs Peel." They knew her name, must have looked in her bag. "We did what we could, I'm very sorry."

"So am I." (Oh, so am I.)

"We'll keep you here for a few days just to be on the safe side."

"Thank you."

"Like us to get in touch with your husband? If you tell Sister, she . . ."

"He's in Egypt."

"Your mother?"

"I haven't got a mother." (How pat it came, but, no, enough's enough, I could not bear to have her come to see me.) "I should love just to be quiet, please."

The doctor smiled: "Being quiet in a London casualty hospital is a contradiction in terms," (what a lovely man) "but we'll do our best."

They let her go home after a few days.

Edwina Farthing folded her in her long bony arms and gave comfort, comfort, comfort.

Up in Scotland Flora Loftus said one night to Archibald, her husband, "I wonder, should I have asked the landgirl's name?"

"No, no, leave well alone," he answered.

A year later on her annual shopping foray, which even the war could not stop, meeting Edith Malone for lunch at the Cordon Bleu in Sloane Street, Flora asked, "How is Ned and Rose's landgirl?"

"They've never had a landgirl," said Edith. "It's Rose who works on the farm."

Flora Loftus stood corrected, held her peace.

FORTY-ONE

When Picot came to write his memoirs and attempted to explain his conversion from the anti-British feelings of a normal Frenchman to the anglophile warmth of his latter years, he found himself describing an incident which took place in Occupied France in the middle of the war, *en route* to London. It had to do with the English taste for milk puddings, he wrote, a taste discovered for him by his guide Mylo Cooper, a brave man.

There had been the rendezvous in a small town where Mylo masqueraded as a plumber, occupying himself over a period of weeks with small jobs such as changing washers, checking cisterns, advising on drains. The local plumber had disappeared into the Resistance; Mylo had access to the man's tools, thanks to a friendship with the plumber's sister, a waitress in a café at the corner of the Place.

The morning after their rendezvous Picot sat with Mylo outside the café watching the *va-et-vient* of police and soldiery at an hotel along the square used by the Gestapo as their headquarters.

Picot was extremely nervous – he did not write this in his memoirs, taking it for granted that his readers would know that anyone engaged in the Resistance would inevitably be tense, to say the least – but on discovering that Mylo proposed to go on sitting around in the café flirting with the waitress instead of proceeding on their journey as they had on previous occasions, his nervousness turned to rage. He had never particularly liked Mylo; now he detested him.

"You are risking both our lives," he said. "We sit here and if we sit much longer someone will remark and inform on us." (In his memoirs Picot had earlier explained that his guide whose job it was to get him safely to England had in mind to help a woman at present in the hands of the Gestapo.)

Mylo answered, "It's possible." Sipped his acorn coffee and exchanged looks with the waitress lolling against the bar counter.

"You know they have her? You have yourself checked?" Picot queried. He had asked this before. Mylo nodded, shifted the bag of tools at his feet to let a customer pass, winked at the waitress who tossed her head.

"How you dare be so foolhardy when so many of us are at risk when she talks," said Picot.

"She won't talk." Mylo rubbed the scar on his leg through the heavy cotton of his trousers.

Picot laughed. "Everybody talks. If not sooner, then later. We should be on our way." Then, since Mylo said nothing, "Is she so special?"

"She is my aunt," Mylo murmured. (She had been so gentle and kind to Rose that morning, made jokes, jollied her up.)

Picot lit his miserable wartime cigarette. "Now you tell me." He sighed.

"Jewish. My mother's sister."

"They all go to the camps," muttered Picot.

"Not this one," said Mylo.

"So where does she go?"

"With us. England."

"Jesu. Holy Mother. Optimist." In his fear and nervous state Picot would remember later that he was tempted to leap up, shout out loud to the people in the café, for all those passing in the street, "This man is English. This man risks my life, arrest this man." Sometimes he dreamed that he had done this, woke screaming, upset his mistress (his wife never woke, she slept like a rock). He debated whether to include this temptation in his memoirs, did not, regretted it later, liking to be thought human.

"If you are so impatient," Mylo had teased, "go on on your own."

"You have the contacts. All in that mad head of yours," said Picot.

"Two, at most three more days," said Mylo.

"Then what?"

"They," Mylo nodded imperceptibly towards the hotel, "move out."

"They move *out*? You *crazy*?" Picot, ever suspicious of his masters, wondered whether they had deliberately entrusted him to a lunatic. It was whispered in London that Colonel P. was not above arranging the disappearance of communist party members. He put this in his memoirs in another context, a later chapter.

"Then she – er – um – joins us and we go on our way," said Mylo, grinning.

"And what is this way? We have missed the boat thanks to your auntie, there is no other boat for a month, the tides . . ."

"Bugger the tides. We walk," said Mylo.

"Over the Pyrenees, I suppose."

"Right."

"And are taken prisoner by Franco's lot on the other side?"

"It's probable."

"*Merde.*"

"Better than being handled by our friends in there." Mylo picked his teeth with a match.

"Handled . . ."

"I am partial to euphemisms."

Picot sighed. "All right. Explain the situation with your aunt. How did she get herself arrested?"

"Who knows? A tip-off? She's in there is all that matters." Mylo's eyes were half closed. He scraped the match along his jaw, he had not shaved for a week. "She's my mother's sister. She has a perfectly good house in Bayswater." He sighed, remembering how Aunt Louise had given them a splendid breakfast (he could smell the coffee). She had lent Rose the train fare home, comforted her after her own aunt's coarse accusations. "She's daft," he said with affection. "Reminds me of Mother."

"Bayswater? London?" Picot let smoke trickle from his open mouth. "And she came back here?" He couldn't believe the idiocy.

"Volunteered. We are a heroic family." Mylo pretended to look modestly down his nose.

"There are heroes in mine, but we are not also fools," said Picot, sneering.

"*Mademoiselle, deux cafés, s'il vous plait.*" Mylo caught the waitress's eye.

Watching the girl move away, swinging her hips, Picot said gloomily, "One wonders what it does to one's guts, this coffee."

"What I did to monsieur the proprietor's drains."

"Which was?" Picot watched the Germans down the street, alert, bored, alien.

"Scoured them out," said Mylo, "but our friends in the hotel had a faulty ballcock; the noise of the cistern kept the gentlemen awake when they wished to nap between bouts of interrogation."

"They believe you to be a plumber?"

"They do." Mylo bent to pat his bag of tools.

"How many more days?" Picot was resigned.

"We should notice some unease tomorrow. Two days later, exodus."

"What makes you so sure?" asked Picot.

"I put sago down all the lavatories, sinks and washbasins. The guard who watched me thought it was soda."

"And?"

"Sago swells," said Mylo.

Telling the story Picot would say, "Of course, I recommended him to the general for the Croix de Guerre," and roar with laughter. In his book he wrote that he had been instrumental in getting a gallant friend decorated for acts of supreme courage and sacrifice, which was re-writing history but more dignified than the truth.

FORTY-TWO

As time went along without news of Mylo, unbearable pain dulled to an ache. It became reasonable to be grateful that fate had robbed Rose of Mylo's child (it had probably disposed of Mylo as well). Her hope ebbed low. The child, she told herself, would have grown up cleverer and more attractive than Christopher, her loyalties would have divided. She told herself harshly that she should thank God for small mercies; she had been spared an embarrassment she was well without.

She surprised herself and used an unexpected fund of common sense, taking pleasure in the predictable and mundane, admitting to a taste for the security and convention she had hitherto despised as evidence of her unloved parental background. With a mix of grief and relief she put her true nature into reverse. She was still too young to know that it is possible to operate on several planes at once.

During the months between the miscarriage and Ned's return she consolidated her defences, teaching herself to manipulate life at Slepe to her own ends, the work among the vegetables and on the farm. The role of mother, host and housewife which up to now had been mere camouflage became, she persuaded herself, her true persona.

When she looked at the Bonnard she saw a picture she liked; it no longer spelled the image of Mylo putting his arms around her preparatory to some delicious act of erotica. In some lights, such as when she was dressing on chill winter mornings, the couple's lack of sensible clothes made her chilly body shiver as she pulled on woolly vest and longjohns. If she looked closely at the girl she could perhaps be disagreeing with the boy, drawing away from him. But more often she dressed in such haste she did not notice the picture at all. Her days were crammed with Christopher's needs. The constant stream of foreign visitors. Instead of country solitude, mooning about dreaming of love, she made friends with the people who worked in the Ministry office in the back wing: at meals she absorbed homesick accounts of life back home in Australia, Poland, the USA, Holland, and even France without necessarily making any connection with Mylo. How was she to know he was really there, or even alive?

When her visitors flirted with her, she encouraged them, boosting their egos and her own, stopping short of going to bed with them, for was she not faithful wife to absent husband? She even stopped discouraging Emily and Nicholas who came to Slepe often, bringing infant Laura, making blatant use of the facilities of Slepe when they wished to economise on their own (they had not had the forethought to stock up for the war like Ned; they had mocked him at the time). Should her visitors' randiness become unbearable Emily could, indeed would, oblige.

Rose was at that time so busy growing a scab over her wound she felt no sense of disloyalty. If there was an occasional mad longing for Mylo, she scotched it.

When Ned did arrive home (wearing major's tabs now and a red band around his hat), he was delighted to find that the wife whose capability he had previously questioned had a firm grip on his estate. He was miffed as well as amused to discover that even after his return Hadley continued to consult Rose about milk yields and pig production, that she was hand in glove with Farthing. He did not say so. (Perhaps it was then he decided that when the war was over he would switch to sheep and cereals about which Hadley knew nothing and get rid of Rose's precious pigs and dewy-eyed Jerseys.) Meanwhile he praised her care of Christopher, laughed at her losing battle with the draughts, promised central heating when the war was over, and applauded her talent for manipulating the guests into helping with the washing-up, tinkering with the innards of the bishop's car and refilling the log baskets.

It was Rose who brought up the subject of money. "You hurt my feelings when you wrote accusing me of extravagance," she said. "As you see for yourself, I have not done too badly."

"I did not accuse. When I wrote I was warning you to be careful, thinking of the future . . ." Ned said touchily.

"I have been careful. Since you complained, I no longer pay the wages in cash; the change hasn't pleased people, who distrust cheques."

"Why not?"

"Never heard of fiddling income tax?" Rose laughed. "It's such a joy to people like the Hadleys. The shopkeepers, too."

"I can't approve. I don't see anything funny."

"No. Well. I stopped your accounts with Hatchards, Penhaligons and Trumpers."

"Good God."

"I thought you would prefer to deal with your tailors yourself – why do you have two?"

"Aren't you being rather . . ."

"Bossy?" Rose met his eye. "Interfering?"

"Yes." He had not expected her to turn out bossy.

"It was you who complained. I acted as I thought best." (Is she teasing me? Ned wondered.) "Perhaps you had better tackle Emily and Nicholas yourself."

"What have they got to do with it? What do you mean?" Ned bristled, this was no child wife.

"Wake up, Ned. Nicholas uses your accounts; he's a great reader, and look how nicely cut his hair is. He's a dodger, you must have known."

"If it's true, I'll put a stop to it," cried Ned, angry now.

"And Emily?" asked Rose mildly.

"What about Emily?" Ned took a step backward.

"Oh, well . . . you know . . . I wouldn't blame . . . I wouldn't put it past . . . I . . ." Rose let her gaze sweep out across the dark fields. She would be gentle with Ned, as he would not perhaps have been with her if he had asked what a cheque cashed for eighty pounds had been used for and she stupid enough to tell him. Ned did not ask what Rose was insinuating; he had already studied infant Laura's physiognomy with trepidation; he watched Rose with respect, undecided on what line to take, then she said, "I should just take it a bit easy if I were you," on a closing note.

"Rose, I . . ."

"It doesn't matter all that much, does it?"

"If you are thinking what I think you are thinking . . ." Ned began.

"I think nothing," and I care less, she thought; if I was in love with Ned it would be different. "It's late," she said. "Let's go to bed." Mylo did not intrude in Ned's embrace. Rose congratulated herself. I shall yet become like Edith Malone, she thought, or Ned's aunt Flora. I have regained my balance, I should be happy.

But standing near the top of the hill in old age, looking out at the view, she remembered that she had nearly lost that balance when a much-censored letter arrived from Spain. What was left of the message read: "Stuck here playing bridge stop je n'oublierai jamais les lilas et les roses stop." Never having heard of Aragon, she had not recognised the quotation. She passed the letter to Ned, who was watching her curiously. He turned it this way and that, and guessed, "One of your guests, d'you think? Shot down and brought out along the escape route? Have you had many Free French to stay?"

"Lots."

"The address on the back is Miranda, that's a prison camp; I've heard of it, chap in my club told me. They get caught coming over the Pyrenees, put in jug, then the military attaché in Madrid sets about extracting them via Gibraltar. Did any of your visitors play bridge?"

She said, "There were several who were keen on cards."

"That would be it, then. Chap must be bored, so he writes to you." Then, "You didn't have an . . ."

"Don't be silly, Ned, I don't have affairs with the visitors. Try not to be idiotic." She had spoken quite harshly to hide the lurch her heart had made, to still its hammering, crush hope, stifle her feeling of guilt and disloyalty to Mylo, who was, she supposed, dead, must be.

How wobbly and wavery her faith had been, Rose thought in old age. Oh, the swings and roundabouts of hope.

It had been about that time, she remembered, that Ned, catching her on a low, weeping at the loss of one of Comrade's puppies, shot by a neighbour's gamekeeper hunting his pheasants, had shown his nicest side. He had telephoned the neighbour in furious rage (he could not bear to see Rose cry), threatened never to invite him to a Slepe shoot, told the crusty squire to bloody fuck off, banged down the receiver. Emily, imposing herself for an unrationed meal, had shrieked with laughter, been rounded on, told to remove herself and her bastard brat from Ned's house, to cease darkening his doors.

Ned's rages were rare and always left him afraid he had gone too far, made himself vulnerable to reprisal. He had been afraid on that occasion that Emily would repay in spiteful measure. The neighbour, from whom he would later buy a Labrador pup, would understand his outburst, condone his spleen. Not so Emily. It was fear of Emily, Rose remembered, which made Ned insist she renew her promise never to leave him and she, sorry for him, aware of Emily's hold, knowing that while keeping up his relationship with Emily he must have her to act as buffer, had promised yet again not to leave him, and she had not left him. It had been quite amusing over the years to thwart Emily and now it was Ned, dead and cremated, who had done the leaving.

FORTY-THREE

From where he sat in the Palm Court Mylo had a good view of people coming into the Ritz from Piccadilly. Each person paused to adjust from the blackout in the street to the bright lights inside the hotel. It was raining outside; people shook their umbrellas as they came in, hesitated, then dodged according to sex through the doors of the cloakrooms. Mylo watched Peregrine Pye, who had just left them, go into the men's lavatory and come out wearing a bowler hat and carrying an umbrella. As he headed out towards the street he passed Archibald Loftus coming in with his wife Flora. "I know that old buffer," Mylo said.

"Does recognising a person make you feel you are really back," asked Victoria, sitting beside him, "at last?"

"Yes, it does." What an understanding girl; he must get to know her better over dinner. It would have been easier tête-à-tête, but Picot was firmly of the party. They were celebrating their safe, though belated, return from France and Spain, had that day finished their debriefing with Pye and his cohorts; there had been no fuss over Aunt Louise. On the contrary Mylo had been congratulated. Mylo smiled at Victoria. "Have another drink?" he suggested. "Picot?"

"No thanks," said Victoria.

"*Un whisky*," said Picot. "I hear, by the way, that the Royal Automobile Club have a store of Pernod. The barman did not know what it was, all the Gaullistes try to get themselves invited there, some idiot spread the news. The indiscretion of my compatriots is appalling. The Pernod won't last two days."

"All the more reason to hurry up and end the war," said Victoria, laughing.

"Where shall we have dinner?" asked Picot. Mylo did not answer; he was watching Ned, who had come in by the Arlington Street entrance, greet Archibald and Flora. They stood blocking the hallway, heads nodding in confabulation.

"Let us start. Flora and I have our train to catch; we've managed to get sleepers, don't want to miss it." Archibald's voice carried into the Palm Court.

"All right," said Ned. "I'll leave a message with the page."

Mylo watched Ned walk towards the restaurant with the Loftuses.

"I can show you quite a passable place in Frith Street run by some Free Greeks," said Victoria. "They have a pâté which resembles liver and sometimes they have venison rumoured to come from Windsor Great Park."

"Sounds fine," said Mylo. "*Ça te convient?*"

"*Oui*," said Picot, "any food is marvellous after prison. Apparently we are persona grata with your boss, Victoria? I had never cared for him until today but now he acts as though he had absolved me of a mortal sin, makes himself agreeable, or at least tries."

"Probably playing a new game with the Free French," said Mylo, laughing. "Playing Party members against Colonel Passy's bureau."

Victoria giggled.

"They are talking of a man called Mitterand who has been over to see the General; he left last week from Dartmouth, my cousin Chantal tells me," said Picot, drinking his whisky.

"Oh," said Victoria, "you are not letting the grass grow." She turned towards Mylo. "Are you catching up on gossip, too?"

But Mylo's eyes were on Rose, who blinked as she came in from Piccadilly. She had no umbrella, her hair sparkled with rain; she had grown it longer to a pageboy cut, its ash blonde was silvery and smooth, her eyes looked dark in the strange light, darker and larger than he remembered. She bent her head, accepting the message left by Ned. She did not go into the cloakroom but walked straight on and turned right along the hall to the restaurant.

"Shall we make a move?" suggested Victoria. "I don't like getting to bed too late these days. The air raids taught me to treasure sleep, and I must get to the office early."

"But there is no raid," said Picot.

"One never knows when they will start again."

"Let's go, then." Picot stood up. "Ready, Mylo?"

"There is a person I have to contact."

Victoria stood up. "See you later, then." She walked away with Picot.

As they climbed into a taxi which had just deposited its fare at the Piccadilly entrance, Picot said, "You did not tell him the name of the restaurant. Shall I run back?"

"No," said Victoria, "it isn't necessary."

No conversational spark lit the table where the two couples sat. Talk had been desultory, continually returning to the subject of food and the dreariness of wartime menus, Archibald's recollections of gastronomic delights between the wars falling flat as a Dover sole. When he embarked on a description of a dinner at Sachers in pre-war Vienna with an aged uncle, Flora Loftus said, "Oh, Archie, do shut up," and Ned looked down his nose, wondering when these famous old gentlemen's sexual powers had waned or whether they had been carried intact into their graves. "I hope to be cremated when it's my turn," he said.

"Put it in your will, dear boy."

"Rose will remember."

The party fell silent while they finished their uninspired pudding.

"Well." Archie looked at his watch. "It's later than I thought, we must rush to catch our train. Come along, Flora, get all your things. I shall be buried to the sound of the pipes on the hillside, that's in my will, one shouldn't leave these things to chance. Flora might boggle at the expense. Come on, Flora, hurry up."

"Don't fuss." Aunt Flora none the less snatched up her gloves and bag, pushing her chair back with her ample behind. "There's plenty of time," she said. "Well, dears, it's been lovely to see you." She reached up to kiss Ned, kissed Rose also. "Pity it had to be for such a sad occasion. I wish Archie wouldn't hurry me so, he's afraid of not finding a taxi, he thinks just because he can't see them in the blackout that they aren't there."

"I'll see you get one," said Ned.

"It's raining buckets," said Archie. "One would have preferred the funeral to be in the country." He had said this at dinner but was not afraid of repetition. "But Edith said – one wonders sometimes what's got into her . . ."

"Henry lived in London latterly. He couldn't stand the house full of noisy children," said Rose. This had not been said before. "So Edith arranged the funeral in London, she thought the funeral at home would disturb the kids."

Flora pursed her mouth. "Did she actually say so?" Her eyebrows rose in shock.

"Yes," said Rose. "They have become her principal interest. She likes them better than she did George and Richard when they were little. With Henry out of the way she can concentrate on them entirely." This had not come out at dinner either.

"You should not say things like that, even if you think them," said Ned repressively.

"Even if they're true?" asked Rose pertly.

"Let's get you a taxi," said Ned to his aunt and uncle. "I have to get back to my office, there's a bit of a flap on. Look, Rose, if I give you the money, will you pay the bill?" He fumbled for his wallet.

"Of course."

"See you later, then, don't wait up." He took money from his wallet and gave it to Rose. "I may catch the night train home," she said, taking the money. "I'll remember to give you the change," she said. "Goodbye." She resumed her seat and watched Ned, Archie and Flora dwindle down the hall until they went through the revolving doors into Arlington Street.

The waiter, hovering with the bill, laid it now in front of Rose. She glanced at it perfunctorily, put money on it and sat back waiting for the man to bring change.

How sordid the table, greasy knives and forks, wine-stained glasses, crumbs, bits of food dropped off forks waved in conversation, crumpled napkins, coffee half drunk. She sipped water from her glass. They had buried Henry Malone in an immense cemetery on the outskirts of London; neither George, who was in Moscow, nor Richard, somewhere in the Indian Ocean, could be there. The rain had persisted throughout the afternoon in a race to fill the grave before the coffin was lowered into it. She had taken Edith, impatient to get back to the evacuees, to Paddington before joining Ned and the Loftuses for dinner.

The waiter brought the change. The restaurant was filling up, it was time she left, others would want the table. She calculated the tip. "There's a note for you, miss." Nobody had called her a miss for ages; she picked up the note: "Waiting for you in the Palm Court," it said.

The blood rushed up into her face, retreated, leaving her very pale. She felt sick, ridiculously weak. Under the starched white tablecloth her knees shook. She stood up. The waiter pulled back her chair, she ran. Mylo held her hands crushed in his: "You are doing your hair in a new way."

"I thought you were dead."

"What is Ned doing here? I thought he was in Cairo. I've been watching you while you had dinner."

"He was. He's in the War Office now, plotting the Second Front."

"You've grown thinner, more beautiful."

"You are thin, too, and, oh, a white hair."

"I've been in prison. I wrote – did you get . . . ?"

"I couldn't believe it was you, it was so censored, something about lilacs, I dared not . . ."

"Are you living with him?"

"He's in London during the week; we have a flat; he's home at weekends."

"Home?"

"Well, it is home."

"And your baby?"

"Fat and well, he's waddling about now."

"That's good."

"Mylo, there's . . ."

"So if I joined you and Comrade in the middle of the night, climbed up the magnolia and in at your window, I might find Ned in bed with us?"

"Sometimes."

"Not always?"

"During the week he's in London."

"With his mistress?"

"Or me . . ."

"That girl Emily?"

"Well . . ."

"Does she blackmail him?"

"Why should she? How did you guess?"

"Her child might be his."

"So it might, but I do not think so. Mylo, there's . . ."

"I love you so."

"And I love you. Mylo . . ."

"Yes?"

"We buried Henry Malone today, that's why we were all here."

"A nice old boy. I'm sorry. How is your mother?"

"So happy! She lives in London, loves every minute of life, has a stodgy lodger, they swim in the emergency water tank in her street when it's hot. And your aunt?"

"We brought her back from France."

"My God! Was she there, how terrible!"

"She was working in the Resistance. She's all right now, staying with friends. Somebody dropped a bomb on her house in Bayswater."

"Mylo?"

"Yes, darling."

"Is this really you? Go on holding my hands like that, tightly, tighter."

"I want to undress you."

"Here? Among all these people?"

"I could and would make love. Even on top of a bus."

"So could I, oh, so could I . . ."

"Does your promise to Ned still stand?"

"Yes. It does." Rose stared into Mylo's black eyes; he was so thin, there were lines now, a sharp line between his eyes. One tear swilled out of her left eye, ran down to her chin: "Oh, darling, I am so happy."

"The first time I met you I asked you to marry me. Within minutes." He touched the tear.

"You said we'd have to wait."

"So you married boring old Ned and are stuck with him and protect him and mother him and defend him from blackmail."

"Oh." How it hurt to hear this. "Oh."

"If it's not Ned's, whose is it?"

"Does it matter?"

"No."

"Secretly Ned worries but she's the spit of Emily and Nicholas. The bishop eventually baptised her; she's called Laura."

"I'm not interested. Where shall we go and fuck?"

"I was going home on the night train . . ."

"Shall I come?"

"Of course."

"What about Ned?"

"Working."

"Why are we wasting time, then, in chitchat?"

"There is so much I want to tell you . . ."

"Can't it wait?"

"I suppose it can . . ."

"Let's be on our way, then." He pulled her to her feet. "I can't really concentrate properly with people around staring."

"Comrade will be so glad to see you."

"Then I shall start believing I am really back."

FORTY-FOUR

The wind was cold at the top of the hill. She looked out across strange country. There is something daunting in a view seen for the first time, its concealments manifold, a challenge that mocks. She turned away, retraced her steps. As she walked she retraced her life.

Why had she not told Mylo, during those days and nights they spent together, about her miscarriage? It should have been easy, but for four days, while their love bubbled and boiled, frothed and spilled over, distilled into an essence of happiness, she could not risk spoiling it.

When Mylo left, she retreated into the familiar minutiae of everyday life at Slepe, drowning herself in domestic detail, relying on it for consolation until he would reappear.

He told her hardly anything of his part in the war; she accepted that he to-ed and fro-ed to France, that other lives would be risked if she talked. Ned, too, made a mystery of his work; secrecy was normal at that time. With the bulk of the population, she relied for news on a diet of newspapers and radio, remained in virtual ignorance. When, after the war, she read its history, she was amazed at what had been going on, that dull men like Ian Johnson, Ned and Harold Rhys had performed feats of courage while she and thousands like her stayed at home complaining of draughts and minor deprivations.

She had told Mylo about the miscarriage when she saw him next. He had telephoned, suggesting blithely that she drive him into Cornwall "for a job", that they picnic on the way, possibly spend the night together, that they use some of the petrol set aside for emergency. (The days when the Germans were expected to invade were long gone; the boot was now on the other foot.) Ned was in London. Rose leapt at the chance. She filled the car with petrol, packed an overnight bag, met Mylo off the train and drove off,

Comrade stood on the back seat, her head thrust through an open window, ears flapped back by the wind, a long and perfect day stretched ahead.

They drove across Devon, left Exeter behind, took the high road over Dartmoor. They were happy; there was no need to talk; sometimes they sang, pleased at the sound of their own voices. They stopped at a moorland pub for a drink, ate their sandwiches in the car near a high tor, watched Comrade chase a rabbit.

"Where are you going in Cornwall?"

"Newlyn. We could spend the night in Penzance. I may find I have to go on to the Scillies."

"Why?" she had asked stupidly. "Whatever for?"

"To catch my boat."

"A boat? You didn't tell me you were off again – you said a job. A boat?"

"'Fraid so."

Taken by surprise she had heard herself whine, "I don't want you to go."

"Don't be silly, darling. It's my job."

"Must you? I shall never get used to this constant wrenching apart."

"I must."

"Can't somebody else go?"

He had said harshly, "Shut up, don't spoil our day. If I'd thought you would be difficult, make a scene, I wouldn't have suggested this outing. I thought it would be wonderful to be with you. I was supposed to go down by train anyway, not joyride with a girl."

"If you want to go by train, I can drop you at the station at Plymouth," she had said acidly, "and go home."

They had glared at each other, fearing and hating each other and what they did. She remembered screwing the top of the Thermos on so hard she had difficulty in getting it off later. Mylo had walked away from her. When she looked after him he was urinating in the bracken. She packed the picnic basket, called Comrade sharply, sat waiting for him in the car with the collar of her coat turned up. When he rejoined her she slammed the car into gear and drove on. Neither of them spoke for some miles.

When the road forked and turned south to Plymouth, she asked neutrally, "Plymouth, then?"

Mylo said, "Not unless you want it that way."

"I don't." She drove on west through Tavistock. After some more miles they both spoke at once, saying, "I'm sorry." Laughter eased their gloom slightly.

Going over Bodmin Moor, Mylo said, "I'm sorry I was so short. I was told some lousy news yesterday."

"What?"

"Victoria. You know, the girl in Pye's office?"

"What about her?" She remembered Victoria's disturbing eyes all too well.

"She got news that both her fiancé and her brother have been killed."

"On the same day?"

"The news was on the same day. They were both in submarines. No great future in them."

"Oh, poor girl . . ."

"It casts a cloud. She's such a splendid girl."

A splendid girl, a splendid girl, a splendid . . .

"Is there anything one can do?" she said.

"You could ask her down for the weekend or something, if your house isn't too full."

"I'll ask her to dinner next time I'm in London." (I could not bear those eyes at Slepe.)

"She'd probably like that," he said.

"Is she fond of that French friend of yours?"

"Picot?"

"Yes."

"She's not keen on him. I believe he made a pass and got rebuffed . . ."

How ungenerous I am, she had thought. "What a horrible war this is," she had exclaimed.

"But today is not horrible, is it? We haven't spoiled it insuperably, have we?"

"No, no."

But it was spoiled. Victoria's sorrow intruded on their day and as she drove over the rise and could see Mount's Bay she matched Victoria's grief with her own, told Mylo about her miscarriage.

What a time to choose; Mylo had gone quite green.

That night they lay in an hotel bed clutching each other, unable to sleep, unable to comfort, unable to make love. In the morning she had driven him to Newlyn. "Wait a moment," he had said. He had gone through the gate on to the quay, returned carrying a box of live lobsters and crawfish. "Take these home with you. They are off a Belgian boat." He put the box on the back seat with Comrade who sniffed, recoiled, jumped into the front of the car in alarm. "Go now, darling, don't look back." He had taken her face between his hands and kissed her fast – eyes, nose, forehead, mouth. "Go, go, go."

Walking back down the hill by the way she had come Rose remembered those kisses, his hands salty from the box of lobsters, his mouth salt from her tears. She had driven as far as Truro before noticing where she was; for the rest of the drive she tormented herself with visions of Mylo crossing to France on a trawler or a submarine or a motor-torpedo boat; getting drowned, shot, disappearing for ever.

Ned had been at Slepe when she got back. "Where the hell have you been?" he had shouted. "Where have you put my corkscrew? I can't find it. I've a bottle of decent wine and I can't find . . ."

"It's there, under your nose," she had said and it had been there under his nose, giving her a shot of one-upmanship (what silly things one remembers) and "Lobsters for dinner," she had said. Ned, seeing the lobsters and hearing where she had been and how much petrol she had used, had said admiringly, "You must be out of your tiny mind."

After the invasion of Normandy a year later, she lay in Mylo's arms in a small flat he had been lent in Chelsea. A new and sinister noise disturbed their copulation. They stood on the balcony and watched the first V1 rocket doodling its noisy way across London to explode in Harrow.

That summer of 1944 he brought her Aragon's poems from Paris, told of the explosion of talent from people bottled up under the Germans, talked to her of Sartre and Anouilh. Growing restless in the country she came often to London, drawn by the fear and excitement of the bombing, the feeling that the end of the war was in sight, the need to walk recklessly on the broken glass in the gutters. Then Mylo was off again, to northern Italy she was to learn later, where he spent the winter with the Partisans and she, with no news of him, grew melancholy, pacing in the park with Comrade where German prisoners of war swept the dead leaves of the plane trees in a grey drizzle, in their grey uniforms, with long grey sweeps of their reluctant brooms, watched by indifferent guards while the wet heavy air pressed the smoke of aromatic bonfires down to nose level.

She went back to Slepe for the coldest winter of the war yet, where she was for once without visitors, they naturally preferring warmer London. Ned, who was by this time in France, complained of the cold, wrote frequently asking for comforts from Fortnum's, cigars and coffee. He gloried in his staff job, his authority and the power he dared not use as he was unable to sort collaborator from Resistance fighter when working with the French. He could not speak the language. He was happily moved to Paris to liaise with the Americans, among whom he made contacts useful to him later in peacetime business.

At Slepe the pipes froze. Rose fetched drinking and cooking water from a well; Christopher caught measles, Farthing slipped on ice and broke his leg, Edwina fell ill with shingles, and Emily, sensing that she might be asked to come and help, dumped Laura at Slepe ("It would be a good thing if she could get measles, save an awful lot of trouble later") and moved to London to live with an American colonel who had a centrally heated flat off Grosvenor Square. Nicholas sulked, closed the Rectory and moved into a pub close to the Min. of Ag.

Struggling with the children, the farm, the shortages and the cold, Rose should have had little energy to pine for Mylo, yet still she watched for the postman, ran whenever the telephone rang, dreamed of a time when worries would evaporate and they would be together.

It was during that horrible winter, Rose remembered as she retraced her steps downhill, that Ned, coming home on leave, extracted yet another renewal of her promise. Finding *Horizon* and the *New Statesman* in the house he accused her of having a "Pinko lover". She would not, he reasoned, have discovered such reading matter for herself, thus insulting her intelligence. "It will be that bugger J. P. Sartre next or the cad Kafka . . ." He had raised his voice (he had not in fact said the cad Kafka, Rose added it later to make a better story), made a scene in front of Christopher and Laura. There had been other indications of infidelity listed but Rose forgot them. She remembered, though, doing something she had never thought to do: she hit Ned, made his nose bleed. Poor Ned. She realised later that he was shaken by Emily's deviation from her norm of availability and infected by a malaise rife among his associates who, returning from the war, found their marriage ties loosened, in some cases bust. While applying ice to his nose she had apologised; by hitting him she was diminished, weakened, more closely tied to him and he, putting his arms around her, had said, "Of course you have no lover. How could I suggest such a thing? You are not that sort of girl. You promised never to leave me; to suggest you sleep around is idiotic. A girl like you would not dream of it."

Instead of being uplifted by Ned's estimate she had been irritated. What did he know of her dreams? Did he take her for gormless, dreamless? (In this mood of irritation, having run out of clothes coupons, she helped herself to his dinner jacket suit and had it cut down by her own tailor into a coat and skirt which she wore with white hat and blouse at George Malone's wedding and later at Richard's.) That she was too meek to be suspect rankled, put ideas into her head which had not been there before, ideas which she was later to put into effect.

Remembering that period, Rose chuckled as she walked downhill. The wind was freshening, stirring the treetops, making her eyes water. In tandem with her irritation she had developed a fondness for Ned and he for his part stopped his nervous requests that she renew the promise. She reviewed life as it might be without him and shied away.

About that time Emily parted with her American colonel, returned to live with Nicholas. Thinking about it in old age, Rose wondered whether her decision to grow up, shut up and stick to Ned was arrived at partly to thwart Emily taking over her husband and home (the idea was there in Emily's mind; one could not be certain whether, given the chance, she would have acted upon it) or had she been daunted, just as minutes ago she had turned away from the unknown, retraced her steps to the known path she had climbed that morning rather than explore new country?

Dogs in the manger are presumably lying comfortably.

FORTY-FIVE

Leaving the open ground Rose re-entered the wood, treading now on beech mast which split crisply under her shoes. Often in woods similar to this she had stood with Ned whistling, then listening for the sound of Comrade hunting with her pup, for the betraying yelp which would signal their whereabouts, their ineffectual effort to capture rabbit, fox or badger. Ned, his patience matched by his admirable Labrador's, would stand beside her. "They will find their way home," he would say. "They always do."

"They may get trapped or shot," she would answer. Never once did Ned say, "Serve them right, if they do," although he must have felt it. She remembered his tolerance; her dogs were always naughty, his well behaved.

It was easier to remember the Ned of the early days of marriage than of later years. Her memory of him in youth was much clearer than that of the middle past when time concertinaed into old age until finally death reduced him to ash, releasing her from her promise.

She could see him on those occasions when at last she found her dogs. He would grin, take off his glasses, polish them with his handkerchief, ask, "Satisfied now?" and they would walk home to an enjoyable tea by the fire with Christopher. But if Laura had come to spend the day, to be fetched by Emily at dinnertime, Ned would watch Laura uneasily, hasten when Emily arrived to offer her a drink, help himself to whisky to keep her company, chatter, laugh a particular laugh, glance towards Rose for reassurance. It was years before Ned was convinced she would not allow him to be gobbled up by Emily.

For her part Emily was content with the role of part-time mistress, that was what she enjoyed. If she extracted the occasional hand-out towards Laura's upkeep, Ned could afford it. Rose knew about it, nobody suffered. When the time came for Cheltenham Ladies' College fees and Ned moaned, he received no sympathy. Rose never fully believed Laura to be Ned's child, At first Ned fostered the myth himself, partly from guilty panic, partly from a liking to be thought a bit of a dog. But, Oh my, thought Rose as she threaded her way through the trees, that promise still meant something in 1948.

Halfway through dinner with Harold Rhys and his new wife and her mother who was visiting for the weekend, Edwina Farthing put her head round the door and said, "The pup's back," but there was no sign of Comrade. Two days later the water bailiff found Comrade where she had become entangled in brambles at the river's edge, been trapped and, when the water rose in flood, drowned. Fond of Rose, the bailiff brought Comrade's body himself, stood awkwardly watching her white face while Ned thanked him for his trouble, offered him a drink. When the telephone rang Rose picked up the receiver, said, "Hullo?"

Mylo asked from long distance, "Does that bloody promise you made to Ned still hold?" And she, watching Ned standing a yard away, said, "Yes, it bloody does."

"That's it, then." Mylo rang off abruptly and she, she remembered as she walked, had broken into terrible weeping. Ned had been kind. He had not offered to buy her a pedigree dog, he had continued to put up with the puppy, and later the puppy's puppy. If he thought her grief exaggerated, he did not say so. He presently took her on trips to Bath and Edinburgh (the exchange control precluding travel abroad), to theatres in London. He stopped quibbling about the expense and installed central heating. He sold his London flat which Rose had always rather looked on as Emily's preserve, and together they chose a cheerful little house in South Kensington which was to be their London base, a London home for Christopher as he grew up. For more than a year he hardly saw Emily. And I, thought Rose looking back, was grateful; I put away thoughts of Mylo; it was as though with Comrade's drowning love for Mylo waned. When a year later she heard by chance from Richard Malone that Mylo had married Victoria, she too said, "That's that, then."

What a lot Emily contributed to the keeping of that promise, thought Rose, treading carefully now down the steep hill; it was a triumph that to this day she was unaware of her hold. But she was not alone; Mrs Freeling also fuelled Ned's discomfort, kept Rose determined to defend him.

While Christopher was an infant and for as long as he looked in any way baby-like, Mrs Freeling eyed her grandchild with distaste. Any baby reminded her of the horrors of procreation and child-bearing she was persuaded she had suffered. But when Christopher grew into what she termed a human being she enjoyed her status of grandparent and looked on Ned with a kindly eye. "Christopher is exactly like his father," she would say. "One can see he takes after you, Ned, he has your eyes, your nose. I can see nothing of Rose in him," and Ned would preen. By contrast when Laura was at Slepe, which she constantly was, playing or fighting with Christopher, Mrs Freeling would stare at the child, draw her son-in-law's attention to her: "Look at little Laura, one would hardly credit that child had a father. She's exactly like her mother, has no resemblance to anyone but Emily, Nicholas of course, but he is Emily's twin. It's odd, don't you think, Ned? Children take after their fathers; Christopher looks like you; Rose looks like her father."

"That's your theory," Rose would say.

"It's a fact." Mrs Freeling clung to her opinion. "I'd say that child might not have had a father. What do you think, Ned?"

(Did she or did she not do this on purpose? Surely she was not clever enough to invent such a tease?) And Ned would flush, say, "Ah, well – I don't know," try and change the subject, while Rose, aware of his distress, suggested an immaculate conception or on one occasion, "Perhaps Emily siphoned up someone's spunk in the bath," disgusting her mother, earning a scandalised but grateful glance from Ned. ("You went too far there, dear." He was never cured of the word "dear".) And Laura, who liked being discussed, would stand close to Ned staring up at him with her mother's bright and wicked eyes. Then Ned, his guilt fuelled by his mother-in-law, would soon be reminding Rose of her promise, if not outright, by hints. Small wonder, thought Rose, descending the hill, that there were no false pretences when Mother died. But let me be honest now, thought Rose grimly, while to thwart Emily was fun, a good motive in its way, that wasn't what kept me with Ned all those years. His insecurity was matched by my need for security.

FORTY-SIX

At the Festival of Britain in 1951, early for a rendezvous with Ned and Christopher up for the day from his prep school, Rose watched the crowds enjoying the gaiety, the atmosphere of optimism. Coming up behind her Mylo said, "Why did you hang up on me three years ago?"

Rose span round: "It was you who hung up. *Why* did you marry Victoria?"

"Because we hung up, perhaps . . ."

"Ned was beside me. I had just heard Comrade was dead, she was drowned, her body . . ."

"Our little friend! So that was it!"

"You need not have rushed off and married Victoria . . ."

"There was no exact rush. You were stuck with Ned, and your child, living in that house. You love that house, I know you do. Getting used to it all. It seemed the thing to do. You didn't expect me to hang around indefinitely." (She had.)

She searched his face: "You have several new lines, more grey hairs."

"I see birds' feet . . . Your eyes . . ."

"Oh, Mylo."

"I love you."

"I am meeting Ned and Christopher for lunch."

"How are they?" He grinned at her.

"Very well. Ned and Christopher have been to the dentist, we are meeting here."

"I love you, darling." He did not bother to lower his voice.

"Have you any children?" She fended him off.

"Victoria has a daughter."

"A daughter. How lovely for you." She stiffened.

"She's not mine . . ."

"Oh."

"She's Picot's."

"But she didn't *like* Picot."

"*You* didn't like Ned."

"What a stickler you are for truth."

"No need to be bitter."

"Is that why you married Victoria?"

Mylo said, "Cut the lunch. Come and spend the afternoon with me. Please."

"If I did . . ."

"I haven't changed and nor have you. I want to hold you . . . come on, just a little fuck for old time's sake."

Weakening, Rose giggled. "What about Victoria?"

"What about Ned?"

"It wouldn't help. It would only make things worse." She fumbled for her resolve.

"Are things bad, then?"

"No, no, of course not. I've got everything I . . ."

"Except me."

"Except you."

"We used to think having each other would be enough for eternity . . ."

"There they are, I can see Ned and Christopher."

"Nice-looking boy."

"Victoria has lovely eyes."

"Yes."

"Mylo . . ."

"Yes?"

"Don't touch me."

"All right, I won't."

"Thank you." She felt desolate.

"Perhaps you would explode if I touched you."

"Yes, I would."

"Good. Some day I will telephone and you will come."

"Here they are . . ."

"Who was that you were talking to, Ma?" asked Christopher.

"Um . . . he's called . . . I think he's called, er . . ."

"I've booked a table." Ned pecked her cheek, took her arm. "All the restaurants are terribly crowded, we don't want to lose it, come on." (If Mylo had touched me, I would have gone with him.)

"Yes, yes, I'm coming. How sensible to book a table." They started walking. Mylo was nowhere to be seen.

"What does that man do, Ma? Where does he live?"

"I don't know, darling. What part of the Exhibition do you want to see?"

"I'd really rather go to the Fun Fair. Who was he, Ma?"

"Who was who?"

"That man . . ."

"I don't know."

"How funny, it looked as though you knew him well."

"Well, I don't." (I don't know where he lives or what he does, only that he's with Victoria. Those eyes!) "He was only asking me something I don't know the answer to."

"This is such an easy place to get lost," said Ned. "This way, I think, ah, here we are, here's the restaurant. I hope they've kept our table. In spite of the signposts."

"Like life, any number of signposts, yet one still gets lost," she had said lightly. Ned had laughed, called her a philosopher. "You didn't know your mother was a philosopher, did you?" He was so proud of Christopher in those days; his fury came later during Christopher's adolescence and later still during the era of long hair and screwball jeans.

She had sat at the table, picked up the menu, while Christopher switched his curiosity to the food. He lost his precocious inquisitiveness as he grew up, growing into the incurious man he was today. If he'd kept it, thought Rose, he might not have married Helen.

She came out of the wood, stepping on to the footpath along the creek. She remembered with a pang how fast her heart had beat as she looked at Mylo that day, how she had felt sick with desire.

I feel sick with desire now just thinking of him. At my age! I've had no breakfast, perhaps I am confusing my hungers. She stood staring at the still water and across the water to the trees on the far side.

FORTY-SEVEN

A few years later, travelling up Knightsbridge on a bus, she had looked down on Mylo walking with Victoria. As she craned her neck to get a better view of him he burst out laughing at something Victoria said and took her arm. The pain she felt was out of all proportion.

In an effort to blot him from her mind she experimented with lovers. If other men could give her enjoyable orgasms, she argued, it would cauterise her pain. Long ago Mylo had suggested that whereas the act of sex with him would be sublime, with Ned or others it would be quite otherwise. She decided she would prove his arrogance wrong.

She had been circumspect, mindful of Ned, not wishing to hurt his feelings, discreet and secret, wary of Emily and Nicholas. She experimented over a period of several years with different types of men. She tried quite hard.

Standing on the path looking across the still water of the creek she remembered ruefully that all that she had learned from these experimental efforts was that the act of sex so joyous with Mylo (tolerable with Ned) became something rather messy, the postures ridiculous if not obscene, at best laughable. "These calculated adventures must cease," she remembered thinking; she could not even recapture the frivolous charm of the tonic brush with George Malone. "I am sorry," she had said to her current experiment, "but there it is."

"But you slept with me last Wednesday," he had complained. He had been angry when she said, "Not this Wednesday, it's early closing." Not finding her feeble joke amusing he cut her for ever after at parties or in the street.

Hurrying along in the rain one day, head down, she bumped into a man walking the other way. "Sorry," she apologised.

"I am not." The man put his arms around her. She recognised Mylo. "Where are you going in such a rush?" He held on to her.

"I was leaving a lover." (This was not the case.)

If she had hoped for a rise, she did not get it.

"Come along in here." Mylo kept hold of her, led her into the lobby of an hotel, made her sit on a sofa. "I saw you belting along the street, waited for you, you walked into me as if I wasn't there."

"You are *not* there," she had said angrily, "*ever.*"

"I am at the moment, darling."

"What?" (I can't bear this, she had thought, I can't.)

"I *am* here, Rose, *now*. What's the matter?"

"I told you. I have just left a lover. I'm late."

He had laughed. "So now we have lovers."

"Yes," she snapped.

"Is it enjoyable?" Amused and teasing, he made her turn to look at him.

"It's terribly boring," she had burst out and Mylo said, "I am glad to hear it." As he examined her face, "You are looking very beautiful," he said. "I like it when your face is wet from the rain."

"Actually I was hurrying because I came out without an umbrella," she admitted.

"You hadn't just left a lover?"

"No."

"Thought not." He held her hands. "You don't lie very well."

"I did have lovers . . ."

"Why?" His voice had been harsh. "Why?"

"Victoria." She whispered the name defensively, then repeated it louder, "Victoria."

"And what about Ned?"

"Ned doesn't know I . . ."

"You know what I mean, Rose, don't prevaricate, what do you imagine I feel about Ned?"

"It's not the same for men."

"A stupid remark not worthy of your intelligence."

"You are hurting my hands." But she had not drawn them away.

"You know I married Victoria because of her child."

"You never said so," she had said huffily.

"You did not give me much opportunity."

"I saw you with her from the top of a bus. You were laughing," she accused.

"Laughing's not a sin."

"And you love her."

"Who said so? Yes, I love her in a way."

"There you are, then." The pain of meeting him made her sulky.

"And Ned?"

"We are friends." Did she at that time admit to herself the love of security?

Mylo murmured, "M-m-m-m friendship, yes."

They had sat there on the sofa in the hotel lobby turning towards each other, her hands in his, searching each other's face, oblivious of people coming and going, bringing a whiff of petrol-fumed rain from the street, muffling into their scented furs as they ventured out. Standing now on the muddy path by the water's edge Rose could remember the smell of the leather sofa. Mylo had asked very gently, "What else?"

She had whispered, leaning towards him, "I cannot bear to think of your cock inside Victoria." And he, still holding her hands, had leaned forward and kissed her mouth. "That won't get us anywhere." She had tried to draw away but he held on to her hands.

After a while he had said, "Listen, darling. It would be better for both of us if we could meet sometimes. We need not make love if it . . .well . . .no, wait, let me speak . . .we can be more normal . . ."

"What's normal, for Christ's sake?" she had exclaimed in anguish.

"Lovers can be friends, my darling. I am not here often. I live in France. If we met occasionally it might stop us tearing each other apart like this . . ."

"*I'm* not torn!"

"Rose, stop it, listen to me. We could lunch together sometimes, go for a walk, visit a gallery, how about it?"

"I don't know." She had been afraid then, tempted.

"Lovers should be friends, too. You know that as well as I do. We have mutual interests. We could discuss books, films, plays. What do you say? Give it a try? Pretend we are civilised?"

"I . . ." Still she feared the unbearable.

"You could tell me about your child, your garden, your cows."

"I have no cows. Ned switched to sheep . . ."

"Those lovely cows . . ."

"Well, it's his farm" – she defended Ned – "not mine."

"Yes, of course, but why should we not talk about it? Your dogs, for instance?"

"I have Comrade's descendants."

"There you are, a safe subject for discussion, there must be others. Give it a try?"

"You are wheedling me."

"I am."

"Won't it hurt?"

"Not as much as never seeing, never knowing . . ."

"So you mind, too?"

"Idiot, you bloody idiot," he yelled at her.

"Darling!" How her spirits had soared.

"Can't get you out of my system. Don't want to, don't even try." (People had stared, looked away.)

"I have tried," she admitted.

"Wasted effort, wasn't it? Waste of lovers. I could machine-gun the lot." This rang true.

"There were not enough for a machine-gun . . ."

"So . . ."

"We should see a bit of sense at our age." She had given in, reaching for the freaky lifebelt of good sense.

"Not always to be trusted, too much sense got you into your fool promise to Ned."

"And your marriage to Victoria."

"Enough." He pulled her to her feet and holding her close kissed her. "Eyes, nose, mouth," he muttered as if renewing acquaintance. "I mind very much that Ned . . ."

"What?"

"What you said about Victoria applies also to Ned."

"Ned mostly goes up Emily Thornby."

"Such coarse words to pass these lips." He kissed her again. "And what about those lovers?" he asked jealously.

"Over. My heart wasn't in it," she said smugly.

"So if I telephone . . ."

"Yes, yes, yes."

"We shall have each to treat the other with care . . ."

"That goes without saying."

"It won't be often, alas . . ."

"It will have to do . . ."

"Resigned?"

"I shall never be resigned."

"Nor I."

As they walked out into the rain she said, excusing her pusillanimity, "I feel I must protect Ned, and there is Christopher."

"And I," said Mylo opening his umbrella, "have to protect Victoria and Alice."

"That's that, then."

"Yes." They stood on the pavement unwilling to part. "So we won't ever turn into one of those awful old couples who hate each other like my pa and ma?"

"I dare say we won't."

"So it's looking on the bright side, is it?"

"Yes."

FORTY-EIGHT

So they met at intervals over the years. Of a generation used to the concept of rationing (food, clothes, petrol), they spaced their joy. In the nature of things each meeting held potential disaster, it being dangerously easy for either of them to feel jealous or possessive, resentful even. They walked a knife-edge, teetering as they nursed a passion, which could so easily have died as an adolescent obsession, into a love conjoint with friendship.

With trepidation they learned to speak of Ned without resentment, of Victoria without fear. Discussing Christopher and his friends or Alice and hers brought the alternative partner into the conversation at a neutral level. But chiefly they discussed books, plays, films. While Rose felt passionately about politics, expressing fury and despair at the lies, hypocrisies and evasions of governments, Mylo distanced himself as his father had and made Rose laugh at her own righteousness. If she had been on holiday with Ned to France, Greece or Italy, she did not tell Mylo how she had longed to be with him instead of Ned, and Mylo took care not to say, "Oh, but you should have seen . . ." or "When I went there with Victoria . . .". She told him about Christopher as he grew up into a mirror image of Ned, to be finally yanked from her orbit into yuppydom by Helen. She talked about her garden, her dogs and cats, her neighbours. And Mylo talked of his work, a freelance like his father, of his interest in abstruse European writers, teasing her into reading Julien Benda, Teilhard de Chardin and Michael Polanyi so that she could keep up with what he was talking about.

When her mother died he comforted her for not having loved her, understood the little problem of the ashes. When Edith Malone died they regretted her passing, reminisced about the winter tennis. When in 1956 during the Suez Crisis petrol was rationed once again and Ned, remembering his wartime hoard, found all the jerrycans empty, they shared nostalgic recollection of their wartime drives. Mylo, asking where all the petrol had gone, for they could not have used up all those gallons, was amused when she confessed to using them over a period when Ned was being parsimonious with housekeeping money, buying instead of petrol plants for her garden. She did not tell him of the scene Ned had made or the wounding things he had said, nor that he had gone off to Paris for an extravagant fortnight with Emily. In her efforts to be fair to Ned, Rose made herself feel quite sick, but she would persist as long as Mylo stayed loyal to Victoria.

Those meetings over the years, two at most a year, often less, were always hard to contrive. Twice she was ill and could not meet him; once she was away with Ned, staying with his relations in Scotland, when Mylo telephoned and they did not see each other for eighteen months. For some reason they never discussed, they never wrote letters, fearing, perhaps rightly, the easy betrayal of the written word.

Always when Mylo telephoned, Rose nearly choked with joy, having superstitiously feared that their previous meeting was the last. While they battled for continuity there was never any certainty, she never felt secure. So when one day in 1960 sitting at a corner table in a restaurant Mylo put his hand over hers and said, "Rose," she was instantly alert.

"What is it?"

"There is a plan – a job in the States."

"And Victoria wants to go?"

"No, she doesn't particularly."

"You want to go?"

"In a way."

"Don't let me stop you."

"Rose . . ."

"You want to go. What's the job?"

"Lecturing, teaching, an interesting university, it's . . ."

"Go on, go. Why on earth not? What's to stop you?" She had controlled her voice while her stomach churned in alarm. "Have a great time, make a lot of money . . ."

"Don't be like that."

She withdrew her hand: "They haven't worked, these civilised meetings, have they?"

"I can't do with half a cake . . ."

"It was your suggestion."

"A bloody stupid one."

"All this popping in and out of my life like a jack-in-the-box doesn't amuse you, then." The finality refused to sink in.

"You never look for *me*."

"No, I don't. Why should I? I've got my life, quite a busy one as it happens. I have Ned, it's my choice, I abide by it. You have Victoria; about time she was considered, isn't it? Time we grew up."

Mylo had riposted, she had struck again.

My word, thought Rose, standing on the bank by the creek

watching the breeze riffle the water, how we hurt each other that day, how we let rip, how well each knew how to wound the other. It was suicide. They had parted leaving the wounds raw. They had not even said goodbye. Split.

It had been a fight to come to terms with her loss. She had become quite ill, grown thin and snappy. When Ned, worried, took her to a specialist he said it was not the menopause, although she was of that age, suggested a psychiatrist. Refusing a shrink, Rose set herself tasks which she called fresh interests. She made a new lily border in the garden, planted more magnolias, took on voluntary work in the neighbourhood, tried hard to like her daughter-in-law, behaved, as Nicholas remarked, like a widow. "Anything wrong, Rose dear? You are behaving like a widow."

"I am easing myself into a role I may never have to play," she had replied, "so that, should the need arise, I can enjoy it." Then she found that she was enjoying her role, was being nicer than she had ever been to Ned, that people came from far and wide to admire the garden. The only failure was her lack of enthusiasm for Helen. Helen's fault, thought Rose, watching a pair of swans cruising up towards her. She should have suppressed her longing for dead men's shoes; one did not have to be a mind reader to know what Helen intended doing to Slepe once she got her hands on it. Well, thought Rose, she's got it now but if she had not annoyed me so I would not have looked after Ned so well, she would have got it years sooner and I, unbraced by my dislike of her, might have moped into a decline, not considered myself cured of Mylo.

So what had she felt when, picking up the telephone nine years later, Mylo's voice said, "I have tickets for Venice tomorrow, pack your bag." She had felt she had come alive again.

"Are you still grumpy?" he had asked.

"I . . ."

"To be honest with you, all those civilised meetings drove me mad, darling. I was like a randy dog."

"And now?"

"Randier than ever."

"What time's our flight?"

FORTY-NINE

The subtle smell of warm drains. St Mark's Square at two in the morning, empty by the light of the moon. Wandering along the narrow alleys. Quizzing the peeling stucco. Leaning over bridges to read each the other's face reflected in the murky water. Mylo's hair grey now, beginning to recede, his face thin and lined. Hers, eyes deep-socketed in reflection, pale (she had had no sun that summer), hair dusty wheat-coloured.

They had leaned towards the water, their reflections joggled into one by passing barges carrying vegetables to the markets. They had sat speaking sparsely, eating prosciutto with figs, large plates of pasta, drinking cold wine at tables by the canals, light dappling their faces. Wandered on to drink bitter espressos near the Accademia. They had swum lazily from the Lido in water soupy with sand and Lord knows what else; they had lain nights rediscovering each other's bodies in a state of happiness neither dared remark on so perfect was it, so tender, such fun.

They were too wise to say, "If we never have anything else ever again, we shall have had this." When strolling along a small canal they heard through the shutters of a room high above the water Paul McCartney sing, "Will you still love me/ Will you still need me/ When I'm sixty-four?" Too wise to catch each other's eye. Too wise when they parted to make arrangements to meet again.

We got it right that time, Rose said out loud to the swans paddling past, their wings cupped over their backs. Stooping she picked a pebble from the path, threw it, broke her single reflection.

FIFTY

Then they exchanged the occasional cautious letter. Just to keep in touch, he said, writing to congratulate her on Christopher's marriage, an event he had learned from a casual meeting with George Malone in New York. "I hope she is a nice girl, that she will make him happy. I remember him in his Moses basket on the back seat of your car with Comrade. You stopped the car to suckle him. Alice, Victoria's daughter, has two children. I don't much care for babies," he wrote.

"Would you have cared for ours?" she wrote on a postcard which she tore up on the way to the post. (Many of the letters she wrote him got torn before posting.) She wrote instead a scrawled sheet enclosed in an envelope, "She is not a nice girl, but she will make Christopher happy." It seemed of paramount importance to be honest, not to pretend to him as she did with the rest of the world that she liked Helen.

Over the years Alice, Victoria's child by Picot, aged twenty-five at the time of the Venetian meeting, played the part of invisible go-between. "How is Alice?" Rose would inquire and news came back that Alice and her family were spending the summer at Cape Cod or, the year that Picot, rich, growing elderly, retired now from his post in Monsieur Pompidou's government, had finally acknowledged parenthood and settled a lump sum on Alice, they, this included Mylo and Victoria, spent part of the summer in the Ardèche. (Not a great success. Picot needed help with his memoirs which Mylo had not been willing to give.) Rose tried to imagine Alice, searched between the lines of information about Alice and her family for Mylo hiding like a sea anemone in the weeds of his stepdaughter's mundane life. Alice was helpful when Victoria was away (where?) and Mylo had jaundice./ Alice had done some useful research for him. What research?/ She kept her mother company while he was in Peru. What was he doing in Peru?/ She was helpful when they moved house. Where to? Where from?

Rose sent her sparse letters c/o Mylo's publishers, distancing herself deliberately. So, sparingly they wrote but did not meet; several times she suspected that he had spent time in England, not made contact. The years flew on or dragged by, according to mood and state of health. When she thought of it, reminded perhaps by a tone of voice in a crowd, a whiff of drains, Rose congratulated herself that their love had ended on such a high, not dwindled as most loves do into habit. "Shall we go to Venice this year? You've never been to Venice," Ned once asked.

"I don't think I could bear the smell. Why don't you get Emily and Nicholas to go with you?" Would Ned admit that he had already been twice with Emily alone?

"I find Nicholas rather trying in large doses. One used to get Emily to oneself – not any more," he answered grumpily. He knew that she knew all about Emily.

"Yes. She cleaves to Nicholas more than ever. Poor you."

Ned said, "What? Can't hear you. Wish you'd speak up, not mumble."

Virtuously Rose held back the words often shouted these days by Harold Rhys and Ian Johnson's wives, "You're getting deaf." *Unberufen*, as Nicholas would have said during the 1939–45 war, that she should grow like those boring old women.

"About time we invited what's-his-name, oh, Arthur and Milly, to dinner," said Ned, dredging round for substitute company.

"All right, if that's what you'd like. I'll ring them up." I must not allow myself to be beastly to Ned.

The note on the hall table in the cleaning lady's script (the Farthings were long since retired, living in a granny flat in the erstwhile evacuees' house) said, "A Mr Cooper will be waiting for you on platform one, Paddington Station, midday – 12 o'clock tomorrow."

When the train pulled in he was sitting on a luggage trolley waiting for her. "I need to talk to you." He put both arms around her, kissed her mouth. "That's better."

"What has happened to you?" He looked terrible.

"Perhaps we could walk in the Park, or is it too cold for you?"

"No, no." She walked beside him to the taxi queue. He looked gaunt, she thought. He has lost weight, his hair more white than grey now.

"Lovely cockatoos!" His face lit up as they passed a group of punks with rainbow hair and painted faces. "In Molière's day it was the women who did that, they were known as *Les Précieuses Ridicules*. Here's a taxi, jump in."

In the taxi he sat looking straight ahead, he held her hand. "Thank you for coming," he said.

They walked under bare February trees in the east wind. "Shall we sit for a while?" They sat on a bench and looked across the grass to the wintry Serpentine. A group of children bounced along the Row on plump ponies.

"Loosen that curb rein, Samantha, don't tug his mouth," shouted the riding instructor.

"How is Ned?" asked Mylo.

"Well. Getting a bit worn. He's over seventy, gone a bit deaf, trouble with his teeth. That sort of thing, otherwise . . ."

"Victoria died," said Mylo quietly.

"Died?" Those lovely eyes.

"It took a very long time." His cheeks were deeply furrowed, what she could see of the stubble mostly white.

"Oh, dear God. Cancer?"

"Yes."

"What can I say?"

"Nothing. Shall we walk for a bit? You mustn't get cold."

"When was it?"

"Nearly a year ago. It's terribly unfair. She never hurt anybody. It took such a bloody long time. She was in such pain. I kept wishing I had the nerve to kill her. She asked me to kill her, she asked me to ask the doctors – I even got the drugs, bought them from a junkie. Alice, her daughter, was being marvellous – you know how they are? Kept on at the doctors to try this, try that . . . It's grotesque what the marvels of modern science come up with to prolong suffering, keep 'em alive. Who enjoys that life? Certainly not Victoria."

"No, no, no, she had such wonderful eyes."

"Yes, weren't they? Wonderful eyes in a plain face. Used to remind me of Comrade."

"So that's why . . ."

"I married her? It may have played a part. You are cold." He took her hands and rubbed them between his. "Haven't you got any gloves?"

"I was in a hurry."

"The shameful thing was that all those months . . . I am so glad to see you, darling . . . the terrible thing was that all the time Victoria was dying I kept thanking God it wasn't you."

Rose stared at him.

"One can't control those obscene and shabby thoughts. Then, too, I had the drugs. I had the drugs without the nerve to administer them.

I should have made the opportunity but there was this – it was not you dying, you see, so I lacked the urgency, the whatever it takes, I just couldn't – anyway, I didn't."

"No."

"Are you glad she's dead, darling?" (Gently.)

"No, oh, no."

"Nor am I, except that her pain is over." He stopped his stride, bent to kiss her. "Are these tears?"

"The wind. The east wind."

"M-m-m. Shall we walk on? We don't need to catch pneumonia. D'you know my Aunt Louise caught pneumonia almost immediately I got her back to England and died? Really, sometimes one wonders – I had to tell you about Victoria, needed to."

"Thank you."

"Then there's Ned. What will you think when he dies? Probably you won't know what to think. There's so little emotion left after a prolonged . . . do forgive me boring on like this . . . then there's your promise never to leave him. What could have been more idiotic? Do you truly believe you stayed with him because of that? Of course you don't. I don't. I think you did promise. I've always accepted that, and it's been useful."

"You think I chose cake?"

"Does it matter now?"

"What are you going to do?"

"Oh, I've been commissioned to write a book about Thailand. I fly off tomorrow."

"It will be nice and warm there," she said sadly.

Mylo did not answer. They were walking now with their backs to the wind.

"Oh, hell!" Rose exclaimed. "We have people coming to dinner and I'd clean forgotten."

"I'll take you back to Paddington, there's a train at two forty-five." He swung her round towards the Bayswater Road.

"What will you . . . ?"

"I have to meet my agent. It's all right, darling."

"Mylo . . ." The wind whipped at her.

"One thing." He still held her arm. "If it had been you dying, I would not have hesitated, I would not have let them stop me, I would have killed *you*," he took her face in his hands and kissed her, "however difficult. Here's a taxi, pop in."

Sitting in the train she reproached herself bitterly. She had said so little, not known where to start with the torrent of pent-up words. As the train put on speed, the voice on the intercom informed her that the bar was open now. The buffet could provide tea, coffee, toasted sandwiches and soft drinks. People stood up and began to push past her, swaying with the movement of the train. Watching them go by she mourned the cold comfort she had given Mylo. I failed him, I failed him, I failed him, her thoughts chugged in time with the train. Contrapuntally she started to fuss about Ned's friends Arthur and Milly coming to dine. Once before she had forgotten people were coming, another pair of Ned's friends, she had made no provision. At the last moment they had taken the surprised guests to a restaurant. Ned had been so cross, made a scene, nursed a grudge, gone on about her incompetence for weeks. I don't think I can bear that again, she thought, not after seeing Mylo today. Then, remembering that the day was Wednesday, early closing for her local shops, she let out a wail. The couple sitting opposite looked at her askance. "Just a twinge." She smiled falsely like a dog about to bite, got up, made her way to the buffet car to buy an expensive paper cup of tinged water, changed her mind when she saw it and had a double brandy.

Arrived, she retrieved her car from the station car park, drove into the town. Surely some shop somewhere would be open? How stupid can you get, she thought, walking up the empty street, all the shops shut on Wednesdays. I am only putting off the evil moment of telling Ned I have no dinner for his friends and him asking whether I have lost my marbles *en permanence*.

As she walked, pulling her shopping trolley behind her, empty and likely to remain so, a Land-Rover passed, pulling a trailer. Catching a salty sniff, she peered into the trailer and beheld – boxes of crabs. The Land-Rover hesitated at the turning into the High Street to let a couple of lorries go by. During this pause Rose reached into the trailer and helped herself.

As the driver of the Land-Rover changed gear and accelerated Rose walked sedately back to her car, her only worry now whether to crush garlic into the mayonnaise she would make and turn it into aïoli, or have it plain.

Presently, the guests departed; duty done, she would gain her bed, shared now with Comrade's great-great-grandchildren (Ned had years ago moved into a separate bedroom) and if she felt like it, weep for Mylo.

And did I weep? Rose questioned, standing by the water's edge. Most unlikely. Our parallel lines had grown past weeping and the theft of the crabs had a curative effect, quite a boost.

It takes a happening like Christopher and Helen squabbling two days after Ned's funeral, their decision to take my dogs with them when they decided to walk off their spleen, allowing them to get crushed by a juggernaut as they argued, probably about me, instead of keeping an eye on my dogs, my company, my last links however tenuous with Mylo, to make me cry.

"I shall catch my death standing here," Rose said out loud.

She stamped her feet on the path to warm them, squared her shoulders.

FIFTY-ONE

Rose was aware that her feet were cold. A fog rolled up the creek, invisible hands pulled a wispy duvet along the water. She watched its advance billowing along quite fast, distorting the few sounds left by winter, twigs dropping in the wood behind her, the cry of a coot across the water. Far above, a plane flew leaving an unravelling vapour trail. Did it come from Thailand?

Fool, I am sixty-seven, not seventeen.

Looking down she found herself shoulder deep in vapour. Her body was chilled, she wanted to pee, she shivered. Irrationally she feared that if she stepped out of sight into the wood she would twist her ankle crossing the ditch, slip and fall. Her walk had been so peopled by thoughts, she had not noticed how alone she was.

She unzipped her trousers, squatted on the path, disappearing below the fog. Standing up she heard a man's voice calling: "Mrs Peel? Mrs Peel?" The sound was muffled but coming closer. "Mrs Peel?" She could see his head and shoulders reared above the fog. "Mrs Peel?" It was the owner of the hotel.

"Here I am," she said, stepping towards him. "What is it?" She did not want him to scent her urine on the path.

"We thought you might have got lost. These fogs roll up from the sea so quickly it is easy to become disorientated." He was irritated, anxious, obviously he didn't want to lose a foolish guest. Any mischance would damage the reputation of the hotel; he blamed her for his anxiety.

"As you see I am not lost, though I may well be disorientated, but thank you."

"You have had no breakfast. My wife was worried." Still he blamed her. The head and shoulders visible above the fog attracted pearly drops from the deafening atmosphere.

"How kind, I am ravenous." And so she was, now she thought of it, walking beside the hotelier. "Do you like being a hotelier?" she asked, hoping to raise their chat to a more frivolous plane. She had to talk; it was not possible to walk in silence, which would have been preferable but ill mannered.

"It has its moments. Would you like the full breakfast or coffee and croissants? My wife . . . We close at the end of the week for a winter break."

"That will be an important moment. Just the coffee and croissants, please. Sounds delicious." She hurried beside him in the fog (I could perfectly well have found my way back by myself). "Ah, here is your cat come to meet us. We met last night and again this morning." She stooped to caress the animal as it did its best to trip her by winding melodiously round her ankles. "She's talkative, too."

"Do you have cats?" Her host's voice was affectionate towards the cat. He had not forgiven her for causing unease.

"Not now. Nor do I have dogs. Nor garden – no ties at all, come to think of it. Nothing to restrain me. It's really rather scary, takes getting used to, being loose."

"Oh," he said, looking at her sidelong. "Um."

"M-m-m . . ."

"I will see about your breakfast; we call it *petit déjeuner*," he rallied.

"Of course you do." (She must not laugh.)

"Would you like it in your room?" he asked.

"Yes, please. And thank you for coming to look for me." (Had an unwary guest once fallen drunk into the creek?) "I must pack my bag. And might I use your telephone? There is a call, maybe several calls, I have to make . . ."

"I will have it plugged into your room."

"And have my bill ready."

"Certainly."

Certainly the bill. One paid the bill, the tally, the reckoning. One settled one's account at the end. "I shall swallow my pride with the croissants." She smiled at the man.

"Er?"

"I may not be able, now that I am free, to pay what I owe." They had reached the hotel now and the fog was lifting. She watched the cat run ahead, pat the door with an arrogant paw, raise its whiskered snout to yowl: "I observe that there's a perfectly good cat flap," she said.

"She's too bloody proud to use it, she won't stoop. We take all the main credit cards, naturally, if . . ." He stressed the last sentence.

"Aha!" said Rose laughing. "Credit! Of course."

The manager wondered what there was that was so funny. "Even Eurocheques," he said.

Avec le petit déjeuner, thought Rose. "Don't forget to charge me for my phone calls," she said.

FIFTY-TWO

The church had been packed. The young couple, popular single, would be popular as a pair. One or both of them had an inordinate number of relations. Although they had arrived early Nicholas, Emily and Laura had been relegated to a pew a long way back.

"That usher can't have known who we are," said Emily as they regained their car.

"Of course he did. That was Richard Malone's youngest. He knows us all right," snapped Nicholas.

"I thought he was still at school," said Emily.

"Time passes, Mama. He left university years ago; he works in the City." Laura spoke from the back seat.

"I thought the bride almost indecently virginal," said Nicholas. "Are those cars ever going to get a move on? I need a drink." The Thornby car was stationary in a line waiting to get free of the village. A number of people had parked inconveniently, causing a jam on the route to the reception.

"It's the mode to be virginal," said Laura.

"Barbara Cartland?" questioned Emily.

"AIDS," said Laura.

"In spite of being stuck at the back I quite enjoyed the spectacle," said Nicholas and tooted his horn. "Don't know many of the people here, though."

"No use hooting, Nicholas, consume your soul in patience like everyone else," said Emily.

"You misquote, Mama; it's 'possess ye your souls . . . ' "

"Don't be such a know-all, Laura, *my* soul is consumed."

Laura raised her eyebrows.

"There was a fine turnout of elderlies," said Nicholas. "The finest collection of lines, wrinkles, scraggy necks, crêpey skin, bags, bald heads, dowagers' humps, arthritic limbs, shuffling, hobbling, rheumy-eyed old crones and cronies I've seen in years. A wedding is better than a funeral for a geriatric turnout."

"Your generation," said Laura caustically.

"We do not suffer from cachexia," snapped her mother.

"And there are others besides us," Nicholas allowed, "there's poor Rose. There were several in the church carrying their years with decorum, not to say panache."

"Move on, Nicholas, can't you see the queue's moving? Rose was not there."

"Of course I can. Shut up." Nicholas clunked into gear. "I didn't say she was there; my point was that she has worn remarkably well, as well if not better than us."

"Look out, Nicholas, you'll hit that car . . ."

"God! Emily. Must you? Actually the old boy who gave the bride away was pretty trim."

"I thought him quite a dish," said Laura. "That shock of white hair with black eyebrows and eyes is stunning. Marvellous figure, too."

"Who was he?" asked Emily. "They should write these things on the hymn sheet. I couldn't display my ignorance to the people near us, they were all strangers."

"No idea," said Nicholas. "I always think, reverting to Rose, that the reason she looks as she does is that she hasn't suffered the extremes of joy, grief, or anxiety the rest of us have been through. A few worries over Christopher, nothing desperate, and Ned. Well, let's face it, Ned wasn't of the stuff to make any woman's face sag, was he?"

"Wasn't she the lucky one?" said Laura on the back seat, finding Nicholas's obsessive interest in Rose Peel entertaining.

"When Rose eventually shows her age she will look like a fossilised rose in a dead flower arrangement," said Emily, ignoring Laura. "Faded, yet crisp. Go on, Nicholas, they are moving again."

"I can see they are. Would you like me to stop the car, change places and let you drive?" asked Nicholas nastily.

"Now, now, you two, don't squabble," said Laura.

"We are nearly there," said Emily, sensing that she had goaded her brother too far. "I too need a drink, we all do. All those uplifting hymns and watching that beautiful pair has made me quite thirsty. That girl, the bride, has extraordinary eyes."

"They run in the family," said Laura.

"I like the looks of the groom; he's improved no end since I last saw him. If I'd been twenty years younger I would have been tempted to . . ."

"More like forty," said Laura on the back seat, "or fifty."

"What did you say?" asked Emily sharply. Laura did not reply.

"All those promises," said Emily after a pause, "are pretty ridiculous. Who on earth can be expected to cleave – correct me if I'm wrong, Laura – cleave indefinitely? It's unreasonable."

"Cleave will do. Is that the reason neither you nor Nicholas ever ventured into Holy Matrimony?" Laura asked a question which had rattled around her mind for a lifetime. Neither Nicholas nor Emily answered.

"Here we are. At last! Now we can get at the booze," said Nicholas. "There's nothing to prevent you embracing that mode of life, though I would think you've left it a trifle late now you've almost reached your half century."

It was now Laura's turn not to answer.

"Fancy having a marquee in winter. I hope we shan't catch our deaths," said Emily. "I personally shall go into the house. Come on, buck up, Nicholas, what are you staring at?"

"I thought I saw Rose Peel's car up there in the yard."

"Don't be silly, she's miles away in some luxury hotel; her car's a mass-produced job, it might be anybody's. Let's find the buffet. I say, there's that old man who – I agree with you, Laura, let's find out who he is."

"She won't be able to afford luxury hotels for long," said Nicholas, parking the car. "I only heard this morning what a mingy annuity Ned left her."

"Everything's entailed on Christopher, everybody knows that." Emily stretched her leg out of the car. "Give me a hand, Laura. Thanks."

"Presumably Ned imagined Christopher and Helen would supplement it," said Laura. "Aren't you going to lock the car, Nicholas?"

"Nag, nag, nag," said Nicholas, turning back to lock the car. "Can you see Rose accepting a penny from Christopher? She *loathes* Helen."

"And we all thought she'd be left rich! Well, well, beggars can't be choosers," said Emily. "She has her old age pension, hasn't she?"

"I can't see Rose begging," said Laura.

"Well, I can't help her, can I?" said Nicholas. "You could have," he rounded on Emily. "You must have known what Ned planned, Ned was in your pocket, you could have pointed out to him the decent thing to do. He may have been stupid but he wasn't all that mean, look what he did for Laura."

"Was Ned my father?" asked Laura, walking between Nicholas and Emily.

"Good Lord, no!" Nicholas burst out laughing.

"What a suggestion," said Emily primly.

"I thought not," said Laura. "I did ask Rose once and she said she thought not."

*

Watching the Thornbys go into the reception, Rose ducked out of sight. She had not foreseen when, by a series of astute telephone calls, she had discovered where Mylo would be at lunchtime, that there would be a large marquee, a hoard of wedding guests. When she had come upon the house by a back lane she had hoped to catch Mylo coming away from a quiet lunch with friends and possibly speak to him. This half-baked plan flew out of the window when, leaving her car in the stable yard, she had rounded a corner, seen the marquee and been almost instantly swamped by a rush of cars bearing bride and groom, parents, guests and various press and onlookers, and, worst of all, Emily, Nicholas and Laura back from the church.

Crouching down behind the wheel, hiding her face until she judged the Thornbys out of sight, she decided that what she had hoped for was not feasible, she must drive away, escape from this potentially embarrassing situation.

Then she thought with a gasp of relief that she had come to the wrong house, had been misdirected, natural enough in the circumstances of the wedding. She had been stupid, she would return to the village and ask again.

She sat up.

While she had ducked out of sight several cars had parked blocking her way out of the yard; she was, to all intents and purposes, trapped. Cursing her luck, she thought all she need do was wait until the owners of the cars came to remove them. But then, she thought, it will take hours and hours and meanwhile Mylo will finish his lunch at the other house and go. Damn Emily and Nicholas and all these people, she thought. Then she thought, What do I care about Emily and Nicholas? I care nothing, nothing at all, all the ways they can hurt me have been incinerated with Ned. All I need do, she told herself, is to go calmly in to this strange house, interrupt the wedding feast, explain my plight, my silly mistake, and ask for whoever owns these cars blocking my escape to come and move them. Easily done. Very easily done. She sat in the car telling herself how easy it would be. So she sat.

She sat in her car telling herself how easy it was to walk in alone to a stranger's wedding party in a rather grand house, wearing her comfortable old jeans and sweater and muddy shoes, barge into a room where everyone was dressed in their high-heeled best and important jewellery, the men in grey morning suits drinking champagne and making yuppy speeches. But never mind that, it would be perfectly simple to find the bride's mother or father or the best man or an usher and explain – I got here by mistake, I am really looking for another house where someone called Mylo Cooper is having lunch. You see I *have* to find Mylo Cooper. With her hands over her face she rehearsed this speech, nearly crying with rage and frustration as she muttered out loud . . .

"Who are you talking to?"

"I was rehearsing a speech."

"So I heard. Did I hear right? You have to find Mylo Cooper?"

"Yes."

"And then what?"

"Perhaps," she said stiffly – her whole face felt stiff – "you could help me find the owners of these cars which are blocking me in and then I can get out. I was rehearsing the speech I have to make to someone responsible, the bride's mother or father or the best man or an usher to ask the owners of . . ."

"I heard that bit."

"Oh."

"Would the bride's step-grandfather do? I gave her away in the church just now."

"Ah."

"I just stepped outside to get a breath of air."

"You are looking wonderfully well, Mylo Cooper."

"You are as lovely as ever, Rose Peel. How did you find me?"

"I telephoned your publisher who put me on to your agent, who told me the hotel you are staying in, and they told me you had a lunch date here."

"Very clever. I saw in *The Times* that Ned is dead."

"Yes."

"It would be untrue to say I am not delighted."

"Ah."

"I intended coming straight on from here to Slepe to gather you up and Comrade's descendants and take you away."

"They are dead too, they were run over."

"I mind about that very much."

"You would not have found me there."

"You would have been looking for me?"

"I can't deny it."

"I am terribly pleased."

"Well . . ."

"I won't say I love you as much as I did at the winter tennis party – isn't it extraordinary that Victoria's granddaughter should be marrying one of George Malone's grandsons? One of the things I love about you is that you don't answer, 'It's a small world,' that sort of bilge – but I will say that I love you differently and more so, much more so."

"Oh. Does she have Victoria's wonderful eyes?"

"Yes, she does."

"I am glad." (His voice had not changed, a little deeper perhaps.)

"I can't think what I am doing standing here while you sit in there in the warm. I am too old to hang about growing stiff, risking hypothermia. Open the door, darling, and let me in. I want to hug you."

She opened the car door, moved over to make room for him beside her. "I have our picture in my overnight bag, I did not bring anything else."

"Quite right. What else would we need? I say, isn't this nice, I love kissing you."

"Not forgotten how?"

"If you must know, I'm as hungry as I ever was. I just space the meals out a bit."

"Do that again," she said. "I very nearly did not come to look for you."

"Pride, I suppose. Thank the Lord you swallowed it. I would never have forgiven you if you had not."

"I might have choked."

"In such a good cause."

"Do you have to go back in there?" she asked presently, listening to the distant hubbub of the party. "Nicholas and Emily are in there."

"So I saw. Pickled in time. Never mind them. I have to say my goodbyes. Then we are off."

Watching Nicholas and Emily circulating among the crowd, Laura reflected soberly that it would be she who would be driving the car home. Nicholas's hand reached repeatedly towards the trays of drinks, Emily's followed suit. They ignored the temptings of vol-au-vents stuffed with shrimps, caviare on strips of toast, and other succulent eats offered by perambulatory waiters. Their tour ended, they rejoined Laura by the buffet. "Having fun?" asked Emily.

"Bored," said Laura, "there's nobody I want to talk to."

"And very few we want to talk to either, but it's not a bad party as parties go." Emily's voice had risen several decibels above her norm. She's tippled into drunkenness, blast her, thought Laura. "Why did none of us marry?" Emily asked the world at large. "*We* would have had the most marvellous parties, the best champagne, not this stuff. *You* could have married, Laura. You could have married Christopher Peel. Why did you not marry Christopher, Laura?"

"I was under the impression he was my brother," said Laura tightly.

"Oooh? Then, when it was too late, you checked with Rose?" Emily's once brilliant eyes focused on her daughter's, still brilliant. "You could have had Slepe, couldn't you? Think on that."

She's not quite as drunk as I thought. "Stupid old bitch," said Laura with wintry intensity.

"Poor Rose Peel. *I* should have married poor Rose," exclaimed Nicholas, ignoring his females.

"Would she have married you?" asked Laura tightly.

"We should have brought her with us today," cried Nicholas, "jollied her up. We used to be so kind to her when we were all young."

"Would she have wanted to come?" asked Laura.

"We teased her, admittedly," said Emily, reminiscence overriding Laura's tone, "but we were very kind. We took her to the party where she first met Ned."

"If I had married her I would have sophisticated her, made much more of her than Ned did."

"Jolly nice for Rose," said Laura, "that would have been."

"Poor Rose. Nothing ever happened to her. I hate to think of her holed up in some hotel alone and palely masturbating when she could have married me – if I'd asked her of course . . . Where's all the drink gone?" Nicholas looked around but no waiter passed.

"You are disgusting drunk and pretty disgusting sober," said Laura.

"Don't speak to Nicholas like that," Emily shouted shrilly.

Laura smiled, mouthed, "Don't speak to your father like that," watched Emily look blankly around in pretence to the people near her, that it was not she who had shouted, but somebody else. "Why did you never marry, Mother?" she asked.

"I could have married, perhaps I should have married," Emily answered portentously, "but there was such a wide choice, one . . ."

"You could have married absolutely anybody," said Nicholas, switching to a fond gargling note. "Even a man like that dishy old example of humanity who gave the bride away. Have we discovered who he is? Does anybody we know know?" Nicholas fumbled for his glasses to scour the room better. "We really should find out."

"You'd better look sharp then," said Laura. "He's just leaving. Look, he's over there with Rose. *She* seems to know him."

SECOND FIDDLE

for Robert Bolt

PART I

AUTUMN

Claud Bannister sat beside his mother, enduring the concert. What right, he asked himself, had an unknown provincial quartet to perform three pieces of modern music for the first time? How was a discriminating sophisticate such as himself to know whether the music was good or bad? I need, he told himself with secret mortification, to read the opinion of the London critics before I dare judge. I am ignorant of music, if not tone deaf. I am neither discriminating nor sophisticated; I have come back to Mother after years of school, university and failed exams without money or qualifications, without even the courage to tell her what I intend to do with my life. What shall I say when she asks me? This music is incomprehensible, he thought, glancing covertly at his mother, yet she seems to understand it. What does she hear which I do not?

On the way to the concert Margaret Bannister had tried, unwisely she now realised, to jolly her son out of his gloomy mood and, failing, had called him "a veritable bundle of resentment" – another of her misplaced remarks, she told herself, exasperated. To hell with it, she would enjoy the music, worry later.

These seats are appallingly uncomfortable, thought Claud, leaning back until the back of his seat creaked, tangibly annoying a bald man sitting in the row behind, a man who as they had come in to the concert hall had called out to his mother in jest, laughed appreciatively at some negligible joke she had made in return, had obviously admired her and been backed in his opinion by his wife who, grey-haired, stout and dowdy, had kindly included him, Claud, with, "How nice to see you, Claud" (remembering his name while he remotely forgot hers). "How seldom we see you, how glad you must be to spend some time with your clever, witty mother."

Clever? Witty? What did all these grey old people know of cleverness or wit?

The quartet scraped to the end of the difficult piece. The audience clapped, the musicians stood and bowed.

"I might grow to like it when I have listened to it a few more times," his mother said to the neighbour on her left. "We finish, thank the Lord, with dear old Bach but they did their best, the brave young things."

Claud scowled at the quartet, stringy and not particularly young, bracing themselves to have a bash at Bach while his mother sat back relaxed, anticipating pleasure. Grey, grey, they are all grey, grey-haired and largely dressed in grey. Claud's eyes roamed disapprovingly over the audience, seeing grey even when the heads were tinted black, auburn, even blond.

His eye was arrested by the sight of a woman three rows ahead, dressed in vivid green, a striped wrap in cyclamen and purple lit with blue slung round her shoulders. He could make out a white neck and above it a shock of dark springy hair; by leaning forward he could just make out a pointed nose and one dark eye. "Who is that?" he whispered in his parent's ear. "What's her name?"

"Hush, I will introduce you presently." That his mother should know on the instant the only person in the audience who was of interest to him added to Claud's sulks. He leaned back in his uncomfortable seat, letting the Bach flow, feeding his resentment (what a bloody evening), disgustedly anticipating the soggy quiches and mediocre wines which would be distributed by benign ladies ("White wine or red? Or rosé? We have rosé, soft drinks too, of course") while their husbands collected donations for the charity in aid of which the concert had been organised. Claud glared at his mother, who was smiling as though amused. What's funny about a boring provincial concert? It's probably in aid of some wretched cretins who would have been happier if allowed to die at birth.

He was presently introduced to the woman in green in the foyer among a babble of voices. She stood with a piece of quiche in one hand and a glass of wine in the other, talking with her mouth full to the conductor of the cacophony they had just listened to.

Claud heard her say, "You know, I simply *loathe* modern music." She sprayed crumbs from a full-lipped mouth, caught Claud's eye briefly, looked away, said, "Hullo, Margaret," leaned forward to kiss his mother's cheek – "I'm spewing crumbs, sorry" – and turned back to the conductor who, Claud remarked jealously, was a darkly attractive foreigner. Margaret Bannister turned, laughing, to speak to friends, leaving Claud to hover and snatch his chance when the guest of honour would be wrested away to be introduced to others. Knowing his mother, he guessed that he would, if lucky, have seven minutes to make his mark before she insisted on leaving. In the event he had ten.

"He's Roumanian," said Claud's mother, as they moved away towards the car. "He probably thinks Laura pronounces love, loathe. She will risk insulting people in public, it's the sort of joke which appeals to her."

"Is she a tough cookie?"

"I suspect a heart of nougat. Would you like to drive?"

Claud guessed rightly that his parent was sick of his ill humour and ready to placate him. Had they reached the moment when he dared apprise her of his future plans? He got behind the steering wheel.

"You should have more confidence in your driving," said his mother presently, as he braked violently at a crossroads.

"By which you mean I should have more confidence in myself?" Claud accelerated, hating the oblique criticism which, he now told himself, had driven his father into leaving home. His mother did not reply. This kind of silence had also precipitated his father's departure. We have not reached the right moment, he told himself.

Laura Thornby accepted another glass of wine but refused the quiche. She stood with her back to the wall, watching the concert crowd thin as they said their goodbyes, collected their wraps and went out into the night where the timbre of their voices sharpened in the freezing air. She thought, as the concert hall doors opened and shut, that she must have imagined the shiver of apprehension she had felt when Margaret Bannister introduced her son. She had felt the draught, she told herself, the night outside was freezing. Her shiver was nothing to do with Claud Bannister.

What a lot he had said in those short minutes. How impetuous to spill such a lapful of hope and ambition to a stranger. What a risk he had taken. And in a crowd! Anyone could have heard what he said. Sipping her wine Laura waited for the evening to end and as she waited she thought of Claud Bannister and was interested in her interest.

"Can we give you a lift?" Helen Peel, her arm through her husband's, slowed as they walked by.

"No, thank you. I have my car."

"Someone said you brought the conductor down from London," said Helen's husband Christopher.

"I did, but he is going back by train."

"So you will be down for a few days?"

"Probably."

"What's his name again, this conductor?" asked Christopher.

"Composer," corrected Helen.

"Both." Laura smiled at Helen.

"D'you mean he wrote that stuff, then conducted it?" Christopher towered over Laura. "You do find yourself the most curious boyfriends."

"So you did not like it."

"Not much. Well, not at all. I'm not up to this modern stuff."

"People said the same about Mozart. Come on, Christopher, we shall be—" Helen started to move.

"But what's his name? I've lost my programme and came without my glasses."

"Clug," said Laura.

"Clug?"

"To rhyme with plug."

"Oh! Oh, all right darling, I'm coming," Christopher Peel allowed himself to be led away. "Is the fellow a communist?" he asked over his shoulder.

"Probably."

"—wouldn't be allowed out of Roumania if he were not."

Helen belonged to the class of English women who are taught to elocute clearly at an early age, thought Laura, listening to Helen's voice calling back, "Goodnight," as she and her husband went out into the cold.

Waiting for Clug to free himself of admirers Laura speculated idly on the gap there would be in her life with Clug returned to Roumania. It had been an agreeable intermezzo, she thought, of just the right length, no time to get bored.

"Are you delivering Clug to British Rail?" The county artistic director came up now. "If it's a nuisance I can easily—"

"No, no, Robert, everything's OK, his bags are in my car. It's no bother."

The artistic director wondered whether he should say something about Clug stopping the night in Salisbury on the way down to see the sights? Perhaps he had better not since Laura appeared to have been with him – well, she had driven him down, hadn't she? Not that that necessarily meant – "I think the concert was a success," he said, looking doubtfully at the thinning crowd, finding Laura slightly alarming.

"Of course it was. D'you think you could extract him from that hive of music lovers? He will miss his train otherwise."

"Of course, of course. I don't think they are as much musicologists as – well – ah – he's a very attractive chap, isn't he? I'll do a bit of tactful disentanglement, shall I?"

Robert shot off to detach the conductor, who stood surrounded by an eager group of women and less eager men.

Laura waved in the direction of Clug, caught his eye, tapped her watch. Clug waved back and put his arm round rescuing Robert's shoulder.

After a while Clug leaned back in the car beside Laura. "Ach, that's good. That boy look at you with calf eye, I see it."

"*Saw* him," said Laura, "not *it*." She turned up the heater. "And it's calves' eyes, not calf. What have you been reading, Cluggie?"

"Woman's magazine. I try to learn all about loathing in capitalismus countries. So much freedom. Now in my country—"

"Loving, Clug, loving. I can't think why I bother."

Clug chuckled. "I go 'ome, so no problem, darling. Loathe, love, same thing."

"Good job you are going."

"So you no longer loathe me?" Clug queried.

"Might be verging on it."

"I observe cruel tone of voice. No need to understand worts."

"Crotchets and quavers."

"*Comment*?"

"My French is as weak as your English."

"You squash. Come to Bucharest," Clug cajoled. "A nice little visit. I fix visa."

"No, thank you. I have told you. No fear."

"Notting to fear."

"Oh God," Laura exclaimed irritably, "do shut up just for once. No fear is slang, it means no thank you, nothing doing."

"We do not do enough," Clug laughed.

"Did not."

"OK, did not. So why not come now? Jost one last night?"

"No. *Non. Nein. Niet.*"

"*Niet*, I understand."

"That's great. Now here's the station. Got your ticket? Got your bag?"

"You come?"

"No, I told you."

"So – you – did." If he wished, if he made the effort, a few words could be accentless. "So a kiss, a final kiss?"

Laura pulled on the handbrake, leaned over and kissed his cheek. "Goodbye, Cluggie."

"Do not get hurted by that calf boy."

"The boot might be on the other foot."

"Yes, that also." He was out of the car now, turning up his coat collar, yanking his suitcase from the boot of the car. "In so situation two get hurt. You betray or he betray."

Laura was out of the car, standing beside him. "I can't see anything reaching that stage." She was amused. "You foresee a non-event."

"You do not see much. Let me stay your place tonight or you come to London?"

"No, Cluggie, I told you. I have to see my family, go to the dentist—"

"I would like to see your home."

"Lovers are apt to get bitten."

"Is it so convention, your familia?"

"If you don't buck up, you will miss your train."

The train, said the man at the barrier, was ten minutes late. Clug put his bag on a seat and, taking Laura's arm, started walking her up and down the platform. Constrained by good manners to see him safely on to the train, Laura sighed. She was looking forward to getting into bed by herself; she found this extra delay an imposition.

"Little Laura." Clug squeezed Laura's arm against his ribs (they were of a height). "'Ow I shall miss you, for me you represent all that is in this country er – er—"

"You have already forgotten what I represent."

"No, no I 'ave not." Clug's aitches froze as they left his lips. "I shall even remember your great uncles, the most lovely uncles in Western Europe."

"Ankles, Cluggie, ankles."

"Votever. When I feel them wrapped round my vaiste I adore them, get most excite, ant your viggling toes, now this young calf will experience this extase."

Catching the eye of a man supposedly reading the evening paper, Laura grinned. "Work that one out, mate." The stranger raised his newspaper, blotting himself away.

"So now this and that with that young so lucky fellow, to start so with a beautiful older woman is bonus," cried Clug. "And a so fonny woman also."

"I'm not starting anything, Cluggie, I'm due for a little rest."

"Rest! Nah! If he start it is better, but it vill be you, I think, no?"

"I think I hear your train," said Laura, laughing.

"Do not forget me, little Laura. I vill remember as you are now for ever. How we loathed!"

"We look like corpses under this fluorescent light – loved, Cluggie, loved. I still can't think why I bother."

"In Venezia the street lights are pink."

"And in Bucharest?"

"Like death also."

"Here's your train. Where's your bag? Goodbye, goodbye." Laura's spirits soared as the train arrived; she felt revivified and looked it, in spite of the fluorescent lighting. Clug climbed nimbly into the train.

"I am still working out how you wrapped your uncle's ankles round a waste—" The newspaper reader brushed past Laura and followed Clug on to the train as it began to move.

"Thanks!" Laughing, Laura blew a kiss towards the anonymous humorist. Leaning from the window Clug, taking the kiss to be for him, blew it back.

Walking back to her car Laura was grateful for the note of frivolity which had rescued her in the nick of time from incipient boredom. If I meet Margaret Bannister's son again I shall treat him in paltry fashion, she resolved. Arm's length should be the rule for a while, safety lay in being casual.

As the train gathered speed Martin Bengough, laying his newspaper aside, began to fuss, patting his pockets, opening his briefcase, rustling through its contents, then half standing up as though he might inadvertently have sat on the elusive object he was looking for. Not finding it, he sighed gustily and sat discontentedly in his seat to stare out of the window into the dark. Reflected in the glass he saw himself and his fellow occupants of the carriage as they relaxed and settled down for the journey to London.

A pair of adolescent boys had brought a travelling chess set; two girls travelling together wore Walkmen clamped to their heads. While one chewed gum and read a magazine, the other had brought out her knitting and clicked the needles frenetically. A white-haired old woman sat with her eyes shut, both hands holding her bag. By himself, in a corner seat halfway along the compartment, Clug was absorbed in a musical score.

Five or six burly young men of the type seen travelling to or from football matches barged suddenly through the compartment on their way back from the buffet car, bringing a waft of cold air mingling with the smell of stale tobacco; they each carried several cans of beer and sandwiches encased in plastic. As they lurched past Clug his fingers tightened on the score and he winced into himself, hunching his shoulders and drawing in legs which had been stretched out.

The train swung round a curve on the line; one of the young men lurched against Clug. "Sorry, squire." Clug looked up quickly, then down again, his fingers gripping the score. As the football fans clanged and bumped their way out of the compartment they were followed by the ticket collector, a tall Sikh in a blue turban. He took each ticket and examined it in silence before politely returning it to its owner. Taking Clug's ticket he said quietly: "You are in the wrong compartment, sir, this is a first class ticket."

"No matter," said Clug. "I move if the train crowds too heavy." The ticket collector returned the ticket and moved on in the wake of the football fans.

Martin, feeling the train begin to slow, stood up, picked up his briefcase and stood by the sliding doors ready to leave the train at the junction which was the last stop before London. The junction platform was crowded with waiting passengers catching this last connection; some of them carried skis.

Martin leaned from the train window, his hand on the heavy brass handle. As the train drew to a halt, he stepped down into the crowd. "Fifth row facing the engine, right-hand side, feels safer travelling second class," he said, brushing past a man swinging himself on to the train.

"Oh, the bugger," said the man without looking at Martin. "I had looked forward to travelling in comfort."

Martin grinned and started elbowing his way through the crowd to the exit. As he paused to give up his ticket, he looked back: the train was already moving and he could see his successor through the window standing near Clug, heaving his bag up on to the rack. Clug was studying his score.

Martin strolled out of the station to the car park where his car waited. He was very hungry. The quiche at the concert had been uneatable; he had swerved away from the wine. He looked forward to the meal he had ordered earlier in the day at a small country restaurant not yet recommended by Egon Ronay, run by the friend of an acquaintance who would be ready to oblige with a late meal.

On his way to the restaurant he stopped at a callbox, reported in and registered the fact that he had a few days' leave. "I have left my umbrella behind," he said.

"If by that," said the voice at the other end, "you mean you are hotfooting after a pussycat—"

"Retrieving my brolly," said Martin equably. "It belonged to my grandfather; he bought it pre-war at Briggs, the umbrella makers in Piccadilly, London, SW1."

"Snob," said the voice, envying Martin his ancestral umbrella with its malacca handle and gold band with the grandfather's name on it. "One day it will get nicked," he said, "I hope. Don't miss your flight, will you?"

Martin replaced the receiver.

He drove back the way he had come by train then, leaving the main road, found his intended restaurant in a village restored to peace and calm by being by-passed. The restaurant was small and comfortable, several tables still occupied by customers lingering over the debris of their meal. He ate a particularly delicious mussel soup, woodcock with matchstick potatoes, watercress salad, and a plain orange compôte. The house wine was so good he wondered whether he could safely drive on. Discovering that there were bedrooms to let above the dining-room, he reserved one, ordered cheese and disposed contentedly of the bottle. Later when he went up to bed he found that the house, which he had not seen in the dark, had once been a mill and that his room was above the mill-race.

He opened a window and peered in the dark at black water channelling towards an obsolete mill-wheel. Further out the main stream slid over a waterfall to crash into a deep pool. This would be a pleasant place to cast a fly on a June evening, but now the air was icy; he shut the window and got into bed.

Listening to the water he reviewed the evening, the last of assignment Clug. And, since Clug spent so much time with her, he had included Laura in the watching.

At the start of Clug's concert tour, at a reception, he had seen them meet. Noted an instant rapport. Since then Clug and Laura had spent all the time Clug could manage together. It had puzzled him that she should take up with Clug when there could be no future in the liaison. She behaved as he frequently did himself, taking up with a girl for a short term, happy never to see her again. Martin grinned, amused to find this affinity between himself and the woman he had been observing for a month. They had spoken for the first time that evening as he got on the train and she, smiling, had let him know that she had known all along and not cared that he watched her while he watched the Roumanian.

He had done more than watch, he acknowledged to himself. By using the ploy of a mislaid umbrella, he would double back to discover, if he could, more about Laura; he was intrigued by her, fascinated. He could perhaps discover why she lived alone, worked alone, had apparently satisfactory but only short-term relationships. A fellow watcher changing shifts had told him that he had come across Laura before, having an affair on that occasion with a visiting American academician suspected by the CIA of sympathising with Chilean lefties. Another colleague remembered that she had had a brief brush with a Hungarian painter in England, like Clug, on a cultural visit. With both these men she had stayed quite openly in hotels, but paid her own way.

What a futile, sneaky life I lead, thought Martin. He wondered, as he had for many months, whether to chuck his job, find a more congenial occupation, or drift on a little longer? He was supposed to be in Washington by the weekend on a fresh assignment. Should he resign now, as he had already suggested he might to his masters, or after the American tour? He liked Washington. He liked the museums and galleries. It was plain that there was no future in a pursuit of

Laura. In the urbane Phillips Gallery, lolling on one of the sofas, he might shed thoughts of Laura Thornby. He particularly liked the Phillips Gallery. Even so, he thought, drifting into sleep to the sound of rushing water, there was no harm in thinking it would be fun to bring Laura to this idyllic place, imagine sharing with her a delicious meal, then bringing her up to this room into this bed. He was wryly amused that in his mid-forties he was still capable of romantic fantasy.

"You are such a sidelong girl," said Claud, aware that Laura was avoiding his eye. They had been introduced at the concert the previous evening, he reminded her; up to then he had known her by sight only, he said.

"I am in my forties." Laura, not the sort to be flattered by being called a girl, continued doing what she had been doing when accosted, picking over the vegetables on the organic stall, much to the irritation of the stall-holder. "If I live to be ninety, which is the current mode, God help us, I am now into middle age."

"You certainly don't look it," said Claud, wondering whether the expression "sidelong" had caused offence.

"One should look one's age," said Laura, her long fingers pinching garlic bulbs. "How much – some of these are powdery?" she asked the stall-holder.

The stall-holder weighed the garlic. "Ninety pee."

"You don't half charge," said Laura, returning the garlic to its heap. "I shall buy the less healthy French kind from my vegetable shop; it's fatter, juicier, fresher, cheaper—"

"Now, now," said the stall-holder, "think of the muck it's grown in, sheer poison."

Claud tried again. "You have allowed experience to etch those delicate laughter lines," he suggested, peering at the skin round Laura's eyes.

"That's about it. How much is the broccoli?" she asked the stall-holder.

Claud resisted an inclination to kick Laura on the shin; she was wearing strong leather boots; talking to two people at once bordered, in his book, on bad manners. "Most women enjoy flattery," he said.

"I am not most women." Laura was now picking over the broccoli. "All right, I'll have a couple of pounds, Brian." She smiled at the stall-holder.

"What an idea!" exclaimed Claud. "You are strikingly original."

"So what shall we talk about?" Laura paid for the broccoli which Brian handed her in a paper bag marked "recycled". Laura added the broccoli to other purchases in a large basket with leather handles somebody had brought her from Minorca. "You get the authentic taste from Brian's veg," she said. "He's been seen scattering the contents of his cesspit over his patch when short of horse shit and his girlfriend, Susie, famous for her skin, quaffs her own urine every morning. She doesn't look more than thirteen; how's that for advertising organically grown food and back to nature?"

Claud followed Laura through the market. "D'you remember my name?" he asked hopefully. It would be nice to get off the subject of Brian and back to himself.

"By association. Lifts? Elevators? Something like that?"

"Elevators?" Claud was at a loss. "Lifts?"

"Miss Otis regrets – is Otis your real name?"

"My name is Claud Bannister," said Claud offended.

Laura laughed. "So it is. I wonder what made me think it was Otis? Got it, you are a writer." She stressed the word, pinning it down. "Banisters, stairs, not lifts."

"You remember that."

"How could I not? You had me trapped in a corner. Undiscovered, but not disheartened, you said."

"Was I so boring?" Claud's voice rose on a note of pain. "I was going to suggest – to offer you a coffee, but if I—"

"Not boring at all. Yes, I'd love some coffee. It's draughty in this market, much as I enjoy it. Shall we go to the wine bar? The coffee is tolerable there." Laura threaded her way through the stalls. Claud followed. "As I remember it, you are writing a novel, have neither publisher nor money, but are determined to succeed. Right?"

"Oh yes, yes I am."

"Why don't you keep a stall in the market?"

Entering the wine bar, Laura unwound her magenta-coloured scarf and unbuttoned her overcoat. She put them on a chair, her shopping basket on another and sat, effectively claiming for herself and Claud a table intended for four people.

Claud sat opposite her and after a moment's hesitation added his anorak to Laura's coat. "What would I do with a stall?" he asked.

"Survive," said Laura, "while you write your books. I take it you are on unemployment benefit?"

"Lord, yes, but I'd lose it if I was caught running a stall. I wouldn't know how, anyway, and what would I sell?"

"Any sort of rubbish. Antiques? Old clothes? Old bottles from tips, your mother's cast-offs. It would pay better than the dole and keep you rich in ideas. You get a cross-section of people in the market." Laura looked through the window of the wine bar which, steaming up, distorted the figures of people passing outside. Catching the eye of a man looking in, she raised a finger and mouthed, "Hi."

"Who was that?" asked Claud suspiciously.

"No idea. Just someone who thinks he knows me. What about an Irish coffee, it's cold enough?"

"Oh I—" (She knew the man, who was he?)

"I'll treat you. Maeve," Laura caught a passing waitress by the skirt, "two Irish coffees, please."

"OK," said the girl, snatching away her skirt. "No need to grab."

Laura put a hand up to loosen the neck of her jersey. "Lovely and warm in here, isn't it?" She looked about at the people coming in from the street; tables were filling up, but nobody challenged her right to the table for four.

"I was awfully pleased to meet you properly last night," said Claud. "I watched you. I wanted to get to know you the moment I saw you."

"Oh?" Laura felt she must pay attention.

"You are so – er – colourful, nobody could fail to notice you." Indeed in her orange skirt, black high-necked sweater and Cossack hat Laura was striking. Claud leaned towards her.

The waitress stretched across the table from behind Claud to place a mug of coffee laced with whiskey in front of Laura. Her bare arm brushed Claud's nose; he could smell her flesh, quite separate from the coffee; he jerked his head back as she set a second mug in front of him. "Croissants," she asked, "or rolls?"

"Have some croissants," suggested Laura. "I shall."

"Oh, thanks. Wonderful." Claud, realising that he was hungry, salivated.

"Butter? Cherry jam?" inquired the waitress.

"Yes, please," said Laura. "You had got as far as colourful. That's a bit better than sidelong—"

"Oh, I, ah—" Claud was undecided. "Er—"

"I love hearing about myself." Laura sipped her coffee.

Claud watched her lips pout towards the mug. He liked the sharpness of her nose, her high cheek bones, extraordinarily bright eyes. "The whites of your eyes are as brilliant as a child's," he said.

"It's all the garlic I eat. Go on."

"Your colouring is dramatic. Your – er – high colour, black hair and eyebrows, and the splendid colours you wear—"

The waitress, returning, thumped a plate of croissants, two tiny dishes of butter and two equally minuscule portions of jam onto the table.

"More, Maeve, more," said Laura, without distracting her gaze from Claud.

"I have switched back to Mavis," said the waitress. "I am sick of the Irish shooting each other all the time. I disassociate myself from that tragic country; the Welsh are more reliable and harmonious."

"OK, Mavis, I'll try and remember," said Laura. "It's all the same to me. I happen to know you were born in Plymouth. Have you a manuscript one could look at?" She darted bright eyes at Claud.

Claud made a protective gesture, hands against chest.

"You will have to learn to accept criticism," Laura grinned. "You can't be pregnant for ever; somebody has to look at your baby."

"My mother almost did; she was trying to tidy my room."

"Tut! Still living at home?" Laura frowned.

"It saves money," said Claud, abashed but unrepentant. He had invited Laura's nosiness, he told himself.

"If you keep a stall in the market, you will be able to afford digs. Maeve's mother, sorry, *Mavis'* mother has a spare room, I happen to know. A cosy sort of loft." Laura gulped the coffee, which invigorated and exhilarated her. Buttering her croissant, she remembered that she had skipped breakfast. This would account for her elevation of spirit; it could not at her mature age be due to Claud's appearance. "How old are you, baby?" she asked, her mouth full of croissant.

"What?" Claud's coffee nearly went the wrong way.

"I said, how old is your baby?" Laura emended.

"Oh, I see. Two paragraphs and sixteen sentences, to be exact."

Claud sucked in his breath. Too late now to confess the true size of his manuscript, an unwieldy pile of much corrected typescript which haunted his nights and plagued his days. It contained, he realised as he looked at Laura, a mass of half-digested ideas, poor jokes, unresolved situations, phony descriptions of love-making and long descriptive passages in no way relative to the plot. What plot? Nervously he repeated: "Two paragraphs and sixteen sentences."

Laura was amused. They laughed. Claud felt immensely relieved. He was saved the risk of showing her his writing; he guessed she would despise it; he would jettison the bulk of it, start afresh.

Laura took off her hat and tossed back thick, springy hair.

"D'you want your bill?" asked Mavis, hovering.

"Not yet, thanks," said Laura. "I did ask for more butter and jam, Mavis. Is that loft of your mother's still to let?"

"Yes, she's upping the rent. There are people who want your table," muttered Mavis.

"Then want must be their master; I get claustrophobia if squashed. I'll bring Claud round to see it. Do bring us our butter, Mavis."

"Those people—"

"Perhaps they hope to share with us?" Laura looked dangerously round. "Who are they?"

Three people waiting near by moved away and squeezed themselves round a table for two, much cluttered with used cups, buttery plates and cigarette stubs squashed into saucers.

Laura munched her croissant and watched Mavis clear the table of its detritus, give it a perfunctory swish with a cloth and take the people's order. "Mavis is an actress. She doesn't go on the dole, she takes this mean job and from this lowly position she observes human nature. She will weave all our mannerisms into her future parts. I shudder to think how I am contributing to some future box office draw. Perhaps you'd rather write plays?"

"No, thank you, that's not my line at all." Claud shuddered at the thought.

"Well, at least you know that."

"That's not a very kind thing to say, not in that tone of voice."

"Who said I was kind? You accosted me, if I remember rightly. But never mind, I will fix you up with Mavis' mum and help you with your market stall."

Claud gulped his coffee. The whiskey in it went ballooning into his brain. Laura had settled his future; he saw himself with a market stall. "As long as I don't have to sell fish," he said. "I can't stand fish. I could work in a loft, though."

"Right, then. All fixed. Jolly good," said Laura. "That bloody Mavis never brought our butter."

"Keeping these chairs warm for us?" asked Brian Walker, coming in from the cold. "Jolly good of you, Laura." He began dismantling layers of outer clothing with one hand, while with the other he deftly hitched Laura's coat and Claud's anorak on to pegs near the door. "Sit down there, sweet Susie," he said to a tiny pink-nosed girl who had come in behind him. "We've come for a plonk and pizza before going home. It's a ball-freezer behind that stall. This is my wife, Susie," he said to Claud. "Let her squeeze in beside you while I fetch us some grub. No use waiting for Maeve, she takes for ever."

"She's switched back to Mavis," said Laura, amused. "I seem to remember hearing she was plain Molly when she was at school. I was telling Claud about your lovely skin, Susie, but now he can see it for himself. Just look at her skin, Claud, isn't it perfect?"

"She tells everyone I wash in my pee," said Susie, wiping her nose with the back of her hand. "Have you got a handkerchief, Laura? Brian's pinched mine. He won't let me use tissues, it's all 'Save the Trees' these days."

"Use this," said Laura, handing her a paper napkin. "I'm told you drink it."

Susie laughed. "You terror."

Brian returned, balancing pizzas and glasses of wine in enormous earthy hands. "Here, treasure, get stuck into that." He sat beside Susie, dwarfing her with his bulk.

Susie bit into her pizza with teeth in proportion to her size and sighed with pleasure. "God, I was cold," she said.

"Claud is going to keep a stall in the market and lodge with Mavis' mum so that he can write his novels," said Laura.

"Laura's a great fixer of other people's problems," said Brian. "What shall you sell from your stall?"

"Antiques," said Claud, answering for himself. "Junk." He was beginning to visualise an agreeable future with a stall in the market close to Brian and Susie, who really did have the most incredible skin, pale and pinkly glowing, as fresh as a small child's. Could one believe?

Laura wrote on the back of an envelope. "That's Mavis' mum's address," she said. "She's called Mrs Kennedy. Let me know how you get on. Bye, Susie, bye, Brian." She slithered into her coat, swung the magenta scarf around her neck, held it across her face so that they could only see her eyes, and crammed the Cossack hat on to her head, tipping it low over her forehead. "See you—" And she was gone.

"But—" Claud clutched the envelope, watched Laura's departing back. "She promised to take me there, to introduce me, to—"

"She's written the scenario, you act it," said Susie, "she's like that. She's not going to fix the rent for you."

"I never supposed—" began Claud, who had supposed exactly that. "I don't understand."

"You are not meant to," said Brian. "What's this butter for, Mavis?"

"Laura asked for it," said Mavis, standing gracefully near the table.

"Will she pay for it?" asked Brian.

"Oh, yes."

"OK, we will eat it. She seems also to have left us a croissant." He split the croissant and shared it with Susie. "Have another coffee?" he suggested to Claud.

"Thanks very much, that would be nice." Claud sat back. He had been in half a mind to run after Laura, make a date to be taken to see Mrs Kennedy's loft or at least arrange another meeting.

"Irish?" enquired Mavis, gaining his attention; she looked bored, as though she was chewing gum, which she was not.

"Welsh," said Claud, banishing her boredom. "Is she always like that?" he reverted to Laura. "She left rather suddenly. I thought she – er—"

"When we warm up we smell of dung," said Brian. "It offends Laura's delicate nose."

Susie snuffled with laughter into her glass of wine.

Claud was uncertain whether Brian was serious; he felt it would be offensive on such a short acquaintance to sniff, yet Brian did look very earthy, his fingernails rimmed in brown, his green wellies streaked with what might easily be manure. Mavis put another mug of coffee in front of him. "Oh," said Claud, "oh dear! She went off without – oh – I must – oh." He clapped a hand to his breast pocket.

"That's OK," said Mavis, standing very close. "She keeps an account here. I'm off soon," she said. "I'll take you home to see my mother if you are really interested in the loft. Have you finished, Brian and Susie? Because if you have I want to clear the table."

"How brutal you are," said Susie, refusing to be rushed. "They don't employ you here to harass us customers."

"They don't know that I do," said Mavis, gathering plates and cups on to a tray. "Come on, have a heart. I want to get home and wash my hair."

"Have you noticed Mavis' hair?" asked Brian, keeping a tight hold of his wine glass. "It really is that colour, she doesn't do anything to it."

"Tangerine," said Susie. "And her eyes are jade, her teeth like little chips of Carrara marble." She nudged Claud. "You hadn't noticed how delicious she is, had you?"

"He was taken up with Laura," said Brian. "Can I pay next week, Mavis dear?"

"Certainly not," said Mavis, snatching Brian's glass and clunking it on to her tray. "Only Laura has a special arrangement, you know that."

"Oh, all right, you great bully." Brian reached for his coat, handed Susie hers. "This should cover it." He gave Mavis a ten-pound note. "Keep the change."

"I'm not proud," said Mavis, laughing. "I won't be a minute," she said to Claud, "if you care to wait."

"I'll wait," said Claud, "thanks." My goodness, he thought, she is pretty; how could I not have noticed?

Brian was buttoning Susie into her jacket as though she was a small child. "Where's your woolly hat?" he asked.

Claud watched them, amused. He felt elated at meeting these new people, Laura's friends.

"In your pocket." Susie let herself be dressed by Brian, who now put a wool cap on her head. "Laura wouldn't let you do this to her," she remarked, sitting doll-like.

"Laura would not let me get a leg over her, either," said Brian.

"I wouldn't let you try," said Susie amiably. "Not over anyone and particularly not over Laura."

"All the same, one wonders what motivates her." Brian gently pushed tendrils of Susie's hair up under her cap with a large forefinger, then leaned forward and kissed her mouth.

"Sex?" suggested Susie, returning the kiss.

"Who with?" asked Claud, watching them.

"One doesn't know," said Brian.

"There are lots of stories," said Susie.

"Nothing you can pin down," said Brian.

"Is she married?" asked Claud. "Or was she, ever?"

"That's one thing that is known: she's not nor ever was."

"Does one know why not?" Claud persisted. He felt a need to know, was there some sadness? "Did some bloke betray her?"

"That's a mystery, but any betraying to be done would have been done by Laura." Susie surprised him by her cattiness.

Claud felt angry with Susie. Laura had left them so suddenly, she had made herself defenceless. Unequal to the task on such short acquaintance, he was grateful to Mavis who, rejoining them, had overheard Susie's remarks.

"You may be wrong there," said Mavis. "My mum has a theory that Laura wouldn't hurt a fly."

Claud recollected his own parent the evening before suggesting a heart of nougat.

Brian said, "An older woman, out of the race, would be a better judge than you, Susie."

"Perhaps she is just self-sufficient," suggested Mavis. "It's not absolutely necessary, as you men seem to think, for every girl to have a man," she added tartly.

"Just nicer," said Susie, getting to her feet.

"See you in the market when you've got your stall," said Susie, now ready to leave. "Brian and I will show you anything Laura forgets to tell you. Bye."

"Goodbye, see yer," said Brian. "Come on, sugar." He pushed Susie out ahead of him.

"Brrr," exclaimed Susie, gasping in the frosty air. "Icicles!"

"Are they really married?" Claud asked Mavis, who stood now beside him, buttoned into an overcoat several sizes too large.

"Common law," said Mavis. "Come on."

Laura, rising from the dentist's chair in the surgery across the street where she had been having her teeth scaled and polished, watched Claud take Mavis' arm as they stepped out of the wine bar. "You certainly see local life from your window, Mr Owen."

"I haven't time," said the dentist, "or the inclination. See you again in six months, Miss Thornby. Next," he said into the intercom.

"You miss a lot," said Laura, ignoring his rudeness.

"Ah, well." He was impatient to see her go.

And what am I missing? Laura speculated as she descended the stairs. What have I missed, she questioned as she wrapped her coat round her against the cold wind, swung her scarf round her neck as she stood on the dentist's doorstep. Far down the street she could see Claud's fair head lean towards Mavis' orange aureole as they broke into a trot to avoid an oncoming car. She turned to walk in the opposite direction, lengthening her stride. I wonder why he is against fish. What would Freud say? More to the point, what do I say? She smiled as she thought that there was really no need for her to miss anything.

Brian and Susie, passing her in their battered old Land-Rover waved, assuming that Laura's smile was for them.

"Found yourself a toy boy?"

Laura, turning, stood nose to nose with Nicholas Thornby who, softly shod, had crept up behind her.

"Looking at you, dear Nicholas," she answered at a tangent, "I can see what I shall look like when I am really old." She stepped back a pace to observe him better. "A trim figure, not too wrinkled but pretty thin on top," she said, amused that he should bother to jerk his stomach in for her, a reflex action.

"You'll be so lucky, your mother and I are uniquely preserved. But who is the boy? He's pretty," Nicholas persisted.

"Claud Bannister."

"Margaret Bannister's boy? He used to be so spotty, I didn't recognise him."

"Ever beautiful, you must have had your share of acne in your day? I know I did."

"It's too far back to remember. Why are you taking him up? I saw you with him in the market. You don't usually go for lame dogs."

"Does he look lame?" Laura wrapped her scarf tighter against the icy wind. "Rather than live on the dole, he's going to run a junk stall in the market," she said.

"How laudable." Nicholas' tone indicated doubt.

"I thought I'd offer him a look round the Old Rectory attics, it's high time some of the debris was cleared out."

"You may have to ask Emily's and my permission."

"I shall, perhaps."

"I don't know what Emily will say."

"She will ask if it's in a good cause and if it's not, she'll be glad of a clearance."

"How well you know her." Nicholas grinned. "One questions whether a toy boy is a good cause." Laura did not respond to this. "But there may be treasures in that attic," Nicholas prevaricated. "One can't be too careful. Priceless Ming vases used as umbrella stands, one reads in the paper," he said, laughing.

"That's not very likely." It was Laura's turn to laugh. "Quite a lot of stuff was put there by me, things the dustmen refused to move."

"Oh those dustmen! Bone idle scroungers."

Laura blinked her eyes, which were watering from the wind, and sniffed, twitching a nose that was a feminine version of Nicholas'. "I know you vote Tory," she said as she stepped aside to allow a woman pushing a double buggy to pass.

"One should not pander to the unemployed," said Nicholas, stepping back close to her.

"So I have frequently heard you say. We are blocking the pavement," said Laura.

"I also saw you chatting to him at the concert the other night."

"I have an idea he once worked in a fish shop," said Laura, sowing a red herring in Nicholas' mind.

"I thought you were interested in that Roumanian conductor (that was pretty trashy stuff, wasn't it?). Isn't it a bit of a comedown to switch to a fishmonger?"

"The Roumanian has gone back to Roumania."

"A communist country, no joy there, I agree. One could see you weren't much interested but he wasn't lame, was he?"

"Not so that you'd notice."

"And this Claud Bannister, shall you lame him?"

"The traffic warden has just stuck a ticket on the windscreen of your car, Nicholas." A man in a tweed hat adorned with salmon flies tossed the information over his shoulder as he elbowed past Laura. "While you stand there gassing like an old maid, blocking the way of legitimate shoppers, you get ticketed. Just wait till they bring clamps to the town!" His voice faded as he hurried out of earshot.

"Damn and blast, that's the third this month," said Nicholas. "Your fault for keeping me talking," he said nastily.

Laura smiled. "Too bad. Tough," she said.

"He's a bit young for a toy boy," Nicholas niggled.

"I heard he was a lift boy in some hotel." Laura tried a fresh herring.

"What versatility! Those tight trousers and bumfreezer jackets. Not my style, alas. I would hardly think—"

"Nicholas," said a tweedy lady burdened with shopping, "that fiend of a warden has stuck a ticket on your—"

"I know, I know," cried Nicholas, furiously. "What's it got to do with you, you silly cow?" He began to move back down the street to his car.

Laura watched Nicholas go with detachment. Then she shouted after him, "I'll treat you and Emily to a booze-up tonight, how about it? A pub crawl?"

Nicholas waved an arm in acknowledgment. Laura continued on her way, leaning slightly into the wind, protecting her face with her scarf, wondering why she felt protective towards Claud, he wouldn't thank me for the fishmonger or the lifts, she thought, but maybe he will when he's famous.

Christopher Peel, sitting beside his wife Helen driving their BMW, noticed Laura as she parted from Nicholas. Craning his neck the better to look back, he reflected not for the first time that there were compensations in having a wife who did not trust one's driving. One could see what was going on without being accused of risking an accident.

"That's Laura in another garish outfit," said Helen, who was suspected by some of having eyes in the back of her head. "God knows why she wears such an outrageous combination of colours; somebody should tell her."

"Why don't you tell her?" Losing sight of Laura as Helen accelerated through the traffic, Christopher slewed his eyes towards his wife. A greater contrast than Helen's clothes with Laura's would be hard to find, he thought, appraising Helen's sensible sludge-coloured sweater and shirt, matching corduroy slacks, dull green waxed waterproof jacket with corduroy collar, brown felt hat. "Sludge," he said, assessing his wife's complexion (nothing worse than a fading suntan with mouse-coloured hair, he thought). "Sludge."

"What?" said Helen.

"Nothing." (I bet she heard me.)

"I wonder what she is doing down here, she hardly ever visits Emily and Nicholas for more than a day," said Helen.

"Oh, I don't know," said Christopher, who knew quite well that Laura came down oftener than was generally known. "Perhaps she feels responsible for the old people."

"Responsible! Laura?" Helen snorted.

"Well—"

"She must be up to something if she's down for more than a day—"

"She's got her pad in the Old Rectory."

"Is she having an affair with that red composer?"

"What red composer? I thought he was the conductor." Christopher betrayed himself.

"Don't be dim, Christopher, the man who wrote that awful stuff we had to sit through at the charity concert; that man."

"How would I know?" (Sitting in the wine bar with that boy. If she'd been on her own as she usually is, I would have gone in and asked her why the hell she—)

"She's an old flame of yours."

"Not that again! Oh God, Helen, why can't you lay off? Any small flicker I may have had with Laura was twenty-five years ago."

"More than that."

"So you know it all. Why don't you tackle Laura yourself? Tell her you don't like her clothes, ask her who she is sleeping with, why she visits her mother, why—"

"No need to fly off the handle." Helen changed gear.

"I am not flying—"

"You are so touchy about Laura."

"It is you who are touchy about Laura, Helen, you never stop, you—"

"I never mention Laura. I just happened to notice her at the concert the other night and to make a small observation just now. No need to blow it up—"

"Christ, Helen, Laura and I were practically brought up together. We were childhood friends, she was constantly in our house, she—"

"She would have married you if your father hadn't put his foot down. I don't suppose your mother had a clue – so wrapped up in herself, her bloody dogs and her ridiculous garden."

"Look, Helen." Christopher raised his voice, shouting above the noise of a lorry Helen was overtaking. "Laura never wanted to marry me, she—"

"Of course she did. Obviously she wanted your money and the house. God knows what *she* would have done with the garden if she'd got her hands on it."

"She did *not* want to marry me!" Christopher shouted, and a hitherto somnolent old Labrador raised its head from among the parcels and packages on the back seat and barked. "When will you get it into your stupid head that there was never any question of marriage between Laura and me? The moment she was old enough, she upsticked and beat it to London. She made a career for herself, she has her own business—"

"A pretty small one—"

"—I don't see why you should be so upset and—"

"It's you who seem to be upset." Helen paused by the traffic lights on the edge of the town.

"Oh, God," said Christopher.

"Actually," said Helen as the lights turned to green, "if you hadn't flown into this silly temper, I was leading up to the fact that I have a small job—"

"For her small business?"

"Yes."

"Then why—"

"I thought you could persuade her to do it for me at cost price or something."

"I could?"

"Yes, you know her better than I, as you've just indicated."

"So—"

"And I don't want to know her better than I do already."

"That makes two of you," Christopher muttered. "What's the job?" he asked. "I don't see why she should do it at cost price, she has her living to make."

"It was just a thought, since you are such old buddies."

Disliking the word buddy Christopher thought, If I told Helen that if it were not for her I would seldom think of Laura, she wouldn't believe me. He watched the road ahead. Perhaps, he thought, I should be grateful to Helen. Glancing at his wife's profile he smiled, then patting her corduroy thigh he said loudly: "You silly old thing, what's the job?"

Helen proceeded to tell him.

Laura, walking slowly in spite of the cold, watched Christopher and Helen's car disappear and thought, Poor old, boring old Christopher. She wrapped her scarf close, pushing it up over her jaw She dawdled, looking into a bookshop window, keeping her eyes down, not wishing to enter into chat with the bookseller, who was in his way a friend. She counted the titles: love, crime, travel, history. By dawdling it was her intention to give Nicholas time to make a scene with the traffic warden, who was lurking within insult distance of Nicholas' car. Either the man had more courage than was good for him or he was new to the town. Only a few years ago Nicholas had tripped a warden so that, lurching against a bollard on the quay, he had fallen into the river. I cannot but admire, thought Laura, watching. The old devil does not resist his impulses; he has a dreadful, endearing, childlike quality.

Nicholas approached his car; the warden, taller and burlier than Nicholas, stood his ground (Laura asked herself which of the two men needed her protection). Nicholas snatched the ticket stuck behind his wiper and tore it across. Obeying an instinct similar to that of a dog confronted by a cat, its back arched, its mouth spitting, the warden shrugged and turned away.

Laura chuckled, ran her tongue over her freshly scaled teeth and, relaxing, let her thoughts return pleasurably to Claud, so fresh and ingenuous after Clug. He was vulnerable in a way Clug could never have been, more importantly so than Christopher in youth. I could protect Claud, she thought, then almost laughed outright as she was swept by an irresistible exultant desire to interfere, manipulate, experiment with Claud – by way of protection.

"You reach it up this thing. I'll go first." Mavis climbed a metal ladder towards a trap-door in the ceiling. She still wore her greatcoat. Claud, watching her climb, resisted nipping her Achilles tendon between finger and thumb. "A well-turned ankle," he said, reaching up but not touching.

"A what? Come on up." She had disappeared.

"Dornford Yates or Somerset Maugham, perhaps?" Claud climbed the ladder.

Above him Mavis switched on a light. "It's pretty basic," she said as he came up through the floor, "just the bed, a table, a chair, the bookshelves. You'll need somewhere to keep your clothes."

The loft was larger than he had expected; cold light streamed through attic windows. Claud went to the window. "Oh," he said, "what a view!"

"Yes," said Mavis, "yes." She stuffed her hands up the sleeves of her coat.

They looked across slate roofs and jumbled chimney pots to the town gasworks, and to the right the river, where boats moored in midstream, swans and ducks cruised. The air in the attic was dry. Claud sneezed and, when he breathed in again, sniffed the faint smell he had noticed when, reaching across the table in the wine bar, Mavis had set the coffee in front of Laura. Fresh flesh. He felt simultaneously a wish to kiss Mavis' throat as it emerged from the heavy coat and something which resembled lust for Laura. Watching the gasometer, he sighed as the twin desires cancelled each other out.

Hearing the sigh, Mavis questioned, "So it won't do? As I said, it's pretty basic." She excused the loft. "It's not even an attic."

"No, no, it's lovely. I could bring some rugs from home. Do you think your mother will rent it to me? What's the rent?"

"Let's go and ask her." Mavis led the way down the ladder. She feared her mother would find the prospective tenant too young; she wanted a steady tenant who would not be likely to negotiate the ladder drunk. There had been an unfortunate incident with a visiting cousin who had slipped and been badly bruised. Since this episode Ann Kennedy had dreaded an entanglement with insurance companies. On the other hand a tenant of guaranteed sobriety might not be sufficiently spry to negotiatc the ladder. It was a worry; she needed the rent. "Don't be surprised if you hear me tell my mother that you don't drink," said Mavis.

"I don't, much. I can't afford to. Why?" Claud rejoined Mavis at the foot of the ladder.

"She's afraid of people falling off the ladder pissed."

"I'm pretty good on ladders, drunk or sober," said Claud primly.

"It's the Irish imagination which foresees possible trouble."

"I thought you were a Plymouth family," said Claud, watching the back of Mavis' head as she descended the stairs ahead of him.

"So what? There are Kennedys born all over. In the United States, for instance. You've been listening to Laura." Mavis, not over-fond of Laura, sounded quite huffy.

"I suppose everyone tells you you have beautiful hair?" Claud attempted to deflect her huff.

"They certainly do." Mavis was unenthusiastic. Then, remembering her mother's need for the rent, she said, "Come on and meet my mum. Mum," she shouted, "where are you?"

"In here," Ann Kennedy answered from the kitchen.

"This is Claud, a friend of Laura's, he'd like to rent the loft, Mum."

"Rent the loft?" said Ann Kennedy, affecting surprise. "A friend of Laura's? Well!" Impossible to tell from her tone whether Mrs Kennedy thought well or ill of Laura. "I'm defrosting the fridge; it's a job which bores me rigid." She waved towards an open refrigerator. "Takes for ever."

"Soften it up with the hairdryer," suggested Mavis.

"Would that be safe?" Mrs Kennedy was interested. "Wouldn't I get electrocuted?"

"It's a lovely loft." Claud hastened to stem the diversion. Suddenly he wanted the loft badly; he could see his typewriter on the table, hear his fingers tap the keys. "I am a writer, Mrs Kennedy."

"A writer," said Ann Kennedy in flat tone. "Oh." She bent to peer into the fridge, "It is beginning to drip, perhaps the dryer – this fridge is as old as Methuselah."

"I am very quiet," said Claud in recommendation.

"Quiet," said Ann Kennedy. "Really?"

"Yes," said Claud.

"There's the ladder."

"I'm pretty nimble."

"I don't doubt."

"I scarcely drink."

"Scarcely."

"I could pay the rent in advance, if it's not too large, that is."

"M-m-m." She peered into the refrigerator.

"Cash," said Claud.

"Cash," said Mrs Kennedy. "Did you tell him the rent, Maeve?"

"*Mavis*," said Mavis. "No, I didn't."

"If you must keep changing your name," said Ann Kennedy in accents of extreme irritability, "why can't you choose one we can all stick to? A decent biblical name like Ruth or Rebecca or Miriam?" Her voice rose as ice suddenly began to clatter noisily on to the ice tray. "Or Mary? What's wrong with the virgin Mary?"

"It's common."

"There's only one virgin Mary," snapped Ann Kennedy, "why not—"

"Because I can't stand the Jews forever killing the Arabs and vice versa, they are as bad as the Northern Irish." Mavis' voice rose to meet her parent's.

"It would be simpler with all this chopping and changing to know you by a number. Number One would suit you fine," Ann Kennedy snapped.

Claud registered that this was a well-established conflict. "Could we get back to the rent?" His masculine calm rather pleased him.

"Of course." Mrs Kennedy stooped to field an oblong wedge of ice which was slipping towards the floor. "Gotcher." She named a rent high in excess of the amount he had expected. "Any friend of Laura's is welcome." She avoided her daughter's eye.

"Great," said Claud. "Perhaps I could move in next week?"

The telephone shrilled in the next room. Before answering Claud's question Ann Kennedy moved away to answer it. Waiting for her to return, Claud watched Mavis standing dwarfed in her immense coat, her face a mixture of surprise and something else. "What's the matter?" he asked, feeling that if he were to become a writer, he must be sensitive to people's moods.

"Nothing," said Mavis, torn between admiration for her mother's bold greed and fear that on reflection Claud might change his mind.

"That was Laura," said Ann Kennedy, returning.

"Oh?"

"Message for you to ring her up or go and see her."

"Me?" asked Mavis.

"No. Mr – er – what's your name?"

"Claud Bannister."

"That's right, Claud. I'm glad she rang. I was a bit bothered about the rent." Mrs Kennedy bent to catch another bit of ice effecting its escape. "So I asked her; she said knock off a couple of quid." Mother's and daughter's eyes met.

"No business of Laura's," said Mavis.

"I'm quite happy with what you—" began Claud.

"No, no. As I say, knock off two pounds. She said either give her a tinkle or come over, she could tell you something about your stall. You didn't say anything about a stall?"

"Well, no. No, I didn't. I could go over this afternoon. Thanks. Would you come with me, Mavis? Show me the way?"

"I have to wash my hair," said Mavis. "You'll find it all right." She pulled her coat collar up over her chin. Claud was reminded of Laura wrapping her scarf across her face in the wine bar. She had looked exotic. Mavis disappearing into the outsize overcoat gave the effect of a tortoise. "There's a bus," said Mavis, "catch that."

Arriving at the Old Rectory, Claud was not in the best of tempers. He had consulted the timetable but arrived to see the bus leaving the square minutes earlier than he expected. On protesting to a youth waiting for a bus in the opposite direction, he had been outraged at the suggestion that he had studied the wrong timetable. "It's winter, zee, you should look for winter times not zummer times." The boy leaned against the wall, grinning. "Ain't no more buzzes til zix thirty or so." Humiliated by the fake yokel accent and the suspicion that he had in fact made a stupid mistake, Claud set off walking, more with the intention of distancing himself from mockery than of reaching Laura.

As he walked annoyance coupled with his imagination spurred him along. Not profligate with ideas, he would use the incident in his new novel: his hero, as yet rather an intangible character, would foot it towards the girl he loved. Naturally he would have to walk somewhere more inspiring than this main road with its draggle of bungaloid habitations punctuated by filling stations. He would set him to walk over a moor, across the Fens or along the Pennine Way, somewhere more peaceable than a main road where cars hurtled past breaking the speed limit, polluting the air with disgusting fumes; he would walk towards his lover, waiting expectantly.

Passing the last filling station, Claud consoled himself for this boring trudge by giving his hero a bicycle, then, growing impatient with the tedious journey, he bought him a car. It was hard to decide on the make. He was snobbish about Fords, averse to Fiats and despised Sunbeams, but by the time he read on a white board half-hidden in a laurel hedge the words, "The Old Rectory", he had bought his hero a second-hand Alfa Romeo. With that little matter settled he could apply himself to his character's destiny in the next chapter.

Claud walked up a curving drive to the front door and rang the bell.

A dog barked loudly. The door burst open. Laura, twenty years older than she had been that morning, beckoned him in. "Come in, come in, are you in trouble? Run out of petrol? Car broken down? Want to use the telephone?" She backed into a dark hall. "Or have you come to read the meters?"

"I walked – I—"

"Walked! Heavens! Nobody walks. The road is lethal. I am surprised you were not squashed like a hedgehog. I'll show you the meter, you're new—"

"Laura – I – you—"

"Oh! You want *Laura*," said Laura's double. "Round the back, try that, servants' entrance."

"Oh – I'm sorry, I mistook, I thought – I—"

"Round the house, the other door." The door so brusquely opened clicked shut in his face.

Repulsed, Claud made his way along an alley which led through overgrown shrubs to a door at the back of the house. There was a knocker. Claud knocked.

"I can see by your face that you met my mother," said Laura, opening the door. "She gets tremendously annoyed if she's mistaken for me, which is a pity because I had an idea that we might prise some junk for your stall out of her; the attic is bulging with tat. Come in."

Claud followed her along an ill-lit passage into a combination of kitchen and sitting-room. Where once a kitchen range had stood was a large open fire, along one wall a gas cooker, sink and refrigerator, in front of the fire a shabby sofa and armchairs. Behind the sofa stood a long deal table, one end obviously used to eat off, the other to work at. A dresser held books as well as china. The room was warm and smelled agreeably of garlicky cooking but beneath this aroma there was a hint of mice. The view from the windows was on to a large neglected garden. Claud felt his spirits rise. "Nice," he said, "it's nice."

"Well – yes – it does. I've walled them off."

"Who?"

"Family."

"Oh."

"I sleep in what was the servants' hall, and my bathroom was the pantry. I'm not here much."

"I got your message."

"I gathered from Mrs K that you've rented the loft. Sit down, do." She pointed to an armchair occupied by a cat.

Claud sat, edging next to the cat, held his hands towards the fire. "Yes I have, it's superb."

"I used to rent it myself," said Laura. "I put the bed and table there, and the chair."

"Really?" Claud was surprised. "What for?"

"Privacy. To escape. I spent my pocket money on it. I lay and dreamed and counted my pimples."

"Oh."

"You know what it's like when family become oppressive, unbearable."

"Well, actually, I—" Claud thought of his gentle unobtrusive mother. "Not exactly, my—"

"Drink? Tea? Coffee? Wine? Did you walk?"

"Yes, your mother seemed surprised. Coffee, please."

"Walking, the lost art." Laura poured beans into a grinder and filled the room with its screech. "Sorry about that, it's French," she excused the grinder. She switched on an electric kettle. "No one in their right senses walks along that road, you should have come over the hill across the fields, or come by bus."

"I missed it."

"People do." Laura poured boiling water on to the coffee, stirred the mix in a jug. Claud, breathing its heavenly smell, found himself telling Laura about his hero who, starting out as a pedestrian, was now the owner of an Alfa Romeo.

"How splendidly vulgar." Laura peered into the coffee jug. "Nearly ready. What's his name, your hero?"

"Justin."

"Oh God!" said Laura. "You can't call him Justin."

"Why ever not?" Claud was nettled.

"You just cannot." Laura poured coffee through a strainer into beautiful but chipped cups and handed one to Claud. "Milk? Sugar? Help yourself. I've got a cake somewhere." She moved to the dresser, where a half-demolished cake sagged crumbling on a broken Worcester plate. "Justin," she said, "is *un*splendidly vulgar."

"Um." Claud gulped his coffee. It burned. He could feel the burn right down into his chest. "I'll have to think about that." He was not prepared to yield, knew that he would and must take care not to tell Laura that the choice of name had hovered between Justin and Crispin.

Laura subsided in a flowing movement to sit cross-legged in front of the fire; she had taken off her boots and was now barefoot.

"You have beautiful feet," said Claud.

"Yes." Laura tucked them out of sight under her skirt. "I know."

"I thought your mother was your *doppelgänger*," said Claud.

"And well she might be," said Laura. "There's a male version too." She did not explain. "Have you seduced Mavis yet?" she asked.

"I haven't had time," said Claud. Two can play at this, he thought, watching Laura's face in the firelight; what does she take me for?

Laura showed her teeth; she had her back to the light and might have been smiling, it was difficult to tell. "Have some cake." She proffered the plate. "That's not mouse shit, it's seed cake," she said as Claud hesitated.

"No thanks." He recoiled.

"Well," said Laura, "since you are here we'd better brave the *doppelgängers*." She reached for a pair of tights hanging on the fireguard and began putting them on.

Claud observed her legs; they were long and peculiarly neat. Her movements as she pulled the tights up over her bottom had a sensuality which brought the word risqué to what he was beginning to think of as his writer's mind. "I would like to seduce you," he said. He decided to give his heroine Laura's body. She had already, he realised, got Mavis' hair in his writer's mind's eye. He had become aware of Mavis and the smell of her flesh in the wine bar, but he had been taken up with Laura, and later all he had seen of her was the enormous overcoat; she had even hidden her hands in its sleeves. "I would like to seduce you," he repeated.

"Fancy that," said Laura, picking up the telephone and dialling. "I am coming round," she said as someone answered, "to explore the attic." Then, "You'd put in a bit of practice before tackling Mavis, would that be it?"

Claud did not know what to make of this. "I don't know what to make of you," he said. Surely at this juncture any woman of Laura's age would laugh and say, I am old enough to be your mother, or words to that effect.

But Laura gave him what that morning he had called her sidelong look. "Just concentrate on Justin," she said. "And what is his lover's name to be?"

"I haven't decided yet." Quickly he dismissed the name he had been toying with, it would never do. Pearl must be dropped back where it came from. Indeed later when he tried to remember the name he could not and even believed it might have been Fleur, or perhaps June.

Laura tugged at her boots. "Coming?" she asked.

★

With his back to the light Claud poured tea from the pot his mother had placed before him. His eye was extremely painful, his head throbbed. Beside the teapot his mother had put a bottle of aspirin. The scene revived memories of the times before his father left home, driven away by his wife's intolerable forbearance.

Claud unscrewed the aspirin bottle, tipped pills on to his palm, gulped them down with scalding tea, drained the cup and refilled it. My pa, he thought, was an incurable alcoholic; he did not last long after leaving Ma's tender care. Perhaps if they could have had a hearty row, a healthy shout when he came home drunk, he would be alive to this day? But *I* was not roaring drunk last night, Claud told himself. I am not an alcoholic. On the other hand recollection of what happened in the Old Rectory is dim, if not zero. "I think I got a bang on the head," he said as his mother rustled the sheets of her newspaper. "I probably have a slight concussion."

Margaret Bannister, an inveterate *Guardian* reader, did not answer. Claud calculated that she had just about reached the leader page after starting at the back with the sports; she was unlikely to reply to his remark until she had worked through to the front page. By that time the aspirin and tea would have begun their work. Thinking this, Claud realised what he had not realised before: that this ploy had evolved over years of his father's hangovers. (Make strong tea, supply aspirin, give it time to work before speaking.)

But what had happened at the Old Rectory? Claud cudgelled his brain. He had followed Laura round the house and in at the door where he had earlier been rebuffed by her mother. On the way Laura had said something he did not quite catch about "disturbing my haunts"; it did not make sense and she had not repeated it. She had pushed open the door, paused in the hall and listened. This in itself seemed odd at the time; any normal daughter entering her mother's house would call out, "I'm here," or, "Anyone at home?" or words to that effect. But Laura put finger to lip, signalled him to follow and then walked fast and quietly along the hall and up the stairs. He had followed her up and along a landing, through a green baize door and up a steep, uncarpeted flight to the attic. Here Laura stopped looking puzzled and pushed open a door, motioning him to follow. He remembered getting the impression that she had expected the door to be shut.

It was while Laura fumbled for a light switch – "Wait there, you might fall over something" – that it had happened.

A bucket was clapped over his head. There was a rat-tat-tat of blows on its outside. The noise was terrifying. He remembered stepping back, falling down the stairs, bumping and banging his head, his nose and his eye as he rolled, tearing off the bucket and scrambling to his feet. Above in the dark of the attic there was the sound of scuffling, grunts, gasps, hisses. It was the absence of voices he had found unnerving. Making no effort to help Laura, he had taken to his heels and fled. As he left the house he heard a burst of laughter.

Sitting in his mother's warm kitchen gulping tea, swilling down the aspirin, Claud felt shame for his pusillanimity as he remembered running down the drive to the road, thumbing a lift from a passing van, being dropped off at a public house. He had sat in the pub trembling with shock (it must have been shock, not fear). At some moment during the evening's drinking (yes, now he remembered drinking. Quite a lot, actually) Brian and Susie had joined him. Yes, that's right, they had talked about his future in the market and given him a lift home. Once inside the door he had vomited. It can't have been very late because his mother had still been up and about. She hadn't said anything. She had watched him clear up his sick; he had been well enough to do that. She had said nothing, absolutely nothing; no wonder his father left home. Claud felt a comradely wave of sympathy for his father, who he usually referred to as "a perfect shit", "a prize shit", "a wimp". Reviving under the influence of the strong tea and aspirin, Claud felt rage and remembered his fury of the night before. He had made a long abrasive speech to his mother before staggering upstairs to bed, the last few steps on all fours. What the hell had he *said*?

Margaret Bannister folded her newspaper and sat down. She had, while reading the newspaper, put butter and marmalade on the table and also made toast. This feminine gift of doing several things at once without being flustered had maddened his father. (Why can't you concentrate on one thing at a time? Have you got three arms, woman?)

"Your education is going to waste." Margaret spoke in derisory quotes. She buttered her toast; the scraping sound jarred on Claud's delicate ear. Normally about as fierce as a lettuce, she sounded jaunty and crisp as she repeated the phrase, "Your education is going to waste," before biting her toast.

Assuming attack to be the best form of defence, Claud snarled, "Mother, you are whining. Why don't you go the whole hog, come straight out, cast your sacrifices in my teeth? No new clothes, no holidays, no decent car, long years of pinching and scraping." Let her whine. Surely she would whine? What if he had come in drunk and been sick in the hall; he had cleared it up, hadn't he? "I am not going to take those exams again." He raised his voice. "I do not want to become an accountant."

"That idea for a career was entirely your choice, as I remember. Pass the marmalade."

Claud lumbered on: "I am going to be a writer and support myself until I get published by keeping a stall in the market."

"So you said last night. Toast?"

"Did I?"

"Yes." Margaret Bannister put more bread into the toaster. "You did."

Keeping in profile, so that she would not get a good look at his battered eye, Claud squinted at his parent. "Did I say all that?"

"Not quite so clearly; your speech was on the slur." His mother caught the toast as it sprang from the toaster, putting one piece in the toast rack, which she nudged towards her son, the other on her plate.

Claud ploughed on. "You can look the other way when you go marketing." He had often raised a laugh among friends at university by describing his mother as "poor but snobbish". He had even sung, "She was poor, but she was snobbish" to the music hall aria after a drink or two. "I am moving out of here." He raised his voice. "I have rented Mrs Kennedy's loft."

Rarely since adolescence had he been so disagreeable to his mother. Why did she not whine? If only she would whine, he would feel less awful, less like his father. There would be the justification to sprint upstairs and pack his bags (he would have to come back for his books and the heavier things).

"You told me that last night." Good God, she was laughing! "Ha, ha, ha, hah!" Helpless laughter! Tears of laughter. "Oh, Claud, if you could see yourself!" She wiped her eyes. "Oh, it hurts to laugh so much, oh!" Her laughter bubbled again. "It was your choice to be an accountant. You wanted security. Security!" Mrs Bannister hiccuped with mirth. "We never were secure in my family, never went in for accountants, and certainly not in your father's. Now there's snobbery for you."

Good God, she must know, must have heard me. "Perhaps I am rebelling against your joint fecklessness," he mumbled, confidence crumbling.

"I think your plan excellent; a stall in the market could be a lot of fun." His mother helped herself to marmalade. "Who put you up to it?"

"I thought of it for myself."

Mrs Bannister raised eyebrows in disbelief and bit her toast. "I bet it was Laura Thornby. She loves to meddle and she would have told you about the Kennedys' loft."

Claud did not reply; his head was splitting. He wished he could remember exactly what had been said the night before. He glanced covertly at his parent; she looked, he noticed with unease, like someone who, having dived too steeply, comes up for a welcome gasp of air. "Did I say anything else?" he queried.

"Just your plans for writing, your market stall, and, oh yes, something about Nicholas Thornby which I didn't catch—"

"Good God, yes! I remember now, he gave me quite a shock—"

"Shock?"

"Well, yes. It's so peculiar. Laura is exactly like her mother and—"

"He is exactly like his sister Emily? They are twins."

"But Mother, it's creepy, the three of them look like triplets, it—"

"Gave you a turn?"

"God knows why."

"God is about the only one who does. One should not of course put the blame on *him*. More tea?"

Claud did not feel well enough to ask her to elucidate her ambiguity. He was disgusted to see his hand shake as he passed his cup; she had made a fresh pot as she talked. "A sure cure," she had been in the habit of saying to his father, "for a slight binge." (Not that Father's binges were ever slight.)

"Mother," Claud heard himself saying, "there is no need really for me to move out. I am sorry I said all that – I can perfectly well stay on here, it's—"

"God forbid!" said Margaret Bannister brusquely.

"What?"

"I said, God forbid, darling." She looked at her son, hardened her heart. "It is not that I don't love having you, but not permanently. Holidays and visits are nice but," here she went quite pink, "you are twenty-three and it is rather marvellous to have my house to myself."

"And not have people throwing up in the hall."

"I was not mentioning that."

"Oh." So that's why she looked as though coming up for air. She'd found freedom. Freedom from him. Claud felt betrayed. "Were you pleased when Father lit off?"

"Of course."

"Gosh." Claud felt awe.

"I have been thinking of moving for some time. I can get a good price for this house," Margaret Bannister said cheerfully.

"Moving? What about my laundry?" It was out before he could stop himself.

"There's the launderette. There's what's she called, Maeve?"

"Mavis."

"Part of the price of independence is dealing with your own dirty linen," said Margaret Bannister. She got up and began to clear the table. Watching her, Claud wished that for once he could confide in her; he had always been so careful not to, but now— "I am very sorry about last night," he began.

"Not to worry, these things happen."

"I didn't break anything, did I?"

"Not that I know of." She was dismissive.

"Good – er – um – er . . ."

"What is it, Claud?"

"I just wanted to apologise." She was feeding the dishwasher plates and cups, just as long ago she had spooned cereal into his infant mouth, patiently mopping when he regurgitated, only the dishwasher was better mannered than he had been. "I only wanted to apologise," he repeated.

"I said, not to worry." She had her back to him.

"We never seem to talk, do we?"

"And whose fault is that?" she snapped. "You long since made it clear that you resent questions and that your life and friends have nothing to do with me, that your affection is minimal, my uses limited."

"Oh."

"Recently it has suited you to live here; possibly you find this place less dull and provincial than you thought. You see it with a fresh eye. I am glad," she straightened her back and shut the dishwasher, "that you have the gumption to risk life on your own. You have no roots here, maybe you are growing them? You cannot expect me to hang around while they grow, and water them by doing your laundry. There's a mixed metaphor for a writer. If we never talk, Claud, it is because you have reduced the snub to a fine art."

Claud pushed his chair back and stood up. "Thanks for telling me," he said. "D'you know once when I was small Dad shouted at me that I would grow up into a completely selfish swine?"

"He must have been drinking."

"No, I think he was sober."

"Perhaps he foresaw your future. Writers need to be selfish."

"I was not at that time proposing to be a writer."

"Well, whatever." She fended him off.

"Did he know the Thornbys?"

"We knew them."

"Are they bad news?"

"—M-m."

"I think it was the old man who put a bucket over my head and pushed me down a flight of stairs."

"That figures." Margaret Bannister switched on the dishwasher. "I really hardly know them," she shouted above the sound of swishing water.

"You must, you have lived here for years."

"You can live in a place without knowing people."

Claud sensed that his mother had no intention of enlightening him. "I only just now noticed Laura," he said.

"Not surprising, she's scarcely ever here." His mother's tone increased Claud's interest. "You are getting to know her now," she said, glancing at her son obliquely. As she did so he became aware of a similarity; his mother's look matched what he had the day before called sidelong in Laura. Yet he failed to put one and one together to see them as much of an age.

"I would recommend a bath," said his mother, cutting short his wish to talk. "A bath that is good and hot, and put a spoonful of Scrubs ammonia in it. It will clear your head wonderfully."

"You used to say that to Father."

"One does so repeat oneself."

He sensed that she was laughing again, that she was a more interesting person than he gave her credit for and that he had missed the chance of knowing her. "You make me feel lonely," he shouted above the noise of the dishwasher.

"Writers are solitary people," she said.

Lying in the bath waiting for his head to clear, Claud reviewed the events of the previous day. Memory was clear up to his arrival at the Old Rectory, after that confused. He remembered reaching the pub where he had asked for a double Scotch to revive his courage. (I really am the most frightful coward, he thought, leaning forward to adjust the hot tap.) Feeling better, he had perhaps unwisely ordered another. (I should have eaten some of that seed cake, he remembered Laura's seed cake.) He heard his voice in the pub saying in confident tones, "The same again, please," yet stop, think, wasn't the voice on the verge of being disembodied? Well? It was after that drink that he had glanced towards the door and seen Laura in triplicate. What had caused most alarm and instability was that this was no ordinary triplication – several times at university he had seen double and once in triplicate – what on this occasion terrified was that Laura in triplicate was no run-of-the-mill vision. One emanation, if this was the right word, was male, the other the female who had shut the door of the Old Rectory in his face. Claud's brain, under the influence of his mother's strong tea, aspirin and the fumes of ammonia, clicked into gear. At breakfast just now he had mentioned Nicholas Thornby "giving him a shock" and now, he recollected, someone in the pub calling out "Hullo, Nicholas" before the Laura in triplicate wheeled round and left the pub as fast and as silently as it had appeared.

How weird, thought Claud, how peculiar. What were they doing? There were three Lauras: one was her mother, the other this Nicholas. Was it then, he asked himself, that Brian and Susie had come into the bar and that had led to the other and fatal double Scotch? Must have been. Made one think. Claud reached for the soap and began to wash. As he soaped his armpits, he remembered that earlier in Laura's part of the Old Rectory he had called Laura's mother her *doppelgänger*, and Laura at some moment had made reference to what sounded like "haunts".

Well, thought Claud, ducking underwater, that explains some of it. He let the water roar agreeably in his ears while he held his breath. I wish my mother had a shower, he thought, sitting up and turning on the cold tap, sponging himself with icy water. Finally he stood up, reached for his bath towel, pulled the plug and dried his torso and legs vigorously while his feet still indulged in the hot water. He then dried his feet one at a time before stepping out on to the bathmat, a slightly old-maidish but commendable habit since it did not leave the mat soggy for the next-comer.

They must, thought Claud, feeling restored and nonchalant, Susie and Brian must have brought me home. Ah well, these things happen, but it still does not explain the bucket over my head, that terrifying bashing and the fall downstairs, does it?

Claud left the bathroom, returned to his bedroom to dress. Yesterday's wear lay scattered. Shoes and one sock by the bed, anorak on the floor, shirt slung over the bedside lamp, jeans. Where the hell are my jeans? Oh dear, at the bottom of the bed, how sordid. And the other sock? Marking a book? Did I try to read? Rather than look further at present Claud turned his back on the bed and found clean clothes neatly arranged in his chest of drawers. What was that his mother had said about the price of independence? Could she mean it? What a viper!

Dressed, Claud shut his bedroom door and trotted downstairs to where he could hear voices in the kitchen. His mother was entertaining Laura.

"Hullo," said Laura. "I brought you the things from the attic, as I promised. What a pity you couldn't wait for them. These will help you make a start with your stall; your mother thinks they are lovely."

"Excellent," said Margaret Bannister, fingering an assortment of objects and small junk spread on the kitchen table. "Cracked, of course, some of them, or chipped; could do with a wash or a polish, most of them. Look at this." She held up a glass. "Bristol, quite pretty."

"What did you do to your eye?" asked Laura, ignoring Margaret's denigrating accent. "What has he done to his eye, Margaret? Your son's got a shiner."

"I have not asked him," said Margaret Bannister. "Look, these nutcrackers work and this spoon might almost be silver, one could clean it."

"Somebody put a bucket over my head and bashed me," said Claud. "Then I fell downstairs."

Laura raised her eyebrows and looked down her nose. "You've been listening to Mavis about Northern Ireland," she said. "She does go on."

"Things like that don't happen in this country." Margaret aligned herself momentarily with Laura. "I'd say this would have been Bohemian before it was chipped." She held up a small vase. "An idea, though, the bucket, for your novel?"

"It's only a little crack, a crack doesn't alter its nationality," said Laura.

"My head was cracked," said Claud, persisting. Laura smiled and went on unpacking the contents of a large basket. "A present from Scarborough," she said, "and here's its twin, a present from Lowestoft, a tiny baby's potty. Oh, this shouldn't be here, I'll take it back."

"What's that?" Margaret was interested.

"Patch box, a good one. Nor should this be here." She pocketed a silver snuff box. "But the rest's all yours." She spread her hands. "All yours."

"So is my black eye," said Claud, "and I think I have concussion."

"You'd know if you had concussion," said Margaret. "Coffee, Laura? I was going to make a fresh pot. If you had concussion you would see double; it affects your eyesight."

"I saw in triplicate last night." Claud stared at Laura. "Clearly, in threes."

"I can't drink Nescaff," said Laura, returning Claud's stare. "Were you pissed?"

"I never touch the stuff," said Margaret. "This is the real thing, want some?"

"Perhaps I won't, I'm late as it is." Laura reached for her coat. Claud helped her on with it. She was not wearing the Cossack hat today; the back of her neck reminded him of Mavis. "I'll see you out," he said.

"Goodbye, Margaret," said Laura, "see you when I come again."

"Where are you going?" Claud followed Laura to her car.

"London."

"Aren't you helping me with my stall?"

"Haven't I helped you enough?" She got into the car.

"Did you put the bucket over my head?" Claud held on to the car door. "And bash me?"

"Oh, Claud, don't be an ass."

"Take me with you."

"Why should I do that?" Laura switched on the engine.

Claud leaned in through the car window and kissed her cheek. "Laura—"

"I suggested to your mother that you should give me twenty-five per cent of the sale of that lot."

"Oh." He had thought she was giving it gratis.

"It gives you a start, doesn't it? With your part of the profit you can buy more stock to carry on with." She brushed her hand across her cheek as though his kiss had been a fly.

"Ah—"

"Brian and Susie will show you the ropes."

"Won't you help me?"

"Shan't be here."

"But—"

"Mavis doesn't always work mornings, she'll give you a hand."

"Did you put that bucket over my head? Did I see you in the pub later? With your *doppelgängers*?"

"You may have done." Laura put the car into gear and drove away.

"Damn you," Claud yelled after her. "Bitch."

"You are getting to be so like your father," said Margaret when he rejoined her in the kitchen.

"What's that supposed to mean?" Claud was surly.

"He too used to find romantic excuses for alcoholic accidents."

"I'm not an alcoholic. I'm moving out," shouted Claud. "I'm off."

"He said that too," said Margaret. "I hope you are as good as your word."

Furious with Laura, Claud rounded on his mother. "You don't believe in me, you have no faith in me, you expect me to be a failure," he yelled. "I tell you this, Mother, if I don't make a success of my writing, if, I say, because I shall, if I am not recognised, I shall kill myself. Now," he said bitterly, leaning close to Margaret so that she flinched with pity at the close-up of his black eye, "now tell me my father also threatened to kill himself—"

"No," said Margaret, "no. He died of a heart attack, he—"

"But he did promise to kill himself. I used to hear him. He'd say he'd hang himself, cut his wrists, overdose. I heard him, Mother. He would have, too," cried Claud, jubilant with rage. "The heart attack happened first, that's all."

Margaret turned away. "We need a vegetable for lunch," she murmured.

Claud watched her go out into the garden in her thin shoes and start picking brussels sprouts, twisting the tender miniature cabbages off their obscenely thick stalks. She looked thin out there, bending in the cold wind, which made her eyes glitter with tears as her cold fingers fumbled at the vegetables, dropping them into a fold of her apron. She had forgotten to take the colander she usually used.

Claud took the colander from its hook. Should he take it to her? She came in before he could make up his mind; he put it back on its hook.

"I wonder, did I leave my umbrella here? I was at the concert the other night, Clug's new Quartet, the Roumanian composer, conductor too, so talented and then the Bach—" Martin looked round the hall, rather shabby and sad in daylight. "A black brolly with malacca handle, a gold band with my grandfather's name on it. Otho Bengough. I put it over there, I think, or maybe not, I was sitting near the back, I—"

"I am only the caretaker, well, cleaner, actually. It's a holiday job before I go on to—" The girl looked pleadingly at Martin with pekinese eyes.

"University," supplied Martin.

"Polytechnic, actually." She blushed.

"Just as good," said Martin. "Who d'you think would have it? The brolly?"

"It can't have been stolen, though—"

"I wasn't suggesting it had."

"Of course not, no; Robert, the arts director, would have given it to Emily Thornby to care for until it's claimed. Though why she should be – er."

"What?"

"Oh, nothing. Oh, well," the girl blushed deeper, "it's just that she's such an odd person to put in charge of – er."

"Lost property?" How very convenient. Was this a sign?

"Yes."

"Apt to confiscate it for herself?"

"Oh, I didn't say that! No, no, it's just that she's funny, er, well—"

"How is she funny?" Martin probed.

"Well, she's a sort of lost person herself. I mean she doesn't fit any usual category, none of the Thornbys do." The girl spoke in a rush. "Actually she's rather terrifying, worse than her brother. Oh, I'll give you their address. Here, if you have a piece of paper I'll write it down. She would never claim to being lost, oh Lord no."

Martin handed the girl a biro. "You don't like her." He found an envelope in his pocket.

"Nobody does." The girl began writing. "Except possibly Laura, that's the daughter. I suppose she has to."

"You have beautiful handwriting." Martin inspected the envelope.

"Oh," said the girl, "thanks. It's no use telephoning them," she said, "their phone's out of order, or was. I've written the number just in case, but often they don't bother to answer. You might catch them lateish—"

"You seem to know their habits."

"Their daily lady works for my mother. She seems to like Laura. You may have noticed her at the concert, in a frightfully green dress, I mean green!"

You don't like Laura. "Thanks a lot," said Martin, "I'll try them lateish." He started back towards his car.

"They've got the most amazing dog," the girl said, following him. "Nicholas has trained him to 'Die for Eastbourne', it's a hoot!"

"Thanks again." Martin got into his car. The Old Rectory, the girl had written in biro, Uttoxeter Road. Why Uttoxeter? he pondered. This place is miles from there.

"Do be careful of the dog." The girl stood by the car. "It bites."

"Kind of you to warn me." Martin smiled at the girl.

"Oh," she said, "not at all." She stared at Martin, thinking that he had a kind face, a mouth which curled up at the corners, slaty grey eyes. She wondered whether he was married. "I am going to study art," she said. "I'm too stupid for anything else."

"I don't think you are stupid. Who put that idea in your head?" Not waiting for an answer, Martin started the engine and drove away. Glancing in the mirror he saw the girl semaphoring that he was heading in the wrong direction. He turned the car at the next intersection and drove back past where she still stood on the steps of the concert hall. As he passed her he waved and shouted, "Silly me," but he thought, Silly interfering bitch; he had liked the green dress.

He circled back to the town (the umbrella could wait) to park in a multi-storey car park. From the top deck of the car park there was a magnificent view of the river, the cathedral-sized church, the market square and distant downland. It was a sign of the age, he thought, as he ran down the steps to the street, that car parks like lavatories often had the best views and, like lavatories, he thought, holding his breath, they stank.

Gaining the street, he slackened his pace to saunter through the town. In the wine shop he dawdled over his choice; in the delicatessen he bought truffle chocolates; in the fruit shop, figs. As he shopped he chatted to the shopkeepers; in the flower shop he chatted while he bought regale lilies. Lastly he spent half an hour browsing in a second-hand bookshop, searching for a book long out of print and engaging the shop owner in desultory converse. Then, laden with carrier bags and the bouquet of lilies, he collected his car and drove fifteen miles to visit his aunt by marriage, Calypso Grant.

"It's not often," said his aunt, "that I get a visit from the Bengough branch of Hector's clan. Come in and share my lunch, you are just in time. Shut up!" she said to a large dog which was barking, bowing and wagging its tail. She reached up to kiss Martin's cheek. "Come in out of the cold."

"I brought you a bottle or two, some chocs and some figs." Martin returned her kiss. "And these." He presented the lilies.

"How extravagant," said Calypso. "I love extravagance. What can I give in return? We will eat the figs with one of Willy Guthrie's smoked hams. You know he married a girl called Poppy Carew?"

"I was at the wedding." Martin followed his aunt into the house.

"So you were. We'll eat in the kitchen."

"I need a little info, Aunt. I've lost my umbrella, mislaid would put it better, and the people who have it are—"

"Are what? Are who?"

"Some people called Thornby."

Calypso laughed. "Everybody knows the Thornbys. They are poison, surely your snooping told you that?"

"You know my little ways." Martin watched Calypso lay a place for him. "They seem to have a daughter who wears green."

"But in my opinion, for what it's worth, she is not poisonous," said Calypso.

Martin asked: "Shall I open a bottle? She was at a concert I went to."

Calypso handed him a corkscrew and began carving ham which stood on a dish on the kitchen table. "I bet you are hungry," she said. "The daughter is called Laura, no doubt you found that out. She has a business in London, no doubt you found that out too—" There was a lack of approval in her tone which Martin chose to ignore.

"Would you know her address?" he asked. "In London?"

"No, but I have the telephone number somewhere."

"That will do. Thanks, Aunt." Martin sat down to his ham.

"I hope you are not in a rush to leave," said Calypso. "Share out the figs, love."

"I have some time off." Martin chose the best figs for his aunt.

"Stay the night," she suggested. "There's a bed made up."

"May I? There's something I have to do later this evening."

"Nefarious?" asked Calypso.

"Just some ends to tie—"

"I like Laura Thornby," said Calypso coldly.

"I have no intention of hurting her," said Martin huffily.

"That's all right, then. I'll give you a key in case I've gone to bed when you get back."

"What made you think I might hurt her?" In spite of himself Martin was edgy.

Calypso chewed her ham, sipped her wine. "Have you really mislaid Otho's umbrella? I remember it well. Never, of course, playing the part of a Trojan horse." She glanced at Martin, who was peeling a fig. "Your grandfather never carried it furled. It looked pretty funny flopping loose when otherwise he was so exactly turned out; he had such a courteous way of offering its shelter when it rained at the races."

"He loved pretty girls." Martin ignored the suggestion of the Trojan horse. Calypso always made one's most delicate endeavours look clumsy.

Calypso smiled, accepting the refusal. "I don't know what he would have been like as a lover, but he was excellent company."

Martin, remembering his old aunt's racy reputation, ventured: "He sympathised with me once for being too young for you and said that he alas was too old; I was about six at the time. It made an impression. Why don't you bridle, Aunt?" he teased.

"Bridling is not my line. More ham?"

"Please." Martin passed his plate.

"I hope you will soon give up your unsporting occupation and find a girl of the right age," said Calypso, referring obliquely to Martin's profession.

"I thought unsought advice was against your principles," answered Martin. Secretly he agreed with E. M. Forster that it was more important to be loyal to one's friends than one's country.

Calypso laughed. "A slip, my dear. The great improvement in your cousin Willy since he married Poppy makes me hopeful for others."

"I shall bear your concern in mind," said Martin. "I am due in Washington next week."

"Another job?" Martin sensed an unsniffed sniff. "Won't your bachelorhood be at serious risk? Those American girls are delicious."

"It has survived on previous assignments." Martin met his aunt's eye.

"All right." She tacitly admitted that she had teased him enough. "All right."

Later that evening, driving through a downpour of rain along the road to the Old Rectory, Martin thought it was pleasant to be free of Clug. What really bugs me, he thought, hesitating in the rain in the darkness of the Old Rectory drive, is why a woman like Laura Thornby should have bothered with Clug when there was so obviously no future in it?

Standing in the shelter of the laurel hedge he reviewed such facts as he had gleaned that day. Brought up by her mother and uncle, school fees paid by someone called Ned Peel, who might or might not be her father. A wickedly mischievous child who had turned into a woman no one seemed to know much about; there was the impression that she was more feared than liked, that she was remarkably secretive. I know why I am secretive, Martin thought, why should she be? There was the emphasis on her wearing bright colours, a linking of her name with Ned Peel's son Christopher (old, very old history this). Her parent was considered a handicap, well, that's not unusual. "A bit lonely, or perhaps I should say solitary." The man in the bookshop. "Not someone you'd care to tangle with." The woman in the flower shop.

Encouraged by a fresh burst of rain Martin shook off his hesitation and rang the Old Rectory bell. There was an instant barking uproar from a well-lit hall. Martin waited, then rang again. The barking increased but nobody came. He lifted the letterbox flap and squinted in. Across a hallway he could see an umbrella stand and in it his forebear's umbrella. Some attempt had been made to furl it and it looked extraordinarily disreputable. His view was blotted out by snapping teeth and hot doggy breath accompanied by choking barks.

Martin withdrew and began circling the house; many people he knew sat asking to be burgled as they watched loud television. At the back of the house light streamed out from a ground-floor window; there was a door with a knocker. He knocked. Since nobody came he pushed and the door swung open to show a large room which smelled of woodsmoke, flowers, garlic, pepper. Martin called, "Hullo? Anybody there?"

A small cat stood up, stretched, lay down again by the fire. At the front of the house the dog still gave an occasional token bark.

If I walk through to the front and retrieve my brolly, I could call it a day, Martin thought. Then he heard a car's tyres crunching on the gravel at the front, the dog's bark changing to a joyful note and voices raised, one of them in song.

"Roll me over, in the clover, roll me over and do it again." Quavering, old, drunk. "Help me out of this, help me out, help!"

"Wait," said a woman's voice.

"I want to go back to the pubby pub pub." Another voice, female, also old.

Martin came softly round the house. A car with its doors open, two old people struggling tipsily, a woman opening the front door, the dog rushing out to slaver over the old people. The woman saying, "Come on, you terrible disgraces, that's the last time I take you on a pub crawl." She tried to lever the old man out of the car. His legs splayed out, folded, he collapsed on to the ground. "Oh, God," said the woman. The old woman was trying to get into the driving seat from the back of the car. "No you don't," said the woman Martin recognised as Laura and snatched away the car keys. The old woman lashed out with her fist and toppled out of the car. Now both old people were on the ground. The dog lavished licks on their faces. "Oh, Bonzo, Bonzo, Bonzo," they chorused, "you love us, boozy Bonzo boy."

"Can I help?" Martin stepped forward.

"Thanks," said Laura, startled.

"No, no, no, no, no," shouted the old man. "Gross interference of personal liberty."

"Put him on the sofa in the drawing-room." Laura raised her voice above the old man's.

Martin caught the old man up and manoeuvred him into the house, deposited him as told, and went back to assist Laura.

"Stop it, Ma, stop it." Laura tried to avoid wildly flailing arms. "No child of mine," shouted the old woman. "Freak! An asp, an asp, an asp."

"You never cherished me much." Laura was patient. "Come on, Ma, don't be impossible, you'll get soaked."

"My name is Emily Thornby," shouted the old woman. "Don't call me Ma." She aimed a blow at Laura's face. Martin caught her wrists. "Where shall we put her?"

"On the other sofa." Laura switched on a light. What a civilised venue, thought Martin, looking about him.

Emily bit his thumb. "Ouch!" Martin snatched his hand away. "Drawn blood?" asked the old man, sitting up and looking interested. "You want to be careful of drunks." He lay back, clutching Bonzo to his bosom. Bonzo snuffled and licked his neck. (What a disgusting animal, thought Martin.) "You love us, Bonzo, even if she doesn't; she has fallen in love with a spotted youth, Bonzo, brought shame on my grey hairs."

"They've mostly fallen out," shouted Emily from her sofa. "Fancy blacking that poor boy's eye; mind this one, Nicholas, he looks dangerous. Who are you?" She stared belligerently at Martin.

Keeping out of reach, wrapping his thumb in his handkerchief, Martin said: "I am extremely sorry. I was passing this way and thought I would collect my umbrella, which I left at the concert." (Why am I apologising?)

"Umbrella," said Emily, "umbrella?"

Nicholas groaned. "God, I haven't been so pissed for years. Thank you, darling." Laura was taking off his shoes.

"Just put some logs on the fire," she said to Martin, "he'll go to sleep in a minute and so will she." She moved across to Emily and removed her shoes.

"Lovely." Emily wiggled her toes.

"Rugs," muttered Laura and went away to return with rugs which she swathed round the old people, propping their heads on cushions. Her actions were tender and considerate. "You are not all that wet," she said, "I'd never get you up to bed."

Martin watched her. She rearranged the logs he had put on the fire and watched it blaze, then stood looking down at the old people swaddled now in rugs, lying quietly. "Better leave the light on in case they get dizzy," she murmured.

Nicholas gave a loud snore and let his arms fall away from the dog, who now leapt from his master's arms and approached Martin, snarling.

Terrified but inspired Martin shouted, "Die for Eastbourne!"

Bonzo rolled over and lay flat.

Laura let out a whoop of laughter: "Oh, how? Oh, where did you? Oh, ho, ho, ho ho." She pressed her hand against her side. "Oh, ho, ho, ho, ho, it hurts."

"I will just get my umbrella," said Martin, "then I'd better push off." He felt acutely embarrassed. This was not how he had visualised introducing himself.

"Yes," said Laura, "yes." Her eyes brimming, she followed Martin into the hall. "Of course," she said weakly. She was still giggling uncontrollably. "Your umbrella."

Martin took the umbrella from the stand and said, "Goodbye."

"Goodbye," said Laura, pulling herself together as she opened the door for him to step out into the rain.

Martin opened the umbrella and held it up; as the rain pattered down on to it, he was surprised to find he was trembling.

His aunt was still up when he got back. "Did you find what you were looking for?" she asked, switching off the television.

"I don't know," said Martin. "I got bitten."

"You'll find Elastoplast in the kitchen," said Calypso. "Goodnight, my dear, I am going to bed. What a risky occupation yours is."

The tone of his aunt's voice, thought Martin, dabbing antiseptic on his wound, exactly matched the smile Laura had given him as he left. In America women did not ridicule with such diabolical accuracy, they were kind to the weaker sex.

"I suppose you talked to Ann Kennedy?" Calypso called from the top of the stairs.

"Who is Ann Kennedy?" Martin answered unguardedly.

"Not a very thorough snoop, are you?" his aunt Calypso mocked. He heard her go into her bathroom and turn on the taps; above the sound of rushing water he heard her voice. "She rents her loft." There was no time, thought Martin dismally as he wound Elastoplast round his thumb, to investigate Calypso's hint. He must leave for the States.

"Pull, for crissakes," Claud yelled, "pull."

"I think – I am – doing – my guts – an injury."

Mavis heaved at the belt of webbing strung under the calor gas heater. "We must get it up before Mum comes in," she gasped. "She's terrified of fire."

On the ladder Claud got his shoulder under the stove and gave it a final heave through the trap-door. The stove toppled over, knocking Mavis on to her back. Claud came up through the trap, righted the stove and trundled it into place on its castors. His legs trembled from the strain of lifting. "Now the place looks civilised," he said, looking at his arrangement of books, typewriter, the box of manuscript, biros, pencils, indiarubber, ruler, dictionary, paper clips. "Ready for the off," he said. "If I type out my two paragraphs and sixteen sentences again, I can carry on from there. Brilliant." He stood looking at his new domain and wound the belt of webbing round his fist. "Where does this come from?" He looked down at Mavis flopped on the floor.

"I borrowed it from the undertaker."

"Oh." Claud laid the webbing down quickly. How many coffins had this webbing abandoned to the worms? "Oh—"

"I'm exhausted." Mavis rolled off her back, crawled to the mattress and sank on to it. "Oof," she said, "this is comfortable." She still wore her overcoat. She lay and watched Claud light the stove. "If you shut the trap-door," she said, "we can see how long it takes to warm the loft."

"Did Laura have one of these up here?" Claud shut the trap-door.

"She had an electric fire. She ran a flex down into the room below; Mum wasn't pleased when she found out."

"Does she come up here?" Claud shrank from the thought of invasion by Mrs Kennedy.

"No, but she noticed when her electricity bill shot up."

"Well, that won't happen with this." Claud patted the gas stove. "Did Laura have to repay your mother?"

"I can't remember. Hey, it would have been much easier to get that stove up without the cylinder." Mavis chirrupped with laughter.

"Now she tells me." Claud stood looking down at Mavis on her back on the bed, Laura's bed, the one she had left here. He rather envied Laura's theft of electricity, tried to imagine Laura on the bed, but it was Mavis there showing her bright teeth, eyes half closed, muffled in that bloody coat. She had dark lashes and eyebrows, he noticed; if they had been pale like many redheads, it would have put paid to her looks. He sat beside her on the bed. "Why do you keep your coat on?"

Mavis held the lapels close together. "I like it."

"Wrap me in it, too." He stretched out beside her. "You smell nice." He nuzzled her neck. "You don't wear scent, do you?"

"No," said Mavis, "no, it's all me."

Claud kissed her mouth. "You taste nice too."

"Tell me the story of your novel."

"I've got an erection."

Mavis clutched her coat about her and crossed her legs.

"Oh, for the happy days of carefree love!" Claud accepted her refusal.

"That generation don't look any happier than us, I can't see that it makes all that difference really."

"It's the idea—"

"Shouldn't you direct your energies into intellectual activity? Sublimate."

"What have you been reading?" Claud inserted his hand between the buttons of the coat and started peregrinating towards Mavis' breasts. "Where are they?"

"Higher up."

"What a lot of clothes you wear."

"I feel the cold."

"The stove is warming us nicely, let me in."

"No."

"All right." He lay beside her. The effort of moving his belongings to the attic had been strenuous. He began to feel sleepy in the increasing warmth. "The shock of being thrown out of the parental home was traumatic," he murmured.

"That's not the story your mother told my mum. She helped you pack, ironed your shirts for the last time, bought you new bath towels."

"What a literal girl you are."

"It will be useful for your novel, though; are all suggestions gratefully received?"

"Not really. I have to work it out for myself; the new schema is one no one has ever tried before."

"Is that so." Mavis in her overcoat sounded sceptical. "What's so original about it?"

"It's about my mother."

"And?"

"Her love life."

"Her love life?"

"You are not to tell anyone." The scent of Mavis' flesh filled Claud with dangerous indiscretion; her exertions had made her perspire, which curiously enhanced her attraction. Again he set his hand to explore the labyrinth of garments, fumbling up towards her breasts from the waistband of her jeans. "However many layers of clothes have you got on?" he asked in irritation as he unbuttoned her coat.

"Vest, T-shirt, shirt and sweater. Your hand is somewhere between the vest and the T-shirt."

"You sound like the guide to Hampton Court maze."

"Go on about your mother."

Claud withdrew his hand. "She's past the age for ordinary sex, right?"

"Is that so?"

"For the purpose of my novel it is."

"OK, go on." Mavis resettled her clothes, rebuttoning the coat so that should he be so minded Claud would have to start again from scratch.

Claud folded his arms behind his head. "She is in love with her machines."

"Her what?" Mavis reared up on an elbow.

"Her dishwasher, washing machine, spin dryer, mixer. They are all more real to her than a man's penis, she has a special relationship with her microwave."

"Your mother hasn't got a microwave."

"Oh, Mavis!" Claud rolled suddenly on top of her, staring at her eye to eye. He could kiss her mouth and throat, but added now to her many layers of clothing were his own shirt and jersey. "I don't believe anyone has been confronted by so much preventive clothing for years and years."

"I am inaugurating a new age of mysterious femininity," said Mavis, her mouth against his mouth. "You are terribly heavy and I am now too hot."

"Take some of it off then."

"No fear."

"New form of contraception, eh?"

"Yup."

"I get it, avoidance of our helpful friend?"

"Might be—"

Claud rolled off her. Tenderly he buttoned the overcoat up to her chin. "I shall start work first thing after breakfast tomorrow." (Susie had said Mavis' eyes were like jade.)

"Is Mum providing?"

"No, I shall eat at a caff or the wine bar when I can afford it so that you can serve me."

"Not tomorrow. Tomorrow is market day. Your stall, remember?"

"Oh shit," said Claud, "shit."

Mavis pulled up the trap-door and stepped down on to the ladder. "I wonder what Laura really got up to in this loft," she said.

As Mavis disappeared Claud felt the space she had occupied flooded by Laura. Why on earth, what had possessed him to tell Mavis about his mother's machine lovers? Surely only Laura's ear, if any, was the one to confide in? Furiously he kicked out at Mavis' head as it disappeared, missed.

At some point during his first night in the Kennedys' loft, tossing restlessly on a bed new to him, Claud realised with chagrin that his hero with the second-hand Alfa Romeo would not fit the scenario of his mother's mechanical loves. In real life Margaret Bannister used a car to reach A from B. She did not consider a car as anything other than a rather boring means of locomotion. It was with household machines that she had rapport. There was the mixer which would only work for her (I know its little quirks), the Hoover which regurgitated particular forms of dust and refused to ingest spiders, the spin dryer which inspired her to raise her voice in song, the washing machine and dishwasher which were as children to be fed, each its own diet. She had, too, a pretty funny relationship with her electric whisk. Would it be possible to weave the whisk into the novel with some esoteric sexual connotation? Sexuality and his mother hardly gelled in

Claud's mind but, Come on, he urged himself, I am a writer, aren't I? I should be able to tease that idea into shape. I am not writing about my living parent, she is merely the blueprint, the toile for the garb of my story. (I must remember not to use phrases like garb for story, they are sickeningly pretentious.)

Unable to sleep, Claud got out of bed and padded barefoot to the table. The pile of paper reproached mutely. With the obstinacy of a procrastinating child it stood between him and progress. He snatched up the heap of paper and tore it across. What he had written would never see print. Just think, he told himself shivering part with cold, part with emotion, what Laura would say were she to set eyes on it. Not for Laura heroes with Alfa Romeos or heroines with, yes he had written it, long legs, wide apart violet eyes, high breasts and tight little bottoms. It's enough to make any intelligent person puke, let alone Laura. What could I have been thinking of?

Claud prised open the window and scattered the shredded bits of paper into the night. Laura need never know. She would appreciate the woman based on his mother and her mechanical familiars, she might even respect his work. I shall dedicate the novel to Laura, Claud promised himself as he closed the window. He went back to lie on the bed, the bed she had installed in this loft when seeking privacy and escape in adolescence.

Half regretting his violent act Claud thought, What an awful waste of paper. Then, My God, it's market day, I must leap up and set up my stall so that I can earn the money to pay for more paper. I owe it to Laura, my muse. Now, now, he muttered, crawling reluctantly out of bed (I was just beginning to get warm again), don't start calling Laura your muse, that's a sure way to get kicked in the teeth. Taking care not to make a noise, Claud opened the trap-door and, creeping down the ladder, tiptoed to the bathroom.

He was halfway through shaving when the bathroom door snapped open and Mavis, tightly wrapped in her overcoat, came in. "What on earth are you doing?"

"Shaving. It's my first day with my stall."

"What on earth for? None of the stall-holders shave in the morning."

"I am shaving. I am different."

"What on earth do you want to be different for?"

"Just get out of here, Mavis, and leave me alone."

"What on earth for?"

"Mavis, if you say that just once more, I'll cut your throat."

"What on—"

"I will, Mavis."

Mavis laughed. "The kettle's boiled, I've made tea, or d'you prefer coffee?"

"Tea. What on earth are you doing up at this hour? Shit, it's catching."

"I am going to help you as it's your first day. I know the market people."

"Oh—"

"I can introduce you, show you the way things get done."

Claud grunted.

"You don't sound very pleased or grateful. I have kept a stall myself from time to time."

"What on—"

"To make a bob or two, dummy."

"Aah." Claud rinsed his razor. "I have my stock ready," he said. "I've priced it, stuck labels on the bits and pieces."

"Clever! Pete will come and look it over."

"Who's Pete?"

"Keeps an antique stall. You'd better be careful not to undercut him, he can be touchy. So can Gladys."

"Does she have an antique stall too?"

"Yes."

"Then what on earth am I doing with one?"

Mavis suppressed a grin at the repetition. "The more antique stalls the better, stupid. People come every week to look for junk. If it's any good, it finds its way to London. The dealers come. You'll get to know them."

"Ah."

"You will put them in your books. Perhaps you've thought of that?"

Laura had; Laura had pointed out his stall would be useful copy. Claud asked, "Any stalls selling machinery?"

"Such as what?"

"Household machines."

"There's one that sells old fridges and mixers, ancient mangles, that sort of thing. Collectors' pieces. Why?"

"Just interested."

"When we've set up your stall, you can look round, get to know where everybody is. I'll mind your stall, if you don't take too long, until I go to work."

"Thanks." Claud followed Mavis to the kitchen where she gave him tea. As he drank he eyed Mavis, wondering whether there might be a place for her in his novel, but always as he watched her it was Laura who was superimposed, the dark woman blotting her out, the two obliterating the memory of another girl, a girl he did not wish to think about from his recent past.

★

Claud enjoyed the early bustle of the market, the setting up of stalls, the unloading of vans, the disjointed conversations between people who knew each other well yet had not met for a week. Everybody seemed to know Mavis. "Hi, Mavis, how's the theatre then?" "Got a star part yet?" "Still on the dole?" "Resting?" "Never! Working in the old wine bar? See you later then, after market."

Mavis showed him how to set up the trestles, found him a place next to Brian and Susie, "Pure uncontaminated organically grown fruit and veg". He was glad of their proximity, amused that Mavis, testing the air with a wet finger, chose a place upwind. She had brought a paisley shawl ("Don't sell this, it belongs to Mum") which she spread over the trestle table, then helped him arrange his wares. As predicted Pete came across to view, followed by Gladys. Neither Pete, who was bearded and bespectacled, nor Gladys, who had tight white curls and awful lipstick, did more than nod when Mavis introduced Claud. They stared at Claud's things making rapid, but minute, inventory. Pete picked up a china mug with a floral design: "I have one like this. I've marked it seventeen pounds."

"What have I put on mine?"

"Sixteen."

"I'll mark it up then." (I am cautious, not cowardly.)

"Good boy," said Gladys. The lipstick had spread on to her teeth.

Pete laughed, his face transformed. "Mine's a bit chipped," he said. "Some wally may buy both." He wandered back to his own stall, taking Gladys with him.

By eight thirty the market was filling up with serious shoppers, housewives anxious to buy the cream of the fruit and vegetables, choose the freshest fish and best cuts of meat; they heaped their baskets and scurried back to their cars, making room for another class of shopper who came to saunter round the stalls, pick over the second-hand clothes, wander among the aisles of stalls picking things up, putting them down again with no proper intention of buying. Rather they came to meet their friends, exchange news and gossip. Small children ran about getting lost, getting found, tripping over the market dogs, who milled around undecided whether to fight or romp, searching always with sniffing noses for a possible bitch on heat. A lame girl pushed a trolley selling mugs of coffee and slices of dubious pizza; there were several buskers, none properly out of earshot of the other, and a man with matted hair selling roast chestnuts. Claud began to enjoy himself.

Mavis disappeared to work in the wine bar; Brian and Susie were busy at their stall. Today Susie wore mittens. Her little pink fingers snipped and snapped up the vegetables, weighing them on the scales, wrapping them in the recycled paper bags. She dazzled her customers with her smile, flashing her neat little teeth. Claud noticed that as she weighed the carrots or potatoes she smiled into the eyes of her customer while a straying finger depressed the scale just a little, just enough, he calculated with respect, to make a considerable increase in her profit. He wondered whether large and burly Brian was party to this trick.

Customers lingered by his stall, putting on their spectacles, peering at the price tags, picking things up, putting them down, moving away, coming back to look a second time. A woman offered Claud sixteen pounds for the mug he had marked up to seventeen; they made a deal at sixteen fifty. Claud felt elated; this was his first sale. He felt he had arrived. He wrapped the mug tenderly in newspaper, took the money.

Contrapuntally while minding his stall he let his mind dwell on his novel. He saw his mother lingering at the stall which sold old household tools. She turned the handle of a frightful old mangle, chatted to the stall-holder. Was she tempted? What part could an Edwardian mangle play in her life? Claud watched his mother and exulted. Laura will love my book; she must be the first to read it. He daydreamed by his stall in the busy market of a crisp and finished manuscript.

"What are you asking for this?" It was one of Laura's doubles; he held a spoon, his thumb over the price tag.

"The price is written on it."

"This spoon has my family's crest on it. I wonder how it got here?" Almost he accused, peering with Laura's dark eyes.

Claud took the spoon from him, looked at the tag: "Six pounds fifty. Sterling silver."

"Plate, actually, it's plate." Laura's double denigrated the spoon, replaced it on the stall. Claud felt the hairs of his neck rise or, he told himself, they rose metaphorically.

"Hullo, Nicholas." Claud's mother had come up behind him. "How are you and Emily? How is Laura?"

"We are all so-so, just about so-so."

Claud was as glad as he had sometimes been as a child to see his mother. "Hullo, Mother. Can I sell you something?" He felt an unusual need to keep her close to him.

"I have been looking at that old kitchen machinery. D'you think it still works? Fascinating stuff."

"Is this your son, Margaret? D'you think he's been pinching our spoons? He's got one here with our crest on it. I'm sure it's ours."

"I hardly think so, Nicholas. I'd no idea you had a crest. Whatever next, should I bow and curtsey? Why don't you buy it?"

Nicholas Thornby moved away. "That's a mischievous old man," said Margaret.

"M-m-m."

"Laura's uncle, or so they say."

"What else could he be?" asked Claud. "The likeness is striking."

"What indeed," said Margaret Bannister.

"Do you think the spoon was his? Most of this stuff comes from Laura; she brought it from their attic." Claud felt uneasy.

"Then don't let on. Let him buy it if he wants it back." Claud was heartened by his mother's robust attitude.

"I think he may have been responsible for my black eye," Claud whispered.

"Oh, I wouldn't go as far as that," Margaret demurred. She wanted to ask him whether he was enjoying his new venture, but did not want to seem interfering. She was afraid of embarrassing her son; he was such a touchy fellow. She felt she should buy something from his stall, but all the little objects repelled her. She felt, standing by his stall, that she was barging in on his independence. She would do better to move away. "I am planning to sell all my outmoded kitchen gadgets to that man over there," she said.

Claud gaped. In his novel she cherished her gadgets, her life was ruled by them; she did not get rid of them. He felt a sharp pang of abandonment.

Margaret went on, "I have so much junk; I shall unload it on him and there's plenty about the house that you may like for your stall."

"That will be lovely," said Claud dully.

It won't be lovely, it will be a nuisance, thought Margaret. She had no confidence in herself as a parent. Other people seem to be at ease with their children, she thought, why can't I? "I shall have a grand clearance, a clean sweep when I move," she said, pretending to be bold.

Claud gasped. He had not realised that her departure was imminent; he had visualised it months, maybe years, ahead, that meanwhile she would be around to provide ideas for the novel. Damn her, he thought, can't she see I need her? Then why can't I tell her? If she were Laura, it would be simple. He watched his mother as she moved away.

"I'll have that spoon." Nicholas Thornby was back. "But I shan't give you more than a fiver. It must have been stolen from us, by one of our dailies perhaps."

"Six pounds fifty," said Claud. "Perhaps it was not a daily." He looked Nicholas in the eye.

"Oh, all right." Nicholas produced the money from his wallet. "Twice robbed," he said. "Don't wrap it up."

Claud took the money and handed over the spoon. He was amused to see that Nicholas had chosen the most worn note from his wallet.

"You gave me this black eye," he said, indicating the bruise, which over a period of a week had faded from purple to greenish yellow.

"I wish I had," said Nicholas Thornby, "by which I mean that I would wish I had if you had stolen my spoon, if you can follow a convoluted train of thought."

"I think I can just about manage," said Claud. He put the dirty note in his hip pocket.

He sold no more that morning and presently packed up his stall and joined Brian, Susie and other traders for lunch in the wine bar. They all sat round a table while Mavis took their orders, standing graceful and pliant beside the table, reminding Claud of the first morning when he had sat there with Laura. Thinking of Laura he hardly noticed Mavis' appetising body in its nylon overall appearing for once without the overcoat. If he had bothered to look he would have seen Mavis' nipples pointing perkily under the nylon as she breathed, but his mind's eye only saw Laura who was not there. He wished he was sitting alone with Laura so that he could tell her that he was regaining some of the confidence lost with the failed exam and the difficulties with Amy. He had not mentioned the failed exam, it no longer mattered; it was the moral disintegration of his failure with Amy which had significance. Thinking of Laura he endowed her with more power than she had, supposing that she had understood his trouble when she urged him to leave home, to write, to keep a stall, that she wasn't taking an interest for amusement's sake but really cared about him, knew about the confidence Amy had snatched from him so ruthlessly, so cruelly. "Damn and blast Amy," he spoke out loud.

"Who is Amy?" asked Brian, looking up from his pizza. "Anyone we know?"

Claud did not answer but ordered an Irish coffee, catching Mavis by the skirt as she passed their table, calling her Maeve. "Mavis, my name is Mavis." She smacked his hand and went away to place his order.

"I am sorry," Claud called after her, "I failed to recognise you without your coat."

Watching Claud settle into a routine at the market precipitated Margaret's plan to sell up and move. She did not trust him to stay in the Kennedys' loft; it was too basic. The bohemian glamour might soon wear off. She could see him moving back into her house bringing habits which did not fit with hers, moods which could be trying.

Since her husband's departure she had secretly looked forward to the time when, his education complete, Claud would flit into the outer world, leaving her to do whatever she wished with an uncluttered conscience. Now she felt threatened. Claud looked like settling in the town he had affected to despise all the years they had lived in it. He was making friends with locals who up to now had not been worth his trouble. Being herself naturally unsociable Margaret had, when her husband embarrassed her with his quarrelsome drinking, kept aloof from people. When he left her she remained withdrawn; his absence made no difference. As he grew up Claud had clearly found home boring, had preferred to spend holidays away with friends, sulked when he had to be at home. She knew that he thought her dull; indeed, in adolescence, he often said so. She had never anticipated his wanting to live near or with her when he left university.

She now saw her solitude at risk. She blamed herself for introducing him to Laura at the concert, so brilliant against the drab background. She felt threatened when, several times during his first week in the loft, Claud dropped in to share her meals, bringing with him his laundry to feed her washing machine, taking the opportunity to have a bath. Her hot water system was, it seemed, more reliable than the Kennedys'. He brought his new friends, Brian and Susie, for drinks; asked whether he could bring Mavis for supper, making it impossible for her to refuse. A mild hint she dropped about independence and doing his own washing he ignored. He was, he said, working hard on his novel, getting inspiration from local colour; he looked round the kitchen when he said this, fingering her electric whisk or fidgeting with the mixer in a way which made her uneasy.

Irrationally Margaret blamed Laura for all this. Mavis, a more obvious cause of potential trouble, worried her not at all; it was the idea of Laura that caused angst. However private and withdrawn she had been during the years she had lived in the neighbourhood, she had not escaped hearing that the Thornbys had a reputation. The old brother and sister were said to be odd, and Laura a mischief-monger; nobody knew why she had not married or what she did when she was elsewhere. She had rented the Kennedys' loft for many years, but latterly had taken over the back premises of the Old Rectory, building a brick partition between herself and the old people. Some person had joked that she had created not a granny flat but a manic's flat. Margaret was on Christian name terms with the Thornbys, as everybody was with everyone these days, a habit caught from America; she greeted them cheerily in public but had no wish to enlarge her acquaintance.

So Margaret made a date with the house agent; her house was eminently saleable. She invited the man who kept the machine and tool stall in the market to call. He came next day and went away with most of her kitchen equipment. The cheque he gave her surprised her by its substance.

She sorted her clothes, ruthlessly reducing her wardrobe to essentials. Oxfam benefited, and the jumble sales more so.

She invited the second-hand booksellers to browse among her surplus books. Systematically she ransacked the house for objects suitable for Claud's stall, packing them in cardboard boxes which she stowed in the boot of her car.

As she stripped the house of belongings, she cleaned it, erasing the patina it had acquired from her occupation, stripping it of its character, preparing it for the imprint of new owners.

When the estate agent brought some people to view, she was in the garden getting it tidy for a spring she would not be there to see. She answered the would-be buyers' questions politely, but when they asked her how she could bear to leave such a charming neighbourhood, such an adorable convenient little house, she did not think it was any of their business and further questions froze.

She knew she was running away and felt guilty. Guilt cemented her determination to escape Claud. When the house agent telephoned the same evening to tell her the people were prepared to buy at the asking price on condition they could move in immediately, she accepted the offer with relief. The prospect of moving away was rejuvenating. She looked forward to it with joy.

"Goodness, what are you up to?" Laura, returned from London, stood in the porch. She looked over Margaret's shoulder into the hall, interested and inquisitive. "Someone told me you were moving," she said. "I wondered whether your house would suit some friends of mine who are househunting. And another thing, have you any furniture you are parting with that I might . . ." She let the sentence drop.

"Why don't you come in?" Margaret stood aside. She guessed that the househunting friends were imaginary, but it was possible Laura was interested in furniture; in any case she could not stop Laura's inquisitiveness without being rude. "Come in," she repeated.

"Thanks," said Laura. "It's a super house, how can you bear to leave it?"

"Quite easily." Let Laura discover for herself that the house was sold.

"Where shall you live?"

Margaret ignored this. "There's a chest of drawers in Claud's room I shall sell. I definitely won't keep that."

"May I look at it? Where did you say you will live?"

"I didn't. D'you mind looking round on your own? I'm rather busy packing things for Claud's stall."

"Of course not. Sorry to interrupt. Has he sold the stuff I gave him?"

"Why don't you ask him?"

"I shall. OK if I look round?"

"Please do." Margaret moved towards the stairs. Let her pry on her own. Why should Claud be beholden to this woman? She watched her climb the stairs, then took a tray and stacked it with a tea set she had thought that morning she would keep. Now she decided to give it to Claud. As she wrapped the cups and saucers in newspaper she heard Laura moving about and thought, not for the first time, that while the outer walls of the cottage were thick, the inside was by no means soundproof. In the past she had heard much she would rather not, not only from her husband but from Claud, too. She could leave these echoes behind.

"How much do you want for the chest?" Laura rejoined her.

Margaret named her price.

"OK, fine, I'll have it. I need one. I found this when I pulled out the drawers." Laura handed an envelope to Margaret. "Snaps of a girl. She's pretty. Friend of Claud's?"

Margaret took the envelope, looked at the snaps. She knew at once that this was an oblique sign from Claud. She did not recognise the girl. This would be the girl he had so often telephoned, who had wrung him out like a dishcloth, taken to hanging up on him, ceased to exist in his life.

"Oh, that's Amy," she said, furious to feel her neck flush, her voice alter. "Well, like a cup of tea? I was about to make one."

"Why not? Thanks." Laura followed Margaret to the kitchen. "You'd never seen that girl, had you?" Laura sat at the kitchen table. "I suppose he was in love with her. I suppose she chucked him. Badly hurt, was he?"

She had made him fail his exams. This was some sort of message; obviously he couldn't bear to talk about the girl, the girl he had called Amy, shouting the name into the unresponsive telephone. Laura was still speaking. "But you never met her, did you?"

"How do you know?" It popped out.

"Your expression. An oh dear that's cat's-mess face."

Margaret laughed. "It always gives me away. You haven't got friends looking for a house, have you? You are interested in Claud."

"That makes two with intuition. Yes, I find him interesting, easily hurt I'd say, vulnerable. One wouldn't want to hurt him."

"I wouldn't suggest you would. How old are you?"

"Forty-five."

"I am fifty-five. I had him when I was thirty-two, rather old to start a family."

"Which makes him twenty-three."

"Yes, poor boy."

"Poor boy, poor boy," Laura laughed. "He needs boosting, jollying up, that's all."

"I've tried. Failed lamentably."

"Your heart isn't in it."

"My heart is battle fatigued," said Margaret.

Laura grinned; she enjoyed teasing people. She watched Margaret making tea, putting out mugs, bending to take milk from the refrigerator, reaching into a cupboard for sugar. "I'll find out what she did to him and let you know."

"I'd rather you didn't." Margaret was repressive.

"It's not good to let things fester. He should have confided in you."

"Well, he didn't."

"He should have."

"Claud's business is Claud's business."

"And you are not interested?"

Margaret shot a spiteful glance at her tormentor, poured her a mug of tea with a steady hand.

She'd like to throw the pot at me, thought Laura. "You'll grow out of this," she said and put two lumps of sugar into her mug, plop, plop.

"What do you mean?"

"You will grow out of wanting shot of Claud." Laura stirred her tea.

"God!" said Margaret. "I don't know what you are doing here. I didn't invite you. I don't know why you are interested in Claud—"

"He's pretty, he's intelligent—"

"You are old enough to be his mother—"

"Sure."

"As his mother I have every right to let him lead his own life—"

"And not tangle with yours?" Laura's eyes sparkled with amusement. "You want to live somewhere where you can twiddle the knobs of your own television, choose your own programmes, go to bed without the fear of being woken by Claud coming in drunk and being sick before he can reach the loo. You don't want to be bothered by his heart cracking about the place over some idiot girl. You are abdicating parenthood."

"You have been spared parenthood," said Margaret, "you prying bitch." She said in friendly accents, "Tell me, was it your uncle who attacked Claud?"

"My uncle?"

"Nicholas."

"Oh, Nicholas. I rarely think of him as my uncle. I couldn't think what you meant for a moment. Yes, it was. He was cross because I gave Claud junk from the attic. It was a mistake to tell them. I should just have helped myself, they would never have noticed. It was my innate honesty."

Margaret sniffed.

"They are funny about possessions," said Laura.

"They are funny full stop," said Margaret. "I've often heard their house referred to as the Funny Farm." This was not true, but it pleased Margaret to say it. She found herself blaming Laura for Claud's drunkenness, his black eye, his being sick in the hall, none of which she had minded much at the time since, compared with her late husband's behaviour, it was mild stuff. "If you are passing anywhere near Claud's loft would you drop some boxes of knick-knacks and china I've packed up for his stall?"

"All right, I'll go. I can take a hint," said Laura, putting down her empty mug. "Where are these boxes?" she asked, unruffled.

Neither woman spoke as they transferred the boxes of junk from the boot of Margaret's car to Laura's. Then Laura asked, "Does Claud want you to leave the neighbourhood? Does he know you are going?"

"There is not room for both of us," said Margaret.

"You do not mean you and Claud, do you? You mean you and me."

Margaret smiled.

"I shall find out about that girl," said Laura, getting into her car.

"Oh, that." Margaret's smile broadened. "She was just the beginning of the rapids."

Laura started the engine, reached for her safety belt. "I am not at all a maternal sort of friend," she said.

"Who wants a maternal friend?" asked Margaret falsely.

"Claud? Perhaps Claud does."

"He's not likely to find one, is he?" Margaret watched Laura go. I wonder what she's after, she thought. Then, turning back into the house, she thought, I can't help him. If I stayed on here, I wouldn't be of the slightest use to him, while Laura will believe in him, give him the courage to write his novel. The trouble with me, she thought honestly, is that I simply cannot believe in this wretched novel, I can't imagine Claud as a writer.

Standing at the sink, rinsing the mugs she and Laura had used, Margaret experienced the feeling of desolation that had assailed her on Claud's first day at school; there seemed little difference between Claud aged five and Claud aged twenty-three. His mix of boldness and timidity was unchanged. At five he had kicked her shins when thwarted, screamed for help if injured, twisted away from her. He had also come running for help and reassurance in time of trouble (he did not do that any more). He had expected her to be there if needed. I always was there, she thought as she dried the mugs and hung them on the dresser.

What am I worrying about? He's a grown man. She unhooked the mug Laura had used. Was there still sugar on the bottom? She rinsed the mug a second time.

Was that lipstick? She looked closely at the mug. She doesn't use lipstick, her mouth is naturally red. Will she and Claud—? Margaret stood holding the mug. I despise possessive mothers, she thought. If Laura should want him and he should want her?

There's nothing I can do, she thought. She shrugged her shoulders and replaced the mug on its hook.

Sly of her to find that packet of photos— It never occurred to me to look for – I defended him, didn't I? I stood up for his independence. Am I jealous? Of Laura? Why did Claud never talk to me about Amy, whoever she is? He never brought her home, Margaret thought resentfully. What am I fussing about? Until Laura came by I was planning to sell up and make my getaway.

Getaway, she thought, there's a word. Then she thought, Laura guessed it all, she understands what I am doing, that it's best for—

This train of thought was interrupted by the sound of Laura returning. Margaret went to the door; Laura leaned from the driver's seat. "On second thoughts, Margaret, I don't really want that chest, is that all right?"

"Yes, of course. Thank you. Don't worry." What am I thanking her for? "Thanks," she repeated. Laura drove away waving.

Closing the door Margaret smiled grimly. "I am doing what is best for me," she said out loud, "as I intended before she interrupted me." I am not letting Claud down, she told herself; I shall be on the telephone, should he want me.

Margaret snatched up the mug Laura had used and smashed it on to the floor, where it broke. Then, slightly shamefaced, she fetched a dustpan and brush and swept up the pieces and tipped them into the dustbin. Washing her hands under the tap, she found herself feeling grateful to Laura for inspiring this small rush of adrenalin.

Laura eased up the trap-door and moved a step higher up the ladder. From this position she could see Claud sitting stooped at the table, one hand clutching a piece of crushed typing paper, the other on his knee, fingers drumming. He did not notice her. He stared up through the attic window. She knew that all he could see from there was the sky, perhaps a gull wheeling past or a rapid flight of starlings; if he wished for a more interesting view, he would have to stand up (or look at me, she thought).

Claud dropped the crushed paper on to the floor, straightened his back, put a fresh sheet of paper in the machine and began to tap; she was interested to see that he appeared confident and resolute. She kept quiet while he chuntered along to the end of a paragraph, stopped, leaned forward to read what he had written, hissed through his teeth and resumed typing. The paper finished, he released it from the machine and, laying it on a pile of manuscript, inserted a fresh sheet and carried on. He kept this up for three more pages before coming to a halt. Then he whistled a shrill note of satisfaction and stood up, rubbing his hands together. As he pushed his chair back he caught sight of her head poking up through the trap-door level with the floor. He stared. Laura did not move.

"You look like someone in a Beckett play," he said.

Laura smiled.

He thought perhaps her eyes were so bright because of the bluish tint of the whites, that he was pleased to see her, that he liked her pointed nose and the way her hair sprang back from her forehead. He thought she looked strange and exciting, that he was pleased, glad, he liked the way she was there not speaking.

He crossed the loft to the trap-door, knelt, then lay, his face on a level with hers. He said, "I thought you had disappeared for good."

"You did?"

"Where have you been?"

"London."

"With that musician, the chap I saw you with at the concert? Is he your lover?"

"No." (Not any more.)

"Ah."

"Ah."

"I have been thinking of you so much." (That isn't true, but I should have been thinking of her, my word yes, I certainly should.) "Missing you," he said. Of course he'd missed her.

"And you? How goes the book? It's new, isn't it? You scrapped the two paras and sixteen sentences?"

"How did you guess? They were rubbish."

"So this is about?"

Claud told her the schema, the character who might be his mother, her peculiar relationship with household machinery, lying on the floor propped on his elbows, his face level with hers. Her hair smelled exciting. It smelled of pepper. "Shall you come up?" he asked.

"If you insist. I am quite comfortable here standing on the ladder, getting a mouse's eye view of your loft."

"It is your loft. I am only here on sufferance."

"Oh, no." She stepped up the ladder. There had been a warm flow of air from the house below fanning up her skirt; she was reluctant to leave it for the austerity of the loft. "Oh, you have a stove. What luxury." She strolled about looking at Claud's things, his clothes hanging limp on nails, his books, the bed which had been hers many years ago. She looked out of the window and was reassured by the unchanged view; she touched the table, let a finger rest for a second on the manuscript, sat down on the bed. "And who else? Who else is in your book?"

"Oh – I – er—"

"Well?" She was sharp.

Claud answered with a rush of words spewed out, speeded by motion. "There's a girl, she bloody intrudes, she's not supposed to be in it but she keeps bobbing up and I do-not-want-her."

"Someone you were – or are – in love with?" Laura spoke lightly, looking away from him, giving him the chance to rat on the bitch. (In what way had she hurt him?)

"Well," said Claud, offhand, "you know how it is, adolescent love, first love I suppose, the usual sort of nonsense. She recurs, that's all, a sort of emotional burp."

"Much in love? It was heavy?"

"Oh God, yes, but I wouldn't give her a second thought now. She doesn't fit the scenario, that's what is so aggravating."

"Sit here." Laura patted the bed beside her.

"I mean," said Claud, obeying, "she played a small and unimportant role in my life, it was quite brief." He spoke protestingly, wishing Amy had been small, unimportant.

"Brevity is neither here nor there. She is obviously someone who needs exorcising. What did she do to you?" Laura probed like a dentist at a raw nerve and leaned against Claud beside her on the bed.

He liked the way she smelled of pepper. He put his arm around her. "You smell so—"

"So what?"

"Different."

"From what?"

"Other people."

"We all smell different. Now tell me about this intruding girl. What was her name?"

"I'd rather not. She was called Amy."

"Shall we take our clothes off and get into bed?"

"Take our clothes off?" Claud sat up straight.

"Yes."

"Undress?" His voice rose in panic.

"Yes."

"It's nearly lunch time."

"I shall treat you as an hors d'oeuvre."

Claud sprang off the bed, undressed, tearing off his clothes, his back modestly turned, his heart thumping in a mix of alarm and excitement. When he turned round Laura was in the bed between the sheets still wearing her sweater.

"You cheated." He scrambled in beside her. His legs felt weak.

"Only my top half—"

"Oh." She was right; below the waist she had no clothes on. "Oh," he muttered, "Oh my G—"

"What was she like, this girl Amy?" asked Laura an hour later, when they had had a refreshing and recuperative nap.

Claud came down from cloud nine. "Must you bring her up, the stupid bitch?"

"What did she do to you?" (The dentist's drill.)

Claud shouted: "She would not take her Walkman off when we made love."

Laura did not laugh. "I can see that that was serious," she said. (I've got the tooth out. God, how it must hurt.)

"You can?"

"Wounding."

"It was."

"Did she perform in time to the music?" (Just a little dab of antiseptic.)

"How would I know?"

"So you threw her out?"

"She threw me. It was her flat."

"Worse."

"Thanks for not laughing. I took a risk telling you."

"You know, I think she fits in the novel. Your mother's machines, a Walkman, quite a small part of course." (Now rinse and spit.)

"Do you really think so?"

"Definitely."

"OK, I'll let her in. I think you are right."

"Good." (Rinse just once more and spit again. In no time you will think you thought of this yourself.) The afternoon sun made a pool of light on the floor. Seagulls shrieked across the roofs, lorries passed grumbling up the street. "Long ago," said Laura, "when I was young,

I got stinking drunk at a party. In the morning when I woke I realised that someone had shared my bed."

"He'd raped you?"

"I don't think it was rape."

"Who was it?" Claud felt his throat constrict.

"There was this smell of hair oil on my pillow, nothing else."

"Hair oil?"

"People used hair oil in those days, dumbo."

"Of course." He remembered his father using some sharp-smelling mix of oil and spirit. "So?"

"So ever since I hope to recognise it on some stranger I may be introduced to."

"But people don't use hair oil any more."

"They don't, do they."

"Did you make this up to make me feel comfortable after telling you about Amy?" Claud was suspicious.

"I wouldn't do a thing like that."

But watching Laura dress Claud thought that's just what she would do.

"Come on," said Laura, "I'm starving. Let's get ourselves lunch, it's not too late."

As he followed her down the ladder Claud felt a rush of gratitude. She had not embarrassed him by asking to read his manuscript. She had not mocked. He felt assuaged, relaxed, masculine and bouncy, positively confident. When she suggested lunching at the wine bar, he agreed. It would be nice, it would round off a successful morning to have Mavis unwrapped from her awful overcoat stand pliant by their table to take their order. "Would it bore you to read my manuscript?" he asked with a generosity which he instantly regretted.

They were walking up the street leaning into a draughty wind. Laura did not answer immediately. She was thinking that it was one thing to possess Claud's body, there was much good work she could do there, but was she prepared to take on his mind? "I would not be bored," she said carefully, "but wary. It's a big responsibility."

Claud felt downcast; he wished he could retract his offer. It was not an offer he would have made to Mavis, for instance, or his mother or Amy, if they had still been on speaking terms. My work is private, he thought, his mind running already on a line roughly parallel to Laura's.

"I should be flattered," said Laura, "but think it over."

"How civilised you are," exclaimed Claud, relieved and ebullient. He pushed open the door of the wine bar. "What shall we eat? Come on, let's sit here where we sat before. Let's harass Mavis."

But Mavis was not there. Her place had been taken by a gangling youth wearing a white apron stretching down to his feet, who looked at Claud with contempt. "Didn't you know," he said, as he looked forward to telling them that everything was off except yesterday's quiche, "didn't you know that Mavis has got a part in a London show? She got a phone call last night and went off at the speed of light, borrowed the rail fare and hopped it. Right, then. You want to eat? Everything's off except the quiche. Might be able to rustle up some salad."

"No matter," said Laura, opening her bag and extracting her purse. "Just take off that silly apron and streak down to the fishmonger's like a good boy, and bring back two dozen oysters. We will eat them with lots of brown bread and butter. Bring half a pound of prawns, too."

"Nobody here can open oysters," said the boy mutinously.

"But I can," said Laura. "Now scoot."

"You bloody Thornbys," said the boy, taking the money. "Bloody, bloody people."

"And bring an oyster knife and a lemon," Laura called after him.

Mavis had arrived early for the train. The wind penetrated her thick coat as she waited for the signal to turn green. She had been foolish to leave home so soon; but she had been consumed by train fever, crazy to be on her way in the Inter-City train which would take her to London where some day, not immediately of course, her name would be up outside a theatre in electric glory.

Terrence had wanted to see her off – he was taking her place in the wine bar – but she had told him to be sure to get to work on time. "Make yourself indispensable," she had said. He would be there now, she thought pityingly, wearing the apron he had stolen for a joke from a café on the school trip to France the year before last.

Her mother had said: "Why don't you ask Claud to see you off? He's only up there typing." Poor old Mum would not understand that part of this joyous departure would be Claud's surprise when he heard that she had gone to work at her true vocation instead of eating her heart out taking orders from all those boring, barely literate vegetable growers, dull provincials who didn't know, wouldn't accept, that she was an actress. Had not Laura pointed her out to Claud in that joking way of hers which put one down? "You wouldn't believe Mavis was an actress." Something like that.

"Goodbye, goodbye," hummed Mavis, pacing the platform, seventy paces to the end, seventy paces back. I have got it all together, she thought with satisfaction. And Claud, how surprised would he be? She had not told him. Nor had she told anyone, least of all her mother, the world's greatest blabbermouth in Mavis' opinion, that the part she had so joyfully accepted was that of understudy. Understudy to an extremely healthy little actress often boringly described by the agent they shared as "a great little trouper".

Mavis turned away from the wind. People were beginning to trickle on to the platform. Not too long now for the off.

I shan't get paid much, she thought, lucky I've saved. Pity I'm not a man, they sell their sperm to make ends meet – a curious piece of information from Terrence who had learned it from a programme on TV. He had added nastily, "Doesn't seem fair, does it, that girls have to prostitute," using prostitute as a verb; he had always sat among the "could-do-betters" at school.

Of course one had done jobs for Laura while at drama school, that was not prostitution. I am a virgin and wish to stay that way, Mavis chuckled, remembering Claud fumbling up from the waistband of her jeans, his hand trapped between vest and T-shirt. "And a virgin I will be," Mavis hummed. Ah! The signal had turned green, cling cling went the telegraph. She could hear the train shriek on the far side of the hill as it plunged from the cutting into the hillside. If that's not sexual, I don't know what is, thought Mavis who, while avoiding personal experience, had read a lot of books. As she snatched up her bags in readiness for the train she felt a surge of excitement as sharp as sex. I shall not be an understudy for ever. She heaved her bags on to the rack. I am not mislaying my virginity. Oh no! she vowed as she settled into a corner seat, not if that's what it leads to, she thought, as her ears reacted to the screams of an infant across the aisle. Oh Jesus, no! she thought as the infant's sibling lost its footing and fell flat, its precarious balance faulted by the train jerking into motion. Claud is not all that attractive, she thought. All that can wait, what cannot wait is my career.

Mavis took cotton wool from her bag and stuffed bits into her ears, a practice she had learned when doing prep while her mother watched soaps on television. Settling in her seat, she stared out of the train window but she did not see the scenery flash by. She only saw herself and her future.

Claud watched Laura open the oysters; at any minute he expected the lethal knife to slip and her bright blood gush. Would it look like ketchup or blood-orange juice as it dripped over the oysters? He had once watched a large red moon rise from a backdrop of oystershell cloud. "Do be careful," he said, appalled by the risks she was taking. The moonrise had presaged a violent storm.

Laura eased an oyster from its shell, pinched a drop of lemon juice on to it and handed it to Claud. "Try that."

Claud bit the oyster, swallowed. "Heavenly."

"Bread and butter, pot boy!" Laura shouted.

"Coming, you great bully." The boy, who had resumed his apron, came rushing from the back of the wine bar, long strides threatening to trip him. He carried aloft a dish of brown bread generously buttered.

They had the bar to themselves, all other lunchers having long gone. "What's your name, pot boy?" Laura offered the boy an oyster. "Like one?"

"Yes, please." The boy swallowed the oyster. "The name's Terrence, not Terry. Thanks." His Adam's apple wobbled in his thin throat. "Looks like you've forgotten me," he said. "I'm the boy you used for that experiment, remember, plaster cast it was."

"Oh!" Laura laughed. "Of course I remember you, you were a wicked little nipper."

Laura and the boy laughed together, excluding Claud from some mystifying intimacy.

"If you'd like to run and get some more oysters," she said, "you can join our feast. I'm feeling rich today."

"I certainly would," said the boy. "You two celebrating something?" He looked sly, his eye resting on Claud.

"Possibly," said Laura, pausing from her work to take money from her bag. "If you run like the clappers, I shall have half a dozen ready for you when you get back."

"OK," said Terrence, and ran, letting the wine bar door slam.

"You have amazingly strong hands," said Claud. Aware that the hands he watched had recently caressed him, he felt a prick of reminiscent desire in recollection of their tenderness. They were not being tender to the oysters.

"It's my work."

"Your work? What work?"

"I don't just fan about doing nothing," said Laura.

"What at? Doing what?"

"I have a business in London."

Terrence, returning with a fresh batch of oysters, put paid to further inquiry.

"How is your um—" asked the boy and prolonged his hesitation.

"My what?" Laura looked up at the boy.

"Mr Thornby." Terrence glanced at Claud. "Mr Nicholas Thornby," he smirked.

"Fine, thanks," Laura answered. "He's busy, he works for several papers now."

"Doing what?" asked Claud.

"He writes articles, reviews books, does travel stuff, that sort of thing. He and my mother work as a team."

"I see." Claud watched Laura and the boy arranging the oysters on plates, alternating the oysters with rosy prawns and quarters of lemons.

"And does your – um – er – still help with your work?" asked Terrence, licking salt from his fingers. "The old man." There was a subterranean impertinence in the inquiry which Claud found disturbing.

"He never did." Laura was brusque. "We lead separate lives," she said, concentrating on a prawn she was peeling.

"Who is, what is, who does he mean by er, and um? What's the mystery?" Claud was irritated by the intimacy which, springing from nowhere between Laura and Terrence, excluded him.

"One can see you haven't had your ear to the ground when you've been at home," said Terrence perkily. "Why, even your mum would know what and who I am talking about." He bit a prawn, crunching it shell and all between large teeth.

"Don't choke on its whiskers," said Laura equably. "What the little sod is hinting at, Claud, is that there's a legend in these parts that my uncle Nicholas is also my father."

Claud gaped.

"It's general knowledge," said Terrence, pouring an oyster into his mouth.

Claud watched the boy's Adam's apple rise and fall. He tried to find something to say and failed.

"It tightens the familial bonds," said Terrence. "These oysters are delish. Everybody knows about the Thornby family."

"Everybody knows the moon is made of Stilton cheese," said Laura. "Eat some bread and butter with your oysters, Terry."

"Terrence," said Terrence.

"Brought you each a glass of stout, that's what you need with that lot." The owner of the wine bar appeared from the back premises with a tray. Laura smiled up at him as he set the glasses on the table. "On me," he said, returning her smile. "Don't stick around here, boy, there's plenty for you to do at back." He looked at Terrence without affection, turned and went away.

"Thank you," Laura called after him. "Great!"

"Who invented this libel?" asked Claud, recapturing his cool.

"It's just something I grew up with," said Laura, "a wartime legend. Nicholas and Emily found it amusing."

"Mr Thornby finds lots of things amusing, doesn't he?" said Terrence. "Hey! He didn't bring me any stout! I seem to remember Mr Nicholas found your work pretty comical."

"What is your work?" asked Claud, beginning to find Terrence's gnatlike presence a trial. "Do tell me if it's not a secret."

"There's no secret. I do restoration work."

"Oh," said Claud, "I see. What do you restore?"

"She makes new noses and fingers for classical statues," said Terrence. "Noses, fingers and cocks, all the things iconoclasts knock off."

"Fancy you remembering such a long word," said Laura, peeling another prawn.

"She makes models from life with plaster casts," said Terrence. "She had me standing in for a putto when I was small, that was a laugh. My mum supposed Mr Nicholas stood in for the mature male statues. She's got a comical mind, my ma."

"Terry, come and clear up back here," came a stentorian voice from behind the bar.

"Dear, dear, must go, thanks for the nosh." Terrence gulped his last oyster and scuttled away.

"What a horrible boy," exclaimed Claud. "Did you really? I mean did he – oh, Lord."

"Are you shocked?" Laura drank deep of her stout. "Delicious Guinness, so good for me."

"Of course not. Yes. No. It seems a bit odd. How did you – er – manage?"

Laura was laughing. "Oh, Claud, you are shocked. Terrence is a mythomaniac, every town has one. Eat your oysters before they die." Claud obeyed, scoffing his last two oysters, tasting only the salt. "It's extremely difficult," Laura was saying, "to make a cast of a child's nose, you have to plug its nostrils and bloody little Terry kept sneezing."

"Nose?" exclaimed Claud. "I thought you meant, I thought he meant—"

"Cocks?" Laura was really laughing now. "Oh, Claud, you are gullible."

Claud did not enjoy being mocked. "Why," he asked, deflecting the subject, "did your uncle, your father, put a bucket over my head and knock me downstairs?"

"Still harping on that! What a worrying bulldog it is. Nicholas and Emily thought I was giving you treasures from the attic. It's piled high with stuff they don't like or need but cannot bear to part with. Do we have to go on about this?"

"No, no. I'm sorry I brought it up."

They finished the prawns and bread and butter, drank their stout. Watching the rim of froth on his glass Claud remembered his terror. When drunk he had thought he saw Laura in triplicate, she had looked so peculiar flanked by Nicholas and Emily, so unlike the woman who now sat beside him, who a short while ago had lain in his arms. "They are your *doppelgängers*," he said.

"No," said Laura sharply. "We are all real, we are each separate. If they make you uneasy, find them a place in your novel."

"Wouldn't you mind?"

"Why should I? They will not be recognisable."

"In that case I'll bear them in mind," said Claud. "One rather good idea would be to insert bloody Amy and her Walkman, don't you think? I think she will fit in nicely." (Already my suggestion is his inspiration. Laura applauded herself.) "Amy might match up rather well with your mythomaniac, what is his name?"

"Terrence," said Laura.

"Oh, Laura, I love you," said Claud, delighted.

"Oysters are supposed to be aphrodisiac." Laura piled the empty shells into a pyramid.

"I mean I love you. Love. Love, not to be confused with lust."

"No?"

"Though of course love and lust are synonymous."

"Like oil and vinegar in mayonnaise?"

"You bring me to earth," Claud cried.

"Was Amy a successful mayonnaise?" asked Laura lightly.

"No," exclaimed Claud, "she curdled. I must have been a poor cook."

(Little does the poor boy know, thought Laura.)

"Of course you weren't," she said. You will be very good indeed before I finish with you, she thought with amusement. "Come on, Otis," she said, "I must go."

"Why Otis?" Claud helped her into her coat. "You called me Otis when I met you in the market. Why Otis?"

"It's just a name I like, a private joke. Otis reminds me of lifts, lifts go up and down. When I first saw you I thought you had spirit which might go up and down. Otis," said Laura, "in case you've never noticed, is a maker's name, you see it on lifts. Am I being pedantic?"

"Not at all," said Claud, at last latching on. "My spirits are high, they swoop."

"Up, up and away." Laura kissed his cheek and was off down the street in a rush.

PART II

WINTER

By vanishing to London Mavis created a vacuum in the Kennedy household. Without her daughter Ann Kennedy became depressed. She went to bed late, got up later still, wasted hours slumped in front of the television. "I know we argued," she said to Claud, catching him on his way upstairs. "We used to spar quite a bit, it kept us on our toes. Now look at me, I am collapsing into old age without Mavis to goad me along."

"I wouldn't say that, Mrs Kennedy, I wouldn't call it collapse." Claud fidgeted, anxious to reach his typewriter and note down an idea for his current chapter before he lost it.

"Call me Ann, you've been in the loft long enough to call me Ann. You can't deny the old age bit. Guess how old I am."

Claud thought he was too wise to guess; Ann Kennedy looked as old as his mother on a bad day, every day. "OK, Ann, thanks. It's not old age. You are lonely, that's all. It's natural to miss her, she's your only child."

"Does your mother miss you?"

"Not so you'd notice. I wouldn't know."

"Thought not. Would you like me to cook you your breakfast now Mavis is gone? It must cost you quite a bit going to the wine bar every morning."

"I quite like the wine bar." His privacy threatened, Claud stiffened.

"With Mavis gone? It would be no trouble to get your breakfast."

My God, she thinks I go to the wine bar because of Mavis. How crazy, she obviously doesn't connect me with Laura.

"I thought you went to the wine bar so you could watch Mavis looking pretty in her overall and have her take your order and say, yes, sir and no, sir."

"She never said yes, sir and no, sir. She was inclined to be bossy and hurry one up so that someone else could have the table."

"Oh, really?" Mrs Kennedy took this as an insult. "Bossy, was she? That's not what other people say—"

"Not bossy in any derogatory sense, Mrs Kennedy."

"Ann. There only is a derogatory sense to bossy, quote me another—"

"All right. Ann. She was bossy in a rather jolly and amusing way. The customers, as you say, liked it." (If she doesn't let me get to my manuscript, I shall hit her.)

"The customers were mostly her friends, they would like it."

"Mrs Kennedy, Ann, I've put my foot in it. I have ruffled you," he apologised.

"I'm not ruffled, I just said—"

"I found Mavis lovely, a stunner." Claud raised his voice, "She was pliant and appealing in her overall and I do assure you pretty, no, not pretty, absolutely competent as well." Claud moved towards the door; they had been standing in the kitchen. Mrs Kennedy barred his way to the stairs.

"Oh."

"I had no intention of insulting Mavis or hurting your maternal feelings. I—"

"That's all right, then. I just thought—"

"It was nice of course to see her in her overall, not totally concealed by that enormous overcoat," Claud carried on, realising as he spoke that he carried on too far. He shifted his weight on to his right foot as though about to walk through Ann Kennedy.

"It's a very good coat, it's the fashion to wear very large coats."

"I know, I read about it somewhere."

"A girl like Mavis, an actress, has to be *à la mode*—"

"Ann." If only she would let him get by, get to the stairs, get to work. "Ann."

"Yes?"

"Don't get carried away."

"I do get carried away. I lie awake nights expecting to hear that she's been raped on her way to rehearsal. London is dangerous."

"More likely on the way back, and she could equally well get herself raped here." The conversation was bolting along a fresh avenue. "I myself was tempted more than once." (Beware of verbal diarrhoea.)

"Am I harbouring a rapist?"

"Only joking, Mrs Kennedy, Ann."

"So I should hope. Now, what about your breakfast? Shall I or shall I not cook it?"

A compromise was reached: she would provide breakfast on Sundays when the wine bar was closed and on market days, since it was only sensible to brave the elements on a full stomach. Claud was to pay for these meals, he discovered later, by listening to dissertations on Mavis pram-bound, Mavis as a toddler, at primary school, at comprehensive and at drama school. As he ate his bacon and egg, grilled mushrooms with kidney and tomato, he learned to say, "Oh, really", "That was nice", "She wasn't stupid, was she", and other such platitudes, while his mind plotted his next chapter, the few sheets of typescript which would increase the pile on his desk.

Some thousands of words later, reading through his work, Claud recognised a minor character taking on the hue of Mrs Kennedy and that the character who had imposed herself as Amy had chameleon-like transformed into an etherealised person with Mavis' face and Laura's body. The characteristics which had been loathsome in Amy were in this paper version funny, sexy and beguiling; he was creating someone he dreamed of at night, confusing her with Laura wearing her jersey and nothing else. He would wake with a shock and an erection and sniff the cold air of the loft for the elusive scent of pepper.

So too his mother, the woman who had chivvied him through childhood, wiped his snot, ironed his shirts and simultaneously endured the vagaries of his violent alcoholic father, changed as he tapped the keys of his typewriter; the real Margaret Bannister disappeared just as in reality she had retreated from the neighbourhood and his immediate life by selling her house and moving elsewhere. So smoothly did she leave that Claud, passing his old home a week after her going, found himself querying whether he had ever lived in it.

He stood in the road staring at the house, noting the small changes already effected by the new owner. His parents' curtains still hung inside the windows, but tied back; there was a new knocker out of proportion with the size of the door; the new owner had whitened the grey slate step; a white cat stared bleakly from beside the scraper, freshly painted black, no longer coated with clods of mud from his mother's gardening clogs. Standing in the road he expected his mother to come round the house carrying the trug which held her fork and trowel, the garden gloves she never remembered to wear; she would be followed by her striped cat who lived under the delusion that it was a dog.

The door opened suddenly and a stranger stood in the doorway. The white cat nipped past her into the house. The woman spoke, articulating clearly. "Can I help you?" (She was grey, one of the grey people.)

Claud became aware that she was nervous, that his mother's cat had been dead some years, that perhaps the picture he had seen in his mind's eye might never have existed. "I am just casing the joint," he said angrily.

The new owner shut the door smartly in his face. Perhaps she would telephone the police? Claud fished in his pocket for a pencil and the notebook in which he jotted escaping ideas. He wrote: "I am only Claud Bannister, the erratic son of the previous owner, no need to panic." He pushed the note through the letterbox. The letterbox snapped at his fingers; it was new, like the knocker. His parents' letterbox had had a weak spring, it got stuck open letting in unnecessary draughts in cold weather. He was assailed by sadness, felt fierce pangs of remorse. He had so often been beastly to his mother. He shouted: "Fuck you, go to hell," bending down and yelling through the letterbox. It nipped his fingers again; he turned and ran, racing down the road to take shelter in the nearest public house.

He went to bed that night rather drunk and dreamed of a procession of women, none of whom were exactly his mother or Amy or Mavis; his dream turned to nightmare as the woman clasped in his arms turned into Ann Kennedy: "Christ, what are you doing in my bed?" He woke trembling, sniffed, smelled pepper. "Laura?"

"Yes."

"Where have you been?"

"London. You were dreaming."

"Nightmare – my mother – then I thought I was in bed with Ann Kennedy."

"Oh dear!"

"Is it really you?" He was fully awake now.

"Yes."

"What are you doing here?"

"Try and guess."

"I often wake and you are not there."

"How is Amy? Amy with her Walkman?"

"Changed, she's quite a raver now, marvellous, kind – gentle too."

"On paper."

"Yes, on paper, of course she's on paper."

"What power you have."

"On paper. How long have you been away?"

"I don't know. A few days."

"How long are you back for?"

"I don't know."

"Laura."

"Yes."

"The people in my book are more real than you and me, Brian and Susie, my mother or the market people."

"So?"

"D'you think I'm going mad?" he whispered.

"I think you are becoming a writer."

"You're not joking?"

"I'm not joking."

"My God." Claud lay back on the bed. "Gosh," he said. "Oh my goodness gracious me, oh my holy heavens."

Laura sniffed.

"You sniffed? Laura, what is it?"

"If you'd leave your book for a moment or two I'd show you."

In Claud's arms Laura sensed a change; he had grown older, more certain, he had matured. It was not a simple matter of a better turn of love-making and good timing. There was a passion and tenderness he had not shown before. She was, while finding this matching delightful and enjoyable, also puzzled. Then she realised with shock what was happening: he was making love not to her, but to this girl he had invented. She gave Claud's neck a sharp nip.

He cried out, "What's that for?" and sprang apart from her.

"Isn't it about time you let me read your manuscript?"

"I am afraid to." He swung his legs off the bed and sat with his back turned to her.

"You are presumably writing a book which you expect will eventually be published?"

"Of course."

"And people will read it?"

"Faceless people, people I do not know or care for."

"Your friends will read it, they too are the public."

"I had not thought. Do you want to read it?"

"Yes."

Claud stood up, picked his shirt off the floor, put it on and went to stand looking out across the roofs to the river. "People are right when they talk of the cold light of dawn. I am full of trepidation," he said. He took the manuscript from the table and laid it in Laura's lap. "Nobody has seen this," he said as he switched on the bedside lamp so that she could see to read. "I suppose I can trust you to tell me the truth."

"Yes." How easily one said yes.

He tapped the typescript. "These are my guts."

"Oh," said Laura, "guts."

"If this book is not well received, if it fails, well, to you it may sound silly, but the truth is I shall kill myself."

"*Feel* like killing yourself."

"No, I shall actually do it."

Laura said: "Oh *hell.*" Setting out to be amused, she had become interested, more interested than was safe. Claud was not like Clug, he would not be going back to Roumania next week.

Claud was speaking. "It's very difficult to explain, Laura darling," (he had not called her darling before) "but it's intense. The people in this book are real. The girl is as real as you, she has your legs for a start, your lovely legs, I love her – no, I can't explain—"

"I think," Laura said, "that I had better not read this." She took the typescript and held it out to him. "Anyway, I should not read it until it is finished."

"OK." He took the manuscript and laid it back in its place on the table. "All right," he said, "I understand. But I meant what I said. I—"

"Yes," said Laura. Then, "Why don't we resume what we were at when I bit you?"

"Oh, Laura—"

"Only this time make love to me not to Amy."

"She's not called Amy any more."

"Well, just concentrate on fucking me. I don't like acting proxy. I'm no good at it."

"All right, Laura, I shall enjoy that." Claud got back into bed. "And later, when it's day, we could have breakfast in the wine bar," he said.

"Stop talking," she said.

"Can we talk now?" Claud asked presently.

"What about?" Laura stared at the dark oblong of the uncurtained window. "Your book?"

"No, you. I want to know all about you."

Laura said nothing.

"Tell me what you did when you had this loft. Did you bring lovers here?"

"I told you. I came here to be private. Ann's husband was alive in those days. A nice man, sensitive. He understood my need to be alone. I bet Ann misses him."

"I don't want to talk about Ann. Tell me about your lovers, I won't be jealous." But Claud felt a rush of jealousy. Had she in this bed done to others what she— "Please tell me, I need to know."

"You need to know!" Laura leaned back, her head on her arms.

"When people fall in love they tell each other everything," said Claud.

Laura laughed. "The more fools they."

"Don't mock. Who did you bring up here? I think I am a bit jealous. Not Brian?" (Susie's Brian, he felt quite hot at the idea.)

"Not Brian," Laura answered gravely.

"Sorry. I am jealous. I admit it."

"A boring unprofitable emotion."

"Who did you bring up here?" He leaned over, his mouth against hers, kissing urgent, questioning kisses.

Christopher had not kissed like this that one time she had allowed him up here. He had not been a fast learner like Claud. Laura kissed Claud back. "That's nice," she said. "Very nice."

"Not boring?" He leaned over her smiling.

"Not at all."

"So who did you bring here? Who lay with you in this bed?" He watched her, trying to read the thoughts behind her eyes, very black in the pre-dawn light.

"Nobody." She remembered Christopher on that wet and stormy afternoon in their teens when she had let him come here to her secret place and they had, for the first time, experimented with sex. She had not let him come again; his presence had disrupted her privacy. He had denigrated the loft. Instead, they had rolled about in his bed when his parents were out and he had declared himself "in love". Great fun was had for a time by both, she remembered, until – until what? For the life of her she could not remember what snide remark, spoken by whom, had caused her brain to click and realise that quite a lot of people believed that she and Christopher were brother and sister and that subtly, by not denying, Emily encouraged the idea.

Looking at Laura, seeing her frown, Claud tried to guess what went on behind those eyes. Laura was not thinking of him. He felt anxious, excluded.

Then her mother's complex relationship with Christopher's father had entered a new dimension. She knew then, she thought, why Ned paid her school bills. It was not goodness of heart, but a guilty response to blackmail. Why else should he have forked out for an expensive education at Cheltenham Ladies' College, and a whole lot more? As she had often done since, Laura found herself admiring her mother's effrontery, her unorthodox method of raising funds for her daughter's education. But at the time, recoiling priggishly from what she thought she saw, she had choked Christopher off, brutally telling him that any warmth she felt for him would freeze to hate if bound by marriage.

Remembering the scene Laura smiled and Claud, watching, wondered.

Christopher, in the heat of first love, imagined in his innocence that love entailed marriage. He had been hurt, angry, refused to accept, become boring, and she had grown mocking, distant and in her turn cross. For not having been in love with him, she felt guilty.

Then in a rage she confronted her mother, and Emily laughed. Thirty years on Laura could hear that laugh. Emily had laughed from relief.

"What a bitch," Laura muttered. Claud strained to hear, but could not.

Suspicious now, she had become aware of a groundswell of gossip. Whispers, suggestive wagers as to her provenance, and it was not Ned Peel who was hinted at, but Nicholas.

Laura closed her eyes and drew a long breath, as Claud watched. She had not this time confronted her mother; she had come here to the loft where she had lain for twenty-four hours, weighting the trap-door with heavy books against intruders. Then, driven down by hunger, she had snatched a sandwich in Ann's kitchen before setting off across the fields to the Peels' house where she had asked Christopher's mother to lend her money. Rose Peel had refused to lend, but had given her five hundred pounds, asked no questions, tendered no advice.

Laura smiled in recollection. She had respected the older woman. Claud longed to know why she smiled, dared not interrupt.

She had cashed the cheque, packed a small bag, and set off abroad, hitching lifts, working her way across Europe, washing dishes or working at au pair jobs until she found herself working for a potter in Provence who taught her her trade.

For several years she had remained in a state of bellicosity and resentment against Nicholas and Emily; it waned as she returned to England, visited her mother and was made as welcome as though she had only been absent for a week. Emily had been charming, Nicholas too; she began to wonder whether she had misjudged them. She even went through a phase of suspecting Ned Peel again. Perhaps Rose Peel had not been so remarkable? She would have been glad to give the money, she would not want her only son to marry his half-sister. She might even, when she gave her the cheque, have thought she needed it for an abortion. Rose would not have wanted that sort of grandchild. She had juggled many mad suppositions rather than face the truth.

Then with acceptance came resignation tinged with hilarity, a philosophy, a mode of survival. There could be no marriage, no great love, no children, but plenty of friendship, good sex and always short-term relationships. Since it was quite difficult to find lovers to fit these criteria, there had not been many. Clug had been the latest.

Then what am I doing? Laura sat up and drew away from Claud. What a crazy idea to seduce Claud and install him in my loft. I must be mad. Here is somebody who breaks all my rules; he could become a lasting responsibility. What a dangerous aberration from my norm.

"I am sorry I nipped you," she said.

Claud had forgotten the nip: "Were you counting your lovers? You smiled."

"My list is pretty sparse." Laura got out of bed and began to dress, excluding Claud as she muffled her body. He would do better sticking to Amy, she thought, and chuckled.

"What's funny?" Claud cried angrily.

"I had a virtuous thought. Come on, get up, when I feel virtuous I feel hungry. Let's go and eat a hearty breakfast." She hustled into her clothes, pulled on her boots. "I crave hot coffee and croissants."

Sulkily Claud reached for his pants. "I crave you," he said.

"Brian built those shelves for me," said Laura, more to annoy herself than Claud. Brian had made a clumsy pass easily parried.

Claud did not rise to this, but with one leg in his trousers hopped to his work table to make a note; he had been seized with an idea, must note it down.

How soon will he bore me? Laura wondered, watching him. "My threshold of boredom is a matter of weeks," she said, but Claud was absorbed and did not hear.

Laura moved to the window and pressed her nose to the cold glass, then blew, steaming it up. She wrote: Christopher, Miklos the painter, Tony from the US, Clug, Claud. She rubbed at the names with her palm. "It's cold out there," she said. "Very cold."

Claud said, "Um," still writing.

Laura clenched her fists, blew again on the pane, clouding it, cutting out the view. "There is no view," she said. "No view."

Claud murmured, "Um, just a minute," writing with one hand, drawing his trousers on with the other.

I'd better get the view in proportion, Laura scolded herself. Time is up! He is becoming more than a toy boy, I have not been careful. "Time is up," she said out loud.

"Nearly finished," said Claud, referring to his notes, as he tucked in his shirt and pulled up his zip.

Laura watched. Thank God, she thought, he does not know that I have come whizzing down from London several times and not let him know. Twice I have watched him asleep and not got into bed with him; another time I drove away without coming into the house, but last night I weakened, was unwary, lost control.

She watched Claud. His features would coarsen, she thought, his looks would improve. A few lines across his forehead and from nose to chin would add interest to the too young face, add beauty. "Oh, come on, Claud," she said impatiently. "Buck up."

Claud threw down his pencil. "You sound just like my mother," he said. "What have you written on the window?" He put his arms round Laura, pinning her arms to her sides, leaning over her shoulder, trying to decipher what she had written. "A list of your lovers? Let me see, don't move." Laura kept quite still, very still. "Oh, darling,

I wish you were like my mother, then I would not be jealous. I am so jealous."

"Put it in your book. Use it."

"I shall. My God, Laura." He blew gently on the window pane. "You have written my name. Look, it says Claud. As if I belonged to a list. What does it mean?" But Laura had ducked out of his arms and made for the ladder.

Margaret Bannister was happy in her new house; there was something astringent about its plain walls, an innocence of atmosphere which pleased. Whoever had lived in the house before her had left no trace.

As she arranged furniture and books, chose curtains, planned the garden, discovered her new village, made cautious friends with neighbours, her spirits rose. She felt an almost unholy glee at having distanced herself from Claud, and with Claud his father, whose memory lurked in the old house riddling her with guilt.

In this new ambience there was little to remind her of Claud or his father. In the old house she had been constantly reminded of scenes she would rather forget.

Open the kitchen cupboard and the door would stick where her husband had torn it off its hinge; in the bathroom was a crack in the mirror where he had hurled a toothglass. Every time she went into the garage she remembered the blow which had blacked her eye. In the bedroom she had too often lain wakeful, wondering what mood to expect when he returned, if he returned, for frequently he did not (I was held up). Long after their separation and his death she had remained uneasy. It was unfair to Claud to associate him with the fears, resentments and pains of her marriage, but she had done so. Now, splendidly free of inhibiting memories, she was free to love Claud without guilt, and remember his father with tenderness for the times of happiness and laughter – for they had shared happiness and enjoyed much laughter before she had developed an exaggerated fear of what she secretly thought of as "the return from the pub". By moving house she had cured the phobia.

As she arranged her kitchen cupboards Margaret dwelt on the good times, recovered her balance. She wished she had moved sooner.

Soon she would be ready to ask Claud to a meal, treat with him on her own terms minus the ghost of his father and the tiresomeness of his childhood, during which she suspected she had been too passive. Doormats make poor mothers, she told herself.

From the safe distance of thirty miles, she thought, without fussing, about Claud's chances of succeeding as a writer, wondered whether he had talent. She was glad that he had the market stall and inclined to put her money on that rather than what seemed to her an ephemeral novel. His writing craze might not last. She was grudgingly grateful to Laura for suggesting the stall; neither Claud nor herself would have had such a simple and original idea.

Before going to sleep – sleep was no problem in the new house – Margaret wondered what it might be like for Laura to have such a young lover and was surprised to find herself envying Laura's enterprise. She knew her husband would have enjoyed a Laura/Claud combination and this increased her fondness for his memory, eased the nagging sense of responsibility for his fatal coronary.

She remembered him an impulsive man. On impulse he had bashed the cupboard, thrown the toothglass, blacked her eye, threatened suicide, walked out on her. But she would not think of all that, rather remember the time he rushed her off to Paris for a lovely week in spring (fly now, pay later), bought her a dress he could not possibly afford, lured her into bed when they should have gone to a stuffy party.

A pity in a way that Claud was not like that, superficially yes, but not really. Claud's father would have made the running, not Laura.

Is there any running? How can I know? I must get another cat, she thought. I am too cautious to take a lover. Then she thought, What about Mavis, so pretty and presumably available? No, no, not with Laura around the horizon. She felt calm about Claud. Now that they were distanced she would not know if he got drunk or came a cropper. She would help by loving him, which cost nothing, and post the odd cheque to Ann Kennedy to subsidise the rent when she could afford it.

She bought a new frame for a snap of her husband taken by a crony, propping the bar of his favourite hostelry, and a matching frame for the snap of Claud taken by Amy whom she had never met, Amy who had made him so unhappy. Father and son were superficially alike. Claud's jaw was more determined, his smile less humorous. Were they really alike? She thought not. In habit, yes. Claud aped his father's trick of pissing out of windows when too lazy to go to the bathroom and she had recently seen him drunk, but that surely was exceptional.

What would he be like as a lover? Presumably he had muffed it with Amy; with Laura sex would be something else again, and any junketing with Mavis would be a repetition of Amy.

When I am completely settled, Margaret thought, I shall ask Claud over to see the house, observe what changes independence and his new career have made. It is weeks, months even, since I left.

Needing exercise Margaret set out for the shops. She would make inquiries about a kitten, have her sleeping pill prescription made up in case she reverted to insomnia, buy whisky to offer, should whisky drinkers call. So far only sherry drinkers had put their foot in the door, hopeful members of the WI which she had no intention of joining. Her husband had maintained that sherry drinkers always called first, true boozers later.

She was surprised, rounding a corner of the lane which led to the village, when an old man she had seen passing the plate in church stepped from behind a tree, opened his fly and exposed his large but drooping organ. Swerving so that her shopping basket knocked her knee Margaret walked on.

Should she have said, "Good afternoon? Nice day, isn't it?" Asked whether he knew of a suitable kitten? Should she have said anything? To say nothing seemed so rude. Had she really seen what she thought she had seen?

In the supermarket she filled her basket with groceries, took two bottles of whisky from the shelf, paid at the check-out. He probably did it to everybody. It might be part of village life, something everyone knew about. She didn't want the village saying, "That new woman at the White House is making trouble." He passed the plate very nicely in church, waited for people to fumble for change.

She couldn't mention her encounter in the chemist, where the girl in the white uniform looked young and lofty as she took the prescription. "Will you come back for it or wait? It will be ten minutes."

"I'll wait." There was a notice-board with lists of forthcoming events neatly pinned. Lists of lectures and films. Curious, thought Margaret, staring at the board, I have never except for my husband and Claud seen a man's penis. Claud had the neatest little thing as a baby, rather like an acorn.

"Mrs Bannister," called the girl in the overall, "your prescription."

Margaret paid. "I don't really need these," she said. The girl looked down her nose. Outside the shop Margaret bumped into Claud.

"Claud!" She was joyously surprised. They hugged.

"Mother! I thought I saw you in there. Let me take your shopping."

"I was going to invite you over when I got straight."

"So you don't want to see me? It's weeks, months—"

"Is it? Time goes so – of course I want to see you. I didn't want to interrupt your work," she lied.

"I'm taking an hour or two off. I thought I'd visit your new palazzo. This is jolly heavy. Buying booze now, that's not like you."

"In case of visitors. Would you like a bottle to take back?"

"Thanks, I would. I'll hoard it for a future celebration. Look, I've borrowed Ann Kennedy's car. I'll drive you home." He put the basket on the back seat, first taking one of the bottles and propping it in a corner. "Get in, here we go! Which way now?"

"Turn right here and down that lane." The old man had disappeared. Should she tell Claud? He had not been circumcised, she had noticed that; both Claud and his father were. "One lives and learns," she said.

"Learns what?" Claud changed gear.

"That's the house there, on the left," she said. She would say nothing. She did not wish to appear inexperienced and naïve. It was wonderful to see Claud. "I've missed you," she said, which was partly true. "This is an enterprising neighbourhood," she said. "There is a whole range of classes and lectures one can join: ecology, sociology, psychology, literature, art, archaeology – I was reading the list in the chemist."

"Which will you take up?"

"I thought psychology would help me most." Claud laughed. In the old days she might have felt diminished. "No need to mock," she said. "Here we are. This is the house. Let me see what I can give you for lunch."

"Anything will do." He wished he had given her warning, she was such a good cook; living alone she probably didn't bother much. "What an agreeable kitchen," he said. "Shall I put your shopping away?"

"Thank you."

"I took you at your word about the whisky."

"I meant you to. What about a risotto?"

"Delicious." He was relieved.

While Margaret prepared the risotto, Claud explored the house. He had been miffed when she moved so suddenly, chose a house without consulting him, left him to come and find her; it did not fit the picture he had composed for himself of a tiresomely possessive parent. She had lived here solo, perfectly happy, for several months. As he went from room to room, finding familiar furniture in new poses, he began to rearrange his picture of his parent. Peering at the newly framed photographs of himself and his father he questioned rather uncomfortably whether he had not perhaps joined his father as a figure from his mother's past? Been cast off?

He shed this discomfort at lunch. While his mother talked about her new neighbourhood, the charms and conveniences of the village, he described the small triumphs of his stall. His book, he told her, was progressing. He was grateful, he said, for the money she sent Ann. Could she afford it? Should he not be independent?

"I like to help if I can," she said. She was pleasurably surprised talking to him. He did not contradict, as he always had on principle, or smack her down when she ventured a political opinion contrary to his own. He was grown more civilised. He even laughed at her jokes. I shall not spoil this by mentioning Laura, she thought. She was reminded of the happier times with her husband.

Tucking into the risotto, salad, fruit, cheese and excellent coffee, Claud forgave his parent her defection. Why should she not live where she pleased? If he made an effort, he could reach her here. He would not stay too long, though, in case the conversation slipped into the personal; she might link him with Mavis or make some reference to Amy. He could not possibly tell her that Amy was transformed into someone quite else. As he listened to his mother the part of his mind which concentrated on his novel began to question whether there were not parts of it mulched with sentimentality. What was it about his mother made him think this? She was having an effect similar to Laura's. Not, of course, the Laura in bed, there was no way he could imagine his mother making use of her legs as Laura did.

Margaret saw Claud smile, did not ask what the joke might be; she was happy that their shaky relationship was improved. She thought enviously of other parents who had secure relationships with their young, a constant exchange of confidences. As they talked she was content to remain in the shallows. It was quite amusing not to ask about Laura, to listen to Claud being cocky and adult, not quite as in love with himself as he had been. She did not, when it was time to go, press him to stay. She watched him drive away, waved at the departing car and as she did so remembered the old man in the lane, poor pitiful creature, and was curiously reminded of Claud new-born, a red and skinny infant, shaken by screams, his balls huge, out of all proportion to his size. She decided to put a pound in the collection next time she went to church and forget the incident in the lane.

She was glad Claud had been the first to make a move, to seek her out; it was almost as if they had quarrelled. Perhaps they had. She hoped he would come again. He is not too like his father, she thought as she washed the dishes. I shall go to those lectures on psychology. I may be too late to learn how to cope with a manic-depressive husband, but I can learn to understand Claud.

Claud, on his way home, felt pleased with himself. He had done the right thing visiting his mother. She was OK. Would it be possible to meld parts of his mother into the small character based on Ann Kennedy? Why not, good idea. An old man standing by a tree in the lane apparently having a leak waved. Claud waved back as he swung round a corner. The whisky bottle toppled but he caught it before it fell. Had she noticed that he had stolen her sleeping pills? He patted his pocket with the bottle of pills in it. She is happy now, she doesn't need these things. I shall keep them just in case I get so worried by my work I lose sleep. I cannot afford to lose sleep. The only loss I will put up with is through Laura.

Helen Peel reminded her husband that ages ago she had given him an errand for Laura. Had he been yet? It was weeks since—

"No, not yet", "Sorry, I forgot", "I'll do it next week", "Thanks for reminding me, I'll make a note—"

"We are into February, I want that god in place by April when the garden is open in aid of the blind – it has a missing hand."

"The blind wouldn't notice anything missing—"

"What a heartless thing to say! What a crude sort of joke."

"It was not a joke, a mere remark."

"I believe your mother was right to call you pedantic." (Helen always referred to her mother-in-law as though she were dead.)

"What's my mother got to do with—"

"Nothing, thank the Lord, but please, Christopher, I am serious. Get that job done for me, I don't want to have to—"

(Deal with Laura yourself.) "OK," said Christopher. "I'll tie a knot in my hanky, make a note, get cracking. Don't worry, old girl, it shall be done."

Why should I run her bloody errand? Christopher asked himself. Because she doesn't like Laura, she's afraid of Laura, afraid of Laura's tongue. Laura had made a sotto voce joke when Helen had the garden open last year in aid of the spastics. It had sent John and Emma into a gale of giggles. He had not heard the joke himself, nor asked to have it repeated. They had told their grandmother and Rose had gasped with pleasure. "What superlative bad taste!" Rose would never laugh at spastics so one guessed the joke was to do with Helen, quite possibly himself. One seldom saw Rose these days, married to that fellow, but she'd always got on well with Laura, there was something deeper than the usual female alliance between those two.

John and Emma in their teens were tiresome enough; what would they be like if they were Laura's children? An alarming idea. Much better to be safe with Helen, one knew where one was with Helen. She would not let John and Emma fall under Laura's influence, or his mother's, for that matter; she knew how to protect her family. Christopher felt warm affection for his wife. Her head was screwed on the right way.

OK, he thought, I'll see she gets the statue's hand fixed. It isn't often she entrusts me with anything to do with the garden. As for John and Emma, there was no proof, but he was sure it was one or other or both who had vandalised the statue. It had been all in one piece when Helen bought it. Christopher chuckled. He did not suppose either of his offspring had intended doing their father a good turn when they chopped the hand off. He looked forward to visiting Laura, was glad to have a valid excuse.

Christopher hummed on his way to the station the following day. A little delay, a spot of pleasurable anticipation, no mad obvious rush to see Laura and perhaps Helen would stop nagging and harping about one's old loves? There was comfortable time to call in on Laura before the directors' meeting. One could catch up with her news. (Had one ever even lagged behind with her news, she was such a bloody clam? Ha, ha, quite a good joke, one could use it again some time.) Make a discreet inquiry or two to find out whether there was still anything up with that wog composer from behind the Iron Curtain. Imagine fancying a communist, it boggled one's imagination. A Red! God! Really! It must be vicious gossip – really what some people's minds – and what about that boy? One had seen her with him. One could find out about him, discreetly, of course. Did he have anything to recommend him? Youth? Christopher stopped humming. Bloody youth. That polished buttercup hair. The features not yet moulded by experience. Where had he read that? In one of Helen's library books? Some soppy woman writer, never read a woman writer, they so often had a pinko tinge.

Christopher caught his train, and all the way to London pictured Laura as she had been and how she might have been had she not – had she not chosen to go her own way. She never had any intention of marrying me, he thought with painful clarity as the train passed Maidenhead. Those few times they had fumbled and tumbled and rolled about in his bed during the Easter holidays when the parents were out had been what she had quite frankly said at the time purely experimental. God! thought Christopher in his middle age, she was a bloody little cock-teaser in those days. It may have been experimental for her, he thought, but for me, he thought, blanching at the memory, well, really, even now after all these years I burn. (Well, simmer.)

Gathering up his *Times* and *Spectator*, putting *Private Eye* into his briefcase – one couldn't really be seen carrying it – Christopher damped his recollections of the unassuaged lusts of adolescence, squared his shoulders, checked his fly, and stepped off the train at Paddington Station. Here he walked fast to the cab rank and, stepping determinedly ahead of a flustered old woman with a heavy suitcase, settled himself into a taxi.

"Where to?" asked the driver.

Christopher gave Laura's business address. The driver turned up the volume of his radio. He was listening to the Test Match.

One wondered why one saw Laura so rarely, Christopher thought as the taxi shot past Sussex Gardens. One needn't wonder, he thought sourly as it jerked to a stop at the lights. Helen would not countenance one's seeing much more of Laura than one did. As the taxi whizzed along the Bayswater Road and dodged nippily into the park one agreed that the other reason one saw so little of Laura was Laura's marked lack of enthusiasm. I shan't tip this man, he drives far too fast, how can he pay attention to what he's doing when his mind is on those jokers down under?

One had arrived.

Christopher fumbled for change. God, these pound coins did one's pockets damage, it was a wonder they didn't shoot down one's leg into one's shoe. "What's the score?"

The driver took the money, did not answer; he was black, Jamaican probably. He turned the radio higher, grinned suddenly at Christopher, shouted, "We's winning, brother!" and drove off.

Christopher made careful way down area steps and walked along a covered passage to the door which had "Laura Thornby, Repairs and Restoration, please ring" on it. Here, in the basement of an anonymous building, Laura plied her trade.

Standing at the door Christopher wondered why this was the only address he had for Laura apart from the Old Rectory, which she seldom visited. Where did she live in London? Not here. This was work, a place of business; there was not even a comfortable chair; did she perhaps live with someone, a man? A lover? Why had this possibility not struck him before? And if she did live with some bloke, how could one find out? People gossiped at home, but here in London nobody noticed what was going on; she vanished into London as into some black hole in space. Christopher put his thumb on the buzzer.

"Who is it?" Laura's voice, tinny and disembodied, whispered through the grille.

"Christopher."

"Christopher who?"

"Christopher Peel."

"Oh! Christopher Peel. One should have guessed. One should have known. Come in, how can one help you?" She opened the door. "Step inside," she said. He had interrupted her at work. He knew better than to rise to her teasing; if he was not careful she would keep it up for hours. One had wept as a child, been reduced to hitting her, pulling her hair out by the roots.

"I am on an errand for Helen," he said. "She has a statue she bought last autumn – it needs a hand."

"It needs a hand. Does one have specifications?"

"Please, Laura."

Laura said, "You'd better come in." She turned and led the way, he followed. "But you can't stay long," she said over her shoulder, "I'm busy."

Christopher tried to remember an occasion when she had not said this.

"All right." She was wiping clay off her hands with a damp cloth. "Let me write it down. Have you got the measurements?"

No messing about, no chit-chat, straight to business. "Yes, actually I made a tracing of the stump, it's a clean break." Christopher fished his wallet from the breast pocket of his pinstriped suit and extracted a piece of tracing paper. "And a photograph of the original."

"Very neat," said Laura, taking them. "Why don't you sit down?"

"I'd rather stand. I have to go on to a directors' meeting. I don't want to sit in some clayey mess."

"Idiot." Laura took a duster from her desk drawer and flipped it across the seat of a chair. "There, sit on that, it makes me nervous having you standing over me. Or sit on this newspaper." She spread a sheet of newsprint across the chair seat. "The *Financial Times* should suit you."

Christopher eyed the newspaper suspiciously. "Another client left it here, it's not my kind of paper." She laid the tracing on her desk and studied it.

Christopher sat uneasily, his hat on his knee. He had never worn a hat until lately, but people seemed to be wearing them again and Helen said he looked right in this soft trilby. Ah, Helen. He looked disparagingly at the hat, hoped Laura would not comment. His eyes ranged round Laura's workroom. Nothing had changed since his last visit: the kiln stood against one wall, tubs of clay covered with wet cloths ranged opposite. There was her desk, the chair he sat on, the chair she sat on; shelves from floor to ceiling held tools and casts. Casts of hands, feet, parts of arms, legs, all ranged in sizes, a variety of heads and bowls which held examples of smaller portions of anatomy, fingers, toes, ears, noses and he supposed penises, though he had never actually seen one.

"I may have one that fits," said Laura. "It would save you a bob or two to have one ready made."

Christopher took this as an aspersion or sideways dig at his frugal spending habits. He disliked the smell of Laura's workshop; the clay dust in the air made him sneeze. Looking about him, he caught the eye of Laura's cat crouching near the warm kiln. The cat was an extremely small pale grey tabby which matched the background. It stared at Christopher. Christopher looked away, discomfited by its amber eyes. The cat yawned, exposing a pale pink palate and useful teeth.

Laura was frowning and leafing through a ledger. Christopher wondered whether the dust in the air made her wash her hair every night; he would have liked to know this small intimacy. Did she shampoo it or only stand under the shower and rinse it through? She looked distant and preoccupied, businesslike in grey denim jeans, a grey sweatshirt. Lit by a harsh overhead light she melted, as did the cat, into the general greyness of the room. He said, "You look so different when you are working."

"And you presumably do not wear that pretty pinstripe when you are on the beach or in the garden." She did not look up as she concentrated on her search. "Ah, this should do you. Number sixty, exactly the right size. Casts I made from Nicholas when I was starting this business. He has beautiful hands."

"Helen does not like Nicholas."

"Helen would not know."

"She might, she's extremely observant."

"All right, since she's so particular, what about these, number seventeen. These?" She slewed the ledger round so that Christopher could see the photograph.

"But those are my hands. I remember."

"Yes." They both remembered an afternoon in the far past. She had laughed as she made casts of his hands one afternoon in the studio she had had in the Old Rectory.

"She'd know—" He was tempted but cautious.

"Rubbish. You were a lot younger."

"She doesn't know, she has no idea I ever—"

"Oh, Christopher, be your age, Helen isn't as stupid as all that. It fits perfectly."

"Well, I won't have it. It would be positively creepy."

Laura said, "OK. Let's see what else." She went on turning the pages. "Mind you, I think Helen is silly to muck about with her statues, she should leave well alone. It's not of course in my interest to lose an order, but—"

"She can't stand mutilations—"

Laura stared across her desk daring Christopher to go on, knowing that given half a chance he would accuse her of mutilating him. He had once actually done so, he had a habit of repeating himself. Christopher dropped his gaze. "She was traumatised in the British Museum as a child." He cleared his throat (all this dust).

Laura snorted. "So she says! Personally I think she is wrecking the garden; it was perfect in your mother's day. It's not meant to be formal and Italianate, dotted about with fake Apollos."

"Helen loathes disorder."

"Your mother achieved a charmed dishevelment in that garden with those loopy clematis and vines, scrambling roses, unexpected lilies. Helen is ruining it. I hear she has dug up the iris beds."

"It's not my mother's garden any more," said Christopher stiffly. "It's Helen's."

"How right you are. Well, who am I to criticise your wife, my client?"

Christopher was silent. He wondered what would have happened to the garden if he had married Laura – he did not like Laura's tone – always supposing Laura had been agreeable.

Laura, for her part, suppressed a smile as she congratulated herself on having evaded this fate. "I prefer you as a client," she said.

"What?" (She had always known what he was thinking.)

"Here we are. Just the job. A recent model. Nice, aren't they?" (Time he made up his mind; this visit has gone on long enough.)

Christopher peered. "Whose hands are they?"

"Nobody you know."

"I hear you are interested in that Roumanian composer."

"I've heard that too; conductor."

"Are you?"

"These are not his hands. The interest was minimal." Laura's patient voice held underlying threat.

Christopher said: "People do gossip, you know."

"I know. Will these do? I haven't got all day, Christopher, and there's your directors' meeting or whatever."

"They look all right." He was grudging. "Sure they are not some criminal?"

"Christopher, your mind! I am not Madame Tussaud."

"I like to know what I am living with. Every time I pass that statue I—"

Laura was laughing. "It's not going to come to life and give you a mason's handshake. These hands have perfectly respectable provenance, I promise you."

"Sure?"

"Sure."

"Very well." Christopher got to his feet. "How soon can Helen have it?"

"I'll let you know. I'll post it and send instructions on how to—"

"I hoped you would do it for us."

"You can manage—"

Still Christopher lingered. "I – er – hear—"

"Yes?"

"Well, Helen, no, to be honest it was me. I saw you in the wine bar with some new friend."

"Claud Bannister."

"So *that's* who it was. Oh. Isn't he supposed to be writing a book? His mother told—"

"I believe he is."

"So you are coming down oftener?"

"Who says?"

"I thought you must be interested when I saw you with him."

"You did?"

"So naturally I thought when you next come down you could fix the hand for Helen. I mean, when I heard, I mean saw, I—"

"What a lot you hear and see."

"What?"

"What?"

"What I am getting at," said Christopher, goaded, "is, are you in love with him? Is he in love with you?"

"He is in love, poor fellow."

Christopher said, "You have lost none of your charm, Laura."

"He's not in love with me, you fool." Laura was irritated.

"Oh, oh, wrong end of the stick as usual. Who is he in love with, then, if it's not you?" Christopher found himself relieved, delighted even.

"Whoever it is may do him harm."

"Would that matter?" (Would she mind?)

Laura did not answer; she watched Christopher thoughtfully.

"I don't believe I've met him since he grew up." Christopher had never been averse to a spot of delving. "I know his mother, of course, just to say hullo. She was a wartime evacuee who was almost not claimed by her parents; one is left wondering what sort of people they were. She married Bannister who drank and left her. One used to see him in the boozer. You must remember him."

"Vaguely."

"They weren't the sort of people we were likely to know, were they?"

"Who?" Laura's eyebrows rose at Christopher's patronising tone.

"The Bannisters, your protégé's parents."

"I'd scarcely call him a protégé." Laura side-stepped Claud.

"Well, whatever he is." Christopher hesitated to proceed.

Making no effort to rescue him from his predicament, Laura waited with her head slightly tilted, her eyes fixed on his face, just not meeting his gaze, a perverse trick he remembered from childhood. He is getting to look awfully like his aged pa, she thought, and smiled, remembering how her mother Emily had teased and manipulated and manoeuvred Ned Peel. "You are getting to look very like your father," she said. "We knew him all right. There's nothing of your mother in you, is there?"

"That's what Helen says, she's thankful."

"Helen would be." Laura's tone was dangerously neutral. "Well now," she said, "it's time you went to your meeting, is it not? You've carried out Helen's little commission, found out that there is nothing between me and the red composer, and nothing between me and Claud Bannister – as though it were any business of yours – so, having ordered a hand for Helen's fake – it'll be a special order, I can't let her have it at cost price – you'd better trot."

"Don't be like that. I'm not prying—"

"What else would you call it?" He's as bad as Nicholas, she thought, forever poking his nose into my life. Has he nothing to keep him occupied?

The small cat, seized by a crisis of digestion, darted now between Christopher's legs on its way to its litter box where, turning its back and lifting its tail, it assuaged its need. Christopher watched the cat's tail shiver, picked up his briefcase and hat, and backed away. "Whew! Whiffy! Phew!"

"It's momentary. She covers it up." Laura was amused by Christopher's repugnance. "The last time I came to see you and Helen I trod in your enormous dog's turd in my best shoes—"

Mulling thoughts of Claud Bannister, Christopher moved towards the door. "No doubt Nicholas will review this oeuvre when it is published," he said, half surprised to find himself aligned with Nicholas.

"No doubt he will," Laura answered lightly, too lightly, Christopher observed.

At the door he bent to kiss Laura's cheek, which smelt of clay dust. "Goodbye," he said.

"Goodbye." Laura closed the door.

As he walked away he heard her tinny voice through the grille. "I like your fancy hat."

Standing on the pavement waiting for a taxi, Christopher felt rage. By hardly saying a word Laura had made him feel a snob for his remarks about the Bannisters, and a fool for prying into her private life; she had not even asked after John and Emma, or shown a gram of gratitude at being given Helen's commission. "Oh, fuck the woman," he cried as a taxi drew alongside in answer to his waving arm. "To the City," he shouted, unnecessarily loudly.

*

Laura sat in the chair vacated by Christopher. He was clever to threaten me with Nicholas. "I never thought Christopher could be consciously dangerous," she said to the cat. "What power weak people possess."

She jotted notes for Helen's order while part of her mind reviewed Christopher's character. Obstinate, patronising, a cultivated reputation for kindness. Perhaps she was wrong to think him weak? I should have let him think he was doing me a good turn in giving me this order for Helen's beastly statue. I should have made him feel good, resisted picking on Helen. I hate her for wrecking that lovely garden. "Oh," said Laura to the cat, who had resumed its position by the kiln, "why do I feel protective? There is no need." She had not imagined the malice in Christopher's suggestion that Nicholas might review Claud's book. The thought converged with a second idea, the idea that Claud in love might become vulnerable to excess. "I don't see why I should feel responsible," she said to the cat, "it cuts across the grain of my nature." The cat purred sleepily, a self-contained animal.

Laura tidied her workshop, put the ledgers back in place, washed her hands at a corner sink, picked up the cat and put it in a wicker cat basket, pulled on a heavy tweed coat. She extinguished the lights and went out, double-locking the door. With the cat on her knee, she travelled by bus to the corner of the street in Chelsea where she lived in an anonymous block of flats. Taking the lift to the top floor she was reminded of Claud by the maker's name. (May his spirit keep up.) She walked along a corridor similar to all the other corridors in the building and let herself into her flat. The flat consisted of two rooms, bedroom and sitting-room, a kitchenette and bathroom. A cat-flap led on to a small terrace; from the terrace the cat occasionally leapt on to the roof. Looking up from the street she had once seen its tiny figure perched high above the street, viewing the world. It was not the sort of cat to catch sparrows or pigeon; it seemed content with its inhibited life, made few demands. She let the cat out of its basket, opened a tin of catfood and fed it. Waiting for it to finish its meal, she picked up the empty saucer, washed it and put it away.

The flat was spick and span, every surface gleaming and dust-free; she had the minimum of furniture and what there was was of fine quality. The bookshelves on either side of the fireplace held books in prime condition. The mirror over the fireplace reflected the only picture in the room, a Boudin of a beach scene near Boulogne. She stripped off her work clothes and put them out of sight. She ran a bath and soaked for a long time, soaping the clay from her nails before shampooing her hair and rinsing it under the shower. She dressed in black velvet slacks and a black cashmere jersey, padding about the room barefoot. She had strong slender feet with unpainted toenails.

When she had mixed herself a drink she would check the Ansaphone for messages, cook herself a bowl of pasta, read a book for an hour or two before going to bed. There she would lie listening to the traffic passing far below in the frosty street. At some time in the night the cat would join her in the bed, for she always woke to find it curled on the pillow. While she slept her turbulent thoughts would swirl and wrestle in her unquiet mind.

Christopher's visit had reminded her of his single visit to the loft in their adolescence, a visit which had taught her the value of privacy. It had taken days to rid the loft of his presence; the idea of his smell in the bed had lingered long after the reality was gone. She remembered shaking the bedclothes out of the window, frightening the nesting seagulls as she flapped them violently in the cool air.

About that time she resolved to have a flat of her own where nobody came other than herself.

In the Old Rectory, even after moving to the back of the house, blockading herself away from the front, she had not been free of her family; just as in the loft she was unable to prevent the occasional intrusion of the Kennedys. Now when she woke there would be nothing in the flat to impinge on her privacy. No book replaced out of line on the shelf, no wrinkle in a rug disturbed by an alien foot, nothing touched by hands other than her own, no lingering scent to revive memory, no trace of another being. She occupied her small flat as closely as a mollusc its shell, did not even share its space with a cleaning woman. All trace of occupation was absolutely hers.

Her lovers had had to put up with meetings in hotels; if they had flats of their own she would visit them there. This way she spared herself the risk of finding a nostalgic trace of a body, loved however briefly, in her bed.

She had not seen Claud for weeks, had stopped driving down the motorway at night to appear unannounced in his arms. It had become too pleasurable. "If I threw away the key of the house I could spare myself this travail—"

Just before she fell asleep she noted a change in the sounds from the street: the frost had given way to rain.

Having climbed the ladder and lowered the trap-door Claud felt secure in the loft. Ann Kennedy's breakfasts were substantial, so for a while his blood cherished rather his digestive system than his brain. He dreamed as he listened to the seagulls circling the roofs as they might Beachy Head, swirling and screaming. Come spring, they would nest against the chimneys, and by the time their eggs hatched his manuscript would have matured into a novel, an exhilarating but daunting prospect.

During this digestive period, staring at the view of the river and the gasworks, Claud saw no view. He saw Laura, Mavis and Amy melded mysteriously into the girl with whom he was increasingly obsessed, who would, digestive process over, guide his fingers at the typewriter. She was so real that at times she ceased to be purely cerebral and he threw himself on to the divan and masturbated as he had in the throes of adolescence, falling then asleep to wake bemused and baffled by the force of his creation, whom he must now try to distil on to paper, so curbing self-indulgence.

He was, too, a little afraid of this enchanting creature, and some days, feeling he must distance himself from her, he turned his mind towards his market stall, busied himself sorting, pricing and packing his stock, forcing himself to stop dreaming so that he could make the money, as Laura had so practically suggested, to pay for the dreaming or, he would correct himself, for the writing, his real work.

She was still there, of course, on market days, his girl; she was not to be conveniently left in the loft. He was aware of her as he listened to the chatter of passers-by, watched Susie and Brian at the next stall, Brian joking and Susie shivering and tipping the scales with her pink mittened fingers, her lovely skin glowing in the winter air. He had, he felt, first-hand knowledge of Susie's skin for, just as his girl had Mavis' hair, she had Susie's skin and Laura's legs. The combination was effortlessly superior to any girl in the market. He hardly noticed, as the weeks passed and in every way his girl became more real, that she grew less and less like Amy, but frequently he worried that as yet she had no name. For he could not bring himself to name her. He knew this was stupid, infantile, superstitious even, but giving her a name would be to let her go, to abandon her to the world of readers.

(Curiously, it never occurred to Claud, otherwise so diffident, to question whether his book would find a publisher.)

So for his readers' use he hit on an acronym, and where all through the manuscript he had left a gap where his girl's name should be, he typed in May. (To make use of Amy back to front was all that she deserved.) He hoped that he would see her passing through the market and looked forward to shouting out, "Hullo, May." An unlikely event, since she lived at least a hundred miles away, but the use of the name May comforted him. If in the course of the book something hurtful and degrading should have to happen to his precious girl, he could imagine it happening to Amy, turned back to front, getting a merited come-uppance while his real girl went unscathed. Having solved this little problem Claud wrote much better than before and gave May a really brutal pasting, which improved the story and made him feel good.

Feeling good, he stopped looking on market day as a bind and began to enjoy it and take a pride in his stall. He took days off from his book and visited other towns, travelling by bus to buy oddities in charity shops or pick through dusty boxes of junk in dealers' back rooms, interesting men who visited the market and sometimes bought from him, giving him good prices for things his mother had given him and even better prices for Laura's original contributions. He was meticulous in the putting aside of Laura's share and looked forward to the time when her part of the stock would be sold and his stall be all his own.

This wishing to be rid of Laura's stuff was in part due to Nicholas and Emily Thornby's visits to the stall. They would linger, picking and fingering, speaking to each other in voices so like Laura's that his scalp crawled, as they hinted in audible asides that this thimble or that silver frame might be or was truly from their attic, implying by a jerk of an elbow or a toss of a pointed nose some possible dishonesty on someone's part, not necessarily Claud's. Claud knew their behaviour to be a tease intended to discomfort. They chuckled and glanced up at him with sliding eyes, always seeming on a lower level though they were both tall, and he, meeting Laura's eyes in their wrinkled faces, felt endangered. Had not Laura lain in his arms, wrapping her legs so cheerfully round him, and had he not purloined those legs for his girl?

There was something so excellent and carefree about Laura's legs and the use she made of them while love-making that he resented these same legs (which were, do not forget, his girl's legs, with whom he was obsessed) having any connection with the elder Thornbys standing there teasing him. Then, while he listened to them, pretending of course that he was busy with another customer, Claud would feel a mad longing for a refresher course of Laura, for it was many weeks since he had waked to find her in his bed wearing nothing but her jersey, and he would feel a fierce lust for Laura which had little to do with his girl, his lover, his obsession. To still these rather strange sensations Claud, one market morning as Nicholas and Emily fiddled with the objects on his stall, began to rearrange it, putting all that was left from the Old Rectory attic on one side. "I'll make things easier for you," he said. "All this came from your daughter Laura, the rest I have collected or been given by my mother."

The old people straightened their backs and stared at Claud. "You are depriving two poor old people of a source of innocent entertainment," said Emily crossly.

"And how is your book progressing?" asked Nicholas, all interest in the stall forgotten.

Claud flushed. "My book?" Had Laura—?

"That pretty girl Mavis, the little actress, told her mother, who told the butcher, who told the baker, who told the milkman, who told us. What is your book about?" Nicholas wheedled.

"Machines," said Claud quickly.

"Machines?" Emily expressed surprise. "What sort?"

"Machines," said Nicholas. "Oh," he said. "Ah."

"No lovely girls?" asked Emily.

"Or fascinating men?" inquired Nicholas.

Claud smiled insincerely, nervously.

"We supposed we had a writer among us with brilliant descriptive powers—"

"Lots of sex," said Emily. "One can't have enough."

"Oh yes one can, Em. Don't listen to her, dear boy."

Claud stepped back, fearing the imposition of intimacy as Nicholas persisted. "Descriptive powers are what matters and what a head start you have lodging with Mrs Kennedy, low slung like a dachshund, with an arse like a Clydesdale mare. That's good, isn't it? Have you noticed her legs?"

"Not particularly," said Claud, recognising the description as exact (poor Ann!).

"Oh, the pity! You must! Truncated legs the woman has, then she produced this almost legless woman, a delicious beauty like Mavis. Is not nature amazing?" Nicholas crowed.

"Or God," said Emily. "Give God credit."

"My sister does not believe in God, but she likes to drag him in to the conversation to give tone," said Nicholas.

"Or Her, don't you think God's female, Mister—" pursued Emily, "Bannister." (She knew his name all right.) "Claud."

"It," said Nicholas. "Definitely It. But to revert to the Kennedys' legs—"

"If you came to visit us instead of Laura – didn't you come to read the meter once? – we could discuss your opus." Emily changed tack.

"His oeuvre," said Nicholas. "We review, you know, or perhaps you don't."

"I expect he has the sense to keep quiet until it's finished," said Emily. "Come on, Nicholas, we really must stop dawdling."

"What was all that in aid of?" asked Brian from the next stall.

"I've no idea," said Claud, but he felt threatened and decided to pack up early and get back to his typewriter and his girl. Laura's relations had put Laura out of his head, but as he let himself into the Kennedy house he thought of her again.

Ann Kennedy shouted from the kitchen, "You're back early. Like some lunch?"

"No thanks," answered Claud.

"There's plenty for two. I used to give Laura a snack if I heard her come in."

Claud paused, one foot on the stair. "What did she do in the loft, Ann?"

"Laura? Nothing."

"Nothing?"

"Nothing."

"Oh—"

"Well, like you, she was pretty private. Always very quiet, just like you, no visitors, no lovers, nothing. Nothing for all those years."

"Oh." (What a lot Ann Kennedy failed to hear.)

"I was glad, of course, that she kept the key; it was nice to feel she had a refuge."

"Oh."

"Even if she didn't use it."

"Yes." Claud waited, but Ann said no more. "Well, I must do some work," he said.

Does she know how often Laura has been here to visit me? he wondered as he climbed the stair. Too late to ask her not to gossip. What does it matter? He pushed up the trap-door. Here I am, he thought.

His typewriter sat where he had left it, the pile of manuscript grown quite substantial, but there was no girl.

The sun shone in splashing the floor with light, the seagulls screamed, but his mind was empty. In rushed despair. He could not remember Susie's skin, he could not remember Amy, Mavis' hair could be any hair on any girl's head, he could not remember Laura's legs, everything was suddenly black and devoid of meaning. What on earth possessed me to think I could write? My confidence is pseudo, he thought. He remembered telling Laura that he would kill himself if he failed. Had he been serious? How then to set about it?

He sat at the typewriter and typed:

Hanging. If I bought a rope, I could swing a rope over one of the beams, stand on a chair and kick off. What did Mavis do with the webbing we used to haul up the stove? The undertaker connection would strike a suitably macabre note. But oh, the gagging purple face, the bulging eyes. I'd prefer to look decent in death.

Claud stood up and examined his face in a small mirror propped on the bookshelf.

Cut my wrists? he typed. I have a razor. But think of the mess. Poor Ann. I could wrap myself in sheets and towels to prevent drips through the ceiling. Have I the nerve?

Overdose? Mother's pills are not lethal, I remember she said so to Pa when he was threatening suicide. She had said they might only make him sick. She hadn't believed him. Really, one's parents! Could I get my own pills? More pills? How many? But don't they pump you out? What indignity. One could, of course, put one's head in a plastic bag to make sure. But that was unnecessarily scary.

Drowning. I hate cold water. Fool, it would be a faster death. Perhaps I should give it priority. Cold kills quickly.

Jump off a cliff. What cliff? Where? We are miles from the sea. Would the church tower do? Could I get up it? Is it locked? Would it be sacrilege? Does God exist? What would I think as I fell through the air? And once again it's messy, nasty.

Throw myself under a train? What about the driver's feelings? (Find out about automatic trains.)

Electrocution. Is there a fire in the house with a long enough flex to reach the bath? Terribly painful. No dignity.

Laughing? People do not die laughing.

Heart attack? It took Father years of drinking to pull his off. Can't spare the time.

Shoot myself? No gun. No nerve. Too noisy.

Hunger strike? You must be joking.

Grief? Despair? Broken heart?

What an *embarras de choix.*

When he had finished the list Claud went over to the bed and lay down, rolled in the foetal position. He was too overwhelmed by despair to search for the cause. He had assumed in his besotted state that all was well, his writing a work of genius. There had been no self-doubts, not lately, anyway.

Lying in his hedgehog position he supposed his confidence gone for ever and began to repeat to himself ways and means of committing suicide.

The trouble, he thought, stretching his legs and turning on to his back, was that each method carried with it an element of failure. He would be too scared to pull it off, he had not thought it through, he would make a laughing stock of himself. Then he thought, That horrible old man was only teasing, why should I be afraid of him? His remark about being a book reviewer was more joky than malign. I must not be paranoid, he was trying to get a rise. What would Amy with the Walkman think of me lying shivering here?

For the first time for months he thought of Amy giggling and joggling in his protesting arms, turning the penetration of her parts into an obstacle course.

Claud began to laugh.

I should have hit her, he thought, bashed her about a bit. He sat up feeling purged.

I am shot of Amy, he thought. Then he thought, I am being too sentimental about May (he did not notice that he quite naturally called his girl May). What I need is more tension, a sharpening of focus if May is to pass muster with the reviewers and of course Laura—

He sprang off the bed, tore the typed list of deaths from the typewriter and pinned it to the wall. "Come on, May," he said out loud. "Let's be having you."

"What we need," he said, turning over the manuscript to chapter one, page one, "is some tightening up, local colour, realistic descriptions of characters. So far I have concentrated on my darling. I shall use Nicholas; describing him will be fun, a good exercise. And I must cut out a lot of blah."

Claud sharpened a red pencil and whistled through his teeth. Outside the gulls had stopped shrieking and it had started to rain. He pulled the wastepaper basket closer to the desk.

All through the afternoon he used the red pencil with gusto.

He tore up whole sheets of typescript and stuffed them into the wastepaper basket. As he worked, despair dwindled to zero. When the winter light failed he switched on his lamp. He worked through the night, making merciless use of the red pencil, tearing and crushing bits of typescript, stamping them into the wastepaper basket with his foot.

At last, when the pubs had long closed and traffic in the town ceased to rumble and swish through the wet streets, and only the church clock dared break the silence, he stood up, stretched his arms above his head, eased his aching back. He felt groggy, exhausted, at peace.

The wastepaper basket was full, the unwieldy pile of typescript reduced to a skeleton, the red pencil blunted.

Swaying with fatigue, he sharpened the pencil. Never again would he ignore it. He stuffed the contents of the wastepaper basket into a plastic carrier bag which he put by the trap-door. He opened the attic window and, standing on a chair, peed into the night. He shut the window, shivering at the cold air, pulled off his clothes and crashed into bed. As he lay down he felt pleasantly intoxicated and thought of Laura, imagining her in his arms. He would pull off her jersey, hold her warmly. Did he not love her? Was she not responsible for the catharsis of the day? Had he in his awful fear and despair invoked her? He could not remember. He reproached himself that drivelling on about his fantasy girl all those weeks he had neglected Laura, pushing her into the background. There was more to Laura than legs.

Claud chortled sleepily, remembering Laura's legs with a sharp prick of desire and the simultaneous thought that Laura would be the last person to tolerate all that mush in the wastepaper basket about Amy/May. She may never know, he thought, but she is responsible for my whittling down of a whole heap of typescript into a work of some coherence. (In his state of sleepy euphoria it did not bother Claud that he was making Laura responsible for a work she had not read.) Thank God, Claud thought, that she refused to read it when I offered it to her. Then he thought paradoxically, I can still love May if I keep her in the proper context. Lastly, he thought before falling into an exhausted sleep, I shall take that bag of rubbish to Laura as an offering.

In her bed in the anonymous block of flats Laura lay wakeful and uneasy. Christopher's visit had revived a host of irritations usually suppressed, reminding her of a past she had put behind her. She did not want to feel sorry for him or made to feel guilty. Useless to think that if she had married Christopher she would have saved him from becoming a bore; it was not marriage to Helen which had precipitated his state, he was inclined that way from birth, taking after his father. She had wasted much breath trying to persuade him that the warmth and affection she felt for him risked turning to hate if knit by marriage. He had refused to accept and she in self-defence had grown mocking and distant.

But she could not forget Christopher's father's long and complex relationship with Emily. She had loved him for his goodness, his devotion to Emily, an extraordinary feat – almost guileless – of keeping faith not only with Emily but with his wife. Had he suffered guilt as he paid her school bills? He had, she suspected, rather enjoyed his situation, thought of himself as a bit of a dog. His wife Rose kept him on a tight rein while Emily, who was never a bore, amused and shocked. If only Helen had been ready to learn from her mother-in-law's example, or taken a leaf from Emily, her life would be merrier, her two children less lumpen. No responsibility of mine, thought Laura, turning on her side, away from the real intruding responsibility, the unwelcome load she could not shed. For if Ned Peel was not her father then most probably, and facing it honestly, as she had taught herself, Nicholas was both father and uncle. And it had not been so much to escape marriage with Christopher years ago that had precipitated flight, but home itself, those two, Emily and Nicholas, who had stuck in her young judgemental gullet.

She had denied them love.

And now, Laura thought as the small grey cat joined her in the bed, climbing up by her feet, its claws making tiny clicking sounds as it proceeded along the billowing duvet coming to rest on the pillow,

Emily has grown old, Nicholas is old too, and my conscience nags and drags because I love them.

"I am responsible for you." She tickled the cat's jaw. "It's easy to love you. I don't mind that." The cat purred, she felt the vibration along her finger. "I lie here counting my responsibilities, listening to the rain. I wish, I wish I could sleep." Outside the slanting rain splashed on the balcony, dripped from the eaves, gurgled down the drainpipe. I would like Christopher better if I could be friends with Helen, she thought. There must be something about Helen I could like. Could I, for instance, get her to admit that she likes her dog better than her children, which I am sure is the case? That would be a start. But she is such a conventional woman. She has no trace of Nicholas and Emily's charm, their total lack of humbug.

"What am I grumbling about?" she said out loud to the cat. "I have fewer responsibilities than most, no husband, no children. I have kept away from Claud. If I work at it I shall soon reduce my feelings for him to a proper level. It's about time I gave him up entirely. He has lasted too long, does not fit my short-term norm," she exclaimed aloud, annoying the cat who snuggled closer into the pillow as Laura, restless, got out of bed and padded to the window to stare out at the rain.

She switched on the Ansaphone to check whether any message needed immediate action.

A new message had been recorded in the last hour, a message from Nicholas: "Emily and I have the flu. We are very ill. Mrs Datchett will not look after us as she says her husband comes first, which is rich since he died three days ago. Does the silly cow think she has the instant entrée into the underworld? One asks oneself would it be too much to invite you to tear yourself away from whoever's arms enwrap you to attend to your familial responsibilities. It is many weeks since you deigned to visit us." Nicholas' voice trailed to a stop.

Laura replayed the message, trying to gauge whether Nicholas sounded ill; he was quite capable of indulging in a jape for the hell of it.

She stood for a while hesitating, then said to the cat, "Come on, puss, responsibilities call." The cat curled herself into a tighter ball.

She dressed and as she dressed admitted to herself that it was many weeks since she had been down to see them, that she had promised herself to tidy the Old Rectory garden last autumn. She had neglected it, and Emily and Nicholas, while enjoying herself with Clug. Clug who had fitted so perfectly into the principle of "short term" that he scarcely left a wavemark. As she dressed, piling on warm clothes, arming herself against the winter night, she thought again of Claud, shocked by the warmth of her thoughts, telling herself that she should have snubbed him, nipped whatever was starting in the bud. She had let herself behave completely out of kilter, been reprehensibly light-hearted, no better than Nicholas, irresponsible, and here she was still eager to meet him, ambivalent, in danger of becoming besotted.

Her anxious mood infected the cat who swished her tail and scratched as Laura put her in the basket.

It might be best, she thought, not to tell Claud she had come back.

Carrying the cat, Laura let herself out of her flat into the deserted corridor and walked along to the lift. As she walked she regretted leaving her warm and orderly flat, her calm London existence. As the lift took her down to the basement garage her spirits, already low, sank lower. She put the cat basket on the seat of the car, drove up the ramp and headed west through the rain to the motorway. She switched on the car radio but quickly turned it off, nauseated by the bonhomie of an early disc-jockey, preferring the hiss of tyres on the wet road and the rhythmic clunk of the windscreen wiper. As her guilt feelings towards Emily and Nicholas hounded her down the motorway, she thought enviously of ordinary, happy, uncomplex families at liberty to love each other. With the coming of daylight she dimmed the car's lights and took note of the passing country. She had last driven up in the depth of winter. Now spring was making a start; there were occasional clumps of snowdrops and aconites in the verges, relics of gardens bulldozed to make room for the motorway, flights of mallard crossing the lightening sky from one reservoir to another. She drove away from the rain into brighter weather.

At the turn-off from the motorway she stopped to fill up with petrol, remove her drab jersey and put on instead a bright red one, topping it with a purple wool cap; if she wore clashing colours in the country, gossips would comment on her get-up rather than the expression on her face. She drove on, hoping that Nicholas and Emily's flu, if it existed, would not have engendered too mischievous a mood and might allow her a few days' peace in her quarters at the back of the house and some therapeutic work in the garden. "I shall make a bonfire," she said to the cat, "and you shall go mousing." She smiled, remembering Claud's surprised eye ranging round the disorderly room when he had come that first time, and that he had half-believed the caraway seeds in the cake were droppings.

Coming to a stop in the Old Rectory drive, she was careful not to slam the car doors. She let herself into her flat and released the cat. The room smelled cold, musty and damp; she crouched by the fire and struck a match, setting light to the tinder. After some initial hesitation the flames caught and roared up the chimney, sweeping with them the clammy air. Laura crouched, feeding the fire with twigs, then logs until the heat built up. The cat came close to roast its chest in the warmth.

She brought the duvet from her bedroom to air and switched on the electric water heater, listening with pleasure to the water gurgle in the pipes. She fed the cat and put fresh water out for it, set a kettle to boil for coffee.

Drinking her coffee, she watched the birds in the garden and planned her bonfire. She would cut back the buddleia and prune the forsythia neglected last autumn; she would trim the philadelphus and rake up the soggy leaves so that the air could get at the grass and the bulbs get a chance to shoot; she would collect the fallen branches from the apple trees; the bonfire would smell wonderful.

But first she must attend to Nicholas and Emily. She let the cat out into the garden, walked round the house and let herself in at the front door.

For a few moments she stood in the hall, listening. Her grandfather's long-case clock tocked in a corner; upstairs Nicholas coughed. As her eyes grew accustomed to the light, she saw the hall table littered with opened letters, a newspaper, a vase of dead flowers. Beyond it the umbrella stand, which she had forgotten until now, had held that shabby but distinguished umbrella belonging to the stranger who had helped her get drunken Nicholas and intoxicated Emily into the house and on to the drawing-room sofas and then Bonzo had ungratefully bitten him. No! It was Emily who had bitten him and when Bonzo had attacked he had said: "Die for Eastbourne." Where on earth did he spring from?

As Bonzo, having heard her, rose from his basket in the kitchen and came hurrying to greet her, Laura began to laugh. She greeted the dog and set off up the stairs in high good humour, resolving as she went to be agreeable to her parents, make light of her responsibilities, enjoy them.

Nicholas and Emily were sitting up in bed when Laura and Bonzo arrived upstairs.

"Darling!" exclaimed Emily. "You came."

"Answered our distress signal. What a trooper you are," cried Nicholas.

Laura sat on the edge of the bed, smiling. "Not dead yet, I see," she said, "nor do you seem to be dying." She leaned forward to peruse their faces, rather flushed and blotchy. "What a couple of old frauds!"

"We are seriously ill," protested Nicholas. "The doctor has given us antibiotics."

"Good."

"He listened to our chests with his thingy; said mine was like a squeezebox, terrible."

"He said my nipples are like a baby's." Emily laughed, her laughter choking into a wheeze.

"Don't laugh," said Nicholas. "It makes you worse. A new doctor, Laura, a personable young man, the very sight of him made Emily feel better. He might do for you."

"Nobody will do for her," said Emily.

"No." Both old people choked with laughter.

Laura poured water and passed a glass to each patient. She wondered what the personable doctor had made of this pretty pair.

"Of course Nicholas was in his own room while the visit went on," wheezed Emily, catching Laura's eye.

"Of course," murmured Laura, surprising a strong rush of affection for the invalids. Look at it this way, she told herself, these two have been faithful for life, give or take a stumble or stray, a slight vagary. Their love may be a deviation from the norm, but it has lasted. They have known what they wanted and stuck to it. Why should they bother? If their mode of life has ruined mine, why should they care? There are many virtuous people who do more harm with their good intentions than this pair of hedonists.

She sat watching Nicholas and Emily lying propped by pillows in the double bed. Bonzo, crawling up over their feet, had settled between them lying on his back, eyes closed, mouth slightly open, tail gently wagging, adding his doggy smell to the fustiness of the sickroom, the tumbled bed and crumpled sheets.

"We wore our best nighties for the doctor's visit," volunteered Emily. "I wore the pink satin job given me long ago by dear old Ned."

"Almost a museum piece. She topped it with her white lace shawl from Peru," said Nicholas.

"Nicholas wore his navy silk pyjamas with the monogram across his tit."

"I bet the doctor was impressed," said Laura. "I suggest," she said, "that you let me make up the bed with clean sheets while you have a bath—"

"Ooh. Dare we risk it?"

"Your nails are filthy and I bet the rest of you is the same. I'll scrub your backs. To be honest, you smell."

"Listen to her!"

"And I'll fill your hot water bottles."

"Just as Nanny did in the long gone nursery days!"

"It will not be the first time I have done it." Laura ran the bath, filling the old-fashioned tub with a mahogany surround, a bath so large it easily held two people. "Come on, in you get," she said.

"The Nazis made people bath before they gassed them," Emily whispered loudly to her brother.

"Careful, careful. Oops, it's hot." Nicholas tested the water with his toe before lowering himself into the bath. "Come on, ducks." He held out his hand to his sister.

Laura took clean sheets from the airing cupboard and made up the bed, turning Bonzo off to do so. She also opened a window to let fresh air blow in. She chucked the dirty sheets out on to the landing, closed the window and turned her attention to the two in the bath. "Let's be scrubbing you."

"You're so bossy." Nicholas dipped down into the hot water.

"I bet the doctor said you could have a bath." Laura took Emily's hands and brushed her nails. "How could you let them get like this?" She did not expect an answer.

"Actually, yes, he did say it could be risked. We rather took it to mean at some future date."

"Hum."

"One wonders whether this is not some ploy of yours to give us pneumonia, get rid of us."

"I wouldn't do that, I love you."

"Ho, ho! She loves us, listen to that," exclaimed Emily. "Love!"

"I think that's enough." Laura straightened her back after sponging Nicholas. "Let's wrap you in hot towels and put you into clean things."

"It's supposed to be people with uneasy consciences who bother about soap. Oh, look at the colour of the water, Emily, that was all us."

"Yuk," said Emily. "You dirty old man."

Laura hustled them back into bed, tucked them in and plumped up their pillows. She took Bonzo downstairs and sent him out into the garden while she boiled a kettle for the hot bottles. Waiting for the water to boil, she wondered how Nicholas and Emily, particular about nice things and a presentable house, could endure so much physical dirt, being both able to lie for hours in a bath without ever using soap or nailbrush. They must have India-rubber consciences, she thought, and warded off feelings of anger and frustration, familiar and useless. Better, she thought, screwing the top on to a hot bottle, to love them as they are, stop judging. She called the dog and went back to her parents carrying the hot bottles.

Nicholas had brushed his sparse hair and put on clean pyjamas. Emily lay against the pillows pursing her mouth. "We hope it's allowed, we changed our minds about my nightie and his pyjamas and put on others. It's all right, we put your choice back in the drawers." She grinned like a child.

(They don't look like – like what? They look like ordinary old people – perhaps they are.) "Should you take your pills now?" Laura asked (but they do look very frail now they are clean).

"About now, yes." Nicholas nodded hard to show willing. "Four times a day the doctor said."

"What have you had to eat?"

"We haven't felt like eating." Emily's pathetic accents would wring the best of withers.

"OK. Lie back, relax, take your medicine, I'll take care of you." Laura dished out pills, popping one into each obedient mouth. "I'll do some shopping, get you some grapes. Has Mrs Datchett really lost her husband?"

"He's not lost. She buried him as Bonzo does his bones," said Nicholas.

"I see that you are feeling better. I'll stay until you are quite well."

"Oh, goody!" said Emily. "Would it be too much to ask you to bring up the television?"

"All right."

"Most noble," said Nicholas. "What a saintly girl."

"I am going to do some work in the garden when I've finished with you."

"Most therapeutic." Emily coughed.

"Any chance of a little nip?" inquired Nicholas.

"Nips don't mix with antibiotics."

"Oh, God, what a life," sighed Emily.

"Don't start complaining or she'll beat it to London and leave us to die, won't you, darling?"

"I – well – might," agreed Laura. "There's not much to keep me here."

"What about—" Emily began.

"Watch it," Nicholas hissed and slapped his sister's hand.

It is admirable in its way, the way they never let up, thought Laura, guessing that Emily was hinting at Claud.

"Some flowers would add nicely to the decor." Nicholas looked appreciatively round the bedroom which Laura had been tidying as they talked.

"I'll see what the garden can provide. What's all this?" she asked, catching sight of an assortment of objects on a side-table.

"We bought them back." Nicholas watched her reaction. "We enjoy picking over his knick-knacks' stall. We think we should support the arts. He's writing a book, your toy boy, did you know?"

"Yes." Laura tossed their dirty nightclothes out on to the landing, suppressing the impulse to hit one or both the old persons, noting that her rare rush of affection was draining rapidly.

"We shall be better tomorrow," said Nicholas hoarsely.

"She's afraid we shall be," said Emily, who read Laura's face better than her brother.

"Don't push your luck, I'm not strong enough," said Nicholas.

Laura carried the sheets and pillowcases down and put them in the washing machine. She made soup and while it brewed she cut branches of forsythia buds from the garden and set a vase where they could see it from the bed. She brought up the television. As she worked, she tried to persuade herself that Nicholas had not actually threatened Claud. She must not become paranoid. What harm could he do?

Presently she went out in her car and did some necessary shopping. When she returned she fed the old people with soup and fruit and switched on the television. They were a little flushed by now, still coughing but beginning to get sleepy.

In the garden she raked leaves into piles, pruned and cut back shrubs, heaping the branches and twigs on to a high pile of leaves. Her spirits improved with the work. When sheets were washed, she hung them on the line to be blanched by the moon, crisped by the frost. She was pleased by the company of the resident robin who discovered treats which she had exposed with her raking.

She filled the wheelbarrow with logs from the store, stacked up the log baskets in the house and brought a load to her own quarters. Her rooms were warm now and homely. Before lighting her bonfire she kicked off her rubber boots and went upstairs to look in on the invalids.

Children's hour was playing on the television; Nicholas and Emily were asleep. They looked old and rather ill, innocent, their mouths agape.

Tired but happy, she returned to the garden to light her bonfire. Crouching beside it, putting a match to dry leaves, she watched the flame hesitate then leap from leaf to leaf and the whole begin to glow as she fed it with twigs, then heavier sticks and branches. As the aromatic smoke swirled up she stacked and padded up the fire so that the whole heap of rubbish would combust and burn through the night, leaving only a ring of ash in the morning. At some time in the night, she promised herself, she would wake and come to the door and breathe in the nostalgic scent of past autumns and winters.

When Bonzo rushed barking at a man coming round the side of the house she automatically shouted: "*Die*—" and Bonzo stopped in his tracks, growling. She said, "Who is it?"

The man said, "Laura, it's me, Claud," and Laura jumped into his arms.

"Oh Laura, Laura, how delicious you smell, woodsmoke and pepper. I saw your car in the town. I was venturing to bring you your share of the stall money and hoping you would be pleased. I brought you crumpets. Are you cross? Are you glad to see me? It is so long since—"

"Why should I be cross?"

"You looked so happy by your fire in the twilight. Have you noticed the sunset, the red sky? And your red trousers and bright jersey, so happy alone I feared to interrupt. Is he going to bite me?"

"No, no. Stop sniffing and growling, Bonzo, stop."

"And I have to tell you the good news about my book."

"Is it finished?"

"No, but it will be. I have pared it down to the bare jokes. Can I kiss you again?"

"Of course. Come in, tell me all your news. Listen, while I settle Emily and Nicholas for the night, will you care for my fire and toast the crumpets?"

"Are they ill?" (She did not notice my joke.)

"Flu, that's all. Then we can sit by the fire and have tea. What time is it?"

"About six. This dog makes me nervous; he looks hungrily at my legs."

"His little way. I will take him up to Nick and Em. Come, Bonzo." Bonzo followed Laura, grumbling. "And when we've had tea," she said over her shoulder, "we can go to bed."

"And I can read you my book."

"And that, too," said Laura. "Or you could read it to me after, that would be even nicer."

While Laura, tired from her exertions in the garden, changed her clothes, Claud made tea and toasted crumpets.

"I have brought you your share of money for the things you gave me for my stall," he said. "I was planning to give it to your mother, or ask her to give me your address in London so that I could send it you."

Laura squatted on the hearthrug. "I am stiff," she said. "Unused muscles ache." She took the envelope of money. "I see that Nicholas and Emily have contributed to your trade; they seem to have bought back a lot of things." She opened the envelope, counted the money.

"Are they mad?" Claud buttered the crumpets.

"Not mad, naughty. What a lot of money!" Laura poured tea, drank. "This is good, I need it. What an astute business man you have become," she teased.

"I enjoy my stall apart from your relations' visitations." Claud had half-expected Laura to refuse the money, tell him to keep it since the stock it represented was back if not in the attic, at least in the Old Rectory; he was after all a struggling artist. But Laura gave no hint of doing so.

Guessing his thoughts, Laura decided that such a move would pander to his incipient weakness; she would give the money to Oxfam. She put the envelope on the mantelshelf. Looking at Claud in the light of the fire she thought he looked older, more vulnerable. His slightly blurred features had sharpened during her absence; he was more adult, his attractiveness increased. "My mother does not know my address, only my phone number."

"So secret? Not even your mother?"

"Particularly not my mother. She could, perhaps, if she'd be bothered, give you my address at work; it's in the telephone book."

"Oh." Claud felt foolish. "Is where you live as private as the loft used to be?" he asked.

"Yes."

"But you will tell me?" He was confident.

Others had been equally confident. Laura did not answer. She sat cross-legged eating crumpets, drinking tea. The firelight sent shadows dancing across her face, invented red lights in her hair. Fat chance, she thought. She said: "I must settle my invalids for the night, then your novel shall have my undivided attention." She kissed his cheek, stood up.

"I thought—"

"We could do that afterwards, surely the novel is the most important?" she said.

Claud thought it too difficult to explain that the novel was the loving and the loving was in large part Laura. He watched her go, then heaped the used tea things on a tray and put it by the sink, hesitating whether to wash up. He decided against; he might break a precious cup, chip the already chipped pot. "No seed cake today," he said out loud. He peered into the bedroom. Laura's gardening clothes lay in a heap, red trousers, yellow shirt, violet sweater. From the centre of the bed the small cat watched. "You'll soon have to move," Claud threatened the cat. The animal's yellow eyes gave nothing away. Claud said, "Shoo." The cat did not stir; he would have liked to throw something, to give it a fright, but he went back to the hearth, stacked more wood on the fire, waited for Laura.

There was really very little of the novel left to read. He could, though, tell her the tale; it was clear in his head. He could read her the few extracts that were left, the excellent description of her legs, the paragraph about Mavis' hair, the description of Susie's skin. I wish she would hurry back, he thought. "I thought you were never coming," he said as she came through the door.

"I am here now," she said, looking down at him. "Shall you start reading?"

Claud reached up to her waist, hooking his fingers in her waistband. "There is hardly anything left of the book to read," he said, undoing the button of her jeans. "But I can quote you the best passage, which is about your legs." He unzipped her fly. "I destroyed so much but it is all there, in my head, ready to flow on to the typewriter." Kneeling, he drew the jeans down from her waist. "Your dream legs keep me awake at night in a state of frustrated lust. Please step out of those, you might fall over into the fire." Trapped by her ankles, Laura stepped cautiously out of the jeans. "You have wonderful ankles," he said.

"Uncles, ankles." (Faint memory of Clug.)

"What?"

"Nothing," she said. (And who else?)

"Oh, Laura." He pressed his face against her thighs, embracing them. "Take off that great sweater."

"Don't knock me over." Laura sat down on the hearthrug. "We could skip the reading," she said, pulling the sweater over her head.

"Shall we? Here? By the fire?"

"Why not? It's comfortable, isn't it?" she said.

"Isn't it wonderful what arms, legs and hands can do, and mouths," Claud said presently, lying with his mouth against her neck, her hair brushing his eyes. "I could weep, I am so happy." He felt the warmth of the fire on his back, contrasting it with the temperature of Laura's body. He could not see her face above his, frowning, puzzled, amused. "I have thought so much about you all this long time."

"And who else?" Laura questioned gently.

"Nobody else."

"Mavis, for instance, or Susie?"

"Oh no. Nobody, unless you count the girl in the book."

"Does she make love like this?"

"Of course. 'These little deaths, this rare love.' I cut that sentence. It was one of the first to go into the wastepaper basket. Oh God, Laura! I haven't given you my present. I left it at the corner of the house when I – what a fool I am! It's the proof that I—" Claud scrambled to his feet, rushed to the door, darted, naked as he was, out.

Laura sat up crossly, feeling the draught of icy air let in by Claud, and pulled her sweater over her head. She was reaching for her jeans when Claud returned.

"Christ, it's cold out there." He was shivering. "Here it is, my present, all for you."

"Shut the door, Claud. What is it?" She took the plastic bag he handed her. "Sit down, get warm, put another log on the fire. Let's have a look. Oh!"

"It is everything I have discarded, all the parings. No, you are not to read them. I brought them to you to prove that I have cut, cut, whittled down, cut, what's the word?"

"Edited?"

"Yes."

"Shall we burn it, then?" She peered at the waste paper.

"Of course, that was my hope."

"Not in here, it would set the chimney on fire. I know, let us put it on my bonfire. Put some clothes on, let's do it now."

They dressed, laughing, excited, and hurried into the garden. Laura seized her rake and parted the bonfire, which flared up, crackled and spat in the darkness. Claud tipped the contents of the bag into its centre, then Laura raked the fire back, piling sticks and leaves high over the paper. They watched the smoke curl into the moonlight, heavy acrid smoke stifling the aromatic scent of the winter burning, making them cough and move away. Then, "Leave it, come in, let us open a bottle of wine," said Laura. "We'll celebrate, find something to eat."

"And then back to bed?"

"Why not?" She felt light-hearted, happy, rash.

As they opened the door the cat skittered out between their feet. Claud thought: Now we can have the bed. The cat disappeared, leaping.

Laura beat eggs for an omelette, mixed a salad, found bread and cheese. Claud opened a bottle of wine. As they ate he began telling her about his book, his thoughts pouring out in a rush, the plot unravelling between mouthfuls of omelette and gulps of wine. Sometimes he searched the meagre remains of his manuscript and read extracts which had escaped the holocaust. Laura listened, surprised, entranced, moved. At last, when the food was eaten, the wine drunk, the story told, she said very quietly, "It's good, it's very good," sighing, "wonderful."

"You mean that?" He was trembling.

"Yes, I do."

"If it fails I shall never write another word. I shall kill myself."

"There should be no such thought." Laura was distressed.

"But there is, there would be."

"You are exhausted, so am I. Come to bed."

"Did you mean it? Do you really think – you just said it's good to comfort me, to console." He was suspicious.

"I did not. It is good. If you write it as you told it and keep the bits you read to me, you cannot fail. I swear it's good."

"You will not betray me?"

"What is there to betray? Of course I shan't, don't be stupid."

"Swear—"

"Look, Claud, I am tired, so are you. What is this?"

"Fear of failure. Fear of death. Same thing. Laura. Promise me—"

Melodrama, thought Laura, sleepy by now. This reminds me of recent Clug. Why do I pick artists? "Come to bed, darling. I promise to try not to betray. Will that do?"

"Why only try?" Claud was excited, excited by his book, by the bonfire, by love-making, by the wine. "Give me half a promise then," he shouted.

"I will give you that willingly." She put her arms round him and held him close. "I am only half a person," she said.

"Laura, you are crying. Why do you cry?"

"It is the smoke from the bonfire." She wiped the tears with her knuckles. I am flawed, she thought, I am in danger. "Listen," she said, "listen to the night. Go to sleep."

"I can hear your heart. Will you give it to me?"

"Not possible."

"Will you marry me?"

"Don't make stupid jokes."

"No joke, I repeat: will you marry me?"

"When I am seventy-five, you will be fifty-three."

"So? Will you marry me?"

"I am old enough to be your mother. Go to sleep." She rocked him gently in her arms, stroking him. What smooth and lovely flesh, how hard the muscles, how fine the flat stomach, ah, there and there, how straight the spine, what delicious knobs. "Sleep now. Stop talking, listen to the night."

"There's a gale getting up, the stillness moves."

"Yes, yes, listen, lie quiet."

"Tomorrow I shall start the book all over again."

"Yes. The final version. Yes."

She watched his face by the firelight flickering in the next room, saw him close his eyes, sleep, let go. She listened to the anxious rising wind as it gathered strength, thrashing up from the south-west, testing its strength on the trees until they groaned and winced. Claud shifted away from her, muttering and mumbling.

She slid from the bed and went to the window. Clouds raced now across the moon, drawing shadow patterns on the grass. The bonfire flared up, smoke beaten down drifted sideways. The little cat rushed suddenly across her line of vision, chasing, careering. The heart of the fire flared, broke open, exposing bits of paper which, catching the wind, escaped. Laura picked her clothes off the floor, tiptoed from the room, dressed, slipped warm feet into cold boots, let herself out into the windy garden. The wind was roaring now, hell-bent, savage. She ran stooping in the moonlight, catching sheets of typescript, stuffing them back into the fire, raking up the sides, dodging the smoke which, changing direction by the minute, caught her by the throat and sent her coughing back, tears streaming down her cheeks.

Months of work, she thought, watching it burn. Will he succeed, will he write what he told me tonight? It was so good, she thought, watching the fire, will he be able to write it down as he told it, sparse, passionate, original? The cat raced past, buffeting a ball of paper, tossing it in the air, snatching it with its paws, patting, waiting for the wind to startle it into flight so that she could creep, pounce and torment.

Laura bent down, snatched up the cat's toy, held it in her hand ready to toss back on to the fire, hesitated, smoothed out the crumpled sheet, read, peering close by the light of the moon. When she had read, she crushed the paper violently between her hands, crouched down by the bonfire, thrust deep into the heart of the fire, cried out in anguish as the fire scorched, sprang back, snatched up the rake and raked up the sides of the bonfire so that all that remained of the paper was totally covered.

Its game spoiled, the cat rejoined her as she let herself into the house. She bit her lip against the pain as she searched for Acriflex to cover the burn. Tears blurred her vision. Gasping a little she tended her wound, muttering to herself, "You fool, you fool," as she covered the burn with gauze. Then she squatted by the fire waiting for the pain to subside, for her equanimity to return. At last she stood up, went to the window, drew the curtains. It would soon be dawn. The wind, decreasing, stroked the branches it had savaged. The fire was almost burned out. There was only fitful smoke.

She felt very tired, consumed by the desire for sleep. She took cushions from the chairs, laid them on the hearthrug. In the bedroom

Claud slept sprawled across her bed, his head thrown back, arms wide, breathing evenly. She took a blanket which had slipped to the floor and, closing the door, stretched out by the fire, covering herself with the blanket, laying her head on the cushions. The pain of the burn was less immediate. Her thoughts under control, she felt the cat creep up past her feet to settle purring by her head. The balance which had tipped was regained. Tomorrow she would care for Emily and Nicholas. As soon as they were well she would return to London to catch up with her orders, the boring awful hand for Helen's fake Apollo for instance. She would scramble back to normal. She fell asleep exhausted.

Laura woke to hear Claud moving about. She feigned sleep. She did not want to talk to him, needed time to recover her composure. She heard him dressing, muttering to himself as he did so. He came into her living-room and, seeing her lying on the hearthrug, whispered, "Oh." She waited for him to go. If she let him know she was awake he would expect breakfast and, worse still, conversation and love.

Claud knelt near her and added kindling then logs to the dying fire. He did not touch her. She listened to him moving about the room, to the sound of paper torn from a pad, a pause while he wrote a message. Then he let himself out. She heard the scuffle as he put on his shoes. Then he was gone.

The slight draught from the briefly opened door counterbalanced the fire which flared up, spitting, as the flame travelled. She was aware of her scorched hand. The burn was not a bad one; her hand had not been long in the fire. She felt uncomfortable from sleeping in her clothes, looked round the untidy room in disgust. Its deliberate chaos usually helped her endure her visits to her family, but not today. She decided that she would reduce her quarters to order before she returned to her obsessively neat flat. Standing chilly and dishevelled, she now keenly wished to get back to London but for a few days at best she must stay and care for Emily and Nicholas. She was ruefully amused by a sense of responsibility quite lacking in her parents.

Claud's note on the table said: "Darling, sleep on. Am off to joyous work. I will come back tonight. Love C."

"He is very sure of himself," she said to the cat.

She ran a bath and as she soaked in the hot water composed a list of mundane things she must do. Finish tidying the garden, clean the house, create order in her disorderly rooms, persuade the cleaning lady to return as soon as her period of mourning was over, stock up Nicholas and Emily's store cupboards and deep-freeze, take their clothes to the cleaners, have their car serviced, make a blitz with the Hoover to rid carpets, sofas and chairs of Bonzo's hairs, and finally bath Bonzo. Making her list she cajoled her normal self to take over. She got out of the bath and dressed in bright yellow trousers, a pink shirt, green sweater. Her hand still pained her a bit, but it would heal. She would not forget what she had read on that ball of paper. She would make use of its memory to counterbalance her feelings (feelings which had been in danger of bolting up a blind alley). She would not stop sleeping with Claud just yet but the terms must be hers, as they had been at the beginning in the loft when she had been the sexual leader.

As she put a fresh dressing on her hand she grimly recalled unravelling the cat's toy, and reading what Claud had written. A passionate declaration, an explicit detailed description of love and not just physical love was stressed. There was a zest of the spiritual. (It was a fine piece of writing; she hoped he carried it in his head to write again.) From past experience she knew it was possible to cope with a live rival if so minded, it could be rather entertaining, but she recoiled from competition with a person as purely imaginary as Claud's girl May. (He had not last night quite got around to May; he had skated and glossed over her as he told his tale.) May, Laura thought, what an awful name. No drama about a name like May. Will May survive? Will he perhaps change May to some grander, more cogent, more dramatic name? The sheer silliness and inadequacy of the name eased her feelings, made her laugh, and feeling better so did her burned hand.

She tried to imagine May, a girl who was, after all, composite: Mavis' hair, Susie's skin, her own legs. It was absurd, laughable.

Then, remembering Claud's rendition of his book and how moved she had been, she dismissed these mean thoughts. Claud had created a girl who came alive, a girl who would linger in the minds of his readers, a person people would discuss, comparing her with other characters in literature. Like it or not May had style. I underestimated Claud, Laura thought. I used him for pleasure. I even suspected him of being a little camp. Then last night, serve me right, I went overboard, was even ridiculously in danger of believing his suggestion of marriage could be serious, not just froth. I could not have been much stupider than that.

Right then, Laura thought, I shall play second fiddle. Playing second fiddle to a fictional character has a certain originality. Having made this decision Laura was almost back to her old self.

Laura applied herself now to Nicholas and Emily; if she filled her days with their needs, she could keep her nights free for Claud. Past experience had taught her that one way of coping with complex feelings for her relations was to tidy their house; this somehow reduced them to manageable size. Out with the dust would go her guilt, and if like dust it reappeared that was the nature of things, though she always hoped there would somehow be less dust than before.

Finishing her attack on the garden, she planned what she would do to the house; there must be an awful lot of rubbish she could throw out. She would make life easier for Mrs Datchett when she came back. But first she tackled her own rooms. The organised chaos which had origins in adolescent protest no longer amused; she packed up cracked, chipped but valuable china for Claud's stall and replaced it with new things from Woolworths. She cleaned out cupboards, scrubbed, dusted and polished, reduced her possessions to a minimum. A lot of things went straight on to the bonfire. She excised objects of personal interest; the rooms must be functional, no more. She had allowed too much to accumulate since building the brick partition; there must be as little left of her self as possible. The cat picked its way about the rearranged rooms in disgust but Claud, arriving each evening to eat supper, sit drinking by the fire before taking her to bed, was in such a state of euphoria over his book that he did not notice the changes. Laura was glad of this; it reduced his hold.

Hearing the sound of the Hoover Nicholas and Emily rose from their bed and, wrapped in dressing-gowns, looked down at Laura working in the hall. They were recovering from their flu but since the weather continued icy they prolonged their convalescence. Laura could look after them.

Emily said: "Look at the dear girl, she is spring-cleaning. Were we as dirty as all that?"

"It's a sign of emotional disturbance, most *hausfraus* are neurotic. D'you think something has upset her?" joked her brother.

"Or somebody. Have you done the whole house?" Emily shouted above the hum of the machine.

"Almost. Bonzo has worked his hair into everything and it gathers in drifts in dark corners." Laura looked up. "Are you better?" she asked as the Hoover moaned to a stop. "Have you taken your temperatures?"

"Normal," said Emily. "Come back to bed, Nicholas."

"There's a parcel of books for you to review," Laura called, "if you want to read."

"Bring them up when you bring our elevenses." Nicholas trailed after Emily. "When shall we tell her our plan?" he asked.

"Let her finish the cleaning. The last time she did this Mrs Datchett free-wheeled for weeks." Emily switched on the television and lay back on her pillows to watch a programme on fashion. "Look at those skirts, Nicholas, right up to their crotches!"

"There is a lot of banging and destruction going on downstairs,"

Nicholas remarked, returning from a trip to the lavatory. "She has the bit between her teeth. I trust she won't destroy anything precious. She is filling bin liners with all things unburnable."

"Having a happy time. Did she bring up the books?"

"I fetched them. Shall we read and compose our reviews?"

"Let's see what there is." Emily seized the parcel.

"She is burning Bonzo's old basket," said Nicholas.

"He doesn't use that one any more."

"And his blanket, probably thinks it full of fleas."

"It probably is. Fleas' eggs last. Do you think she is making the house ready for the undertakers?"

"In which case we have a surprise for her, but no need to be morbid, Em. I say, let's have a look." Nicholas reached for the books. "I love the innocent smell of a new book. What shall we be this month, mean or charitable?"

"Let's damn with faint praise." Emily relished their power. "Oh, darling, you do look fierce, what's that sack for?" Emily clutched the duvet to her breast as Laura came into the room. "What are you up to?"

"I am degenerating into a dutiful daughter," said Laura lightly. "Actually I am collecting empties to throw out, bottles, cartons, that sort of thing. Why do you never throw anything away? Look at all this." She opened a cupboard. "Gosh—"

"It might come in useful."

"For what?" Laura snatched up paper, small boxes, empty tubes of toothpaste, old jars of face-cream and broken combs, dropping them into her sack.

"Mrs Datchett is going to be pleased if she ever comes back," said Nicholas placatingly. "Especially if she only wants to do light work. Sit down a minute, Laura, and talk to us."

"When I've finished this. She is coming back. I have been to see her." Laura continued her clearance. "Don't worry. What's all this?"

"We have something to tell you," said Nicholas.

"Let her finish her wave of destruction," said Emily. "Have you had a go at your part of the house, Laura?"

"Yes. That wasn't too bad. What are all these?" Laura sat back on her heels. "What are they?" She sniffed at a box of empty bottles. "They smell – er – funny."

"There was a shortage of bottles in the war; one returned the empties to the barber. One did the same with Fortnum's jars," said Nicholas. "One didn't always keep up the impetus."

"The war ended in 1945," said Laura, still thoughtfully sniffing. "This was hair oil," she said, puzzled.

"Penhaligon's best. Has it kept its scent?"

"You have not used it for years and years—"

Laura held a bottle to her nose. "Oh—"

"Stop sniffing like that, Laura. What's the matter?"

"I think I will get your elevenses." Laura dropped the bottles into the sack. As she carried it downstairs she thought, It can't be. It's my nasty suspicious mind. She tipped the sack into the dustbin.

In the kitchen she filled the kettle to make coffee and washed her hands. It was so long ago, she thought, I may be wrong. I wish I was. Why did I not realise at the time? What good would it have done?

She remembered the party, Nicholas and Emily's birthday. Everybody drank too much. She remembered waking next morning, the smell on the pillow. Christopher had been at the party with his mother and father, good old Ned – but Ned used that stuff from Trumpers. She remembered it well, it was quite different from— Did anything happen? Nothing? Surely nothing. I'd know if it had, would – I – not? One does not forget smells or what might have—

It was at least twenty years ago. Laura washed her hands again, made the coffee, carried the tray upstairs. Halfway up the stairs she stopped as twenty years of suppressed memory snapped. She remembered waking in her bedroom. The door closing as Nicholas left the room. The smell of his hair on the pillow, the stickiness on her nightdress and inner thighs. A mistlethrush had been singing outside in an apple tree, as one was singing now. Had the birdsong unlocked her memory? Her head had been aching. It was clear now. Had she wept? She remembered her heart thumping as it thumped now. She had bathed, oh yes, she had bathed and later Emily had accused her of taking all the hot water. Plotted to kill Nicholas? Contemplated suicide? She had forced herself to forget, buried her terrible anger deep, an anger which welled up now almost choking her as she stood on the stairs gripping the tray.

In the garden a robin chirped up in the lilac bushes in contrapuntal harmony to the mistlethrush, just as it had then all those years ago.

She continued up the stairs.

"What was it you wanted to tell me?" She laid the tray across Emily's lap.

Emily pursed her mouth. Nicholas paced the room. Laura sat on the bed at Emily's feet. "You look better," she said, "both of you. You have recovered from your flu." It was less easy to like them when they were well. "You look positively spry," she said. "What's the secret? What have you to tell me?" She watched Nicholas. "Nicholas—" she began.

"What?"

"Nothing." What would be the use of asking him if he remembered the incident of all those years ago? If he did and he habitually trolled beds, I would feel no different, no sadder than I do. I did not, thank God, get pregnant.

Nicholas was speaking. "What did you say? Sorry, I missed—"

"You never listen," Emily shouted in sudden exasperation.

"Hush, Em," said Nicholas. "I was saying, Laura darling, that we have decided to have a living-in couple to look after us—"

"What a good idea," said Laura. "Where will you put them?" (Is there such a thing as circular incest? She considered her own question in all its permutations.)

"Well, darling, since you are never there, we thought the flat at the back. We will knock down your joke wall, of course."

"Of course," said Laura. "Is that what you wanted to tell me?" She suppressed a shiver.

"I don't like your tone of voice," said Emily.

"It won't be worrying you for long, Mother."

"But you will come and stay with us," said Nicholas.

"There will be no reason to." Laura kept her voice level.

"But you are Emily's child, she's your mother."

"And what are you, Nicholas?" Laura asked. "What are you to me?"

Nicholas did not reply.

"Your coffee is getting cold," said Laura. "Drink it up."

"It would choke me." Nicholas put the cup aside.

"Tell me this, Nicholas. When I was collecting those empty bottles just now did you, too, remember a party years ago?"

Nicholas stared at Laura.

If I were writing a book, thought Laura, I would write that his mouth is working but it isn't and I don't feel anything, no extra pain, nothing. "I think I have stunned myself with housework," she said. "Of course I will get out of my bit of the house. You have no need of me, I have no need of you. It's a pity, but there, never mind."

"We thought," said Emily, "that with your business in London, your flat wherever it is, and the men you live with whoever they are, that it is a terrible bore for you just to come down from a sense of duty."

It is, thought Laura, but this time Nicholas begged me to come, said you were dying. "Wolf, cry wolf," she said. (Surely it is better to be facetious than to accuse?) "Nicholas," she said cruelly, "what's the matter, you are looking funny?"

Nicholas stood with his back to the light, his hands clenched to fists in his dressing-gown pockets. She could see his black eyes reflecting her own. "Is this happening to us?" he said, ignoring Emily. "An ordinary family?"

"I hope no one will ever call us that," protested Emily with her usual sharp spirit. "We are too remarkable. What's the fuss about?" She looked from Laura to Nicholas. "We only want your rooms for servants or whatever they like to be called these days. I suppose they will consider us ordinary. Am I missing something?" she asked. "Some nuance?"

"No," said Laura, exchanging a glance with Nicholas, "I don't think you are missing anything."

"A few days ago you said you loved us." Nicholas ignored his sister.

"So I did." Laura stood up. "Finished your coffee?" she asked. "I'll see to your lunch. I bought fish."

"Laura." Nicholas followed her out of the room.

"It's all right," said Laura, "nothing's changed."

"Oh dear," said Nicholas, "oh dear, oh dear."

Laura started down the stairs with the coffee tray. The cups rattled annoyingly in their saucers. Nicholas caught up with her in the hall. "It would be such a gross betrayal if you said anything to—"

"Don't worry, Nicholas," she said, "I told you nothing has changed. Worse," she said, pushing open the kitchen door, "can't be worse."

"That's what you think," said Nicholas. "Oh darling, I do love you."

"And that's a pity too. Go back to Emily, Nicholas, go!"

I shall put this out of my mind, she thought, washing the cups at the sink. I shall walk over the hills this afternoon and exhaust myself. I shall come back and have supper with Claud and go to bed with him and if May is in bed with us, it bloody well can't be helped. At least I shall get those two old grey people out of my mind. "And tomorrow," she said to the cat, "we shall go back to London and stay there."

Laura sat in the wine bar. She was wearing a snuff-coloured skirt and a bitter chocolate jersey. At her feet in its wicker basket her small cat glowered.

Since she had been in in the autumn the bar had changed hands. The new owners kept it dark, compensating for the lack of light with soft musak and a line of rich gâteaux served with Viennese coffee, hoping to attract a classier clientèle than the market people who, with their loud talk and noisy camaraderie, had been apt to treat the bar as a club to the exclusion of others.

The market people had moved up the street to a new establishment, Terrence informed Laura, which served sausages of all nationalities with a fine variety of pickles and mustards. "They can make as much noise as they like there. You won't find people like Brian and Susie here any more. They've moved up the street, chips with everything."

"When did this happen?" Laura sipped her wine.

"Last week." Terrence idled by her table. "I was offered a job there, but I've better things to do."

"Oh?"

"I am going into private service. Would pussy like a saucer of milk?"

"No, thank you." Laura looked up. Above the long apron, spotlessly clean, Terrence sported a striped waistcoat. "I like the waistcoat."

"My uncle brought it from Germany; some count's footman sold it to him. It's got his crest on the buttons."

"Very nice. Shall you be happy in private service?"

"I mean to be."

"Doesn't it depend on the people?"

"No problem, it's just an old couple."

Terrence had grown taller during the winter, more robust. His face had filled out so that his teeth were less daunting. The probability occurred to Laura that the old couple might be Nicholas and Emily, that Nicholas and Emily might need protection, or conversely Terrence. But she was on her way to London. Nicholas, Emily and Terrence must fend for themselves. She raised her paper and pretended to read.

"I plan to get Mavis to work part-time with me," said Terrence, ignoring the hint. "It's a local job, see."

"Very nice." Laura folded the paper to the leader page. Was the thought of Terrence living in the rooms where she had made love to Claud abhorrent? She had been stupid to allow him to keep coming there; it would have been better to have stuck to the loft where somehow she had always kept the upper hand, contained her love (if that was what it was). If she had not had an assignation with Margaret Bannister she would have paid her bill and left.

"When I have some experience I shall go to a school for butlers and move on to the States. They pay terrific salaries there. You get your own car, the lot."

"That's all right, then," said Laura.

Terrence moved away to position himself by the bar, ready to swoop on customers as they came in.

He's a sly fellow, she thought. I've never much liked him. Why doesn't he say he is going to work for Nicholas and Emily? Perhaps he is not telling me because he resents my teasing him when Claud and I ate the oysters. Does he think I might put a damper on his plan? Will his smell obliterate the faint echo of Claud in my bed, of us lying by the fire? I must look on his presence in the Old Rectory not as a barrier but as a protective shield. I wonder how he will get on with Bonzo?

Laura looked at her watch. Unpunctual people irritated her; Margaret Bannister was late. She tapped a spoon against her empty glass, and gave Margaret another five minutes.

The street door swung open and Helen Peel came in. Laura raised her newspaper too late; Helen had seen her. "When am I going to get my hand?" She advanced on Laura, sat without being asked at the table.

"Soon," said Laura.

"I suppose you have been looking after Emily and Nicholas." Helen always knew it all. "They have had flu."

"Yes."

"She and Nicholas are bloody spoiled, never lift a finger, do they?"

"No."

"I hear that they are going to have a living-in couple. Putting them in your part of the house. I suppose you know all this?"

"Yes."

"Can't imagine how they can afford it, they must be living on capital. Aren't you worried?"

"No."

"They can't make much from their articles and reviews."

"No."

"Where's that boy?" Helen snapped her fingers. "Here, Terrence, stop picking your nose and bring me some coffee."

"Yes, ma'am." Terrence grovelled, "Your usual chocolate gâteau with your coffee and whipped cream, ma'am?" He winked at Laura. "Or will madam have wine today?"

"Coffee, of course. D'you suppose he's making fun of me? They normally call one love or ducks. What d'you think, Laura?"

"Yes."

"Oh." Helen looked surprised. Terrence set coffee, cream, and a large slice of cake before Helen. "D'you think I should eat this? Christopher says I am losing my figure."

"Lost."

"You are a comic." Helen laughed indulgently. "Were you waiting for someone or do you want to be alone?" She examined the chocolate cake. "What a large slice."

"Yes."

"You are not making yourself very agreeable." Helen forked cake into her mouth. "Monosyllabic as ever."

"Cat got my tongue." Laura leaned down, picked up the cat basket and moved to go; as she did so Margaret Bannister came in, full of apologies. Laura led her to a table out of earshot of Helen. When she had ordered wine for Margaret, she said: "I asked you to meet me so that I could give you this. It's money Claud made on his stall."

"I don't—"

"It's my share of the stuff I gave him to start off with. You remember, a job lot from our attic? I thought of giving it to Oxfam, but I think if I give it to you to spend for Claud that would be best."

"I don't understand." Margaret looked suspiciously at the glass of wine Terrence placed before her, hesitated, then raised it to her lips, drank.

"Claud is writing a book, Margaret." Laura turned her attention to Claud's mother. Claud had inherited her looks but was not yet as bruised by life. "Claud is writing a book," she repeated.

"I know that." Margaret thought that she had never particularly liked Laura, or might not have liked her if she had ever got to know her well.

"It is going to be very good. He is in full flow and may not have time for his stall."

"It's just a phase," said Margaret dampingly.

"It may turn out to be a very long phase; he is extremely talented, Margaret."

"Oh." Margaret swallowed a mouthful of wine. "How do you come into this?" Nothing irritated her more than being told about Claud, talented or otherwise, as though she were ignorant of his character. The more so since she suspected she was ignorant. "Of course he is talented," she said.

"He read me a bit of his work the other day; I thought it wonderful," said Laura. "I am off to London," she said reassuringly. "I shan't be down here for ages. I have not the time to give it him myself."

"You could have posted it." Margaret put the money in her bag. "There was no need to make me come all this way from my new house. I am not living here any more, you know."

Laura let this rudeness pass. She could not explain to Margaret her need to see her. She was not sure herself why she had desired the meeting. Was it part of her farewell to the neighbourhood? "How is the new house?" she asked politely.

"I like it very much. I like the garden, the village is delightful, there is so much to do. Evening classes, lectures." Margaret already regretted her rudeness, felt the need to give something to Laura. "I can plan my days," she said, "without having to consider other people. Claud, for instance," she smiled at Laura, "and shades of my late husband." She drank her wine. Perhaps she was giving too much? "My new house has no memories. Perhaps you cannot understand that?" she said.

"I understand very well." Laura signalled to Terrence to bring more wine. She thought of her London flat which held only herself. "You have found freedom," she said, "for the first time since you married. You will turn feminist next, go soap-boxing."

"You are making fun of me," said Margaret, smiling. "I can't think why I am talking to you like this. I hardly know you."

"What else have you found?" Laura searched Margaret's face for traces of Claud. How would Claud use his mother in his writing? Did he know his mother? "Tell me," she said, "what else?" She was surprised to find herself so interested.

"I have not stopped loving Claud or his father – but Claud—"

"You don't lose your maternal instinct just because you move house."

"But you find a new perspective, see things differently!" Margaret wondered whether a childless person such as Laura could have maternal feelings.

"How so?"

"I am taking a course of psychology; when I finish I may be able to explain it better. To start with I have befriended someone who needs it. I feel maternal about him."

"A young man?" This was interesting. "A replacement?"

Margaret leaned closer to Laura. "An old man," she said, "so lonely he flashed."

"Like a glow worm?" Laura puzzled.

"No. His thing. To get attention. The only attention he got was passing the plate in church and that was negative. He is the most wonderful gardener. It wasn't sexual, it never is. He's like a child."

"Second childhood? Very old?" Laura frowned.

"He can still dig an excellent trench." Margaret spoke quite seriously.

Laura crowed with laughter. Margaret's substitute for Claud seemed totally out of character. "What an amazing thing to do," she said, "it doesn't seem like you at all."

"Why not? I was not much use to Claud." Margaret spoke stiffly. "Like any normal person I need something to keep me ticking. This poor old man will be the minimal replacement I can manage." She drained her glass.

And I have no replacement. Laura sucked in her breath. Perhaps my empty heart will silt up, she thought, wishing now to get away. She signalled to Terrence to bring the bill, said that she must be off or she would get into a jam on the motorway. The brief moment of intimacy was over. She was anxious to leave.

They left the wine bar together. Laura waved at Helen, who shouted after her, "Don't forget my hand," so that other customers, looking puzzled, examined their own hands. Helen was gobbling a second slice of gâteau.

"I don't suppose she has a very happy life, in spite of Christopher Peel's money. All those statues must mean something. Perhaps they represent the beautiful people she had hoped her two boring children would be, and are not? My evening course on psychology may explain that too. It's amazing what one learns." Margaret had now changed, or half-changed, or was prepared to change her opinion of Laura, would have liked to prolong the meeting, have another glass of wine, get a little drunker.

"Well," said Laura, "maybe." She did not wish to discuss psychology. "Thank you for meeting me. And for taking charge of the money."

"See you soon, perhaps?" suggested Margaret. It would be nice to be friends with someone who thought so highly of Claud, someone who seemed to understand what you said.

"Not for a long, long time. My mother is getting a housekeeper, she will have no need of my visits."

"Ah." They walked along the street to Laura's car: Margaret now wondered whether she was not relieved that Laura would not be around? There were a lot of things she would like to ask, though. What sort of life did she lead in London? How did she manage? How did she know that Claud had talent? What made her so sure? What was Claud like in bed? She was sure Laura had been to bed with him. She did not give the impression that her sex life was ended; did she have a lover in London? What was it like for a young man of twenty-three with a woman of forty-five? Or for a woman of forty-five with a young man of twenty-three?"

"It must be nice," she said.

"What?"

Margaret said, "Nothing," but she thought rather wistfully that Laura was getting something much more enjoyable with Claud than what she had experienced with Claud's father. "He was so often drunk," she muttered, and hoped Laura had not heard; she should not have drunk so much wine.

"Here is my car," said Laura, who had heard and would presently ponder on the risks of amateur psychologists. She put the cat basket on the back seat.

"Will he find a publisher?" When Margaret was anxious, she looked like Claud.

"I am sure he will."

"Will you find him one?"

"Claud's work has nothing to do with me, Margaret, you must know that."

"It's true that he used to say that writing was what he wanted to do."

"Well, then—"

"There were times when he was sulky and unpleasant." In her mind Claud's mother multiplied the one scene with Claud into many.

"Now he is doing what he wants, he is happy, he will change."

"You don't know much about psychology."

"Maybe not. Well, goodbye. I must be off." Laura kissed Margaret's cheek. She got into her car. Margaret walked ahead along the street. From behind she resembled Claud. It was something about the hunch of her shoulders, the length of stride.

Margaret stopped to look in a shop window, hesitated, went in. It would be easier to forget Margaret than her son. What a strange woman, Laura thought with amusement, withdrawing from her own child. How could she do it? And withdrawing, deciding to ration out her affection on some old pervert, as though affection (love, if you like) were a commodity like the vegetables Brian and Susie weighed out in the market. But she would not stop loving Claud, Laura thought jealously, she had no need to. She was settling down, if she but knew, to the enjoyment of her maternity. Lucky Margaret, thought Laura, I cannot do that.

She switched on the ignition and pulled out into the street. Terrence, standing in the doorway of the wine bar, waved. "Bloody cuckoo!" Laura shouted, but she returned the wave in case she should decide that she was grateful to him for filling the gap left at the Old Rectory.

"Bloody Nicholas and bloody Emily." She changed gear to overtake a van and speed on her way out of town. "They can't hold me any more. I shall fight free from the tentacles of conscience," she shouted over her shoulder to the cat imprisoned in its basket on the back seat. "I," she shouted, "can ration my love for them." Nicholas, Emily, Helen, Christopher, Margaret and insolent Terrence would be tucked away out of sight in the cubby-holes of her mind to be thought of occasionally with love or affection, just as she thought of the American professor, the Hungarian painter, and of Clug. The immediate problem was to reduce Claud to similar, manageable size, find a secure cubby-hole for him.

Laura stopped to buy petrol, have her oil and tyres checked.

Had the djinn escaped from the bottle? Who would help her get it back? Up to now she had always been able to control her emotions, always kept love affairs light-hearted, enjoyable and brief, aware of the inevitable soon-to-be-arrived-at parting. (She had never permitted any suggestion of continuity.) She had kept a sloppy timetable with Claud, visiting him too often in the loft and lately allowing him to visit her every night in the Old Rectory. She had not toyed with love, not stopped when she still could have without pain.

And above all there had not been enough jokes. Jokes were the essence. Claud took everything seriously, he did not for instance compare well with Clug in that field.

Laura circled out on to the main road and increased speed. She had been in danger of losing her grip, she told herself irritably, and trod hard on the accelerator.

As she drove she savoured her last night with Claud. He had been caring and passionate, he had made love better than ever before, she had been physically and emotionally delighted, their union had been excellently synchronised, she could not fault it.

She had been a little puzzled by this notable success, she remembered now, until Claud, lying spent, his head on her breast, had volunteered that the last difficulty, the last tiny hitch in the composition of his novel was overcome.

"And what was it?" She had stroked his throat with her finger. "This awful hitch?"

"My girl's name, of course," he had answered sharply.

"Oh?" she had asked, sleepy, relaxed, content.

"May will not do at all."

"No?"

"Her name, of course, is Lydia."

"Of course. Excellent."

"She still has your legs."

She had not noticed help was at hand.

Laura, braking carefully, glancing cautiously in her rear mirror, drew into a lay-by and switched off the engine.

A man driving past said worriedly to his passenger, "Do you think that woman is all right? Should we stop and help? Phone at the next phone booth? She is hooting with laughter."

After wiping her eyes, Laura thought delightedly of Lydia, that thanks to her she was free. She was no longer even second fiddle. All the way up to London she let off little snuffles and spurts of affectionate healing laughter.

PART III

A YEAR LATER

A year later, if she thought of Claud, it seemed right to Laura that an affair begun in a spirit of jest should end on the same note. Her life in London was so remote from the atmosphere of the Old Rectory and the tightly interlocking society of the country town that it had been relatively easy to let thoughts of Claud dwindle to manageable proportions. If she had been in danger of making herself ridiculous, she was the only person to be aware of it.

Her work kept her busy; she made several trips abroad, going twice to Brussels, once to Milan, and once to Lyons. She went on holiday as she had often before to stay with hospitable friends in Tuscany, where she dallied agreeably with a fellow guest who was at a loose end between divorces. She found his company relaxing and enjoyable. Reminded briefly of Claud as she straddled her new acquaintance, she thought how much easier it was to be agreeable to people who made no demands, were not intense.

Every two or three months she telephoned her mother (a duty call). She learned that life at the Old Rectory carried on much as usual. The acquisition of living-in help had not made much difference. For reasons of her own Emily was for some time coy about naming her minions, letting slip only by degrees that the live-in housekeeper was Terrence and his aide, Mavis, who lent a hand when she felt like it.

It transpired that Emily had hoped that Mavis would couple up with Terrence, but Nicholas thought Terrence was homosexual, which knocked that little plan on the head. Fortunately Bonzo had taken to both the young people.

Laura did not speak to Nicholas.

On her return from one of her business trips there had been a letter from Claud forwarded from the Old Rectory. He asked her to meet him for lunch on a day already past to celebrate the acceptance of his book by a publisher.

Laura had not (being so splendidly distanced) even known that the book was finished. She had presently dialled Ann Kennedy's number. Ann answered.

"Yes," Ann had said. Claud's book was to be published; he was getting a good advance. He had been to London to meet with his editor. Happily Mavis had been home – yes, resting – she had gone with him to see the editor to give moral support. He had been nervous, poor boy.

"How fortunate," said Laura, "for Claud." Was Mavis filling the gap? Was Mavis' precious virginity at risk? Would she, Laura, mind a Mavis/Claud linkage or Mavis' virginity kept or lost? Neither eventuality moved her in the slightest.

Ann said she would tell Claud to ring Laura when he came in from the market. Claud was making rather a good thing out of his stall, quite a respectable amount of money. Mavis gave him a hand sometimes.

Laura noted with amusement the change in Ann. Claud, no longer in need of bolstering by his mother, was earning real money.

When later Claud telephoned, Laura asked, "How did you get my number?"

"I braved your mother. That terrible dog tried to bite me."

"All you have to do is shout, 'Die for Eastbourne'. He isn't really ferocious. Tell me about your book. I am so pleased. So happy for you. I told you it was good, didn't I?"

"You did, you did."

"When is publication?"

"May."

"I can't wait for the reviews."

"If I get bad reviews I shall kill myself."

"Don't start that again, start a new book."

"I have."

"Oh, good. What is this one about?"

"It's a sequel to *Lydia*. Surely, I told you my novel is called *Lydia*?"

"No."

"Well, it is. Wonderful title, isn't it? If you create a character as I have with Lydia, you can write a series. My editor is all in favour."

"Oh."

"I scrapped all that crap about machines and my mother and the girl wearing her Walkman, you knew that?"

"No."

"I'm sure I told you."

"Does she, Lydia, still have—"

"Your legs. Well, yes. I can't scrap your legs, they are an integral part. And Mavis' hair, of course."

"Susie's skin?"

"I've let Susie's skin lapse."

"Oh, why?"

"Well that carry on with—"

"Drinking her pee?"

"It's not really on, is it?"

"It's your book."

"Oh, Laura, I am working terrifically hard; the book, the new one, is flowing. When I get my advance I shall invest in a word processor."

"My, my. Shall you move out of the loft?" She could not visualise a word processor in the loft, it was far too grand.

"If the book gets good reviews I shall move, but until I'm sure—"

"You will get good reviews."

"Promise?"

Laura crossed her fingers. "I am sure you will."

"Mavis wants me to write television scripts for her."

"Does she indeed."

"She thinks my dialogue is very good."

"Really?"

"I incorporate a lot I overhear in the market into my work."

"Is that so?"

"What is so, Laura, is that I shall badly need you around when those reviews come along."

"As an integral somebody?"

"Laura!"

"A joke, Claud."

"But you will be there?"

"In some capacity."

"Wonderful."

Putting the receiver back in its cradle, Laura thought that of all the people down there in the country the only one she missed was Bonzo.

Claud walked along the street in a state of elation. The sun shone. At breakfast in Ann's kitchen he had read the review of his novel, *Lydia*. His first review.

The words sensitive, witty, stylish, percipient, talented, waltzed through his brain. He was happy in a way he had never been happy before.

He was an author bursting on to the literary scene. *Lydia* was welcomed in print, the arts critic of a prestigious newspaper had generously praised his book. Happiness! His editor had telephoned him from his home before leaving for the office. Congratulations!

The bookshop had three copies on display in the window. "Local author." Claud went into the shop. He needed the excuse yet again to feel the book, sniff its newness, the special smell of an unread book, see the photograph of himself on the back, read the blurb (which he knew by heart), approve once more of the jacket (rather eyecatching and startling), discuss the pillar-box-red binding.

Had the shop seen the review? Indeed yes, wasn't it good? Now we must wait for the Sundays. Would he like to sign the copies in stock? Of course. Claud signed, laughed joyously, exchanged pleasantries, did not quite dare to ask if they would order more than these three—

He continued on his way. Ann had asked him to call at the fruit shop since he was too excited to work, and buy her six bananas and two pounds of Cox's apples, here's the money, no doubt she would soon be seeing him on television. (It was a pity she never read a book.) Passing the newsagent Claud bought two more copies of the paper. He would send a cutting to his mother, who only read the *Guardian*, and keep one for himself. Mavis had said he must keep a cuttings book. He was to meet Mavis in the wine bar to celebrate. It was lovely to sit at a table with Mavis. People commented audibly on her looks, the colour of her hair. Today, with luck, they would point him out to each other as a writer (if not today, they would soon). Alas that Terrence would not be there to wait on them. Since discovering Claud had written a novel that was about to be published, Terrence affected to have read Proust. Let him now read *Lydia*, but his own copy.

Carrying Ann's bananas and apples, the extra copies of the newspaper, and his happy head high, Claud continued on his way, running into Nicholas and Emily outside the post office.

"Hullo," said Nicholas, "our local author."

"Hullo," said Emily, "felicitations."

"Hullo," said Claud, exploding with smiles. "Have you seen the marvellous review of my book in *The Times?*"

Nicholas looked unusually intelligent. Emily smiled slyly. "Nicholas Shakespeare is so kind," she said.

In London on the bus, on her way to her workshop, Laura also read the review. By coincidence it shared among others on the arts page a preview of a series of concerts to be conducted by Clug the following autumn. It was a long time ago that he had conducted at the charity concert where she had met Claud. He had grown greatly in international stature since and Claud had become a writer. To pick up where one had left off was as far from Clug's mode as her own. He would not, she thought, be sending her free tickets.

She was mildly irritated that her feelings for Claud were not as dispassionate as those she held for Clug. It would be churlish, though, to put off congratulating him. When she reached her studio she dialled Ann Kennedy's number and asked for Claud.

"He is out," said Ann. "I can give him a message. Shall I do that or will you ring again later? He is celebrating with Mavis."

"Just give him my congratulations, tell him how happy I am for him."

"Will do," said Ann.

As she worked Laura found herself worrying as to what Nicholas and Emily would say about Claud's novel. During the pre-publication months it had occurred to her several times to suggest that they should give the book a puff, but on mature thought she had decided that such a move would invite mischief; she rather hoped that *Lydia* would escape their notice.

During her lunch break she went out and bought a copy of a weekly Nicholas wrote for and a copy of the woman's magazine which occasionally employed Emily. She scanned the reviews on Claud's behalf with some trepidation. *Lydia* had not escaped their notice.

Nicholas praised the book highly but briefly. "A brilliant first novel."

Emily's piece was longer. While damning with faint praise, "Claud Bannister is a witty leg-fetishist," Emily hedged her bets by using expressions such as "for discerning readers" and "a good read to tuck up with"; her one-and-a-half paragraphs might, probably would, be construed by the charitably-minded as a recommendation.

Laura was relieved for Claud; they could have done so much worse. It was pretty safe to expect kindness from the Sundays.

She had promised to stand by, but she did not think he would need her support. She would not telephone. She would write a thoughtful, affectionate, congratulatory letter.

She supposed that there would be a word processor now and that he would move out of the loft. Would Lydia's successor keep the same style of legs?

How nice to be a writer, thought Laura, to kill off, alter, or totally transform a character as Claud had transformed Amy and not have to wait as lesser mortals such as herself for time to dull recollection.

When she found the parcel containing the hand for Helen Peel's Apollo hidden under a stack of out-of-date telephone directories, Laura felt a fool.

The parcel should have been posted at least a year before. If anyone had asked her she would have sworn that she had despatched it; she had even, when doing her annual accounts for the income tax, thought that Helen was more than usually dilatory in not sending a cheque.

Since the fabric of her life depended on meticulous attention to detail

Laura was shaken. She wondered whether this unconscious act of self-sabotage might not indicate that she was starting the menopause. She had long since decided to be sensible about the menopause, but if it did things like this to her it would play ducks and drakes with her well-ordered existence.

Continuing with the annual clearance of her workshop, a practice she normally enjoyed, she found herself irrationally cursing Helen for not reminding her, for not sending Christopher to harass her, for letting her forget. She remembered now that when she had last seen Helen, Helen had reminded her, a reminder that she instantly forgot since her thoughts had been busy with Claud. There had been far too much thought of Claud, she told herself angrily. He had lasted too long in the first place and he was now only having a come-back thanks to his novel.

Laura threw the telephone directories into the bin. Damn Claud, she thought, slamming the lid on the bin. She would take the hand down to Helen during the coming week, grovel, fix the hand on to the god for her, tell her not to worry about the bill. Helen would be embarrassed and she, Laura, would feel better. This really is menopausal stuff, she thought.

Having fixed Helen, she would call in on Nicholas and Emily for a surprise visit. There would be no time to see Claud. He had moved on in his life, as she had in hers; thoughts of Claud were retrogressive; she never bothered to think of Clug or other lovers like this; it was nice to meet them occasionally on a friendly basis, but they were "over", were they not?

She finished cleaning the workshop, looked round at the order she had reduced it to with satisfaction and left.

That afternoon she walked through the parks to Trafalgar Square, spent an hour in the National Gallery, had dinner with friends and went to bed. The following day being Sunday she would sleep late as she usually did, wander out to buy the papers and, depending on the weather, decide how to spend her day.

In the event she was wakened early by some American friends she had not seen for over a year, who drove her down to spend the day near Oxford. When she got home, it was late. She was tired and rolled into bed after feeding the cat without bothering to listen to possible messages on the Ansaphone.

It was Monday evening before she thought to bother about messages. She had had an unexpectedly busy day; clients with urgent orders from abroad had kept her late at work. She was tired when she reached her flat, had a leisurely bath, washed her hair, changed her clothes, poured herself a stiff drink of whisky, put her feet up on the sofa and switched on the Ansaphone.

The first two messages were routine; she sipped her drink. Then there was a blank, then a loud screechy voice which she did not recognise started an incoherent babble about not knowing what to do and would she come at once. A second voice interrupted, "Here Mum, let me," and "We got your number from your mother, Laura, what an old bitch, can you come, it's about Claud, he's—"

"No," said the first voice very loud this time. "Tell her what he is doing, he—"

Laura placed the voices as those of Ann and Mavis.

"He's not doing anything," said Mavis' voice.

"I hate these machines," Ann squeaked. "He might kill himself, Laura, he won't talk to anyone, his mother is coming."

There was a pause, then, "Mavis, d'you think this will reach her? Shouldn't we call the—" Laura gulped a mouthful of whisky. The machine was still running.

"Laura Thornby is not here at the moment," it said in Laura's voice, "but if you care to leave a message, she will get back to you as soon as she can."

"I am sorry to bother you," said Margaret Bannister's voice, "but Claud is behaving very oddly; he has shut himself up there and—" Here the voice which had begun calmly choked. Mavis took over, excited, almost laughing. "Mrs Bannister says his father was a manic depressive."

"No, I said he was an alcoholic; any psychologist will tell you that an alcoholic is not necessarily a manic depressive, though sometimes—' Margaret sounded cross and assertive. The machine clicked, then repeated, "Laura Thornby is not here at the moment, but if you care to leave a message, she will get back to you as soon as she can." Then a man's voice asked whether she was in a position to come and measure up for a foot repair on a statue on a fountain in Tewkesbury recently damaged by vandals. A letter with full particulars would follow, thank you.

Laura took another gulp of whisky, looked up Ann Kennedy's number and dialled. "Hullo," said a masculine voice.

"Ann Kennedy, please," said Laura. "This is Laura Thornby."

"You'd better talk to Mavis," said the man.

"Who are you?" asked Laura.

"Laura?" Mavis came on the line. "At *last*!"

"What the hell is going on?" asked Laura.

"We have been trying to reach you ever since yesterday," said Mavis, gasping. "Claud's gone bananas."

"What's—"

"It's the Sunday papers."

"What?"

"The reviews! Claud's book! Haven't you read them, don't say you missed—"

"No."

"Oh!"

"What do they say?"

Mavis let out a sound between a giggle and a shriek. "I'll let Martin read it. I just double up every time, it's so funny. Here he is."

The masculine voice said, "It's only one review. Shall I read it to you?"

"Please."

"It's quite long, I'll pick out the offending bits. Here goes. It says, 'Even the most average of readers deserves better than this', and um, here it says, 'If there were a prize for the booby of the year, Claud Bannister's novel would win hands down', and here it remarks on 'paragraphs overloaded with disintegrating vowels which would lie more happily in the WPB than on the printed page'. He's having a ball, this reviewer."

"What is really happening?" Laura took what she recognised would be Claud's mother's definition of a tight grip. "Is it serious?"

"Hard to tell. I don't know the man. I gather he was psyched up, all joy over his reviews, very very happy, then yesterday morning this. He shut himself up up there and won't come out."

"Ah."

"Making a meal of it."

"Oh."

"Wants to see you though, shouted something to that effect to Mavis."

"Is his mother there?"

"She was, but she went home, said his father did this sometimes. Brave lady."

Laura did not know what to make of this.

"I'd say it would be a good idea if you could manage to come down," said the man quietly.

"Not a laughing matter? Mavis sounds—"

"No," said the man. "No laughs."

"I'll be there in an hour and a half," said Laura.

Traffic was still pouring out of London on to the motorway; it would be rash to hurry. On the back seat the cat mewed in her basket, annoyed by the interruption to her routine. Laura found herself gripping the wheel unnecessarily tight as her mood swung between anger and fear. Why should she feel responsible? What was there to be afraid of? She was guilty of encouraging Claud to write. What was injured pride doing to him? Was he not an upper and downer, had she not on first meeting him called him Otis?

Overtaking a car she gave herself a fright by passing too close, nearly hitting it; the driver blasted his horn. Laura broke into a sweat. She should not have drunk such a strong whisky.

When she walked into the Kennedy kitchen, she said, "Well? What's happening, what's going on?" aggressive from nerves. Ann, Mavis and Margaret Bannister were sitting round the table. A man she vaguely recognised but could not place leaned against the wall.

Ann Kennedy said, "You are responsible for putting Claud in my loft, you get him out of it." She was belligerent, her normal easy temperament in abeyance. Laura braced herself for a statement that the house was respectable, but Ann said no more.

Mavis said: "He's got a gun." Her eyes were shining, thrilled.

Margaret Bannister said, "I thought I'd better come back as you were coming down. He won't speak to me. This is all so ridiculous. He should have joined a proper profession with a pension to look forward to, not been encouraged to fan about in an attic."

The three women stared at Laura, anxious, excited, accusing. Mavis emitted a little splutter of mirth. "We thought we'd wait for you before sending for—" began Ann.

"Fire, ambulance, police," chanted Mavis. Theatrical London had done marvels for Mavis' self-confidence.

"I'll go up," said Laura.

"I will come with you," said the man who had so far not contributed, and pushed himself away from the wall.

"This is Martin Bengough," said Ann rather formally. "He's a great help."

"Hullo," said Laura. She wanted to ask what Claud had said or done, whether he had threatened – she decided it would be a waste of time. "Come on, then," she said to Martin. "I don't believe he has a gun," she said, climbing the stairs. "I feel sure he can't shoot."

"That's good."

"I know you, you were one of the people who used to shadow Clug." She climbed on, hurrying.

"Yes," said Martin, keeping up. "I was. I've been in Washington since then."

"He loved it," said Laura, reaching the top landing. "Here we are, he must have put something on the trap to weigh it down. There's no bolt. I suppose they tried?"

"Told them to bugger off or he'd throw himself out of the window."

"I don't think he would care to do that—" She started up the ladder.

Martin stood below, looking up at her; she was wearing grey jeans and a black cotton jersey. She had admirable ankles. Clug had been right.

"He has weighted it with something. I shall have to ask you to help me heave, I'll give him a shout first. Claud," she shouted, "Claud? It's me, Laura."

There was no reply.

"Come on," said Laura, "help me." She swung sideways on the ladder so that Martin could join her. He put his left arm round her to balance and pushed up strongly with his right. A heavy weight on the trap-door shifted. "And again," panted Laura. Martin put his head down, stepped higher on the ladder and heaved. His mouth was full of Laura's hair; the trap shuddered and gave way. "Let me go first," he said, "if he's got a gun."

"Don't be stupid." Laura climbed past him into the loft, pushed aside a load of books which Claud had used to block their entry. Claud lay face down on the bed, fully clothed. There was a whisky bottle empty by the bed and an empty bottle of pills.

Laura found Claud's pulse; Martin opened the windows wide, then picked up the pill bottle. "Nitrazepan," he said, holding it to the light. "Mrs A. Kennedy. Two to be taken at night."

"I can feel his pulse," said Laura. "Help me roll him on to his side. He must have stolen them."

Martin rolled Claud over, pulling one leg up in the recovery position. "He is stinking drunk," he said.

"And drugged?" Laura pushed up Claud's eyelids; she was not sure what she was looking for.

Martin said, "I don't think these are killers." He showed Laura the bottle.

"It's the combination," she said. "D'you think you could call a doctor? I'll stay here."

"Half a mo," said Martin, kneeling on the far side of the bed. "What have we here?" He scrabbled under the bed. "Look!" He held out a handful of pills. "He spilled the pills. I don't suppose he swallowed more than one or two." He smiled at Laura across Claud's body. "My bet is he's just plain stoned." He watched Laura with interest. Her face was grey and taut as she stared back at him. She said, "Black coffee, d'you think?"

"I'll see to it." He left her with Claud.

When he came back she had covered Claud with blankets and was sitting beside him, holding his hand.

"I told them downstairs the panic's over." Martin poured a mug of coffee. "Let's try him with this." He heaved Claud up, propping him with pillows. "Mavis seemed quite disappointed. Will you hold the cup?"

Martin held Claud, while Laura held the cup to his lips. Claud mumbled something, belched, went back to sleep.

"No good," said Laura, "it might choke him."

"Matter of time," said Martin.

They resettled Claud on his side. "I don't think a doctor is necessary," said Martin.

"No," said Laura. "What did his mother say?"

"She says his father used to do this, it's hereditary. She's gone home again."

"Didn't she want to see him?"

"Said not, something about other commitments."

"I don't know why sensible people seem so heartless," Laura exclaimed passionately. "She is not a heartless woman."

"Shall you be sensible?" Martin thought she looked ugly with fatigue and fear.

"I shall sit with him." She was defensive.

"I wasn't suggesting you were sensible."

"He might be sick." She ignored his remark.

"So he might." Martin smiled at her across Claud's body, then looked away. Claud began to snore.

"Were you in love with him?" Martin caught Laura's eye.

Laura flushed, then as he watched she grew very pale and thoughtful.

Below them in the house there were sounds of Mavis and her mother going to bed, doors opened and shut, the lavatory flushed. In the town a clock struck the hour. Martin wound his watch; the excitement was over.

"Everyone gets at least one very bad review," said Martin.

"I should have warned him if I had been around," Laura said.

"But you weren't."

"No."

Martin wandered about the loft. He picked up the books Claud had used to block their entry, replaced them on the shelf, moved to Claud's desk and began riffling through some typescript. "This will be his next book—" He began to read.

"Leave it alone," said Laura savagely, then, as Martin spun round startled, "it will be all right when he has torn most of it up. It has to be sieved, largely forgotten."

Martin observed her defensiveness, her intensity. "Like life?"

"Yes, of course."

"So you did love him?"

Laura did not answer but took her hand away from Claud and folded it with the other in her lap.

"And you feel guilty and think you have betrayed him, I suppose."

"Guilt is a fact of life," she said.

"And betrayal?"

"That, too. Actually," said Laura conversationally, "what triggered whatever my feelings may have been was my inability to share."

"With Mavis?" Martin made a wild guess.

"With Lydia," said Laura and began to laugh.

"Who is Lydia?" Martin saw that laughter became her, made her eyes glitter.

"Lydia is his girl, the heroine of his novel. She has Mavis' hair and did have Susie who sells organic vegetables in the market's skin. Actually he dropped Susie, he was never too keen on her recipe for beauty. Lydia is a composite girl."

"Does she have anything of you?" Martin watched her.

"Some mention, I believe, of my legs."

"Bravo! Her character, though, what of that?"

"She has the character to suit her creator."

"Creator?" Martin's eyebrows queried the use of the word or Laura's intonation.

"A writer's use of Godwottery, if I can use that word in an explanatory sense. He is in love with her, she is his perfect woman, a woman who will never hurt him. But a critic has attacked her, hence this." Laura gestured towards Claud. "When Lydia is threatened, he reacts like a rabbit eating its young to conceal them from the enemy. Claud kills himself."

"Not very successfully," said Martin. "Bit on the bogus side, something of a bosh shot I'd say."

"Well, no," Laura murmured. She leaned over Claud, peering into his face: "Can't get it right first go, can he? It's like the first draft of his book," she whispered. "You stupid, stupid fool."

Laura sat beside the bed keeping watch. Martin settled in the chair by the desk, his back to the window. She had shaded the light from Claud's face. Neither of them spoke.

Laura listened to Claud's breathing, deep and regular now with only the occasional snore; from time to time she felt his pulse. Time passed slowly. The town was asleep.

Martin watched Laura, remembering her with Clug, an attractive intelligent woman having a good time. It had been an uncomplex job; she had been easy to track in her brilliant colours. They had, he and the others, watched for the clothes rather than her face. They had learned not to be foxed by the muted colours she wore to work. Her face, which had lit with merriment when she explained Lydia to him, was again blotted with anxiety and fatigue with dark smudges under her eyes. She was very different to the woman he had addressed briefly, breaking the rule of anonymity, as he boarded the train to follow Clug and she, catching his joke, had blown him a kiss. She looked half-dead now, sitting there beside Claud, who had this weird obsession for an imaginary girl. On the other hand, was he too not verging on obsession over Laura? Might the Laura he guessed at not be as imaginary as Lydia?

He tried to gauge her attitude. She had been angry when she called Claud a fool, loverly almost. Would she, if the occasion required it, have given Claud mouth-to-mouth resuscitation? The thought of such an intimacy appalled him. He imagined her covering Claud's mouth with her own, inhaling and exhaling his sour, stale-whisky breath, and was utterly disgusted, closing his eyes to blot out the inner vision, rearing away from his thoughts. When he looked again, he was surprised to see that the moment of passion when she had called Claud a fool was superseded by what looked remarkably like boredom.

Still Laura showed no inclination to talk. Martin looked around seeking inspiration. He must get her to talk.

He noticed a list pinned above the desk, got up to read it. "Here's a list of methods of suicide. Do you think it was long planned?" He brought the list to Laura.

"He threatened once or twice, as people do." She took the list. "It's all negative," she said. "He wasn't keen."

"Perhaps he meant it, though."

"I took it to be histrionics when he threatened."

"As his mother did."

"She is not an easy mother; I don't think he is an easy son. She is probably right to go home. If she or Ann had been really worried, they would have sent for help."

"They sent for you."

"But not official help. I should think Mavis worked everybody up. They were not to know that he had got pills and whisky; they obviously under the drama thought he was making a scene, then sulking."

"Which, in effect, he was."

"Yes."

Silence reasserted itself. Laura seemed content to sit with her thoughts, but Martin felt a strangling desperation, a longing to shout and yell at her. He had waited so long to get to know her. What was going on in her mind? They had been up here hours, the world would wake up soon, he would lose his chance. He must take a risk. He said: "Do you think while we wait for young Claud to surface that you could pretend that you and I are alone in a compartment in a train?"

"Why?"

"On the assumption that strangers meeting in trains can speak intimately, since the odds are they are safe to speak the truth because they will never meet again."

"If you are bored, you can push off, go home, I am quite all right." (I do not need you, her voice implied.)

Martin ignored the snub. "What do you say to my suggestion?" His tone indicated that she might be chicken.

"Intimacy is not my genre," she said, yet the idea of the train appealed to her, it had an irresponsible attraction; perhaps this man would prove truthful. "All right," she said, "I'm game."

"Shall I begin? My name is Martin Bengough. My job in this country, which incidentally I have just chucked, has been to follow people like your conductor friend Clug when they visit and see that they don't spy on military establishments and so forth, but stick to their allotted programmes."

"Jolly boring."

"Usually yes. With Clug one got music and the bonus of watching you."

"And discovering that I am not a military establishment."

"Exactly."

"Still pretty dire."

"My aunt Calypso Grant thinks it's disreputable."

"A bit harsh. You have to live and as I remember there was more than one of you."

"Twelve of us."

"My, my! Twelve people to spy on poor little Cluggie! Is that what we pay taxes for? Gosh." Martin winced. "Sorry, go on."

"I was enchanted by you. I wanted to get to know you. When I passed Clug on to the next fellow for the last time, I doubled back here, made use of a silly ploy. I pretended to have lost my umbrella. I had left it in the concert hall on purpose. The caretaker girl told me that your mother would have it; this was splendid, I was able to come to your house, a legitimate excuse. You had been out with your parents, had difficulty with them when you arrived back—"

"I remember. They were legless. You were most helpful. My mother bit you. She can be naughty."

"I bear the scar," said Martin.

"And you knew the password for Bonzo."

"The caretaker girl had warned me that he was fierce, told me about the Eastbourne bit." Laura laughed. Was she relaxing? "There now, we have made a start on our train journey. Were you in love with Clug?" Martin asked.

"Lord, no." Laura was amused.

"I rather thought not. You don't allow yourself to fall in love." (He would not tell her that she had been watched at other times with other men.) "But you do go in for pleasure, I believe. Nobody gets hurt." Should he go on, or had he gone too far, too fast?

"And?" She gave nothing away.

"You strayed from your norm with this one." He glanced at Claud. "Got hurt, probably. Feel responsible for him, perhaps?"

Bloody man, thought Laura, blast him, it all comes back, the struggle of a year exposed. She snapped, "What else?" (What other truths would he dare to present her with?)

"You never allowed yourself to marry or have children." He watched her face.

This self-confessed spy was aware of Nicholas and Emily yet she rather liked his open face with its honest grey eyes. He should have the guts to go on with the idiot game he had started. She hoped he was capable of hurdling the difficulties, or was he craven? "Is that all?" she asked.

"A précis."

"And?"

"I hoped during the last year, which I have spent in the States, to forget you. When I got back I came down here looking for you. I have been and am obsessed by you." (Was she listening?)

Between them on the bed Claud emitted a porcine snort. Laura, pushing her thick hair back with one hand, leaned forward to stare at Claud. She said, "Yes?"

"I didn't expect to find you in these circumstances."

"No?"

"Watching your ex-lover revive from a suicide attempt makes it rather harder to come out with a – an – er—"

"What?"

(An offer, a suggestion, a proposition? What had he to offer?) "I thought you and I might—"

"What?"

"Love," said Martin. The word spoken out loud threatened them both.

Laura shrank into herself, drawing her knees up, hunching her shoulders as though a weight threatened to crush her.

Martin thought: We have here two failures, hers and mine. Could two failures constitute one success?

Laura said: "I would not suit you. I am emotionally parsimonious."

"Must it be so?" Martin asked.

"I am only half a person," Laura said gently, for he seemed an agreeable sort of man. Then she said: "I don't think your train is getting us anywhere." Then more firmly she said, "I think I shall get off it now. I see no destination." Then she said, "Oh look – he is waking up."

Claud had opened his eyes.

*

Claud, focusing on Laura, said, "Laura!" in a surprised voice. "Great!" and went back to sleep.

Martin thought Laura's relief tangible. Her shoulders relaxed, she sighed, smiled, shook herself. "The longer he sleeps, the better," she said. "He's OK now."

Martin felt he must recapture her attention. While Claud slept she had at least listened. He asked sourly, "What happens when he finally surfaces?"

"Gallons of tea and aspirin, and a boiling bath with ammonia in it. Could you organise that?" She got to her feet. "Lord, I am stiff." She rubbed her knees, stretched.

"Why the hell should I? He is your lover." Martin's rage bubbled up. "Is that what you have been planning," he shouted, "while we have been sitting here? Why should I organise his bath? He's nothing to do with me, he's yours. I thought you were worrying whether he was going to die of alcoholic poisoning, that you were feeling remorse, minding about the stupid sod."

"All right, don't run his bath," said Laura equably. "I was worried. I was thinking while we played trains and so on that it would not be too awful if he did die." She had shed her concerned appearance. She looked as he had first seen her in Clug's company, relaxed, distant, self-contained and bloody attractive. Martin drew in his breath. "I must tell Mavis – or perhaps you would, oh no, you won't, will you – to buy him another wastepaper basket, for he will destroy most of that." Laura pointed to the typescript on the desk. "Then he will carry on with his next book and life with Lydia. And it will be all to do again," she said. "Next time, next book, next rotten review, you'll see."

"I shan't see, I shan't be here," said Martin loudly.

Laura did not appear to hear. "I shall apologise to Ann for lumbering her with such a dodgy lodger and she will defend him. She will make it clear that his behaviour is in some way my fault, that no good comes of an affair between a very young man and a woman old enough to be his mother, that I am to blame for this little caper. The same goes for Margaret. Oh," Laura swept her hair back from her face with both hands as her voice sank to a whisper, "I thought that if he should die, I would be free of him, but you can only get free of live people, that's what resuscitation is about." She began to tremble.

Martin pushed her gently down on the edge of the bed and sat beside her.

They sat with their backs to Claud. Martin pretended not to see tears pouring from Laura's eyes, dripping off her chin on to the black cotton jersey. He took her hand and held it. He said, "Let's get back on the train for a bit."

"All right." She leaned sideways away from him and wiped her face on the sheet. Claud might not have been there. She stopped crying.

Martin said, "Did you seduce him or did he seduce you?" He was painfully jealous.

"I came up the ladder one day and got into bed with him. There was an element of surprise. It's getting light outside, look, little pinkish clouds."

"Go on."

"I wanted to teach him how to make love. So many men never learn."

"You did that?" Martin held her hand (it would not be difficult to put a pillow over Claud's head and hold it there).

"Yes. Listen, the birds are beginning to sing."

"Then what?" (Better to let the bastard live.)

"Then I found it was not all talk and sex, he could write. It was so good, I helped him burn the first draft. I got burned myself." She held her free hand up and turned it about. "There's a scar somewhere."

"There will be."

"Then he fell in love with his girl. He truly loves her, she is part of him. He said if he got bad reviews, he would kill himself, suicide threats, tiresome emotional blackmail. Sitting here all night I have been thinking he's a selfish bastard. It would not matter if he did die. I was so angry I almost wanted him to. I knew he wouldn't, that he was merely stupefied with whisky and there was Lydia absolutely alive and perfectly sober."

"Were you perhaps feeling guilty for seducing him?"

"No! We had a lovely time. How could I feel guilty about that? Wishing him dead, which I did for other reasons, is betrayal, though."

"I wish," said Martin, "that you would give me the chance of betraying you."

Laura looked astonished. "Why?"

"You haven't taken in a word I said," Martin yelled. "I love you, I want you. I want to stop you wasting yourself on this ass." He glanced contemptuously over his shoulder at Claud.

"But I have," said Laura. "I thought that was obvious. All I have had this night is a small hiccup of responsibility."

"I thought you were torn in two."

"It isn't being torn in two that matters, it's being shredded into little pieces so that you can never get back together, that matters."

"And you are back together?"

"Yes. I am." She seemed wonderfully calm now, cheerful.

"What about me? Give me a chance to love and betray," (or play the clown) "please."

"No chance. I am getting off your train." She was friendly, cheerful, composed. Perhaps he had not seen her weep? She was slipping away from him, he had never held her. "Listen to the birds," she said. "It's time for me to be off."

"God! I feel awful! Woeful, oh," cried Claud. "Ouch! I feel terrible."

Laura leaned over Claud. Suddenly exasperated, she said: "I bet you do. Listen to this, Claud. You have written a bloody good book, stop whingeing about one idiotic review and get on with the next. Tear up what you have written so far. Got that?"

Claud nodded and, since nodding hurt his head, groaned.

Laura stretched her arms above her head. "Right, then. I'll send Mavis up with tea. If she's not awake she should be." She moved to the trap-door. Martin followed her. She started down the ladder. "Goodbye, Claud," she shouted, "goodbye." She jumped the last yard of ladder and began running down the stairs. "Wake up, Mavis." She banged on Mavis' door. "Wake up, it's over to you."

Martin could hardly keep up, she ran fast, leaping two steps at a time. "See Mavis swamps him with tea," she shouted over her shoulder, "and get aspirin from Ann." She had reached the hall and was fumbling with the latch, opening the front door. "Dear God!" she cried, "I forgot my cat was in the car. How could I have forgotten her? Oh, puss, you have made a mess and no wonder, who could blame you?" She let the cat out of its basket and tipped the contents into the gutter. "Oh, hell and damnation!" she exclaimed. "It can't be true! I left Helen's Apollo's hand in London. I shall have to post it." Then, noticing Martin standing at a loss, she snapped, "Why have you not put the kettle on? Claud is dehydrated, he needs tea."

"He can wait another few minutes. Where are you going?" Martin raised his voice. He was thirsty and tired by the long watch, desperate.

"Back to London. He needs tea," Laura reiterated.

"Fuck his tea."

"Oh!" Laura began to laugh. "Oh-ho-ho-ho-ho."

Martin caught her wrist. "There's a delightful restaurant about ten miles from here in an old watermill. There's a stream. Will you come there with me? We could have breakfast?"

She freed her wrist. "I got off that train," she said. "Go on, put the kettle on, he's dehydrated."

Martin watched her car dwindle down the street. He thought, I shall not go on with this, as though the decision to part company was his. There was nothing to build on except imagination.